DRAGONFIRED

BOOK THREE OF THE DARK PROFIT SAGA

J. Zachary Pike

Edited by Courtney Rae Andersson

Cover Design by James T. Egan of Bookfly Design
Map Artwork by Foreign Worlds Cartography
Interior Illustration by Wolfordeer Colony Studio
Interior Design by Eira Brand of Zipline
Published by Gnomish Press, LLC, October 2023 and
Distributed by Riyria Enterprises, LLC.

Printed in China

Version 1.0.0

Gnomish Press, LLC
P.O. Box 64
Greenland, NH 03840
GnomishPress@gmail.com

Published by:

GNOMISH
- P R E S S -

Distributed by:

RIYRIA
ENTERPRISES

ACKNOWLEDGEMENTS

This trilogy has been, up until this point, a lifelong task. I began drafting the earliest concepts of the story when I was sixteen. Then titled "A Fine Hunt," it was a shadow of The Dark Profit Saga. I've changed immensely as a person over the course of writing it, and it'd be impossible to acknowledge everyone who has helped me grow and shape my craft. But I'd be remiss to not list those who have been most instrumental in making it something I can stand by today.

Courtney Rae Andersson of Elevation Editorial is an excellent editor, and this work is better for her attention.

Kelsea Reeves served as my sensitivity reader for this book and gently made me aware of where my ignorance could cause harm, as well as pointing out where my attention had avoided it. I thank her for it.

My beta readers submitted invaluable feedback that helped make this a better book. A special thank you to my cousin Hillary Poisson, who went out of her way to hunt typos too numerous to count. Mike Tibbals was as fastidious as ever in tracking details, and I received invaluable feedback from Victoria Balbes, Aleisha Kirby, Geoff Griffith, Scott Serbin, and Jasmine Wahlberg. Thank you all.

Thank you to my first readers from decades past: Al, Eric, Erin, Kristin, Nick, Ryan, and Warren, who suffered through the work that would become Orconomics before it had any economics and were still encouraging. Thank you to Charles Hang for sending and answering financial questions.

Thank you to my fellow authors for encouragement and inspiration. Thank you to Josh Cole for good chats and coffee. Thank you to Phil Tucker, TL Greylock, Mike Shel, Dyrk Ashton, Davis Ashura, AC Cobble,

M.L. Wang, Alec Hutson, Michael & Robin Sullivan, Matt Presley, John Bierce, and my many other friends in publishing.

Thank you to my family; my wife Becky, my lovely children Grace and Madelyn, my wonderful parents Dale and Carol, my sister Erin, my brother-in-law and friend Jacob, and their children Liam and Naomi, to Cindy, Danielle, Emma, and Jeff, to Uncle Bobby and Gary, Hillary, Elizabeth, and Christian, and to all those that I love whom are too numerous to mention.

Thank you to my patrons and most dedicated newsletter fans, many of whom suggested names for characters in this book.

- The infamous Shadow Stallions were given reader-submitted names. Team founder Jimmy Greensleeves was a bard played by Bobby Chatterjee in my short-lived newsletter RPG. Patron Brittany Wallace submitted fashion-questionable thief Forbiddance. Stu Reeve played Brooker of House Oscogen, though he neglected to wield a trout during the game. Patron Mason Murray submitted Mirara, only to find that I cut her language proficiencies down to "Great Eagle."

- The bard and cleric who helped Kaitha and crew take down the Swamp Hag of Fenrose Heath were reader submissions. Cleric Mirnen MacLeod was played by patron Jasmine Wahlberg in the newsletter RPG. Bard Ghunny Craftson was played by Tom Wright.

- Several of the ruffians who killed poor Hristo Hrurk were names for players of the newsletter RPG; Moxie Glum was played by Knut Ivar Hellsten, Kriss Rodgerson was played by Christopher Rodgers, and Drif Matuk was played by Chris Douglass.

- Hristo Hrurk himself was retroactively named after Hristo Kotsev, who runs my Bulgarian publisher Artline Studio. Behold the power of the Retconomicon!

- Geoff Griffin is a longtime reader and patron who suggested the names of three characters through multiple promotions. The idiomatic "Jack Cowfarmer" was inspired by a character he played in my newsletter RPG. Sister Erika, Quartermaster of Tandos, and Selena Wardroxan, student of omnimancy, were also submitted by Geoff.

- A couple of Jynn's other students used suggested names as well. Meryl Sabrin was played by Aleisha Kirby. Balorox Brightstar was played by Vijay Rampal.
- Izek Li'Balgar was named for the son of patron Victoria Balbes, who also—at least long ago—had a distaste for wearing hats.
- Jesh Watters was named for patron Josh Watters, who also repairs arcane devices.
- Nik Demilurge, Senior Vice President of Investment Banking at Consolidated Acquisitions Unlimited LLC, was once a cleric played by Nick Hohnstein.
- Kethador Lounala of the Giant Slayers was named for a character played by Keith Cohan.
- Sixth Age explorer of the Winter's Shade Weevil Half-Burrow was played by Mark Boettcher.
- Gnurg Slayer Great Zen was played by patron Scott Serbin.
- Davos Luria, the low-ranking pyromancer who nonetheless bested Laruna, was played by David Lurie.

To borrow from Tolkien, I don't update half of you as often as I should like, and I update less than half of you as often as you deserve. Your support means more than you know.

Finally, thank you to all of my readers. I published Orconomics determined to finish the trilogy no matter how many readers I had. On the other side of it, I am certain that thousands of readers enjoying my work and engaging with me has been a key factor in finishing The Dark Profit Saga, and I am eternally grateful for it.

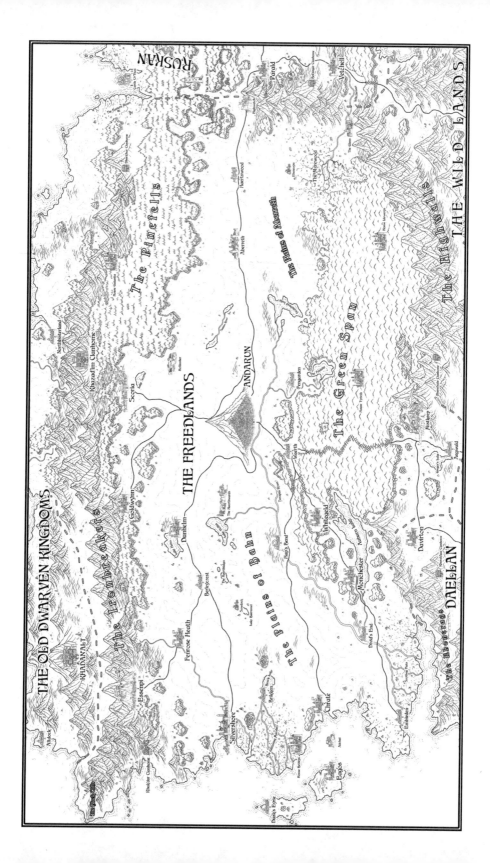

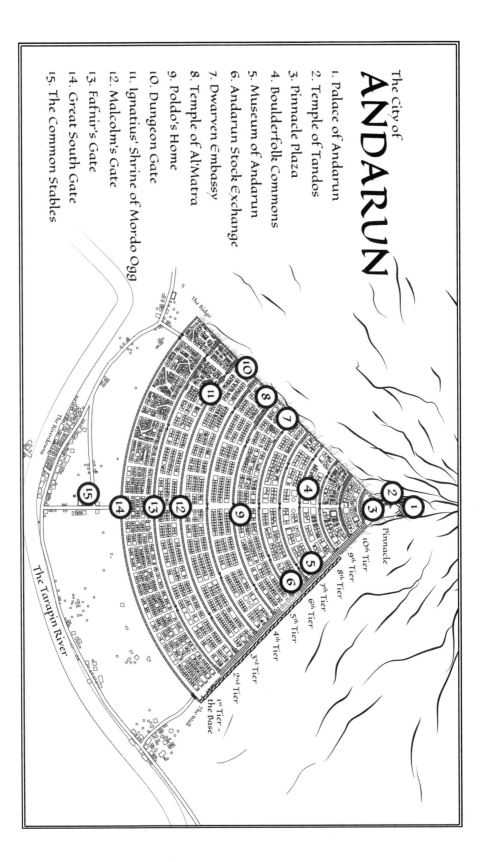

The City of
ANDARUN

To

Becky.

Rebecca to those who aren't close, a treasure to those who are.

Especially me.

──PROLOGUE──

The destinies of mortals flow like water droplets down a window. Fates splash together in short, staccato spurts, rivulets gaining momentum as they merge with others until they rush down in rivers toward a foregone conclusion.

In the case of the water droplets, said inevitability was to spatter against the moldering sill of the window of Jerald Fisher's room. In the case of Jerald Fisher, it was an untimely death.

Jerald could not sleep on the night he met his fate, as he had a lot to do in the morning. The contact had put in a last-minute request to push the meeting until tomorrow, but that conflicted with his other plans. Jerald had other things to do early in the morning. The horses needed to be saddled, the rent for his room needed to be settled, and—most critically—he needed to get out of thrice-cursed Sowdock.

On a map of the Freedlands, Sowdock was a speck on the shore of a smudge between the Haerthwards and House Bethlyn. Its population barely met the qualifications for a hamlet. A handful of villagers eked out a living dragging fish in from the murky depths of Lake Baerussel, while a small band of armed Tinderkin were paid by the Dunhelm Fish Company to keep away bandits and wandering monsters. A pair of House Gnomes ran a small tavern that sold ale and home-brewed liquor to the mercenaries. They kept a spare room above the stills to rent to travelers imprudent enough to attempt a direct route from Hap's Bend to Silvershore. Judging by the geological stratifications of dust that covered the tiny apartment, Jerald was the first such fool in a long time.

Still, it suited Jerald's purposes. Since fleeing Andarun, he never stayed anywhere for more than a few nights, and Sowdock made the practice easy. Tonight marked his fifth evening in the hamlet and, consistent with Nove's principles of universal irony, he was sure it would be his last.

Jerald glanced over the ciphered note again, the sharp letters written in thick, straight strokes. His own translation was written in flowing script next to it. "Delayed by complications. Meet tomorrow," Jerald muttered. Tomorrow was too late.

The mercenaries had told him that another traveler had been seen at Sowdock's edge two days ago, and they'd found three more sets of hoofprints out of town. It could have been a coincidence, of course. But the coincidences were piling up, as were the bodies. What was left of them anyway.

It started when Jerald learned that the Great Eagle had disappeared. The Agekeepers wanted to interview the bird who had carried both King Johan and his predecessor at the moment of King Handor's demise. It was for their histories on the fall of Highwatch, Brother Arturan had said. Yet when they went to locate the bird, they found that the eagle had died in a dragon attack shortly after Johan's coronation.

The Agekeeper's tip had the stench of malfeasance about it, an intoxicating aroma to any good journalist. A veteran town crier operating on Andarun's Second Tier, Jerald followed his nose and started asking around. True to the old Agekeeper's word, he confirmed that the eagle that carried King Handor and Johan the Mighty on the late king's final flight had gone missing. Yet, before Jerald could pen his script for the morning's cry, the dragon struck again, immolating a farmstead on the outskirts of Andarun, and with it the woman who translated for the eagle's union.

This was something big, big enough to mean a small fortune and moving up a tier or three for the town crier who figured it out. Jerald enlisted a couple of apprentice hollermen to help him uncover the truth. Medina got a tip that a bannerman who saw Handor fall took his own tumble off the New South Gate. Pinderman found out that the nestkeeper at the eagle's aerie drowned in the Tarapin. They were definitely onto something.

And then, suddenly, they were in the middle of something.

Pinderman disappeared one day without a trace. Medina left a trace, or—more accurately—a residue on the cobblestones. The thrice-cursed dragon must have caught her walking home late at night; her neighbors heard a reptilian roar and a scream before the alley outside her apartment went up in flames.

Their disappearances helped Jerald see the big picture a little more clearly, and it was a sign pointing out of town. He moved from hamlet to hamlet under a false name, avoiding bannermen, parties of heroes, or anyone else who might want to check his NPC papers. Two days out of the city, he overheard a barmaid tell a traveler that the Dragon of Wynspar had torched the Agekeeper's Cloister at Waerth. Jerald had a sure bet as to the whereabouts of Brother Arturan at the time.

The old town crier sucked his teeth as he looked over the note. How much did he trust this contact? His mysterious benefactor had promised him safe passage to Silvershore and a set of forged NPC papers. That was enough to secure passage on a boat down to Highport or Knifevale, which was the best chance he had of seeing another holiday. But if the contact couldn't come through on the promises, or worse, was lying...

Jerald made up his mind and grabbed his rucksack. He'd leave a ciphered note at the meeting spot before dawn, and let the contact know the deal was off. He spared a sheet of vellum and an old quill for the purpose as he shoved his notes and journals back into the bag. He'd need to hire a fisherman to carry him across the lake and risk a day's travel through the wilds, but hopefully be back on the road by the weekend. It was a good plan, a plan with no reason to fail, and a plan that he desperately needed to work, all of which, unfortunately, made it a plan on a collision course with Nove's principles of universal irony.

Written by the greatest of the Fifth Age's philosopher-scientists, Nove's theories sought to explain the nature of irony in the universe through mathematical formulas. His work led to his famous principles of universal irony, laid out in several seminal works across a long and storied career. Nove's penultimate work on the subject, the *Omnibus Defectum*, laid out the mathematics that doomed Jerald Fisher's plan, and with it Jerald Fisher.

Nove's fourth principle of universal irony proved, by way of substitution, that planning increases the possibility of an unforeseen outcome. This was widely recognized well before Nove's time; an old Tinderkin proverb said that every wedding held at least one disaster, and the best anyone could hope for was that it wasn't the choice of spouse. Yet it was Nove who first mathematically proved that the old adage held true precisely because so many people put so much planning into weddings. The great philosopher-scientist demonstrated that planning builds expectations for things to go right, which proportionally increases the ironic potential for things that go wrong. Blocking off avenues for expected problems only creates the sort of ironic ripples in the fabric of reality that lead to truly spectacular misfortunes, whether in wedding planning, military exercises, or—unfortunately for Jerald—desperate escapes.

Perhaps if Jerald had kept Nove's principles in mind, he would have done the sensible thing and grabbed his bag, made a comment about how doomed he was, and fled into the night. Yet, the town crier was too busy plotting his course and considering possible risks to mitigate, right up until an unholy shriek rent the night air. A second later, there was a thunderous whumph, like the gods' own fireplace igniting, and orange light washed into the room through the shed's lone window.

Jerald rushed to the glass pane and looked out into the night. The inn was burning impossibly fast; the thatch of its roof was already an inferno. A couple of flaming mercenaries ran screaming for the lake. The shadow of something sinuous flitted past the moon.

He was found. The thrice-cursed dragon was here.

With a desperate cry, Jerald grabbed his satchel and burst out of the doorway. Heat and smoke stung his eyes as he sprinted through the burning hamlet with all the strength in his legs. A reptilian screech echoed above, but the town crier could go no faster with the satchel weighing him down. He hurled the bag of notes into a thicket of bushes, planning to retrieve it once the creature was gone. He still had a chance, as long as he could reach the safety of Lake Baerussel's chilly waters. The lake lay like a black mirror just ahead of him, gleaming with the orange light of the flames, drawing closer with every frantic step.

Then something above Jerald roared, and a startled voice from above screamed a curse. He looked up in time to see something oblong and trailing flames fall from the sky, illuminating a pair of leathery wings and a face that seemed more teeth than scales. The burning projectile hit the ground and erupted in a bloom of white-hot flames that washed over the town crier and drowned out his final scream.

—CHAPTER 1—

A tormented howl echoed through the mists of the mire. In the thick fog, the deep wail seemed to come from all directions at once. It carried notes of menace and agony in equal measure; the sort of baying that made night watchmen stand at the ready, prompted children to pull the covers over their eyes, and reminded late-night travelers why inns on the Heath could get away with charging such exorbitant rates.

"Ohhhhhhh..."

Yet the ominous howl held no fear for the robed figures huddled amidst the standing stones. Twelve mossy obelisks rose from the swamp like the jagged teeth of a long-dead titan; six shadowy figures lurked between the stones in a way that suggested said titan could have done better with its flossing. Sconces ringed the stone circle, cradling green flames that danced to the rhythm of the hooded figures' chant.

"Come... come... come... come..."

As they spoke, the infernal howl became a moan, dropping in pitch even as it grew in volume.

"Ooooohhhhhhh..."

As the moaning approached the circle, the robed figures' chant changed and accelerated in response.

"Come and see! Come and see! Come and see!"

Now something tall and grotesque was taking shape in the dark mists: a hulking shadow against the moonlit gray. It shuffled its bloated and bulbous form forward on thick legs. Tattered rags covered most of it, but what graying flesh was visible was pocked with boils and open sores. One crimson eye shone from beneath a mass of oily hair. It grinned, its smile like a barricade of sharp, blackened teeth.

"Ohhhh!" the hag moaned.

One of the congregants, a stout figure in an ill-fitting robe, shuffled aside to part the group and reveal what lay at the center of the ritual circle: a tiny bassinet. The chanting grew in insistent fervor. *"Come! Come and partake of thy dark need!"*

"Ohhhh!" The monster scuttled into the circle with sudden, unnatural speed, looming over the bassinet. The tiny figure swaddled within shook and whimpered. *"Ohhhh... I really shouldn't!"*

"Oh, thou must," intoned the robed figures. *"Partake of thy dark need."*

The bloated monstrosity hovered over the bassinet, talons waving at the ends of her long, spindly arms. "Oh no! I couldn't," she croaked. "I been eatin' too much as is, and I'm supposed to be watchin' my figure."

The robed figures intoned the next part of the ritual automatically, *"What speakest thou? Thou lookest wondrous. Partake as it pleases thee!"*

"Well, I wouldn't want to be a bother!"

"It is for thou that such was prepared. Partake!"

A hungry light flared in the creature's eye. "Well, if you insist..."

"Nothing could please us more. Help thyself," they responded.

A clawed hand peeled back the blanket of the bassinet, revealing a face like a bug-eyed weasel with a skin condition. "Eh?" gasped the hag, reeling back at the sight of an unexpected Kobold scurrying away from the bassinet.

"We got her!" shouted Burt as he fled.

The hag screamed in fury, rearing back. A crackle of dark energy bloomed around her outstretched hand, then dissipated in a flash of silver and crimson as a streak of light rent her palm in two.

"Take her down!" cried Kaitha of House Tyrieth, her hood pulled back to reveal a copper-skinned face framed by auburn locks. The Elven ranger had already nocked and drawn another enchanted arrow.

The hag lashed out in retaliation, a hateful sneer barely covering her jagged teeth. A blast of orange flame interrupted her strike and lit several of her oily rags alight. The creature fell back with a wail, its baleful eye seeking the source of the fire. They fell upon Laruna Trullon, who was already readying another blast of fire.

Sneering, the monster reached for the solamancer with a clawed hand. It drew back when twin flashes of steel severed several of its outstretched talons. Gaist, free of his disguise and wearing his signature black cape and red scarf, launched another flurry of blows with twin short swords.

"This is entrapment!" the hag shrieked. She clutched the stump where her hand had been with her remaining, mangled appendage. "I ain't eaten no baby! And I wouldn't 'ave, 'cept you offered!"

"What about teenagers?" shouted Laruna.

The hag's lone eye had a hunted look. "Only bad ones!" she protested, searching for some sympathy. Finding none, she turned to flee.

Unfortunately for the monster, the other false cultists were joining in the attack now. A cleric in silver armor raised her hand, and an intricate circle drawn in golden light bloomed on the ground around the monster. The lines and runes forming the ring thrummed with power as the monster neared them, and she staggered back as though she had run into a wall.

A robed bard—pink-skinned, sandy-haired and bespectacled—had produced a lute from the depths of his robes and now played with enthusiastic vigor, though beyond his confidence there was no clear sign this was having any effect.

The final cultist, the stout one with the ill-fitting robes, flipped up his arms to throw off his garments. Unfortunately, the uncooperative clothing tangled above his head, and he staggered to the side with a muffled swear, clutching at the billowing fabric uselessly.

His absence made little difference. Swords sang. Silver arrows flashed like lightning amidst clouds of enchanted flame. Holy magic flared with divine light. The lute added ambiance. By the time the unlucky hero finally struggled out of his oversized disguise, the swamp hag was little more than a steaming pile of rags and gore.

"Thrice-cursed bones!" swore Gorm Ingerson, throwing his robes into the muck.

"All right, so it wasn't great for a first quest back," Kaitha conceded as the midmorning sun burned the last of the fog away.

"It was a bloody disaster," Gorm grumbled. The Dwarf perched on a toppled standing stone, nursing a tin mug of coffee and a wounded ego as he watched the guild at work. What had been a ritual ring and then a bloody battlefield was now a labor camp, mere hours after the death of the Swamp Hag of Fenrose Heath. Guild clerks and carters swarmed over the monster's corpse like ants over a fallen beetle. The workers wore smithing leathers, vented masks, and thick goggles to protect them from noxious fumes and residual sorcery as they searched for every last scrap of loot.

"You got that right," said Burt, leaning against the stone by Gorm's feet. One paw held a tiny mug of coffee, the other clutched the smoldering remnants of a damp cigarette.

"We did a lot of good," Kaitha insisted. "We exposed the corrupt aldermen's smuggling ring, tracked down their connections in the evil cult of Nuryot Sabbat, apprehended their High Circle, and killed their patron hag. That's good work."

"Aye, ye did all that." Gorm wasn't about to let recent triumphs foil a good sour mood.

"Look, I'm sorry about the robe," said Kaitha. "But it turned out all right. We just learn from our mistakes and move on."

"Oh? And what did ye learn?" asked Gorm.

His acerbic sarcasm eroded Kaitha's resolute smile a bit. "I meant, maybe next time you could just fight in the disguise."

"Next time I ain't doin' the burnin' henchmen uniform ruse."

"You got the right side of that wand, buddy," said Burt. "At least nobody asked you to be the bait."

"I still don't understand your problem with the henchmen uniform ruse," said Kaitha. "It's a classic."

"It ain't just the ruse... it's all of it." Gorm grimaced. "It's different than it used to be. Decipherin' coded letters. Investigatin' who's shippin' what where. Gettin' all political and caught up in power struggles. And then a game of mummer's masks."

"It's an intrigue quest," said Kaitha. "Most of them are these days. A little more research, some extra running around, maybe brush up on dialogue and persuasion skills, but it's not that different."

The Dwarf swigged his coffee and watched a trio of guild carters carefully excavate the swamp hag's purse. "Used to be ye just did your paperwork and then went down some hole swingin' your axe. Maybe that's what I'm good at."

"Now you're just moping," Kaitha told him.

"Look at this quest, running around chasin' them cultists. I barely helped at all. I was the most useless member of the party."

Someone cleared their throat behind them. They turned to find the sandy-haired bard, smiling and cleaning his glasses.

"Second most useless," Gorm whispered to Burt.

Kaitha hushed him before addressing the hero. "Leaving already, Ghunny?"

"Aye." Ghunny Craftson's Scorian accent was almost as thick as Gorm's. "There's rumors of owlverines or Dire Badgers hittin' the farmlands north of Fenrose Heath. Somethin' big and hairy and in need of killing. MacLeod and I are hopin' to beat the rush."

He jabbed a thumb over his shoulder at Mirnen. The dark-haired cleric of Musana led two saddled and packed horses up behind the bard. "The solamancer said you wouldn't be interested, but we wanted to give you the chance to make some easy coin and rank."

"We'll pass," said Gorm. "We've business on the way back to Andarun."

"Fair enough," said the bard. "Well, wherever ye go, be sure to tell them our deeds. We'll sing yer praises as well. Social proof an' all. Key to buildin' a brand!"

"Ye're under no obligation," Gorm called after the retreating pair, earning him an elbow in the ribs.

"All right, what was all that about?" Kaitha demanded once the other heroes were out of earshot.

"Most overrated bard I've met, which is a feat," Gorm said. "I'd rather not have such singin' anything about me good name."

"Not that. What is all this moping about how your skills aren't up for this?" said the Elf. "I've seen you chase a hint of intrigue halfway across a continent. We took down a thrice-cursed liche last year, and that quest was about as straightforward as a landshark's burrow. You can say you were rusty on your first time hitting the quest board in years, or say you were off your game, but don't pretend it's a lack of guile or cunning," Kaitha told him. "That's ridiculous."

"And I hope you ain't really longing for the old days of runnin' blindly down a burrow, axe swingin'," added Burt. "Speaking as a friend whose family comes from down said burrow."

Gorm took a deep breath, another sip of coffee, and a moment to weigh their words. "Fair enough. I just... I just thought last year would go different."

His mind trod familiar paths through recent history. The berserker known as Pyrebeard had enjoyed wealth and renown over the course of his career, but he'd thought the course of that career ended decades ago. Much more recently, he was promised a return to his former glory in exchange for running a quest with the Al'Matrans. It turned out the job was a sham perpetuated by Johan the Mighty, Champion of Tandos. After he watched the guild slaughter an innocent tribe of Orcs and murder his friends, Gorm and his companions fled into the wilderness. They uncovered a liche's plot, allied with the scattered Shadowkin tribes, and redeemed themselves by saving the Freedlands from an undead army. Riding high on the wings of such success, Gorm swore to bring down King Johan and the guild's corrupt regime.

And then the world had politely coughed and turned back to the way things were.

"We were supposed to fight Johan," he said. "We were supposed to all be in this together."

Kaitha sighed. "We are in this together."

"Then how are we questin' again?" Gorm asked. "How are we back to bein' worried about a career, and findin' loot, and slaughterin' monsters?"

"We proved that hag was guilty," Kaitha interjected.

"Aye, we did the quest." The Dwarf waved away the point like an irritating gnat. "But we're trackin' hags, not takin' on the king. How is it we're workin' for the guild again?"

"People still need protecting," Kaitha said, "regardless of who runs the Freedlands."

"Aye, I know... I just..." Gorm sighed, unwilling or unable to have the same argument again.

He'd expected a big confrontation with the king. He'd spent the first month after the liche's defeat preparing for a climactic showdown. For half a year, he was wound tighter than a coiled spring, waiting for Johan to make a critical misstep. He'd plotted with Asherzu, the new chieftain of the Guz'Varda Tribe, to find or plan the maneuver that would expose the king's evil scheme. Through it all, Gorm was certain that no adversity could crush their resolve.

Instead, a steady stream of peaceful, mundane days had slowly eroded it.

"Johan is popular." Kaitha sighed. "He's rebuilding the city. The economy is coming back. You can't 'save' a kingdom from a monarch that it wants."

Gorm shook his head. "This ain't about popularity and money."

"Most things are," said Burt with a shrug.

"Things are changing," Kaitha insisted. "I mean, look. Burt came on a guild quest, and nobody has tried to kill him."

"Unless you count that whole 'monster bait' scheme," the Kobold grumbled.

The Elf ignored the remark. "Progress is slow, but that doesn't mean it isn't happening. It just takes little steps."

"This ain't about a toddler learnin' to walk! It's about fighting!" Gorm said. "I didn't think we'd be done by now, but I sure as drake spit didn't think we'd be running guild quests while Johan eats tea cakes on the throne. I never imagined the Shadowkin would go corporate! I don't know how it ends, but I swore I'd see this through. For Tib'rin and Niln."

"We're here, ain't we?" Burt's hackles were up. "Lady Asherzu has other priorities, Lightling, but she sent me to help you and advise you and, apparently, to be monster bait. And I got you that lead on some info about Johan, right?"

"We just passed up that owlverine job so we can investigate it," said Kaitha. "We're still with you, Gorm. But we can't ignore life beyond this... this need for justice."

"Aye." Gorm gave a sad sigh and nodded. "But I can't move beyond it. I ain't got time in the day or fire in me belly for anything else." He looked at the dead hag. The crone may have been Human once, or even a Gnome, but long years of service to Mannon's demons had warped and twisted her into a giant monster. "Even for the good stuff. So aye, my whole heart ain't been in this quest. I'm distracted. And by Khazen's Shield, I'll never understand how anyone else can be otherwise knowin' that bastard's on the throne."

Kaitha bit back a retort and let it out as a low hiss through gritted teeth. "I understand how you feel," she said. "I hope Burt's new informant can help."

"Only one way to find out," Burt said, stamping out the final embers of his cigarette.

"Aye," said Gorm. "How soon can we leave?"

Kaitha shrugged. "The field paperwork is done, and this is Mirnen's gig, so she'll handle arbitration. I think we can leave as soon as we round up the other two."

They looked across the worksite at the other members of their party. "Gaist looks set to go," Gorm said, nodding to the weaponsmaster standing motionless next to their horses.

"And the mage?" asked Burt.

Their collective gaze swiveled to the lone figure on the far side of the swamp, orange robes obscured in the cloud of steam that rose around her. The air above her flickered with heat and occasional tongues of flame.

Kaitha sighed. "I'll go check in on her."

"We need to talk." The sprite spoke in a high, tinny voice straining to get to the bottom of its range, like a mouse trying to do an impression of a lion.

Laruna Trullon glared at the tiny messenger hovering in front of her, squinting in the pink glare. There was a humanoid figure no taller than her little finger somewhere amid the light, but it shone so brightly when it was delivering its message that it looked like a tiny star with wings.

Billows of steam rose up from the water around them, vaporized by the sorcerous heat rolling off the furious mage.

"Throndar has been doing a lot of thinking," the sprite continued. "Throndar cares very deeply for you."

Laruna rolled her eyes as she seethed. Throndar's barbaric habit of referring to himself in the third person made it sound like the magical messenger was engaging in gossip rather than reciting his own words.

"Yet Throndar has seen the signs now. When you skip out on an ox Throndar slaughtered for the one-month anniversary of our meeting, you show you do not value him. When you make fun of him for caring about our one-month anniversary, you show Throndar that his feelings do not matter to you. And when you get angry with Throndar for expressing this, you show him that you are not ready for a relationship."

The solamancer's fists clenched so tightly that her nails bit into her palms, the curse on her tongue held back behind clenched teeth.

"You will probably call Throndar names. You will say he is weak. Throndar of the Plains of Ice is not weak! He is aware of his feelings and, more importantly, the impact of his feelings upon others."

Laruna bit her lip. She wasn't going to call him names. She had screamed a few choice insults the first time she'd heard the recording, but now that she knew the barbarian had predicted as much, she wasn't about to give the universe the satisfaction.

"Throndar did not wish to do this over the magic talking lights, but Throndar wishes a lot of things were different, and you are seldom here. Throndar hopes you will find what—"

"Are you still listening to that?"

Laruna's eyes swiveled to where Kaitha stood several yards away, though the afterimage of the glowing sprite was a large purplish blotch in the middle of her vision. "He broke up with me using a messenger sprite," she growled.

"Two weeks ago," Kaitha said. "And listen, don't take this the wrong way, but didn't Hogarth end things with you the same way?"

"No, he just ran off and left a note," said Laruna. "Most of them do. You're thinking of Gord of the Fjord."

"Yes, that must be it," said the Elf diplomatically. "My point is, you've let more than a few barbarians slip away over the course of the year, and it's never seemed to particularly bother you."

"Yes, well, Throndar was different," Laruna protested.

Kaitha raised an eyebrow. "Was he?"

The solamancer's mind briefly became a slideshow of well-oiled abdominal muscles, tiny fur loincloths, and windswept mullets. She searched for the difference that set her latest barbarian apart and, after some introspection, found it had nothing to do with Throndar at all. "I didn't make it into any of the circles again," she muttered.

"What?"

"There are thirty-six circles with a pyromantic focus, from the Circle of the Unbound Phoenix all the way down to the Circle of the Errant Candle. Joining one is the easiest way to become a pyromancer. And those stuck-up, self-loving sons of gorgons... well, I couldn't get into any of them." It took conscious effort for the mage to unclench her fists and let out a long sigh. "I failed another trial a couple of days before we left."

"Oh, Laruna. I'm so sorry." Kaitha gingerly made her way across the steaming turf to embrace her friend. "But that doesn't make any sense. You wield fire better than any other mage I've ever seen."

"No, I weave more fire than any other mage," Laruna said. "But the trial isn't to conjure a lot of flames. It's to take the fire away from another pyromancer—pull it from their hand, or redirect a spell, or even just draw heat from the weave around them. And I couldn't even take the flame from thrice-cursed Davos Luria."

Kaitha smiled helplessly at the name.

"The acolyte attendant of the Circle of the Errant Candle—the lowest-ranked pyromancer on Arth. He can barely conjure sufficient fire to fry an egg, but what little he has, I couldn't take." Laruna ground her teeth at the memory, and flames flickered in the air around her head.

Kaitha took a discreet but meaningful step back.

"Sorry," said the solamancer, willing the fire away. "Taking the flame from a pyromancer is like trying to dig out a sandpit with a stick. I was out of my mind after Davos failed me. That's why I blew off Throndar's anniversary cow roast."

"I suppose that makes sense," said the ranger. "I know that must hurt. But the first part of healing is moving past it. So let the sprite go, and then let the matter go—"

"And then I just move on?" Laruna asked. "Just like that?"

"In one sense. In another, we all do," Kaitha said with a grin. "The horses are ready. Let's not let troubles with men distract us from work."

The solamancer nodded, pushed down her lurking anger, and dismissed the messenger sprite with a word and a wave of her hand. It winked out of existence with a tiny sigh, taking Throndar's farewell with it. Together, the mage and the Elf headed back toward the horses. A thought occurred to Laruna as they passed the loot team's sorting table and its array of distressingly moist treasures. "Speaking of troubles with men..."

Kaitha's face hardened. "I was specifically speaking of not getting distracted by them."

"Fair enough, but I wondered if we should ask around with all these guild workers here." Laruna nodded to a cluster of clerks. "They hear a lot, and they might help with your search. Gorm said that people saw a Troll walking around Chrate a few months ago."

"I'm not searching," said the Elf forcefully. "I'm done. I've moved on."

Laruna shook her head. "I know you're angry, but he's our friend."

"Is he?" Kaitha asked. "I mean, I made a mess of things, but do you realize what I did trying to find him and tell him I'm sorry? I was the one who told Gorm about Chrate, and we went there for a month. I went to the Myrewood three times. The mountains, the desert, the Pinefells—I searched everywhere, and followed every lead. I gave up so much to tell him I'm..." She caught herself and looked down at her wrists, clad in simple leather bracers. "It's apparent that he's moved past our... whatever it was. I need to move on as well."

"Maybe," said Laruna.

"No, definitely." The Elf swung her hand in an emphatic chop, as if to physically cut the debate short. "He didn't show up, Laruna. I asked him to, I needed him to, and he wasn't there. That's how you know someone is... someone cares. They're there when you need them to be. When it's really important, and you really need them, they show up."

Laruna recalled the kind Troll, and the steadfast protection he'd provided them in the wilderness. "He did show up, many times," she suggested. "Maybe now he just doesn't know you're trying."

Kaitha winced, stung by the idea. "Maybe." She gave a hopeless shrug. "But after a while, it's just too hard to chase someone that doesn't want to be found. It's over." The Elf's declaration was meant to sound final, but a tremble in her voice betrayed her. "It's over," she said again.

"Oh, why can't lovers ever be together? Why does fate conspire against them? Why are the gods so cruel?" Queen Marja of Andarun wailed these rhetorical questions at a pitch that made the crystal chandelier hum and set teeth on edge. Yet the eruption was as short as it was shrill, and moments later Her Highness sank back into the strata of silk throws and cushions that covered the royal couch. The queen's eyes remained locked on the pages of *The Gnomish Knave* by Tayelle Adamantine, her lips moving with a faint hint of a whisper as she read.

Preya Havenbrook, royal baker and Marja's most trusted aide, didn't need to hear the monarch's words to know what they said. She stood silently next to the queen's couch, patiently holding a silver tray with a filigreed cloche. It wouldn't be long now, judging by Marja's place in the latest book.

Preya could time her day by the pages. The contours of the queen's favored stories all fit into the same, well-worn groove. Early in the book the protagonist and the object of her desire—this time a Scribkin duchess and a Tinderkin rogue—experienced an instant and undeniable attraction. Their lust was invariably complicated by circumstances such as prior engagements, other lovers, disapproving families, ongoing wars, infernal magic or—in the infamously complex *The Warlock's Daughter*—all of the above. Yet it was never too many chapters before the lovers found themselves alone in a bedchamber, a barn, or some other conveniently private location to consummate their acquaintance.

As intense as the encounter was for the reader, it was invariably fatal for Adamantine's characters. A sudden interruption would follow the private encounter with clockwork regularity. This led to a prolonged period of devoted pining, leading to a penultimate moment of hope when fate seemed to be about to allow the lovers their happiness. This glimmer of optimism always heralded some fatal misunderstanding, tragic confusion, insidious deception, or a patriarchal sorcerer hurling fireballs from the back of a manticore—it must be said that *The Warlock's Daughter* stood out in many ways as a marked departure for the author.

Whatever the misfortune, Preya knew the outcome. It should be arriving any page now.

"No!" shrieked Marja. "Not Willam!"

Preya had studied patisserie under the notoriously strict Ovenmaster Barzi Ur'Plante, who was said to keep his kitchen so clean you could eat off the plates. Technically, the floors were probably also clean enough to eat from, but nobody would ever dare utter it for fear that word of the joke might be overheard by the ovenmaster. Seven years at the baking academy under Ur'Plante's iron gaze had given Preya just enough discipline to not roll her eyes at the queen's shock.

Of course Willam was dead. One of the lovers always died by chapter fifteen. The only thing left was for young what's-her-name to realize that Willam had become Will-was, wax poetic about what would never be, and then take her own life.

The appeal of books about lovelorn suicide was a mystery to Preya. She and Mr. Havenbrook loved each other of course; it took a lot of love to stay together for thirty years and three children. They'd saved enough to buy a little cottage on Drakehead Lake and planned to retire there together. Certainly she'd grieve if the fates took her husband before their plans came to fruition, but a few months in a black veil after a modest funeral would be the extent of it; nobody would catch Preya Havenbrook yelling for a poisonous snake or a vial of nightshade. She'd take that retirement money and get herself a little apartment on the Teagem Sea, where the wine flowed freely and was poured by well-tanned young people in grass skirts. No doubt Mr. Havenbrook would pursue a similar hypothetical course of action should the fates be cruel, and good for him.

The characters in Ms. Adamantine's books lacked this pragmatism. Invariably they would decide life couldn't be endured without the person they'd just met a few weeks ago and turn grieving into a terminal exercise. It was for this particular reason that Preya was in the royal chambers and not the palace kitchens. She noticed a fatal-looking soliloquy on the pages of the queen's book and readied her cloche.

"Oh, why? Duchess Anne," sighed Marja. "Why?" She set the book down with one hand, while the other probed the air next to her. Her thick fingers found a couple of chocolate walnut tea cakes on Preya's waiting tray.

The royal baker kept her head bowed. Her thoughts wandered past the guttural sounds of her morning's work going the way of Willam and Anne. For Marja, the tea cakes were as much a part of the book as the love scenes or inevitable suicide, and she expected them to arrive with the same precision timing.

Preya startled when the queen suddenly stopped eating: judging by the weight, at least half a tray of tea cakes remained on her platter. With more than a little worry, Preya risked a glance at the queen and asked. "Do the cakes not please you today, Majesty?"

Marja's face was cinched up like a drawstring bag, her mouth a tiny pout amid an expanse of caked foundation, running mascara, and chocolate walnut crumbs. Her red-rimmed eyes glared across the room.

Preya looked to see what had drawn the queen's ire, but the chamber opposite the couch was empty save for a lady-in-waiting trying to shuffle out of the queen's field of view.

Yet Marja didn't notice her staff's unease. "Life isn't fair," she said aloud.

"Indeed, Majesty," said Preya, and meant it.

"My Johan was supposed to be here today," the queen said.

Preya was well aware. Had the king been sequestered with Marja in the royal chambers, the royal baker could have spent the day working on plans for Alluna's festival next month. Yet Johan had sent his apologies—again—sending Marja back to her novels and Preya back to the kitchen.

"Have I lost his eye?" she wondered aloud.

"Oh no, Majesty." Preya joined the chorus of ladies-in-waiting denying the king's lost interest. This was sincere as well; the king's passion for his wife was infamous. The two could scarcely pass in the hall without creating a scene that would make Tayelle Adamantine herself blush. Such frequent and uninhibited displays of affection were shocking to most of the royal staff, most of whom had grown accustomed to royal marriages that were appropriately chilly and distant. The maids had a system of knocks and taps on the walls they used to track the movements of the royals and ensure that no unfortunate staff members got stuck in a room with the young newlyweds.

Mr. Havenbrook and Preya had enjoyed a similarly vigorous time in their marriage, back in her day. Yet Preya's mother told her once that even the most pure and unassailable feelings had to change over time; that the metamorphosis of passion to devotion didn't happen in spite of true love, but because of it. Love was the granite core of her marriage, the rock-hard center left over after a steady stream of long nights working, changing diapers, and bickering over bills had eroded the passion. Preya had once assumed that this shift was inevitable, though the queen's books forced her to acknowledge that such love could also be cut short by a double suicide or a murderous warlock riding a monster.

"Well then, why does he stay away?" pouted Marja. "Why is he off with all of those heroes and stodgy businessmen?"

None of the assembled women were dumb enough to answer that. Preya gave a helpless shrug. Everyone knew the king needed to attend to his duties. The Heroes' Guild needed help contending with the Red Horde and an active dragon. Business leaders required attention to matters of the economy. The king personally attended work on his top-secret project in the rearmost chambers of the Royal Archives, built in the mountain itself—the ones even the maids were forbidden from visiting.

Yet the queen took such mundane tasks as an affront. Once trapped in an unhappy marriage to the late King Handor, Marja had withdrawn from the world into an endless parade of romance novels, where heroes were always swarthy, bosoms constantly heaved, and love subjugated the laws of nature and bent history to its whim until it drove its victims to suicide. King Handor's death and Johan's proposal had given the queen the chance to return to reality, but it was apparent that Marja would prefer that reality come and visit her romantic fantasies.

Preya thanked the gods that true love wasn't that way, but there was no helping someone who wanted it to be. Just as Marja's steady diet of tea cakes had left her with the figure of a walrus, the queen's addiction to romantic tragedies had left her unable to find any joy in a relationship that wasn't either in a state of melancholy desire, simmering tension, or wild abandon. Johan's distraction was intolerable to the queen—almost more so than her loveless marriage to Handor. At least a chilled marriage gave Johan a plausible reason to not show up whenever she longed for him to come and ravish her.

"Why does he stay away?" A single tear carved a gorge through Marja's makeup as she read aloud from her book. "Wherever could he be? 'Tis not just his absence that pierces my heart; 'tis the question of whether his heart still beats for me, or whether it still beats at all. Oh ignorance! Oh mystery! You cut at me as a knife! I cannot bear not knowing!"

—CHAPTER 2—

Ignorance is a commodity.

In any economy where knowledge has value, ignorance does as well. Brokers make money by knowing key information; they make fortunes by ensuring that other brokers remain unaware or unsure of the same information until after critical trades. Governments rise and fall based on the careful cultivation and utilization of mass ignorance. The wealthy and powerful pay handsomely for secret messages, opaque business structures, or secure locations. And no location was more secure than Adchul.

The ancestral home of Arth's most elite lawyer-monks perched atop a crag of rock jutting from the ocean halfway between Eagos and Chrate. Most of the island was surrounded by the monastery's formidable walls, hewn from the same black granite as the sea-swept stones around it. Yet the isolated location, treacherous currents, and imposing fortifications didn't give the fortress of Adchul its unmatched reputation for seclusion; rather, ancient rites and clauses of attorney-client privilege and universal nondisclosure shielded the monastery's inhabitants. Any crystal ball or scrying pool set to peer at a spot within three miles of the island would only display a curt cease and desist notice.

Behind high walls and safely cocooned offshore in an impossibly complex web of shell companies, limited liability entities, and corporate structures, the lawyer-monks' tenants were completely insulated from any outside threat—murderous, sorcerous, or litigious. It was perfect protection, provided you could pay for it.

Or, Duine Poldo reflected, provided they'd let you stay.

The Scribkin stared glumly out the window of his chamber. The sparse furnishings and bare stone walls suggested that it was the sort of accommodation that normally came with a set of striped leisure wear, included bread crusts and water, and offered daily entertainment that mostly involved hitting rocks with hammers. The window offered a view that was only marginally improved: black seas roiling beneath a gray sky all the way to the horizon.

"How long do you think we have?" he asked without turning.

A Wood Gnome wearing a red squirrel's pelt squeaked by way of answer. The Gnomes of Clan Fengeld, or Domovoy, communicated with taller folk using a dialect of Imperial that was actually nuanced, complex and— Poldo had been surprised to discover—copiously laced with profanity and lewd remarks. Usually most of this subtlety and swears were lost in translation, in part because a Wood Gnome's tiny voice sounded like a nest full of baby birds to anyone larger than a household rodent, but mostly because many people considered Domovoy to be a more destructive variety of household rodent.

Still, after all this time working with the Wood Gnomes, Poldo was able to understand them well enough. "A week will not do," he said. "The sailing will be too difficult by then, and we won't catch a boat. If we can't stay until spring, then we'll have to catch a boat by tomorrow."

Another Wood Gnome piped in.

"Yes, I'm sure they are aware of that," said Poldo sourly.

A third Wood Gnome, a woman wearing a brown rat's skin, chittered something and thrust her fist in the air.

Poldo blanched. "Well, I... I, ah, I probably wouldn't phrase it as such."

Brown Rat repeated herself emphatically.

"Where would you even get a cucumber that large? But, ah, no—look, I appreciate the, ah, the sentiment. We are all frustrated with the lawyer-monks, but—"

Red Squirrel came to his rescue with a chirruped question.

"Yes. It will be a most difficult meeting." Poldo stood. "Not many can win a dispute with the lawyer-monks of Adchul, and even less can do so after contracts have been signed."

A few of the tiny men and women chittered and waved their fists in the air.

"Thank you," said Poldo. "I'm afraid I do not share your confidence."

He stepped up to a simple mirror propped against a wall and preened as best he could. He wore a fine suit tailored by Llewyn and Dorfson, but the cuffs had begun to fray. His silver hair was past due for a trim, and combing it back only made it look like a misshapen mane. The luxuriant mustache beneath his bulbous nose could be kept in fine shape with a pinch from a tin of Vinn's Fyne Gentleman's Wax, but there was no such cure for the crow's feet at the corners of his weary eyes. He polished his spectacles, adjusted the kerchief in his suit pocket, and headed back to his simple desk.

"One more thing," he asked, picking up the eviction notice. "Did they ever give us a reason for terminating our stay?"

Red Squirrel chirped and shook his head.

"I imagine they wouldn't." The Scribkin spoke brusquely as he headed out the door and into the hallway. The Wood Gnomes scattered like leaves in an autumn gale. The tiny men and women moved in near silence and out of sight, but he was certain his diminutive entourage was never far away.

Red Squirrel dropped onto Poldo's shoulder as he passed under the archway that led into the courtyard and squeaked a question in his ear.

"I couldn't say for certain why we'd be evicted, and I suspect that's what they're counting on," said Poldo with a grimace. They walked into the courtyard, the black spires of the monastery rising like the pylons of a tomb city all around them. They walked past Adchul's western shrine, a small hut filled with scrolls dedicated to Emilveber, a minor god revered by bureaucrats and lawyers. Several robed monks waited in a neat line to pay their respects, one at a time, at a small window.

Red Squirrel chirruped.

"Yes, I definitely have my suspicions as to why," Poldo said, walking past the line.

The space between the shrine and the western wall of the courtyard was a small shock of green amid the blacks and grays of winter in Adchul. At the center of it, working the earth with hands like spades, was a Troll.

The Troll looked much like what you would get if you poured a potion of hair growth over a small mountain. Most of him was covered in fur the color of lakeside granite. Upon closer inspection, his shaggy coat displayed spiraling patterns of gray and blue wandering across his chest and shoulders like moss over a boulder. His stony skin was visible only around his gnarled hands and on his face, which looked like an amalgam of an ape, a skull, and a drawer full of knives.

Poldo recognized the toothy countenance as a friendly smile. "Good morning, Thane," he called.

"Good morning, Mr. Poldo," rumbled the Troll. "Business to attend to?"

"I suppose," said the Scribkin. "Hopefully I'll be done soon enough to assist you in the... the..." Poldo looked at the Troll's small garden. The green shoots and leaves brought to mind an adolescent's facial hair, with wide, bare expanses between thin patches of green. Yet, given the snow encrusting Adchul's ramparts and the bitter cold in the air, the fact that there was any growth at all was surprising. Had the plants been there yesterday?

"Do you suppose it's common for flowers to grow that quickly? In winter?" he asked faintly.

"If you care for them well." Thane's voice seemed absent as he gently stroked the stem of a bloom that Poldo couldn't name. The Scribkin would almost swear he could see the leaves growing fuller at the Troll's touch.

"I just... I always assumed you were planting for... uh... the spring." Poldo was reaching the extent of his horticultural experience, which until last week had been limited to pouring water on houseplants.

"I've always had a gift for gardening." Thane shrugged.

"I... I see," said Poldo. "Well, perhaps you can give me a few pointers later."

The Troll nodded and smiled, but the young plant held most of his attention now.

Poldo sighed, a wistful smile twisting up his mustache. It was rare to see his friend and bodyguard at peace. The life of a Troll living among society was likely filled with rejection and scorn, and in particular an encounter with an Elf that Thane had admired seemed to have left deep scars. Clearly, he was haunted by a painful past, and would have been more so if the present would stop butting in with new trauma.

The last thought proved extraordinarily prescient when Poldo turned to find a hunched figure staring at them. The lawyer-monk clearly held considerable seniority; the combined weight of the medals, pins, and other insignia hanging from his robes had bent the man over double. A small, floating desk hovered through the air beside him, periodically dipping as though struggling to support the reams of parchment stacked atop it. His leathery face was shrouded by his heavy hood, yet the shadows couldn't conceal the monk's disgust and revulsion as he stared at Thane.

Poldo stiffened. No, there was no question at all in his mind as to why they faced eviction from Adchul.

"You know," he muttered to the Wood Gnome on his shoulder. "When I was young, I learned that in business it is usually best to keep one's language professional, no matter the circumstances."

He gave a nod of greeting to the lawyer-monk, who returned it warily.

"And now that I am older and wiser, I've learned that you can do so and still stick it to the bastards," he muttered, before raising his voice and arm in greeting. "Good morning!" he called to the lawyer-monk.

The old Human grimaced, but his shoulders fell like a deflating sail. With a heavy sigh, he crossed his hands in front of him and launched into Adchul's traditional greeting. "The following is a wish of a good morning between myself, Brother Atticus, hereafter 'I' or 'me,' and Duine Poldo, hereafter 'you.' This is a non-binding greeting that does not guarantee or obligate either party to provide a morning of any quality, good or otherwise..."

Poldo allowed himself a petty, satisfied smile as his thoughts drifted back to a sign he'd seen in the small archway down by the docks. It was painted in simple blackletter that read:

YOU DON'T HAVE TO TAKE A VOW OF SILENCE TO WORK HERE, BUT IT HELPS.

The lawyer-monks spent their days meditating on the great disciplines of voiding liability and channeling leverage, and their sacred Master Agreement taught that careless words and idle chatter carried potential risk. Dinners at Adchul tended to be a quiet affair.

"... Nothing said in this disclaimer or greeting constitutes legal advice." An enchanted quill on the old monk's floating desk quickly worked over the surface of a piece of parchment, documenting every word. "You agree not to discuss legal matters with me without first signing a contract including an agreed-upon rate and fee schedule..."

The Troll had taken note of the monk and his monologue. "Did you forget how much they hate it when you say, 'good morning?'" he asked Poldo.

"No," said Poldo brightly. "Thane, I'm afraid your job is likely to become more challenging. We will be leaving Adchul."

Thane frowned. "I thought you wanted to remain for at least another year."

"Indeed, but circumstances are changing," said Poldo.

"I see," said Thane with a long sigh and a glance at the lawyer-monk. The Troll was no fool, and he held little illusion as to why they had a hard time finding permanent lodging.

Brother Atticus droned on. "... You further agree to release me from any liability for any damages, emotional distress, or financial harm that comes as a result of this conversation..."

"We will find somewhere stable." Poldo reassured his bodyguard with a warm smile and a friendly pat on the shin. "Somewhere better."

"Not safer," Thane said sullenly. "The Hookhand still has assassins looking for you back on the mainland."

"They've yet to put a scratch on me with you by my side," said Poldo. "I'm more worried about his lawyers piercing our corporate veil and finding their way to Mrs. Hrurk's Home. But all of those concerns are for another day. If the lawyer-monks won't see reason tomorrow morning, we'll want to leave as soon as possible. Pack your things and make your preparations. I'll head to the docks to see if we can arrange passage on short notice."

"I'll be ready in the morning." Thane stroked the short plant with a long sigh. "I'm sorry for the trouble."

"You have nothing to apologize for, my good man," said Poldo brightly. "Let's save blame for those that deserve it. Speaking of which..."

He turned to Brother Atticus, who was just completing his greeting. "And so, with the aforementioned understood and with your implicit consent to a verbal agreement, I wish you a good morning as well, as defined in subsection forty-two, paragraph 'r' of Adchul's Master Agreement."

"Thank you, Brother Atticus. I have truly enjoyed this conversation," said Poldo with both honesty and malice. "And now it is with equal pleasure that I must bid you good day."

Oopa of Many Hues was having a very bad day.

Usually a bad day meant that the olive prices rose right after she unloaded a barrel at the market, or that a client skipped out in paying for the information, or—on one horrible occasion—that the family goat got loose in the silk market. When it comes to expensive tastes, nothing beats a goat in a silk market.

But today was worse. She longed for the days when her worst problems were an empty purse, a half-eaten bolt of fabric, and a nanny goat with a bad case of indigestion.

A crossbow bolt ricocheted off the sandstone wall next to her, reminding her that the current problem—the very insistent problem—was a quartet of armed men with crimson robes.

Another shot zinged overhead as Oopa sprinted around the corner and into Kesh's Dawn Market, her many-colored cloak trailing behind her like a rainbow banner. Merchants and shoppers shouted in surprise and anger as she shoved them out of her way, then screamed as she toppled a table covered in brass vases. Her pursuers leapt over the fallen vessels, so Oopa overturned a cage of squawking imps, knocked down a stack of clay pots, and went out of her way to crash through a fruit cart. Then she tossed her rainbow cloak over a mannequin, kicked it over, and ran in the opposite direction.

It was all to no avail. A glance behind her revealed the red-robed men continuing their dogged pursuit, unfazed by the makeshift diversions and obstacles. Worse, now the noctomancer selling the imps was giving chase as well.

Oopa's eyes darted to a stack of crates leaning against a white stone building. A burst of quick leaps took her to the top of the pile, and another took her onto the clay-tiled rooftops. She climbed up to the steeple of the roof to get her bearings, and quickly dropped onto her belly.

Below her, where the courtyard of most complexes would be, a pit of thick, black mud burbled and congealed like last night's stew. She caught a glimpse of a crest on a banner hanging above the muck; an Imperial serif wearing a crown of gemstones.

An old proverb from before the birth of the Empire said, "the man who would hold court with dragons will wear a jeweled crown." Most scholars believed that it originally was meant to say that power brings wealth, but most scholars don't get to direct policy. Emperors and empresses throughout history had interpreted the wisdom to mean that taming and working with dragons or dragon-kin would surely lead to riches and authority.

The only problem with this theory was dragon-kin.

Dragons themselves were believed to be sleeping beneath mountains across the globe since ages past. They rarely surfaced—only a handful of times during entire ages—and those that did seemed more in the mood to burn cities and eat livestock than to hold court. That left the ambitions of Imperial dreamers to drakes and other dragon-kin, which were universally ill-tempered, stubborn, and deadly. Many of the Empire's finest men and women had lost their lives in attempts to ride wyverns, or lead Stone Drakes to war, or even just to convince a Flame Drake to light a stove.

More recent emperors recognized that dragon taming was a waste of serifs and knights, and relegated the task of taming dragon-kin for the Empire to criminals and exiles. For the most part, these souls met the same fate as their nobler predecessors, but the criminal mind often has a certain ingenuity that's incompatible with a proper education. Eventually, an innovative and desperate dragon-tamer discovered Mud Drakes.

Mud Drakes were dimmer than most dragon-kin. Their thick scales deterred most threats, and their dull minds couldn't process any that remained, so they seldom got defensive. As ambush predators, they had no instinct to chase prey. They got disoriented when walking for any distance at all, and thus were as easy to lead around as beasts of burden. It was almost impossible to get hurt by a Mud Drake, provided you didn't stand directly in front of a hungry one with its muzzle off.

And the only place the royal Mud Drakes had their muzzles off was in the Imperial dragon tamers' stables.

Muck oozed around dark, bulging shapes in the mud below. Once happily concealed within a mud pit, Mud Drakes remained perfectly still until prey wandered into range.

Oopa took a deep breath. She glanced down to the street on the other side of her and saw red-robed figures awkwardly trying to scale the crates. Another was taking aim with a crossbow—

One of the ceramic tiles next to her exploded with a plonk. It was the sound of a last chance quickly evaporating.

Oopa kicked at a couple of tiles to loosen them up as she scrambled to her feet. She half-crawled, half-sprinted along the gable of the roof as the first red-robed figure clambered up onto the tiles. The man's pursuit was brief and ended with a scream over the chalky sound of sliding terracotta, followed by an undignified plop and a chorus of reptilian bellowing.

Oopa didn't have time to glance backward. She launched herself into the air as she reached the edge of the roof, and a crossbow bolt slammed into the tiles where she had been a moment earlier. A split second later, she slammed into the top of the building across the street and scrambled over the edge.

This rooftop was flatter and didn't have any precipitous drops into drake-infested pits. The building was on the edge of one of Kesh's famed waterways, just a few streams down from Ogdin's Canals. She used the gleaming, white pillars of Ogdin's Cairn to orient herself, then plotted an escape route back to the sewers. The route would take her across the canal to the Sandmills and through the bustling slums of the Dockman's Quarters.

That meant that right now was as quiet a moment and as high an altitude as she would enjoy for quite some time.

After a moment's thought, Oopa ducked behind a set of abandoned falcon cages and pulled a small, round stone from a pouch on her bandolier. She tapped on it impatiently, growling to herself as the magic took a moment to fire up. Then a tiny, rose-colored light bloomed within the glassy surface.

"I went to the Crimson Grove. It was a risk, but I saw the trees and they're full," Oopa whispered to the stone. "I mean, they're laden with fruit. That's because they grow year-round. They're always in season! And the growers aren't happy I found—"

A sudden shout rang out from a nearby roof. She looked up to see a pair of red-robed men emerging from a stairwell, brandishing their long, curved blades.

"Have to run!" she said and tapped the stone once more. It flared pink in her hands as she sprinted toward the north side of the rooftop. Her muscles tensed and stretched as she launched herself off the edge of the roof, out over the canal. She glanced down as she leapt. The water was an azure slash through the sand- and bone-colored streets of the city. At its edge, she saw a flash of red.

The final pursuer. The one with the crossbow.

The bolt hit home before the thought did, punching into Oopa's back with enough force to flip her over in midair. Something pink and bright flitted past her face as the messenger sprite flew above her, speeding off toward its destination.

Then she rolled in the air again and lost sight of her final message. Trailing blood, she plummeted toward the dark water below.

The crimson olive dropped into the amber liquid with a faint plop.

It began to spark and fizz on contact with the fluid, dancing above the flashes of light like a mad imp dancing over flames. Its wild jig sent streams of tiny bubbles to the top of a fluted glass, which the waiter placed in front of an ancient Scribkin wearing horned spectacles and enough foundation to whitewash a fence. Cracks and fissures spread over Merrin Fumple's face as she smiled and lifted the glass in a toast. "Imperial flame olive," she said. "Adds some punch to any drink, and it's doubly good on a chilly day."

The Gnome took a sip. Light flared and a cloud of steam erupted around her.

"Whoo. Ha ha!" Smoke curled from the corners of Merrin's grin. "A bit pricey, but you only live once."

Heraldin Strummons wore a smile that didn't touch his eyes. He suspected that Merrin had lived at least three Human lifetimes, and spent them draining the coin pouches of countless hopeful musicians. Still, a dozen of those aspirants had become famous, and if Heraldin wanted to be the one to round out a baker's dozen, he needed to make a good impression. "Worth every penny," he said with as much enthusiasm as he could muster, then added, "You know, they use Imperial flame olives to make explosives."

"Do they?" Merrin asked with a smile. "Is that why they're so hard to get?"

"I would guess so." Heraldin had no idea about the state of the olive market, but his penchant for fighting with glass chem-bombs kept him in contact with the alchemical industry. "Their oil costs more than liquid gold, but to the right buyer it's worth the exorbitant price."

"All I know is you can definitely use them to make amazing snacks and cocktails. You should try one while they're still in stock." She took a sip that set her silver eyebrows alight.

"I'm good with my moonwater," Heraldin said. Moonwater was much like river water, as far as Heraldin could tell, except that it was served with a slice of grundant on the rim and cost two giltin for a glass.

Everything was like that at Salvatore's, an upscale restaurant tucked between even more upscale buildings in the center of the Sixth Tier. All of the dishes boasted exotic names, elegant garnishes, and extravagant prices. Heraldin suspected the dim candlelight wasn't so much to set the ambiance as it was to obscure the numbers on the menu.

"Moonwater does sound good," Merrin said. "I think I'll try one of them as well."

"Be my guest." Heraldin managed to force the words through a brittle grin.

Merrin was always the guest at lunch. That was, Heraldin understood, a key part of the arrangement. If some aspiring bard wanted Merrin's time, they bought her a meal. If the hopeful minstrel was worth talking to again, Merrin would buy the meal next time and call it square. Of course, if a hopeful bard wasn't worth Merrin's time, she'd call it even anyway; the musician got a shot pitching to a top industry agent, and Merrin got the most expensive thing on the menu.

She liked to have a few drinks. She liked to make small talk about her grandchildren. She liked flirting with the waiters—especially Halflings, it was said—and speculating about whether or not she was too old to have a little fun. She had a loud laugh that she employed often and took quick notice if nobody joined in. It was all a game to Merrin, the sort that cats play with doomed mice. As the bard playing the part of "rodent" for the afternoon, all Heraldin could do was try to keep the game from ending prematurely or in tragedy. Eventually, he knew, the conversation would turn to his work.

Their turn to the matter at hand coincided with the arrival of Merrin's third cocktail. "You must have brought me out to pitch the ballad of the liche-slaying heroes of Andarun," Merrin said as she inspected her glass. An illusionary ship sailed across the surface of her deep blue drink.

The comment caught Heraldin off guard. "Well, I mean someday I hope to do it—"

"It's such a great story," said Merrin. She capsized the boat with a long sip. "Six heroes, thought to be criminals, return from exile to save the kingdom and slay the overlord of an undead army. And the liche and one hero are father and son? That's the sort of twist that makes for the best epics."

"Ah, yes," said Heraldin. "And I look forward to writing it, once I get the—"

"I mean, who else is going to get the rights, with you being one of the heroes?" Merrin said, peering at Heraldin through her thick glasses. "You've got first swing on the biggest ballad of the age!"

Beads of sweat bloomed on Heraldin's brow. "Ah, well, it should make getting them easier—"

"You don't have them yet? No problem. It'll be easy." The Scribkin waved the concern away with a fork. "They say most of your partners are back working with the guild by now. That means they'll have agents, and agents love money. Trust me on that one, I know." She gave a barking laugh. "Just go to their agents to sort out the rights. Everyone will want a cut, but that's the business."

The bard cleared his throat. "Actually, some of my companions are unrepresented—"

"What? Oh, good thing you're all friends, then. Call in a personal favor. You need to get those rights. Oh, the food!" The shriveled Scribkin smiled as a waiter placed a plate of lettuce and tentacles before her. "Ah,

Salvatore's always has the best mentalopod. It's dangerous if it's too fresh, but if you wait too long the brain squid isn't even wriggling anymore. The chef here always gets it right."

She pointed to one of the faintly purple, severed appendages pulling itself across her plate toward freedom.

"Never was one for Arakian food," Heraldin said, then quickly changed the subject. "Anyway, did you read the draft I sent you?"

"Hang on. I want to enjoy this." Merrin held up one hand to pause the conversation while another maneuvered a fork to strike.

The bard averted his eyes as the old woman wrestled a struggling tentacle into her mouth. He could stare at his own plate of roast griffin shank and parsnips, but he couldn't ignore the sounds of laborious chewing and the faint echo of an inhuman shriek at the back of his mind.

"Mm. Perfect," said the Gnome, dabbing her lips with a napkin. "Anyway, yes. I read your ballad."

Heraldin's face lit up. "And?"

"It's done."

"Of course. I wouldn't send an incomplete song."

"No, I mean, it's been done. A lot. A thousand times last summer." She pointed a fork at Heraldin. "It's like every other story I've forgotten this year."

"Right. It's a timeless tale," Heraldin attempted.

"Only in the sense that it's never going to have its day," said Merrin. "Listen, kid, I know ballad writing looks easy, but there's a lot to a good story. It's not enough to just give any old Jack Cowfarmer a magic sword, send him off to fight some scargs, and... and... and... and... and... and..."

Heraldin startled. Merrin's eyes had gone wide and so dilated that they were almost black. She picked up her fork and began jabbing it mechanically into her own arm.

"Merrin? Merrin, are you feeling well?" Heraldin asked, snatching the fork from her hand.

"Whoo!" said Merrin a moment later, shaking off the spell. "All right. All right. I'm better now."

"What was—"

The Scribkin brushed his concern aside. "Some of the livelier mentalopod put up a fight on the way down. Tickles your skull from the inside." She saw the prong-marks in the leathery skin of her forearm and laughed. "This one's got spirit."

"Ha... ha." It took a great effort for Heraldin to keep his face from screwing up into a grimace. "You were saying?"

"Right. Ballads," said Merrin. "Listen, you can't just write down a random story, call it a ballad, and get a contract. You need a story behind the song. Something extra. A little il'ne se la. Not the old farm-boy-saves-the-world routine."

Heraldin winced and shook his head. "I think if the right audience heard it—"

Merrin cut the bard off. "Think so? Go busking and see if you find that audience. You can sing whatever you want to the street urchins. But if you want to play to big audiences and have other bards license your ballads, you need something more."

"Ah." Heraldin's face fell.

"Like the rights to the greatest story of the age. That would fill an auditorium, right? Kid, when you get those rights, you call me. I'll buy you dinner." Merrin smiled at him, but her eyes were cold iron.

"I see," said Heraldin.

"Good. Now then, how's the griffin tonight? I usually... usualleee... alleee... leeeeee..." Merrin's words trailed into a high-pitched whine. Her face went blank again, her eyes dilated to black voids.

"Is it the squid?" Heraldin asked, then leapt back as the Scribkin grabbed a knife and held it aloft.

"Alleee...." slurred the Gnome.

"A little help!" Heraldin called, fending off Merrin's clumsy stab with his fork.

The agent lurched from her chair and started marching toward the kitchen with the plodding determination of a giant golem. A couple of patrons gasped, and much of the restaurant's table staff rushed over.

"The brain squid's too fresh, Janisss!" The head waiter shouted to the Naga in the kitchen while trying to dodge wooden swings from the spellbound Gnome. "Too fresh!"

Heraldin grimaced as a busboy tackled Merrin to the floor. By rights, a plate of botched mentalapod and the ensuing fracas should have been the biggest disaster of the evening, but it paled in comparison with the agent's implicit ultimatum. His musical career and financial comeback were on hold until he could convince his former companions to let him write a ballad about them.

There were a lot of reasons to think that they'd be reluctant to grant such a request.

For starters, they'd heard Heraldin sing.

"That's a dealbreaker." Burt stared into the deep blue of a cold twilight before dawn from the safety of Gorm's rucksack. "Lady Asherzu would never agree to it."

"Ye could talk her into it." Gorm rubbed his hands together and stepped closer to the dying cookfire to ward off the creeping chill. Winter had come to the Plains of Bahn, though the snows had held off for now. Instead, a deep cold whipped across the scrubland and fields on northern winds, nipping at exposed skin and burrowing through the thickest cloaks. "Ye know as well as I do that if she revealed what she knows about Johan and Bloodroot—"

"I know that it'd be her word against a hero-king that every other Lightling considers almost as holy as Tandos' divine rump." The Kobold rummaged around in Gorm's things. "And we both know she'd lose that fight."

"It'd be an excuse to investigate Johan," Gorm pointed out.

"It'd be an excuse to investigate our corporation as well, and the bannermen are really good at finding bad things Shadowkin have done. Especially the things Shadowkin haven't actually done." The Kobold held up Gorm's flint and steel, tail wagging. "We'd be lucky to come out of it only losing the company, and the lady ain't doing anything that puts the business in danger."

"I'd say havin' a king who hates Shadowkin is a pretty big threat to all of ye, not just that new company of yours."

"Yeah, but that's nothin' new, is it?" Amber light flared in Gorm's backpack as the Kobold lit a cigarette. "King Oven introduced noncombatant papers just so he could make it legal to kill us for not having 'em. King Felik spent years makin' it easier and easier to take those papers away. You know what King Handor did to the Orcs at Bloodroot. Every Lightling king would rather see us dead than prosper, and Johan's just the latest one. And despite that, the lady's found a way to make money on the right side of the law."

Gorm eyed him sideways. "This is about more than gold," he said.

"That's something that you only hear people with lots of gold say." The red eye of Burt's cigarette flared with sudden intensity as he took a slow drag.

Over the cookfire's dying light, the sky heralded dawn's imminent arrival with a faint blue glow on the horizon. Gorm rubbed his arms and willed the sun to come faster and end third watch; he hoped to be on the road before long. "We were supposed to strike back. We were supposed to change the way things work."

"Ha," said the Kobold. "The world doesn't change. Not for the better, anyway."

Gorm sucked at his teeth. "It... it used to. I mean, I know things were bad. I know I done terrible things. I fed the guild's monster and helped perpetuate an endless war. It wasn't good."

"This is where one of you Lightlings usually says, 'but.'" Burt glared at the Dwarf askance.

Gorm left the conjunction unsaid. "I remember this time we went to the dungeon of Mathrax the Foul. Kidnapper. Slaver. Specialized in snatching kids and... and doin' things to 'em in front of a crystal ball." His hand tightened around the axe at the memory. "Built up a small army of mercenaries and assassins to protect his whole operation. Anyone who got too close to the truth would be found face down in the Tarapin. Same thing happened to the quest contact."

"Sounds like a bastard."

"A basement full of them," said Gorm. "And they knew, Burt. Every cutthroat, every thug working for Mathrax knew what happened in that basement. And we can talk about how hard life was for those mercenaries, or how society was unfair to them, but there's no amount of sufferin' that would excuse that kind of evil. And when my party got there, and they tried to send our corpses floating down the river, well... all the nuance and complications of this mad world didn't matter. We were just a party of heroes, doin' what's right, savin' folk who needed it. A force for good protecting the innocent by slayin' evil. It was as perfect a moment as I've ever lived—where my purpose and everythin' I wanted and what the world needed most all lined up. Moments like that... that's why I took up professional heroics."

Burt took a drag from his cigarette and nodded, which was as much approval as he'd ever allow for guild heroes.

"I thought... I thought fightin' Johan would be like that again. Our side so clearly in the light of justice, his so clearly in the wrong. I thought we'd be back in one of them perfect moments. But it ain't. It's all complex. All the people and their needs and dreams are all strung together, caught in the same web."

Burt shrugged. "Why do you think the Red Horde and League of Night and all them other villains want to burn it all down? It's way easier to tear a kingdom down than fix it. Utopia's never gonna happen. At least total annihilation might be possible."

Nothing sparks reluctant optimism like an encounter with someone even more bleak. "Well, I mean, it ain't all bad," Gorm fumbled.

"It ain't much good." The opening of the rucksack smoked and fumed like the maw of a deflated Flame Drake. Burt could puff his way through a whole packet of Shireton's Best rolled pipeweed in less than an hour when he got worked up. "The rich and the powerful take from those without, but if you flipped the script and took from them, they'd call you just as bad."

"Ye can't seriously—"

"I ain't in the Red Horde. Do you think the lady would have me as her hand if I thought the way they do?" Burt waved the concern away. "But I still understand why they think burning down the kingdom would be a good start. Everything seems stacked against people, Gorm. Everything seems wrong. And there's no way to fix it. We can't win, Gorm. Not in this world."

"Feels that way." The Dwarf let out a long breath.

"Hard to see otherwise," said the Kobold. He held up his cigarette. "Look at this. You think Shireton's Best only employs fat, happy Halflings in green fields like the woodcut on the packet? Nah, they pay the poorest folk pennies to break their backs, just like every farm out there. I know. I got cousins who used to work the fields out by old Aberreth."

The Kobold took a long drag from the cigarette. "So what should I do? Get everyone to stop buying cigs and food, so those poor souls can nobly starve? Or maybe I force those farmers to pay better? Well, I ain't the king, and if I was a king who did that, everyone with money and power would call me tyrant. Kings like that don't last long. So I smoke, and I eat, and I try to do what I can to get those poor sods in the field some better treatment. It ain't much, but it's what I can do. The key is to get over it. Just go with the flow."

"Hard to find comfort in that when we're in the sewers," Gorm grumbled.

"If it makes you feel any better, I hear Johan goes crazy knowin' that the Shadowkin are running a big business."

"Annoyin' him don't seem like enough."

"It's like the Tinderkin say: 'The best revenge is a life well lived,' right? Live it up and stick it to the thrice-cursed bigwigs at the top."

"This ain't about revenge," said Gorm. "It's about justice."

"Yeah, well revenge is a lot easier than justice." Burt blew out a long ring of smoke through his nostrils.

"But if ye'd—"

"If we'd do what you wanted, we'd be Dwarves thinking like Dwarves." Burt jabbed his cigarette toward Gorm. "But if we were Dwarves, we wouldn't need to do anything. We'd be sitting pretty, knowing the king would keep us safe as long as he had someone green or furry to kick around. We ain't alike. We're on the same side, but we ain't the same. Just because you think something makes sense doesn't mean we're going to do it. You don't understand what you're askin'."

Gorm's lips drew into a thin line as he stamped the chill out of his toes. "Aye, I guess not."

They stamped and smoked for a bit, trying to get warm in the icy silence.

"M'sorry," Gorm mumbled eventually.

"Cigarette?" A bony paw extended from Gorm's rucksack, holding a Shireton's Best.

Gorm smiled at the offer; a conciliatory cigarette from the Kobold said a lot. Specifically, it said, *I want to offer you something, so that you know we're still good friends, but I also know that you hate cigarettes.*

"Nah," the Dwarf said, waving the offer away. "Not sure how ye can stand smokin'."

"Suit yourself," said Burt. "Look, I know it feels like things are moving slow, but I think this informant's gonna pan out for us. Get things moving. And you gotta realize it's a big deal that the lady is paying attention to this at all. She's got a lot going on. Big-time, important stuff."

——CHAPTER 3——

Asherzu Guz'Varda, Chieftain of the Guz'Varda Tribe and—more recently—CEO of Warg Incorporated, stared dispassionately at her officers from the head of the table. "Honored cohort," she said. "I must ask you: is it really the place of this most revered board to review humble expense reports?"

A Goblin in a cobalt suit cleared his throat. A wooden plaque in front of his seat said "Izek Li'Balgar" in thin, white letters. "Ah, usually not, honored one," he said. "But Borpo of the Skar'Ezzod has been most insistent about the reports—"

"Costs that bring rage and shame!" interrupted a huge Orc perched atop a tiny office chair, like a siege engine teetering on a farmer's cart. Borpo wore a fine suit and tie that strained and frayed as the muscles beneath it bulged and flexed. "We have labored many nights, and we still see costs such as these? And often with no trail of paper to follow to the irresponsible spender?"

"We must spend money to make money." A Slaugh in a slick suit seated across the conference table raised her webbed hand. "Is not a market that has gone down the ideal time to invest in—"

"We cannot invest money that does not reside in the budget, Guglug!" countered Borpo.

"We would have more money to invest if the expenses were better managed," said Freggi of the Water Horse Clan. The Goblin's words only seemed to incense both the Orc and the Slaugh.

"The expenses are the investments!" croaked Guglug.

"Unreported expenses cannot be controlled!" bellowed Borpo.

"Honored ones, please," said Asherzu of the Guz'Varda. "We must hear each other's words if we are to move forward. There must be a way to solve this problem."

"I will take the head of anyone who does not save his receipts!" Borpo produced an axe from beneath the table and held it aloft dramatically.

Asherzu sighed and rested her forehead against her fingertips. "Borpo..."

"Or her receipts." The warrior shot the chairwoman an egalitarian grin.

The CEO's unchanged expression suggested that mild sexism was the least of her   concerns. Borpo quietly slid his axe under the table and eased back into his seat.

Asherzu let her breath out through her tusks. Not for the first time, she regretted ever thinking that leading a tribe would have prepared her for running a business.

In the early days, she had been enamored with the idea of a corporation. When the tribe split away from the Red Horde, they were joined by other tribes of Orcs, clans of Goblins and Gnolls, families of Slaugh, and other Shadowkin and monstrous people. These groups identified with the Guz'Varda Tribe's cause and ethos and allowed Asherzu to advocate for them to the Lightlings. Yet tribes are—by definition and by nature—tribal, and the elders of all gathered knew that it was only a matter of time before differences—cultural, political, or petty—fractured their alliance. Shadowkin customs offered no way to merge or centralize ancient family designations without losing more than was gained.

Yet the Lightlings had invented structures for people of any ancestry to work together in common purpose and share rewards based on contributions: the corporation. At Asherzu's suggestion, the tribes all sent wise-ones, shamans, and chieftains to join the Working Association Research Group, or the WARG. After six months of research and debate on the ideal way for the tribes to collaborate, the WARG had recommended forming a joint company for the benefit of all the member tribes and even produced a charter to launch the corporation.

Of course, finding and structuring leadership and employees for such a corporation would take time, and there was already a joint venture featuring each tribe's top talent in the study commission itself. By a nearly unanimous vote, the tribes and clans converted the WARG into a corporation. The WARG rider was attached to the charter, deeds for tribal assets were drafted and transferred, and a new kind of company was born under the name Warg Incorporated.

In theory, Warg Inc. was the top business talents of Shadowkin tribes collaborating to recapture wealth that had been taken from their peoples over centuries of looting by the Heroes' Guild. Yet in Asherzu's experience, every day was a reminder that reality is always much messier than theory allows for.

"I will ensure that we can see to the matter of the expenses," Asherzu told the executives seated around the conference table. "Let us focus this time on our mission."

"Do we have a mission?" asked Pogrit, matriarch of the Fub'Fazar Clan of Gnolls.

"No, and that is the problem we must solve," said Asherzu. "Lightling corporations all have missions."

"Such as the ones they give their heroes," said Borpo, nodding.

"Like 'kill twenty Bloat-boars?'" suggested Guglug.

"Or 'bring me five Dire Muskrat spleens?'" Izek said.

"Our company does many things," said Asherzu loudly, trying to steer the conversation. "Warg owns shares in two tanneries, four blacksmiths, an armor shop, thirteen corner grocers, three mercantile caravans, a grundant orchard, inns, breweries, and more. And that does not count our new investment banking group. We hold all these companies, but what do we actually do?"

The others at the table stared blankly. "The finances?" croaked Guglug.

Asherzu nodded, watching the gears of understanding grind into motion. "That is our day job. But what do we do?"

An uncomfortable silence bloomed in the room.

"So we're not talking about the muskrat spleens?" said Izek.

"No, we are not."

"Well, that is the sort of mission I have heard the Lightlings speak of," said Borpo.

Asherzu tried to force a smile as she stared at some of the most respected Shadowkin in the Freedlands. It struck her once again that experience can be a double-edged sword. Some people learned and practiced the fastest, most efficient way to get from point A to point B, which was all well and good until a company needed to get to point C. Her father, in his wisdom, had once remarked that the only difference between being on track and stuck in a rut is the intended destination. "I meant a bold statement that echoes our purpose to the ages," she told the board. "A declaration of why we exist."

"I usually leave that sort of thing to the shamans and priests." Guglug waved a webbed hand dismissively.

"As a company," Asherzu growled. "Why does Warg Incorporated exist?"

"We have the charter," said Izek. "We wrote it not half a year ago. Is that not our mission?"

"Yes, correct!" Asherzu felt a glimmer of hope. "That is the sort of mission we are looking for. But it is too long. No one can recite the whole thing—that was not a challenge to do so, Borpo."

Borpo sat back down, deflated.

"We need a mission statement that captures the spirit of the charter, but remains short enough that you could speak it to another on a trip down the stairs," said Asherzu. "A quick way to say why we all come to work each morning."

Izek stuck a hand in the air. "To make money so we can buy food."

The Guz'Varda chieftain rapped her fingers on the table. "That is true, in part, but it does not inspire passions."

"I, for one, am very passionate about not starving," said Izek.

Asherzu sighed. "I meant that a statement such as that will not motivate people."

"It will once they get hungry," offered Freggi.

The CEO took a deep breath.

"Perhaps we should agree to let the agency of advertisements help us with this 'mission statement,'" suggested Pogrit gently. "They say they are good at this sort of thing."

"They say they are good at everything," grumbled Borpo. "It's just more expenses."

"Your words are wise, Honored Pogrit," said Asherzu, without even trying to hide her relief. "Let it be so."

A rumble of agreement went up.

"And if there is nothing else..." Asherzu let the sentence trail away hopefully; she was already inching her seat away from the table.

"Your pardons, honored one," said Izek, shattering Asherzu's hope of escape. "We wish to say that the new brokerage group is having... difficulty on the Wall."

"Of what sort?" said Asherzu.

"We cannot make trades as quickly as the Lightlings do," said Guglug. "There is always an excuse for extra paperwork."

"And when we do trade, the prices never seem to be as good," said Izek.

"It should not be so," said Asherzu. "Our agreement with the kingdom says we are citizens, with all the rights and obligations of any Lightling."

There was an uncomfortable silence around the table, of the sort one hears when everybody knows the answer and nobody wants to be the one to say it.

"It is true," Asherzu insisted. "If the Lightlings on the Wall do not know it, we must make them see it."

A couple of the assembled Shadowkin nodded weakly, but the chieftain could see the doubt in their eyes. More drastic action was necessary.

"You will see as well," she told them. "I will go to the Wall with Izek and Guglug tomorrow, and we will make trades together. I will show you the path of the aggressive seller."

"I hope that you are right, Lady," said Guglug, doubt still evident in her frog-like eyes. "It is good that we have all the rights that can be written down. But I fear that even with the ink long dry, we Shadowkin are not treated the same."

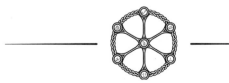

"Nonsense," said Mother Maeven. "We do not treat Shadowkin differently than any of our other tenants."

"I think you'll find that our documents are quite explicit on the subject," said Father Snade.

"Your Troll employee was not a factor in our decision to evict you," said Father Gaul.

Poldo glared up at the three senior lawyer-monks, though it was hard to make them out in the dim light of their chamber. The room looked like the mad vision of what a crypt builder would do with an endless supply of books. Massive tomes lined every arched wall, filled each cubby in the gothic pillars, even rested in the sculpted hands of robed gargoyles and cherubs. Neat stacks of books covered the floor around the office at the center of the chamber. The senior lawyer-monks' desk was set above the lone chair for clients that Poldo now occupied. The desk itself was a mahogany juggernaut, wide enough to give three lawyer-monks ample space, and surrounded by great drifts of scrolls and periodicals to the point that they seemed to be sailing amid a stormy sea of paper.

"I wonder what did lead to your decision, then," Poldo said. "The rent has been paid on time, we are quiet and courteous, and no provision in our agreement has been broken. The only reason I can see to evict us is that Thane is my bodyguard."

"Really?" said Father Gaul. "It never occurred to us."

"And frankly, I think it is a bit small-minded of you to think that way," added Mother Maeven.

Poldo took a deep breath, if only to stop his mustache from twitching. The lawyer-monks stared back at him impassively; at least, he thought of them as impassive. He couldn't be sure, as their faces were entirely concealed by the long, crimson hoods draped over them, and most of their hunched bodies were obfuscated by enchanted quills, ledgers, contracts, and office supplies that swarmed around the lawyers like flies around cattle. "Nevertheless, it seems probable to me that our eviction is due to traveling with a Troll."

"It is not," said Father Gaul. Poldo suspected he was a Dwarf; he was wider than the other monks and hints of a long beard occasionally flashed in his dark cowl. "We explicitly said as much."

"You'll find it on clauses six, nineteen, and thirty-four of your eviction notice," added Father Snade. "As well as clause one hundred fifteen of our Master Agreement."

"Writing a statement down doesn't make it true," snapped Poldo.

"But it does make it agreed upon," retorted Mother Maeven. Normally the sister spoke with a melodic cadence that suggested she was Elvish, but now there was nothing but iron in her voice. "And while the law cannot say what truth is, Mr. Poldo, it can be certain of that which has been negotiated and agreed to by all parties."

"That statement does not reflect upon the truthfulness of the lawyer-monks of Adchul in negotiation or preparation of your documents," chimed in a small voice from beside Poldo. The high disclaimer sat at a tiny desk near the guest seat, her hands neatly folded in front of her. "Philosophical remarks should not be taken as statements of position or intent."

"Then tell me the reason," said Poldo. "I've seen the way your brothers and sisters shy from Thane. If not for fear of him, then why evict us?"

"The nineteenth clause states that we may issue notice of eviction without submitting a reason," said Father Snade.

"Which we are choosing to do," said Mother Maeven.

"Ah, but the sixth clause says that you agree to treat us fairly," said Poldo. "And you haven't evicted any of the other tenants yet. You can say you are not acting against the Troll, but we are the only ones you are evicting without cause."

"Who said we are acting without cause?" said Father Gaul. "Not giving a reason is not the same as not having one. Why, we might plan to convert your chamber into an apiary."

"This does not represent a statement of intent nor a commitment to build an apiary," chimed the high disclaimer.

"Perhaps we need the space for new brothers and sisters," said Father Snade.

"This statement is hypothetical and does not reflect actual membership numbers at Adchul," the high disclaimer trilled.

"Or maybe we wish to renovate the space into more offices," supposed Mother Maeven.

"Building plans are confidential and cannot be disclosed," added the high disclaimer.

"You know none of those things are true!" said Poldo.

"We know all of them are defensible," said Father Gaul.

The high disclaimer sang out, "This is not an admission of knowledge related to the truthfulness of previous statements!"

"If you believe otherwise, we could always take this up in a court of your choosing," Mother Maeven purred.

The lawyer-monks leaned in like jungle cats sighted on a small deer.

"No, that won't be necessary." Poldo stared each of them in the cowl, one by one. "We all know the truth, and we all know what was agreed upon."

"If you say so," said Father Snade with clear disappointment.

"I am sure you will still wish to retain our legal services, even if you are no longer boarding with us," said Mother Maeven as she turned back to the papers on her desk.

"That will not be necessary," hissed Poldo. "I shall send word of my new counsel within a month. You will provide them with all necessary documents."

The lawyer-monks seemed surprised. "Mr. Poldo, we must advise you that choosing another firm is not in your best interest," said Father Gaul.

The most infuriating thing, Poldo later reflected, was that this was true; the lawyer-monks of Adchul had no peers, and any other firm he retained would inherently increase his risk of exposure and legal action against himself and his assets. Yet the Scribkin was already deep in a crimson-faced rage, and at that moment what was best for him and what was best seemed diametrically opposed. "Noted!" he barked. "Be that as it may, I'm sure I shall find less cowardly counsel much more to my liking. I must bid you good day!"

"That is disappointing. Good day, Mr. Poldo," said Mother Maeven. Snade and Gaul muttered "good day" as well, and the high disclaimer launched into the customary denials of responsibility for the quality of Poldo's day. She was still trilling about words that didn't mean what they said when the office doors closed behind the Scribkin.

Fury powered Poldo through the Halls of the Sacred Offices. His legs worked like the pistons of a steam engine as he drove past startled lawyer-monks and clerk initiates. Yet by the time he was back in the courtyard, the full extent of what was happening caught up with him and the next task loomed large. Quite literally, as Poldo stood shorter than Thane's knee.

The Troll was working in his garden, a rare expression of tranquil contentment resting on his toothy face. Thane had saved Poldo's life when they first met and earned himself a job as the Gnome's bodyguard. He'd kept Poldo alive for over a year, despite the best efforts of several assassins. That alone indebted the Scribkin to the Troll, but it was their friendship that gave the Gnome pause now.

"It's just so rare to see him happy," Poldo said to the Wood Gnome scampering up his shoulder. "He's spent so much of our time together worried about what people will think of him, or remembering what that Elf did to him. And yet here, he's... he was at peace."

The Wood Gnome chirruped.

"I know." Poldo leaned against a stone pillar. "I'll tell him. But he's going to blame himself, and I... I thought he could use one more moment of joy."

The Gnomes watched in silence as Thane stroked at a budding plant with a finger, coaxing a small flower to bloom.

Yet such peaceful moments seldom last, and business waits for no one. Another Wood Gnome landed on the Scribkin's shoulder and chittered a couple of interesting tidbits of market news.

"Oh? We shall have to sell our Imperial bonds and shift them into the commodity markets. And I think we can turn a tidy sum going short against Conglomerated Silversmiths." Poldo sighed. "I'm afraid we shall have to ask Mrs. Hrurk to make the trades."

The Gnome squeaked.

"She must hate going on the Wall." Poldo pushed himself away from the pillar and stepped lightly into the Troll's garden. "But unfortunately, the market waits for no one, and if we delay we risk missing an opportunity."

To Gorm Ingerson, few feelings stung as much as being late for an only chance. He dreaded that fraction of a moment when icy fear running up his spine crossed paths with his heart plummeting into his stomach. The sensation called back memories of returning to Bloodroot and finding the remains of the decimated Guz'Varda Tribe, and his dear friend Tib'rin the Goblin.

In this case, the connection to those traumatic memories was only made stronger by the burned-out husks of buildings. Smoke and ash stung the Dwarf's red-rimmed eyes as his party surveyed the wreckage. A faint, sulfurous stink pricked at his nose.

"And we're sure this was Sowdock?" he growled.

"Yes," said Kaitha. "This is Lake Baerussel, and Sowdock was the only town on its shores. There's no other hamlets for miles."

Gorm nodded. "So what could have done this?"

The ranger pursed her lips and scanned the muddy scrubland around the charred wreckage. "There's no prints—foot, hoof, or paw—to suggest raiders or the Red Horde. No sign of a fight, either. It seems impossible to be an accident, though—fire wouldn't leap across all of these buildings without help. And I don't smell chemicals, which eliminates the most popular alchemical combustibles."

"So, no party of outsiders, probably not an accident, probably not alchemists." Gorm nodded. Her analysis lined up neatly with his gut. "Magic?"

"It wasn't just some hedge mage or rogue apprentice," said Laruna. "The weave hasn't been altered enough for that. A more experienced caster weaving a complex spell might have done this, but they'd be putting a lot of effort into concealing their methods."

"Our arsonist didn't seem too concerned with discretion." Kaitha stared at the smoldering ruins of an inn.

"But it's possible this was a spell?" Gorm said.

Laruna pursed her lips as she worked her fingers through the air. "It's possible. It'd take someone more skilled at forensic sorcery in a full laboratory to tell."

Gorm nodded at the blackened skeleton of a barn or large house. "Could one of them foreign sorcerers tell much if we brought back some o' that wood?"

"Yes, exactly," said Laruna, a moment before the Dwarf's words registered. "Wait, what?"

But the Dwarf was already trundling off. A few quick chops with his Orcish axe split a charcoal stick as long and wide as his forearm from a former rafter. "So all this may have been the work of a wanderin', very skilled wizard."

"Perhaps. Or maybe..." Kaitha let the unspoken suggestion hang in the air.

"Aye, I know what you're suggestin'," said Gorm thoughtfully as he wrapped the charred wood in a burlap sack and tucked it into his saddlebags. They'd heard the town criers and listened as the rumors swirled among the guild community. It was the most obvious answer, once you set aside the fact that it didn't make much sense. Gorm had a hard time doing that. "Do ye suppose the dragon came this far from the mountain just to torch a fishing village?" he asked.

"The dragon has been very active of late," Kaitha suggested. "And erratic."

Gaist cast a sidelong glance at the Elf that said her suggestion seemed unlikely.

Gorm shared the weaponsmaster's doubts. He turned his gaze eastward, where a distant mountain appeared as little more than a hint of purple on the horizon, so faint that it may have been more wish than Wynspar. "This is a long way from Andarun."

Kaitha shrugged. "Who can say why a dragon does what it does?"

"Certainly not witnesses," Burt said. "Nobody got out of this."

"Probably not," Gorm agreed. "But let's go check."

They tied the horses to a ruined fence and trudged into the blackened hamlet. It certainly looked like a dragon had hit it; few forces on Arth had the firepower to reduce buildings and bodies to soot with such efficiency. Half of a former building was a copse of charred timbers, the other was dunes of gray ash. Bits of misshapen metal were strewn throughout the debris; a half-molten stove with a flaccid pipe, a sword blade that had warped under the heat that burned away its grip, a silver puddle that may once have been some cheap cutlery.

Yet Gorm found that if he looked at the destruction a certain way, he could see a clear pattern in the ash and soot. The scorch marks and far-flung debris all radiated away from a blackened center next to the lake, like the iris of a dead titan's eye staring into the sky. Nothing recognizable was left anywhere near the center of the blast, but near its northern edge Gorm made an interesting discovery.

Laruna looked down at the twisted shape. "It's a piece of metal. We've found several like it."

It looked like a breaking wave sculpted from steel and soot. Its long, irregular curve was marked by undulating shapes and jagged edges where a great force had ripped it apart. Down the center of the wave, Gorm could see that something had been imprinted on the metal.

"This one's different," Gorm said. "More ripped up. Somebody fetch a sheet of parchment. And charcoal."

The paper took a while to find. Charcoal was close at hand. Within a few minutes, Gorm was pressing the page against the warped metal and scrubbing it with a hunk of charred tavern. As the paper blackened, a portion of a warped, skeletal face came into relief. A thin, wobbly diagram of a flame surrounded the distorted skull.

"What do ye suppose this means?" Gorm asked. "A secret gatherin' like the Leviathan Project? Or maybe the sigil of some dark cult? Or even a portrait of another liche?"

Laruna glanced over his shoulder. "It's the symbol for 'flammable contents.' You see it in alchemy labs all the time."

Gorm scratched his beard and surveyed the blackened town. "But what does it mean?"

"It means you can't cast pyromancy or deal with lit flames around—"

"Specifically," the Dwarf said loudly, "what's a steel barrel of flammable liquid doin' in the middle of nowhere? And could it have done all this damage?"

The heroes' collective gaze drifted over the shallow crater and the ruined remnants of the town beyond it. Gaist shook his head.

"I don't know." Kaitha sucked a fast breath in between clenched teeth. "We'd smell alchemist's fire or bane oil if they were in the barrels. And even then, this blast is far too big..."

"Faeflame?" suggested Gorm.

Kaitha dismissed the idea with a wave. "Leaves green soot."

The Dwarf's brow furrowed in concentration. "Arson's Friend?"

"Only comes by the vial, and that's if you can find it. I haven't seen it in the market for years." Kaitha shook her head. "Seems unlikely."

"Aye." Gorm scowled and tried to think. He looked to the mage. "Any ideas?"

"Don't look at me." Laruna shrugged. "I've never needed another way to light enemies on fire."

"Looks like another matter for a foreign sorcerer," said Gorm.

The solamancer opened her mouth as if to say something, then shrugged and walked away.

Gorm heaved a sigh and looked out over the ash. There wasn't much left of Sowdock to search; there hadn't been much of it before the fire either. "I suppose we're done here."

"Not quite!" Burt's head popped up from a knot of charred bushes, wearing a rare grin. "I sniffed out something you're going to want to see."

The nose of any breed of Gnoll, from Bugbears to Kobolds, was as keen as a bloodhound's. Knowing someone's diet from a waft of their breath or sorting through the textured scents of a hallway to deduce who had passed through it were nothing to a Gnoll. They could smell fear, and guilt, and a hope that nobody would look in the cupboard anytime soon.

Other children wondered how mothers always knew; Gnoll pups held no such uncertainty.

Feista Hrurk glowered down at her three paint-spattered progeny as they stood in the center of the kitchen of Mrs. Hrurk's Home for the Underprivileged. Dogo whimpered as thick tears rolled down his face. Little Terrie was staring back with a defiance that was both enraging and familiar to Feista. Rex leaned indifferently on his crutch, waiting for the consequences to fall so he could get back to ignoring them in favor of his adventure novels. It was enough to make Mrs. Hrurk wonder why she had been so excited for him to learn to read.

"Do you know what I need to do today?" she growled, eyeing each of the pups in turn.

If shrugs made a sound, the response would have been deafening.

She counted off tasks on her paw. "I have to negotiate a contract with the carpenter for the new apartments. I have to go to the fishmonger to make him actually deliver the salted fish we bought for the winter. I have a new family of Goblins arriving this weekend to prepare for. I do not have time to repaint Mr. Zug'Gath's apartment."

More shrugs. Feista recalled vaguely that she had once been similarly indifferent to the toils of her parents, though she was certain she hadn't been this bad. Her father would have ripped her throat out. She might have done the same to her ungrateful brood, had Aubren not burst into the kitchen.

"Carpenter's here, ma'am!" said the young Human. "And the postal courier has been by as well. Just bills—your letter didn't come," she added, answering Feista's unspoken question.

Mrs. Hrurk's shoulders fell at the news despite her best effort not to get her hopes up.

"But the Wood Gnomes did hand off a note from Mr. Poldo." Aubren handed over a slip of paper covered in tiny stamped letters with a conciliatory smile. "That's something, right?"

"Oh, it's always something with him," said Feista, but her treacherous tail wagged vigorously and undermined her feigned annoyance. She read the note eagerly. When she noticed the pups grinning, she suppressed her smile and leaned against the counter to keep her tail still. "Now Mr. Poldo has asked me to go to the Wall to make a trade. There's no time for your mischief today."

"But apparently there's time to lecture us," grumbled Terrie.

Mrs. Hrurk stared daggers at her daughter. Had Feista ever spoken to her own mother with such insolence? Yet the girl had a point. There wasn't time to teach them a lesson. "Since you are so interested in painting, you will repaint the hallways outside Mr. Zug'Gath's apartment yourselves. Flat gray, as it was before!" she added quickly.

The boys groaned. Terrie bristled. "That's not the sort of painting we—"

"Oh, I know what you like to do," Feista snarled. "But you'll never make a real mark on the world if the bannermen haul you off for painting silly symbols on the neighbors' walls. So you'll fix your mistake, and apologize to Mr. Zug'Gath!"

"And if we don't?" Rex asked, doubtlessly emboldened by his sister.

"Must I ask Vilga of the Fire Hawk to make sure you keep your honor?" she asked.

The trio of pups blanched, their tails involuntarily tucking beneath their legs. Feista and her pups had discovered that her Goblin bookkeeper's grim efficiency had many applications beyond managing the accounts. Mrs. Hrurk wondered what else Vilga was good at, though the children had apparently decided that ignorance was bliss. "No, Mother," they muttered.

Aubren and Feista watched the children scuttle out of the kitchen. "Anything I can do to help, ma'am?"

"Yes. I'll need you to handle the carpenter while I head to the Wall," said Feista.

"Oh, I... I haven't done much negotiating," confessed Aubren.

"Everyone negotiates," Mrs. Hrurk said. "The trick is getting better at it. Just stay calm, hear what he has to say, and let him know what we know and what we'll accept."

The girl still hesitated. "But what do I know about carpentry?"

The Gnoll grinned. "We know he's been whining that material costs are up. And we also know that the lumber yard says wood prices are where they were a year ago, and the blacksmith says he raised the price on a bag of nails by a penny. You can do a lot with that information."

Aubren thought for a moment, then smiled. "So he's been lying."

"He's been exaggerating," said Feista with a shrug. "Food prices are rising. I'm sure his lunches and coffee grow more expensive, and his laborers feel the same pinch. He's told half the truth, and hopes that the gap in our understanding will let him raise prices by..." She did some mental calculations as she checked her slim, black briefcase. "I would guess around eight percent. Show him what you know, and you should be able to hold him to three or four."

"That's all it is?" asked Aubren.

"That's all," said Feista, pulling her cloak around her. "Most of negotiation is just showing up with the right information."

Information is power.

Not in the conventional sense of power, like armies and heroes and enchanted weapons. Never bring a book to a knife fight. But the right information, known at the right time, deployed with care and precision, can best any weapon. If you know where your enemy sleeps, there doesn't need to be a knife fight at all.

The right knowledge could raise armies or raze cities. It could make careers or shatter lives. It could change lines of succession. It could bring down kings and the people in powerful places.

It was the latter sort of information, specifically, that Gorm Ingerson pored over with his companions amidst the ashes of Sowdock. He had never met this Jerald Fisher, but the late town crier's foresight or luck had preserved his investigations into a number of suspicious deaths and disappearances. An old Dwarven proverb held that secrets were like daggers pointed at their target; these journals were more like a battery of trebuchets pointed at the Palace of Andarun.

"Everyone who saw Handor die, everyone who looked into it..." Gorm said.

Burt nodded. "No loose ends, as they say, right?"

"And the dragon..." Kaitha stared at the horizon, trying to fathom the unsaid possibilities.

"There might not be a dragon at all," Laruna said.

"Of course, we all know there's a dragon beneath the mountain," said Kaitha. "I mean, we know there is a dragon down there, right?"

Gaist shrugged.

The Elf frowned as she pushed her memory as far back as it could stretch. "I feel like we've always known there was one down there. I just can't recall anyone who's ever seen it up close and lived. But the attacks—"

"They're all here," Gorm marveled, flipping through the pages. "Every time the dragon's struck in the past year. Dayle. The Base. The Agekeeper's Cloister at Waerth."

"You think Johan's in league with the dragon?" said Laruna skeptically.

"I still ain't sure the dragon was here, or that there even is one," said Gorm. "But I'm bettin' that the bannermen will say that's what did this to Sowdock." He waved a hand at the general destruction around them.

"They might be right," said Laruna. "Dragonfire isn't like other flames. It burns hotter than any other fire, enchanted or chemical. And it'd be easy for forensic mages to tell if a fire is created using mundane or magical tools."

"Well, that's why we need a wizard to look at the wood and that chunk of barrel," said Gorm.

"And we'll find one back in the city," said Burt, jerking a thumb over his shoulder. "Speaking of which, we'd best make tracks before the bannermen get here."

"Or better yet, we'd best not," said Kaitha. "Lead my horse. I'll cover our passage."

"Aye!" Gorm started toward the horses with the others, but Kaitha held him back a moment.

"I know you're excited, Gorm," she told him. "But we can't move too fast here. We need proof."

"And we'll find it," he assured her. "But for the first time in a long while, I can see all the signs pointin' in the same direction."

"It's not proof," Kaitha reiterated.

"But it's a good story, and it's easy to follow. That may matter just as much," said Gorm. "Who benefited most when Handor died? Who was with the king at the time he did? Who would want to silence an eagle that was the only other witness? And who has the most to lose if an Agekeeper and some town criers go digging into the story?"

——CHAPTER 4——

"The Doom of the Bloodworm of Knifevale! The Slayer of the Lion of Chrate! The man who took down the Necromancer of the Ashen Tower!" A herald in gold and blue livery ran across the stage, crying adulations into a hollow drake's horn. The bony spindle was enchanted to carry the man's voice over the blaring trumpets, the thunderous drums, and the roar of the adoring crowd. "You know him as the foremost Hero of the City, the Champion of Tandos, the one who drove back Detarr Ur'Mayan's army, the leader of the free Peoples of the Light, and your king! Please welcome His Majesty, Johan the Mighty!"

The crowd thundered in response. The masses rose to their feet as one, a swelling tide in the sheltered bay of Andarun's Grand Opera House. Faint pink lights flared in the orchestra pit, a telltale signal of the sprites that the town criers gathered there used to help remember the event. Above them, the occupants of one of the state boxes dutifully rose to their feet, clapping politely.

One of them was swaying.

"Hooray! Hooray fah Johah!" Weaver Ortson's words were a slurry of mumbled praise and dripping sarcasm. The Grandmaster of the Heroes' Guild in the Freedlands rocked back and forth like a tree in a breeze. The goblet he raised in mock salute would have dribbled wine everywhere had he not had the foresight to drain it as soon as it was filled.

"Sit down, man!" hissed an ancient Dwarf from the seat next to him. Looking at Fenrir Goldson called to mind a barrow king in a suit, with his emaciated frame, skin like spotted paper, scraggy remnants of a long white beard, and a disdain for all living mortals. "Good gods, Ortson, have you no dignity?" he rasped.

"I'd think you know better than that by now." The leathery Halfling next to Goldson gave a short laugh. Bolbi Baggs was merely ancient, which made him the younger of the duo that helmed the Goldson Baggs Group. "But do sit down, Ortson. The king is about to speak."

Weaver slumped into his velvet chair and looked with bleary eyes at a gleaming figure standing in the middle of the stage. King Johan's heavy armor was decorated with enough gold to gild a palace. His flaxen hair and crimson cape blew in an otherwise imperceptible wind, the product of expensive magical glamours. The mages had done well with the cosmetic enchantments; the deep, purple scars that a liche's magic had left across the king's face were barely noticeable, even with the opera house's heavy lights beaming down on him. When he laughed, it was like the clarion call of a trumpet leading to war. When he spoke, almost every mouth in the great auditorium fell silent.

Almost.

"This drivel again?" Goldson hissed to Baggs a few minutes into the king's speech.

"The gods will smile upon us if he's just here to review familiar themes." Baggs swirled a snifter of brandy as he watched Johan raise a fist to the crowd. "For all we know, he'll be letting us know about another terrible merger we're to do, or disrupting trade with the Empire for no good reason again."

Goldson snorted.

As a king, Johan approached the kingdom's levers of power much the way a barbarian with a sledgehammer might approach a Gnomish steam engine: quickly, brutally, and without any consideration for the way things were supposed to work or the wreckage he left behind. Companies were told what business decisions they would make. Nobles were given new duties on whims. Guildmasters and union leaders found themselves scrambling to respond to royal edicts. Those that didn't comply found themselves publicly scorned and sometimes privately sequestered in Andarun's dungeon. Those that did roll along with the edicts endured a different sort of punishment, which mostly involved struggling to stop losing giltin hand over fist while maintaining ostensible compliance with the king's decisions.

All of Andarun's high society dreaded these sudden decrees. And everyone knew Johan's favorite medium for delivering them was the Speech.

The topology of the Speech followed the same well-worn contours every time Johan gave it. It had all the structure and preparation of a stream of thought, and it poured out of the paladin king in a torrent of quips and jokes, wistful remembrances and nostalgic entreaties, boasts and bravado. Yet beneath the gleaming smiles and trumpeting laughter ran an undercurrent of discontent.

"When I slayed the noctomancer Detarr Ur'Mayan or the council of Orc warlords, I didn't need to worry about their paperwork." Johan smiled wistfully into the distance as he spoke, as though he could see better times just over the far horizon. "We knew what was right back then! Things were simpler."

The crowd cheered. Weaver toasted, presumably cued by the applause rather than any agreement with—or awareness of—Johan's words. Goldson and Baggs shifted in their seats, bracing themselves for what would come next. Such an appeal to selective nostalgia and general righteousness was almost invariably followed by some decree or suggestion that wouldn't fix the problem, but certainly seemed connected to today's woes in the minds of the enthralled masses.

"That's why it's time for me to go back to professional heroics," Johan said. "To assemble a team, and fight for justice once more! Andarun, meet your new heroes, the Golden Dawn!"

The crowd erupted into their most ecstatic cries yet as curtains parted and five new heroes walked onto the stage. Stage lights gleamed on golden armor emblazoned with suns and rays of light.

Baggs smiled at his partner. "No new edicts for us," he predicted. "And much better than the tax hike you feared, Goldson."

The old Dwarf scowled down at the stage. "They look like a bunch of ragged miscreants in expensive armor," he growled.

"That's professional heroes for you," said Baggs.

Goldson shook his head and muttered something lost in the roar of the crowd, unconvinced. The audience didn't quiet enough for the Dwarf to speak until Johan was done introducing his new party and started heaping superlatives on them.

"What is the matter, Goldson?" Baggs asked, troubled by his partner's pensive expression.

"Do we know who these people are?" Goldson said.

"Who cares?" said the Halfling. "I'd have expected you to be happy to skip the details. Or at least no more unhappy than normal."

Goldson shot him an impatient glare. "Our firm, Mr. Baggs, has long enjoyed a special relationship with the crown and the guild. When Handor was king, we knew the kingdom's position on everything. We advised. We provided support, and in most cases, we earned a decent margin on it," said Goldson. He nodded down to the five heroes standing behind the king. "Who are those lot? Why are we financing them? What opportunity are they pursuing, and why weren't we presented with it? Does this pertain to the king's secretive business in the Royal Archives, or does it mean he has new plans for our, ah, joint venture?"

Baggs' mouth set in a deep frown as he listened. "It's been apparent for quite some time that Johan is the proverbial tiger that we have caught by the tail, Mr. Goldson."

Goldson sipped his drink and nodded in agreement.

"Still, I think you'll agree that in such a situation, the key is, metaphorically speaking, to not get caught and to not let go." Baggs took a sip of his own brandy. "Our only course is to ride the beast as best we can."

"Of course. But I should like to better know where we're going," grumbled the old Dwarf. "Johan's loyalty to Handor always had its limits. We should assume his alignment with our interests is... similarly constrained."

"Naturally," murmured the Halfling. He spoke up and turned to the drunken guildmaster. "Weaver? What do you know about this so-called party of heroes the king has assembled?"

Weaver Ortson was refilling his glass and sloshed a little wine onto the crimson carpet at the mention of his name. "Jus'... jus' shigned the papersh," he slurred.

"You do know something, though," Baggs pressed.

"Jus' shigned some papersh..." Ortson shook his head. His hands trembled as he poured. "I jus' shigned..."

"Thrice curse it, man! What did you sign!" barked Goldson.

Yet Ortson said nothing useful. It was unclear whether this was because the guildmaster possessed a particular determination to keep a secret or because he was inebriated to the point of amnesia. It was also irrelevant; all of the bankers' attempts to badger the man only yielded incoherent mumblings and some stains on the carpet.

"Leave him," Baggs growled to Goldson eventually. "He's useless to us like this."

"As if that's different from the norm," grumbled the Dwarf. He stared down at the stage, where the king promised that he and his party of heroes would protect the people from the threat of the Red Horde. "Something is afoot, Mr. Baggs. Uncertain times are ahead."

"I suspect you're correct, Mr. Goldson," said Baggs, turning back to the stage with a grimace. "And nothing is worse for the market than uncertainty."

Feista Hrurk's favorite thing about trading on the Wall was the uncertainty. The possibilities. The *potential*. The sense that, as much as the bankers and brokers wanted to know what the market would do next, anything could happen here once the bell rang and commerce was set loose upon society. She took a deep breath and savored the thrill of the market. It felt like an electric tingle buzzing from the fuzz on her ears down to the tip of her tail.

She watched the traders and brokers mill about in the shadow of the great stone edifice. The Wall was constructed such that its top remained mostly level, while its bottom dropped with each tier of the city down the mountain. It towered over the buildings and streets down at the Base, but was no taller than a hedge fence up on the ninth and tenth tiers.

On the Sixth Tier, the Wall was still taller than many of the buildings next to it—even taller than the great dome of the Andarun Stock Exchange. The exchange's clerks had erected a great signboard above the trading grounds, built with long slats that could have numbers and letters slotted into and out of them. A large crew of Kobolds, House Gnomes, and

Goblins dashed over a network of ladders and girders surrounding the sign, swapping out letters and numbers as prices rose and fell.

From her vantage at the edge of the trading grounds, Mrs. Hrurk could watch entire markets move. Her keen eyes tracked power and wealth as it migrated across the economic landscape. She could practically hear the pulse of society with every ebb and flow of the prices. The market itself seemed alive.

And like any living organism, it was messy. Traders and brokers pushed and shouted and waved packets of parchment in the air in a ritual that was some strange crossbreed of an auction, a melee, and a stampede. Buyers, candle-runners, and onlookers were caught up in the boil and added to the general confusion.

It put Feista in mind of Muskie's Fish Market down by the Riverdowns. The only difference was that they sold paper instead of fish up here, and the sellers were convinced they didn't stink as much. Feista knew otherwise; having a dog's nose was a blessing and a curse.

First up on Mr. Poldo's list was a way to short Conglomerated Silversmiths, though Mrs. Hrurk was too savvy to risk shorting outright. Feista's ears perked up to hear better, and the thrum of the crowd separated into a thousand conversations, deals, and shouts. A man was angry about the price of the dragon's hoard. A woman was yelling that she wanted barrels of tannin. A financier was hawking stock loans and short sales.

The last one sounded promising. She pushed through the crowd to a heavy Halfling in a garish purple suit with a matching top hat. "Stock loans! Get rich today! Pay tomorrow!" he hollered.

"You sell options?" Feista barked at him.

The Halfling looked her up and down, his red mustache drooping under the weight of a sudden frown. "You sure you're in the right place, honey?"

"No, I'm not sure," said Feista, working to keep her hackles down. "If you do put options, I might be, but if you keep asking dumb questions, I'll have to take my money elsewhere."

The Halfling held up his hands in apology. "All right, all right. Sorry. It's just that options are complicated, right? And there's, you know, minimums."

"I'm optioning on eight hundred thousand giltin today, if I can find someone who doesn't waste my time. Do you, or do you not, sell put options?" the Gnoll growled.

The financier perked up immediately. "Oh, um, yes! Yes, I'm your guy. Put and calls, short selling, derivatives, you name it. What do you need, darling?"

"Mrs. Hrurk," she said.

"T. D. Swabber." He held out his hand, mistaking her correction for an introduction.

Feista suppressed a sigh. "A pleasure. I'm looking to buy put options on ten thousand shares of Conglomerated Silversmiths. Three-month time frame, strike price of eighty giltin per share."

"Are you sure you—"

"Mr. Swabber, I've got deliveries coming to the home, contractors working on the kitchen, and three pups doing their best to destroy everything I manage to build. I am very busy. If it was just a short against the box I could have sent sprites to make the trade, but my partner doesn't think there's much chance of a bounce and they haven't figured out how to make a sprite that can handle the per-share cost yet, so I have to be here. That's an opportunity for you to earn a decent commission, if you don't waste my time trying to figure out if I know what I'm doing. I do."

"My apologies, hon—Mrs. Hrurk," said Mr. Swabber. He counted off his fingers as he ran through some quick mental accounting. "That's a two thousand and forty-four giltin fee, plus a ten percent commission."

"Two thousand forty-four!" barked Feista. "Did you not hear that I know what I'm doing? That's almost double the going rate! A thousand for the fee and a flat hundred giltin commission is more than fair."

T.D. Swabber grimaced. "One thousand? That's below the rate I'd charge a... uh."

"Yes?" prompted Feista.

Mr. Swabber's eyes had been drifting upward, but he quickly locked them onto Feista's. "Uh, nothing."

"You were going to say a Lightling. You charge more for Shadowkin." Feista pointed a claw at the Halfling.

"No! Uh, no, I wasn't." The Halfling glanced up to someone behind her with a nervous smile.

"You were. Next you'll tell me I have to wait for the paperwork to go through."

Mr. Swabber took a step back. "No, no I won't! I—Look... eleven hundred for the fee, one hundred giltin commission, I'll do it right now. You'll be done before the hour is up. Okay?" He glanced at something above Feista's head on the last word.

"Deal!" Feista grabbed his hand and shook it. Only then did she turn to see what had distracted the financier. "Oh."

Mrs. Hrurk stared up. An Orcess in violet and yellow silks stared down at her. The Orcess' hair was done in long braids, interwoven with chains of green and orange beads. A small retinue of Shadowkin traveled with her, including an Orc built like a mountain fortress.

"That was finely done," said the Orcess.

"Thank you," said Feista nervously. Something about these Shadowkin seemed familiar.

"And thank you for giving my people a lesson on the path of the aggressive seller. I am Asherzu, Chieftain of the Guz'Varda and CEO of Warg Incorporated."

"Ah." Feista's tail involuntarily tucked between her legs in the presence of the most well-known Shadowkin in Andarun. Mr. Swabber, tailless though he was, had a similar reaction; the Halfling's cheeks flushed, and he ran off with a mumbled excuse about tracking down a candle-runner.

It took the Gnoll a moment to remember her manners and introduce herself. "I am Feista Hrurk. Um, of the Hrurk, proprietress of Mrs. Hrurk's Home for the Underprivileged."

"It is good to meet you, Feista of the Hrurk," said the chieftain. "I am here with the board of Warg Incorporated, to show them how we might better negotiate on the Wall. Honor us with your time, Gnoll. Tell us of your methods while you wait for the Gnome to finish your trade."

"I... I would be honored," said Mrs. Hrurk, her head spinning.

"As would we. And I am sure that Izek has insightful questions for you." Asherzu smiled at Feista, yet her tone suggested that things would not go well for Izek if he didn't have questions.

A Goblin near the back of the group swallowed hard and stepped forward. "Uh, what fee would you have accepted had he not taken your offer?" he began.

"Eleven or twelve hundred is standard," said Feista. "I wouldn't have accepted above that."

"Ah. And the commission?" piped in a Slaugh next to Izek.

Feista answered his questions as best she could, still stunned that the executives would speak to her, let alone ask her questions. She discussed her information and analysis with them until Mr. Swabber returned with drafted orders and a tall Human that wore a long coat beneath several satchels, scroll tubes, and belt pouches. On his head, the man wore a candle-runner's distinguishing hat—a cap with a lit candle in a brass setting on the front of it.

"It seems that your trade is ready to execute," said Asherzu, eyeing the candle-runner as he set up the small, portable desk he carried. "Your insights are wise and your knowledge is mighty, Feista of the Hrurk. I offer you my card."

The chieftain held out a small, cream-colored rectangle with her name and Warg Incorporated's address stamped on it.

"Uh, thank you," said Mrs. Hrurk, patting her pockets even though she knew she didn't have a card to offer back.

"The home you spoke of running does not seem a good use of your power, noble as it is," said Asherzu. "I would be honored to have you at my side. Send a sprite to our office should you wish to have a new job."

Feista was stunned. A tumult of thoughts swam in her mind, but the ones that bubbled up to her mouth were all a litany of excuses that she stammered to the chieftain; she had the pups to think of, and the people at the home relied upon her, and the renovations in the kitchen needed constant attention, and—

Asherzu dismissed these concerns with a wave of her hand. "Yes, surely each of us has a destiny to attend to," the Orcess said. "Call upon me if ever you decide to seize the one awaiting you in finance."

"When observed from a close perspective, how can destiny be distinguished from coincidence?"

Jynn Ur'Mayan posed the question to a small, plain room crammed with desks, most of which were occupied with students in gray robes.

The omnimancers-in-training took notes in small ledgers as the archmage lectured.

"Up close, fate looks like tiny connections. Moments of serendipity. Tragic accidents. And yes, coincidences large and small," Jynn continued, pacing back and forth in front of the students. "Yet theoretically, from a distance, one could see a continuous chain running through otherwise disparate events to a planned conclusion. Time streams toward these destinations as though through grooves in the great loom, and it takes tectonic forces to change the fates of those caught in the stream. Across history, there have been few people who have tried to harness such powers."

A student near the front of the class raised her hand. "The Order of Twilight?"

"Indeed, Miss Sabrin, to some degree." Jynn gave a small smile. "In its heyday, our order dabbled in low magic. But they learned well not to toy with it lightly after they saw the folly of their predecessors."

A few of the more advanced omnimancers in the room sucked their teeth and raised their eyebrows. "The Sten?" a young wizard ventured.

"Quite right, Mr. Brightstar." Jynn stepped in front of the large table covered in a wide variety of esoteric devices, stone totems, wands of varying lengths and shapes, and a few items covered with heavy gray blankets. "According to the early work of Nephan, the Sten believed that Arth and its destiny were inexorably woven together. As water erodes a stone, so stone becomes a channel for the river, and so the river carves a canyon. The cause and the effect shape one another. Thus, the Sten believed that by shaping Arth, they could shape their fate." From the table, the archmage picked up a small, granite totem carved in the shape of a turtle with a tree etched into its back. "They made spirit stones to attract the souls of the dead and speak with the voices of their ancestors." He nodded toward a twisting array of copper tubes wrapped around colorful crystals. "And they crafted subtle tools to change the flow of fate, and bring them better fortune."

"Didn't many ancient peoples make grave markers and good luck charms?" asked a skeptical mage from the back of the class.

Jynn's smile turned brittle as the class tittered. "Many cultures did, Miss Wardraxon—"

"Wardroxan."

"Selena," Jynn amended. He often had difficulty pronouncing names from Faespar. "Still, there is reason to believe those made by the Sten actually brought them great fortune."

"Before they were wiped out." The young woman's skepticism was evident.

"During the eons they reigned over Arth, yes," said the archmage.

It was Selena's turn to look nonplussed. "Even if they were fortunate during that time, how do you know it was low magic and not just random coincidence?"

"That is the question I posed, yes. Low magic is often subtle and hard to detect. But sometimes it isn't." He paused for dramatic effect, pulled off one of the cloths draped over a sculpture at the center of the table, and smiled in grim satisfaction as a couple of students gasped.

It looked like a copse of tiny trees, carved from black granite and arranged on a stone serving platter. Branches stuck out from the spindly trunks at precise angles and merged into others. A black sphere hovered in the center of the miniature wood, flat and featureless save for a faint blue light that glimmered at the edge of the orb. The sphere intersected the trunks and branches perfectly, so that it looked like a careless god had neglected to mend a hole in reality.

"This," said Jynn, "is a prophetic vault. It doesn't react to high magic, and no force can move it from its position amidst the sculpted branches. No scrying can see the inside. It has been sealed for over a week, and its contents will remain locked within, held exactly as they were until the prophecy I wrote comes true."

"What did you prophesy?" asked Meryl Sabrin.

"'Upon the gong, as our time in course wanes, the seeker of answers shall stand and wait, and so the vault shall open again,'" Jynn answered.

Confusion and distaste pulled Balorox Brightstar's features toward the center of his round face, scrunching it into a puzzled scowl. "That could mean anything."

"Exactly!" Jynn beamed. "Note the esoteric language creates plausible fulfillability, allowing for multiple scenarios where the prophecy could successfully be completed. It also creates uncertainty in the listener, which helps diffuse Novian counterforces and defend against competing prophecy."

"Competing prophecy?" Meryl asked.

"Of course," said Jynn. "Just as surely as wizards duel with fireballs and lightning bolts and other forms of high magic, the masters of low magic once clashed to shape the future with prophecies and counter-prophecies."

Fifteen chairs screeched and groaned as fifteen mages in training leaned forward in their seats, drawn to powerful knowledge as moths to a lantern.

Jynn held up his gloved hand, a single finger raised in warning. "But remember, low magic is the power that gods and demons wield through their temples and cults. This is the battleground upon which cosmic forces fight for the world. It is easy to create unintended consequences when you may not see the results for days, or years, or even within your lifetime. And to make an error with low magic, or to attract the wrong attention, can be the unmaking of a mage, or a whole order, or even an entire people."

"You think that's what happened to the Sten?" Meryl looked with worry at the table full of arcane apparatuses.

"Who can say?" said Jynn airily. "Hubris can bring the mighty low."

"So we're not going to use low magic then?" Selena looked disappointed.

"What? Oh, no. Of course we will." Jynn chuckled and waved the concern away. The classroom filled with relieved laughter. "But we'll be very careful. And we have tools to ensure that we won't run afoul of any existing destinies. A wand of ebony and nornstone, for example, can help us measure the latent fate in our immediate proximity." He picked up a midnight wand that was so long it nearly extended from the tips of his fingers to his shoulder. He held it out as if bestowing a sword to the class. Midnight runes glimmered along the wand's length in a blue so deep they could only be discerned from the dark wood by the reflection of the glowstones above. "It should be a small matter to determine if local events are totally mundane"—he pointed to the base of the wand with his free hand—"or the signs of Arth-shaking prophecies that could define the end of the Seventh Age." Here he indicated the notch at the end of the wand. "All we need to do is channel air and fire to—oop!"

A blinding burst of blue light flashed as soon as the archmage channeled magic into the wand, leaving nothing but a colored smudge across the vision of those who hadn't closed their eyes fast enough. A thin tendril of black smoke rose off the wand's tip.

"What does that mean?" asked Balorox.

"It means that many of the Order of Twilight's relics have stopped functioning after millennia of neglect." Jynn waved the wand up and down to extinguish any residual flames, then set it back down with a shrug. "Regardless, our use of low magic will be ethical and sensible, and as the next generation of the Twilight Order, we—"

The archmage was interrupted by a sudden flurry of banging on the wall to his side, accompanied by a muffled storm of angry Ruskan.

"One moment," Jynn told his students with a short-lived smile. He stepped up to the wall, grabbed a broom that seemed to have been propped against it for no other purpose, and banged on the wall with enough fury to match the assailant. "Enough, Mrs. Ur'Kretchen!"

"You talk too loud! You always screaming! And you magic my apartment!" bellowed the creature on the other side of the wall, ostensibly an elderly woman but possibly a greater demon. She had a gravelly voice, a thick accent when she spoke Imperial, and—if the plaster shaking off the stone wall was any indication—a siege mop. "Too loud always, and always magic! Make cat go crazy!"

"I assure you we've done no. Such. Thing!" Jynn growled, smacking the wall with his own broom handle to punctuate each word. "We do not care about your cat!"

Another Ruskan tirade broke out, though Jynn could hardly understand it. He had forgotten some of the mother tongue since his childhood, and he suspected his mother never would have allowed him to use the sort of language that Mrs. Ur'Kretchen was employing in the first place. Yet it was moot profanity; slipping back into Ruskan was usually a sign that the old neighbor's fury was abating. The banging stopped, heavy footsteps shuffled away from the wall, and somewhere in the adjacent apartment a cat yowled.

"Ahem. My apologies." A sheepish grin flitted across Jynn's face as he returned the broom to its corner. "Another reminder that we're all looking forward to the order raising enough funds to afford a proper tower."

The faces around the classroom pulled into deliberately blank expressions; students of omnimancy did not need another reminder that the Order of Twilight lacked the amenities of those of the Sun and Moon. Their newly reinstated school received a pittance from the Academy of Mages, and just as the Twilight Order walked the gray boundary between noctomancy and solamancy, they also balanced between meager progress and insolvency.

Jynn struggled to find the right words to bring his lecture back on target, but he was saved when the great bronze bell at the Temple of Musana marked the hour and the end of class. "Next lecture I'll share what we've begun to uncover in our studies of Stennish artifacts!" he shouted over the shuffling of parchment and quills. "And look!"

The students followed his gaze to the prophetic vault, where the black sphere of nothingness had disappeared in a cloud of glittering particles. A small porcelain plate balanced amidst the sculpted branches, bearing an egg and herring sandwich. Jynn carefully reached between the stone rods, picked the sandwich up, and took a theatrical bite. "Still fresh as the day I made it—after a week!" he proclaimed to light applause. "And now, who has the question?"

He scanned the classroom for a standing student, as he had written in his ledger of experimental prophecy, but found none. The mages assembled remained seated, leveling questioning glances at one another.

"Nobody?" Jynn's brow furrowed. "There should be a someone looking for an answer amongst you. I specifically prophesied a seeker would be standing."

Someone cleared their throat at the door. Jynn turned as a familiar figure stepped into the room.

"Well, I did have one question," said Heraldin Strummons.

"What now?" Burt asked. He stretched as the party walked up the road to the New South Gate. Mount Wynspar reared up before them, the great city of Andarun spilling down its front like a frozen waterfall.

"Now we do some investigatin'," said Gorm. Winter was settling onto the mountain and the surrounding plains, which meant sunset came earlier each day. As the Dwarf took in the city, the sun's last rays bathed the Wall in amber light, and across the tiers lanterns began to flicker to life. "We need more information, and we need to be discreet."

Kaitha sighed, conjuring a cloud of frosty mist in front of her face. "I have a couple of appointments. But I don't have another quest lined up yet. I'll put in some discreet inquiries about that eagle."

"Yeah," said Laruna. "I need to talk to the Academy about the pyromancers, but I can ask about alchemical fire while I'm there."

"Take half that charred log to your Academy folk," said Gorm. He looked back over his shoulder. "And for ye, Burt?"

"I've got paperwork and meetings." The Kobold leaned out of Gorm's rucksack, puffing a cigarette as he considered the city. "The chieftain will want an update on your suspicions."

"We'll need her help once we find proof," Gorm said. "We can't take on Johan without the Shadowkin."

"Let's start with getting the proof, then," said Burt. "Lady Asherzu ain't going to stick her neck out on the word of Lightlings alone. We've seen how that goes."

"Aye." Gorm grimaced as he started walking toward the city in renewed earnest.

"And what will you do?" Kaitha asked him.

"Look for evidence," he told her. "Sniff for clues. There's a couple of old friends I want to check in on."

The Elf held back a laugh, but he could see it dancing behind her eyes. "Something about the way you say that makes me think they may not be happy to see you."

Gorm shared a look with Gaist. "That depends on how accomodatin' they are."

"We cannot invest money that does not reside in the budget, Guglug!" countered Borpo.

—CHAPTER 5—

"Go away. We're closed!" called the acolyte, her voice muffled by the thick oak door of the Temple of Al'Matra.

"No ye ain't." Gorm pounded his fist against the door with the rhythmic obstinance of a battering ram. "Not for me."

Another acolyte spoke out, his voice cracking with worry and adolescence. "Uh, the high scribe was very clear that you're not to—"

"You're not supposed to say that!" hissed the first acolyte.

"Eh?" said Gorm, pounding harder. "If'n I need to have another chat with Pathalan, I can start knockin' on the door with me axe!"

"No!" cried the Al'Matrans in unison. A hurried, hushed argument played out on the other side of the door. Eventually the door swung open, and the pair of acolytes grudgingly bid Gorm enter. The taller of the two, an Elven woman, nodded to a pock-faced young Human, indicating that he should guide Gorm to his destination.

The adolescent acolyte nodded back to the Elven one, gesturing for her to accompany the Dwarf. Scowls broke out, then escalated into a full-on pantomimed argument that Gorm ignored and brushed past.

Tension filled the Temple of Al'Matra whenever Gorm Ingerson walked through the door. Acolytes and scribes spoke in hushed whispers in the moldering hallways. Clergy members moved to their destinations with a bit more urgency. Scribes suddenly found excuses to check the records in the deepest recesses of the temple archives.

This air of unease was in part because the Temple of Al'Matra seldom had any visitors. People in need of divine aid had a lot of gods to choose from, and most of the other deities were sane, or at least more sane than the All Mother. Most Al'Matrans in the temple chose to serve there because, if you could put up with the dingy accommodations and the occasional silly task, the meals were free, the beds were warm, and you had to be at least ostensibly respected as a clergy member in city business. For almost everyone who could afford their own room and board, there were better temples to pray at. The temples of Fula or Erro, in particular, provided very favorable ratios of blessed comfort to required devotion.

Yet among the thin ranks of regular visitors to the Al'Matran temple, Gorm Ingerson was the most well-known and least welcome. He was loud, smelly, brash, and all the other typical complaints the followers of an Elven goddess might mutter about a Dwarf in their sanctuary. Yet those minor offenses faded in the shadow of his worst sin: the berserker had very strong opinions about the way the temple should be run.

"This floor's gettin' disgustin' again," groused the Dwarf, stamping through rows of crumbling pews. "When was the last time ye dusted in here?"

"I-It's just that not many p-people come into the sanctuary," said the adolescent acolyte, rushing to catch up with him.

"It ain't about impressin' visitors. It's about respect!" Gorm traced a thick finger along the edge of an ancient seat. It squelched, and his fingertip was black when he held it up. "And the roof's leakin' again?"

"It's the statuary, sir," added the Elven acolyte, hurrying after them. "The All Mother insists we keep them on the upper terraces, but they're made of heavy granite and the wood in the roof isn't what it once was."

"Ain't no excuse for lettin' leaks go," growled Gorm. "Nor allowin' the dust to build up, nor toleratin' them mushrooms growin' in the floorboards, nor leavin' that giant rat in the sanctuary."

A dog-sized ball of fur and bones gave a rasping cough and half-limped, half-skittered toward the door.

"Oh, that's just old Scabbo," said the Elf. "He's too far along to be any harm, and since we got scargs in the basement he likes to hang around up…" The young Human lost momentum as Gorm turned the full force of his glare on the acolytes.

"Hire a hero to clear out them scargs and the rat." Gorm pointed a finger at the pair like it was a crossbow, and they shrank from it as though it might actually fire. "Fix the leaky roof. Weed the hallway. And dust and sweep the sanctuary. I told the last acolyte all of this!"

"Yes, we know," said the Elf meaningfully.

"They started the two of us on door duty after she quit," added the young Human, with as much reproach as he could muster.

"Then get it fixed, or I'm going to have actions with someone."

The acolytes shared a confused look. "I beg your pardon?" asked the Elf.

"Ye and I are havin' words now, but actions'll speak louder." The threat in Gorm's voice was as subtle as a ballista. "If necessary."

The Human paled. "Ah, that won't be… I'll send word to the high priestess, sir, but I honestly don't think the All Mother feels disrespected if the sanctuary is a bit… uh… decaying."

"Ain't her I'm worried about." Gorm made his way over to his usual spot in front of a bronze sculpture of a man with long robes and a melancholy expression. The memorial to High Scribe Niln of the Al'Matrans was likely the cleanest spot in the goddess' temple, well swept and meticulously polished.

"Uh, right. Right," said the acolyte. "We'll just leave you to it, then?"

The Dwarf didn't look up from his inspection of the statue. "Aye, and see that someone cleans the rest of the sanctuary come morning."

Gorm settled in as the acolytes scurried out. There was a well-built chair set up near the sculpture for his visits.

"Hello Niln," he said, settling into the chair.

The statue of Niln responded as one would expect.

"Sorry I ain't been in as much lately. I been busy. And I… I get tired sometimes," he confided in the statue.

Niln waited in expectant silence.

"A year ago I thought we were almost there… like we were right on the edge of avengin' ye," Gorm mused eventually. "Rightin' the ways ye and Tib'rin and Zurthraka and all the Guz'Varda was wronged. Expected next time I came to see ye, I'd be tellin' ye Johan was dead and we avenged ye. Course, I can't say that yet. Maybe that's what kept me away."

Gorm looked around at the All Mother's crumbling sanctuary. Scabbo wheezed at him from behind a rotten pew. He sighed. "A nation ain't like a dungeon, right? A society ain't like a monster. Ye can't just kill it, take its money, and celebrate with some ale. My whole career I been doin' jobs where the final solution was me axe, and once the targets were gone all me problems were solved. Especially the financial ones."

A lump rose in his throat. "But then I met Tib'rin. Changed me life, he did. And as he helped me get to know the Orcs and Goblins and other folk, I realized what a horror that was. That the ones I was killin' were people too. That ye can't treat 'em as monsters. And I... once I saw what I'd done, the whole thrice-cursed world looked upside down."

He sat in silence for a time, remembering the shame of it. The statue of Niln waited patiently.

Eventually, he took a deep breath and continued. "But the whole thrice-cursed world was made by people. Friends and families, hard workers and folk who do their best to be honorable. And ye can't tear society down without destroyin' them too. That's why the Red Horde have the wrong of it. They want to kill the ones in power, to burn their homes, to orphan their children, and then to take back the money so that callous, murderous people won't be in power. But they would be. It'd just be a new batch of 'em."

Niln looked solemn as ever.

"How can ye save the world when the world seems like the problem?" Gorm asked. "How do ye solve a problem when the only visible solution is the same problem again? How can ye save a kingdom from its own king? Or from the people that keep him king? It's hard, Niln. It takes a long time. And in the meantime, the others are back to old careers or startin' new ones. The Guz'Varda and the other Shadowkin are takin' to business. Thane... gods, I searched for him so long, and no trace of where he's gone to. I know everybody's got to try an' get by, but I just thought we'd fight through the problems instead of workin' around 'em or runnin' away."

The statue of Niln looked down on him in sympathetic silence.

"I suppose ye know what it's like, fightin' battles that nobody else is fightin' for a solution nobody can see. But ye... ye were stronger than me in that regard. Every day ye got up and dove headfirst into a fight for somethin' everyone else doubted, and ye took on a world that was too much for ye."

He looked up at the bronze visage of his old friend. "I never gave ye enough credit for that. With Tib'rin I... I got to say goodbye. To tell him how much I learned from him, how he was a good friend. And ye... ye were ripped away thinkin' I thought ye a fool. Because I did. A nice enough one, but a fool. Wasn't 'til after ye were gone that I realized how strong ye were, in your own way. In a better way than me."

Niln's smile was contrite. Serene. Forgiving.

"But I learned from ye, sure enough," said Gorm, standing. "Me friends all think I'm barmy, just like I once thought ye was. But ye showed me, and now I'll show them. There's a way to bring justice. There's somethin' more here. And what we found in the ashes of Sowdock, it's going to change the world, Niln. To save it. Even if I don't know how, I'll keep marchin' toward it. No matter what comes."

He grinned up at Niln, who seemed to be smiling back at him. "We're gonna shake the foundations of the world, ye and Tib'rin and I. Just wait." And with that promise, Gorm strode out of the sanctuary of the All Mother and left the bronze statue of the high scribe alone in the dim light of the waning candles.

The echoing clanks of the Dwarf's iron-soled boots faded. Soon the only sound in the sanctuary was the wheezing snuffle of Scabbo grubbing about for mushrooms and roaches. Eventually, the old rat tired and shuffled off to sleep somewhere beneath the altar. Even the crickets stilled. For most of the night, nothing disturbed the solemn silence around the statue of the high scribe.

Then the acolyte responsible for singing the matins hour came in, saw Niln's face, and screamed at the top of his lungs.

"Such a reaction belies a lack of control, do you see?" said the old pyromancer. "Control is everything."

Laruna stared at the ancient woman from across an alabaster table, doing everything in her power to wear a serene smile. It was not working.

Her face was trying to twist itself into a mask of rage, suitable for loosing the screams that she was holding in her heaving chest. As hard as she fought to will her treacherous features into something serene, the most she could manage was holding them in a manic, rictus grin.

"I... am... controlled," she rasped through her teeth. "See?"

The old woman's heavy-lidded eyes followed an errant spark that flicked away from Laruna. Embers of latent sorcery popped off the young solamancer's head like infernal dander, singeing the silk cushions in the fine chambers of the Order of the Sun. "I see a lot," she said deliberately. "I do not see control."

Laruna sucked in a deep breath. This was the Ember of Heaven, she reminded herself, the mightiest pyromancer to come from the Empire this age. When she had been the Flame of Heaven, the Ember had served the Imperial Court for decades and earned praise from all corners of the Empire and the Free Nations alike. It was said that no foe but time could snuff out the Ember, and she seemed to be giving time itself a bit of a hard go. The years had marbled her rich walnut skin, turned her raven curls silver, and turned her famously curved figure into something more uniformly spherical. Her new moniker made it clear that she couldn't wield as much magic as she did in the legends of yore. Yet, while her youth and power were waning, her mastery of pyromancy was undiminished. It was said that she could steal the flame from a dragon's mouth.

It had taken all of Laruna's influence as a Hero of the City, some of her recent wealth, and a not insignificant amount of pleading on the solamancer's part to arrange this consultation. Now it took every ounce of her self control not to blow it up in a writhing ball of flame. She took a deep breath and tried another approach.

"Archmage, I can weave spells with excellent technique," she said, channeling fine threads of fire into a complex formation. "I know the eighteen forms of Zhut So Tsi. I can cast spells of the eighth order of—"

"What is that to me?" The Ember's voice dripped derision. "You speak like a noctomancer, all cold and damp, collecting spells and forms like a child pinning insects to a corkboard. We are of the sun! We cast from the heart!"

"I thought you told me I needed control!" snapped Laruna, weaves of pyromancy flaring around her fist as she pounded the table.

"You do. And the fact that you see casting from the heart and losing control as the same thing tells me that you are not ready." The Ember's voice was firm, but not unkind. "You need to learn life's lessons before you wear the pyromancer's robes."

"Then teach me!"

"I cannot," said the Ember. She cut off Laruna's next demand with a wave of her hand. "Nobody can. You must discover some things for yourself."

It wasn't the denial that did it, Laruna reflected. She never really expected a mage like the Ember to train her, or to play matchmaker for an apprenticeship. It was the way she wasn't allowed to speak, the quick dismissal of her thought before she was able to give it voice, that drove her over the edge of rage.

Fire suddenly wreathed Laruna as she leapt to her feet. "Enough riddles! Just tell me what the pyromancers want from me, or—!"

"I see that you are angry." The Ember spoke levelly, neither without fury nor at the mercy of it. "That's good. I am angry too. When your rage comes you wield the fire, Laruna Trullon, but who is wielding it in that case? You? Or your anger?"

The flames around Laruna billowed like a funeral pyre. "What are you talking about? You just said we're both angry!"

"I am not my anger. I am the fire." No sooner had the words left the old pyromancer's lips than the flames around Laruna drained away. The younger woman's fury remained, but all the heat, all the fire, all the magic sluiced from her grasp and pooled in the Ember of Heaven's waiting palm, where it glowed as bright as a small sun.

Laruna stared in stunned silence at the brilliant light dancing in the Ember's hand. Her anger still boiled, but the magic that usually accompanied it felt as distant as the far continents.

"And until you are the fire as well, you will not wear the pyromancer's robes." The old woman closed her palm, and the light winked out. "You do not need power, or technique. You need to master yourself. That is what holds you back."

Laruna startled at the words, an old memory blooming in her mind. "What? Like personal growth?"

"Yes. Exactly."

"Like an epiphany?" A small smile twisted the solamancer's lips as a plan germinated and hope took root.

Now it was the Ember's turn to look confused. "I suppose..."

"I can work with that," said Laruna. "I know how to do personal growth."

The Ember of Heaven leveled a hard stare at her. "I'm not sure you do."

"I can. I know what I have to do," said Laruna, now grinning ear to ear. Her mind raced as she scrambled to her feet; she'd need books, and arcane chalk, and she had to find Kaitha. The solamancer was so excited that she made it halfway to the door before she remembered proper protocol and turned back to the nonplussed Ember of Heaven. "Thank you, Archmage," Laruna said, bowing as she backed out of the room. "Thank you for meeting with me."

"It is the very least I could do." Jynn spoke every word with the precision and force of an assassin's crossbow bolt. "You can be certain that I would like to do less, but the gods alone know how many more classes you might have disrupted if I didn't agree to see you this morning."

If Heraldin noticed the naked hostility in the archmage's voice, he hid it well. "Right. Sure. You know, friend, I admire what you've accomplished in the last year. You're really starting something special here. Great office, too. What is it you're studying now?"

"The effects of low enchantments on probabilistic causation," said Jynn.

"Sounds complicated! Maybe dangerous," said the bard.

"There are certainly risks of unintended consequences," muttered the omnimancer.

"Well, it's amazing work. And what a fantastic office." Heraldin waved a hand at the small room. Most of Jynn's office was dominated by the large, ebony desk that the wizard sat behind, but the space that remained was lined with glass cases that brimmed with curios and oddities. There were seven gems in various colors set on a blue velvet backdrop. Strange creatures with too many legs and orifices hung suspended in jars of green fluid. One of them opened several of its eyes and stared at Heraldin as he leaned too close.

"Aha. And the eyeballs in a jar. Ha! Great! It's hard to get over how well you're doing," the bard managed, working to keep up an optimistic front.

"Apparently," said Jynn humorlessly.

"You're probably wondering why I came calling," asked the bard.

"I'm fairly certain it's because I failed to place appropriate boundaries in an experimental prophecy," said Jynn. "What I don't know is why you think you came here."

"A business opportunity."

"No."

"You don't have to work at all." The bard's smile was implacable, but notes of desperation crept into his voice, and his eyes kept darting to the thing watching him from the jars. "No involvement whatsoever. I just need you to sign over the ballad rights for your part in our adventure—"

"Absolutely not," Jynn said. "Anything else?"

"At least hear me out!" the bard pleaded.

"No," said Jynn.

"Why not?" Heraldin's voice cracked. The thing in the jar was starting to wave its legs.

"To begin with, I've heard you sing."

Heraldin rolled his eyes. "Yes, fine, but with glamours and backup singers—"

"What is more," Jynn continued, "while some may consider the tragic events of last year entertaining, I do not wish to relive them. I have enough painful ballads written about my family, as you may recall."

"But this one would be different," Heraldin tried.

A shout in the hallway rang out, drawing Jynn's eyes to his office door.

Heraldin leaned forward over the desk, as much to move away from the leering thing in the jar as to hold the archmage's attention. "This ballad will be good for your personal brand!" he insisted.

"Oh?" Jynn's nose crinkled in irritation. "Which part? When my father turns himself into an undead abomination and wipes out most of the Freedlands' armies? Or tears down the walls of Andarun? Or when he tries to kill the king? There are more than enough people who resent my heritage already, and I have endured more than sufficient time in the public eye for it."

"But—"

"Enough. The last thing I need is a bunch of third-rate troubadours caterwauling about my father's rampage across the Freedlands." Jynn waved Heraldin away with a gloved hand. "Although when ranking unwelcome events, it only narrowly beats old associates barging in with random requests! I'd ask—"

Yet the wizard's request was lost in the thunderous bang of his office door being kicked in by an iron-soled boot. Gorm Ingerson surged into the room like a one-Dwarf barbarian horde, trailed by an apologetic omnimancer. "Jynn! You're from Ruskan, right?"

The archmage stared agape at the Dwarf. "What?" he hissed.

Heraldin leaned over the desk to whisper, "You know, for someone who claims to study destiny and probabilistic causation, you really don't seem to know much about Novian teachings."

"I'm sorry, sir!" burbled the omnimancer. "We tried to stop him, but he won't listen to us."

Gorm spoke over the mage, as if to emphasize her point. "We need to know if it was magic fire or somethin' else that burned this here wood." The Dwarf drew a mistreated hunk of charcoal from somewhere in his grungy robes and waved it at the wizard.

Jynn's brow knit as his eyes swiveled between the three figures babbling at him. "What?" he said again.

"We?" asked Heraldin.

Gorm snorted and jabbed a thumb over his shoulder, where the shadows by the door shifted and unfurled into the shape of Gaist. The young omnimancer gave a frightened squeal.

A frost seemed to settle on Heraldin's countenance, and he greeted the weaponsmaster with all the warmth and cheer of a midnight blizzard. "Oh. Hello."

"He's on me quest," said Gorm.

"Of course he is," said Heraldin.

"I couldn't stop him either, sir. He just ignored me," said the apologetic omnimancer, but nobody paid her any attention.

"Still not speaking to me, I see," the bard said airily.

"I thought he didn't speak to anyone," said Jynn.

"Oh, this is very different," said Heraldin, his eyes narrowed to slits.

Gaist stared at the archmage impassively.

"Oh, is that how this will go?" Heraldin sputtered.

"All right, quiet!" Gorm thundered. The room fell quiet, save for a muffled burble from the many-legged thing in the jar, and even that nameless creature shut its eyes and went still when the berserker leveled a threatening glare at it.

With a satisfied snort, the Dwarf turned back to his former colleagues. "The rest of the old party and I have been adventurin', and I think we found evidence of something big. Too big to talk about in front of pryin' ears." Gorm nodded to the young mage, who gave a grin of abject terror and looked pleadingly at Jynn.

The archmage sighed and dismissed the omnimancer with a wave of his hand. The door slammed behind her.

Suspicion crinkled the corners of Heraldin's eyes. "By 'big,' do you mean extremely profitable, or do you mean it's related to your schemes to upend the kingdom?"

"This ain't about money," said Gorm.

"I suspected as much." Heraldin slumped back in his seat. "And it must be suicidal as well, judging by the company you keep."

Gaist looked at the ceiling pointedly.

"If we can prove it was magic or alchemy that burned this wood, we'll prove all them dragon attacks ain't a dragon at all. And if it ain't a dragon, we've plenty of evidence that whoever or whatever it was has been servin' Johan's interests well. But we need to know what burned this here log." Gorm waved the charcoal for emphasis. "And Laruna said I'd need a foreign mage to tell me what kind of fire it was, and I remembered ye was from Ruskan originally. So I'm callin' in a favor."

Jynn stared blankly for a moment as his vocabulary reconciled with Gorm's casual relationship with the Imperial tongue. "Forensic," he said, emphasizing the last syllable. "You need a forensic mage."

Gorm shrugged. "Aye, fine. Ye never struck me as particularly healthy anyway. Can ye do it or not?"

Jynn sighed again and rubbed his temples. "To clarify, if I run some... investigative enchantments on that bit of charcoal and give you the results, you and Gaist will leave and take the bard with you."

"We didn't come together," said Heraldin.

Gorm gave the man a sidelong glance. "Deal."

"I'm not just going to walk out of here because it suits you!" snorted Heraldin.

"Didn't say ye would," said Gorm darkly.

Jynn stood and spoke over the bard's protests. "Very well, I will take you to the laboratory if it will get this over with and let me return to my work. But rest assured, this is the absolute last favor I will do for you."

"You can say it's the last time, but it never is, you know? You just want it to be." The Tinderkin scratched her wrists as she spoke to the small ring of attendants seated in the basement of the Temple of Oppo in Tamanthan West. "I just... I just..."

A smattering of encouragement broke out around the group as the middle-aged Gnome wiped away her tears and collected herself. Kaitha smiled and nodded.

"But I'm taking it one day at a time," Sepra said. "One day at a time. And I'm glad I've made it this far, but... it's just hard, you know?"

Kaitha did know. Everyone seated around the small, stone room did. They broke into light applause and encouraging smiles.

"Thank you, Sepra. Well done," said Brother Mattias. The old priest of Oppo had kind eyes that sparkled from the recesses of his leathery brown wrinkles. His thin, white beard settled on the southern crags of his face like snow on the Ironbreaker Mountains.

As Sepra sat back down, Kaitha glanced around the circle to see who would speak next.

The temple was like the deity it was dedicated to: modest and inconspicuous. Most houses of the Humble God were just rented buildings with an olive laurel nailed above its door; Oppo's Fourth Tier temple had once been a restaurant specializing in Imperial food, and the building still smelled faintly of turmeric and grundant. A few small oil lamps illuminated a ring of the old restaurant chairs set out in the middle of the room.

A ruddy-faced Dwarf with a black beard volunteered. "Eh, I'm Glod Boforson," he said, standing.

"Hi, Glod Boforson!" said the attendees in unison.

"It's been two years, eight months, and twelve days since my last hit of elixir," Glod intoned.

Kaitha joined in light applause. That was part of the script; the mantra. Everybody said it differently, of course. One had to switch in his or her own name, and the details were important. Yet the script was essential. One's name. How long since the last relapse. What used to be hard. What was still hard. Why it could be endured, and what made going on worthwhile. A reminder to take it one day at a time. An expression of gratitude, and then you were done. Every recital ended with a short burst of applause and rote affirmations.

"My name is Cherri Fullweather," said a pale Halfling after Glod sat down.

"Hi, Cherri Fullweather!" came the chorus.

"It's been three months and two days since I had elixir," said Cherri, and now the applause was accompanied by approving murmurs. It was always hardest at the beginning.

After Cherri came Lann, a Human addicted to aetherbloom, though he had fallen into relapse that week. Different parts of the script came into play when he announced as much, tears streaming down his face. The priest offered encouragement. A new pledge was given, and a sponsor for the pledge identified. Tears were shed at a couple of moments, but in the end it seemed Lann was back on the right path.

Then it was Kaitha's turn.

She took a deep breath as she stood. "My name is Kaitha te'Althuanasa Malaheasi Leelana Ter'ethe…" she began.

As she said her name, Kaitha took the time to think about what she would share. She had to stick to the script. She knew the script. She liked the script.

"...Liliea Musanatila Bae Iluvia Daela..."

The only trick was getting her life to fit into the script. She could say the words as she was supposed to, but they weren't entirely honest. And everyone agreed that if you weren't going to be honest, there was no point in showing up to these things. Yet if she was honest, things didn't just veer off script—they took a hard right and plunged off a cliff. Sweat beaded on her brow just thinking of it.

"... Asanti Tilalala nil Tyrieth," she finished.

The circle radiated uncertain silence.

"Hi... Kaitha," said the old priest, and the others followed his prompt.

"It's been a little over a year and a half since I had salve," said Kaitha. "I don't know the exact number of days because I... I wasn't really trying to stop, you know? I just kind of had to."

"It's important to make a decision," offered Cherri Fullweather. The others in the circle murmured in agreement.

"Yes, well, I made a decision not to go through withdrawal again." Kaitha paused and took a deep breath. Things were already starting to go wobbly. "I'm still adventuring, which is risky without salve, but they make these new emergency surgical sprites that deploy on impact. They're supposed to be less addictive than salve."

"Ye had to use 'em yet?" asked Glod Boforson.

"No cause yet."

"Ah. Well, they're definitely less addictive," Glod remarked.

Kaitha nodded. "Good. I can't... the addiction and withdrawal were horrible. And it wasn't just what it did to me. I was in a sort of... well, it wasn't a relationship. It's complicated, but it was something. Whatever it was, I hurt him. I mean really hurt him."

"Many of us hurt the ones we care about in the throes of addiction," said the priest.

"Yeah," said Kaitha. "But I put four arrows in his throat and eye."

The members of the circle on either side of the ranger scooted their chairs, slowly and carefully, away from her.

Kaitha shook her head. "And then he left, obviously."

"Under his own power?" Cherri sounded confused.

"And whatever we had, or almost had, I... I realized that was what I always wanted. But it's gone. It's gone, and I can't bring it back. And I try to distract myself with work, like another quest can take my mind off things, but I've killed a liche and saved the city. I've slain the toughest monsters on the guild boards. I've earned all the highest honors a hero can get. There's nothing left to strive for."

Kaitha's voice quavered as she tried to recover. The script lay in burning shambles around her, but she had to plunge ahead. "I get quests and endorsements, but they don't give me anything I didn't have before, way back when I started drinking and taking salve. I made it to the top. Twice. And there's nothing here but myself and... and an emptiness. A nothing that's bigger than anything I ever had."

She was talking faster now, as though her words could outrun the tears welling up from her depths. "And it's not even a craving for salve, though gods know I want a hit. It's nothing I can get. I just felt this void even back when I was taking kicks all the time, and I wanted... something. Something I never had, and I couldn't name back then. But now I can name it. It's him. Everything was better when he was there, and then I..." Her voice broke at the memory. "I drove him away. But now I don't think there's anything that can fill the hollow, and I just want to forget everything. I don't want to remember."

The silence of the circle was interrupted by Cherri violently blowing her nose into a handkerchief.

"Uh, but I'm taking it one day at a time," Kaitha added, and then sat down to a spatter of uncertain applause.

"This seems like a good time to break for refreshments," said Brother Mattias, prompting a small stampede toward a table by the door. There were always refreshments at meetings like this; if you wanted people to grapple with their inner demons and surface old pain in front of several strangers, it helped to have pastries and coffee. The members of Kaitha's chapter of Siblings in Perpetual Sobriety seemed especially eager for the distraction of hot drinks and cheap tea cakes tonight.

Kaitha wasn't hungry, and she felt worse than ever, but the old priest caught her before she could leave the temple. "I wanted to say I appreciate how you spoke up, today," he told her. "I know that wasn't easy."

The ranger thanked him with a joyless smile.

"And of course, you are welcome to come for as long as you need. Always," said Brother Mattias. "But I think you may benefit from speaking to a therapist."

"I'm seeing two," she replied. "They both agreed I should come to this group."

"Ah." Kaitha recognized the pained look on the priest's face, the wince of a man who wanted to be of more use than he could. "Well, there's also a group up on the Sixth Tier for Elves who may be experiencing dark thoughts."

"Yes. They're the ones who recommended me to my second therapist," she said.

Brother Mattias' wince deepened. "Right. Yes."

They stood in the awkward silence of two people who don't want a conversation to end poorly, but are just about ready to let it so long as it ends soon.

The priest broke first. "Well, you come as long as you need. Sometimes, all you can do with troubles like this is face them head-on and see them through."

Kaitha nodded as she pulled on her cloak. "I will."

"And you're keeping the dark thoughts in check?"

Kaitha bit back a retort and frowned at him.

"Good." The old priest smiled. "We'll see you soon. And in the meantime, I pray that you find what you're searching for."

—CHAPTER 6—

"It should be in... in this drawer, I think. Or maybe... where did I put that?" Jynn muttered to himself as he rummaged through an old alchemist's cabinet at the back of his modest laboratory. "Perhaps in the chest?"

Gorm drummed his fingers on the countertop behind the wizard and eyed the various apparatuses laid out across its surface. Mortars and pestles, thin glass tubes, beakers, and a small runestone sat in no particular order around the charred hunk of wood at their center. The archmage's dog, a motley ball of scruff aptly named Patches, napped by a potbelly stove. "This going to be long?" he asked.

"It will take longer if you keep distracting me." Jynn extracted a length of copper pipe from the chest and peered down its length.

Gorm shrugged and looked at Gaist. The weaponsmaster stood at rigid attention near the back of the room, staring straight ahead. Or rather, he was staring pointedly away from something. Gorm glanced to see what it was, and immediately regretted it when he met Heraldin's gaze.

The bard gave a hopeful smile. "Have you given any more thought to the ballad rights for our adventure?" he asked.

"No," said Gorm, and his tone added that he didn't plan to.

Heraldin pressed on anyway. "It could be mutually lucrative for us to—"

"I've heard ye sing," the Dwarf said with an air of finality, then stood up to have a look around the rest of the laboratory.

The room was in the basement of the Veluna Heights apartment complex, building C, and as such it was decorated in the painted-cement-and-exposed-pipes motif popularized by budget-conscious landlords across the multiverse. Beyond the cheap and minimalist construction, however, it looked like the typical lair of a powerful wizard. There were stacks of papers everywhere, bookshelves buckling under the weight of arcane grimoires, appropriately dribbly candles, and all the other trappings of a brilliant mind bent around the secrets of the universe at the expense of a tidy office.

Gorm had seen many such studies over the course of his career, and that made him uneasy; most of the mages he'd paid a visit to had been necromancers, demonologists, and other rogue spellcasters who'd gone villain. They all favored a particular motif.

"Lot of skulls in here," he remarked, trying to keep his concern from his voice.

"What? Oh, yes, I suppose," said Jynn.

A specimen on a musty desk caught Gorm's eye; a tiny, red-skinned humanoid with a pointed nose and cloven feet. It hung limply between two wire stands, suspended by metal hooks pushed through its bat-like wings. Its multifaceted eyes were dull and lifeless. "An imp?" Gorm asked.

"Yes, of course," the archmage said without looking up. "I'd assumed a hero of your reputation would have seen many of them."

"Aye, but not dead," said Gorm, nonplussed. "Ye can't kill demons! Well, ye can, but when ye do they evaporate back to whatever hell they came from. It's some inner-dimensional... I mean, their bodies are all attuned to some sort of... Well, I don't know how exactly ye mages say it happens, but even if ye chop a demon's head off, ye can't be sure they won't be back lookin' for revenge some years later. Never seen a corpse before."

"Ah, yes." Jynn smiled and glanced over at the tiny body. "My father's notes detailed a way to use shadow and death to bind a demonic entity to this reality, preventing it from reconstituting in its native dimension."

"And your father taught you this spell?" asked Heraldin.

Loose scrolls and dried herbs tumbled from a drawer as Jynn rummaged around in it. "Not directly. He devised the basic weaving pattern in the late stages of the Leviathan Project and documented it in his journals. I suspect he was looking for a way to more safely dispose of summoned demons, but the technique is also useful for studying the physiology of extraplanar beings."

Dwarf, weaponsmaster, and bard exchanged concerned glances. "Interesting," said Gorm "You're still doin' research on Project Leviathan then?"

"Among other things." The wizard pulled a small runestone from the drawer and waved it triumphantly in the air. "Aha!"

"Are you studying... anything else yer father looked at?"

"Oh, here and there." Jynn's disinterest was too firm and quick to be genuine nonchalance. "Picking at old notes and his remarks. And his work on the soul-bound has deep implications for our study of low magic; combining the souls of the deceased with that of a fallen extraplanar being to resurrect an enhanced incarnation of both is—"

"Evil?" interrupted Gorm.

"An abomination?" ventured Heraldin.

"Fascinating," said Jynn firmly. "And it may have many practical applications, such as... well..."

"Raising an army of hellish, demonic creatures using the souls of the dead?" asked Gorm.

"World domination?" said Heraldin.

"What exactly are you implying?" demanded Jynn.

"It's just that... it all seems a bit... ah..." Heraldin pursed his lips as he searched for the right word. Failing to find it, he went with the obvious one. "A bit evil."

"A bit?" Gorm prodded the dead imp with a gloved finger.

"Bah." Jynn waved the argument away with his gloved hand. "I'll not be governed by the whims of the public and their outmoded labels."

"And who does that sound like to ye?" asked Gorm.

"Well, I... I... Oh." Jynn's eyes glanced to an ornate case set on a cabinet across the room, where a long, purple crystal sat on a rune-encrusted stand under a glass cover. "Yes, I suppose it does sound a bit like my father."

"It'd be a perfect impression without all that hair and flesh on your face," said Gorm.

"Aha. Well, an unfortunate turn of phrase on my part." The wizard's grimace was fleeting and rueful. "I suppose we all take after our parents in some ways."

"It is vitally important that you, in particular, do not," said Heraldin.

Gaist nodded.

"Fair enough, but to study is not to follow, is it?" Jynn set the runestone on the table, placed a wire tripod with a porcelain dish above it, and reached for a spiraling glass tube. "I'm no more a liche than a botanist is a tulip, or a herpetologist is a toad."

Gorm snorted. "Every liche used to be a mage. Ain't never met a toad who used to be a wizard."

Somewhere above them an explosion thundered. Panicked shouts and arcane chants rang out from the classrooms above.

"Then you haven't spent enough time with amateur omnimancers," Jynn hissed through his teeth. He pinched the bridge of his nose, eyes shut and brows furrowed, and began to count down from ten. An omnimancer somewhere upstairs rang the all-clear before the archmage got to six.

"Still, if ye ain't trying to dominate the world or be immortal, why look into your father's work at all?" Gorm pressed. "What would people say if they knew what ye were doin'?"

"What would the guild or the bannermen say about this experiment you requested?" The archmage nodded to the hunk of blackened wood. "Do you have the proper manifests and contracts to show that you've rightfully looted construction debris on your adventure?"

"Uh—"

"Yes, unsanctioned and illicit, just as I suspected," said Jynn, twisting the last pipe into place. "And yet I trust your judgment, to the extent that I will do you this favor, and you trust my discretion. As former colleagues and old friends, I hope I can expect the same from you."

"What would Laruna say?" asked Heraldin.

The faintest flicker of concern crossed the wizard's features, a hint of remorse that barely registered before he steeled his expression. "I trust your discretion as well."

"Aye," said Gorm, shooting a warning glare at the bard. "Aye, you can."

"Good." Jynn broke off a piece of the charcoal, dropped it into a bottle, and poured a vial of blue liquid on top of it. Then he inserted a glass pipette into the container, set the whole ensemble on the table, and wove threads of fire and water over the complex apparatus. Fluids bubbled through twisting tubes. Steam whistled from a copper device. Pipes and vials trembled as a thick, purple goo formed a viscous droplet on the end of a delicate spigot, and the whole table shuddered when the oily substance finally dropped onto the porcelain plate above the stone rune. It bubbled and writhed on the white enamel, like a shapeless leech in its death throes, until it suddenly went rigid and deflated with a sad little *pfert*.

"Hmm," said Jynn.

"Is it supposed to do that?" asked Gorm.

The wizard didn't answer. Instead, he added another lump of charcoal to the bottle, poured in another vial, wove the same spell. The alchemical show began an encore; bubbling, whistling, trembling, shuddering, writhing, *pfert*.

"What does that mean?" Gorm was growing impatient for some hint of interpretation.

"We can rule out sorcery with a high degree of certainty, but also mundane combustion," said Jynn, his brow furrowed. "Even a campfire has enough arcane structure bound to the weave to indicate a topological pattern in a manifested thaumatic gel. There are very few ways to leave no signature."

"Speak plainly," said Gorm.

"This wasn't burned by natural or magical fire." Jynn looked up. "But more, it was burned by something so destructive that it... uh..." The wizard worked his fingers as he grasped for an apt metaphor. "It cauterizes the weave, so there's no way to tell for sure what caused the fire. It's almost like it was made for secrecy."

"Aye, see, that sounds like Arson's Friend," said Gorm.

"I beg your pardon?"

"Arson's Friend," the Dwarf reiterated. "Potion that was popular with the rogues back in the day. Comes in little, bright red vials, if I remember correctly. Doesn't burn especially big or hot, but what it did burn couldn't be traced back to any source. The chemical seared out all the traces."

"It could be that," said Jynn slowly. "But it could technically also be disruptions in the weave, or sorcerous interference within my laboratory, or just a fluke of the test."

"Aye, that's why people use Arson's Friend," Gorm affirmed. "Ye knew what it probably was, but ye couldn't be sure. Hard to track. Hard to make stick at court or a guild tribunal."

"It sounds like a definite possibility," said Jynn.

Gaist nodded thoughtfully.

Gorm's brow knit. "But... if I remember, Arson's Friend burns itself out quick—too fast to spread unless ye throw more than a few vials around. And the rogues and thieves I worked with said it was more pricey than gemstones. They didn't use it for startin' big fires as much as destroyin' evidence and such. It'd take a barrel of the stuff to burn down a whole village, but I've no idea where someone would get even a vial of it." Gorm grimaced. "Ain't like the General Store is going to advertise a potion used to dodge the law."

"Well, not advertise, no." Heraldin rolled a pair of green glass globes in one palm, grinning as he watched the chemicals within them swirl. "If you call it 'Arson's Friend' they'll throw you out and call the bannermen on you. That's its street name. But any reputable alchemist would sell it as Imperial flame olive oil."

Jynn's eye locked on the bard. "Imperial flame olives?"

"Yes. Small red olives imbued with fire." Heraldin pinched his fingertips together as if holding up one of the fruits. "People use them in drinks, funnily enough, but they're in high demand because—"

"Come with me!" The archmage started for the door. Patches leapt from his bed and trotted after his master in case the sudden activity meant that there was about to be a treat, a walk, or in the very best of cases, both.

"What?" said Heraldin, his fingers still holding the imaginary olive.

"Where are we going?" asked Gorm, hurrying after the mage.

"To my office!" said Jynn, already pushing out the door and into the dim hallway beyond. "Come on! Hurry!"

"Not sure what the rush is. Always a rush for me, always somethin' terrible if I don't hurry," grumbled Friar Brouse. He scratched his thin beard. It was the only part of Brouse that could be referred to as thin, and one of the few bits that wasn't covered in the heavy yellow robes of a theological support friar. "Everyone always comes callin' with a so-called emergency, and I says 'is it really an emergency,' and then they says 'of course it is,' but then it's spilled jam on the altar or sommat like that. Sommat like this," he added accusingly.

"It's an emergency," said Sister Varia. The priestess of Al'Matra was wearing a long green and white robe, accented with simple silver jewelry. "It's very concerning."

"Nobody's running around. No shoutin' or people carrying water to a fire. No ghostly apparitions or demonic incursions." Brouse set his work bag on the grungy floor of the temple and removed a tattered, black briefcase from it. Inside the case, an array of crystals sat in neat rows in a black velvet setting, each with a small plaque beneath it. The one labeled "Al'Matra" was glowing green. "Oh, it's an emergency, they says, but it's got none of the hallmarks of an emergency, so far as I can tell."

Sister Varia stiffened a little bit. "The high priestess and the high scribe are both very concerned about this matter."

"Ha! 'Very concerned,' she says. The high priestess and the high scribe should both know that I don't come running for 'very concerned.'" The portly Human snorted. "If your goddess isn't dispensing fiery justice or trying to stop a fated end-of-an-age sort of prophecy, she can wait until after breakfast like everybody else."

"It's almost noon," protested a nearby acolyte.

"Had a late call last night at the Temple of Dogs," snapped Brouse, giving the young man a nasty look.

"We are sorry, sir." Sister Varia did her best to smooth things over with the portly friar. "They thought it was very pressing."

Brouse cast a sidelong glance at the young Elf. "All right," he grumbled. "I'm here now, ain't I? Save the apologies for whoever's handling my bill.

In the meantime, what's wrong with the statue of, uh..." He paused to read the plaque at the base of the sculpture. "High Scribe Niln?"

"It's his face," said the acolyte.

Brouse considered this. "Good lookin' enough to me. Maybe a bit mousey."

"It looks fine. It's just... different."

"Different from how he looked when he was alive?" asked Brouse.

"Different from how he looked yesterday," said Sister Varia. "Brother Aphius discovered him this morning."

"Hmph," said Brouse. He reached into his bag again. Holy symbols, translucent crystals, bundles of herbs, strings of beads, and the other tools of a theological support friar lined the interior of the case, neatly arranged within an intricate system of pockets and straps. He selected a few from the bag and laid them on the floor.

The copper coil spun. The blueish crystal flickered with inner light. A string of beads between two yew twigs swung back and forth with metronomic rhythm. The crushed leaves were crammed into a long pipe, which Brouse lit with a match.

"There is no smoking in the sanctuary," chimed Sister Varia.

"Incense," said the friar around the pipe. "Helps soothe angry spirits and align cosmic waves."

"Really?"

"Probably." Brouse puffed furiously as he stared at the string of beads, conjuring blue-gray clouds around his head. "You're getting higher than normal causal waves here, but that's just population destiny. Seen it all the time."

Sister Varia looked confused.

"It's all the people in the city. Get so many fates crammed together, does funny things with predestination, it does." The portly man waved away her question and the smoke in his eyes. "And the latent fate around here is..."

He glanced down at the bluish crystal, which had sputtered out in a plume of azure smoke.

The friar shrugged. "Well, it's probably high as well. Doesn't matter though. Aside from that, everything in here looks mostly normal."

"Normal?" the priestess exclaimed. "The statue moved!"

"No, some metal moved, and it happened to be part of a statue," explained Brouse. "Spatial distortion from your standard predestined event can warp materials. Maybe some warrior down the street realized his true power, or some mage figured out some whizzbang secret. Or something. Point is, your basic fluctuations in fate can twist a hunk of bronze, and you might think it looks like he's moved."

"He—he's got an entirely different facial expression!" protested the priestess.

Brouse shrugged and waved his strange device at the Al'Matrans. "These readings don't lie. No magic. No concentrations of power from any known deity or fiend. No recent miracles. This is just mundane, everyday destiny. See it all the time."

"You don't know that." The priestess drew herself to her full height and then stuck her nose up a little more. "The gods work in mysterious ways."

Brouse grunted and rolled his eyes. "Drake spit. No they don't."

"I beg your—"

"They do the same thing over and over," said the support friar. "The sun rises, the seas wave, rivers run downhill, plants grow, animals eat each other, people eat the animals and plants, and then kill each other even though they're full. Happens every day. Nothin' mysterious about the gods' ways; they work in repetitious and predictable patterns. Sometimes to mysterious ends."

"Ah! But our goddess works in obsessive, irrational patterns!" the young acolyte said, with the eager gusto of a lawyer revealing a brilliant new piece of evidence. His look of triumph withered under the priestess' glare.

Brouse shrugged and started packing his bag again. "Oh. Fine. Her. I'll give you that one. But even if we've got no idea what their holinesses are plotting up there, we can see how they're doing whatever it is down on Arth. And they don't seem to be up to anything here."

"You can't—"

"The beads in this here causal numenometer would be dancing a jig if any god in the hall so much as blessed your lunch." Brouse waved the device at the priestess before shoving it in his bag. "The smoke in my pipe would be turning purple if it was a wizard messing with the weave. This is your standard act of fate, and given that all that's happened is a bit of bronze shifting by an inch or two, it probably ain't a big one. No emergency. Send for me if he hops down from the pedestal or eats a pigeon. That sort of thing." He picked up his bag and touched the tip of his cowl.

"But..." The priestess pursed her lips. "It's just... creepy. I really feel like something meaningful is happening here."

"Well, feelings and meaning are your realm, your grace," said the support friar. "Never pay much attention to that sort of thing myself. We just keep the water holy and the eternal flames lit. There's not anythin' here needs me."

"If you say so," said the priestess uncertainly. She looked up at the bronze cast of the most recent failed incarnation of the Seventh Hero of Destiny. The statue of Niln held a book in one hand, while the other was raised from his side in an upturned fist, as though bracing himself against the winds of a storm. His face was twisted into a manic grin.

"It does seem a little odd." Thane looked around as he and Poldo made their way down the winding, scrabbly path toward Adchul's dock.

"What does?" huffed Poldo. The path zigzagged down a steep slope toward the water, making a pattern almost like slanted stairs for a Troll of Thane's height. A Gnome such as Poldo, however, had to run back and forth for several yards to descend the same amount as one of the Troll's steps, and Poldo was almost winded trying to keep up with the Troll's leisurely pace.

"That we're leaving now. It doesn't look like a good day to sail," Thane said.

Poldo looked down the path. The sky and the sea beneath it were both a dull gray, and an ominous shadow darkened the distant sky. A steady wind kicked up small whitecaps on the ocean and chilled the Scribkin through his thick, black coat. The weather shook him a bit, but he was reassured by the stout Dwarven ship that waited at the dock, banging against the pylons with an irregular rhythm as it rocked in the surf. It was nothing like the sleek Elven schooner that had brought them out to Adchul months before; this boat was wide, low to the water, and covered with enough steel to arm a battalion of knights. Instead of masts, thick pipes extended from the middle of its deck, belching black smoke into the air.

"Fortunately, we're not sailing," he told Thane with a nod to the boat. "Our ship has runic forge-engines, and it's probably watertight belowdecks. Most ships catch the wind and race the storms, but Dwarven vessels ignore the weather."

Thane nodded reluctantly. "It still doesn't seem like a particularly good day to begin a voyage."

"It isn't a particularly good day, but soon every day will be a particularly bad one, and this is the last scheduled delivery this week." Poldo clutched his hat against the wind and stared with naked envy at the bevy of Wood Gnomes riding in the Troll's fur. "The winter storms will start in earnest by Highmoon, and they'll last well into next year. The lawyer-monks said that when spring finally settles the water, the kraken and sea wyrms start their mating seasons, and there are few captains mad enough to brave the waters at that point. There will be few ships in Adchul until Bloomtide."

"And that's longer than the lawyer-monks would care for us to stay?" asked Thane.

"Burn what they care for," wheezed Poldo. "It's too long for me. Besides, it's a short voyage. If those clouds hold and the currents are favorable, we'll have dinner in Chrate this evening."

A profane shout rang out. The Dwarven sailors had noticed their passengers approaching, and now they pointed and cursed, backing away from the Troll.

Thane wavered at the edge of the dock. "And did you—"

"All your information is on the manifesto I sent the captain," said Poldo, wheezing as he stumbled past Thane and onto the wooden planks. "It's their problem if they didn't read it carefully. Come on."

The Troll hesitated, then took a deep breath and stepped carefully onto the old timbers of the dock. The wood groaned and screeched in protest, but the noise was drowned out by the thundering of iron boots on oak. The Dwarven sailors pushed back up the gangplank as one, watching their passengers warily from beneath iron helms.

Poldo ignored them. "It will be nice to be back on the mainland again. Better food, more to do, much easier to conduct business. I hope to find a sprite from Mrs. Hrurk waiting when we arrive in Chrate."

Thane paused near the gangplank and looked out over the water. A bitter wind blew from the north, carrying droplets of seawater that felt like needles of ice. The Wood Gnomes hanging from the Troll's shaggy coat huddled closer together for warmth. "Did she take that job with... with the Orc company?" he asked absently.

"Warg Incorporated," said Poldo, bracing himself against the gust. "I should hope she will, and I've encouraged her to do so. Possible news of her career is just another reason to look forward to the letter. Why, imagine where she could go after landing a job with Asherzu Guz'Varda! One could easily see business travel bringing her to Chrate or Monchester. We might even be able to meet her there, if her schedule allows. It would be good to see her again." Despite the bitter cold, Poldo found himself smiling at the thought. Unfortunately, the Wood Gnomes also saw him smiling, and several of them were giving him impertinent grins. Poldo cleared his throat and brushed the ice crystals from his mustache with a deep scowl.

Fortunately, the Troll didn't seem to notice. The Troll didn't seem aware of anything, for that matter.

"Thane?" asked Poldo.

There was no response. The Troll stared to the east. He wasn't searching for something, or scanning the horizon, or even staring blankly as his thoughts wandered. Thane watched a point across the waters with the determined focus of an opera enthusiast with bad balcony seats. Poldo followed his gaze out across the gray water and saw nothing but a dull mist.

"Thane?" the Gnome repeated.

"Uh... right. Yes." Thane shook his head. "What were we discussing?"

The Wood Gnomes started to chitter something, but Poldo cut them off with a raised voice. "I was merely pointing out that we might have a chance to see Mrs. Hrurk if the fates align."

"Ah. Good." Thane wore a smile that never reached his eyes. "It would be nice to meet her."

Poldo nodded. "And perhaps there is someone else we could try to meet."

The Troll flinched, prompting some squeaks of alarm from the Wood Gnomes in his fur. His hand rose up to his face as his gaze drifted back to the east. "I... I doubt it," he said.

"Thane, I am sure that if your Elf met you under different circumstances, she wouldn't have... uh..." The Gnome struggled to find gentle words for a violent act.

"Put an arrow in my eye?" said Thane.

"Not to put too fine a point on it," muttered Poldo.

"Oh, it was quite sharp."

"She might not have shot you under different circumstances," the Scribkin said firmly. "You told me she first saw you with a dead man in your hands, and no way to know that the corpse was her would-be assassin. How would she react to anyone after such a first impression?"

"I didn't think it was a first impression." The Troll shook his head. "I just... I thought that we had been connected, somehow. That even if she hadn't seen me, she knew me. I was wrong."

He loosed a sigh that sounded like a rockslide in a gravel pit. "And since she didn't know me, what was I doing? What was I to her? A monster lurking at the edge of the darkness? A beast to be slain or evaded? And all that time, I thought... Well, I was a fool. A deluded fool."

"Everyone makes mistakes." Poldo patted the Troll on his furry tree trunk of an arm.

"Not everyone perpetuates mistakes for a year. Not everyone chases their folly across Arth," Thane said. "Not everyone still aches to make things different. But I can't... and I couldn't face her now."

Poldo nodded. "Perhaps it is best to move on after all then."

"I think so. And I am trying." Thane looked out to the east once more, staring beyond the ship bobbing determinedly on the water. "But it's not easy to forget her, or to let go of whatever I thought we had. Sometimes it feels like it's still there, somehow."

"That sounds difficult," said Poldo.

"I will be fine." Thane shook his head and started for the gangplank of the ship. As one, the Dwarven sailors backed away from the approaching Troll, and the ship tilted away from the dock as the crew pressed against the far rail. Poldo was about to shout at the lot of them, but Thane silenced him with a look. "I will be fine," the Troll reiterated, stepping onto the deck and righting the ship. "I just hope she's happy, wherever she is."

—— CHAPTER 7 ——

Kaitha's face was a mask of misery, and tears were beginning to well in her eyes. She willed her facial muscles to flex deeper, to drag the corners of her mouth down so far they hurt. Her face already ached to the point where her eyes were watering.

Yes, she decided as she stared at herself in her bathroom mirror. She could frown.

It struck her that such a scowl might not be considered natural. Was it a sincere frown? Did it matter?

She glanced down at her sink. It was a freestanding fixture sculpted from Elven porcelain, with an elegant swoop that widened at the top. It reminded her of a swan gargling whenever she ran its silver tap. There was a small shelf set just above the sink on thin silver wires, and on the shelf a pamphlet lay propped against a clay mug so that she could read it. Near the top of the paper, a woodcut of a somber-looking Elf sat next to a headline that read:

THAT WHICH IS NOT IMMORTAL IS STILL IMPORTANT.
A Helpful Guide to Managing Dark Thoughts.

She assumed the man was intended to look sympathetic or caring, but he just seemed smug to her. With a snort, she looked down the page to a section entitled "Are You on the Dark Path? Take this Quiz to Find Out."

The first question asked, predictably, if she could frown. It didn't mention anything about being convincing or sincere. Besides, the frustration she felt at the old priest of Oppo was real enough.

Brother Mattias' question still echoed in the dim and uncooperative corners of her consciousness. "And you're keeping the dark thoughts in check?" He'd tried to sound encouraging, or conversational. He'd failed.

Kaitha's grimace deepened at the memory. Manners held that it was a very personal question to ask an Elf if they were experiencing dark thoughts, yet Brother Mattias took it as a given that she was struggling and had jumped straight toward asking if she was still holding on. She didn't look that bad, right? Yes, she'd cried a bit, but so had the Halfling who had just given up elixir. Kaitha had been without salve for over a year, and had practically rebuilt her career in that time. She was due a little leeway if a tear leaked out now and again.

Or had he seen something else?

The frown test had never seemed that convincing to Kaitha. It was based upon the well-known fact that Dark Elves constantly giggled or laughed, even when murdering people. Especially when murdering people. They may have been the most creatively vile of the forces of evil, but you couldn't say Dark Elves didn't enjoy their work. It was said that so long as an Elf could frown when asked about dark thoughts, they weren't yet beyond redemption. Of course, this was said by Elves who needed a fast and easy way to demonstrate that they shouldn't be hauled off to the gallows by an angry mob.

Prior to the Seventh Age, it was thought by many northerners that the term "Dark Elves" referred to the color of their skin, and that the malady of the Elven soul that drove them to evil was inexorably linked to the ebony complexion of the south's Sun Elves. This misunderstanding was convenient for, and thus further popularized by, the Wood Elves, High Elves, and other Elven houses of the Freedlands whose skin ranged from tawny bronze to snowy pale. Yet, their deception was dependent on pervading ignorance, and that ignorance could not survive the increasing trade with the Empire and the Imperial cultural influences that the Sixth Age brought to the Freedlands. Once the rest of Mankind learned the uncomfortable truth that Elves of any heritage had the capacity to become Dark Elves, the houses of the Freedlands had needed to explain a lot about their nature in a short amount of time—often the exact amount of time it would take to light the pyre around their stakes.

Kaitha scowled again, but wasn't sure how much the facial expression could really prove. It seemed unlikely that Dark Elves were unable to make a face for a moment. Perhaps they couldn't sustain it for long without breaking into laughter?

She continued to grimace and snarl at herself for several minutes, then moved on to the next question. "Have you attended a temple ceremony or said an earnest prayer in the past month?"

Kaitha pursed her lips thoughtfully. How earnest were her prayers? She followed Tandos, of course, as did most Elves in martial professions, but she didn't consider herself faithful to the god so much as open to occasional dalliances with him. Did invoking the god's name when worried or before meals count as being earnest?

Dark Elves, it was well-known, were godless. Yet that had little to do with their religious observance. It was more unique that no god was observing them. Every temple taught that, in principle, a major or minor god from Arth's extensive pantheon represented every person, whether or not that person worshipped a god in return. Atheists were watched over by Null, a minor deity whose adherents were known mostly for criticizing other temples and being first in line for weekend brunch. Shadowkin who forsook the traditions of their old gods often found themselves embraced by temples of Fulgen or Oppo. The Dark Elves remained uniquely unclaimed by any temple or cult. Once an Elf went down the dark path, they were well and truly forsaken.

Kaitha recalled speaking with Niln the Al'Matran on the road to the Myrewood, and how he had told her that she was touched by the All Mother. The thought brought some measure of comfort. Al'Matra was said to be mad, but the goddess would have to be a few disciples short of a clergy to choose Kaitha for anything, and you couldn't say much better about most of the mortals that joined her temple. Still, as long as she and the queen of the gods had each other, she couldn't be on the dark path.

Probably.

It occurred to Kaitha that if Al'Matra was her best hope, she needed to plan for contingencies. She looked at the mantra printed on the small pamphlet and read it aloud, though she was fairly certain she could recite it from memory by now.

"Just because it's not immortal doesn't mean it's not important. Impermanence is not insignificance. That which is fleeting is still worth feeling. Our memories matter while we have them. I will not lose hope. I will—"

A knock at the door to her apartment interrupted her whispered litany. Kaitha scowled, but stepped into the main room of her apartment. It was smaller than the suite she used to have, but it was still an elegant Elven studio on the Eighth Tier. The decorations and paint were done in swirling, floral forms. The bathroom was opposite her bed, which was separated from the rest of the apartment by a thin screen decorated with paintings of hawks and falcons on swooping branches. The rest of the room was a small kitchen and an emerald couch that looked through her balcony doors out over the city of Andarun. Opposite the bedroom was a sturdy oak door, and behind that was Laruna Trullon, grinning hopefully into the spyhole.

"Hey," the mage said by way of greeting as the Elf opened the door. She started at the Elf's appearance. "Hey, are you all right?"

"Yeah, I'm good," Kaitha lied, swiping a hand across her eyes. "It's nothing. What brings you here?"

"I had a question." The mage's eyes were eager and bright. "About our adventure last year."

"Sure. Got another quest?" asked Kaitha, gesturing for Laruna to sit on the couch. "More undead?"

"No, no, no." The solamancer remained standing. "You told me you had an epiphany, right? Like back on the plains, right before you stopped, uh..." Laruna froze, but the edge of the conversational cliff was about three paces behind her.

"Yes," said Kaitha softly. "That was when I realized I had a problem with salve. It was the first step."

"Right," said Laruna. "But it was because of a dream, right?"

"I think it was more of a withdrawal-induced hallucination," said Kaitha.

Laruna waved away the distinction. "Visions, dreams, same thing."

"Is it?"

The mage leaned closer, her face a mask of manic optimism. "You met a turtle and a bird or something, you talked to them, and then you reached some inner insight."

"Well, yeah," began Kaitha. "It was a tortoise and a falcon, but it wasn't so much a dream as—ow!"

"Sorry," Laruna leaned back and held up a single strand of auburn hair. "Thought you had a loose hair on your tunic."

"Oh."

"Well, that was what I wanted to know!" Laruna thrust her hands into her pockets in an unconvincing display of forced nonchalance. "Thanks for the talk, but I just remembered that I've got a lot to do. I'll let you know when a good quest pops up. Keep me in mind for the same!"

"But why—" Kaitha began, yet the solamancer was already out the door before the Elf could finish her question. The slam of her front door reverberated through the living chambers.

"Why would she keep my hair?" the ranger said to her empty apartment.

"Don't you think that's a little strange?" shrieked Queen Marja. "Don't you think that looks odd to the servants and commonfolk?"

Preya Havenbrook, servant, commonfolk, and royal baker of Andarun, stopped inspecting the tea cakes on her tray for just long enough to duck under a flying platter. She stood atop a small stepladder that made it possible for a Halfling to work on the Human-sized counter in the middle of the royal confectionary in the Palace of Andarun's labyrinthine kitchens. She was back to the frosting again before the china shattered against the far wall.

"What does it say when a king shuns his beloved! What do people think when a man spurns his marriage bed for... for paperwork!" the queen roared. Her eyes were wild and her face crimson as she eclipsed the door to the royal confectionary like a blood moon. "Why would anybody be reading dull papers instead of spending time with someone they love? The nobles must wonder if you even care for me at all! Do you?"

King Johan the Mighty stood in the door opposite Marja's, the only other exit from the room. He wore an apologetic smirk as he opened his hands to the queen. "My love, of course I—"

"You swore your love was true, and nothing could keep you from me!" Her face was crimson between the rivulets of mascara running down her face, and her hands grasped for any unfortunate crockery within reach. "You said you dreamed of me!"

"I do! My love, I surely do!" King Johan dodged a hurled teacup. It shattered against the great stove. "You just need to be pa—"

"I have been patient!" Marja hollered. "What about our honeymoon to the Teagem? What about our state trip to Eadelmon?" She fumbled at the shelves, and a lady-in-waiting dutifully pushed a saucer into reach. "We were supposed to travel the world! It was supposed to be like the romance tales! But no! You spend all your time smoking with those suited buffoons and playing at hero with those louts in golden armor. I went looking for you last night and the servants told me you were studying records in the Royal Archives! The Royal Archives! We could have been together, and you were reviewing old paperwork!" She punctuated the accusation by hurling a porcelain gravy boat. It sailed past Johan and crashed onto the stone floor behind him.

"My love, there was a shipment I had to see to—"

"Oh, so it was those strange crates you had shipped in from Umbrax! Do you think that makes it any better?" Another teacup sailed over the king's head.

Johan held his hands up. He backed out of the kitchen, but not quickly enough. "I know it doesn't. I know. But I just have this one... enterprise that I need to see to—"

"It's always one more thing! It's never me!" shrieked Marja. "Is this our love story?"

Preya's piping bag trembled a little, drawing a wavy line through the otherwise pristine pattern frosted onto the apple grundant tea cake. They were already talking about love now, and the pair were both in the bakery of the royal kitchens. A bead of sweat formed on her forehead, but a servant's duty was to remain invisible, and Preya was nothing if not disciplined.

Johan and Marja's encounters reminded the baker of the lottery games that they played during fairs in Mr. Havenbrook's hometown; the ones where you dropped a stone down a board full of pegs or had a maiden toss an apple into a circle of buckets or, perhaps most applicably, where the farmers made a grid in the field using chalk dust and then sent a well-fed cow out over the field of green grass and white numbers. The king and queen bounced through the chambers of the palace as they shouted and crooned to each other, but it was only a matter of time before the cow of the cosmos relieved itself on an unfortunate room and all the servants within it. The rooms of a castle built into the side of a mountain lacked the sort of windows and spare doors that could give desperate servants an escape when simmering conflict erupted into fiery passion.

"My love, I dream of the day when I can spend more time with you," crooned Johan. "But I have responsibilities. A sacred duty to serve the people—"

"Oh, who cares about the people?" snarled Marja. "We were supposed to be in love! I wasn't supposed to be back in my chambers reading my romance books while you muck about with the citizens!" She hurled a mixing bowl for emphasis. It trailed billowing white clouds of flour and salt as it sailed over the king's head and out into the main kitchens.

"We will be together more!" said the king. "But with the economy where it is, and the dragon attacking... I just need a little more time for some plans to reach fruition. Once all this unpleasant business is settled, I can take some time away from all of this... governance." His lips curled when he said the word, as though it carried an unpleasant taste. "Then I can focus on you, my love."

Marja went from crimson to purple in a flash, but a moment later much of the color drained from her face. "Where my love goes, what am I to do but follow?" she whispered.

The king's smile grew brittle. "Uh, I beg your pardon?"

"If you must govern, why not govern together?" Marja wore a hopeful smile as she strode into the confectionary. It gave the lucky baker near the door a chance to make a run for it. "I... I could rule alongside you, just like Isabellin and Archar in *Lady of the Haerthwards*, or Elenor and Roland in *The Bandit King of Faerun*."

"Ha! Well, I don't think that would—"

"Why not?" The queen still wore her hopeful smile, but there was iron in her eyes now. "The queen can issue proclamations and make judgments. My decrees carry as much weight as yours. That's the law, right?"

Sudden concern—almost fear—flashed on the king's face, but Johan recovered quickly. "Ha! No! I mean, yes. Of course you have the authority, my love, but what kind of husband would I be if I made you use it? You shouldn't have to sully yourself with such matters to see your beloved."

"But I wouldn't mind if—"

Johan strode across the room, meeting Marja across from the table that Preya worked at. "Ha! I know you wouldn't! But I can't let it come to that. We need to take the opportunities we have now, and spend more time together!"

The kitchen girl took the opportunity to flee the confectionary. Unfortunately for Preya, the king and queen had come together at her table, one on either side of her stepladder, and both seemed oblivious to the royal baker nervously frosting tea cakes beneath them.

"Do... do you mean that?" Marja said in a quavering voice.

"I do. I have missed you, my queen." The king embraced his wife, catching Preya between his golden plate armor and the voluminous folds of Marja's dress. The stepladder fell away as the royal couple pressed together, and the baker was left dangling between a frock and a hard place.

"Oh, Johan!" squealed the queen.

Preya cleared her throat nervously, her feet kicking in the air, her arms pinned to her side. Unfortunately for the Halfling, Johan and Marja never spent much energy thinking about the little people. "The kingdom can wait," Johan crooned. "Let's rekindle our love, as Madren and Haela did in—"

"—in *The Milkmaid's Cottage*," Marja finished with him. "Oh, yes, Johan. But when? Now?"

"No time like the present!" trumpeted Johan. "Ha haa!" A sweep of his arm brushed the carefully constructed tea cakes from the counter and dropped Preya to the floor. The baker suppressed a grunt of pain as she landed on the stone tiles, tea cakes raining down around her with sad little plops.

The king heaved the queen onto the table effortlessly. The old oak groaned in protest as Marja leaned back and emitted a high-pitched squeak, like wind escaping a novelty bladder. She laughed as Johan whispered something presumably salacious in her ear. Preya Havenbrook couldn't hear it; the Halfling was already sprinting for the door as fast as her legs would carry her, clothing and pieces of armor raining down around her.

"Ugh. Nobody wants to see that," said Gorm Ingerson, his lip curling into a sneer.

"Why is it so... pink? And quivering?" Heraldin's face twisted up in disgust.

"It's been a while," said Jynn. "Things build up."

"It's unnatural, s'what it is," Gorm grumbled. The three of them stared at what had recently become the most reviled sight in Andarun. A small oak drawer was set in the wall of the archmage's office between two windows. As Jynn reluctantly stepped toward it, the drawer rattled and shook with manic energy, loosing flashes of rose-colored light as it threatened to break open. A brass plaque on the front said, "INBOX."

"I thought all this fancy new magic was supposed to make life better," said Gorm.

"There are always bumps on the road to progress," said Jynn distractedly. He sidled up to the inbox cautiously, as though it might strike at any moment. It flew open as soon as he touched the latch and erupted into a cacophony of shrill shouts.

"A special offer for you!"

"It's almost Mordo Ogg's Day!"

"Mr. Ur'Mayan, an invitation!"

"Report from the fifteenth of Frostfall!"

"Is your sorceress satisfied?"

"A Mordo Ogg's Day Sale at the General Store!"

"Silence!" barked Jynn, waving a hand over the drawer.

Most of the sprites' shouting died down, save for one hopeful cry of "I am an Umbraxian prince..."

Gorm edged closer and peered into the inbox. Within it, dozens if not hundreds of messenger sprites were packed into a trembling mass of arms, legs, and wings. Their tiny, glowing faces swiveled toward the archmage with laser intensity, but they managed to fall mostly silent. A thought struck the Dwarf as he considered the tiny couriers. "Mordo Ogg's day was weeks ago," he said, unable to hold the reproach from his voice.

Jynn pursed his lips. "It has been a while," he repeated tersely, then looked down at the sprites. "Now, I want the sprite from—"

The tiny shouts began anew, the sprites shaking in frenetic desperation.

"The sprite from Oopa of Many Hues!" Jynn shouted over the din. "From her report on the fifteenth of Frostfall."

A chorus of disappointed groans and sighs played out over the susurration of a multitude of tiny feet shuffling, but one excited sprite pulled itself from the mass and began hopping up and down atop its peers. "Report for the fifteenth of Frostfall!" it piped. "Report for the fifteenth of Frostfall!"

Jynn beckoned it to his desk, and began to shut the drawer over the protests of the sprites within. He paused as it was halfway shut and snarled into the opening, "And if any of you are about sales for any holiday, promotional offers, or marital enhancements of any kind, consider yourselves dismissed!"

A collective sigh of relief rose in a pink cloud from the mouth of the drawer as the vast majority of sprites within evaporated. The remaining stragglers sulked as Jynn slammed the inbox shut and turned back to his chosen messenger. "Now then," he said. "Report."

The sprite hunched down as if to avoid attention and whispered into its own hand. "I went to the Crimson Grove," it said in a voice that, though high-pitched and piping, was clearly meant to resemble a low whisper. "It was a risk, but I saw the trees and they're full. I mean, they're laden with fruit. That's because they grow year-round. They're always in season! And the growers aren't happy I found—" The sprite stood up straighter and gave a rasping cry, like a child imitating a distant shout. "Have to run!" it concluded, then turned back to Jynn expectantly.

"That's clear as mud," Gorm said.

"Out of context, I suppose it is." Jynn unlocked the drawer of his desk with a thread of magic and began rifling through the papers inside. "My father spoke to me three times after his death. Once at the Ashen Tower, once at Highwatch, and once as I defeated him in Andarun. And in the first two of our encounters, he mentioned Kesh, and claimed the olive markets there are the greatest example of depravity in the world."

"The merchants there are said to be ruthless," said Heraldin.

"Perhaps, but ruthlessness was a virtue to my father." A shadow passed over Jynn's face. "As was an inquisitive mind; if he mentioned it twice, he intended for me to investigate. So I sent hired agents to find anything amiss with the olive sellers."

"And what did they find?" asked the bard.

"Mostly what you'd expect." Jynn pulled a folio from the drawer and set it on the desk. "Merchants gouging prices, tampering with scales, hiring bandits to steal from one another, that sort of thing."

"In other words, bein' merchants," interjected Gorm.

"Indeed. Ah, here." The wizard produced a slip of parchment from the folio and scanned it quickly. "Yes! We found a few suspicious threads to pull at, and I kept Oopa on to investigate them. By my notes, last week she went to the Crimson Grove to investigate the scarcity of Imperial flame olives on the markets. And according to her message, their rarity has nothing to do with a lack of production or seasonal cycles. On the contrary, the groves are full, and flame olives are always in season."

Heraldin's brow screwed up. "Then why are they always so expensive?"

Gorm grinned. "Somebody's buying them up."

"Exactly," said Jynn. Which means that someone has cornered the market on the key ingredient of Arth's most potent flame oil."

"And if we find out who's buyin' all that oil, we can find who's makin' all the Arson's Friend," said Gorm. "We follow the trail far enough, and we'll find our so-called dragon. And I'm bettin' we'll find Johan and them Goldson Baggs bastards sittin' there as well."

"The olives," said Jynn.

"What?"

"The olives," the archmage repeated. "They'd likely transport the whole olives. The oil is too volatile to make the journey up from the Empire."

Gaist nodded.

It made sense to Gorm. He hadn't traveled with a group carrying Arson's Friend on a quest since he was a newblood, when he witnessed poor Topher Guggins slip and fall on a vial. The guild coroner had to scrape the old thief off the ceiling. "I suppose you're right. Haulin' barrels of Arson's Friend across the desert would be suicide. One errant arrow from a bandit would vaporize a caravan."

"Even carrying the olives is dangerous," said Jynn. "They can combust if they're exposed to too much heat or jostled too hard. Transporting them must involve some amount of magic or engineering, and they're still safest to move by sea."

Gorm scratched his beard. "So our culprit is bringin' huge amounts of olives, in secret, up to somewhere near Andarun usin' magic, Gnomish gadgets, or boats."

"Or all three," said Jynn.

"That'll take a sophisticated smuggling operation," said Gorm. "Now all we need is a way to track 'em."

"Ahem."

Dwarf, wizard, and weaponsmaster turned in unison to the bard, who had steepled his hands at the edge of the desk. "It sounds like you're in need of a particular set of skills and connections. Skills and connections that I, as it happens, have. And you three, as we have discussed, have something that I need as well. This seems the makings of a good deal, doesn't it?"

"Absolutely not," snapped Gorm. "Out of the question!"

Gaist shook his head forcefully.

"I'll keep your share of the royalties at ninety basis points. That's above average for a ballad," Heraldin shot back. "The contract will be as generous as they come. All you have to do is sign over the rights."

"Counteroffer," growled Gorm. "Ye help me, and I don't take ye down to the docks and use ye as bait to fish for the great Tarapin."

"This is how the people will learn of the moments you single-handedly fought the liche, buying time for Jynn to weave his ultimate spell!"

"That never happened," said the archmage.

Gaist shook his head.

"Sounds wrong to me," agreed Gorm.

"It doesn't matter what really happened! That's the key to a great ballad," said Heraldin. "You have to make it more interesting than reality. So sensational that it's more fun for people to run with it than go digging for the truth. The bigger, the better!"

"See? This is why me answer is no."

"Really?" Heraldin looked dubious.

"That and the fact that I don't trust ye. And the fact that I've heard ye sing."

"Come now! Your investigation has brought you to a point where you need someone with ties to smugglers that you can trust, and I—one of your closest friends—"

"One of my professional acquaintances," amended Jynn.

"One of the bards I don't always want to kill," interjected Gorm.

"Closest friends," Heraldin repeated loudly and leveled a pointed glare at Gaist. "And I happen to be just such a connected individual. I'm a former bodyguard of Benny Hookhand, the most prolific smuggler in Andarun! And you only knew you needed me because Jynn is investigating olive markets on the recommendation of his father. And I need the three of you, and the intellectual rights to a recent bit of your biographies. It's too perfect to be a coincidence! This is destiny! Don't deny it! Seize the moment!"

Gorm snorted. "Ye think—"

"I'll do it," said the archmage.

Gaist whirled to stare at Jynn.

"Ye what?" asked Gorm.

The bard sounded almost as surprised as the Dwarf. "You will?"

Jynn looked at his desk for a moment, ruminating on something far from oil prices and music rights. When he looked back up, there was steel in his blue eyes. "Yes."

I accept your generous offer without reservation.

Feista Hrurk wrote in a neat, tight script. She was watched by a small group of Wood Gnomes from the corners of her office in Mrs. Hrurk's Home for the Underprivileged. One of the Domovoy on the bookshelf next to the desk, a silver-haired woman in a white rat pelt, looked down at the letter and chirruped a question.

"Um, yes, thank you for asking," said Feista. "I've thought about it a lot, and this is what I want."

Mr. Poldo told Feista that it took him a while to be able to understand the speech of the tiny men and women who formed the backbone of his businesses; Wood Gnomes' voices were as soft and high-pitched as rodents. The Gnoll imagined it was easy for most people to mistake the Domovoy's speech for fighting rats or agitated squirrels, but for someone with a dog's ears it was easy to make out what the diminutive Gnomes were trying to say. The only tricky parts were sorting out the Wood Gnomes' thick accents and getting past their prolific cursing.

White Rat gave a small shrug and went back to sharpening a pencil into a spear. The Wood Gnomes here were in Mr. Poldo's employ, and they mainly served as translators for the coded messages that she and the Scribkin exchanged about the running of the house. Otherwise, they stayed around Feista's office and didn't cause much trouble, provided she knocked on the doors and left them a saucer of milk on weekends.

Still, it paid to be polite to someone who knew where you slept. Feista bowed her head with a friendly smile before she turned back to her letter and, after steadying the tremble in her paws, continued writing.

> Attached please find my executed agreements. Per the instructions in your offer letter, I will arrive at work on the 23rd day of Frostfall at the Warg Incorporated main office at Sixteen Wrothgar Way on the Fifth Tier.

The pups would be fine, she told herself. Mr. Poldo had assured her that replacements could be found for working around the home, and the gods knew Aubren was ready for more responsibility. This was a dream career for Feista. A once-in-a-lifetime opportunity. Her grandmother once told her that when life gave you lemons, you grabbed them as fast as you could and shared them with all of your family so that nobody got scurvy. Granny Zelvia came from a time and place where lemons were as rare as diamonds, and still much better to eat.

With a deep breath, Feista tucked the letter and signed contracts into an envelope and sealed it with wax. Then, with a nod to the Wood Gnomes, she stood up, turned around three times, and left her office.

She found Aubren cleaning the dining hall downstairs. "I need the letter courier to get this when he stops by," the Gnoll said, holding up the thick envelope.

Aubren looked worried for a moment. "He's already been by, ma'am. And no, it didn't come," she added, answering Feista's question before she could give it words.

Feista brushed away her disappointment and focused on the letter she did have—the one she needed to get to Warg Incorporated. At times like this, Feista wished she could rely on more relevant matriarchal wisdom than "sour on the tongue, no more bleeding gums." Still, you had to work with the generational role models you got, and if anyone could say anything about Granny Zelvia, it was that she never gave up. "I'll be out for a while then. I need to either chase the courier down or deliver this to the Fifth Tier."

"What? Now?" asked Aubren.

"No time like the present," said Feista. Fate had given her a treasure, and she planned to squeeze every drop out of it. She grabbed her cloak, told Aubren to watch the pups, and burst through the front door with so much enthusiasm it threatened to fly off its hinges.

The door swung shut. The clank and thud of Dwarven and Human footsteps faded in the halls of the building that housed the transitional Tower of Twilight. Patches eventually abandoned hope that the guests' departure heralded an imminent walk to the park and went back to his bed. Jynn Ur'Mayan stared at the back of his office door, his body motionless while his mind rifled through his life's work, which recently had extended to include his father's life's work.

Jynn had locked cabinets filled with information on Detarr Ur'Mayan's projects, along with the soul of Detarr Ur'Mayan himself. Aya of Blades had provided some insights back during the liche's invasion. The omnimancer had acquired the collection of Teldir of Umbrax through an estate sale. He'd even issued a guild quest to retrieve the lost writings of Win Cinder, though few heroes signed on and they'd yet to return.

Since childhood, Jynn had known about his father's joint venture with the kings of Ruskan and the Freedlands. Teldir's papers noted that the goal of their collaboration was a way to escape death, either by achieving true immortality or at least securing a return from the dead. The kings had assembled five wizards and started a project named for Mannon's great escape from death at the hands of the gods: the Leviathan Project. The project wasn't necromancy—it was explicitly stated not to leverage necromancy in the contracts Jynn had found—but the participants were given wide leeway to skirt the borders of the dark arts in pursuit of new solutions. His father worked on soul-binding, but other mages took other avenues of inquiry. Aya of Blades researched cures and potions created by the ancient masters of low magic. Win Cinder had tried to entice or ensorcel a minor god to steal souls from Mordo Ogg's threshold. Teldir tried to bind souls into golems, as one might enchant a magic weapon.

Detarr Ur'Mayan once called the Leviathan Project "unsightly work," which meant that it was the sort of endeavor that usually brings villagers with torches and pitchforks. The five noctomancers hired henchmen and thugs in quiet arrangements to avoid attention, and many assumed they had gone villain. But they hadn't—the noctomancers were operating under full royal authority and protection. At least, until Az'Anon the Black made a grave mistake.

Jynn wasn't sure exactly what Az'Anon did wrong. Whatever it was, it frightened the other four noctomancers on the Leviathan Project and turned the kings of Ruskan and the Freedlands against them. Days after the project's charter was terminated, the Heroes' Guild was on a hunt for its participants. The deed had marked the beginning of the wizard's descent from being Az'Anon the Black to becoming the Spider King, dabbling in true necromancy, and threatening Andarun. Yet Jynn could find no record of what, exactly, he had done.

There would be records, of course—guild contracts and documentation for the justification of the quest—but those were kept under the protection of the royal archivists. Such papers were sealed in the Royal Archives of the Heroes' Guild Great Vault beneath the Palace of Andarun, and not available to the public, not even an Archmage of the Academy of Mages. This point had been made emphatically and repeatedly clear in Jynn's prior correspondence with the royal archivist in the guild office on the Fifth Tier, who advised the wizard that such records were not to be released to the public until the sun froze over and the Pit released the dead.

That left Jynn with no good options left. He had no way to locate and speak with the mages of the Leviathan Project, living or dead, except perhaps his father. And while Jynn had risked much to pursue Detarr's knowledge, using necromancy on a warded phylactery was a bridge too far, and too interwoven with explosive counterspells. The omnimancer's research on the project had been nearly at a dead end for months.

Then Gorm showed up, with evidence linking his father's remarks to the dragon attacks. And Heraldin was there, perhaps summoned by Jynn's own experimental prophecy, with a way to further investigate the issue. Two of the few people he knew, arriving on exactly the same day, with information related to Detarr Ur'Mayan's coded words. Looking back, had he not been recruited by the Al'Matrans, he would never have met Gorm and Heraldin, would have never found his father's work, foiled his father's schemes, or found Patches. The litany of serendipity went on and on.

It was all coincidence, Jynn knew. Yet he also knew that coincidence and destiny are much the same, in the way that raindrops and the ocean are the same; one might have been more vast and powerful and dangerous than the other, but they were made of identical components, and in sufficient quantities the lesser became the greater. Too many convenient coincidences were a sign of fate, but if you saw the hand of destiny at every coincidence, you'd wind up looking as silly as a captain trying to sail a schooner across a puddle. The trick, the essence of low magic, was to know the difference.

Eventually he stood and pulled a slim volume off his bookshelf. About halfway through the thin leather journal he found the most often cited quote of the Third Age omnimancer Salam Abdus.

> Note, dear reader, that destiny is like a cat that you wish to call to you. Give it your attention, try to coax it into place, and it shall have naught to do with you. Play coy as a maiden, and it shall surely come running. Yet turn your back on the bastard at your deepest peril.

Jynn took a deep breath. Regrettably little remained of Adbus' teachings; he was most famous for this observation being quoted in Nove's

Lex Infortunii, wherein the great philosopher-scientist noted that shortly after writing the quote, Abdus was eaten by a Dire Ocelot.

Still, the archmage could see that wisdom remained in the ancient omnimancer's words. It would do little good to meddle in matters of destiny—his experiment with the prophetic vault had shown him the folly in that. Yet it seemed like folly to ignore the confluence of events that had brought him so close to his father's work. If fate had really brought him this far, perhaps it might take him further still. Perhaps even into the Royal Archives. It was just a matter of being in the right place at the right time, without using magic to do so.

Predicting the future is notoriously fraught, but predicting a wizard's course of action is relatively simple. The likelihood that a mage will do something can be expressed as a ratio of the power or knowledge of secrets gained against the effort and risk of gaining it. Since Jynn stood to gain insights into his destiny and possibly access to his father's research without engaging in any actual low magic, his decision was easy. The only question was where he should be until his next meeting with Gorm and Heraldin.

"Come, Patches," he said, fetching a leather leash from the shelf between two arcane tomes.

A sudden, frenetic cacophony erupted from the bed beside his desk; the scrabbling of claws on wood playing under earnest panting. Patches skidded around Jynn in a tight circle, his paws flailing in all directions, his tail wagging hard enough to bend his body into alternating right angles.

"Yes. Yes, it is time for walkies," Jynn assured the dog dancing about his feet as he pushed the door open. "Perhaps all the way down to the Fifth Tier."

——CHAPTER 8——

Laruna didn't expect Jynn Ur'Mayan to step through the door.
She expected her father, as she was standing in her childhood home, or maybe the magefinder from the Academy who had found her among the ashes of that very house. Yet it was Jynn who strode into their thatched hut, looking sharp in the rich purple robes of a noctomancer.

"What are you doing here?" Laruna demanded. "Why you?"

"Oh, Laruna," said Jynn, looking startled. "Um, it is good to see—"

"You're an omnimancer now. And an archmage."

"Ah, yes." Jynn sounded confused, but his robe changed instantly and, after a moment's indecision, a black glove appeared on his left hand. "Do you remember when we were together?" he asked, and looked behind her.

Laruna turned, and found the back half of her old house was now, in fact, the Plains of Aberreth. Another Laruna and Jynn were lying in the long grass, watching the stars dance above them. He was smiling as if in conversation. The other Laruna was staring at the sky with a conspicuously blank expression. She whipped around, and the Jynn in the house was gone.

The wizard in the grass looked back and forth from the vacant-eyed Laruna to the one still standing in the hut, confusion plain on his face. His robes flickered from purple to gray uncertainly, as if waiting for her to decide which he should be wearing.

Laruna set her jaw. She could feel her anger rising for some reason, but the important thing was to stay centered. "Let's start with some questions," she said, striding into the grass.

Her body double melted away, leaving a space next to the reclining wizard, who recovered admirably. "I... come and lay in the grass with us. With me," said Jynn.

The solamancer stopped at the wizard's feet, bent down, and said, "Now listen. This can be a fun little chat, woman to metaphysical presence, or it can get really nasty, really thrice-cursed fast. And it all depends on how quickly you drop the act."

Jynn's smile went rigid, and his eyes darted left and right as if looking for an exit. "I'm not sure what you—" he began.

"Last warning," said Laruna.

"I just wanted to taaARRRRRRRGH!" Jynn's protest turned into a shriek of pain as Laruna traced arcane sigils in the air.

"Let me know when you've had enough," the mage said, patterns of light and fire dancing around her fingers. Similar threads wove around Jynn's wrists, ankles, and neck. "You're the spirit that gave my friend some life-changing wisdom, and I'm here to get the same."

"I'm not supposed to break character!" whined the wizard as he scrambled to his feet.

"And I bet I'm not supposed to invoke the Binding of Forseth either," said Laruna. "But here we are."

Jynn's eyes widened at the mention of the spell, and he raised his hands as a courier might when confronted by an aggressive dog. "All right, all right, I know these dreams can be frustrating, but if you just listen to your heart youaaAAAAARGH!" The threads of sorcery around the wizard's extremities flared with crimson light. His features bulged and distended and dribbled down like a painting splashed with turpentine as he screamed.

"My heart is telling me that if I make this spell intense enough, this smug little spirit will answer my questions," Laruna said, her voice rising above the shrieks. "Let's see if it's right."

"No! No, please!" The wizard raised his hands above his warping head in surrender. "I'll talk! Anything you want to know! Just stop!"

"Good." Laruna gave a nod of satisfaction and toned down the power she was weaving into the spirit's bindings. The red light died away, and Jynn collapsed back onto the ground. "First off, I want my epiphany."

"Ugh. Gods. I hate dealing with mages." The wizard shook his head and patted his face to dislodge the residual effects of the spell. It took a particularly vigorous slap to get his nose back in place. "I was here for that."

"What do you mean?" growled the mage.

The spirit shot her a look that could have curdled milk. "I'm. Trying. To give you. An epiphany," he hissed.

"Good. Say it. Or whatever," said Laruna.

"I can't!" snapped the wizard. "This isn't some spell you can read from a book or diagram you can study. If I just tell you what you need to know, it'll sound pithy and trite and you'll dismiss it as nonsense! You can't be told it! You have to live it!"

Laruna snorted. "No, I won't. Just tell me."

"Thrice curse the gods, this is why mages are the worst!" snarled the wizard. "All the books in your blighted Academy can't keep you from being such blazing fools. As much as you wish it were different, you're still a mortal, and your mind works like a mortal's! If I could just tell people their innermost secrets and have them believe me, my job would be a walk in the celestial gardens." Jynn shook his head and muttered. "Instead I've got to plumb the subconscious for all these set pieces and characters and whip up these elaborate visions to try to drill some wisdom into your thick skulls."

Magic flared around Laruna's hands. "Well, you'd better find a better way to—"

"Yeah, fine. The spell. I get it, believe me." Jynn waved a hand at the light binding his other wrist. "Let's go back to your place, and I'll show you what I can."

"Quickly."

"Oh, of course." Jynn's voice dripped with acrimony as he gestured at the scenery. The grass rapidly receded into the dirt, which became the floor of Laruna's childhood kitchen once more. A malnourished fire flickered weakly in the potbelly stove, and the table was set with the cracked clay dishes she remembered from childhood. Thick bundles of garlic and onions dangled from hooks in the walls, prompting a frown from the solamancer.

She nodded at the offending vegetables. "We could never afford that much food."

"Oh, where is my focus?" Jynn's double tried to affect sarcasm, but it was clearly very hard to do while his vocal chords, and the rest of him, were undergoing a rapid transformation. Within a couple of seconds, the spirit had shifted into a younger version of Laruna, not yet a teenager and dressed in hand-me-down rags. With a dirty face and wild curls, she looked exactly as Laruna remembered herself, with the exception of the sorcerous bindings flickering around her limbs and neck.

"You're doing me now?" Laruna said flatly.

"Somebody's got to if we're going to try to show you some memories," grumbled the younger Laruna. The girl opened her mouth and emitted a musical series of chimes.

The kitchen door swung inward and a vision of Laruna's father stuck his unshaven face into the room. "Yeah?"

"We're gonna take it from the top, but I'm gonna add some running commentary," said the young Laruna. "See if we speed this up a little."

The vision of Jek Trullon scowled. "We're not supposed to break character."

"Yeah, obviously. Binding of Forseth." Young Laruna gestured at the magic around her neck and nodded at her older self.

"Oh! Right then!" The vision of Laruna's father winced in fear, then gave the solamancer an apologetic nod and ducked back out of the room.

"Here we go." Young Laruna extended her arms and began to weave a tiny flame, juggling the glowing ember between her hands. "Ooh. Look at me, I can magic! I just figured out some basic pyromancy and I think I'm special! Ooh!"

Laruna scowled. "I didn't sound like that."

The child feigned shock. "Oh, does my performance lack verisimilitude? Have I failed to suspend your disbelief? I wonder how that could have happened!"

Laruna's brow furrowed hard enough to grind her teeth together. "Just get on with it."

"Magic, magic, magic! I make fire!" said the little girl.

The door burst open. Jek stormed in, his performance considerably more convincing than the spirit playing his daughter, right down to the flecks of spittle dribbling off his chin as he let loose a familiar scream. "Fool girl! What do you think you're do—!

"Freeze!" said young Laruna, and Jek went as still as a statue mid-shout. She turned to her older self. "All right, look at him. What do you see?"

"It's my father," said Laruna, glancing at the apparition. "He's going to go fetch the whipping stick."

"Right. Anything else?"

Laruna thought for a moment. "No, just the stick. He only used his belt when—"

"Yeah, yeah, right. But stop thinking about what he will do, and start looking at him. What do you see right now?"

Laruna struggled to find the words, in part because anger and pain were pushing a lump up in her throat as she stared at Jek's frozen visage. "He's mad at me again," she said. "And even though I'm just a kid, he's gonna beat me with everything he's got. Because that's all he has—beating people weaker than him. And I was only weaker because I was a child. He's a powerless, simple-minded, cruel, good-for-nothing fool. Ma and I were the only decent things he ever attained, and he should have loved us... he should have..."

"He was all of those terrible things, and still is," said the spirit gently. "But you knew all of that already, and this isn't about him. There's something else. Look closer."

Laruna turned to glare at the sad excuse for a man in the doorway. He reeked of alcohol and chicken droppings, and he was wearing his favorite hat, the one Laruna had never been allowed to touch. His mouth was pulled back in an angry shout, and in his eyes, a familiar spark.

"Oh," asked Laruna. "You mean how he's scared of me?"

"Right!" said the spirit.

"No *spug*," said the solamancer. "He was scared of everything he didn't understand, and that makes the world a terrifying place for someone so ignorant."

The vision of young Laruna looked nonplussed. "You knew?"

"Of course. It was always easier for him to get violent than do the right thing, but he only ever picked a fight that he knew he could win. But he was scared that if I could weave, he wouldn't be able to pick on me. Wasn't wrong, either. Once I came into my power, I made all his fears come true."

On cue, the little hut went up in flames like dry kindling. Her father screamed in abject terror, the way he did in Laruna's more satisfying memories, and scrambled for the door.

"And you know he was afraid of you?" the spirit said again.

"See for yourself." Laruna gave a contemptuous snort as her father's specter stumbled from the shack and fled into the darkness of the dreamscape. "He never spoke to me again after that night."

"Fine. Hold that thought. Next!" The young Laruna snapped her fingers. The house melted away, and Laruna was in the Tower of the Sun, in the ivory and gold Chamber of the Proctor, crimson and orange banners hanging from every vaulted window. The younger Laruna was a bit older now, her shoulders hunched and her faced pocked by an awkward adolescence. She slouched in front an old man wearing heavily decorated robes and the potent scowl that teachers reserve for their least favorite students.

"Proctor Tightwort," glowered the adult Laruna.

The vision of the teacher didn't seem to notice the solamancer. "You will not advance in classes," he said to her younger self, his white beard trembling as he shook with anger. "Not casting as you do! If you can't learn to weave properly, you will fail, I assure you!"

"Oh, no, you can't fail me," the teenage Laruna deadpanned. "But I can magic so good. Magic, magic, magic." The teenager waved her hands and flames swirled up around her like a rising tide.

"You shall not pass!" shouted the proctor, slamming his staff down on the marble floor.

"And freeze!" said the child mage again. "Now, look at his face. See it?"

"Yeah, he's scared too," said Laruna, examining the proctor's frozen visage. The fear was evident in his watery old eyes. "They're threatened by my power."

"Is that it?" asked her younger self. "Well, let's go see who else felt that way." She snapped her fingers, and they were off again. They leapt through her classes, to her early adventures in professional heroics, to her days struggling in the Academy. Each memory flitting by brought a new frozen face from her past. Some were angry, some defiant, some even tried to look friendly, but every visage revealed a spark of fear or a wary unease. By the time they reached Laruna's time with Hogarth the Barbarian, she was growing impatient.

"Yes, I know Hogarth was scared of me," she growled at her double, now an adult as well. "They were all scared of me. People fear what they don't understand. What they can't control."

"Sometimes," said the spirit with a shrug. "But sometimes, they understand what they fear very well. These aren't strangers to you, are they?"

Laruna scowled at the question. "Well... no, I mean... yes, I knew some of them very well, but..."

"Why do you suppose the people who know you best are frightened of you?" asked the spirit.

"Well, I wouldn't say those are the people who know me best," Laruna began.

"Oh?" asked the other Laruna. "Have it your way, then."

And with the words, they were back on the Plains of Aberreth, looking up into a starry sky. And the other Laruna was lying on the ground, staring up into Jynn's eyes. "Oh, here we are—" the spirit began in singsong pantomime.

"Don't," growled Laruna, the gorge rising in her throat. This was hallowed ground. This was a sacred place, a rare memory of real happiness, and the spirit's mockery felt like a desecration. "Don't ruin this."

The vision of a past Laruna and Jynn froze. "But look," said the spirit out of the corner of her mouth.

Laruna looked. This was the night Jynn had professed his feelings, that he'd opened up as much as he ever had. Everything had felt perfect. And yet, now that she'd studied it on so many faces, she could spot a familiar spark in Jynn's eye.

"Why?" she asked, drawing closer to the frozen memory of the noctomancer. Her stomach dropped and her head swirled. "Why here? Why now, when we were so happy? Why would he—"

"Now!" shouted the other Laruna. "She's distracted!"

There was a sound like chimes in a hurricane. The dream world bubbled and puckered and then bled away in a rush as the spirits fled. Laruna tried to correct the spell, but she had lost her balance and she couldn't stay lucid enough to correct the weave. With a frustrated cry, she plunged into blackness.

And then she pushed herself into a sitting position, draped in a night slip and covered in a cold sweat. She sat on the bare floor of her apartment at the center of a circle she had drawn in chalk and salt. The arcane incense had nearly burned out, but its prickling scent filled her nostrils with every breath she heaved.

"Why?" she whispered. "What was there to be afraid of?"

"If you're not afraid right now, you're a fool," Heraldin hissed. He hovered at the doorway to a nondescript office building on the Ridgeward side of the Third Tier. "Keep your guard up. We're entering the domain of one of the most insidiously evil forces the world has ever known."

Gorm peered past the bard through the doorway. The office beyond was aggressively taupe and harshly lit by blue-white glowstones hanging from the ceiling. A few clerks in starched suits were scattered amidst seemingly endless rows of nondescript desks, like lonely buoys in a foggy harbor. Their expressions were dull and joyless as they wordlessly shuffled and shifted papers from inbox to blotter, blotter to outbox. Occasionally, one of them would pound a page with a large stamp.

The Dwarf turned back to Heraldin with a skeptical grimace. "Afraid of what? Looks like any other office," he said.

Gaist nodded.

"Don't be fooled by its commonplace appearance," said Heraldin. "This is no ordinary workplace."

"Where are we, anyhow?" Gorm asked.

"The Thieves' Guild." The bard's voice trembled with trepidation and perhaps a hint of sorrow.

Gorm's face screwed up in confusion as he looked back at the clerks shuffling their papers. One of them appeared to be sleeping. "What? Really?" he asked. Memories of the Thieves' Guild surfaced from the dark corners of his mind. A raucous bunch of hooligans and cutthroats swashbuckled and caroused through his memories, stealing and extorting and sowing chaos across the Andarun of yesteryear. Yet that had been in the days when the Jade Wind was at the peak of her career and the Pyrebeard was just an up-and-coming Dwarven warrior. "I ain't heard nothin' of them in years."

"Decades," said Heraldin.

"What happened to 'em?" Gorm asked, watching the waxen husks of employees stamping their documents.

The bard glanced about, his eyes wide and cautious. He leaned in close to whisper to Gorm and Gaist. "Private equity."

"Private equity?" said Gorm.

A sinister susurration passed through the office, as though the walls themselves muttered dread secrets. The glowlamps flickered and swayed in a wind Gorm couldn't feel, casting deepening shadows about the office.

"Quiet!" Heraldin hissed, pulling the Dwarf back from the doorway. Gaist dropped into a low crouch, a mace and short sword suddenly at the ready.

A few of the workers' heads swiveled mechanically toward the door, but they gave no other indication that they saw the heroes in the doorway.

"Get off me!" Gorm growled as he waved Heraldin's hands away. "Are ye seriously tellin' me ye got your pantaloons in a pinch because some rich folk bought out the guild?"

"Not just any rich folk," said Heraldin. "Private equity. The Dark Money. It moves like a predator through the undercurrents of the market, and once it has a business in its tentacles, it slowly drains the very soul from it."

Gorm peered back into the beige hell. It certainly looked devoid of any spiritual vitality. "By investing in 'em?" he asked, still skeptical.

"I believe you've heard of the Ten Cent Transportable Edibles Company?" Heraldin asked.

"Ten cent beef rolls?" asked Gorm.

"Once, yes. The Ten Cent Transportable Edibles Company made their good name selling beef rolls throughout the city, and by all accounts built a considerable fortune," said the bard. "But their good name and that fortune is what private equity firms wanted, and a few years ago the Dark Money bought up their stock and took them private. The new owners implemented processes and procedures, replaced the accountants, and charged Ten Cent a considerable management fee to 'keep things running.' And then, they started loading it with debt. The Dark Money borrowed huge sums, put the debts on the Ten Cent Transportable Edibles Company's balance sheet, and used the funds to pursue another acquisition."

Gorm shrugged. It all sounded complex and esoteric, and not especially relevant to his favorite nostalgic snack. "Don't see why—"

"How does a company survive shouldering enough debt to buy an even bigger company? They cut costs. They strive to make things predictable! They stick it to the customer! Under the burden of Dark Money's loans, Ten Cent Edibles fired all of their vendors and moved to a franchise model. They started buying day-old buns from a wholesaler in the Base instead of baking their own. They somehow found a way to source lower-grade meat. The art of making a good beef roll was reduced to a handbook of cost-cutting procedures dictated to contract franchisees. And when all of that wasn't enough—"

"They raised their prices through the roof," the Dwarf finished, looking back into the office. He thought he saw something creeping through the shadows on the beige walls, but it could have been a trick of the eye in the sputtering light of the cheap glowstones.

"I heard they started charging for condiments last summer," said Heraldin.

"Ye gods." Gorm stared in horror as visions of climbing prices and deteriorating beef rolls flashed before his mind's eye. "That's criminal."

"No, it's not. Disgusting, amoral, an abomination unto a city's favorite meal on the go, yes, but all very, very legal." The bard shook his head and looked back at the clerks mindlessly stamping their paperwork. "So it was with the Thieves' Guild thirty years ago. When I was but a lad in stockings, they were the greatest rogues in all of Arth. Their guildmasters were said to sit atop a mound of loot that rivaled the Great Vault of Andarun. By the time I picked my first lock, the top thieves in the guild had sold their interests to private investors and retired to some ivory beach on the

Teagem Sea. The Dark Money plundered the thieves' wealth and saddled the guild with debt to fund new ventures, new acquisitions. And once the guild was nearly bankrupt, the new managers took steps to reduce costs."

"Never thought of petty crime as havin' much expenses," said Gorm.

"It doesn't," said Heraldin. "In thieving, reducing costs means cutting risks. They started by forbidding employees to carry weapons on jobs to reduce payments for survivor benefits. Then there were lists of restricted targets and procedural handbooks for safer operations. Eventually, they forbade employees from stealing to slash budget line items for bribery and bail."

Gorm's face screwed up in confusion. "How's that work for thieves?"

"It doesn't." Heraldin gave a rueful chuckle. "No self-respecting vagabond could abide their strictures, and they bled talent like a stabbed mark. Their fall led to the rise of Benny Hookhand and Fish-legs Lemmy and Sue the Golem—all of the gangs and crime rings that rule the city's underside today were built by ex-guild operatives. Only the dregs remained, operating a crumbling shell of the Thieves' Guild."

"Bones," swore Gorm, watching the nearest clerk review a slip of parchment. A fly landed on the woman's face. She didn't so much as blink. "What are we doin' here, then?"

"Selling information was always part of the Thieves' Guild's business," said the bard. "It's still a good place to learn about the comings and goings in any market—stock, commodity, underground, or black—and one where we don't need to worry about any competent thief recognizing us. It's our best bet to find out who is moving the flame olives about, and where. But be on your guard! Don't speak of anything you love, any business you frequent, and art you admire, lest the Dark Money learn of it! Private equity's greed and power know no bounds!"

Another sibilant whisper echoed through the office.

"Aye," said Gorm, warily. "Aye. So what do we do?"

"You've bought information before, yes?" asked Heraldin. "Paid gold for rumors at taverns and such?"

"'Course."

"It's just like that, without any soul." The bard stepped carefully into the room. "Come on, you'll see."

They sidled up to a pine desk near the front of the pack, indistinguishable from every other save for a small, brass plaque that read "CUSTOMER INQUIRIES" and the two chairs set in front of it. Heraldin slid into one of the seats with the oily grace of an informant sidling up to a back-alley bar. Gorm followed his lead, and Gaist stood behind them, alert and wary.

The customer inquiry attendant, an olive-skinned Human with mousy hair and a tweed suit, gave no indication that she noticed the three men who had arrived at her desk. She didn't so much as look up from her current sheet of parchment.

Gorm looked to Heraldin, who gave an encouraging nod and cocked his head toward the inattentive attendant. The Dwarf cleared his throat and attempted the customary greeting for purchasing covert intelligence. "I hear you're the one to see for information."

He was pleasantly surprised when she responded in turn, albeit without looking up from her parchment. "I might be. If the price is right," she intoned, her voice flat and emotionless.

This was more familiar territory. Gorm dropped a heavy purse of coins on the table with a smirk. "I trust this will be sufficient."

The attendant stamped her document with one hand and used the other to tap one of several small sheets of parchment that had been nailed to the front of her desk. It read, "THANK YOU FOR USING EXACT CHANGE."

"Er, I don't know—"

She rapped her finger on another page, headlined "STANDARD RATES." Below it was a long list of esoteric terms and figures.

Gorm read aloud as he glanced over the rate table. "Intermarket exchange rates, three silver multiplied by one-half risk factor. Commodity or labor sourcing, seven giltin multiplied by three times risk factor. Associate identification, thirty giltin multiplied by risk factor." He shot Heraldin a desperate look. "Eh, I don't... I mean, can't I just say what I'm looking for and get the price?"

The attendant sighed heavily and nodded.

"We're lookin' to find out who's been movin' Imperial flame olives from Kesh into the Freedlands, and where the shipments are goin'," said Gorm.

"Commodity movements, rare goods, company identifiers only, multiple destinations," the clerk declared mechanically. She consulted a small slip of parchment in one of the piles on her desk. "Risk factor of... three." Another pause to slide some beads around an abacus set beside her outbox. "Sixty-eight giltin, four silver, and two copper."

"Right." Gorm counted out the coins and arranged them in neat piles.

The attendant looked over the payment, gave a small nod, and began wordlessly writing on a sheet of parchment covered in woodcut text. When the form was filled out, she pounded it with two separate stamps, placed the document in her outbox, and rang a small bell. "Responses," she said, as though this was somehow self-explanatory, and returned to the documents she had been examining earlier.

Gorm had bought information from thieves in taverns countless times, but he couldn't make any sense of how this was supposed to work. He watched in bewilderment as another clerk stopped at the customer inquiry desk, put the contents of the outbox into a leather satchel, and shuffled back into the depths of the office. "Do I pay ye or—"

"Responses!" she reiterated, pointing at another nondescript desk.

"Come on." Heraldin nudged Gorm as he stood. The Dwarf gathered up his coins with a shrug, and the three heroes went over to the desk indicated by the attendant. It had another small plaque. This one said, "CUSTOMER RESPONSES."

They waited in uncomfortable silence. The quiet was oppressive and heavy, only interrupted by the occasional pounding of a stamp or the turning of a page. The minutes stretched into an awkward eternity, and Gorm could not tell how much time had passed before a wrinkled Tinderkin in a rumpled gray suit hobbled up to the desk.

The old clerk held two sheets of parchment; one was the form the inquiries attendant had written, and the other was covered in promising-looking script. "Payment," he said evenly.

Gorm placed the coins on the desk. The Gnome counted the money, made a note on the form, and adjusted his spectacles to read the script on the second page. When he spoke again it was in a ridiculous accent, like a bad mummer trying to affect a hoodlum from Chrate. "Word on the street is you lads want to know about movin' Imperial flame olives into the Freelands. Well, I got sources that says they seen 'em comin up from Kesh through Mistkeep and Waerth by unmarked cart. An' the talk about Fengarden is there's an unusual number of said unmarked carts runnin' through their city and round the Drakehead. Common practice to avoid customs at the Riverdowns. But nobody's seen 'em enterin' the city nor passing through the village at Eastgate, and the crews rebuildin' Aberreth aint talked 'bout 'em neither. Might be bound north for Scoria or Goldwynn if they're stayin' off the King's Road, but no word. That's as far as the guild ears will get ya."

His performance done, the clerk cleared his throat, scooped up Gorm's coin, and added in cold monotone, "No refunds."

"So, what, the olives just make their way around Drakehead Lake and disappear?" asked Gorm.

The clerk gave a shrug and a nod as he gathered up paperwork and stood.

Gorm thought about where the shipments could have gone. "Any word of the shipments in Hollinsher or East Upshore? Or could the carts be unpacked somewhere?"

"Inquiries," the clerk said with a perfunctory smile before he turned to hobble away.

"Should have known," Gorm grumbled.

"I doubt they know more anyway, friend," said Heraldin. "And I am eager to be out of here."

Gaist nodded, still glancing around the room.

"Aye, can't disagree there," said the Dwarf, already making for the door. "And it seems a good lead. The trick is followin' it."

With the three customers gone, the Thieves' Guild office returned to its quiet work. Clerks processed, indexed, cross-referenced, and filed tips from field observers. Managers assembled briefings from collected paperwork. Senior staff monitored these reports to see if adjustments were necessary in risk profiles or quarterly projections. Every guild member went about their duties wordlessly, completely focused on scrupulously following process. Few things survived from the pre-acquisition era of the guild, but creative and memorable punishments for breaking guild policy had endured.

And so the response clerk quickly went to the back office with Gorm's payment and paperwork. A guild accountant counted out the payment, checked it against the total on the inquiry form, and returned the paperwork to the clerk with a receipt of payment. The clerk deposited the inquiry, the scripted reply, and the receipt into a new folder, signed a pre-printed attestation of veracity, stamped everything with his seal, and put the entire packet into the inbox of a desk marked "POST-OPERATIONAL OPERATIONS."

The senior clerk of post-operational operations opened the file, reviewed its contents, and paused as she was placing it in an outbox marked "TO FILE." Something echoed faintly at the back of her mind, like the call of a miner lost in a deep cave. She reviewed the description of the customers and nature of their request, then consulted a ledger of guild procedures. A few loose memorandums on process updates were in the back. One of them, dated from the prior Bloomtide, had a list of topics and the descriptions of a dozen people. She compared the memo to the inquiry form, made a note on the file, stamped it, and placed it in a different outbox labeled "ESCALATIONS."

Thus Gorm's paperwork was diverted from the river of paper flowing into the depths of the guild's archives. Instead, it cascaded from desk to desk, collecting notes and stamps and additional papers, until it arrived at the Office of External Communications. A communications clerk bound the folio with a red ribbon, put it into a briefcase, and carried it to a courier waiting by a nondescript carriage.

The carriage took the clerk up to a beige, windowless building wedged between two law firms on the Seventh Tier. Suite forty-two of the building was empty aside from a single desk, and behind the lone desk sat the shadow of a figure reading from another set of documents. The courier placed the bound folio on the desk with trepidation before fleeing the room. Before the sound of the courier's hurried, retreating footsteps had completely faded, the man behind the lone desk cut the red ribbon and opened the folder.

He picked up the inquiry form and read. Then he read it again.

He set the paper down. He took a deep, meditative breath, and trembled as though fighting to suppress a scream. The struggle contorted his fine features for a moment, and then he lost. An expletive forced itself from his lips in a spray of spittle.

"*Spug!*" swore Benny Hookhand.

——CHAPTER 9——

"**P**ardon my language. I am not used to this—*bones*!" Poldo swore again as his seat shifted and nearly dropped him. His stomach lurched as the cobblestones swayed below him.

"You all right?" Thane asked over his shoulder.

"Yes, fine, thank you." Poldo righted himself. "I am not used to this height. Perhaps, though, a few adjustments to the straps? For stability."

A Wood Gnome chittered an order, and the Domovoy on Thane's shoulder sprang into action.

"And you're sure you don't mind? It's just hard to move quickly on these, aha, relatively short legs." Notes of apology rang in Poldo's voice as he stared up at Thane. "And I never learned to ride, living in the city as I did..."

"I don't mind," said the Troll, though he was preoccupied with the leather harness around his arms. Wood Gnomes swarmed through his shaggy fur, making adjustments to the straps. Those strips of padded leather connected to Poldo's seat, an apparatus halfway between a plush seat and a haversack on the Troll's back.

"And, as you well know, coaches tend to attract unwanted attention," Poldo continued.

"And I'm good at avoiding it, yes." The Troll gave his limbs an appraising stretch. "It fits well."

"I should hope so, given what that leatherworker charged," said the Scribkin. "Are you ready to travel for Mistkeep then?"

Thane straightened and took a breath of the salty air. West of them, dark clouds rolled over darker waves that crashed against the rocky coast. North of them, the city of Chrate perched amid the rocks. Black smoke spewed from the maze of crooked chimneys that crowned the port city.

"Yes," the Troll said. He took another breath, and his subsequent grin was equal parts pure joy and daggerlike teeth. "It will be good to be back in the deep forest."

"Will it? Uh, excellent." Poldo, for his part, had enjoyed his brief hours in a city, even one as dingy and soot-filled as Chrate. He'd found a teahouse that brewed a decent cup, and for a few blessed moments he'd been able to relax and pretend he was back on the Pinnacle of Andarun with a cup of Spelljammer's green blend in hand and the jewel of the Freedlands spread out before him.

Yet Poldo knew they couldn't linger too long. The fiasco with collateralized threat obligations had left a lot of people very angry at Poldo, many of whom had ample wealth and meager morals. At least a few had quietly placed bounties on his head. He wouldn't be safe in Andarun without a king's guard, and Chrate was far less safe than Andarun. The port city was a nest of skullduggery and grift, an orgy of thieves, spies, and assassins plying their trades against each other.

Whenever he walked into Chrate, the Gnome was like a plump chicken strolling into a den of wolves, albeit a chicken that walked around with a Dire Bear watching over it. Poldo preferred not to put his bodyguard out by provoking constant attempts on his life. They'd spent a night in the decaying port on their way to Adchul those many months ago, and poor Thane had barely slept for all of the would-be assassins creeping through the window and shimmying down the chimney. On this trip, they'd only been in town long enough to purchase Thane's harness from a dusty antiques shop, drop it with the leatherworker, and have a cup of tea while waiting for the modifications to be complete.

The Troll gave the straps of the harness a couple more experimental tugs. Poldo's seat didn't shift. "Let's be off," he said.

Poldo sighed. "Yes, let's. We've a long journey ahead. My luggage?"

A pack of Wood Gnomes carried his briefcase and bag up behind him and, through no small feat of acrobatics, climbed the Troll and hung the baggage on the saddle's luggage hook. Once the tiny Gnomes had taken up positions in Thane's fur, Poldo rapped on the small, wooden desk built into the front of the seat. "All secure!" he called.

"Hang on," said the Troll. He stepped off the road and moved through the forest beside it. Leaves rushed by as the Troll reached his stride, but somehow the huge Shadowkin managed to not disturb them, and he moved through the forest with eerie silence.

They were only a few strides along when Red Squirrel hopped up onto Poldo's desk and chittered a question.

Poldo shifted uneasily and thought for a moment about the tasks ahead of him, "Ah, yes. Let's draft a reply to Mrs. Hrurk, shall we? I'm sure she'd appreciate an encouraging note before she starts her new job tomorrow."

Red Squirrel squeaked and leapt back into the Troll's fur. The hair by Thane's left shoulder rustled, and Poldo heard the briefcase open and close behind him. A moment later, six Wood Gnomes were arrayed in front of a sheet of paper and a set of tiny stamps, each with one letter. One chirruped that they were at the ready.

"Thank you. Ahem. My dear Mrs. Hrurk... uh..." Poldo tried to find the right words, and found it unusually difficult. He cleared his throat again, but failed to dislodge a thought tugging at the back of his mind. Raising a finger to stay the eager transcribers, he leaned sideways and shouted up to the Troll, "You're sure you don't mind this?"

"Why would I mind?" Thane rumbled.

"Well, it's just that I..." Poldo rapped his fingers on the wooden desk resting between the Troll's massive shoulder blades. "I feel a touch guilty riding you in a saddle."

"You're not riding me," Thane said. "I've put you into my backpack."

Poldo leaned back. "What? No, this used to be an officer's saddle in the Sky Knights. The Sun Gnomes used it to ride Great Eagles."

"Well, it was a cow and a couple of trees before that, but I wouldn't put it out in the pasture." Poldo could hear the grin in Thane's voice. "Whatever it used to be, it's my backpack now. I hope you don't mind riding in it."

The Scribkin bristled a little. "Well, that doesn't seem very dignified."

Thane shrugged, shifting the desk and its occupants. "At least nobody is trying to saddle you," Thane said.

Poldo barked a laugh at that despite himself. "Ha! Yes. Fair enough, I suppose."

"Forget what is fair," said Asherzu Guz'Varda. "The Wall is not fair. It is not even-handed or forgiving. It does not care about you at all, and if you throw yourself off its highest point tonight, the traders will still come back in the morning and buy and sell like you were never there."

The Orcess smiled at the workers seated in the rows of chairs before her. From her place among their ranks, Feista Hrurk cleared her throat and glanced around the gathering hall at her fellow recruits, a motley collection of Shadowkin with fresh suits and nervous faces. All of them looked almost as terrified as she felt.

"And the best thing about the Wall is how unfair it is," Asherzu continued. "The Royal Court is fair. The arbiters of the Heroes' Guild are fair. They were not always so; years ago they came and slaughtered us at will, and that was unfair. They stole our wealth and left us destitute, and that was unfair. And then they set up a system of noncombatant papers to 'allow' us to live in their gutters, and that was unfair."

The chieftain paced back and forth in front of them, raising her voice as if to call to those in the back even though there were no more than two dozen hires in the room. "And then a year ago, we worked with their king to make the NPC program apply to all, and the Lightlings discovered fairness again. Now they see that it would be unfair to punish the Humans for the evils of their parents. It would be unfair to take gold the Elves earned plundering us, unfair to penalize Dwarves for making investments in our suffering, unfair to take from the Gnomes just for doing the best they could while following the unjust laws of their time. And now, and only now, the kingdom and the Heroes' Guild cannot do what is unfair.

"But the Wall, the market..." Asherzu grinned as realization dawned on the audience and an undercurrent of soft laughter flowed through the room. "The market is not fair. The market is not concerned with keeping us as we are, with preserving a status quo. The market is a battlefield, as merciless and cold as any your ancestors fought upon. Fought and won."

She spread her hands to the assembled recruits. "You will fight alongside us. You will bring glory and honor to your people, prosperity to your families, and dismay to your foes. Your mind is your only weapon on the Wall. Sharpen your cunning, seek out every weak spot in the competition, and bring tears of despair to all that oppose us!"

The assembled Shadowkin stood, whooping and cheering. Feista bounded to her own feet, her tail wagging furiously as she clapped. While they were still cheering, Asherzu took a small bow. "I see great things for all of you at Warg Incorporated," she said. "May your gods smile upon you this day."

The applause surged as the chieftain stepped out of the small room, flanked by her massive brother and a gaggle of assistants. Feista thought she saw Asherzu wink at her as the Orcess left, but it was too quick to be sure. When the Gnoll turned back to the front of the room, a Slaugh in an ill-fitting suit hopped up to the podium. "Thank you, Chieftain," he read from a small sheet of parchment. "Next, we will cover our axes and flails policy, harassment and animosity, and then we will move on to the healing plan."

The rest of Feista's orientation was slow and overwhelming at the same time; standard procedures, benefits and policies, conflict resolution guidelines—duels to the death were strictly forbidden during working hours. It was like drowning in porridge until suddenly, thankfully, it abruptly ended, and they were allowed to take a lunch break in the small park outside.

She found a spot near a fountain where some of the other recruits were gathering. Clutching her small bundle of bread and salted fish, she found a spot between an Orcess who was going into Sales and a Goblin who had accepted a job in Human Resources.

"So you'll do payroll and settle disputes?" Feista asked him.

"Oh, gods no," said the Goblin. "That's Hireling Resources. In Human Resources, we try to figure out how to extract the most wealth from all of these Lightlings in a sustainable way."

"Like plundering their homes?" asked the Orcess.

"That's old thinking," said the Goblin. "Pillage a town's gold, and you'll be rich for a day. Make a town systemically dependent on services that only you provide, and you'll be rich for a lifetime."

After lunch, Feista was fetched by a young intern. He had a mottled green face pocked with spots that could have been acne or some sort of intentional modification—it was hard to tell with Gremlins. The intern led her up three floors of stairs into an open floor, illuminated with the pale blue light of glowstones and packed with rows of shining pine desks. Only about half of the seats in the room were occupied. A mahogany desk faced the others at the front of the room, and behind it an Orc bulged out of a fine suit. A polished brass nameplate on the desk said "Borpo Skar'Ezzod" twice; once in Imperial lettering, and below it in Orcish bone glyphs.

"I am Borpo, the Bloodied Fist, first among the Skar'Ezzod, Senior Elder of Finance and Analysis at Warg Inc. You will be my direct report," Borpo told Feista as the intern skittered away. He grasped her paw in a meaty hand and shook it vigorously. "Together we will bring honor and glory to Warg Incorporated!"

"Uh, yes," said the Gnoll, trying not to wince at his crushing grip.

"Come. Let us review your duties!" Borpo spoke every word with force and gusto, as though emphasizing a punch.

"Yes," Feista repeated.

He walked her past all of the empty desks to a green door. Behind it was a small, windowless chamber lined with bookshelves, each of them brimming with folios of parchment. Four desks were in the middle of the room. Three of them were completely empty, while the fourth had a brass nameplate that said "Feista Hrurk."

"You will be in our analysis team," said Borpo. "The analysis team will find the weaknesses in our opponents' stocks, the cracks in their armor that will bring down their bloated corporations. You will provide the brokerage and finance teams of Warg Inc. the insights they need to stand against the Lightling companies."

"Yes, but... where is the rest of the team?" Feista asked, looking at the cluster of empty desks.

"You are the first of your kind!" boomed Borpo. "Opportunity is before you, and now you must grasp it!"

"But I—I mean, I've never done—"

"Asherzu Guz'Varda has spoken highly of you!" said Borpo, and now there was a hint of danger in his thundering voice. "What is more, she believes it is a failure of Finance that we had no Analysis Department before today. And given how wise our chieftain and CEO is, I am sure this will work out very well." There was enough vitriol in his last declaration to curdle milk.

Feista felt her tail instinctively curling beneath her legs, and willed it to straighten. "Uh, right, but—"

"Excellent. Then we have an understanding. I expect your first report tomorrow. Glory and honor!" With that bold and disjointed declaration, Borpo strode back out of the Analysis Department.

Feista took stock of the day as she watched him go. She had only a vague sense of her job, a boss that seemed to resent its existence, and no team to rely upon. On the other hand, it was apparent that she still had Asherzu's confidence, and that clearly still counted for a lot. There seemed to be plenty of good research materials here as well, and there were some papers in her inbox that seemed like a good place to start. And then, in her pocket...

She pulled out the neatly folded slip of fresh parchment. The message had been transcribed by Wood Gnomes afield, then chittered to a sprite, flown to Andarun, and relayed to Gnomes at Mrs. Hrurk's Home for the Underprivileged, and was finally stamped out and left on the front table this morning. Mr. Poldo had devised it as an extremely secure way of sending letters, and as an added bonus, most of the correspondence only took a single night to arrive.

Mrs. Hrurk who is dear to me,

I greet you with happy smile! Your new job reaches my ears. Very happy!

Feista sighed. She had to admit that Mr. Poldo's ingenious use of Wood Gnomes was secure from interception, but much was lost in two rounds of translation. Usually the coherence.

I have knowledge of nervousness in new task. Fear not! I had new job too, long time ago, and you are my superior. I am confident you will be best at business!

There is hard work you are very good at. There are smart things you are very good at. There are no things you cannot do.

I stare ahead to the time when I hear of your success.

Biggest hopes,
Duine Poldo

"There are no things you cannot do," she said to herself as she tucked the note back into her pocket. With a determined nod, Feista Hrurk sat down at her new desk, took the top piece of paper from her inbox tray, and got to work.

"This is no time for sittin' around!" Gorm growled, fists on his hips. Gaist cast a long shadow over his shoulder. Both Dwarf and doppelganger glared down at the bench before them and the recumbent figure occupying it.

"I respectfully disagree." Heraldin lay in the shade of the lone maple that marked Duflo Park on the Fifth Tier. The bard kept the brim of his wide hat pulled low over his eyes. "And I'd know better than you. I'm both a former participant in your insane quests, and something of an expert on leisure. I can say from experience that I find the latter much more agreeable."

"We know where the flame olive oil is goin'!" the Dwarf insisted. "We're on the cusp of exposin' Johan for a liar and a killer!"

Heraldin lifted his hat an inch to watch an Elf in a well-tailored dress walking along the street. "And when you do, you owe me your ballad rights."

"If and when your information pans out!" Gorm jabbed a figure at the bard, distracting him from the retreating Elf. "And not a moment before."

"Then the sooner you start, the sooner we'll all get what we want." Heraldin pulled his hat down over his eyes again. "I look forward to your return."

"I thought ye might want to do your part," grumbled the berserker.

The bard lifted the edge of his hat a fraction with a flick of his thumb. A single, irritated eye gleamed up at Gorm from the tangle of shadow and hair beneath its brim. "I did my part."

"We ain't done—"

"I found you the source. I led you to the information," growled Heraldin.

"Aye, but—"

"I fought the undead. I stood against the liche. I rescued the downtrodden. I spent a year in the thrice-cursed wilderness. I fought for the Orcs. I quested for the Elven Marbles. I have done much, much more for this city than this city has done for me, my friend, and now? Now I want to play music and drink in excess and sleep the mornings away. I have earned it. I did my part." The bard pulled his hat down with theatrical emphasis. "I bid you good luck."

Gorm threw up his hands in exasperation and looked at the weaponsmaster. "Will you talk some sense—er, stare some sense into him?"

Gaist cast a sidelong glance at the lounging man and shrugged in such a way that suggested this was an old fight he was unwilling to start again.

"I saw that," sniped Heraldin. "Not everyone is so eager to shout zahat'emptor."

Gaist's eyes narrowed.

Gorm's limited grasp of language failed him. "'My hat is empty?'" he hazarded, based on his knowledge of Old Dwarven and Root Elven.

"'Only my honor remains,'" the bard translated, staring at the weaponsmaster. "It comes from the old tongue of the Imperial people around Arak. It's the battle cry of Arakian men who have nothing to live for. They call it a way of life, but it seems to me the battle cry of those who'd rather die than live another day."

Gaist shook his head fiercely and turned away.

Gorm took a step back. He'd stepped into some muck between the bard and the weaponsmaster. If their fight was about Arakian culture, he suspected it cut at an old wound for Gaist. Iheen the Red, the adventurer Gorm had once quested with and that Gaist now emulated, hailed from Arak and wore the red scarf to honor its warriors. This was a line of inquiry that had already cut deep, and applying pressure would only make it worse.

"All right, enough of that," the Dwarf said, waving a hand between the two. "Heraldin, I'll not force ye to come, though we could use your help. Is there anything we could say to get ye to join us?"

The bard's face softened a bit. "My friend, do not take it personally. Questing is not for me."

"Ye were one of us—one of the Heroes of Destiny."

"Yes, but not by choice. The first and last person who got me to leave the comforts of the city on an insane errand was Niln, and he did it with a royal writ and the threat of death. Your place is in the heart of battle. Mine is here, on a comfy seat dreaming up rhymes about your brave deeds."

Gorm nodded. Heraldin was a competent fighter and a decent lockpick, but at his heart, he was still a useless bard. "Aye, fine. Suit yourself. Come on, Gaist. I know who's probably looking for work."

"I need a quest." Kaitha's words were like sandpaper on skin, rasping, raw, and irritated. "I have been in this gods-forsaken city for days. I need something to... I need to go questing."

The woman across the table spread her hands wide. "Kaitha, my jewel! The Jade Wind is back on top!" The agent's raven curls glittered with pearls and gems, and golden chains dangled between the many piercings scattered across her warm umber face. "We're at the Pinnacle! Breathe it in. Savor it!" She gestured expansively at the crowded tables around Spelljammer's Cafe.

Andarun's premier teahouse was packed to bursting, and even its outdoor seating was crowded with patrons. Great iron braziers set around the cafe blazed with enchanted flames, warding off the bitter cold and lighting up Pinnacle Plaza. Similar lights were flaring all over the city, treating Spelljammer's customers to a spectacular view.

Kaitha took a deep breath. Loribartalebeth of House Araka was a supportive and professional representative, but she oozed a well-oiled optimism that left the ranger feeling greasy. It was a demeanor common among agents; the persistent smile of someone who takes a cut of the loot without risking a cut from blade or claw. "I'm enjoying the success, Lori," she growled. "I've enjoyed it. It has been sufficiently savored. So much so that I'm ready to do it again. There has to be another contract coming up."

Lori shrugged and changed the subject. "Did you see what happened to the old statue?"

Kaitha looked out the window. Across the square, the Dark Prince gazed down at her from atop his stone pedestal. A ring of bannermen stood around the sculpture, a bulwark against a small crowd. "No. What?"

"Somebody drew all kinds of magic symbols on the cobbles around it," Lori confided. "All dark and spooky looking. The bannermen don't know who, but people whisper someone is trying to bring back the Sten."

"Like an evil cult?" Kaitha leaned forward, interested.

Lori gave her a skeptical look. "We'll see. It'll be weeks before they sort anything out and get in paperwork for a quest."

"Then let's talk about something else," said Kaitha. "Preferably something with an available contract."

"It hasn't been a week since you got back from dealing with the High Hag of Nuryot Sabbat," laughed the Sun Elf. "You need rest! Relaxation. Maybe a trip to the hot springs. Take my advice—"

"I don't need advice. I need a quest."

"Trust me. It's my job to keep you happy."

"It's your job to get me jobs. I'll be happy if you do it."

A shadow flickered over Lori's face for half a breath, like a wisp of cloud blowing past the noonday sun. Her grin returned as quickly as it faded. "Well, I did line up that one gig for you," she said, reaching beneath the table.

Kaitha grit her teeth. "Not the gruel."

"Premium breakfast grains," Lori corrected as she produced a rolled-up parchment from the satchel beneath her seat. "I just got a proof of the box art."

"This isn't what I meant."

The agent unfurled the scroll and rolled it out on the table. A woodcut showed Kaitha brandishing a bow and arrow behind a bowl of porridge. The printed ranger's hair whipped dramatically in a wind that didn't seem to affect the steam rising from the bowl. Her steely gaze was locked on the gruel in a way that suggested she was more likely to shoot the cereal than eat it, a sentiment that the flesh and blood Kaitha shared. Large block letters at the top of the print screamed "HEROATS," while a smaller font next to the ranger's face declared "HER OATS ARE HEROATS!"

The agent tapped the paper. "Beautiful, right?"

Kaitha squinted. "Something about it is…"

"Well, it's not perfect." Lori waved dismissively. "Maybe too nostalgic. But just imagine how good it could look if you'd pose for the woodcut artist."

"No."

"Heroats is an institution. Everybody who's anybody has done licensed box art for them. And now they want you! This could be big!"

The ranger shook her head. "I'm not posing. I need a quest. A real job."

"Someone with your profile needs to focus on brand expansion into other verticals. Like premium breakfast grains. Killing monsters and saving people is small time stuff."

"That's the job! That's literally what I do." Kaitha had to set her tea down lest she spill it or club her agent to death with her cup. "Killing monsters and saving—"

Lori cut her off. "You want to help people, I know. Listen, not everybody has bugbears in their basement. And when they do, the bugbears almost always have papers and pay rent! But everybody needs a nutritious breakfast to start the day."

The ranger stared at her agent flatly. Her agent grinned back.

"I'm not doing it."

"This pays twice what the hag quest paid, for one printing. If boxes with you on them sell fast enough, they could be doing another run next week. There isn't a monster on the upside of Wynspar that could get you anywhere near this payout."

"This isn't about the money," said Kaitha.

That turned out to be the one statement that could darken the Sun Elf's mood. Lori's grin melted, then congealed into a determined scowl. "This is what I have for you—"

"I want a quest."

"You and everyone else," hissed Lori. "My friend, there's never been a shortage of professional heroes, but since the Shadowkin reforms, former NPCs are flooding the quest boards. The market for talent is crazy right now. There are Orcs twice your size questing for half your rate."

Kaitha snorted. "Yeah, but do they have experience?"

"They're getting it, and fast," Lori shot back. The Sun Elf shook her head and reconstituted her toadying smile. "Listen, you're the Jade Wind.

You're more than a commodity; you're living history and a brand unto yourself. That bit with the liche removed any doubt that you're the best of the best. But in this market, it takes a while to line up work for someone of your stature. It's going to be a while before I have another job for you. And in the meantime..." The agent glanced meaningfully at the woodcut on the table.

The ranger grimaced. Her head throbbed.

"Just think about it." The Sun Elf pushed the woodcut across the table. "Anyway, I hate to do this, but my next appointment just arrived. Grab a scone to go, on me."

Kaitha startled and followed the agent's gaze to the door of Spelljammer's, which was fully eclipsed by a nearly square profile.

"You can't be serious," said Kaitha.

"Daring... adventure!" rumbled a familiar voice. A hulking Ogre pushed out onto the patio and made for Lori's table with all the grace and tact of a dreadnaught pushing through a fleet of fishing skiffs. His meaty, tattooed arms jostled tables, startled patrons, and sloshed tea as he lumbered toward the Elves. A one-eyed Human clad in black leather and a Gnome with his hair dyed an eye-watering shade of pink followed in Brunt's wake, righting toppled chairs with muttered apologies.

"You're repping Brunt?" Kaitha asked.

"Mr. Brunt," corrected Lori. "Like I said. A crazy market."

"Boundless... opportunity!" Brunt erupted.

"Promise me you'll think about the premium breakfast grains," Lori whispered, then turned her attention to her next clients. "Mr. Brunt! Mags! Timbleton! So good to see you! Let me order a pot."

Kaitha managed to bid her goodbyes without making any untoward remarks, took the Heroats artwork, and left the cafe.

It was late, and the day had been long and fruitless. Exhaustion weighed her every step by the time she made it back to her building. "It's all the same," she muttered to herself as she staggered up the stairs.

It wasn't even the good kind of stagger. She'd had many pleasant stumbles up these steps in the past, the sort where her grin was as lopsided as her gait and every bump or trip seemed incredibly amusing through a chemical haze.

Not tonight. Tonight her bones ached with every clomp of her leather boots on the steps. She felt the sort of weariness that made friends remark that they were getting too old for something or other, but as an Elf, she wasn't getting too old for anything. She wasn't aging. Or changing.

"Everything just stays the same."

She shook her head as she unlocked her door. Dark thoughts lay down that path. She just needed some sleep. But first...

An old memory compelled her into her bedroom closet. She pulled a small chest from the back shelf and blew the dust off it. Then she set it on the table and opened it.

The box held an ornate knife, expired licenses, contracts for her favorite quests, and other mementos that were only as valuable as the memories they inspired. And near the bottom, tucked beneath a poster advertising a hefty sum for slaying the Hydra of Gauntcragge, was a roll of parchment bound by a red ribbon.

She opened the aged scroll and read. "Her oats are Heroats."

It was the exact same woodcut they'd pitched back in twenty-four. They hadn't even bothered to update the slogan after five decades. Kaitha tossed the new proof back in the box with its older twin and headed to the balcony. From her apartment on the Eighth Tier she could look out at most of Andarun, a river of lights and rooftops spilling down Mount Wynspar. It was beautiful, but her eyes were drawn westward, past the Ridge to the stars shining over a horizon that she couldn't see.

This was familiar too. How many nights had the Jade Wind spent staring at the black emptiness above and trying to fend off the crushing despair? How many nights had she turned to drink to help in the fight? How many times had she used salve to escape it? The emptiness was always with her; it had never left, except...

Except when she entered that garden, and when its king had followed her from it. And she'd felt him there, known that he...

He was never coming back, Kaitha reminded herself. She turned and walked back into her apartment. He'd had more than enough chances to meet her, and he chose not to. That was answer enough to any questions that might linger.

The hollowness inside her grew a little at the thought, a space in her heart that might have been full, but turned out to have been empty all along. Thane was no help. Success was no cure. There was only one way to appease the gnawing void, and nobody else was going to give it to her. She scratched at her aching wrists as she approached the closet door. Her heart was pounding in her ears; steady and loud, irregular and ringing like a bell.

Kaitha paused to consider this cardiovascular oddity, and realized that the sound wasn't so much her heart as a small, pink sprite banging against the glass doors of her balcony. She shrugged off the urge with the aid of the distraction and opened the window.

The messenger sprite flitted inside and settled on her table. "Kaitha of House Tyrieth?" it trilled.

"I am. Say your message."

"Lass, it's me," said the sprite in a high-pitched grumble. Kaitha couldn't help but smile as the sprite hunched over and glared at her in an approximation of Gorm's mannerisms. "Get geared up and meet us at the usual place in the mornin'. Me an' Gaist think we know how to find where them barrels are headed. We're on the trail."

——CHAPTER 10——

"I thought you covered your tracks." Cigar smoke curled from the edges of Johan's grin. The wisps evaporated up into the haze that hung in the small, sparse room in the rear corridors of the Palace of Andarun. "You said that you were immaculately careful."

Weaver Ortson froze, his tumbler of spirits halfway to his lips. The king's smile was congenial and teasing, but cold fury lurked in his voice like a shark in dark waters.

"Careful only goes so far," said the Gnome across the table. The Tinderkin was a recent addition to the king's secretive meetings, to Ortson's chagrin. The guildmaster thought of the Gnome as a sort of viper with a topknot. His face was adorned with a black goatee, silver earrings, and a series of scars and cuts that crisscrossed each cheek. He didn't wear suits or even a business-appropriate jerkin, but instead came dressed in black leather armor and wielding a bladed hook. And he spoke out of both sides of his mouth, in the most literal sense.

"What I meant to say," the Gnome said, "is that every precaution was taken, but Your Majesty knows how tenacious Gorm Ingerson can be."

A shadow flicked over Johan's face at the mention of the Dwarf. He pointed at Flinn with the burning end of his Daellish cigar. "So I do know, Mr. Flinn! Ha ha! What I would like to know is, what do you plan to do about it?"

"Oh, I got plans, but it ain't time for 'em," rasped Mr. Flinn. His face contorted as though he'd taken a bite out of a lemon, and then he added in smoother tones, "Contingencies are in place, though at this moment the best course of action is observation."

Ortson glanced meaningfully across the table at Goldson and Baggs. The financiers were watching the conversation with a distant disdain. Baggs shrugged at the guildmaster.

"Contingencies! Ha! I'm glad to hear it," said the king. "But I'd be more glad to hear specifics."

"I thought you'd want to keep your hands clean," said Mr. Flinn, and then after another spasm, "What I meant to say is—*I know what I meant to say!*" The Tinderkin's hook hand jerked up to within an inch of his own face, and he stared at it like a gladiator staring down an opponent. After a labored moment, the Gnome grabbed his own arm, flared his nostrils, and pushed it back down to the table. Then he looked up with an expectant smile, as though the outburst had never happened.

"Are you all right, Mr. Flinn?" asked Mr. Baggs. "You're acting a bit odd this evening."

"More so than usual," Mr. Goldson added into a tumbler of whiskey.

Ortson dropped the charade altogether as he turned to the king. "Is he quite mad?"

"Ha! Perhaps. Mr. Flinn is a man of two minds about almost everything." Johan smiled and nodded at the Gnome across the table. "I'm sure you remember that Mr. Flinn assisted us with assembling Al'Matra's heroes and cleaning up the matter at Bloodroot."

"I'm sure I don't," harrumphed Mr. Goldson.

"We do our best not to get bogged down in the details of such matters," said Mr. Baggs. "It makes our lives easier."

"And keeps our liabilities limited," added Goldson.

"Eh? See? Keeping their hands clean," growled Mr. Flinn.

Ortson, though, had a deeper knowledge of the mercenary companies operating in the Freedlands, if only for the sake of keeping tabs on his competition. "Wait, this is the same Mr. Flinn from the Silver Talons! The one we hired for Bloodroot, and to bring in Ingerson."

"Well, I wouldn't say that." Johan's smile brimmed with cruel amusement. "It's true that Mr. Flinn has let us down on occasion. But since those unfortunate incidents, Mr. Flinn has disbanded his mercenary organization and formed a most useful... partnership with another entity."

"Who?" demanded Mr. Ortson.

"It's best that we don't know," said Mr. Baggs coldly.

"You got that right," growled Mr. Flinn.

"Needless to say, he has—or rather, they have—become central to several of my plans." Johan stared at the twitching Gnome. "Their combined service has been unerringly helpful. Until now."

"Sire, we don't know that Ingerson has actually found anything," Mr. Flinn said.

"He's found enough to make him curious about things he should know nothing about!" snapped Goldson.

"He knows enough to ask questions," added Baggs.

"Curiosity is not proof," said Mr. Flinn. "Questions are not evidence."

"Optimism is not a strategy," countered Goldson.

The Tinderkin squirmed in his plush velvet seat. "So long as Ingerson can't trace our path, he poses no threat."

"So long as he's looking where he doesn't belong, it's a concern," pressed Baggs.

Flinn's face twitched and distorted as he literally wrestled with another outburst. "True enough. But if we were to pause the shipments—"

"Absolutely not," said Goldson. "The... strategy has been driving revenues across multiple lines of business."

"Were operations to cease, we'd see declines in everything from weapon sales to training contracts," said Baggs. "There isn't enough revenue in looting to offset losses like that."

Mr. Flinn gave a placating smile. "Gentlemen, I understand your concern in the short term, but in time—"

"The markets don't wait, Mr. Flinn!" thundered Goldson.

"As they say, profits delayed are profits denied," said Baggs.

"That's not what they say," Ortson muttered into his drink.

"Who cares what the common folk say?" the ancient Dwarf hollered. "We need things to continue as planned!"

"Though, of course, we don't need to know what that plan is," Baggs added cautiously.

"We need to demonstrably not know what the plan is," said Goldson. "But we still need it to happen."

"Of course, of course, gentlemen," Johan said magnanimously. "I shall ensure that things will stay on schedule."

Mr. Flinn's eyes widened. "But sire, if the Dwarf finds the facility—"

"You've taken precautions, have you not?" Johan's eyes gleamed dangerously as he glanced at the Gnome. "Circuitous routes with unmarked wagons and such?"

"'Course we did! We ain't newbloods," blurted the Tinderkin. He took a moment to get hold of himself. "But, as Your Majesty knows, Gorm Ingerson and his fellows have a regrettable habit of surpassing expectations. It's only a matter of time before—"

"Ha! Exactly!" said Johan. "All the Golden Dawn and I need is a bit more time. A few more shipments. Ingerson doesn't know what he's looking for, and if by some chance he stumbles upon it, what will he do? Tell the town criers? Appeal to the nobles? Starting a movement takes time that he doesn't have. Ha! We'll have won the day long before he manages to find more than a couple sympathetic ears."

The co-conspirators around the king exchanged worried glances. Mr. Goldson puffed long trails of blue smoke from his pipe in agitation.

"Ingerson truly does have a regrettable habit of surpassing expectations," Mr. Baggs said.

Johan's smile didn't move, but his eyes narrowed. "We only need a little time, gentlemen. And if Ingerson... overperforms again, well then, Mr. Flinn likes to plan for contingencies, as I recall. In the meantime, we have a lot of work to do."

The moon was already rising, and Feista Hrurk wasn't halfway through her work.

The briefcase she dragged up the steps to Mrs. Hrurk's Home for the Underprivileged bulged with paperwork that Borpo was expecting first thing in the morning. There were reams of calculations yet to be made and reports yet to be drafted, but the last of the sun's light had long since faded, and she had put off a crucial ritual for far too long.

Warm light and pandemonium washed over her as she opened the front door. Two of her children careened into her like fuzzy catapult stones, and by the time she got back to her feet, Little Rex was making his way across the hallway for a hug. Her son's lame leg couldn't move fast enough to keep up with the rest of him, and his tail was wagging so hard he could barely stay upright.

There were stories to hear, and nightgowns to don, and bedtime tales to recite. The pups yipped and danced around her heels, all in a futile effort to cram a day's worth of love into the precious moments before bed. And then, wretchedly fast, the best part of her day was over. The children were all asleep, and the briefcase called to her from where she'd set it in the hall.

It would have to wait. The home had business as well. Aubren needed to talk about issues with a fishmonger that was raising his prices. Vilga had a stack of paperwork Feista needed to sign. There were a slew of new applications from people of all sorts who couldn't stretch a giltin between rent and food.

The stars and moon were bright in a black sky before she staggered into the study, hoisted the briefcase onto her desk, and collapsed into a chair.

She pushed through the mountain of paperwork at a glacial pace. The problem was that she had to keep flipping back and forth between pages to compare the figures she needed. Often by the time she found the number she was searching for, she had forgotten why she needed it. It was like trying to understand a quilt by sorting through a stack of cloth scraps.

The thought of her old family quilts sparked a thought. Her mother and grandmother had never stitched a fancy blanket; Gnoll quilting was more about scavenging fabric than creating elaborate patterns. Feista's one heirloom was a covering made from six neat rows of trouser fabric, leather armor, and hide scraps, all cut into perfect squares. As a pup, she had lain in her bed comparing one patch to another, and remembering the tales of her grandsire sneaking through dungeons to snag cloth and armor from the corpses of unwary heroes.

She needed something like that. A grid of squares for comparison...

It took a few minutes to locate a ruler and a charcoal nib, but soon enough Feista had drawn several neat rows and columns onto a large piece of parchment. She listed companies of interest down the first column, and then the relevant metrics and projections across the top. It took well past midnight to find and transcribe the figures into their corresponding squares, not to mention run her calculations, but soon she had all of her numbers spread out on a single sheet.

Feista grinned down at the grid, triumphant. It was like a map of her portfolio, each risk and opportunity as clear and grand as the view from the Pinnacle. From that lofty perch the Gnoll could survey projected revenues, expense issues, and holdings. With such a vantage she could easily draw inferences about any company's projections based on performance, or exposure to the key stocks and funds, or potential tax burden on gross income.

Feista blinked. Gross income. But now that she considered it, hadn't Blackheart Securities provided revenue? As did Syrinx & Sons? But the Vellum Court and Royal Foresters Fund had both listed their gross income. A pit formed in the Gnoll's core, and her stomach dropped into it. She had mixed two values in the same column, and now all of her calculations were suspect.

All of the joy and exuberance leaked out of Feista in a prolonged groan. She'd have to recalculate all of her numbers. At this rate, she wondered if she'd get to bed at all. She dropped her head into her paws and tried not to weep.

A pink glimmer rippled across the thick pane of her window. Feista glanced up as a messenger sprite squeezed through an old pipe fitting and fluttered over to a pack of Wood Gnomes playing a game with peanut shells. A letter from Mr. Poldo had arrived.

The prospect of a note from the Scribkin cheered Feista a bit, and she made herself a mug of black tea as she waited for the Wood Gnomes to stamp out a message using tiny, metal letters and a pad of ink. Soon a pair of Gnomes deposited a transcription of Poldo's message on her desk.

Mrs. Hrurk.

I am hopeful for your great happiness. Hairy Mountain and I journey far in woods, and not too much trouble. It is very easy to not have much trouble with Hairy Mountain at my side.

Have found broker for trades of the foundation for house of poverty? Now you must be busy with new job. Tell me who to send trades with, and I will see foundation's treasure to great prosperity.

Please send me sprite with more news of big job. I have big pride for you!

With much sincerity,
Duine Poldo

Peas: If you are too much working hard, perhaps consider Gnomes of Appropriate Size? They are always most useful for basic tasks and taking less time.

Feista looked up from the paper. "Gnomes of appropriate size?" she said aloud.

White Rat emerged from behind an inkwell and chirruped in response. Behind her, many more Gnomes suddenly peeked out from the nooks and crannies of the study, all staring at the Gnoll.

"Is that what you call yourselves?" asked Feista. "That's how you say Wood Gnome?"

White Rat shrugged and nodded with an affirmative squeak.

Feista smirked. "I suppose that makes the rest of us too big?"

The tiny woman gave a massive eye roll, to the effect that this was an obvious point. A few of the other Wood Gnomes muttered under their breath.

"All right, I was just asking," Feista said, paws in the air. An idea was forming in her head. "Mr. Poldo suggested that I ask for your help with my work."

As one, every Wood Gnome suddenly discovered a fascinating patch of wall or ceiling to stare at. White Rat chittered something that was both unintelligible and yet also clearly an excuse.

"I'd pay you, of course," said the Gnoll.

The number of Gnomes on her desk tripled before she had completed her sentence. Round, eager faces smiled up at her from beneath a variety of rodents' skulls.

"It's just that it's not really a simple task," sighed Feista. "The calculations are fairly complex." By way of example, she sketched out a sample equation above the column for estimated tax burden. "See, you need to use the number from the fourth column and the tax rate from the nineteenth."

Rat Pelt clapped three times and barked something. The Wood Gnomes all but disappeared, and Feista's parchment trembled under a swirling morass of blurring Gnomes. A few high-pitched squabbles rose above the din, but when the dust and paper settled a few moments later, the entire column had been erased and filled in with corrected figures.

Feista stared past the paper, her mind's eye locked on the amazing possibilities behind the fresh pencil marks. "Wait, what if we apply the new numbers to the rest of the columns?" she asked, filling out new formulas above each column.

Rat Pelt squeaked and clapped again. A sort of organized chaos erupted on Feista's desk, like a tornado setting the table for tea. More than one brawl broke out regarding math and the order that it should be done in, and the Gnoll thought she would have to intervene at one point. Yet a sheet that would have taken Feista over an hour to fill out was completed and double-checked in less than a minute.

The Gnomes stared up at Feista with wide smiles. She stared back with wide eyes. "This changes everything," she breathed. "This is going to make my life so much easier."

"You probably shouldn't say things like that." Duine Poldo leaned forward in his saddle, or Thane's backpack, to speak into the Troll's ear. The birches and maples of the Green Span drifted by them, sun-dappled and painted the colors of a flame by autumn's touch.

"I'm sorry?" rumbled Thane.

"I don't mean to be rude," said Poldo hurriedly. "It's just not wise to make such statements aloud."

"I shouldn't say our next lodgings will be better," the Troll said flatly.

"Well, not that specifically," conceded the Gnome. "It's the nature of the statement, not the subject."

"We slept in a bramble thicket," said Thane. "It couldn't get much worse."

"There again," said Poldo. "You're setting expectations. Don't you remember Nove's principles?"

Thane's tectonic shrug rocked Poldo's desk like a wave at sea. Several Wood Gnomes poked their head out of the Troll's fur to discern the cause of the disruption. "Who is Nove again?" he rumbled.

"Nove? The great philosopher-scientist? The most famous scholar of Essenpi?"

"The name does sound familiar." Thane looked skyward and worked his fanged maw as though tasting the word. "I can't help remembering that he sold weapons. Or maybe toiletries."

Poldo's brow furrowed, but then a thought struck. "You mean Nove's razor," he told the Troll. "That's one of his principles of universal irony."

"That sounds right." Thane nodded.

"Nove defined the ratio of matter to irony in the universe as a constant, and from that constant he derived several useful principles," continued Poldo. He quickly launched into a history of the philosopher-scientist before his bodyguard could respond.

The Gnome's lecture wasn't due to any devout adherence to Nove's teachings; Poldo was just desperate for any topic of conversation that didn't involve plants or gardening. Thane had an enthusiasm for horticulture that most men reserved for money or vice. He had told Poldo that he had once been a gardener, and had proven it by coaxing a garden from the anemic soil of Adchul. The long months on that tiny, salt-sprayed island had given the Troll time to focus on his plants, but deprived him of variety.

Now Thane dashed through the woods with the eager energy of a child at a harvest festival. Between the forest's autumnal glory and the wide array of flora they encountered, the Troll erupted in gasps of delight and gushes of gardening monologues with the regularity of a geyser. It was enough to bore the boots off a botanist. It was more than enough to drive Poldo to discussions of philosophy and metaphysics.

"And so, Nove's first principle of universal irony is best observed by avoiding statements that set expectations for the universe to upset." Poldo noticed that a few of the Wood Gnomes riding in Thane's fur were listening to his speech with interest. The rest of the Domovoy had made themselves conspicuously absent.

"So you think we won't find an inn tonight because I said I expect to?" Thane made no attempt to hide his skepticism.

"We're less likely to," corrected Poldo. "It's about odds, not certainty. There can be no irony in a certain universe. And our universe is most uncertain."

"Is that a crimson willow?" asked Thane.

"Although the philosopher-priestess Bregit wrote that even an absolutely certain universe would be sufficiently complex to appear uncertain to all but the gods!" Poldo interjected hurriedly, trying to divert his bodyguard from the tree. "Even so, judging by the temples' histories, our universe is most uncertain. And so Nove's principles stand."

Thane sighed as he pulled his eyes from the willow, but then a thought struck him. "Although I didn't say I expected to find an inn last night, or the night before, and we've spent both nights sleeping in the open."

"Yes, I remember." Poldo reflexively reached for his aching back. Noting that Thane was eyeing a thick shrub in its golden fall plumage, he quickly launched into an explanation.

Poldo noted that though Nove's second principle appeared to deal with the universe's cruel sense of timing, it actually held that space was no kinder. Straightforward derivations of Nove's second principle demonstrated that the desirability of an object decreased the likelihood that it was within a given radius of those desiring it.

"The actual math includes several complex functions, but it's easiest remembered with the proverb of the town guard," Poldo said. "A town guard is almost never around when a crime is committed against you, and yet is almost always present to observe a crime you commit."

Thane shook his head. "That can't be right," he rumbled. "If it's true for you, it's not true for the person you committed crimes against."

"Well, the analogy isn't perfect—"

"Or what about the inns?" continued Thane. "If they had been built where we are not, wouldn't they be on more traveled roads then? Or are you suggesting that innkeepers only set up shops where people don't go?"

"Aha!" Poldo rocked back in his seat, triumphant. "I'm saying that building inns makes it less likely that travelers will go there, which is ironic for both the innkeepers and the guests."

Thane glanced back over his shoulder with a dagger-toothed grin. "So all inns are doomed, then?"

"No, you're speaking in certainties again. Nove's principles relate to the angle of trends, the arcs of probability curves. They don't apply in a certain universe."

"Well, then, why bother observing them at all?" asked Thane. "If the principles don't always apply, it seems silly to do anything about them."

"They apply often enough. It's mathematically proven." Poldo waved his hands as if to shoo the question away. "Regardless, Nove's teachings are easy enough to observe. You just always assume the worst case is the true one."

"That sounds like a miserable way to live." Thane pushed a low-hanging branch out of the way. "I don't want to go around assuming the next day will be worse than today. Besides, it can't always be the worst case. If it was always bad, it wouldn't be ironic, right? There's no irony in a certain universe."

"Of course! That's actually the basis for Nove's sev—" At this point, by some twist of Novian timing or arboreal resentment, the branch that Thane had pushed aside slipped through his fingers. The Troll instinctively ducked under the arc of crimson leaves, but in so doing he exposed Poldo, and the Scribkin's instincts were only of use behind a desk. The branch caught the Gnome full in the face, filling his mouth with leaves and his eyes with stars. A chorus of tiny squeaks of dismay rang out from the Wood Gnomes as Poldo nearly fell from his perch, followed by sighs of relief as he slumped forward in his seat.

It was still a fierce blow, and Poldo didn't fully recover his faculties until well after the Troll had set him down on the ground and the Wood

Gnomes had fetched him a canteen of water. He thanked them all and waved away their concern once he felt able to stand, and then spent a few more minutes consoling his guilt-ridden bodyguard. All in all, it was nearly a half hour before they were ready to move on.

"And let's stop at the first inn we find," Poldo remarked as Thane lifted his seat into place.

"So you're confident we'll find one," said Thane affably, trying a little too hard to return to their prior conversation.

Poldo took a deep breath. "Let's say I'm hopeful. And then let's say no more of Nove's principles. Or trees and plants, for that matter. I've had my fill of both."

"I'm surprised you've stuck with it as long as you have," Kaitha said to Gorm, but she didn't take her eyes off the road. "I thought you said it was all crazy nonsense."

"It is crazy nonsense," Gorm muttered without looking up from his copy of the Books of Niln.

"But you're still reading it." Kaitha narrowed her eyes and leaned forward against the pile of mossy boulders.

The goat bleated.

"Well, I don't read it all the time," said Gorm. "Just now and again."

"So why now?" Kaitha asked, giving the Dwarf a sidelong glance. "We're in the middle of the plan."

"What else should I be doin'? It don't take more than one to spot the carts comin' out of Andarun."

The eastward flow of carts, wagons, and caravans along the river had slowed to a trickle. Most of the day's long-distance travelers were already well on their way by now, and the wandering merchants, tinkers, and Tinderkin were undoubtedly trying to ply their wares within the city walls by this point. Gorm and Kaitha had seen a caravan carrying materials and workers to the reconstruction of Aberreth, and a few traders making a late start for Scoria, but otherwise the road had been mostly quiet.

"You're supposed to be watching the goat," Kaitha said.

"The goat and I have an understanding." Gorm cast a murderous glance at the malformed creature. Its yellow eyes stared in opposite directions with strange, coin-slot pupils, yet Gorm had the sense that the ill-tempered beast was constantly watching him. The horns sprouting from its head were twisted and asymmetrical, as was its gnarled, lumpy body. Its upper and lower jaw never seemed to point in the same direction, and they scissored back and forth as the goat considered the rope that tethered it to a spot beneath Gorm's boot.

"You have an understanding with a goat." Kaitha laid the statement out without comment, as though hoping it would collapse under the weight of its own absurdity.

"Aye. It doesn't chew the leash, and I don't straighten out his face."

The goat bleated defiantly, but it took a step away from the rope.

Kaitha shrugged. "That doesn't explain why you're reading Al'Matran prophecies again."

Gorm shifted, finding a different part of the mossy boulder to lean against. "I dunno. Some of the stuff happenin' reminded me of Niln's books."

"Niln prophesied about olive markets?" The ranger smirked.

"No. Well, sort of. Several Al'Matran prophets wrote a lot about olives, and Niln wrote a treatise on their works. But that ain't why I'm reading. And then some of the prophets wrote about someone striking down a king, and old Handor is only just cold in the grave."

"Kings die all the time," said Kaitha. "Especially Human kings. I've seen at least a dozen come and go."

"Fair enough. I can't point to anythin' and say it's definitely happenin' or not. The All Mother's scriptures are as clear as bog muck." He thumped a finger on the open page. "Like here. Ye read it one way, and the prophet Aseph makes it sound like the Seventh Hero dies when he meets the Dark Prince. Ye read it another, and it sounds like it's actually the Dark Prince who bites it. Ye flip forward to the end of the chapter, and they're both alive and kickin'. So what actually happens when the two meet?"

"They're probably not going to meet, right?" said Kaitha. "Because one of them is made of stone and the other is wishful thinking by Al'Matran scribes. It's all nonsense, remember? For every halfway decent prophet in that temple, there's at least ten more who couldn't predict what's for dinner if they held a menu. And no disrespect to Niln, but he was wrong about... well..."

"Almost everythin'," Gorm finished for her. "Aye, I know. But it ain't the odds, it's the stakes. If Niln's work is true, somebody could be tryin' to bring back the Sten, or worse, they could summon Al'Thadan. And Mannon's greatest ally gets called back with his eyes on Andarun. It could be the end of the—"

"Wagon!" hissed Kaitha, pointing at a cart similar to the one they'd seen in the Riverdowns rolling up the road.

"Right." Gorm closed the book. "Gaist in place?"

"He's good at standing still." The Elf pulled up the hood of the long, ratty cloak she wore, concealing her fine armor entirely. "Wait for it."

The old cart rumbled up the road at a lazy pace. When it had nearly reached the rock that Gorm and Kaitha were hunkered behind, the ranger signaled the Dwarf.

Gorm lifted his foot, releasing the rope. The goat immediately bolted across the road, with Kaitha hot on its hooves. The wagon driver jerked the reins and swore, but the Elf had left him plenty of room to maneuver between the goat and the apparent shepherd chasing it across the road. The wobbling wagon rolled on its way with a few extra curses.

"Clear," Kaitha shouted over her shoulder as she jogged to where the goat had paused. The goat, for its part, was so distracted by the carrot it was munching that it didn't even object when Kaitha picked up its leash again.

"Ye sure?" Gorm called doubtfully.

"Trust me," Kaitha hollered. She snapped her fingers to get the goat's attention and, once she was reasonably certain that it was looking in her general direction, pulled another carrot from her belt pouch. The goat tried to lunge for the vegetable, but she kept its leash short as she placed the carrot in the same cranny as the one before it. Then she began the laborious process of hauling the struggling animal back across the road.

Gorm met her halfway and grabbed the goat by the horn. "I ain't sure this is gonna help us find the wagon."

The goat planted its feet stubbornly, but the only effect was to carve shallow grooves in the road as the heroes dragged it back to the rock.

"The shipments have to come through here," said Kaitha. "They don't head toward the city or they'd pass through Eastgate, nor do they go to

Aberreth. If they're using the roads, they have to head this way. And the goat is the key to finding them."

"The goat's the part I ain't sure about," said Gorm, repositioning himself behind the rock.

"Well, here's another chance to watch and learn," Kaitha said with a smirk. She pointed to another wagon rolling toward them. It traveled at a snail's pace and was taking a small eternity to approach.

When the wagon was finally in position, Kaitha gave the signal once more. The goat bolted back toward the carrot, the Elf played the errant farmer once more, and both ran across the road. But this time, the wagoner didn't take the ample opportunity to maneuver. Instead, he hauled back on the reins with all the desperation of a man trying to avoid going over a cliff. The horses whinnied in protest and skidded to a quick stop. The wagoner sat with his head tucked down between his shoulders, as if trying to retreat into his own chest cavity. He stayed in that pose, holding his breath, for several moments after Kaitha had crossed the street.

On Gorm's signal, Gaist took the opportunity to sneak around the back of the wagon. He carefully slit the canvas near the back, just large enough to peek inside. Satisfied, the weaponsmaster backed away and nodded to his companion before disappearing back into the shadows.

The wagoner didn't move on until the Elf waved to him and demonstrated that the goat's rope was clearly in hand. Only then did the cart roll onward, leaving a cloud of dust and muttered curses in its wake.

The ranger was all smiles as she sauntered back across the road. "Now there's a man who knows he's hauling explosives."

Gaist was beside them suddenly, nodding as he watched the retreating cart.

"Aye," said Gorm. "That's our wagon."

The goat, finished with its carrot, bleated once and sprinted away. It carved a crooked path across the grass field, its legs flying akimbo in chaotic patterns as it ran, so that it looked like it was floating on top of a melee toward the nearest cabbage patch.

"Speaking of unleashing horrors upon the world," Gorm muttered.

"Finding our mark is worth the deposit on a rented goat." Kaitha nodded toward the retreating wagon. "Let's see where this leads."

—— CHAPTER 11 ——

"It's something to do with the dragon," said Feista Hrurk. She studied the grid of numbers spread over the sheet of parchment. The figures stared back at her, as plain as the fur on her snout and as inscrutable as a whisper on the wind. Something in the numbers made her uneasy, but it was hiding behind the bars of the grid. "It's strange... just off somehow."

A few of the Wood Gnomes lounging about her desk sat up straighter. White Rat stood and launched into an impassioned, if inaudible, diatribe of squeaks.

"No, no, I'm not saying the math is wrong," said Feista with a wave of her paw. "I'm saying... something else is. The companies must have reported bad data or... or the market could... well, it must be bad data."

She sat back in her chair and steepled her claws. The Analysis Department office was as still and dim as a tomb, but she had grown accustomed to the quiet solitude. If she was honest, it was a nice change after spending years wrangling pups and tenants in sixteen-hour shifts. She let her mind return to the numbers; she had caught a rotten scent, and she wasn't going to let go until she had tracked down the problem.

"Show me the top five hundred shareholders of the dragon's hoard by volume and how many shares they own. The total value as well."

The Wood Gnomes on her desk flew off as though blasted by a gust of wind. A storm of frenetic activity rippled across her shelves as books and binders were plumbed at impossible speeds. Moments later, the tiny workers began to return, and the system broke down entirely.

Spotted Mouse and Brown Rat had a collision as they went for the same spot. Gray Squirrel tripped over the fighting pair, and the squabble became a brawl. It would have devolved into a full melee had Feista not clapped her hands.

"All right, all right. This is how mistakes get made." Feista's tone became more calm and slow, and yet more dangerous—a voice that would have sent her pups scrambling for their beds. "Let's try it with the drum, shall we?"

She pulled the old instrument from beneath her desk and set it between her legs. Its top was yellowed with age, as were the leather strings holding it against the wooden base. The drum's colorful beads had dulled with time, but the beats it made as she tapped expertly on its surface were still crisp and loud.

"Right. You can hear it, can't you?" Feista pointed to a cluster of Wood Gnomes. "All right, you three are on a research team. Take the top two shelves. And you, Gray Squirrel. Yes, you. You're on point writing the first column..." She continued distributing tasks until everyone in the assembly had a job, then sent the research teams back out with her request.

"Write on the strong beat, move on the slow beats. You perform your tasks in step." Feista tapped out the tempo on her drum, and the Gnomes began to bob and sway to the music. "Remember? Researchers, get the information. Then you relay it to the writers. Writers, fill in the first two columns. Then the math teams calculate the remaining columns and write them in. Then next line, and repeat."

With their instructions clear and their tempo set, the Gnomes moved with the rigid precision of Lightling waltzers. The numbers materialized beneath their feet in perfect time with Feista's tapping, spreading across the grid like frost over a windowpane. "Yes!" said Feista. "With the rhythm. You all go in rhythm."

White Rat watched the dance from the arm of Feista's chair. She squeaked something like a compliment and pointed at the Gnoll's instrument.

"Oh, this? It belonged to the great-grandsire of my great-grandsire's grandsire, Finnen Yarp." Feista ran her free fingers across the beads of the drum while her other paw kept the beat. "He led the war drums for the armies of the Eight United Clans, back when they almost took the Ironbreakers, and he told our family's history in these very beads."

An impressed chirrup erupted from White Rat.

"Well, some beads very much like it. This is a replica my grandsire made after the original was lost."

White Rat squeaked.

"Oh, yes, I'm certain it isn't a real war drum. The original would have Finnen Yarp's ears hanging from it."

The Gnome's chitter had a distinct air of incredulous horror.

"Well, it's an old burial custom!" The question put Feista on the defensive, and she could feel her hackles rising. "The ancestors did it so he could hear the drums forever. Anyway, how do you people honor your—"

She noticed the Wood Gnomes scattering a moment before the door to her office burst open. Borpo shouldered his way into the room behind the ringing wood. "Mrs. Hrurk! With whom do you speak?"

Feista's eyes searched for any exposed Domovoy, but found none. Wood Gnomes that couldn't stay out of sight often wound up underfoot, even if it took a few stomps. "Uh... just—just speaking to myself! Who else could it be?" She gestured lamely at the three empty desks around her own. "It helps me think."

"And are you playing a war drum? In the office?" Her boss had found an advantage, and there was a note of eagerness in his voice.

"It, uh, also helps me think." The Gnoll cleared her throat and tried to reassemble her composure. "I wasn't aware there's a rule against drums in the office, sir. I saw that you keep one on your shelf."

"That is different." The huge Orc's perpetual scowl deepened. "I do not play it in the office."

"Then why—"

Borpo's fists flew into the air, and his flexing muscles strained the threads of his suit. "It is for the purpose of inspiring excellence as a visual decoration! Music can be distracting to others in the work environment!"

"I'm sorry, sir. I'll make sure my war drum is silently inspiring from now on."

Her supervisor stared at her from beneath the manifold creases of his knit brow, struggling to find the high ground once again. Failing that, he changed the subject. "I expect your analysis of the current threat market by the end of the day," he growled.

"Yes. It's in your inbox."

"So quickly? You must take the time to prevent mistakes!"

"I did triple-check the numbers, sir." Feista fought to avoid sounding smug, but it was a losing battle.

"It is very fast," Borpo muttered to himself, shouldering his way toward the drawer.

"Perhaps the drum helped." It was a mistake to say it. Feista saw the miscalculation before the words were out of her mouth, but they spilled out like papers from a dropped file.

The Orc half-turned back to the Gnoll. His eyes narrowed to crimson slits as he glared at her, and his massive jaw worked as though chewing the retort before he spat it at her. "You will regret this insolence!" he hissed. "My eye is upon you!"

He slammed the door with enough force to shake every book and binder on Feista's shelves. It took her a moment to push away the fear and the thrill creeping up her spine. Her voice shook as she stowed her drum. "Let's... let's be a bit quieter, shall we?"

She resumed her rhythm with a pencil tapped against the corner of her desk. The whispering of papers filled the room as the Gnomes took up the dance again. Numbers poured into the grid, and soon enough the tiny workers were gathered around the lines and triple-checking the sums.

Feista looked at the bottom line and sighed. "No, there must be an error. You have too many digits there."

White Rat chirruped a reply, filled with doubt and fear.

"I appreciate that, but we need to check it again. This can't be right." The incredible sum spilled out of the bottom of the neat grid and down into the margins of the page. Feista turned her attention to the lines above it, scanning for anything that might be out of place. "Maybe we've included something that doesn't belong here."

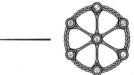

"Doesn't make sense." Gorm leaned against a jagged boulder already slick with water as he waited, peering across the barren, rocky terrain. "Nobody builds in the Winter's Shade. There shouldn't be anywhere to go out here."

"Shouldn't be." Kaitha kept her gaze locked on the distant wagon. "That's different from 'isn't.'"

Gaist nodded at something on the horizon.

"What do ye see?" The Dwarf peered out around the boulder at the distant, obscured silhouette of the wagon. Four indistinct figures circled the cart—mercenaries, Gorm knew. The hired swords had met the cart on the road to Scoria on the first night out of the city, and the next morning they had taken an unexpected turn off the road and into the barren, rocky fields of the Shade.

"They're moving again," Kaitha said. "They stopped to wedge a rock in a gap in the road, but—"

The wagon lurched. All four mercenaries dove to the ground. The world held its breath for a moment, waiting for the cart to erupt in a fiery bloom. When the barrels within failed to conflagrate, the heroes took the opportunity to dart into a cleft in the stone ahead of them.

"Guess they didn't set that rock right," Gorm said, his lips twitching up into a smile. Few Dwarves could completely suppress their hereditary smugness when Human stonework failed.

"They can't go much farther," the ranger said as they crouched down. "We're almost to the foot of the mountain, and it'd be suicide to haul those barrels up the north face of Mount Wynspar."

"There's some who say it's suicide to pass through the Winter's Shade, but that didn't stop 'em," said Gorm.

While the southern slope of Mount Wynspar housed the most diverse and vibrant city in the Freedlands, its northern crag had watched over a wasteland for ages. The Winter's Shade was gray and desolate, abandoned by even the carrion flies. The Sixth Age explorer Weevil Half-Burrow once claimed the blighted area was defined by the mountain's shadow on the winter solstice, and the name had worked its way into popular legend.

Or perhaps shoved its way in; popular legend grew quite crowded around the Shade. It had been decades since any foolhardy farmers had tried to work the gray, dead soil, but local mythology was full of tales of crops that bled and fruit trees that screamed and burst into flames a year after they were grown. Heroes sometimes crossed over the cursed land in an effort to shave time off a quest, and every year or so a party taking the shortcut would go missing without a trace.

"Plenty of people survive the Shade," Kaitha's quiet reassurance sounded like it was intended as much for herself as for Gorm. "At least there's no monsters."

"I can deal with monsters," he said. "A good axe will solve just about any monster problem. Not so for creepy old curses."

The Elf wasn't listening. "No game or birds, either. Or insects. Or plants..." She suppressed a shudder. "Well, they... they can't go much farther."

"Let's hope not." Gorm eyed the lengthening shadows of the stones and crags around them. "I don't want to camp in these wastes again."

The driver and his mercenary companions climbed over the wagon like ants over a fallen biscuit, inspecting each barrel for leaks. The three companions had little to do but stare into the gloom and wait for the painstaking review to run its course.

The Dwarf suppressed a chill. "My people say this place was cursed by the Sten in the War of Betrayal."

"Oh? According to Elven legends, this is where Tandos struck Al'Thadan down," said Kaitha.

Gorm's brow furrowed as he tried to cram Elven theology into the confines of his worldview. "So... Al'Thadan's blood made the land barren?"

Kaitha shrugged. "The mages say it was just the amount of power it takes to kill a god. To wipe a whole people from Arth and banish their pantheon from the weave. It twists the whole weave around it, and curses the place it punched through."

"Low magic," said Gorm, recalling his conversations with Jynn.

"Probably." Kaitha gave a ragged sigh, the sort that usually precedes or follows a long cry. "It all just seems terribly sad to me. All that death... all those souls..."

The Dwarf gave her a sidelong glance. "Aye. The War of Betrayal was the worst of what Mankind can do to one another."

"So far." The Elf wrapped her cloak around her like a shawl and glanced back toward the imposing face of the mountain. "But people are full of surprises."

"It is easy to think that your current understanding of trends can be used to predict things, but market forces have consistently shown that circumstances return to the mean," Duine Poldo said. "And so I'd urge you to... to, ah." It occurred to Poldo that the regular patting of stamps hitting paper had ceased. He glanced down.

Three of the Domovoy were taking Poldo's dictation using the set of tiny lead stamps Poldo had made for them. Another kept the stamps well-inked with a brush and Poldo's inkwell. All four stared up at him from the table that served as their makeshift desk at the back of The Wandering Monster, a roadside inn and tavern along the way from Waerth to Mistkeep.

"Is there a problem?" said Poldo.

Red Squirrel cleared his throat and chittered a curt reply.

"Condescending? Is it?" Poldo lifted the page and replaced his glasses. After reading for a few moments, he shook his head and crumpled the paper. "It is. Along with everything else I wrote," he said, throwing the mangled letter next to several similar balls of paper.

The Wood Gnomes below sighed and grumbled under their breath as they pulled another sheet of paper out and re-stamped the now-familiar salutation, "My dear Mrs. Hrurk."

Poldo sighed and looked out across the common room of the inn. What The Wandering Monster lacked in amenities, it made up for in grime. Still, it had a warm fire, cold grog, and a quiet corner by the window where Poldo could work. "I don't mean to sound like I'm teaching an apprentice, but..."

One of the Wood Gnome's squeaked.

"Well, of course I trust Mrs. Hrurk's judgment." He picked up the latest letter from the Gnoll and shook his head. "But these numbers that she sent make no sense. The Heroes' Guild regulates how those shares are issued. It's audited by the royal lord of accounts. Everyone knows this isn't possible."

He sighed and looked out the window next to him. The long shadows of the trees on the boulder outside the window told him the sun had almost finished setting. "I just need to tell Mrs. Hrurk what everyone knows without sounding like I'm teaching her the obvious."

Red Squirrel piped up.

"Well, yes, I suppose it's technically possible she's correct, but given the controls in place, it's exceedingly improbable." A thought struck the Scribkin. "Maybe that's how I should say it."

The Wood Gnomes winced and shook their heads.

"Or not. This is very difficult to say." Poldo sank back into his seat.

Another squeak.

"Look, I'm sure your compatriots did the math correctly, and I know she said she has checked it many times, but—" Poldo felt his ire rising a bit. "Listen, I think decades of experience in finance should count for something, shouldn't they? Can we just take my word that the most trusted fund on Arth is not insolvent? Or shall we litigate the color of the sky next?"

Approaching footsteps interrupted the Wood Gnomes' response. A slender Human in dark armor was headed toward Poldo's corner of the tavern. The Domovoy grabbed their stamps and dove into the briefcase just before the dark figure addressed the Scribkin.

"Duine Poldo?" the woman said. She had the sort of dark, glassy eyes that said their owner has seen a lot of death, and the sort of twisted smile that added she had enjoyed it. The bolt end of a crossbow protruded from the gap in her long, black cloak. "At last we meet."

Poldo rapped his knuckles on the table three times and sighed. "Yes, and I'm afraid you have me at a disadvantage, miss."

"I do," said the assassin. "I like it that way."

"I presume you also like to keep things 'nice and neat,'" Poldo said.

The assassin's brow furrowed. "Uh…"

"Discreet as well, I presume? Clean kills, no witnesses, just a body in a ditch and a stack of unmarked bank notes," said Poldo. "That sort of thing. Your lot seems to prefer it that way."

"Yes," said the assassin slowly, though clearly nonplussed at the infringement upon her monologue. She pressed on. "Now, why don't you—"

"I don't suppose you'll reconsider? Or tell me who sent you?"

"No," hissed the killer. "One more word out of you and I'll bolt you to that chair."

Poldo shrugged and leaned back in his seat. Had it been novel, such an assassination attempt would have shaken him. But oily assassins with ample precautions and scarce humanity were becoming rote.

"Now, I do like to keep things clean, as you said, and there's all these witnesses around—" The assassin flicked her crossbow to point back at the tavern's other patrons, inadvertently giving Poldo his chance.

As soon as the crossbow wasn't trained on him, he gave the table a fourth knock—the signal knock—and dove to the floor. The assassin swung the crossbow back around just as an arm like a hairy tree trunk punched through the window, grabbed her by the head, and yanked her into the gloom outside.

Poldo picked himself up and dusted himself off. "Gods help us if we ever meet an assassin who prefers things be a messy spectacle," he muttered as he began to pack up his briefcase.

Screams of "Monster!" and the thunder of footsteps leaving the tavern were almost loud enough to drown out the shrieks and grim sounds from outside.

The Gnome ignored the cacophony and made his way to the front of The Wandering Monster, where the tavern's proprietress and her husband cowered behind the bar. "Sir!" whispered the tavern keeper, a Human short and stout enough to be a Dwerrow. "Sir! There's a Troll, sir! Get to cover!"

"Yes. Oof. He's with me," grunted Poldo as he scrambled up a bar stool. Once perched on the seat, he took out his wallet and began leafing through the bank notes. "I'm afraid that, in the course of stopping an attempt on my life, my bodyguard was forced to break one of your windows. I'll gladly pay for it."

The blood drained from the woman's face until it was as pale and pasty as a lump of bread. "You brought the Troll upon us?"

"I've hired him, if that's what you mean," said Poldo. "Now, a window such as that must be at least forty giltin—"

"You can't stay here!" snapped the woman, clambering to her feet. "You'll have to leave."

"And take the beast with ye!" said her portly husband, standing beside her. The man's face was two beady black eyes peeking out over a bristling yellow beard; he looked like he was most of the way through swallowing a sheaf of wheat.

Poldo snorted. "What? Why? Thane's done no harm."

Behind him, another window shattered as the killer crashed through it and into the front room. The tavern keeper's husband shrieked and dove for cover.

"To the innocent," Poldo added.

Thane's face, apologetic and spattered with crimson, loomed in the broken window. "Sorry!" he said. "I was swinging her by a leg and I think her boot must have slipped off."

"It's fine," Poldo called, trying to avoid the tavern keeper's eye.

"Let me get that." The Troll reached in and began tugging at the remains of the assassin. "I can get carried away when... well, you see."

"It's really fine!" Poldo called. "He's just very protective of his friends, is all," he added to the proprietress.

"Oh, it wasn't just her boot! Her foot came off at the knee." Thane held up the offending appendage. "I knew I had a good grip."

"Extremely protective," said Poldo, rubbing his temples.

"He's a Troll," she whispered. Her eyes were wide for emphasis, but otherwise she let the argument stand on its own merits.

"Now listen, I would be dead many times over if it weren't for that Troll," Poldo said. "He's as good and loyal as—"

"Oh, stuff it with that nonsense," the tavern keeper hissed. "All you city-folk are always tellin' us that Orcs are friendly, and Gnolls are sweet as puppies, and Goblins don't stink. Well, I'd like to think thirty years runnin' a tavern on the edge of the woods may have taught me sommat about them Shadowkin, and I know they're thieves and bloodthirsty killers to a one!" Her voice rose in volume until she was cut off by the hollow thud of a body hitting the oak floor.

Poldo turned to where Thane had dropped the ex-assassin. "Sorry, I... I forget sometimes that... I'll just—" The Troll disappeared from the window.

"Thane, no," Poldo began, but the Troll was gone. Fury boiled up within the Gnome, so much so that he shook until his stool wobbled. "Well, I can see my gold is no good here," he hissed. "I shall take my leave, madam."

The tavern keeper nodded in satisfaction as Poldo climbed down off the stool. The action must have dislodged a thought, because she demanded, "Oi! What about my windows!"

"I suggest you fix them, lest more vermin creep in to tend the bar!" snapped Poldo, pausing at the door. "Good day, madam!"

Outside, the Scribkin followed the nickering of nervous horses to find Thane sitting by the inn's stables. "I think we'll be better off making some more progress and camping on the road tonight," Poldo offered with forced cheer.

The Troll sighed and started to put his desk-pack on. "I'm sorry," he mumbled. "If I hadn't been there—"

"If you hadn't been there, I'd be rotting in the woods." Poldo took a deep breath and tried to calm himself by staring at the last of the season's foliage. The Green Span was gray and brown now, and those sparse leaves that remained were gilded by the amber light of the setting sun. "You've nothing to apologize for."

"I..." Some memory struck Thane, and he shook his head. "I just wish things were different."

"If by 'things,' you mean those witless bumpkins running the inn, then I do as well." Poldo strapped himself into the desk. "I'd change a lot about them."

"They're just set in their ways." Thane waited for the last of the Wood Gnomes to scamper up his leg before he set off down the road. "It's hard for people like that to deal with... well, with me."

"The problem is their smug, smarmy overconfidence! They won't give a new idea a chance, let alone a new person. They can't accept what it would say about them if a new person brought something good to society."

"If they... they didn't see things the way you wanted them to..." rumbled Thane.

Grim realization came upon Poldo like dawn over a battlefield, and he was horrified by what he saw. "We never give anyone different a chance..." He caught Red Squirrel's eye peering out from the Troll's fur. "I never gave her a chance."

The Wood Gnome chirruped and nodded.

"I just dismissed Mrs. Hrurk's insights because... well, because she's not an old analyst like me. Her information is sound and her logic can't be faulted, but I..." Poldo shook his head and gave a bitter chuckle. "All the world's evils are so much easier to spot in someone else."

"Never gave her a chance," the Troll repeated, lost in his own thoughts.

"Well, all the world's evils are only possible to fix in ourselves," the Gnome said. "Let's draft a new letter to Feista. And then a letter to Emblin and Stormbreaker. We also must tell my broker to divest ourselves of all our shares of the Dragon of Wynspar's loot."

Several more Wood Gnomes peeked out of Thane's coat, squeaking a chorus of surprised questions.

"I am absolutely serious. I'm putting my faith in Mrs. Hrurk, and that means our shares in the dragon's hoard must go," said Poldo. "Every last one."

─CHAPTER 12─

"There's far too many for that," hissed Kaitha.

"No more than a dozen." Gorm peered over a boulder. Across the rocky slope, men and women in red and white robes carefully unloaded the wagon. The explosive barrels were loaded onto small carts that workers wheeled through a wooden gate into the side of the mountain. Beyond it, a strange fortress loomed over the basalt plateau. A new fort bulged from the ruins of an ancient one, like a Dire Hermit Crab living in a discarded helmet. Old Stennish ruins were carved into the northern crags of Mount Wynspar, covered with carvings of flowing angles. Wooden palisades and freshly painted walls poked through the gaps in the crumbling ruin and hung out its yawning doorway.

As the workers pushed their cargo into the wooden facade of the fort, more people came streaming out the wide door.

"Okay, maybe two dozen," said Gorm, dropping back behind the stone. "Still, we can take 'em. Ye drop in, I sneak round that ravine there, and Gaist runs round the other way. Then we knock 'em all out."

"Before the alarm goes up." Kaitha's voice was level, but her brows rose on a tide of skepticism.

Gaist shook his head.

Gorm scowled and scratched his beard. "Well, ye... ye use a few arrows—"

"Arrows are for fatalities, Gorm," said Kaitha. "We can't kill anyone."

"Lass, these are the people conspirin' to fake the dragon attacks. They're unloading explosives that was smuggled to a secret site where they ain't supposed to have one. They ain't innocents."

"Maybe. Or maybe they're just day workers at an industrial forge we know nothing about. Or researchers looking into the curse of the Winter's Shade," the ranger said.

"Ye know those ain't the case. They're wearing Tandos' colors."

"Exactly my point! Shooting people is the sort of thing you want to be really certain of, and that goes double for clergy in the king's patron temple!" Kaitha hissed. "Johan is itching to declare us villains. If you're going to kill some priests without cause, you might as well do up the paperwork for our executions while you're at it."

Gaist inclined his head and blinked, conceding the Elf's point while maintaining a posture that was very clearly pro-fatality.

Gorm opened his mouth, then clamped it shut again with a snort. "I suppose ye got a better proposal?"

"Look. There are other entrances to the complex." She pointed to Mount Wynspar's northern face. Several gates and doors were visible farther up the mountain, some no larger than a Halfling's hole, several as big as a stable's gate, and one opening as wide as a street built inexplicably high in a sheer cliff face. "We can find one with fewer guards, get in, and see what they're hiding. If it's nothing, we sneak back out. If it's as bad as you think it is, we gather proof to use as leverage."

"Simple as that?" snorted the Dwarf. "We just stroll in and have a look around?"

She smiled in a way that got his guard up. "Well, we could just walk if—"

"Don't ye say it," Gorm growled.

"Every one of them is wearing red and white," Kaitha insisted. "We each get a set of robes, and we can walk right in the front door."

Gaist slapped his forehead.

"Ye know I hate the henchman uniform ruse," the Dwarf hissed through his teeth.

"I know it, but I don't understand it. How can anyone hate the henchman uniform ruse? It's a classic," said Kaitha. "It's page one of the *Heroes' Guild Handbook*. Everybody knows the henchman uniform ruse."

"Aye, including most henchmen," grumbled the Dwarf.

"It still works! If you keep your distance and don't draw attention to yourself, even cautious henchmen will fall for it," said Kaitha, already starting along the rocky path toward another entrance.

"They can't possibly all be that stupid," Gorm muttered, trundling after her.

"There you go underestimating people again," laughed Kaitha.

They found a small spring on the outskirts of the facility. A strong flow of crystalline water burbled from the rocks and, more importantly, a steady flow of young Tandosians lugged pails back and forth from a side entrance to the bubbling water. Several rocky outcroppings and patches of scrub brush surrounded the spring, perfect for lying in wait or concealing unconscious and recently disrobed Tandosians. It wasn't long before Gorm, Gaist, and Kaitha wore a set of crimson and white robes each.

"See? Easy," Kaitha remarked. "And it hardly took any time at all."

"Ain't inside yet," grumbled Gorm.

"That's a small matter," the Elf said. "Just adopt a posture of purpose."

"What?"

"Half of blending in is looking like you belong. So we need to look like we have a job to do."

"I thought that's why we stole these buckets," said Gorm, lifting a pail.

"The buckets will just cause questions. And you don't need them to have purpose. Watch." The Elf straightened up and set her features in a sort of determined discomfort. "I just pretend I have somewhere to be, and I need to be there fast."

"It's the chamber pot, from the look of ye."

Kaitha scowled. "Fine. We'll try the buckets."

"Whatever suits ye," Gorm grumbled, tugging at his costume. His red and white robes bunched up around parts of his anatomy that rarely grazed the surface of his consciousness, but now screamed for attention with every chafing step. "Long as I can get out of this ridiculous outfit sooner rather than later."

"It's not that bad," said Kaitha.

"Easy for ye to say." Gorm tugged a wad of fabric from somewhere intimate. It immediately wormed its way back into the wretched position, like a determined sleeper unwilling to be roused. "Everything fits Elves well."

"My robe doesn't—" The ranger looked down at herself. The robes she had stolen were far too short for her, yet they somehow accented her lithe form while showing off the almond skin of her ankles and wrists. "Well... I can't help it."

"How unfortunate for—gah!" Gorm nearly leapt from his skin at the sight of a Tandosian woman stepping out from behind a rock. His axe was already in hand before Kaitha dropped a hand on his shoulder.

"Stop!" she hissed. "That's Gaist!"

"What?" Gorm looked.

The Tandosian woman stared at him from beneath heavy, lidded eyes. With a noncommittal nod, she pulled at a crimson scarf in the folds of her robe.

"Gods!" The Dwarf bit his tongue and shoved his axe back into his belt. "Ye scared the tar out of me," he added, trying to conceal his weapon in the folds of his ill-fitting robe.

"He's blending. You should try it," said Kaitha.

The doppelganger nodded.

"By turnin' into a woman? Or walkin' like I need to use the loo?"

"Gorm—" Kaitha bit back a retort and let it out as a long sigh instead. "This is the best plan we've got."

"It's the one we're goin' with, anyway," said Gorm, handing Kaitha and Gaist a pair of borrowed pails. "Let's just get to it."

They stepped out of the rocky crag and made their way down the trail to the small doorway in the side of the mountain. It opened into a large hallway with branching pathways.

"Which way?" Gorm asked.

"Follow the water drops," said Kaitha, nodding to a trail of splashes leading down one hall.

"Fair enough." Gorm's skin crawled as they walked through the ancient corridors. Much of the original stonework of the ruined hallway was obscured, either by some long-gone calamity or by the shoddy woodwork that the current occupants had used to shore up their crumbling facility.

Yet parts of the old carvings peeked through, revealing intricate patterns of fluid shapes that reminded the Dwarf of swaying branches or bubbling streams. The corridor was like a forest river born of stone and filled with hastily constructed flotsam.

Their tunnel quickly merged into another corridor, and then another. Somewhere along the way, the trail of their predecessors literally dried up, leaving them wandering in the dark. The three heroes tried to stay to side passages and avoid Tandosian patrols, but soon enough they heard the shuffling footsteps of a priest approaching. Even in the syrupy, amber torchlight, it was clear that the newcomer's robes were finer than those the heroes stole. They kept their eyes to the floor and nodded as the old Elf strode by.

"Praise Tandos," said the robed Elf.

"Praise Tandos," Gorm and Kaitha murmured, sharing a significant look.

Yet that seemed to be the wrong response. The Elf stopped and gave them a quizzical look. "Are you new?"

"Uh, yeah," said Kaitha, setting down her bucket. She let a strand of auburn hair dangle in front of her face just so she could demurely brush it behind a pointed ear. "Did I... did I do something wrong?"

"Okay, well, yes." The Elf's patronizing tone suggested he was doing Kaitha a favor; his grin said he was hoping she'd return it. "You can't just say 'praise Tandos' again. You need to say the second part."

"What?" asked Gorm.

The Elf's eyes flicked to Gorm for a moment, then back to Kaitha. "You remember. I say 'praise Tandos,' and you say—"

"Good night," said Kaitha. She punched the leering Elf in the throat hard enough to choke off any reply. The surprised man reeled back as if to run, but Gorm caught him with a bucket of water to the gut. The woman usually known as Gaist caught the staggering Elf in a sleeper hold and covered his mouth until he went limp.

They worked in silence. A small storeroom nearby held empty barrels that carried the biting aroma of flame olives. They bound the unconscious Elf with his own belt and left him behind a tall stack of the emptied casks.

"So it's the Tandosians after all," Gorm said as the trio of false acolytes peered out into the empty stone corridor.

"Some Tandosian-affiliated worshippers, yes," Kaitha agreed. "Could be a cult, or some obscure sect."

The Dwarf shook his head. "This is Johan's doin'. I got a feelin' in my bones."

"I'd rather have proof in my files," said Kaitha as they slipped back into the hallway.

They made it past another turn and halfway down the hall before they encountered another Tandosian, a pale Human with hair that resembled used straw bedding. "Praise Tandos," Gorm barked before the woman had a chance to do so first.

"And his divine work," said the Tandosian automatically. Yet she stopped them when they moved to pass her. "And the next bit?"

"Oh, sorry. It's just that she needs help," Gorm said, nodding to the hallway behind the woman. She turned to see who the Dwarf was talking about, earning herself a neat blow to the back of the head from Kaitha.

They dragged the woman back to the same storage room and laid her beside the Elf. "Glad I'm wearin' this silly getup," Gorm remarked as they retraced their steps. "Otherwise this might get violent."

"No alarm has gone up," Kaitha hissed. "And we've learned their password."

"Passwords." Gorm emphasized the plural. He held up an empty bucket. "And I've spilled all me water in the fights."

Gaist turned her pail upside down. A single drop splashed on the stone floor.

"It's fine." Kaitha said, holding up her own empty vessel. "Nobody will notice."

They had only gone a little farther before they encountered another pair of Tandosians. The pair wore simple robes and carried empty buckets on their way to the well. "Praise Tandos!" said the taller of the two.

"And his divine work," said Kaitha.

"For his glorious deeds," said the second Tandosian.

All eyes turned to Gaist.

"Uh, we don't need to do the whole routine, do we?" Gorm asked. "It's just these buckets are heavy and all..."

"Oh, the master's invocation is very important," said the first Tandosian.

"Especially with us bein' new," said the second. "A big site like this, how could we know even half the people here?"

"If the temple wants to avoid infiltration, we need active security measures." The taller Tandosian spoke with the rhythmic authority of someone reciting training materials. "Why, for all we know you're some mercenaries doin' a uniform ruse."

"Or even doppelgangers." The second Tandosian whispered the possibility loudly, as though it carried special scandal.

The first Tandosian stared down at Gorm's hands. "Come to think of it, why are you carrying empty buckets away from the well?" he asked.

Gorm, Gaist, and Kaitha shared a meaningful look.

A few moments later, they were bearing the prone pair of inexperienced Tandosians back toward the storeroom. "I told you the buckets would only bring questions," Kaitha said.

"I already agreed to ditch 'em, didn't I?" Gorm said. The Dwarf labored under the dangling legs of a recumbent acolyte, while Gaist held up the victim's head.

"Yes. Fine. Thank you." Kaitha took a deep breath as she shifted the acolyte thrown over her shoulder. "At least we know there's something good down here. Otherwise they wouldn't be doing so much to keep people like us out."

"Let's hope so," Gorm growled. "The question is, how long can all this nonsense with the thrice-cursed invocation go on?"

"It shall endure for ages to come!" roared Borpo Skar'Ezzod. "It is a most dependable asset! All of the Lightling banks rely upon the mighty stability of the dragon's hoard!"

Feista shrank back into her chair, as though she could push herself through the leather and out of the meeting.

"Is that not the problem that your employee has called our attention to?" asked Asherzu Guz'Varda. She stood at the window with her back to those assembled in her office, hands crossed behind her.

"The problem is that the Gnoll you burdened me with is asking questions that need no answers, when she should have been looking at plunder funds and hedge companies!"

Feista shut her eyes and tried to will her tail not to tuck itself between her legs.

"We prefer that you not ussse such agresssive language, Mr. Ssskarr'Eszzod," said Ms. Thyssisss, a young Naga from Hireling Resources. Her upper body was that of a young Gnome with brown hair, a smart red blazer, and reptilian eyes. Her lower half coiled around her chair several times.

"At Warg Inc., we pay respect and honor to all of our employees," said Mr. Meister, the head of Hireling Resources. The Gremlin's deep blue scales nearly matched his navy suit, which made the bright orange bristles of his bushy mustache and slicked-back crest stand out like bonfires against an evening sky. "We don't like to hear our team members referred to as 'burdens.'"

"Then perhaps you will fire this fool, and solve both of our problems!" Borpo shook his fist in the air while he shouted, as though throttling an imaginary underling.

"Borpo, enough," sighed Asherzu, rubbing her forehead.

The large Orc snarled. "It will be enough when you finally—"

The floorboards ominously creaked under a shifting mass. It was sometimes easy for Feista to forget that Darak Guz'Varda was present; the chieftain's brother-turned-bodyguard was usually as still and silent as a signpost. And like a signpost, he was there to remind people where the boundaries were. If you were aware of Darak, he was aware of you; that alone was enough to make Borpo sit down quietly.

"Were her figures wrong?" asked Asherzu quietly, still staring out the window.

"What?" Borpo's black brows bunched, twisting up in the middle of his brow. "They must be—"

"Did you check? Was the mistake in the sources, or the arithmetic?" said the chieftain.

Feista bent down to feign scratching her leg, then grabbed her tail and pulled it back behind her.

Borpo's fists clenched as though wringing a neck, and the threads of his suit stretched and snapped under the strain. "Why should I check math that is clearly wrong? Why would—"

"If only to correct an employee, that would be enough," said Asherzu, finally turning. "What is more, if what she says is right—"

"It cannot be right!" snarled Borpo, and Darak took a step forward this time.

Feista flinched and covered her face. Free of her grip, her tail tucked itself back between her legs.

Asherzu waved her brother away without taking her eyes from Borpo. "We must act on facts, on information. We must succeed by spotting what others miss, by finding what larger firms pass over. Yet you continue to rely on feelings and common perceptions. We have spoken before of this on several occasions, have we not?"

"But—" said Borpo, deflating a little.

"Three timesss, Lady," said Ms. Thyssisss, consulting a file in her lap.

"That have been documented," added Mr. Meister.

"And yet here we are again. Such failure to improve is unacceptable! Your demotion shall be swift and merciless, and the analysis team shall no longer report to you." Asherzu made the proclamation as one might hand down a death sentence on the battlefield.

The Orc paled. "But... but why—"

"Come along," said Mr. Meister, guiding the Orc toward the door.

"And when next I see you in the tribe meetings, I expect your beard to be a finger length shorter," said Asherzu as Ms. Thyssisss slid up beside Borpo.

"But... no! Please!" Borpo said to the Gremlin and Naga. "Talk some sense into her! Surely my concerns do not warrant such punishment!"

"Pehapsss if it wasss a sssolitary isssssue," said Ms. Thyssisss, "but we have documented your offensssesss exssstensssively." She took him by the arm and guided him toward the doorway.

"Mr. Meister—Gabor, come now!" pleaded Borpo. "Did I not share roast boar and fine grog with you after the last company feast? Are we not brothers in arms? How can you do this?"

Mr. Meister shrugged. "As we like to say, you don't have to be cold-blooded to work in HR. But it helps!"

The Gremlin and the Naga shared a laugh as they led the Orc away. Feista was still trembling when she turned back to the CEO. To her surprise, she found Asherzu grinning.

"Finally, a way to pull that thorn from our side," the chieftain said to her brother.

"For a time, anyway," said Darak. "Borpo will find a way back to power."

"Of course. His persistence is what makes him valuable. But, by the fallen gods, it is nice to have some respite from his scheming." Asherzu looked back at Feista with a warm smile. "I am sorry you were forced to endure such a display. Please, accept my apologies, and tell me more of your findings on the dragon's hoard."

"Uh..." Feista's stomach was still firmly lodged in her throat. "I... uh..."

"Please. Do not be nervous," said the Orcess. "Boldly explain your findings, and then know that we will check them. And if they are wrong, well, we shall all learn something."

"Y-yes, lady," said Feista. "I am not scared of being wrong."

"Then why is your tail—"

Feista shifted in her seat and swore to herself that she'd cut off her thrice-cursed tail someday. "I worry because I do not know what all of this means, Great Lady. Because people yell or go white with terror or... or get demoted at the mention of the dragon's hoard being overvalued. And it is still a theory! What will happen if it is proven? I am scared of being right!"

"Do not worry." Asherzu idly picked up a warg skull from her desk and stared into its empty eyes. "If you are right, your findings might be exactly what this company needs."

"How can that be?" asked Feista. "Lady, it would be a disaster."

Asherzu's smile mirrored the skull's fanged grin. "For those who fear to tread new paths, it would be. But for those with bold hearts, with the strength and courage to dance with the thunderstorm and carve new paths with the lightning..." She set the skull down and turned her smile to Feista. "Well, for us, the future is always bright."

"Glowing with a light beyond mortal comprehension," said Kaitha.

"Filling the halls of eternity with glorious radiance," the guard said automatically.

Gorm squirmed and tried to discreetly adjust his makeshift robes. "Sowing... uh... blessings an' justice in... erf... in equal measure."

"And so bringing light unto the darkness."

"May it be so." Gorm held his breath and tried not to stare at the guard as he waited. Sweat beaded on his brow and chafed under his ever-bunching robes.

"Always and forever," finished the guard, a black-bearded Dwarf in a simple red and white tabard. He leaned against the doorway that served as his post and nodded appreciatively to the disguised heroes. "Good, good. Ye two are learnin' fast, for new ones. Though your friend needs to speak up more."

Gaist, still cloaked in the form of a small woman, shrugged and nodded.

The old Dwarf nodded at Gorm. "Plus, you're still tryin' to wear Human robes. One of the Elves put ye up to that?"

"Aye. One did." Gorm gave Kaitha a sidelong glare as he scratched at the robes furiously.

"Har! They never tire of that bleedin' prank," said the guard amiably. "Don't worry. Sister Erika's the quartermaster—she can set ye up with a nice tabard. Much more comfortable. There aren't many Dwarves here, but there's enough that they'll have one in your size."

"And where's she set up again?" Gorm asked.

"Right down in the lower barracks." The guard turned to nod at the correct hallway, giving Gorm an opportunity to punch him squarely in the jaw and slam his head into the stone wall.

A few minutes later, Gorm admired his new tabard as Gaist and Kaitha dragged the unconscious Dwarf back down the hall. "This fella was right," he said, enjoying a cool breeze below his belt. "This is much more comfortable."

"I'm ever so glad," hissed Kaitha.

"Why are ye sayin' it like you're angry, then?"

The Elf snorted as they arrived at the storage room. "We finally got the whole invocation right! We could have actually made it past a guard peacefully, and you knocked him out!"

"I needed to get out of those robes," Gorm said. "'Sides, what's one more guard knocked out at this point?"

He pulled open the door to the storage room, which at present was primarily used to store unconscious Tandosians.

"I suppose it doesn't matter," said Kaitha, working to maneuver the latest victim into the room. "Gods, at this rate we're going to take down every guard in the thrice-cursed building."

"That's what I bloody said we should do," grumbled Gorm.

"Well, I guess you got your way!" the Elf snarled back. A prone Tandosian started to groan something, but she silenced him with a swift kick. "Can we just get back to finding out whatever it is they're hiding here?"

The trio quickly returned down the now-familiar passage to the unfortunate Dwarf's station, where they adopted a posture of purpose and walked determinedly into the adjacent hallway. The new corridor was long, bathed in golden light by glowing crystals set in wall sconces, and otherwise empty. The sounds of bustling crowds grew as Gorm and Kaitha made their way through the passage, punctuated by an occasional growl or roar. Gorm rested his hand on his axe as they stepped up to the next guard station.

"Praise Tandos," Kaitha began with a wave to the two guards stationed at the doorway.

"Yeah, yeah. Go on through," said a Human guard with a wave of her mailed hand.

Their sudden nonchalance was enough to give Gorm pause. "Uh, but the invocation—"

The two guards shared a knowing look and a derisive snort of laughter. "Look, I can tell you must be new," said the senior guard.

"Yes," said Kaitha.

"Which means the only reason you'd be coming to the dens is if you been assigned to the burn teams," the guard continued.

"That's us," said Gorm, eager to avoid her suspicions.

The guard nodded and held up two stubby fingers. "Right. So first of all, your orientation has already started on the other side of the dens. And second, you probably ain't got enough time left on Arth to waste on the invocation! Ha!"

"So how's about we do you a favor and skip it?" the second guard chimed in.

The pair of Tandosians shared a good cackle at the joke. The heroes feigned concern and scurried on through the doorway.

The cavern beyond was bigger than a city square, and brimmed with almost as much activity. Grubby attendants wheeled carts loaded with the corpses of farm animals across the rough-hewn floor. A small army of acolytes carried brooms, buckets, and raw cuts of meat between six large cages carved into the sides of the stone. Across the way, the cavern sloped up toward a wide mouth, through which gray light and a dull drizzle seeped in from outside. Near this entrance, Gorm could see a pack of people standing around something large and indistinct.

Gaist nudged him and nodded to a ramshackle shed set against the wall behind them on high supports. A network of rickety walkways spiderwebbed across the cavern's ceiling from the door of the hut.

"That looks like a supervisor's office if I ever saw one," Kaitha muttered.

Gorm nodded. "Aye. Ye and Gaist check it out, and I'll see what this so-called burn crew's about."

"Be quick. We may not have long." Kaitha and the doppelganger peeled away from the Dwarf and made for the stairs to the office.

Gorm continued on toward the pack of acolytes near the cavern's entrance. The closer he got to the crowd, the tighter he gripped the handle of his axe. Many of the nervous-looking Tandosians wore leather masks and green goggles of the sort that Scribkin often wore when tinkering with unstable machinery. A heavyset Human woman near the center of the circle was shouting instructions at the group. Behind her, an Elf dressed all in leather was seated on top of a lumpy, brown form, like a leather blanket thrown over a great stack of crates. His goggles were topped by a strange contraption, at the center of which was a large gemstone that roiled with crimson and amber light, like a ruby that was burning from the inside.

"Now," the instructor barked as Gorm joined the rear of the group, "when Brother Laylo is good and ready, he can think that the beast should lift him, and the gem will transmit the instruction."

Gorm looked around the group nearest him and found a likely looking stooge, a skinny Imperial Human who was trembling like a leaf. He nudged the young man in the ribs and asked, "Hey. I got in late. What's she talkin' about?"

The Human didn't respond. His eyes, wide with terror, were locked on Brother Laylo and slowly rotating up. Gorm turned to see what had captivated the young man.

"Oh," he said, watching Brother Laylo rise into the air on the back of a long, serpentine neck, just behind a reptilian head that stared at the acolytes with undisguised malice.

—CHAPTER 13—

"Perhaps this is what we're looking for," said Jynn, craning his neck. Across the street, a shifty-eyed Human in a long trench coat loitered outside the Heroes' Guild office on the Fifth Tier.

Patches tugged on his leash to get closer to a tuft of weeds poking up between the cobbles. The suspicious man was likely not what Patches was looking for. The archmage's dog was completely occupied with his perpetual search for things to sniff, eat, widdle on, or some combination thereof.

"I'm not sure if the royal archivist is a Human, especially not one so young," Jynn mused. "His use of Sixth Age formalities in correspondence led me to suspect that he was an Elf, though now that I say it, it seems more likely to be an official tradition rather than a cultural idiom. Still, the man acts as though he has something to hide."

Jynn wasn't entirely sure what the royal archivist was out to conceal, which admittedly was a key part of the job description. Yet the recalcitrant official had cut off all correspondence with the archmage months ago, and none of his contemporaries would answer inquiries about the Leviathan Project or Detarr Ur'Mayan. Clearly, someone was hiding something.

The man in the trench coat perked up and smiled as a Tinderkin woman in a broad hat exited the guild office and nonchalantly walked over to him. They exchanged a surreptitious nod and, once around the corner from the office windows, a quick kiss.

"Oh," said the wizard flatly. His lip lifted in a sneer of contempt at the banality of a secret romance. He'd brought Patches down to this street to allow the universe to unlock the secrets of his father's work, and all that creation had taught him so far was that the Heroes' Guild office on the Fifth Tier was a hotbed of interoffice trysts.

Patches happily pulled something from a gutter and ate it.

Jynn checked his sigils again with a tired sigh. They weren't much; just simple lines of chalk and salt drawn at key points around the guild office. Using any low magic at all was dangerous; the greatest risk of inviting destiny was that it might accept the call. Still, he needed to tempt fate—quite literally—to grant him insights beyond the love affairs of lonely clerks. The sigils represented a small attempt to amplify the flow of destiny.

He tugged his dog along toward the nearest rune, but the leash suddenly went slack in his hands. The wizard glanced up to see a blur of gray and brown streak around the corner, and then Patches was gone.

Nobody can curse like a wizard, which is why they tend not to swear much. You have to watch your mouth when your language and gestures can warp reality or unleash blasts of eldritch energy. Still, Jynn had more than a few choice words for his dog as he ran down the street, one hand holding his robes up above his knees and the other waving the detached leash.

Patches was out of sight by the time Jynn skidded around the corner. The archmage felt a surge of panic as he looked around the busy street for some sign of the dog, but a joyous bark from his left put him on the right course quickly. He sprinted down two more streets in pursuit of the happy yapping—practically a marathon by the standards of the typical sedentary wizard—and so his lungs burned and his eyes watered by the time he found Patches seated by a park bench, furiously nuzzling a familiar woman in orange robes. Jynn backpedaled to a halt far too late to avoid her.

"Oh. Hello," said Laruna, still scratching the dog's ears. She gave the archmage a small smile that didn't quite reach her eyes. "I thought you must be around if Patches was here."

"Ah. Yes," said Jynn. He glanced around the street, noticed her smile was faltering, and only then realized that he'd failed to return it. He yanked his lips into a manic grin and barked, "Hello!"

"It's good to see you," she said, some measure of cheer returning to her face.

Jynn searched for the right words. Feelings were rising unbidden from the back corners of his mind, and it took a significant degree of mental exertion to keep them boxed up and where they belonged. After too long a pause he settled on an emphatic, "Yes!"

"What brings you out this way?"

"Uh..." Jynn wasn't sure what the best thing to say was, but he was certain the worst was anything close to "using ancient magics to research the forbidden demonic sorceries that my father—a liche, if you'll recall—spent his life and unlife developing for the purpose of raising the dead." What would she think of him if she knew he was dabbling in Detarr Ur'Mayan's studies, or trying to leverage the magic of the Sten? He looked around the street again for some excuse before his eyes settled on Patches, still trying to nuzzle the solamancer's knees into submission. "Just... walking the dog!" he said, and thrust the leash forward like a talisman.

Her face fell, and he wasn't sure why she was disappointed. "I see," she said. "Well, if you're busy—"

"Oh, very!" blurted Jynn, reattaching Patches' leash.

"Ah. Well, perhaps we could talk another time." Laruna stood.

"Yes! Another time! I would like that!" Jynn's inner self shrieked for him to reduce his use of exclamation marks, but he was too preoccupied with trying to control the maelstrom of unwelcome emotions raging through his mind.

"Good," said the solamancer unhappily. With a nod and a final scratch of Patches' ear, she turned and walked away.

Jynn watched the mage go, trying to organize his thoughts. It was some time before he shelved enough of his errant emotions to turn back. His stomach still roiled as he walked back to check on his sigils by the guild office, but he gritted his teeth and renewed his focus. The runes needed to be precise, the wizard reminded himself, if the universe was to show him what he needed.

"If there's any one thing you need to know, it's this: keep hold of the Eye of the Dragon," barked the Tandosian instructor. "That gem's all that's keeping Brother Laylo alive right now. Or any of us, really."

Most of the assembled Tandosians took a step away from the dragon-kin. Gorm remained in place, studying the beast and its Elven rider with curiosity. He often regarded claims about charms or crystals and magical protection with a healthy dose of skepticism, but he couldn't think of any other reason for Brother Laylo to be comfortably reclining on the back of a Storm Drake while retaining all of his limbs.

"You lot may have heard that the gem lets you speak to dragon-kin or some such nonsense," the instructor continued. "And maybe for your dragons of legend, it could work like that. But most drakes are dumber than a pile of rocks, and even if they could understand you, why do you think they'd care? When was the last time you worried what a chicken or pig was trying to tell you? Nobody listens to their breakfast."

Regardless of its intelligence, the Storm Drake had developed an interest in the shouting woman by its side. Its reptilian eyes locked on her, and its brilliant blue dorsal crest rose up in unmistakable hostility.

The instructor didn't pay the drake any mind. "What the gem does is allow Brother Laylo to exert his will on the beast. To feel as it feels, and to send his own thoughts back to it."

A slight scowl appeared on Brother Laylo's face, and the drake's aggression paused. The creature looked confused for a moment, then conflicted, and finally its dorsal fin sank back down as it turned away sullenly.

"As long as the gem stays with Brother Laylo, we remain safe." The instructor's lips curled up in a wry smile. "Until, that is, we talk about the flame olive oil. Mounting your fuel on a Storm Drake is finicky business, which is why we usually use the Wind Drakes or Mountain Wyverns. But Stormies are faster and can go farther, so sometimes we have to use this fella here. The key to remember is that the lightning comes from their mouth or the underside of the wings, so the canister must be positioned—"

Gorm was genuinely curious as to how the Tandosians mounted volatile explosives onto the back of a reptilian thunderstorm without vaporizing half of their secret fortress, but at that moment a commotion broke out across the great cavern. Bruised and disoriented Tandosians were staggering through the tunnel Gorm had entered by, several of them nude and all shouting to raise an alarm.

"Time's run out," he muttered to himself, looking around. The other Tandosians were momentarily distracted by the ruckus, but soon enough they'd focus on finding the interlopers.

Unless, of course, there was a bigger distraction.

He hefted his axe and hurled it expertly. The Tandosian next to him saw the attack, and turned to accuse the Dwarf. "You—!" the surprised student gasped.

Gorm grinned and pointed as Brother's Laylo's headgear clattered on the floor alongside the Dwarf's axe. Brother Laylo himself was clutching a small gash across his forehead, apparently unaware that the cut was at the spot formerly occupied by the enchanted gemstone. By the time the dazed Tandosian realized what he had lost, he was staring into the cobalt eyes of a Storm Drake, its dorsal crest extended to full height and crackling with energy.

Gorm punched the accusing acolyte in the gut and dove into the crowd, moments before Brother Laylo disappeared in a burst of brilliant blue electricity. Searing light cast scattering Tandosians in stark shadow. Silhouetted students fled for the doorway. Carters began frantically rolling the wagons of explosive barrels away from the chaos.

Amid the mayhem, Gorm caught the eye of the Tandosian instructor as she scrambled toward his fallen axe. Something like recognition lit up in her eyes, and she began to shout something.

"Mistake," muttered Gorm under his breath.

The other Tandosians were too distracted to pay attention, but the drake was working to isolate a target in the milling chaos around him. It found one in the screaming instructor. Before the Tandosian could finish her sentence, the drake grabbed her in its powerful jaws and hefted the woman into the air with a whip of its tree-trunk neck.

Gorm took the opportunity to scoop up his axe and another prize. "Time to go!" he laughed, already sprinting for the exit.

"Just a moment longer," murmured Kaitha. Her fingers danced across a long line of leather folios in the drawer of an oak filing cabinet. There were several such cabinets in the small office set above the great cavern, but she gravitated to the one with a heavy lock on it. The prone supervisor on the floor had unwillingly provided her with a key, and now the secrets of the Tandosians paraded beneath the ranger's gaze.

Blue lightning crackled outside the window again, and the sounds of pandemonium escalated as one might expect. A beastly roar rose above the din. Gaist waved urgently toward the door.

"I know! I just need a little more time." Kaitha pressed her lips into a thin line as she flipped through the pages. Most looked like mundane invoices and memorandums; documents that might have yielded clues with the sort of painstaking study that was made impossible by rampaging dragon-kin. None seemed relevant to her search, until—

A folio near the back of the drawer caught her eye. The first document had King Johan's signature beneath a thick wax seal, and seemed to lay out the charter for a secret project. Beyond it were missives, maps of Andarun and Mount Wynspar, a receipt for a captive wyvern, and— critically—several invoices to an Imports, Exports & Stuff of Andarun for hundreds of barrels of flame olive oil.

"Success," she breathed, just as the door burst open. A burly Human stood in the doorway, wearing a red and white tabard and a look of genuine shock upon seeing an Elf rifling through the paperwork while monsters ate his colleagues. His eyes fell upon the unconscious supervisor in the office, and then the rest of him fell backward over the railing, propelled by Gaist's boot to the chest. The guard's final shriek cut through the cacophony below, signaling that it was an appropriate time to be elsewhere.

With a nod of assent to the doppelganger, Kaitha shoved the entire folio labeled "Project Reawakening" into her satchel. Then she readied her bow, nocked an enchanted arrow from her Poor Man's Quiver, and ran out onto the catwalks that hung above the caverns.

The arrow turned out to be unnecessary. Few workers were still up in the suspended walkways, and those that were remained entirely focused on the chaos below. Two more drakes had been loosed, and now the three dragon-kin stormed across the stone floor, driving gaggles of screaming Tandosian workers before them. Clerics, paladins, and knights of Tandos were gathering at the edge of the cavern, trying to formulate a plan while avoiding being fried by bolts of enchanted lightning. Only one figure within the pandemonium seemed unconcerned by the tumult, and he had already broken away from much of the action as he sprinted toward the wide mouth of the cavern.

Kaitha grinned and pointed. Gaist nodded in affirmation, and together the ranger and weaponsmaster sprinted along the walkway above Gorm. Kaitha vaulted over the railing of the catwalk onto a high outcropping of rocks, then skidded down the rough slope to a steep drop. Another leap took her onto a pile of crates, and then it was a few simple hops to the ground. A moment later, Gaist dropped to the floor beside her.

"Hey!" the Elf called as they ran up alongside the sprinting Dwarf. "How goes it?"

"It's been interestin'!" Gorm huffed. "Ye two find anythin'?"

"Got some documents that look important." Kaitha patted her satchel with a wink. "You?"

"Nabbed a magic dragon rock." Gorm held up a red gem that occupied most of his fist.

Somewhere behind them, a drake roared. Another flash of electricity cast the entire cavern in pale blue and black. Kaitha could feel her hair rising into the air, errant sparks of static playing beneath the auburn strands.

"Also, I set a few angry drakes loose next to some highly flammable barrels," the Dwarf admitted.

"That doesn't seem like a great idea," breathed the Elf. They were only a few feet from the mouth of the cavern now, but it lacked any stairs or ramp by which to descend.

Gorm gave a small shrug. "Least they ain't set off any—"

A thunderclap sounded behind them. The walls of the cavern were bathed in fiery crimson for a split second before a wave of heat and force carried them out the mouth of the cavern like leaves on a summer wind.

Kaitha rolled in the air so that her forward foot hit the slope below first, and she let the momentum carry her in a frenetic sprint down the shale. But even her Elven grace quickly found its limits, and she wound up twisting her ankle and falling into an ungainly roll down the hill. Above her, several perturbed drakes launched themselves from the smoldering remains of the dens and took off into the sky, trailing smoke behind them as they fled.

It was several minutes before Gaist walked over and helped the ranger to her feet. The doppelganger had resumed the familiar form of Iheen the Red, though he still wore the robes of the diminutive acolyte of Tandos. He looked like an onyx giant crammed into a child's dress.

As soon as the ranger could stand and her ears stopped ringing, she staggered over to the crater that marked Gorm's landing. "Sometimes it's like you've never even heard of Nove," she told the Dwarf as he righted himself.

"More like I don't see what worryin' about some dead sage will help," Gorm grumbled. He shoved the gemstone, still clutched in his dusty hand, into his belt pouch. "Ye two good to go?"

"Yeah." Kaitha tested her ankle as she looked back at the cavern. Flames danced within the mouth of the mountain, making Wynspar look like an angry demon preparing to rain fire down upon the unrighteous. "We've got to move."

Gaist nodded.

Together, the trio hobbled down the slope, avoiding the frantic Tandosians running about the site. Above them, sparks rose into the gray night sky. Most of the lights were embers, red and orange specks dancing on currents of heat. Several, however, were a brilliant pink, and once they reached sufficient altitude, they flew south over the mountain.

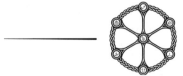

"Messenger sprites, sir," said the clerk, an Imperial woman in smart, severe robes. She set a scroll on the black leather surface of a cherrywood desk. "From the north site. I think you should read the transcription."

One of Weaver Ortson's eyes opened slowly. The other was lost in the folds of his mottled, unshaven face as it rested on the desk like a lump of moldy suet. His monocular gaze fell upon the empty bottle next to him, swiveled up to the stacks of unfinished paperwork on his desk, and finally found the clerk standing before him.

"Fnerf," he said.

"Sir?"

He sat up, stretching a long trail of spittle from his lips down to the desk. He wiped his mouth, rubbed his eyes, and tried again. "I did not wish to be disturbed, Maive."

"Yes, sir. But this s-s-seemed important." The clerk's voice wobbled as she walked the tightrope of explaining something very obvious to someone very powerful.

Ortson grumbled and cleared his throat as he picked up the scroll and broke the seal. The words on the parchment hit him with the full force of sobriety, a day-long hangover packed into a singular moment of despair.

"How..." His lips flapped uselessly as he wrestled with the message. "How long—"

"They flew in moments ago, sir."

"And who else has—"

"Nobody, sir. Just us in Special Projects and you." The clerk thought for a moment. "But presumably the temple and the king have been alerted as well."

"That's what I thought," said Ortson, already struggling out of his chair. He swung his arm in a wide gesture that sent his glass sliding along the desk. "Send for my carriage!"

The glass of amber liquid slid along the bar into the waiting hand of Heraldin Strummons. He raised the whiskey in a toast of thanks to the barman and turned around to survey the taproom of the Winking Cyclops.

It was a bar of Heraldin's favorite sort, a run-down tavern on the Ridgeward side of the Sixth Tier. The drinks were strong, the beer was cheap, and the tips were usually good for a bard with daring tales. Such establishments were perfect for earning some coin and spending it well.

The bard's brow furrowed as he caught a glimpse of a familiar face in the crowd; a misshapen nose crisscrossed with scars beneath a mop of furiously orange hair. The man had acquired more crimson lines on his face since Heraldin had last seen him, and the bard had changed as well—he was no longer possessed by an animate hook, for example. Beyond that, Heraldin now had a sense of integrity, albeit a flexible one, and so he took it as his duty to warn the proprietor of the Cyclops about the danger lurking in the crowd.

"Don't look," he muttered to the proprietor. He leaned back on the bar in a manner that might be mistaken for relaxing by someone who didn't understand how spines work. "Your bar is in danger."

"That so?" The barkeep had the physique and temperament of a Dire Bear. His face was set in a laconic scowl that suggested if anyone was going to be frightened at the Winking Cyclops, he intended to be doing the frightening. He polished his glass in an unconcerned manner. "How?"

"That there is Rod Torkin, safecracker and demolitions expert for Benny Hookhand." Heraldin nodded toward the scarred man, who had arrived at a table with four other rough-looking individuals. "The man's a genius for getting through vault doors and complex locks. And there—sitting next to him—that's his sister Bettel Torkin. She specializes in magic locks. If those two are here, they're either plotting their next hit or—worse—in the middle of it now."

The barman glanced over to the group of rogues, and then smirked. "Very funny."

"This is no joke, friend," Heraldin insisted. "I'd know those faces anywhere."

"More like you'll spot 'em anywhere, even where they ain't." The barman picked up a glass and started rubbing it. "They ain't criminals. Them's Rod and Grettel Sparklit, and the group they're with is the Golden

Dawn—King Johan's new party of heroes. If they're plotting anything, it'd be how to stop these dragon attacks and sort out the Red Horde."

"Those are Johan's new crew?" Heraldin couldn't hide his skepticism.

"Sure as you're born. 'Course they ain't wearin' the fancy gold armor, but it's them all right." The barkeep cast a sideways glance at Heraldin. "Don't be jealous, eh? Great hero like His Majesty's bound to work with more than one party. And you're already famous for helpin' him take down that liche. Save some monsters for the new folk, and enjoy your liquor. You've done your part, aye?"

"I suppose I have," said Heraldin. But as he stared at the five members of the Golden Dawn whispering and plotting with one another, he grew more and more certain that the alleged Sparklit siblings were, in fact, the famous Torkin Twins. And, he reflected as he grimaced into his whiskey, less certain of everything else.

"Well, we... uh... we can't know for sure they were a party of heroes," Weaver Ortson said, mopping sweat from his brow. "But ransacking a dungeon full of dragons certainly does sound like our folk."

The faces looming from the dark smoke around the table remained stony and, for the most part, unhappy. Goldson and Baggs were there, naturally, as well as Athelan of House Bethlyn, High Priest of Tandos. The Tinderkin with the hook leaned against the back wall of the room, watching Ortson sweat with the patient air of a lone wolf following a wounded stag. King Johan sat directly across from Ortson, the dim light gleaming off his golden armor. Johan's scarred face was still locked in its perpetual grin, but his eyes were dark as they prowled about the room.

"I thought you had taken precautions to bar heroic activity in the Winter's Shade," said High Priest Athelan.

"It was unsanctioned, of course," said Ortson.

"That doesn't justify your lapse in control," the Elf countered.

"And the lapse doesn't excuse your temple's lack of security," snapped Ortson.

"Enough," said Johan. The king fell into a brooding silence that smothered any protest from the assembled conspirators. The quiet was almost unbearable by the time the king let a low growl escape his lips. "It's Ingerson. The Dwarf was following the Imperial flame oil." The king glanced back at the Tinderkin in the shadows.

"We took the usual precautions, sire," said Mr. Flinn.

"Surpassing expectations," muttered the king. "Tell me, Ortson. Are you familiar with *The Warlock's Daughter*?"

Weaver thought back over his sorcerous acquaintances. "Which one, sire? I know a few warlocks who—"

"The book, Ortson. By Tayelle Adamantine. One of Marja's favorites."

The guildmaster was familiar enough with Adamantine's work to know that he didn't want people thinking he read it. "I wouldn't say that I am, sire," he answered truthfully.

Similar denials of varying degrees of sincerity rose around the table.

Johan shrugged. "Marja loves them. In *The Warlock's Daughter*, do you know what keeps the hero and his love apart?"

Weaver thought back to what he knew of Adamantine's books. "A double suicide?" he ventured.

"No. Well, yes. But I meant what indirectly caused their deaths."

"Indirectly, sire?"

"What doomed Gaelan and Yvette was optimism," said Johan.

"And a fireball-wielding warlock riding a manticore," offered Athelan. "Uh, I've heard," the high priest amended with a crimson blush.

"It was optimism!" Johan sat up again with a measure of his usual buoyancy. "It was planning for the best. Ha! They might have escaped the warlock had they hoped for the best and planned for the worst. Reckless optimism is the path to failure. Optimism such as thinking a petty regulation will keep Ingerson out of our business or some mid-rank priests will keep professional heroes out of ancient ruins." The king glared at Weaver and Athelan in turn.

"Of course, sire," said the high priest. "It won't happen again."

"Not if we plan for the worst-case scenario. Ha! So let's assume Ingerson breached the site. How bad could it be?"

"The worst possible outcome is that the interlopers found the Eye of the Dragon," said Athelan.

"Or retrieved sensitive documents," said Goldson.

"Right. So if we assume Ingerson looted those, what then?" Johan posited.

For a moment, the only sound around the table was the faint rush of blood draining from every face. Then, all began to speak at once.

"He could expose everything," said Ortson.

"We'll be run out of the city," said Baggs.

"Or run up the gallows," grumbled Goldson.

"If people found out about this—" gasped Athelan.

"No, no." Johan shook his head. "Ha ha! None of that will happen."

The uncertain quiet set back in as most of the table tried to reconcile what they'd just heard. Baggs piped up. "Sire, the people expect a government to behave with a certain level of... ah..."

"Basic decency," offered Ortson.

"Exactly! Ha! They expect it! They believe it's happening." Johan held up a mailed finger. "It would take a big event to convince them otherwise. And there is little that people hate so much as big events that show them they were wrong. If we provide a different story, a better story, they'll fall over themselves to believe it."

Most of those gathered still seemed nervous. "Sire, the truth will come out," said Athelan.

"And our story will be waiting for it in the yard." The king's smile grew, pushing his scarred flesh away from his pearly teeth. "When stories clash, people believe the one they find most reassuring. Our job is to make sure we have the better tale before Ingerson tries to play his hand."

Urgent murmuring broke out around the table.

"It's a massive risk," said Goldson.

"It could work, though," offered Baggs.

"I'm not sure there is a choice," Athelan said.

"What are we talking about?"

The last remark was interjected with volume and force from the doorway. Queen Marja waited for those assembled to turn their stunned gazes upon her before she swept into the room, dressed for an evening ball.

"Uh, my dear—" began Johan.

"I'm the queen!" Marja delivered a quick riposte to an argument that hadn't been made yet. She grabbed a chair from the wall and wedged it between the king and Bolbi Baggs. "You said we'd rule together! I belong at these meetings."

"Indeed you do, my love! Ha!" Johan scooted his chair over to make space for the queen. "We were just discussing the import rates on non-staple grains."

Several nervous glances passed over the table; with a brain like a sieve and a mouth like an open spigot, the queen was the worst sort of confidant.

"Why are you talking about grain at a time like this?" Marja demanded. "Did you know the dragon burned down another one of those shanty villages not two weeks ago? You should be doing something about the attacks! You're supposed to keep me safe! And the kingdom, too."

Johan tried to placate his wife. "My dear, please believe that—"

"No!" snapped Marja. She took a deep, shaking breath and, lip quivering with nervous energy, stared up at Johan. "I am queen! I will... I will be part of ruling. And... and I won't allow any other business until you and I have decided what to do about the dragon."

Anger flashed in the king's eyes. "Marja, I—"

"I won't!" Marja declared. "I can stop things, too. I am the queen, and royal by birth!"

Ortson watched Johan's face carefully. A shadow passed over the paladin's scarred features, not of anger or malice, but disappointment. With a resigned sigh, the king pulled his hand down over his face, but when he looked up, his smile had returned as though applied like an ointment. "Of course, my love. But let us discuss it in the morning."

Marja was undeterred. "Why not now? Everyone is here."

"Well, everyone needed to discuss import tariffs on non-staple grains. I would not plan a defense of the kingdom without the Golden Dawn," Johan interjected. "We shall call them to gather in the morning, and we will plan a glorious proclamation that will be on people's minds and tongues for weeks to come."

──CHAPTER 14──

"It had better be a big deal to get us up at this hour," grumbled Burt.

"It's the biggest scandal in at least two ages," Gorm said. "And I called ye all together because every one of ye had a role to play in discoverin' the secret."

He glanced around the desk at the confidants gathered in Jynn's laboratory, nodding to each as he mentioned them. "Burt's been our contact with the Shadowkin united by the Guz'Varda."

"Unofficial liaison," corrected the Kobold.

"Kaitha, Gaist, Laruna, and I found evidence that Sowdock wasn't burned by a dragon. Jynn helped us figure it was Imperial flame olive oil that the false dragon was usin'. Heraldin discovered how it was being sourced."

"Don't forget to sign over your ballad rights before you leave!" The bard held up a sheaf of paperwork and a quill with a helpful smile.

"Since then, Kaitha and Gaist joined me in tailin' a wagon carrying that olive oil into the Winter's Shade. And what we found there is hard proof that Johan's a fraud who killed his own people. We'll need all of your help to move forward. And when we do, all of ye will be in danger. Ye understand?"

The Dwarf looked at each of his old friends in turn. Each nodded back to him. "What did you learn?" Jynn asked.

Gorm took a deep breath. "This goes back, back to when Handor was king. Johan, who was Champion of Tandos at the time, took an enchanted gemstone from the Great Vault beneath the Palace of Andarun."

"Impossible," said Jynn. "That's part of the Royal Archives, and guarded by the Heroes' Guild and bannermen. Nothing goes in or out without proper requisitions."

"Requisitions that were easy for the Champion of Tandos and confidant of Handor to get," said Kaitha, setting a stack of papers on Jynn's desk.

"So he took this. The 'Eye of the Dragon.'" Gorm set the enchanted gemstone on the desk next to the paperwork. "With this here magic jewel, the Temple of Tandos spends years catchin' wyverns and drakes, and usin' the gem to learn to ride them. And all the while, they been developing fire weapons usin' flame olive oil from Kesh. Oil that leaves no trace, and thus can't be proven to not be from a dragon."

"They'd need a lot of oil to simulate such an attack," said Jynn. "And Imperial flame olives only grow in a very small area. They'd have to... they'd... they cornered the markets on flame olives for the flame olive oil."

"Aye," Gorm said. "With the help of the Goldson Baggs Group, they bought all the means of production a decade ago. With the help of the Temple of Tandos, they concealed their facility in Winter's Shade. When the price of flame olives skyrocketed, they used Goldson Baggs' market analysts to spread lies about seasonal growin' patterns and cover up what they'd done."

"We have invoices and correspondence to prove it." Kaitha added more paper to the pile.

"It took time for them to work out how to use the dragon-kin and the flame oil. The first test attacks were few and far between. But once they got operations runnin' smoothly, they spent years more attacking the Freedlands' own cities and eliminatin' competitors and inconvenient public figures under the auspices of the Dragon of Wynspar."

"You think he's framing the dragon?" asked Heraldin.

"I think there ain't a dragon at all," said Gorm.

His words reverberated like whispered thunder in the office. An unsettling silence fell on the room.

"But..." Laruna stammered. "But everyone knows there's a dragon beneath Wynspar."

"What everyone knows and a giltin will get ye a fish on market day," said the Dwarf. "Think a dragon would tolerate grown drakes roostin' in its mountain? Every legend I heard of 'em says they're as territorial as they are greedy. If there was really a dragon below Wynspar, it'd have wiped out Johan's plans before they started."

Heraldin shook his head. "So... all these years... the dragon stirring..."

"I knew Handor was a bastard, but I never thought he'd kill Lightlings like that." Burt shook his head, waving off clouds of blue cigarette smoke.

"Ain't much evidence Handor knew," said Gorm. "Seems like it was Johan's idea from the start. It's all there, plain as day in the documents. And now we have the bastard king by the throat!"

"Probably," said Jynn.

"Ye think he can deny it?" demanded Gorm.

Gaist pointed to the Tandosian documents for emphasis.

"I'm aware of the evidence," the archmage told the weaponsmaster. "But only a fool would underestimate the king."

"We have proof!" Kaitha said.

"He has the kingdom," Jynn countered. "The people love him. The temples see him as one of their own. The Wall is having its best run in years. They will be reluctant to give up their prosperity and security for something as insignificant as the facts."

Gorm shook his head. "That ain't how it works."

"It is. I've lived it," said Jynn. "For all my father's evils, he did not kidnap Princess Marja. Yet people still tell each other the story of how Johan saved her. The public would rather have a hero for a king than a royal assassin, and contrary to what the Agekeepers say, it is public preference that writes history."

"And the people won't prefer his story once they hear it was him that's been torchin' their towns and blamin' an imaginary dragon!" said Gorm.

"And what if the dragon is imaginary?" asked Jynn. "How many billions of giltin are invested in the Dragon of Wynspar's hoard? What do you think happens to that gold if there is no dragon and no mountain of treasure for it to sleep on? Will the banks and their investors accept that their fortunes are invested in a lie?"

"Some things are hard for people to believe, especially if they're true," Heraldin added.

"But... we have proof!" Gorm protested, though the fuel had been pulled from his fire. "Every town crier would leap at the chance to holler about a scandal like this."

"Not if the executives at the Town Crier Network are concerned about their stocks," countered Heraldin.

"That's madness!"

"Yes, but it's also the norm." Jynn retrieved the Wyrmwood Staff from a corner of his office. "We're not saying we shouldn't share the information you gathered, but we need to proceed cautiously."

"Johan could claim that we are trying to frame him, to bring down the kingdom." Heraldin steepled his fingers and stared at Jynn's desk as though it were a thrones board. "So long as he maintains the dragon is real and we're interlopers, the evidence won't matter to people whose fortunes are on the line."

The wizard ignored the commentary and began twisting reality around his fingers. "No, we cannot rush to the first town crier we find with the evidence." The space in front of Jynn pinched into an onyx surface haloed by a faint blue corona. "We can store the evidence in this pocket dimension while we plan. Until we've carefully considered how to deploy this information, we must keep the evidence safe."

"We'll have to act soon," said Heraldin. "If Johan knows what you took, if he has some inkling of the evidence we hold, he'll be forced to make a move soon."

"You think he'll have us arrested?" asked Kaitha.

Heraldin shook his head and pursed his lips. "No. Moving against us publicly would only give us a platform, a stage to make our case. And if he felt he could risk discreetly assassinating us, he'd have attempted it long ago."

Gaist shrugged his shoulders, then lifted his hands up in the manner of a smith offering a fine sword.

"He's right!" gasped Heraldin.

The others looked uncertain. "He is?" asked Gorm.

"Johan doesn't have to discredit our evidence; he needs to make sure nobody pays it any mind." The bard grinned triumphantly. "That's his move. He won't waste words denying our story; he'll just give the city a bigger one!"

Gorm shook his head. "That can't be right. The bloody King of Andarun has been stagin' attacks on his own people and killed one of the mages' dignitaries for investigatin' him. What could be bigger than that?"

"I shall lead the Golden Dawn to slay the Dragon of Wynspar!" trumpeted Johan the Mighty.

A shockwave of gasps and whispers rolled through the throne room, radiating away from the dais where Johan and his party posed. Wearing enchanted armor and triumphant grins, the Golden Dawn stood with fists to their hips and feet set apart, as if preparing for an aerobic workout. The king's chosen heroes looked for all the world like the heroes of antiquity come to life.

Weaver Ortson was a hero of a more recent age, one where men and women of valor were better versed in stagecraft and public relations. The guild's arch-choreographers had instructed the Golden Dawn carefully on the most inspiring poses. Staff beauticians and illusionists had applied makeup and magical glamours to each member of the party. The guild's top illuminancers wove enchanted mists and glowing orbs around the room to ensure that the king and his fellows were put in the best possible light. Under Ortson's direction, the guild's combined efforts ensured they looked like legends striding in from the mists of history and tracking glory all over the present's carpeting.

Now the guildmaster sat in the shadows behind the throne's dais, nursing a glass of Elven white and watching the theatrics with a critical eye.

"Never before has our kingdom faced a peril like the Dragon of Wynspar." Johan spoke with all the ostentatious solemnity of a bejeweled sarcophagus. "But never before have we had a warrior king, a slayer of necromancers and liches, a hero for the ages upon the throne! Ha haaa!"

The throne room burst into cheers. Weaver Ortson sipped his wine; he had made it something of a private game to drink whenever the king told a falsehood at these functions. In Handor's days, the guildmaster would take a swig of whiskey or down a cocktail for each lie, but even Ortson's battle-hardened liver couldn't withstand the combined might of hard liquor and Johan's mendacity. He'd even watered down the wine for this particular spectacle, and he was already well pickled halfway through the production. The king droned on, and Ortson dutifully drank.

"And though the dangers are great—"

Sip.

"I must put your safety ahead of my own—"

Sip.

"For my only ambition has ever been to serve the land and people I love!"

That whopper was worth downing the rest of the chalice. Ortson was halfway through it when a high-pitched squeal startled him into spilling the remainder. He glared at the queen through the wine dribbling down his brow.

Marja took no notice of the sodden guildmaster. Her eyes were the size of dinner plates, set on the gleaming figure of her husband. Her lips squeezed into a small, crimson singularity of a smile, occasionally leaking squeaks of anticipation.

Ortson reflected on Marja's change of heart as he mopped the wine off his face. The queen had opposed Johan's plan until the king idly mentioned that it was like something out of a storybook. The remark had affected an immediate change on the queen's demeanor. At first she fell into a sort of dreamy trance, walking through the palace with heavy-lidded eyes and a bewitched smile. As Johan's announcement of the plan approached, the queen returned to reality, or at least to a reality tangent to Ortson's, and insisted on participating in the production. Now she waited in the wings of the throne room with the other staff and stagehands, waiting for her cue.

Ortson startled. Her cue!

"And those I love mean everything to me!" Johan ad-libbed. The king's tone sounded like he had left the safety of the script behind several sentences ago, and was now unhappy to find he had doubled back on himself. The guildmaster coughed and waved to the queen's attendants, who loosed their grips on the queen's arms.

"Joooohaaaaaan!" Marja shrieked, bouncing up the stairs like an excited lapdog. She launched like a cannonball at the king as she crested the dais and crashed into his arms. "My love! You cannot! It's too da-a-angerous!"

"I must!" Johan's face showed evident relief that the show had reunited with the script. "The kingdom needs me—needs us—to be strong, my love!"

"But what will I do without you?" Ortson pantomimed along with the queen's lines as he refilled his chalice. "How can I endure our time apart? For so many years I was without love, without hope..."

"This one's for Handor's memory, then," muttered Ortson, raising his cup in toast. Now that the queen's monologue had started, it was likely to be his last drink for a while. The queen's melodramatic praises of her husband and bemoaning of her suffering turned the guildmaster's stomach, but he couldn't call them lies. Marja believed her own tripe with all the blind fervor of a mad cultist. Her ravings were just as intolerable as a mad cultist's as well, so Ortson turned his attention elsewhere.

His eyes were drawn to the Golden Dawn, and not for the first time he found himself wondering who they were. Weaver never faulted Johan for not wanting to share a stage with Ingerson, but even so, the guild was full of talented heroes who would line up to fight at the king's side. Instead, Johan had dredged up a bunch of base-dwellers, claimed they were chosen by Tandos, and strong-armed Ortson into bypassing most of the guild's protocols and procedures to get them in the party.

He'd protested, of course. Stood on his principles, or at least hopped on them long enough to make a brief show. But then he'd met the Golden Dawn, seen the silent menace in their smiles. They may not have been killers by profession, but Ortson would have bet that they could have won international amateur competitions. They all looked unsettling, but none more so than the mage...

The Dawn's raven-haired noctomancer turned to look at Ortson as though he'd spoken her name. The guildmaster almost jumped off his stool and turned back to the king and queen, who had nearly finished their lines.

"I just don't know how I can live without you!" Marja pantomimed a sob through a wide smile.

"Nor I you," said Johan. He plucked a silk handkerchief from the queen's dress. "Grant me this kerchief as a token of our love, a boon on my perilous journey. I swear I would give my dying breath to return it to you."

Ortson's brow knit. The king was off script again, though he had to admit it was a good addition. The crowd whispered appreciatively, and the queen herself seemed elated at the king's oath.

"And return it to you I will!" Johan's words seemed to be for Marja, but he was staring at a point in the ceiling so intently that the queen and several nobles turned to see who was sitting in the rafters. "My party and I will slay the foul beast! I will come back with a dragon's head and a dragon's hoard! Ha haaaa! For this is the greatest threat of our lifetime, and the chance to stave it off will be a quest of the ages, a saga for bards to sing of!"

"A bloody disaster, any way you look at it," said Duine Poldo.

"Uh, right..." said the town crier.

Poldo looked down at the royal proclamation, printed in thick letters on a sheet of cheap parchment. The town crier had a thick stack of them to hand out to travelers along the road from Waerth to Mistkeep.

"And this was announced just this morning?" Poldo said.

"Uh... y-y-yes. News arrived by sprite just after lunch." The town crier's lip flapped for a bit, as though he was trying to drink from a stream without using his hands. "S-sir, th-there's a—"

"I'm aware," said Poldo. The announcement included an outdated woodcut of King Johan, as well as an advertisement for The Furkin's Firkin, a tavern up the road that presumably owned a printing press and employed an independent town crier.

Town criers had once been official employees of city-states and kingdoms, but after the downfall of Boss Wool and a corrupt ring of nobles in Scoria, the citizens of the Freedlands began to embrace the idea that a press operating at the beck and call of the powerful cannot be trusted. Enterprising journalists had recognized the value of independent voices in public discourse, and so founded a wide network of small presses and town criers' associations across the land. Of course, if there is value in anything, enterprising businesses will try to conglomerate with it, and soon thereafter large corporations began buying up the new companies. Now there were just a few big names in town crying—the Town Crier Network, the Collaborative Guild of Journalists, and the salacious Wolf's Howl all came to mind. The remaining independent town criers were employed by small presses based in remote villages, popular inns, and one particularly enterprising brothel in Chrate. Most of these small shops lacked the resources to cover anything more complex than disputes between local merchants or stories of unusual farm animals. As such, they paid to have most of their news brought in via sprite from the bigger town crier networks. Now a town crier anywhere on Arth could tell you what happened in Andarun yesterday.

This particular town crier, however, was currently focused on the here and now. Or more accurately, he was focused on the Troll looming high above him and what it might do in the next thirty seconds. "It... It's a Troll, sir," he squeaked, frozen to the spot.

"Quite aware," Poldo said. He gave the lad a handful of silver pieces and a nod that served as permission to scamper away.

Thane, for his part, had stooped to read the proclamation over the Gnome's shoulder. "Why would it be a disaster for the king to slay the dragon? I mean, for anyone besides the dragon."

"There's no certainty that he will slay it, for one thing," Poldo said. "The king is battle-hardened by all accounts, but I don't recall that his companions have completed any major quests. And a dragon! Heroes today fight drakes and dragon-kin, yes, but nobody has fought a proper dragon for centuries. Legends say that a flap of a true dragon's wings can blow men from their feet. A swipe of a black dragon's tail can level houses, and a blast from a red dragon's flaming breath can melt clear through stone."

"Yes, well, *legends*," said Thane. "According to legends, I should eat rocks and naughty children, and my breath can kill a village."

"I'd believe it after you ate that garlic stew the other night," quipped Poldo. "But then, the Wood Gnomes' breath was just as deadly."

"The garlic? It was the beans I regretted," rumbled the Troll. The bushes around them buzzed with the tiny laughter of the hidden Wood Gnomes.

"Quite," chuckled Poldo, who had been banished to the far side of the camp after the ill-conceived meal.

"But that just proves my point," said Thane. "The myth is that I belch out poisonous fumes, and the truth is I use too much garlic and beans in my stew. You can't trust legends."

"Not fully," conceded Poldo. "But the same legends say you can hide yourself as a rock, and that you're a fierce combatant, and nobody would dispute that. There is some truth in every story, and the Agekeepers say there's much in the stories of dragons' might."

A Wood Gnome clambered up to Poldo's shoulder and chirruped a question.

"Oh yes, though I don't remember most of the histories. I recall that the last true dragon on record was when Queen Jorgette of Ruskan sent a small army of adventurers after a young dragon in Faespar back in the Sixth Age. A much smaller army returned with its head." Poldo turned back to the flyer in his hands. "Sending six heroes into an ancient dragon's lair... well, I'd be surprised if the guild doesn't declare them all statistically dead as soon as they set foot in the dungeon. And if the king dies, that leaves ruling to Marja. That would be an undesirable situation by all accounts—including Marja's, I'd wager."

"True. But what if the king has found a way to win?" said Thane, helping the Gnome clamber up into the seat of his backpack.

"Even worse," said Poldo dourly. "People didn't invest in the Dragon of Wynspar expecting to actually see its hoard. They invested for the exact opposite reason!"

Thane's face scrunched up as he started down the road. "That doesn't make any sense."

"It's counterintuitive," said Poldo.

"What does that mean?"

"It's when something doesn't make any sense, but it's still how things are," said the Gnome. "The dragon's hoard fund is a safe place to store money, an asset that always grows more valuable because no hoard adjustor could ever get close enough to say otherwise. Or it was. Mrs. Hrurk's analysis says there couldn't possibly be enough treasure deep in Wynspar to pay everyone out as much as they think they own. Everyone has bought more treasure than there could possibly be."

The Troll shook his head, nearly dislodging a Wood Gnome who had climbed up for a better view. "That doesn't make sense either. You've always said the banks and investment firms are watching where people invest and how much. You said that's their job."

"It is their job. They should be watching the money, but I suspect what they're all actually doing is watching each other. Everyone assumes everyone else is keeping track. Looking at the competition suffices for due diligence."

"So it's counterintuitive," said Thane.

"No, this time it's just straightforward stupidity and greed," muttered Poldo. He glanced back at the northern horizon, where the distant silhouette of Mount Wynspar might have shown were it not for all the trees. "If the dragon falls and it isn't sitting atop an impossibly large hoard of treasure, a lot of Arth's businesses will be facing a sea of red ink and a lot of uncomfortable questions."

"I mean, it don't make any sense," Gorm growled. "There ain't a dragon. Even if he could find the biggest, nastiest drake on Arth and call it a dragon, even he can't fake a dragon's hoard!"

"Well, he could claim the hoard was smaller than expected," said Jynn. "Or say that the dragon's fire destroyed—"

"He could say the fairy king of thrice-cursed Faespar took it, but a missing giant pile of money gets people askin' questions!" Gorm leaned against the tower railing and glared down at the procession below them. "Everybody's got loads invested in that dragon's hoard. There ain't any amount of storytellin' or fancy talk that's gonna keep people's attention if all their money up and disappears, right? But the thrice-cursed king just gives that gods-forsaken laugh—"

"Ha haaa!" Johan's laughter rang out like a trumpet from the middle of the square. Several actual instruments bugled in reply, signaling several wranglers to whip their teams of oxen, pulling the thick chains behind the beasts taut. The chains pulled on a bronze ring held in the mouth of a life-sized dragon's head, all cast in bronze and mounted on a massive doorway set into the Ridge. Metallic squeals of protest rang out from black iron hinges, each as long and wide as a war-wagon axle, as the Dungeon Gate began to lose its tug-of-war with the beasts of burden toiling in its shadow.

Gorm watched the oxen work from above. He leaned against the thick oak rail at the top of the northern guard tower, a ceremonial crossbow dutifully propped in his hand. "If all Johan's gonna do is fake a dragon's death, he's just buyin' time before the inevitable. There's got to be another angle he's playin', something else he's working at. Some reason for the delay."

"Probably," agreed Kaitha. "But there's not much to be done about it yet. If he comes back with no dragon, we'll be ready to take our story to the nobles and town criers."

"And if he does manage to find one, we'll need time to find a new strategy," said Jynn.

"There's little we can do but wait," said the ranger.

"Look! There's Mountain Thunder!" Heraldin, focused on the ceremony below them, pointed to a party of heroes assembled near the king's podium. "They got a premium spot. High visibility. Good lighting. Still out of range of thrown produce. And yet we're stuck up here."

"It's because they took down that rock gnurg that came down the mountainside," said Laruna. "They say if the Great Zen hadn't gutted the beast it could have broken through the Ridge onto the lower tiers."

"Fair enough. But it doesn't explain why Kethador Lounala and the Giant Slayers got top billing. They almost had a party wipe against a griffin last month." Heraldin scowled down at the young party of heroes positioned at a prime spot. Despite the chill in the morning air, the plaza around the king was packed with nobles, rulers of city-states, prominent business people and officials, and more than a few popular adventuring parties. The elites milled and chatted between the dais that the Golden Dawn stood upon and the well-guarded barricades near the edge of the Dungeon Gate's plaza. "Half of the heroes down by the stage are thrice-cursed newbloods!"

"Are you actually jealous of people's position at this farcical event?" Jynn raised an eyebrow askance at the bard.

"Well, I... not jealous, per se. I don't need to be right next to the king at the center of everyone's attention, with adoring fans and agents and merchandisers staring at me," Heraldin said. "But sticking us on top of the watchtower? It's an insult! We'll be lucky if anyone in the crowd can even see us up here. No, we'll be lucky if they don't!"

The streets beyond the king's podium teemed with throngs of people, kept from the Dungeon Gate's plaza by the Golden Dawn's podium. Men, women, and children of every variety swarmed the streets and rooftops. Eager faces peered from every window. Andarun's citizens were drawn to spectacle like ravens to a battlefield. With this much of Andarun's upper crust gathered in one place, people assumed any related event would likely be historic, hilariously embarrassing, or—in the best-case scenario—both.

"It used to be very prestigious to man the guard towers when the Dungeon Gate was opened," said Kaitha. "I remember being thrilled the first time I was selected."

"Yes, well, just in case anyone today mistakes being stuck up here for some sort of honor, they put the Shadow Stallions in the southern tower." Heraldin gestured across the plaza, where five adventurers in mismatched armor were crowded on one side of the ramparts to make room for a Great Eagle perched opposite them.

Jynn perked up at the name. "They must be fairly well-known if I've heard of them," he said. "I recall someone saying they exceeded everyone's expectations."

A couple of the Stallions noticed the Heroes of Destiny staring and waved.

"More like outlived them." Kaitha returned a wave to several of the oddball heroes while speaking out of the side of a smile as big and brittle as a mummer's mask. "Everyone assumed that any party Jimmy Greensleeves assembled would be wiped by a band of Goblins, but they've somehow beat all the odds and managed to achieve mediocrity. Nobody has any idea how."

Jynn squinted across the plaza. "Is that Elf waving a... fish?"

Gaist raised his eyebrows.

"That'd be Brooker of House Oscogen," said Heraldin. "He's the Stallions' ranger."

"Self-proclaimed ranger," interjected Kaitha.

"But why is he holding a fish?" Jynn said, tentatively returning the wave.

"And who's the Elf with the pink hair?" asked Laruna, nodding to a pale Elf in tattered leathers and long, fuchsia braids.

"Forbiddance of House Virteuth," said Heraldin. "She's their thief."

A confused silence fell over the Heroes of Destiny.

Laruna opened her mouth, then closed it, then tried again. "How does one remain inconspicuous with that hair?"

"It really is a miracle they've survived," said Kaitha through her teeth.

"I see," Jynn said. "The, ah... the Sun Gnome looks normal enough." He nodded to a stout woman with skin the color of brick and hair that matched her silver armor.

"Oh yes, Mirara looks normal," said Kaitha. "And then she opens her mouth and you realize she only speaks Great Eagle."

The Sun Gnome leaned in toward the giant raptor and emitted a screech loud and piercing enough to be audible over the Dungeon Gate's rumbling groans. The eagle cocked its head to look at Jynn and hissed.

"And that's who Johan is comparing us to," said Heraldin. "He may as well spit in our eye."

Gorm snorted. His eyes were still locked on the figure parading back and forth in front of the Golden Dawn. The opening gate and the whispering crowd drowned out anything Johan said, but it seemed to Gorm that the king's speech was drawing to a close when Johan waved his flaming sword in the direction of the dungeon. An eruption of thunderous applause confirmed his suspicions a moment later, and the Golden Dawn began making their way off the stage and toward the dungeon.

"Here's what really bothers me," said Kaitha. "I know the heroes running in just about any party from Scoria to Mistkeep, even if only by name and reputation. Bones, even the Shadow Stallions have made a name for themselves. So why hasn't anybody heard of a single member of the Golden Dawn?"

"Oh, I've heard of a couple of them," said Heraldin. "Just not under these names."

"Ye have?" asked Gorm.

"Oh, yes," said the bard. "I'd know Rod and Bettel Torkin anywhere, no matter how fancy the armor or glorious the titles. They worked for Benny Hookhand. I'm less familiar with their fellows, but I'd wager they're no more qualified for heroics and no less specialized in some crime or another. Rod and Grettel Sparklit are blade names. I'd imagine they're all using them."

"They're using what?" said Jynn.

"Blade names," said Gorm. "Professional monikers." Many heroes operated under a *nom de l'arme*, either because their given name wasn't the sort to strike terror into the hearts of villains, or because it was, and they'd prefer something less menacing on the mailbox.

"Like the Jade Wind?" the wizard asked.

"No, that's more like an honor title, a brand," said Kaitha. "A blade name is ostensibly like a given name. Like when Niln had you called Jynn Ur'Gored," she added, nodding at the archmage.

"Right. But usually more contrived or pretentious," added Laruna.

"Oh. Like Heraldin Strummons," said Jynn.

"Exactly," said Gorm.

"What?" said Heraldin. All eyes swiveled to the bard, who sputtered, "What did you just say?"

The collective gaze of the group swiveled back to Gorm. "Well, I mean, with your past and your dealin's with the unsavory, well... I guess we assumed that ye took a blade name."

"I had several aliases, yes," said Heraldin. "But naturally, the Al'Matrans found my given name when I was recruited."

"Yes, but they knew mine as well, and they still allowed me to call myself Jynn Ur'Gored."

"And you all thought this was a fake name?" Heraldin said.

The rest of the table suddenly found the action below the watchtower irresistibly engrossing. Gaist pointedly avoided eye contact with the bard.

"It just... you know... sounds really..." Gorm struggled to find the right words. Unfortunately, the wrong words had already been used.

"Contrived or pretentious?" said the bard flatly.

"Uh..." Gorm glanced at Kaitha and signaled for help.

"Oh! Uh... so this Grettel and Rod Sparklit..." The ranger came to the Dwarf's rescue. "You think they worked for Benny Hookhand?"

"Yes, the Torkin Twins are among the greatest safecrackers on Arth," said Heraldin, still glaring at Gorm. "Bettel was a hedge mage and an artificer who could crack any magical lock. Rod added demolitions and brute force. The two of them could get through any barrier—stone, metal, or magical. Any thief this side of the Highwalls knows that if you need to get into somewhere you shouldn't be, the Torkin Twins could get you there for a hefty price. And yet, Johan is taking them into the dungeon, under blade names, dressed as heroes."

"Why would he do that?" asked Kaitha.

Gorm looked down at the gilt thieves and ruffians masquerading as heroes as they marched into the open maw of the Dungeon Gate. Johan glanced up and, though it was hard to be certain, it looked to the Dwarf like the king winked. "No way to be sure," he said as the great gate began to swing shut behind the paladin's party. "But I got a bad feelin' about it."

——CHAPTER 15——

"It's like a knot in my stomach," Feista Hrurk said as she wrapped a hard cheese into a cloth. "I can hardly take the suspense. I dread the arrival of news of the king's quest."

"Whatever for?" said Aubren. The young Human sliced apples over a bubbling cauldron of porridge. "You said yourself, Warg Inc. has been making gold hand over paw with all that fancy math you did."

Mrs. Hrurk was forced to concede that point. Thanks to the Gnoll's warning, Warg Inc. had divested itself of its shares of the Dragon of Wynspar a mere day before Johan announced the Golden Dawn's quest. It wasn't until after the quest that most banks had bothered to calculate how much treasure the dragon would need to have in order to realize their investment. Their staff analysts must have reached a similar conclusion to Feista, because shares of the Dragon of Wynspar hoard plummeted over 30 percent within a day, and trading had been volatile since. She'd seen a chart of the hoard's share price that looked like an unforgiving mountain range, with more jagged peaks and deadly drops than the Ironbreakers. And because almost every company in the Freedlands was heavily invested in the dragon, or invested in a company that was, few stocks traded on the Wall were doing much better.

Warg Inc. was one of the lucky few. Investors all over Arth were in a state of animal panic, stampeding toward any stock that wasn't tainted with the dragon's hoard. When Asherzu announced that Warg Inc. had divested from the dragon's hoard well before the king's announcement, she may as well have danced in front of a herd of Mammoth Bison in a red tunic. The traders had charged—quite literally; Feista and Asherzu might have been trampled without Darak there. As it was, they'd stood behind the mountain of an Orc and watched a river of equity flow into their company.

Feista took a deep breath. Many analysts said that it was hard to believe Warg's sudden fortune, but she found it more difficult than most. "You're right," she said with a smile to Aubren. "I just... well, every sprite the king sends up from the dungeon could be carrying news that the dragon is dead and its hoard exceeded every projection. Which would be wonderful for the city, but not so much for Warg, and a disaster for me."

Aubren clucked her tongue. "If you don't mind me saying so, ma'am, you worry too much. The bank will be fine, and you will too, no matter what happens to the king and the dragon." And with that, she rang the bell to signal that breakfast was ready.

The kitchen erupted in activity around Mrs. Hrurk. Children charged in through the back door on their way to the dining room, trying to get a whiff or a taste of breakfast before the kitchen staff carted it out to the other boarders. Feista caught a brief glimpse of her own pups among the pack. Only Little Rex paid their mother so much as a glance, and only because his bad leg slowed him down a bit. Staff and volunteers began loading trays with bowls of the hot mash and carting them out to the boarders. Aubren darted through the chaos like an Imperial dancer, shouting orders like the emperor himself.

Feista kept packing her lunch, feeling grateful that she didn't have to participate in mealtime anymore. There was no way she could have taken on the job at Warg and kept Mrs. Hrurk's Home for the Underprivileged running without Aubren's help. And now that she did have the job, she could afford all manner of new niceties for the home. Aubren bought fresh fruit for the tenants, and had called on the grocer to arrange for fresh milk and eggs to be delivered weekly. She'd even hired a party of young guild heroes to clear out the giant rats attracted to all of the nice new food in the larder. And there was a little gold left over to send the pups to a school up the street. Little Rex was even good enough at sums to help the Wood Gnomes.

All of the success felt good. Better than good; she felt like some god or another was smiling down on her. Yet she couldn't shake the feeling that she was pushing her luck, that sooner or later the universe would come to collect its due for her happiness. She'd been this happy before, back when Hristo Hrurk was still alive. He hadn't made much as a lift operator, but he'd been so proud to work at Goldson Baggs, and so fiercely devoted to his family. He might not have left his job had he not worried for Feista and the pups; might never have had to take that fateful walk to buy bread; might never have encountered those guild heroes in the street...

Feista took a moment to compose herself, then went and checked her inbox. There were a few bills, but no couriers had delivered anything of importance. Feista was used to the disappointment; these days she presumed that the letter hadn't arrived yet. She only checked when she thought of Hristo, and a pang of guilt struck her for not checking more often.

"Oh, Mrs. Hrurk, did you see the letter for you?" Aubren asked, walking by the office with a tray of dirty bowls.

Feista's stomach dropped, and her tail reflexively curled between her legs. "A letter?" she asked.

"Well, a note," said Aubren. "A sprite arrived from Mr. Poldo late last night. The Wood Gnomes were going to leave it with the deliveries, but I asked them to take it straight up to your room. Did you see it?"

Relief, and more than a little guilt, spread through Mrs. Hrurk. Still, the thought of a letter from Poldo brought a wide grin to her face and set her tail wagging hard enough to shake her hips. "Thank you, Aubren. I'll be sure to read it before work."

"Times like these, it's good to hear from an old friend," said Gorm.

"Right," said the acolyte.

"Well, not hear. More like see. Ye know what I mean." The Dwarf's speech was slurred, and he was trying to lean on Burt for support. This was not going well, as the Kobold was barely taller than his knee and built like a bunch of reeds draped with a rat pelt. "I jus'... I jus' wanna see him."

"I understand, sir, I really do," said the miserable Al'Matran. "And High Scribe Pathalan gave us permission to let you pass. It's just that we're undergoing, ah, routine maintenance, and the sanctuary is closed."

"Tha's good!" said Gorm. He pushed the Elf aside as though opening a gate and staggered into the Temple of Al'Matra, Burt at his heels. The Dwarf shambled forward a few steps, paused as a thought struck him, grabbed the acolyte by the arms, and shifted him back into position in front of the door. "Maybe ye got rid of the mushrooms an'... an' the rat," he said, staggering into the sanctuary.

The acolyte chased after them once the shock had worn off. "It's just that... uh... well, we have cleaned up a bit, and nobody has the heart to bother old Scabbo these days, but really, that's not the issue. You should know that we didn't change... the... the..."

"The what?" asked Burt as Gorm wandered into the Al'Matran sanctuary.

"Uh... the..." The acolyte's jaw flapped uselessly as he stared into the sanctuary.

The Al'Matran hall of worship had been cleared of most of its furnishings, as well as the mosses and mushrooms. Ornate censers and braziers arranged around the room bathed the floor in warm light and filled the air with aromas of cedar and incense. The lights and incense burners were part of an elaborate, esoteric diagram covering the floor, linked by lines of salt and chalk that Gorm was currently trampling over as he made his way across the room.

The acolyte, however, didn't notice Gorm's trail of destruction. His eyes were fixed on the bronze sculpture at the center of the arcane lines. Niln's serene likeness greeted the visitors with outstretched hands.

"Something wrong?" Burt asked the dumbfounded acolyte.

"It... uh, but he... where is... where's his smile?" stammered the Al'Matran. "Look at his face!"

Burt squinted up at the statue. "I dunno. Looks happy enough to me," he said with a shrug.

The Elf's only reply was a squeal of terror before he sprinted away.

"Yeah, nice talkin' to you," Burt called after him. With a snarl and some muttering about pinkskins, the Kobold pulled a limp cigarette from his vest, lit it in a holy brazier, and pulled a long drag as he wandered over to Gorm. "All right, big guy. Here's Niln. This is what you wanted, right?"

"Yeah." Gorm sat in front of the statue, staring with bleary eyes at Niln's feet. He took a deep breath. "Yeah," he repeated softly.

"Feels like we didn't need to come all the way just to talk to a ghost. He's just as gone out there as in here."

"No, no," Gorm slurred. "It's different. Lost a lot of friends in my career. Iheen, Tib'rin, Ataya... all of 'em gone, each one leavin' a hole in me heart. But Niln... what with his books and this statue, it just... it just feels like he's here with me, ye know? In some little way. Ain't much, but it's the most I got."

Burt sighed, but his expression softened. "Yeah. Take your time, Gorm." The Kobold pulled a small flask from his vest and poured himself a thimbleful of Teagem rum. Drink in one hand and smoke in the other, he settled down next to a warm brazier and closed his eyes.

Gorm sighed again. It wasn't a matter of finding the words; the apologies, the excuses, and everything else he wanted to say battered the back of his teeth like floodwaters against a dam. Yet he couldn't bring himself to look into the high scribe's sad bronze eyes. So he sat in silence, slowly sobering as the evening drifted on. Eventually, an admission leaked out. "I failed ye," he said.

Niln looked down with a benevolently blank expression.

"It ain't that I gave up. I still... still haven't. I won't. I want to fight. I want to make it right." Gorm squeezed his hands into fists and wiped salty tears from his eyes. "But I ain't enough. Every lead I chase goes nowhere. Every plan I hatch gets us nothin'. Johan just... well, the world seems set up for him to win. And nobody else seems to care."

He shook his head. "The Shadowkin say I can't fix all their problems; if I came in and rescued 'em I'd be part of their problem. Light's Folk think Johan's a hero, and tellin' 'em otherwise only makes 'em hate ye and love him more. Nobody cares about the truth provided the lies are more comfortable. Even Burt's gone cynical. Well, more cynical."

"I'm a realist," Burt called.

Gorm sighed. "Now Johan's going to slay his fake dragon, and then he'll be even more of a hero. City's already full of people who don't care about his crimes. What will they let him get away with after that? And I don't want to give up but... I don't see the way forward."

He looked up at the statue. Niln seemed to stare down at him with benevolent understanding.

"Is this what it was like for ye?" Gorm asked the high scribe. "Knowin' where ye needed to go, and no idea how to get there? I always thought ye didn't know what ye were doin' because... well, because ye were a young fool, but now... Ye were tryin' to make the world right when the world's doin' everythin' it can to stay wrong. And all ye could do was give up or stumble around in the darkness, looking for the way forward."

There was a fond warmth in Niln's cold, bronze face.

"And ye never gave up," Gorm told him. "Even when ye stopped pretendin' to be a guild hero, ye were goin' back to find your place at the temple. Ye kept tryin' to find your way. And it's inspirin', but..."

Gorm fell silent. Niln waited patiently.

"I been readin' your scriptures again," he said eventually. "And the old books ye collected for me. Know half of 'em by heart by now, but they... they just don't make sense. If there's somethin' I'm supposed to see in the prophecy, I missed it. Or it ain't here yet. Or it's all nonsense, just as daft and useless as... as everythin' else I tried."

Someone cleared their throat. Gorm glanced back, and saw that the entryway was packed with worried Al'Matrans, all staring at him and the statue.

"I'd better go," Gorm said. "The king's been down in the dungeon for three days, and he should reach the dragon soon. If he sends a sprite back tomorrow, maybe we'll get some clue as to what he's plottin' behind all this nonsense. And then... well, then I'll keep on fightin', once I figure out how to do it. And wherever this goes, however dark it gets, I'll fight."

The statue's smile was all gentle acceptance.

"I swear it to ye, Niln." Gorm's voice cracked, and the next breath he drew was long and ragged. "I'll see it through to the end."

He dusted the salt from his knees as he stood. Burt hopped up and fell into step beside him as they crossed the sanctuary. They tried to push their way into the temple's lobby, but the crowd of Al'Matrans glommed onto them like dungeon slime on an adventurer's boot. The priestesses and scribes peppered Gorm and Burt with questions as they forged a path to the door.

"Did you see him move?"

"Was he like that when you arrived?"

"Notice any tears on the statue?"

"Perhaps bloody ones?"

But sobriety had snuck up on Gorm under the cover of his melancholy, and now his emotions were coalescing into curmudgeonly determination. "What are ye lot on about? Don't ye have work to do? Such as cleanin' out this sanctuary, for one!" Before anyone could answer, the Dwarf shouldered an unfortunate scribe out of the way and stormed out of the temple. Burt stepped over the prone Human, careful not to spill his drink, and scampered along in pursuit.

The clergy of Al'Matra sagged as the pair left the temple, disappointed that they hadn't any answers as to what happened with the statue. They quickly went rigid again as they realized, virtually in unison, that in their eagerness for answers they had left the statue unmonitored. The acolytes and priestesses crept back to the sanctuary door like mice approaching a sleeping cat. The first scribe to peek around the door shrieked in terror.

The statue of High Scribe Niln was staring directly at the door, his mouth set in a wide grin. One of his eyes was squeezed shut, as if to give the shocked Al'Matrans a mischievous wink.

"Are you trying to make a joke? Is this supposed to be clever?" Laruna's brow knit as she glared at the apprentice manning the registrar's desk.

The hapless solamancer behind the desk withered under a glare as dry and heated as the desert sun. "I... I, uh, sorry miss. I thought you were making a joke as... I mean, no, of course not. My apologies."

Laruna snorted. "Just enroll me in these classes and then we can both move on."

"Yesss..." said the clerk, finessing an unspoken "but" into a prolonged sibilance. "Have you, maybe, considered some courses that are more, ahem, rigorous?"

"These classes are what I need."

"Of course, of course," stammered the clerk. "It's just that, well, an illustrious hero such as yourself might be more interested in plumbing the mysteries of existence, or the latest weaves for refracting light and heat. These classes are more focused on... basics."

"They're what I need," she growled again.

"People may think it strange to see a grown woman—"

"They're what I need!" snarled Laruna, with enough force and heat to send the apprentice diving behind his desk for cover. She took a deep breath and tried to calm herself. "I need to fix some... basic things," she said evenly. "I can handle people giving me strange looks."

A legion of dour faces stared at Weaver Ortson. The throne room was packed with people, and every one of them wore a fine suit and a deep scowl. The only sounds in the great, stone expanse were the sibilant hiss of the sand falling in the hourglass, and an occasional cough echoing through the chamber. He felt naked and exposed, a rigid grin his only defense against the impatient stares.

Ortson glanced at the hourglass. There was just under a minute to go by his judgment, but it felt like a small eternity. A glass cloche was set on the table next to the timepiece, and in it a small, pink sprite waited patiently.

Industry leaders and nobles were ready with their own sprite stones, preparing to issue buy or sell orders the moment the sprite spoke. Agekeepers and town criers lined the walls, quills ready to record history in the making. Queen Marja, on the throne behind Ortson, was watching the tiny, glowing figure with manic concentration.

All eyes were on the sprite. Unfortunately, according to Nove's fifth principle of universal irony, that only served to further delay the announcement.

Anyone who has had a birthday party, opened holiday presents, or watched a clock for the end of a particularly painful class knows that time seems to pass more slowly while waiting for a desirable event. The philosopher-scientist applied a more rigorous methodology to this axiom, using Nove's Constant to devise a mathematical model that showed how attention and anticipation delay events and distort time. Nove's writings on his fifth principle of universal irony posited that enough people watching a pot over a fire could actually postpone the water within it from boiling indefinitely.

Nove famously attempted to prove the theory in a grand experiment involving a cauldron of water, a bonfire, and an arena full of students, with tragic results. The combined attention of thousands of philosopher-scientists in training suppressed the water from boiling for well over an hour, nearly long enough to rule out any other conceived explanation for the delay. Yet, just before the designated time passed, a sudden distraction arose. Sources disagree on whether it was the call of a passing waterfowl, a flatulent professor, or the confluence of the two, but some noise caught the collective attention of the student body, causing them to momentarily ignore the pot. The sudden shift in perspective and expectations caused ripples in the Novian counterforces at work in the pot, releasing all of the pent-up energy in one horrible instant. The boiling water vaporized in a violent explosion that shattered the cauldron. Three graduate students were killed and many more injured by the shrapnel.

Though the attempt to conclusively prove Nove's fifth principle in a laboratory failed spectacularly, most great minds on Arth accepted it as true. Ortson Weaver certainly found it credible as he sweated under the collective glare of the assembled nobles and merchants. It took a small eternity for the last grains of sand in his hourglass to finally fall.

"Thank you for your patience, ladies and gentlemen," the guildmaster announced. "The, ah, notice period for the announcement of the king's messenger sprite from the dungeon of Wynspar is over. As you can see, this is the same sprite that visited the throne room earlier today, and many witnesses can attest that nobody has been privy to the information within."

The hush only deepened in response. Ortson could practically hear their fingers quivering above their sprite stones.

Weaver nodded to a noctomancer standing behind the throne. The wizard had lank hair, a quill in his front pocket, and eyes filled with contempt for anyone who didn't know sorcery. He lifted the cloche and wove a glowing ring of air and shadow with an expert gesture of his long fingers. The magic drifted down over the sprite, so that she was standing at the center of a temporary magic circle.

"I have—!" The sprite's voice boomed like thunder and ended in an ethereal screech.

"Sorry," mumbled the wizard. He wove a few strands of air to modify his magic circle.

"I have a message for Weaver Ortson!" the sprite said, and now its voice was appropriately amplified for the entire audience to hear.

"Has the message been played before?" Weaver shouted. He was one of those unfortunate people who conflates volume with decorum.

"The message has not been relayed!" chimed the sprite.

"Excellent," said Weaver. "Well then, play the message, and be ready to play it again."

The sprite immediately popped up and into motion. "Hello? Hello? Has the message started? Yes, right? Ha! This is Johan, Champion of Tandos. We've reached—what is that?"

The sprite's voice changed a bit. "What are you—arghhh!"

The crowd let out an audible gasp as the second speaker cut off in a scream.

"What is that?" shrieked the sprite. "No, no, no—aaaiiee! Bettel!— Aaaaarg!" The sprite paused to let out a hideous, bestial roar, unlike any creature Ortson had ever heard. It was followed by another death scream, and then a grim gurgling. Another voice chimed in, sounding more like Johan's, but ragged and rasping. "Tell Marja... tell Marja I love her! In this life or the next, we will be together—aaarrgh!"

Ortson's next three heartbeats lasted an eternity in the stunned silence of the room.

"Shall I play your message again?" asked the sprite.

The throne room erupted. Marja screamed and fainted. Financiers hollered orders into their sprite stones. Green and red sprites cascaded up toward the windows, bathing the world in otherworldly light. Bannermen began shouting for order. They may as well have gone down to the docks and yelled at the Tarapin to stop flowing.

Only Weaver Ortson remained motionless. Questions raced through his mind as he stared at the messenger sprite waiting patiently on the table. "Shall I play your message again?" it repeated.

"I'd rather eat a boiled basilisk than listen to that farce one more time!" snarled Duine Poldo as he stormed up the streets of Mistkeep. "I'd be sick to my stomach either way, but at least with the basilisk I'd be spared all of the dismal theatrics!"

"You was starting to look a little ill for a while there," Thane observed.

"'Oh, we have standards to keep. Oh, we require more paperwork for NPCs of a certain size!'" mimicked Poldo. "I've never seen such principled slum lords in my life! It's like the lawyer-monks all over again. These landlords, the lawyers—they're all papering over their bigotry with a thin layer of documents and formalities."

"This time was a little different," said Thane, peering at a plaque on a gate.

"How so?"

"I could understand what these landlords were saying," chuckled Thane.

The Scribkin scowled as they crossed a cobblestone intersection. "You seem awfully cheerful, given the sort of treatment you've endured today."

"This? This isn't anything. Usually when people try to keep me at a distance there's more screaming and running involved." The Troll brandished a fanged grin as a Domovoy popped out of his fur and chittered something. "And the Domovoy get poisoned or people trying to stomp on them. We can handle a bit of extra paperwork."

"Paperwork that would take months to procure. Paperwork they know you can't easily get. Paperwork they wouldn't ask for from a Human or a Dwarf," huffed Poldo. The street's gentle slope was becoming more pronounced as it sloped up toward the Highwalls. It might have afforded them an excellent view of the city had Mistkeep not been enshrouded by its famed, eponymous fog. "And then these gutter scargs use the missing forms to turn away Andarun giltin! For Mistkeep real estate, no less! They wouldn't last five minutes in the upper tiers' real estate market, let me say that!"

"But we did find a place." Thane peered over the wall ahead of them. "This place, specifically."

"Well, pardon me for not beaming with hope for Mankind's future just because we found a landlord who's more greedy than stupid," said Poldo. He could still feel his mustache bristling at the memory of the realtors he'd met with over the past few days. "It's probably a shack made from old crates."

"I think you'll be pleasantly surprised." Thane pushed open a small wooden gate set in a stone wall and ushered Poldo into a small, sloping yard bordered by the stone wall and some evergreen shrubs. A charming cedar cottage sat in one corner, with a lean-to roof extending off one side.

Thane admired the mossy slopes as Wood Gnomes streamed from his fur to fan out across the yard. "It's nice," he said.

"Very nice. One wonders why it was available to... oh, bones." Poldo slapped his forehead.

"What?" asked the Troll.

"It's got to be infested. Or maybe haunted," said Poldo. "Nobody would let a place like this out for rent unless it's got some sort of monster and they don't want to pay the guild for an adventurer."

With Novian punctuality, a sudden flurry of activity rattled the bushes nearest Thane. A squealing rat the size of a dog burst from the foliage, harried by the spears and blades of the Wood Gnomes in pursuit. It hopped and bucked around the yard before it crashed back into the hedge and expired with a final scream.

"And there you have it," said Poldo. "It's got monsters."

"So do you," said Thane with a grin. The Troll started toward the house. "Come on. It's nothing we can't handle."

There were other creatures, of course; a single giant rat wasn't enough to throw off a landlord. The Domovoy cleared several more of the massive rodents from the yard, and dispatched a flying snake in the upper eaves. Thane found a young yeti cowering in the root cellar. He carried the snarling creature by the scruff of its neck to the eastern gates and set it loose in the mountain cliffs outside the city walls. Poldo discovered a clan of pixies had taken up residence in his bedroom. He negotiated a deal wherein the pixies moved to the now-vacant attic in exchange for a truce with the Wood Gnomes and a ban on mischief.

Cobwebs lined the hallways. A thick layer of dust coated the scant furnishings. A skeleton lay crumpled in the closet, and the ghost in the kitchen wouldn't stop wailing until they sent for an undertaker to bury the bones. Poldo and his team tackled each challenge, one by one, until the house was free of monsters and approaching cleanliness.

By the next afternoon, when the setting sun had burned much of the fog away, the cottage felt considerably more homey. The exhausted Scribkin and Troll sat side by side on the upper slope of the yard, looking out over Mistkeep. The skyline framed the majestic shape of the Star Tree growing from the center of the city, its leaves glimmering deep blue and a warm, orange glow emanating from the boughs within. Even with the dead of winter fast approaching, the tree's magic kept the mountain's ice and snow at bay.

"Beautiful, isn't it?" said Poldo.

"Hmm? What is?" Thane murmured.

Poldo saw that the Troll's gaze had turned northward, across the Green Span. "What's on your mind?" he asked gently.

"I just... I was thinking about her again."

"I see." The Gnome let his gaze drift back to the Star Tree, its dusk-colored leaves alight in the amber glow of the dwindling sun. "How so?"

The Troll's sigh sounded like a geyser. "Do you remember when you said you never gave Mrs. Hrurk a chance? You didn't listen to what she told you about the dragon?"

"I do," said Poldo. "Thank the gods I had you to help me find my senses and listen to her. I might be bankrupt had Mrs. Hrurk not convinced me to divest myself of the Dragon of Wynspar's hoard." Poldo nodded to the northern horizon. "But what does that have to do with your Elf? And you?"

"I... I see the same problem in myself." Thane's great mouth worked as he turned a thought over in his mind. "I didn't... I never gave her a chance."

"A chance for what?" asked Poldo.

"To meet me. To see who I am, and decide if she wanted me to stay." Thane looked at his hand. "So many times, she asked me to come out, begged me for the truth. And I never trusted her with it. I never let her decide about me, because I was scared she'd... she'd... well, you know."

"To be fair, I'd say she reacted about as poorly as you feared," said Poldo. His eyes turned to the shrubs, where the Wood Gnomes were constructing a sort of long house from rat pelts and snake bones.

"I'd say I gave her reason to. The first time I let her see me, I was drenched in blood and mauling a corpse. Would she have screamed if I revealed myself in my garden? If I answered when she called me, would she still have drawn the bow? If I had let her see me, if I had trusted her to choose, if I had let go of my fear..." The Troll shook his head. "If I had done things differently, I think she would have as well. But I never gave her a chance."

Poldo put a hand on the thick fur of Thane's arm. "Perhaps you should tell her that."

The Troll's face froze, and Poldo could see a flash of fear behind his crimson eyes. "She... she does not need me, not the way her party did when I found her. And I... I am not ready."

"Perhaps in time," said the Scribkin.

The Troll smiled down at the Gnome. "Perhaps." He leaned back and took a deep breath of the mountain air, as cool and crisp as a burbling spring. "Fate brought us together once. It may do so again. Until then, she's made a new career for herself. She's living a good life. She doesn't need me to... well, she just doesn't need me."

"What do you need, though?" asked Poldo.

Thane took some time to think about it. "I have a home here, and friends. I have a job, and neighbors, and a whole city to explore. And apparently, I still have more to learn about myself."

"All good things," said Poldo.

"Very good things," rumbled the Troll. The setting sun glinted off his broad smile as he looked out over the city. "I think what I need is to enjoy them."

──CHAPTER 16──

"You know. Take the win. Bask in the victory for a moment. Celebrate," said Burt. "Lady Asherzu is taking a few of us out for dinner tonight to celebrate our recent gains and give the king a Naga's salute."

"A what?" Gorm looked up from a pile of eggs over charred gristle and wiped yolk from his beard.

"A Naga's salute? You know, something like, 'he looked like a brave warrior, though I only ever saw his back?'"

The Heroes of Destiny exchanged confused looks. They sat around a small table in a musty diner, attacking plates of burned and steaming breakfast fare with widely varying degrees of enthusiasm.

"That doesn't sound like much of a salute," said Kaitha.

"That's the point," said Burt. "Look, it's a Shadowkin thing. Saluting an honorable foe after he's fallen brings you honor, and gloating over the recently dead can actually dishonor you. But the Naga are the thrice-cursed best at paying false honor to a hated foe. We're gonna do it their way to praise your bastard king down to the depths of the abyss."

"Prematurely," said Gorm.

"See? That's my point!" The Kobold waved a fork at the Dwarf. "My people know a victory when we see one. Wins come so few and far between, you can't miss 'em. Just enjoy it while it lasts. Stop tryin' to make this into some sort of... of...."

"Some sort of intrigue," Gorm sighed.

"Exactly!" the Kobold said. "Trying to make this all cloak and dagger. Talkin' about secrets and conspiracies! Callin' for meetings at obscure little holes-in-the-wall!"

"Now hold on!" Gorm said. "Road Brothers' Diner ain't some obscure hole-in-the-wall!"

"It's a franchised hole-in-the-wall," said Heraldin.

"Not helpin'," Gorm grumbled.

In fact, the Road Brothers' Diner may have been the original hole-in-the-Wall. Mark and Larry Road made their name slinging eggs, hash, and charred meat from a stand built into a crook of Andarun's most prominent architectural feature down at the Base. They leveraged that success to forge a deal with a real estate magnate, and over the decades signs bearing the red road sprouted up and down the city and across the Freedlands. Now they ruled over a greasy empire that stretched from Silvershore to the Highwalls.

"Road Brothers' is the only place that serves a decent breakfast above the Fourth Tier." Gorm prodded his fork angrily into a charred, pink mound, then tried to hide the fact that it broke one of the tines. "Though it doesn't hurt that this place tends to be a bit..."

"Empty?" said Kaitha.

"Abandoned?" suggested Heraldin.

"Gods-forsaken?" said Burt.

Gaist pointed at Burt and tapped his nose.

"Private," Gorm finished with a glare at the weaponsmaster. He snorted at the empty dining room. A one-eyed Gnoll napped next to the grill. "Road Brothers' is always busiest down on the lower tiers. Folk up here are too snobbish for it."

"We prefer our meat... identifiable," said Jynn.

"Ye'd rather pay two giltin for a bowl of sliced fruit and a lukewarm tea?" Gorm said.

"But you admit that you were looking for a private spot." Burt's tail thudded against his chair in triumph.

"We're just taking precautions," said Gorm. He nodded to Kaitha, who pushed a brown paper parcel wrapped in twine across the table.

"There's a key and instructions in this packet," said the Elf. "If something happens to us, and the time is right to move against Johan—"

"How much help do you think we'll need to outmaneuver a corpse?" Burt interrupted.

Gorm and Kaitha shared a look, and he knew she shared the same thought as well. You couldn't survive as a hero as long as they had without a sense for this sort of thing. Just as a seasoned sailor could feel the weather about to change or a veteran alchemist could discern when to duck behind a blast shield, experienced professional heroes felt it in their gut when a nemesis wasn't fully dead. Gorm had seen too many villains leap back up for a final strike or escape through a hidden passage to believe Johan was truly gone.

"We should be so lucky," the Dwarf told the Kobold. "But we probably ain't."

"Luck's got nothing to do with it," protested the Kobold. "You all heard what that messenger sprite said! The whole party's a pile of monster dung by now."

"I hope so," Kaitha said. "But you need to acknowledge the possibility that Johan may be alive."

"I'd love for that smarmy bastard to be rotting in some monster's gullet, but I seen Johan fight," Gorm said. "I saw him take on Az'Anon alone back when... well, I saw him fightin' the monstrosity Az'Anon alone, and he came out on top. They say he slew Detarr Ur'Mayan with barely a thought. Dueled him as a liche, one-on-one. Same for countless drakes, griffins, slimes, gnurgs, ye name it. There ain't much on Arth that could take him down that fast, if there's anything."

"Well, apparently there's something that can," Burt countered.

Kaitha nudged the envelope toward the Kobold. "Just take the key. There's instructions on how to get evidence of Johan's crimes. Important evidence."

"Then take it to the town criers," Burt said.

"That could be exactly what Johan wants," said Kaitha.

"The whole city is on his side right now," said Jynn. "The public loves nothing more than a hero who died in their defense. If Johan's allies can convince the people that we've been fomenting insurrection against a martyr, we'll be the ones branded criminals."

"Tell Lady Asherzu what we said, and keep it safe," Kaitha continued. "If nothing's wrong, you can laugh at us for years to come for being so foolish."

Burt stared at the envelope. A conflict played across his face as he weighed the idea that the king might be alive against the likelihood that the Shadowkin would have the upper hand for such a prolonged period, and found both scenarios equally improbable. "And you're really sure Johan was up to something?"

"That quest was as rotten as last month's fish," said Gorm. "No reason to take it, other than distractin' the public from what we found. No dragon to fight at the end. No reason for a hero as experienced as Johan to die."

"The entire expedition was a charade," said Jynn. "The deaths of the Golden Dawn could be as well."

"But that sprite... the damage to his honor, or his image as some mighty paladin... why would he do that?" asked Burt.

"I suspect that answer will probably lead us to the reasons for the false dragon attacks," said Kaitha.

"Maybe," sighed Burt. He slipped the packet Kaitha had offered into his vest, but given that the packet was almost his size, the maneuver was about as surreptitious as covering a rhinoceros with a tablecloth. "Maybe not. There's still a chance Johan is carrion worm food."

"Trust me, nobody wishes for Johan to be gone more than I do," said Gorm dourly. "But in order to believe that, ye have to think one of Arth's most powerful heroes died on a false quest against a fake monster. Any way ye look at it, it just don't add up."

"We've triple-checked the math, sir," said the accountant.

Weaver Ortson looked up from the memorandum. "And the auditors have seen this?"

"They went through everything, sir." The badges and bars covering the silver-haired Tinderkin's long, black robes put her among the most senior ranks of guild accountants, but the uncertain grimace she wore could have belonged to any bookkeeping apprentice about to deliver bad news to a client. "We'd, uh, we'd be happy to be wrong, but given the king's reported position within Wynspar, the presumed threat rating of the dragon, and the... well, that horrible sprite, we couldn't really come to any other conclusion."

"Hmm." Ortson scrubbed a hand over his unshaven jowls and scoured the memorandum for any possible error. "This is Johan the Mighty, after all. The man slew Az'Anon and Detarr Ur'Mayan in one-on-one combat, and survived a duel with a liche not two years ago."

"I'm well aware of the king's impressive record, sir. We wouldn't have delayed a proclamation this long were it anyone else. But after two weeks with no word, His Majesty's chances of survival..." The Gnome trailed off and gestured at the parchment in Ortson's hand.

Ortson let out a deep sigh and read the memorandum again. It proclaimed in the straight, precise letters of a Gnomish printing press:

Let It Be Known That on This Day,

the 11th of Al'Matra,

the Party Known As

The Golden Dawn

and Comprised of:

His Majesty Johan the Mighty, Paladin of Tandos,

Dagnar Firdson of the Bharad'im Clan, Warrior

Fenlovar of House Tyrieth, Cleric of Tandos

Agatha of Chrate, Mage of the Order of the Moon

Grettel Sparklit, Lawful Rogue, and

Rod Sparklit, Bard

Has Been Declared

STATISTICALLY DEAD

by the Accounting Department of the Heroes' Guild of Andarun.

These heroes of the realm have met their end in the line of duty, and are hereby **HONORABLY DISCHARGED** from their quest.

The rest of the page was filled with a rationale for the decision, tables listing comparable cases, models used, and an index of probabilities that all pointed to the same terminal conclusion.

"Guild law says we have to make the declaration within two weeks of last contact," said the accountant. "We can't put it off any longer, sir."

"So be it," sighed Ortson. He signed the document, dribbled some wax next to his signature, and pressed it with the seal of the Grandmaster of the Heroes' Guild. "It is done. The king is dead."

"I'm sure that was hard for you, sir," said the accountant.

"It was a rum by the Teagem compared with what comes next," he said, standing. "Summon my carriage."

The short ride to the palace gave Ortson time to splash his face with enough perfume to mask the reek of liquor. His face was still damp when the ornate guild carriage rode through the palace gates. A muttered word with the royal guard sent bannermen running to deliver ill tidings, leaving the guildmaster to deliver the most baleful message of all.

Attendants and an acolyte of Tandos met the guildmaster by the throne room. They guided him into a passage that was opulently decorated yet also covered with thick cobwebs. The grotesque webbing lined the walls and ceilings, and thin strands of it crossed the room and stuck in Ortson's sweaty hair.

"The state of this hall is a disgrace!" Weaver sputtered, brushing a thick white strand from his face. "What are the bloody servants doing if not cleaning the royal halls?"

"I'd say we all have had more pressing matters of late," said the acolyte archly. "With the news you bear, I'm surprised you have the attention to spare for such mundane matters."

Ortson scowled. "Of course not."

"Indeed. The queen awaits."

The webbing subsided as the guildmaster and the attendants reached the royal dwelling. Marble statues and opulent furnishings were all dusted and polished as well as Ortson had come to expect others to expect. Yet despite the servants' attentions, the air felt as still and empty as a tomb inside the waiting chambers, and Weaver was relieved when one of the royal handmaidens summoned him into the queen's presence.

Queen Marja reclined on a long, sturdy couch, flanked by several of her ladies-in-waiting. Ortson presumed that she had anticipated his news, as she was draped in a black gown and veil. What he could see of her eyes shimmered with tears. "What news, Mr. Ortson?" she asked him.

"A thousand pardons for the intrusion, Your Majesty. I have an announcement." Weaver bowed as he stepped into the room. "It is as we feared. My lord and king is declared dead."

"No!" cried Marja. She turned away from the guildmaster and stared out the window at the falling darkness.

"Ah, I'm afraid so. Uh." Ortson shifted uncomfortably when he glanced at the queen.

Marja faced the window in a pantomime of wistful sorrow, but her face was set in a tight smile, and her eyes darted back and forth as though reading words written in the evening clouds. "Our destiny was written in the stars. It's just like Gaelan and Yvette," she whispered. "Or Madren and Haela, or Edward and Bel—"

"Your Majesty? Are you... are you well?" said Ortson uneasily. Hadn't the king mentioned a couple of these stories at some point? He was sure Johan had made a comment about Marja's affection for tragedy.

A couple of the royal attendants smiled apologetically and shrugged, as though the queen's enraptured monologue wasn't entirely unexpected.

"And just like those poor souls, Johan and I are star-crossed lovers who cannot be apart," said Marja, staring out the window. "They say that not even death can stop love."

"Well, not in a metaphorical sense," said Ortson.

"No. Not a metaphor. It's true."

Ortson winced. "Majesty, I believe there are laws against that sort of thing."

"I know what I must do!" Resolve crystalized the queen's smile. Her fervent stare could cut diamonds.

"Announce the king's death to the people?" tried Ortson, in the hopes that the unmoored conversation was drifting back to the general vicinity of sanity.

Marja turned to them and grinned. "We need a snake!"

"A... snake, Majesty?" asked a lady-in-waiting.

"Not any old kind, mind you," the queen admonished her. "I think Haela used a swamp viper..."

Weaver's brows shot up. The ballad of Madren and Haela's was regarded as one of the greatest romances on Arth, but it had a body count that rivaled the grimmest battle sagas. "Your Majesty! Surely not!" he blurted. "This cannot be the way!"

The queen paused to reconsider. "Well, I do hate snakes. And I hear the venom is quite dreadful. Well, then a dagger—mmm. But I don't want it to hurt..." She drummed her fingers on the armrest of her chair.

"My queen, I beg you! Come back to your senses?" cried a lady-in-waiting.

"Baker!" said the queen. "Where is my royal baker?"

A gray-haired Halfling stepped from the pack of attendants. "Majesty, please, listen to Mr. Ortson—"

"Baker! You will make me poisoned tea cakes!"

The royal baker shook her head. "Majesty, no! I could never—"

"Oh, it will be simple, my dear." Marja waved a dismissive hand at the baker. "Tell the apothecary I want it to be painless. And nothing that will make me spasm or anything—I don't want to be making a funny face at the funeral. Then put whatever he concocts in the icing of some tea cakes."

"But, Your Highness—"

"Don't you see?" said Marja, staring up at the ceiling as though it were a starry sky. "This is how it was meant to be! This is the end of my story with Johan!"

"But... but I could never harm Your Majesty!" blurted the royal baker.

"Baker. Dearest baker. Don't think of it as hurting me," Marja told the shaking Halfling. "Think of it as helping me find my true love once more, beyond the mortal veil!"

The Halfling shook her head, "No, my queen, I really cannot—"

"One of us is eating poison tonight," Marja growled.

"Lemon or raspberry icing?" asked the Halfling.

Ortson and the royal attendants threw themselves before the queen as the royal baker scurried away. They implored her to think of the people, to put the needs of the nation first, to not succumb to grief in the darkness. The ladies-in-waiting assured Marja that she would find love again. The advisors told her the palace needed her guidance.

Their words flowed over the starstruck queen like waves over a boulder. Marja sat, unmoved and unmoving, her eyes locked on the clouds outside her window. She gave no sign that she was aware of her surroundings at all until the baker returned with a cartload of tea cakes, each frosted with a delicately piped skull. A small placard placed at the front of the tray read: "DEADLY POISON. DO NOT EAT. PLEASE." in a transparently desperate attempt by the baker to stop the queen. But Marja ignored the sign and clapped her hands together as the deadly pastries rolled before her.

"And now, the hour of our reunion is at hand. I am coming, dearest Johan!" Marja put a hand to her forehead and gave an exaggerated swoon as the baker pushed the cart forward. Ignoring the pleading of the assembled ladies and servants, Marja selected a pastry with pink frosting and held it up for consideration.

"The love of my life, the light of my soul, is gone!" she declared to the tea cake. "With nothing left for me in this world, I must leave it, and meet my dear Johan in the next. And so with one bite, mmph, I... with two bites—mrph— I bid... I..."

"Majesty, no." Ortson's breath caught in his throat as he watched Marja unmake herself with growing gusto.

"With two... I mean, three cakes—erph mmmh—I bid the world— mpprh—farewell. This world holds nothing for me but one more cake... mph... I mean two more... and my memories of sweeter days, my love for Johan, and these four cakes and... and..."

Marja lost track of her monologue and lurched forward. She attacked the remaining tea cakes with gusto, sending a spray of crumbs and toxic frosting across the table. The queen made it halfway through the tray before she gave a little choking noise, looked up with unfocused eyes, and flopped face down on top of the remaining pastries.

The crowd watched the spectacle in stunned silence. Weaver Ortson stepped toward the fallen monarch slowly. With a deep breath he lifted her arm and felt her limp wrist. Then he turned back to the royal attendants and said, "I... uh... I have another announcement."

"Another one dead!" laughed Ignatius, looking at the shrine of Mordo Ogg. The red light in the skull's eyes flared a little brighter for a moment. The crooked old priest squinted at the glow, as though reading something in the pattern of flashes. "Oh. A star-crossed lover. Well, good luck to you," he added somberly as the light faded.

As a priest of the god of death, Ignatius supported people's right to die however they chose, and also their right to die even when they didn't choose. Mordo Ogg's clergy were mostly concerned that death kept happening; the who and how and why, if there could be a why at all, were extraneous details. Usually.

Yet something about the idea of young lovers killing themselves never sat well with the old priest. He'd seen enough couples go off to the next life to know that when people who truly loved each other died, there was grief and longing and pain, but also a notable absence of mutual death wishes. You had to pity any soul whose greatest hope in the afterlife was to continue an obsessive, self-destructive relationship. Ignatius sighed and shook his head.

Then the old priest's moment of reflection was gone in a literal flash. Ignatius' glee returned as the pulsing light in the shrine's eyes resumed. "There goes another! Ha! And you too! Lots of deaths recently! Usually means more on the way! Like that one now! And three at once! Guess you really should have fixed that leak in the boat! Ha! And two more! Ha ha!"

"So eight in total then?" asked the host.

"Yes. We are eight," said Asherzu Guz'Varda, glancing back at her party. Most of Warg Inc.'s senior leadership team waited in a small lobby at the front of the Treant's Taproot.

"Thank you," added Feista Hrurk as the Elf hurried away.

"And he will bring us food?" Pogrit of the Fub'Fazar muttered.

"Not yet," said Burt. "First we have to tell him what we want."

"Well, obviously we want food," said Izek Li'Balgar. "Otherwise we would not have come!"

"Right," said Mrs. Hrurk, unsure of what to say. She glanced at the Kobold for help, but Burt only shrugged. "Uh, but we have to tell them what kind of food."

"Why must we plan the meal?" demanded Guglug. "Is that not what the cooks are for?"

"Patience," said Asherzu.

Feista sighed. Warg Inc. was led by some of the most brilliant figures among the Shadowkin. She'd heard legends of Pogrit the Black-Maned and Wise Freggi back when she was a pup on her father's knee. Yet most of the board knew little of the city; war and hardship had forged their legends in the deadly wilderness or on Arth's battlefields. Even though they lived in Andarun now, they rarely ventured outside the Shadowkin communities.

As a city Gnoll, Feista was beginning to appreciate why.

"I will demand the food, and he will bring it," said Darak.

"That's not how a Lightling restaurant works," said Burt.

"It is how Garruck's Ham Hut works," grumbled Darak sullenly.

"Look, I know Lightlings have some strange customs, but trust me," said Burt. "I used to eat here all the time in a prior job. It's top-tier dining for Seventh Tier prices. And so swanky, the staff have h's in their ums."

"They have what?" said Feista.

"Ahm," said the host as he reappeared. "If you would follow me, I will take you to your, ahm, table."

"See?" said Burt, rubbing his paws together. "This is gonna be good."

The host led them into a dining room furnished with oak and brass tables and chairs. The walls were covered with a small armory's worth of weapons, shields, and plate mail, with a few monster heads and other trophies interspersed among them. Feista noticed more than a few Goblin totems and Orcish Gaists up on the wall, but she put it out of her mind. She had seen nicer restaurants, but only from the back alleys when she was picking through their trash. It was a rare opportunity to eat at such an establishment.

They were directed to a large table near the back. A few couples and groups were spread across the handful of tables; closest to Asherzu's party sat a group of several Dwarves who had clearly been enjoying the wine list.

Feista sat and picked up the menu. Her tail wagged as she read over the list of river fish, mollusks, chicken, and lamb.

"Why is the writing so hard to read?" Freggi of the Water Horse Clan turned the menu on its side, and then upside down, in an attempt to decipher the script.

"It's calligraphy," said Burt.

"It is confusing and hard to see." Izek squinted at the menu. "I cannot tell what letter this begins with!"

"Why would anyone write in such a way?" Guglug demanded of Mrs. Hrurk.

Feista sighed. As a younger person and a lifelong city-dweller, she was often called upon to defend the customs of the city. "It's cultured."

"It's sophisticated," offered Burt.

"Sophisticated?" snorted Pogrit. "A repeating crossbow is sophisticated. A permanent shapeshifting hex is sophisticated. This is silly writing that cannot be read."

"Right, but people can read it, right?" said Burt. "If you're in the know, you know how to read it. It's like fashion or trends. If you've got enough status, you'll know how to follow along."

"So it is an otherwise useless skill that gives you status?" asked Izek.

"That's..." Burt paused. "Well, yeah, that's a pretty good description of sophistication, actually."

"Seems foolish to an old dog like me." Pogrit scoffed at the idea.

Still, Feista noticed that the old Gnoll and the other board members began to study the menus with renewed interest. And their collective opinion of Lightling food seemed to brighten considerably when a Scribkin waiter brought the first round of ale and wine, along with another curiosity.

"You said that we must ask for food," Darak said, pointing an accusing finger at the basket.

Burt didn't look up from the menu. "We do. Just give it a minute."

"But they have brought us some sort of... tiny loaves," said Darak.

Izek picked up one of the long, thin pieces, speckled with garlic and parsley, and gave it an inquisitive sniff. "Yes, bread," he said. "Rods of bread."

"Yeah, they do that," said Burt.

"We did not ask for the bread!" declared Darak.

The Kobold finally set down his menu. "All right? So? The bread's free! What about it?"

Izek moved in a blur. The bread in the Goblin's hand disappeared with a sound like a log going through a sawmill, and a similar spray of dust and debris.

"Hold on!" said Freggi.

Izek froze with his hand just above the breadbasket.

"How can this be?" Freggi demanded. "If they gave free bread to everyone, that would be all people ate!"

"People will come and stand in line just for this bread!" said Pogrit.

"We do not need to buy food at all!" suggested Guglug. "We will just eat this bread."

"No, that's..." Burt shook his head. "You only get the bread because you're going to buy other food."

"Ahh." Pogrit gave the other Shadowkin a sly nod. "That is how they entrap you."

The Goblins and Slaugh nodded back sagely. Darak and Asherzu looked less certain. But all of them reached for the basket.

"If I may." Asherzu raised a glass of ruby wine after the bread was little more than crumbs. "Today, we gather to honor Mrs. Hrurk. These are hard times on the Wall, but her analysis has kept our firm strong! And as the city mourns its king—"

"To a degree," muttered Burt.

"We can take courage from our strength!" The chieftain cast a warning glance at Burt. "So I honor you, Feista Hrurk, for your keen insight! And I honor all of you for your hard work. Because of your efforts, Warg Inc. is mighty, and grows in strength and market capitalization by the day!"

They drank. Their celebration was muted at first, but wine and ale loosened their tongues, and soon much of the table was sharing old battle stories and laughing.

Halfway through her wine, Feista noticed that Asherzu and Burt were having a conversation of their own. They spoke without directly looking at one another, in tones so quiet and low most of the rest of the table couldn't hear it. But Feista's ears were to sound what a spyglass was to sight, and she couldn't have avoided eavesdropping at this distance had she wanted to.

"And you are sure we should forego the Naga's salute?" Asherzu muttered to the Kobold.

"Gorm thinks the king's death is a ruse," Burt said.

"To what end?" asked the Orcess.

"The bard thinks the Golden Dawn are a bunch of crooks. More so than other gold-hounds. Specific ones. And everybody thinks the king went down there for some sort of mischief. They aren't sure what it is, but it's like the old saying: an Ogre has two fists, so when the first one hits you, you know the second ain't far off."

"And so for now he wishes us to play along and try to avoid speaking ill of the king," said the chieftain.

"Yeah. And he gave us the packet. Just in case."

"Just in case." Asherzu nodded and glanced at Mrs. Hrurk, prompting the Gnoll to feign interest in Izek's war stories. The rest of the table listened with delight to the old Goblin's tale of an elaborate headdress that got caught on a passing adventurer's saddle.

"And if the strap had not broken, my neck would have," Izek told them. "Since that day, I never wear a headdress!"

The table's laughter was cut short when their waiter returned with a slight clearing of his throat. "Ahm, so sorry to disturb you. Would you please lower your voices a little? A few guests have complained, and given the state of the kingdom and the king's uncertain fate..."

Feista cleared her throat when it became clear that the Scribkin intended to leave the rest of his sentence unspoken. "Oh, uh... a thousand pardons," she said.

"Thank you," said the Gnome. He gave a toothy smile, and the waxed tips of his pointed black mustache rose up like a pair of spears. "Now, have we decided on our order? Perhaps a round of appetizers?"

"What is an 'appetizer?'" asked Guglug, her frog-like features twisted in a confused scowl.

"It's a small dish served before the meal," said the waiter.

"Is that not what this bread was?" asked Freggi.

"How much food is to be eaten before the food arrives?" said Pogrit.

Burt slapped a paw over his forehead.

"It, ahm, helps stimulate the appetite," suggested the waiter.

"I am already hungry," said Darak.

"Why else would we have come?" said Pogrit.

"We'll skip the appetizers," Feista told the waiter. "I'll have the braised haardvark."

The Scribkin gave her a grateful smile and took the rest of their orders. Conversation was slow to resume after he left.

"Why would he say we are too loud?" asked Darak. "We are not so loud as the Sons of Fire." He nodded to the inebriated Dwarves at the next table, currently in the middle of a traditional mining song. Feista's eyes lingered on their table for a moment, held there by something elusively familiar.

"Yeah, Lightlings can be like that sometimes. They want you to be quieter or... you know. Not make a big fuss out of things," said Burt. "You just gotta roll with it."

The Kobold's answer prompted resigned sighs and nods from most of the table, but Asherzu looked frustrated.

"Why must we roll with this?" the chieftain demanded. "We are citizens of Andarun, NPCs the same as everyone else. Why must we be quieter?"

"Well, I—uh..." Burt gulped and flapped his jaw wordlessly before his searching eyes landed on Feista. "You want to help me out here?" he asked.

Feista didn't, but now Asherzu's violet eyes were locked onto the Gnoll with all the sudden intensity of a mountain thunderstorm. "Uh... sometimes in the interest of keeping the peace—"

"What good is an unjust peace? Why keep it? No, this will not stand." Asherzu raised a hand to summon the waiter.

Feista's tail curled under her chair. Most of the others feigned sudden interest in their cutlery. Burt began grabbing bread. "I'd eat while you can," he advised.

"Yes? Is everything well?" said the waiter, sliding back up to the table.

"The Sons of Fire are louder than we were," Asherzu told him. "If we were too loud, and they are louder still, you must ask them to lower their voices."

"I... ahm... I really don't think that will be necessary." With Novian timing, the Dwarves hit an especially boisterous chorus, and the waiter nearly had to shout to be heard over their song.

"But what of the state of the kingdom? Is it not true that the king is declared dead?" said Asherzu. "Will other guests not be disturbed?"

"We, ahm... we all handle our grief differently, do we not?" said the waiter.

"Then why did you ask us for quiet?" said Asherzu.

The waiter held his empty tray like an improvised shield. "Ahm... madam, I-I-I do not appreciate what you're implying." He looked to Feista as though she could help.

"If we all remain calm, I am sure we can work through this," said Feista.

"I am very calm," said Asherzu levelly. "I am calmly asking why I must remain so calm when the Sons of Fire are allowed to sing at the tops of their lungs."

The Dwarves, for their part, were no longer singing. A few of them had taken notice of the confrontation. One of them gave Feista a helpless shrug.

"I... ahm... I am feeling very threatened right now," sputtered the waiter.

"Why are you threatened by a question?" asked Asherzu.

The Scribkin pointed an accusing finger at Darak. "Him! He's looking at me like he wants to kill me!"

"This is how I look at everyone," Darak rumbled.

"To be fair, you do want to kill a lot of peop—ow!" Burt cut off when he caught Asherzu's elbow to his ribcage.

"We are citizens of Andarun dining out," said the chieftain. "We do not solve our problems with violence. Nobody need feel threatened by us."

"Usually," Burt grumbled, rubbing his bruised chest.

"Nevertheless!" The Scribkin was starting to alternate between several shades of crimson as some alchemical mix of embarrassment and anger bubbled under his skin. "You... you have been very aggressive! I'm just doing my job!" He looked to Feista for help.

But Mrs. Hrurk's gaze was locked on the Dwarves' table, or rather, an object on the wall behind the nonplussed Dwarves. "That's Finnen Yarp's drum," she said.

"Ahm—" the waiter began.

"That's my ancestor's war drum," Feista said, pointing to a tattered instrument hanging between an imitation great axe and a stuffed cockatrice. "You make it so clear that we're not welcome here, so clear that you don't respect us, and now you have our ancestral drum, an heirloom stolen from my tribe, nailed to the wall amongst your cheap trinkets!"

The waiter struggled to react to this new line of attack from his flank. "I—ahm... you may be mistaken—"

"Those beads tell the history of my clan! I know them better than you know your mustache!" snapped Feista. She pointed to a couple of scraps of tattered gray dangling from the base. "Those are Finnen Yarp's ears! That's my family's drum!"

"Ahm, I am sure we purchased that—"

"Bones to what you bought!" barked Feista. "How can you buy someone's heritage!? Generations of my people lived and died by that drum, and you dare hang it on your wall so Lightlings can stare at it while they eat overpriced fish and cheap bread!"

The Scribkin's mustache bristled. "How dare you—!" he began.

Mrs. Hrurk did not remember much of what transpired next. There was shouting, and the crash of a chair on the floor as someone stood too quickly, and a high-pitched wailing that she had thought was a child but turned out to be the waiter. Then something massive closed around her like a snapping jaw, and the world became a blur of black and crimson.

It was some time before her senses came back, filing in one by one like embarrassed schoolchildren returning from a headmaster's office. First, she felt the irregular, gentle drips of a light drizzle falling on her fur. Then the earthy smell of damp cobblestones drifted into her nose. She heard concerned murmurs and the pattering of rain. When she opened her eyes, Chieftain Asherzu and the senior leadership of Warg Inc. stared down at her. Finally, her memories came crawling back, hobbled under the weight of her shame.

Feista sat up, mortified. "Did I say—"

"You did," said Asherzu, kneeling next to her.

"And did I—"

"You might have, but Darak restrained you. The Gnome is unharmed, save for his honor."

"But were we—?"

"We were. Right out on the street." Burt blew a plume of cigar smoke up toward the night sky. "Should have grabbed more bread while we could."

Feista looked around at the other Shadowkin, each smiling down at her with sadness and worry in their eyes.

"A thousand apologies!" Mrs. Hrurk said. "I should have controlled myself. I should have—"

"Remained silent?" asked Asherzu. "Set aside your feelings? You did that before, and yet what did it buy us but poor treatment from the waiter? Do not be sorry for standing up for yourself. Our fight is clearly not over." The Orc chieftain looked up and across the street at the restaurant, marked by a square black shingle with a silver root running through it. She turned back to the Gnoll with a thin-lipped smile. "It is good to see the fight lives in you. We just must seek more productive ways to let it out."

Feista looked at the restaurant where her heritage was currently providing ambiance for wealthy diners. Shadows of revelers danced in the amber light spilling through the Taproot's frosted windows, and she could hear the Dwarves singing their drinking song. Her paws balled into fists. She tried taking a deep breath, but it became a low growl on the way out. "Someday I'll make this right," she swore to herself. "I don't know how or when, but... someday."

"Yes," Asherzu said, "But for now, let us find some food."

"Garruck's Ham Hut," rumbled Darak.

"Ah, a proper restaurant." Pogrit's tail wagged at the thought. "We will go there and demand food, and eat quickly."

"It will be much better," agreed Guglug.

"Though, I will miss the free bread," said Izek.

Feista thanked them for their kindness, but excused herself and headed for the steps down to the Sixth Tier. She'd lost all taste for the city tonight, and her appetite was gone.

——CHAPTER 17——

"It isn't snack time anyway," said Matron Yen. "That comes after class."

"But I want a cookie right now!" demanded the novice in front of her. His apple-cheeked features were set in a five-year-old's best approximation of menace. "You give me my cookie, or else!"

"No, Rilard. Not until snack time," the matron repeated, unmoved. She stared at the boy with immutable calm, even after he loosed a scream and burst into flames.

"Ah, see class?" the solamancer said to the other assembled novices. "Rilard has lost control, and he thinks magic will make it better. It won't." Matron Yen waved a hand, and the boy's flame winked out, leaving him teary-eyed and pink-faced but otherwise unharmed. "But that isn't channeling magic. What was he doing?"

"Letting anger channel," Laruna chorused with the novices. She remembered the phrase from her own Basic Command and Control classes well over a decade ago. She reflected that her experiences with the subject were much like young Rilard's as she watched the novice slink to the anti-magic circle in the time-out corner.

"That's right," said Matron Yen. A touch of silver frosted the gentle instructor's raven hair, yet she wore robes less decorated than Laruna's own. "Now, what are we feeling?"

"Scared!" piped up another young novice.

"Sad," said a girl of no more than four.

"Angry!" Rilard snarled from the corner.

Laruna didn't respond aloud. In such a rudimentary class, her answer was always going to be some form of "embarrassed," "ashamed," or "worried that somebody past the age of puberty might see me." But, she noted, she also felt a hint of annoyance with Rilard. It struck her as odd, because the boy was only acting as young Laruna did all three times she took this class. She recalled what it was like, to be drowning in shame and embarrassment and fear—yes fear—that the world would reject and attack her as her father had. And she became rage itself, and then the fire came.

"Good," said the matron. "Knowing how you feel is the first step to controlling yourself."

Laruna nodded and took a deep breath through her nose. Her new therapist had recommended breathing exercises, just as she had suggested taking this class again. Laruna felt things were going well with Dr. Tritchwater; they'd made it three entire sessions without Laruna burning down her office. This happy thought reminded her that she needed to write an apology to Dr. Sloomp and check in on the insurance paperwork.

"It's okay to be angry," said Matron Yen. "We all feel angry. Or scared. Or sad. That's not bad. What's important is what we do with those feelings. Do we let them control us?"

"No, Matron Yen," recited the class.

"What do we do with our feelings?"

"We feel them!"

"And?"

"We know that it is okay to feel this way."

"... dis way," finished a few children who had fallen out of synchronization.

"And then what?"

The last bit was hard for the smaller children to remember and pronounce, but Laruna carried the chorus. "We use them to channel and mold the energies of the universe."

"... the unicorns."

"Very good. It's 'universe,' Matilda. Now, close your eyes. Even you, Rilard. No peeking. Good. I want you all to think of someone who has made you feel sad or angry. Somebody who has hurt your feelings."

Laruna closed her eyes and turned her gaze inward, to the memories of her father and his rage; screaming at merchants, hollering at the Farmer Tennen, threatening Mother, and berating Laruna herself. In each scene, Laruna could now see that Jek Trullon was afraid—of being cheated, of losing respect, of being left by a woman who was his better in every way, of being bested by his daughter. The mage had come to realize that Jek wasn't a cruel man who delighted in misery; he was the sort of violent coward who reflexively erupted at any perceived slight or threat.

"Do you see that person?" asked Matron Yen. "And it's okay to think of me, Rilard, but there's no need to point."

Laruna stared at her father in her mind's eye, and found she could no longer look on him with proud contempt. It wasn't that he looked any less vile through this new lens, but because he looked a lot more like Laruna herself.

How many times had Laruna lashed out when frightened? How often did she use volume and violence to get her way? The idea that she had anything in common with her father, that she had inherited any trait from the man, twisted her insides around until her anger was leveled directly at herself. Usually this self-loathing was a harbinger of self-directed profanity and an outburst of flames, but now she held her anger and hatred at arm's length. The rage was there. She felt it. It was not her.

"Now, I want you to try to forgive that person."

Laruna's nostrils flared. Fury rose within her like a wave, but she was as a seabird, floating atop the rage as she watched it rise, and crest, and tumble away into nothing against the shores of time. "I am not the anger," she whispered.

"Remember, forgiving that person doesn't mean you like them. It doesn't mean you have to talk to them, or be their friend. Though I do hope we can be friends, Rilard." There was a gentle smile in Matron Yen's voice.

Laruna heard the boy mutter something and shuffle his feet.

"It means letting go of the anger, of the hurt. You still know you felt it, and you still remember it, but you won't let it control you. Because hanging on to the pain keeps hurting you. It holds you back. Releasing it sets you free, and freedom is power."

As the only adult in the class that wasn't teaching it, Laruna initially surmised that the task of letting old hurts go was more challenging for herself than for children. Then again, she realized, when she was only six, she had already known what a monster her father was, and Jek Trullon had given her plenty of pain to contend with. How long had it festered in her? How different would her life have been had she let that all go when she left the old fool behind?

How different would it be from now if she released it today?

Forgiveness is an act of iron will, and it takes a strength of mind and heart that Jek Trullon had never mustered, a fortitude that had eluded Laruna Trullon for all of her years. But here and now, the fourth time learning the lessons of Basic Command and Control, with the memories of those she had scared and hurt swimming in her mind, with the distance she had rent between her and... well, everything, Laruna found the strength. And she let go.

"Did we all do it? Did we try?" asked Matron Yen.

"Yes, Matron Yen," recited the children. Laruna could not speak.

"And how do you feel?"

A cacophony of mixed emotions rang out in the class.

"I feel better."

"I'm still a little sad."

"Like I don't need to stay angry."

"I want that cookie!"

Laruna smiled, silent tears bubbling from her closed eyes and streaming down her face. Her anger was still there, as were her memories of pain, but they were distant, far below her; she had left them behind as a seabird lifts itself from the surf and soars toward the burning sun. She was no longer the rage, the fury. The fury was a tool, no, a fuel, and it would come when the fire needed it.

She whispered her answer so low that nobody could hear it over the cacophony of eager children.

"I am the fire."

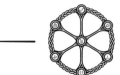

"Yet the flames that burn the brightest fade the fastest," said High Priest Athelan. The Elf nodded at hundreds of ivory candles beside him, arrayed in a candelabra as massive and glittering as an inverted chandelier. The massive fixture gave off as much light and heat as a funeral pyre, but without the unpleasant smell. In case his metaphor was not obvious enough, the Tandosian patriarch added, "So it was with their Majesties Johan and Marja, for cruel fate has taken both Andarun's mighty king and beloved queen far too soon."

The former rulers of Andarun lay in state on either side of the blazing candelabra, or rather, Marja did. Johan's casket was empty save for a jewel-encrusted broadsword and a red cloak. The box reminded Weaver Ortson of the king's armor; covered in gold, ornate to the point of bad taste, and lined with crimson velvet. Marja's casket was true to its honoree as well; draped in elegant silks, beveled with silver inlay, and built double wide.

"Crueler still, our monarchs had not had time to produce an heir to succeed them," the priest continued. "Pray for wisdom and guidance for all as we navigate these uncertain times."

Ortson rolled his eyes. In these uncertain times, the one thing the guildmaster could count on was that the nobles and dignitaries gathered in Andarun's throne room needed no primers on recent royal genealogy.

Tradition held that there were twelve days between a monarch's death and the royal funeral, with no dancing, music, or drink. This period of abstinence was ostensibly for mourning. More practically, the cessation of dances, revelries, grand balls, and other social obligations gave the nobility a chance to scheme and maneuver before official talk of succession began. The Duke of Dunhelm and Duchess of Waerth were spreading rumors of bygone trysts to undermine each other's lineage. Houses Tyrieth and Bethlyn were dropping distinctly unsubtle hints about the ages when Elves ruled. Several Gnomish clans were trying to unite around pushing for a Halfling king. It was like watching the opening moves of a game of thrones, only played between several dozen sides and all at once.

Ortson had neither concern nor patience for the identity of the next monarch. Nearly a fortnight of mandatory sobriety had sheared away all vestiges of the guildmaster's blissful ignorance, honing his mind into a diamond-tipped point that was leveled squarely at the king's empty casket. Johan's last messenger sprite trilled in his memory, playing out the last moment of the Golden Dawn like a tiny, grim mummer. Every repetition of the macabre performance brought new questions with it.

How had the king, moments after his final, anguished cry, managed to send the messenger sprite? And why did the king only speak at the beginning and end of the message? Why was he silent as the rest of the Golden Dawn fought and died?

Or was he silent at all?

The guildmaster's mind kept going back to the horrible cry of whatever creature had ended the Golden Dawn's short career. Weaver Ortson had fought drakes, griffins, abominations, dark cults, demons, owlverines, and every manner of dire beast before he hung up his sword and took a job in the guild's administration. But he'd never heard any sound like the hideous roar that the sprite had imitated, burbling and screeching and thunderous all at once. Yet despite the unique and alien nature of the shriek, something about the call tugged at Weaver's memory. There was a familiar cadence beneath the warped call, less like a bestial snarl and more like—

"Ha-haaaaaa!"

The last note of the trumpeting laughter hadn't faded before the gasps and screams of the mourners drowned it out. Ortson attempted to wheel about in his seat, but the Duke of Dunhelm fainted dead away and fell into the guildmaster's lap. By the time Ortson had deposited the limp noble on the floor, Johan the Mighty was already limping up the steps before the great candelabra.

The king shrugged aside the attentions of concerned bannermen. His golden armor was grimy and dented, his hair a tangled mess, his face a splotch of soot split by a white crescent grin. "I have returned, my good people! I nearly lost hope, as my journey home took every ounce of... my... my..." Johan's triumph faded as his eyes fell on the second casket at the foot of the throne. "My queen!" he gasped, rearing back in shock. When he rocked forward again, momentum sent him stumbling toward his wife's coffin. "How? How can this be?"

Looking back and forth between the weeping king and the doorway he had entered by, Ortson was inclined to wonder the same thing.

"She could not bear to live without Your Majesty," cried Athelan above the astonished whispers of the assembled mourners.

"No! Marja, no!" sobbed the king, falling beside the queen's coffin. He pulled a silk handkerchief from his belt and draped it over the ornate cover. "I swore... I brought it back, but I was too late, my love! You were taken too soon!"

Weaver's gaze swiveled to the back of the room again. Behind rows of stunned mourners, several bannermen stared with slack-jawed confusion back at Ortson. Weaver surmised the guards were also wondering exactly how the king had managed to travel from the dungeon to the funeral without word of his emergence preceding him.

"Now this cursed dragon has taken everything from me!" Johan sprawled over Marja's coffin now, his hands and face pressed against its top, his pauldrons grinding into the wood with every pronounced sob.

"Our joy at your return is eclipsed by this tragedy," said the High Priest of Tandos. Weaver's eyes narrowed. Athelan was a famously taciturn man, preferring to communicate via thin-lipped grimaces over speeches. The priest's reluctance to spare a word for his fellow man went beyond a desire for a frugal tongue; the old Elf was a miser of words. And here he was waxing poetic about Johan's return and Marja's death with such force, such precision, such timing, that it seemed almost rehearsed.

The guildmaster would have mulled over this point longer, but the king suddenly pushed himself up to his elbows and looked around the room with wild, red-rimmed eyes. "Where is Guildmaster Ortson? Weaver Ortson?"

Ortson's mind flashed back to a quest early in his career, when he had been creeping around a small hill that had suddenly opened a huge, yellow eye right next to him. Then, as now, his instincts froze him to the spot. But back then, the Balemound had gone back to sleep, whereas the king kept calling until every eye in the throne room had turned on the paralyzed man.

"Uh... sire?" Ortson, lacking any other conceivable course of action, raised his hand.

"My old friend." Johan's face split into a wide grin as his eyes fell on the guildmaster. "You must do a task for me."

"As... as Your Majesty wishes."

Johan grinned. "This kingdom faces a threat greater than I ever imagined. The dragon has killed my whole party, and almost myself, and now it has taken my love. If any of us are to survive its fury, if we are to slay a beast of legend, we will need more than just professional services. We will need heroes of destiny!"

"Yep. Definitely destiny." Theological Support Friar Brouse pointed up at the statue of Niln with half of a scone. "See it all the time."

"That's what you said last time!" High Scribe Pathalan called to the traveling monk from the far side of the Al'Matran sanctuary, one sandaled foot out the door in case the sculpture tried anything funny. "You said it was just latent fate shifting reality or something."

Several of the attendant priestesses and acolytes clustered behind the high scribe murmured in agreement.

"See it all the time," said the friar again, as though this statement was in and of itself a sufficient response. He took a bite of scone and chewed thoughtfully as he watched the bronze likeness of the previous high scribe.

"Really? Statues just move all the time?" demanded the current officeholder.

"Ain't movin' now," Brouse observed, spraying crumbs over his yellow robe.

"But he did! He grinned for weeks, and then he looked all calm and normal when the Dwarf visited, and since then he's been... winking at us." The high scribe shuddered. "Goddess, I swear his eyes are following me."

"Just an illusion. People always see things," muttered Brouse. He looked down at a gyroscopic contraption that was slowly rotating several colorful beads around a dish of blue liquid. "Nothing unusual in the weave."

"Well, there might have been when we called you three weeks ago!" snapped Pathalan.

"Hey! You think you're the only temple that's got holy relics acting up?" Brouse glowered back at the cowering Al'Matrans. "You lot have been making calls all month. And some of the big ones got real emergencies, too. The marble glowmoths over at the Temple of Fulgen are actually starting to glow. Every fresco showin' anything past the First Age is turning black. I had three different temples calling in statues, paintings, or relics bleeding last week. Serious stuff."

He pulled a blue crystal from his bag and tapped it twice. It flickered with a cerulean light, then made a sound like a bumblebee on a griddle and expelled a cloud of azure smoke. "Thrice-cursed bones! And I can't get a bloody nornstone to work for the life of me! Between the temples' whining and artificers' swindlin', I got enough problems to give a god a headache. I don't give a fig leaf about some statue making faces at—gah!"

The torches in the sanctuary flickered, casting dark shadows across the room. When they flared back to life a heartbeat later, several Al'Matran's screamed. The statue of the former high scribe was smiling up at the ceiling above the empty throne at the center of the sanctuary, looking as though he anticipated the goddess herself was about to crash through the roof and land in her old chair.

"See?" demanded Pathalan. "It's got to be a ghost or… or dark magic. Something sinister!"

"Ain't looking at you now, is he?" asked Brouse. "Hrmph. No magic. And no haunting, neither." Brouse scratched at his beard and looked back and forth from the spinning beads to Niln's face. "I still say it's destiny. You get this sort of thing when people are about to have big, life altering changes thrust upon them."

"Do you?" Pathalan's voice oozed sarcasm and doubt.

"Depends on how big and life altering the change is, how many fates are woven into it, that sort of thing." Brouse waved a hand about his head, as if he could fan away the bothersome questions. "Usually more subtle and less spooky. But yeah. All the time."

The current high scribe stared up at the face of his former rival. "How often?"

"Beg pardon?

"Within the last year, how often have you seen this?" the high scribe reiterated.

Brouse stared blankly. "Well, I did mention all that other strangeness over at them other temples," he grumbled.

"But moving statues? Shifting when nobody's looking? Inanimate objects making direct efforts to communicate?"

"Not... as much," said Brouse. And then, with defiance, he added "This year."

"The past decade, maybe?" the Elf asked.

"Well, maybe not often," conceded the friar.

"But you've seen it before?"

"Not 'seen,' per se." Brouse sucked air through his teeth. "But you hear about it, right? Like the old legend of how Lady Tiaga followed a path of whispering trees to find her clay army, or the story about how the Stennish statues bowed their heads and wept blood when Issan marched on Andarun."

There was an expectant pause that extended into a strained silence. When High Scribe Pathalan broke it, he spoke in the punctuated rasp of a man who is one inane response away from embarking on a homicidal spree. "So... you heard about things like this in legends from ages past?"

Brouse's years in support work had rendered him impervious to such hostility. "Yeah, and other places. Those are just a couple examples everybody knows. It's not like you're familiar with all of the people who almost had a destiny."

"You can't 'almost' have a destiny," protested a young scribe. "You either have a destiny or you don't."

"No, everybody has one," said a junior priestess. "Just most of them are dull, so we don't talk about them. Nobody wants to hear that they're destined to retire from accounting when their eyes give out, move into a small pensioner apartment, and play dice with the other old folks for the rest of their days."

The theological support friar scoffed and pulled a piece of thick twine strung with stone beads from his case. "That's no destiny."

"Well, it isn't much, but my grandad seems to enjoy it fine."

Brouse thrust the string of beads up toward Niln as though it was a lantern. "Fine for him, sure enough, but a destiny has a purpose. A mission. And you aren't born with it," he snapped, wiping the smug smile off the acolyte's face. "Maybe some prophecy or scripture out there calls for the seventh daughter of a seventh daughter, or a lad with red eyes and white hair, or a low-born king, but even if you're one of them, you aren't the only one on Arth, or the only one who will come along."

"So what is destiny at all then?" asked an acolyte.

Brouse snorted at some inscrutable reading in the beads and shoved them back in his case. "Destinies are places where the weave twists, like them whirlpools in the river. They show up at certain times or under particular circumstances, and if the right sort of person gets caught in their pull, they'll be drawn toward the middle. Past a certain point, there's no escaping it. But before then, people can pull themselves out."

"They just walk away?" asked the priestess.

"Sure, or fail in a task, or reject a calling. The Elven armies were led by some nameless general before Issan took over and stood against the Sten, but the nameless fool didn't take the chance to kill the Dark Prince. And who knows how many young ladies chose not to climb the desert paths that Lady Tiaga braved? History's full of people who might've saved the world if they hadn't decided to take over the family business or see how things worked out with a lover." He thought about that for a moment. "I mean, history's not full of people like that. But they were there. You get my point."

Pathalan grimaced up at the statue. "So all this is happening because someone's getting close to... what? Finding an army? Or leading one?"

"I leave that for the gods to sort out." Brouse gave a noncommittal shrug. "There's all kinds of different fated verses and prophetic whatsit out there waiting for their respective chosen one, or the stars to align, or the sun to hit some gem just right, and different gods are always angling to get different ones fulfilled. That's why they're always muckin' with things. And it's probably why all you temples have this strange stuff going on."

"You think the gods are behind this?" Pathalan, like many members of the clergy, had a strong faith that the gods were responsible for much of the past, and an even more emphatic belief that they almost never had anything to do with the present.

"Probably. They're usually behind this sort of silliness." Brouse cast a suspicious eye at the clergy. "Shouldn't a bunch of priestesses and clerics know all this? What are they teaching you here?"

The assembled clergy suddenly took a great interest in the floor and ceiling. A few acolytes cleared their throats. "The All Mother's teachings are less practical than some other gods,'" said High Scribe Pathalan with well-rehearsed understatement.

"You'd think so, wouldn't you?" said Brouse darkly.

"But what do we do about the statue?" asked an acolyte.

The monk shrugged. "Got any young priestesses with a secretive past? Portentous birth marks? Unknown lineage coupled with a vague sense that life should hold something more?"

"Alithana has a weird mole and acts like she's better than everybody," offered one acolyte, earning herself a smack on the head from a nearby priestess.

"Well, I'd keep my eye on her, then. Or anyone else who might fit the bill." Brouse began packing his suitcase back up. "Seen destiny in action before. Something's coming to a head, and we won't know what until we're on the other side of it. With luck, it's just someone who needs to realize they're actually capable of slayin' a bugbear or avengin' their mum or something."

"And without luck?" asked Pathalan, edging away from the statue.

"Then a real hero of legend might rise," Brouse said.

"That seems like a good thing," said Alithana. "The world needs more heroes these days."

"Nah, the world needs more caring people willing to do hard work for the common good." Brouse grabbed his pack and grimaced up at Niln's face. "But bein' nice and sacrificing for others don't get you in the Agekeeper's scrolls. To be a legend? To have some big, reality-warping destiny, a hero needs somethin' really horrible to stand against. You don't get that sort of hero without a darkness that might destroy all of Arth."

─CHAPTER 18─

"A vile foe that menaces all of humanity... fate of the world rests in the balance... great shadow falls over the entire world..." Heraldin skimmed the scroll, murmuring key passages to himself as he read. He had to squint to see in the gloom of the tavern; even at midday, only a few veteran rays of light managed to fight through the dark clouds hovering over the city and the layers of grime on the glass.

Gaist hovered in the shadows next to the bard's table, apparently content to let the paper speak for itself.

Beneath the boilerplate sections on doom and gloom, respectively, the parchment outlined a job.

MANDATORILY ASSIGNED IMPERATIVELY NECESSARY QUEST

LET IT BE KNOWN THAT THE HERO

Gaist

AS ONE OF THE SIX HEROES OF THE CITY, IS HEREBY SUMMONED BY HIS ROYAL HIGHNESS,

Johan the Mighty

KING OF ANDARUN, CHAMPION OF TANDOS

AND

Weaver Ortson

GRANDMASTER AND HIGH COUNCILOR OF THE HEROES' GUILD

TO UNDERTAKE A MAIN QUEST TO SAVE THE KINGDOM AND SLAY

The Dragon of Andarun

The Party shall assemble at the Palace of Andarun by the 24th of Al'Matra's month, at midday, to be charged with this holy task, and shall enter the dungeon before the First of Tandos.

"This must be the king's big move," said Heraldin. "The one that Gorm anticipated would come when the king returned."

Gaist nodded.

"And that means a guild courier is likely somewhere with a similar letter for me," the bard said.

Gaist didn't disagree.

"Interesting." The bard sat as still as the weaponsmaster for a long, silent moment, his eyes staring through the page to some vision on the other side. Then Heraldin vanished in a brightly colored blur, leaving a couple of giltin clattering on the table and a very surprised weaponsmaster staring at his seat.

The bard made it two blocks Baseward before Gaist caught up with him, and that was only because Heraldin was sticking to the shadows and the back alleys. "I knew that cloaked figure outside my apartment was up to no good," the bard said as the weaponsmaster fell into line. "I just assumed it was a debt collector or one of Benny's old thugs, maybe even an assassin. I had no idea it would be this bad."

The doppelganger stared at him through narrowed eyes.

"Yes, I meant it. And I mean to avoid it," said Heraldin. He checked across the street, then took the Ridgeward gate down to the Second Tier and dove back into the alleyways.

The weaponsmaster was at his heels, cloaked in a silence that said volumes. Heraldin pressed his lips into a thin line and ran on, cutting off any further unspoken conversation. Snow and slush coated the cobblestones, and a chill wind howled through the alleys and stung the bard's face.

The bard didn't slow until he reached a shady-looking jeweler's at the Baseward edge of Sculpin Down. A slate outside the ramshackle window read:

THE RUBY TIGER
Fine Jewelry for Every Encounter

- **Elemental resistances**
- **Spell warding**
- **Martial prowess**
- **Engagements**
- **Weddings**
- **Marital prowess**

All sales final. Enchantments not guaranteed.

Heraldin pushed open the door. The small room beyond it was barely large enough for the bard and the weaponsmaster, and featureless save for two black doors on either side of them and a front counter of sorts. It was built more like a small fortress than a storefront. A sheer face of black iron panels and bars extended from the floor to the ceiling, with necklaces and rings barely visible through barred windows. A small hatch was positioned in the middle of the wall, above an empty desk and below a hand-sized panel that slid open as Heraldin and Gaist stepped into the shop. A yellow eye surrounded by gray skin stared out without much enthusiasm. "Yeah?" said a gruff voice with a thick Daellish accent. "What you lookin' for?"

"I was hoping to have this appraised," said Heraldin. He pulled a coin from the depths of his pockets and held it up for inspection. One side of the copper coin showed a roaring tiger, and the other had the number "42" etched into its flat face.

"Let's see." The hatch above the desk flipped open, then shut again after Heraldin pushed the coin into it. The eye disappeared, and there was a satisfied grunt.

Gaist glanced at Heraldin, but the bard pointedly avoided his eyes.

Erratic and muffled mechanical sounds emanated from behind the iron wall; the turning of tumblers, the clicking of locks, the creak of panels and doors on hinges. "To the left," grumbled the voice just as the lock of the left door audibly clicked.

Heraldin thanked the shopkeeper and walked into the left chamber of the shop. It was larger than the storefront, though not by much, and better furnished with a wooden table and two small chairs. When the bard locked the door behind Gaist, a panel in the wall dropped to reveal a small cubbyhole. Inside was a long, flat, ironclad box with a plaque on its face with the number "42." Heraldin's coin sat atop the chest.

The bard pocketed the coin and set the box on the table. There was a brass lock with a keyhole next to the numbered plaque, but he ignored it and produced a set of lockpicks from his belt. When he caught the weaponsmaster's quizzical gaze, he explained with some smugness, "I had old Uthgar customize this one for me. I keep the key to this box on my person, and using it will trigger a poison needle trap. In order to get in, you have to pick the real lock." He inserted a lockpick into the hole of a missing screw and gave it an expert twist, popping a false panel off the back of the box and revealing another, smaller keyhole.

"There's no key for this one," Heraldin said as he set to work. "It has to be picked."

Gaist rolled his eyes.

"No interruptions," Heraldin hissed, working the picks with the minute precision of a surgeon operating on a pixie. "I must concentrate!"

For over a minute the only sound was the tapping and clicking of the bard's lockpicks dancing with the tumblers. When the final, sonorous click rang out, the top of the box popped up. Heraldin lifted it to reveal several pots of pigments and unguents, a selection of brushes, a folio of documents, three full coin purses, a small mirror, and an unsettling mass of hair.

"I'll miss being Heraldin Strummons," said the bard, rifling through the papers. "It was nice to be myself for a while."

Gaist said nothing.

"But you need to read the signals," said the bard. "See which way the gutters are flowing, and get out before it all goes down the drain." He selected a booklet from the set of papers, a set of NPC documents for a Daellish visitor.

The doppelganger shrugged.

"No, don't try to talk me out of this."

Gaist gave him a wry stare.

"You know what I mean. At this point, there are two possibilities." The bard propped his mirror against the side of the small chest. "First, Gorm could be right: the king may be up to something dastardly, he's sending us directly into a trap, and this quest is just a well-documented excuse for our deaths. Or the second possibility is that there really is a dragon down there, Johan's sending us to fight it, and we're dead anyway."

Heraldin pulled a false beard and matching mustache from the gray and black mass of hair, dislodging a couple of eyebrows as he did so. "Either way, things are getting... epic." The bard's mouth wrinkled at the taste of the word.

Gaist furrowed his brow.

"No, I like to sing epics," Heraldin corrected. "I like to tell other people about them over a mug of beer. But I don't want to live in one. One minute it's all business as usual, and the next the world has gone upside down because of fighting gods or demon lords or ancient prophecies. Few survive that sort of thing, and some that do envy the dead."

He dabbed some glue from a small pot onto his cheeks, then set about rearranging his face. "Mark my words, we have no idea how this is going to go, except that it's much, much worse than whatever you're thinking."

Gaist leaned against the wall and watched the bard begin to metamorphose into a Daellish merchant. Mid-transformation, Heraldin turned to the weaponsmaster, causing half of the false mustache to sway disconcertingly from his face. "What?" he demanded.

Gaist was as still and solid and blank as the wall he leaned on.

"No, what?" snapped the bard. "If you're going to nonverbally communicate something, just nonverbally communicate it!"

The weaponsmaster stared back at him.

"Well, it's not so easy for most of us," Heraldin grumbled, looking back at his reflection. "And I don't need to join this quest! I don't need to help. The city will be fine without me. Or not. It doesn't..." Heraldin shook his head. "Well, it matters, but why does it fall on us? This is between the king and Gorm, but you and I could leave! We could—"

Gaist remained silent, but his sudden scowl cut Heraldin off as effectively as the loudest shout. The bard fell silent, but only for a moment.

"Haven't we done enough?" he asked, looking at a reflection trapped halfway between his own face and a new one. "We spent years in the wilderness. We killed a liche. We drove back the undead. We helped the Guz'Varda, and the rest of the Shadowkin, and then saved the city. When is our debt paid? When can we just rest? When can we enjoy what we've earned?"

A huge hand landed on his shoulder. He looked at Gaist and saw his own weariness reflected in the weaponsmaster's eyes. But he could also see embers of purpose and resolve burning there, reminding Heraldin of a fire that he had briefly felt in his better moments. And now that he saw it, the bard found that the same embers still smoldered somewhere within him despite his best efforts to extinguish them. To his own despair, he realized that he had developed a conscience over the course of his adventures. And now that Gaist had given his fledgling moral center a voice, of a sort, Heraldin was sure it would allow him no joy or rest until it was satisfied.

His false mustache fluttered in a long sigh. "I know," he said. "I wish I didn't, but I know."

The faintest hint of a smile played beneath Gaist's crimson scarf as the bard peeled off the false facial hair and carefully repacked his disguise.

"Come on," Heraldin told the weaponsmaster, sliding the box back into the cubby. "Gorm told us what comes next. Let's go and get the right thing over with."

Gaist shifted subtly; not enough to block the door, but enough to indicate the door would be blocked if the bard kept walking.

"What now?"

The weaponsmaster raised an eyebrow.

"Fine!" said Heraldin. He pulled the box back out and set about replacing the false documents and the purse of coins. "I wasn't going to use them, you know. I just... I would have felt better with a little insurance on hand. Old habits die hard."

Kaitha stared at the vial of golden liquid on her dining room table.

The salve inside the bottle sang to her. It whispered of delights that she had once known, hinted at joy that had slipped away, promised to reveal secrets that she had forgotten.

Chief among those lost secrets was how the bottle had arrived in her apartment. Kaitha could not recall buying the salve. She was sure she had been shopping for an entirely different purpose—though she couldn't recall what—and had been surprised to find the potion in her bag upon returning to her apartment. But now it was there, smoldering in the lamplight, waiting to provide sweet, sleepy warmth to anyone who needed it.

A part of Kaitha knew these tricks, these clever little ruses she set up to absolve herself and place the guilt for her transgressions firmly with circumstance. Part of her screamed that she had worked so hard to come this far, and she couldn't give in now. It willed her to stand, to walk across the room yet again, to flee from the apartment and the infernal bottle that filled it.

But she paused at the door, her hand on the handle without turning it. How far had she come, really, the other side of her asked. How many days of emptiness had she endured just for the right to endure another one? How many priests and therapists and support groups had heard her struggles and passed them along? How many times had she searched for the only one who made it different, calling to someone who would never reply? What did it accomplish? Why not take the happiness the bottle offered her if it was the only bit she could find?

She walked back to the table and froze with her hand on the bottle. Gorm had warned her that Johan would strike soon, that the whole party would need to assemble as soon as the king revealed his scheme. The weight of responsibility pressed her hand to the table, and she set the bottle down.

The Elf shook her head. She needed to leave.

She almost made it to the door before her doubts came rushing back with the desperate intensity of a carnival barker about to lose a fare. Why bother? What could she and Gorm really change? What could Johan actually take away from her when her life was this empty?

He could take a lot more away from other people, she reminded herself as she set her hand on the door. Others were depending on her.

Others who would be gone soon. The party would wither and perish as all mortals do, and the memories of them as well, replaced by different mortals with new concerns, while she—

"No!" Kaitha growled. "Impermanence is not insignificance!" She moved to open the door handle, and found that she wasn't grasping it anymore. The bottle was in her hand, and she was back at the table. She dropped it like it was made of fire and backed toward the door.

Though, there wasn't really a good reason to be scared of it. She had functioned just fine for years using salve, hadn't she? Yes, she'd had some minor problems when she was cut off, but there was little chance of that now that she was back on her game.

"Minor problems?" she laughed, incredulous at herself. She'd nearly died out of desperation for the stuff! She would be gone if it weren't for—

The memory of Thane drew her out of her inner debate and pulled her gaze to the window. She couldn't see past the glow of the city, warm and golden as a campfire's circle, but she sensed a tugging from the darkness beyond the city lights, a call just beyond hearing, a longing for something forgotten.

Kaitha lost track of how long she stood suspended between the window, the door, and the bottle on the table, trapped like a boat caught in crossing eddies. She could have stayed rooted to the spot and wrestling with her own thoughts all night if the bannerman hadn't knocked at the door to her apartment.

She wore the heraldry of the royal chapter, with the crested hat that marked her as a courier. The bannerman greeted the ranger by name without warmth or malice, deposited a gilt envelope in the Elf's hand, and left with a curt bow. The door thudded shut again as Kaitha carried the message back into her apartment.

Kaitha opened the envelope and read it.

She sat down and read it again.

She stood up once more. Gorm would want to talk about this before they spoke to the king, and there wasn't much time. "I can make it one more day," she told herself as she pulled on her cloak.

She paused by the table on her way out. The vial of salve was still there. It could just as easily be in her rucksack, and nobody would know. She picked up the bottle.

"I have to make it one more day," she snarled. With a snort she strode to the window, wrenched the glass open, and hurled the bottle out into the air above the street. The ranger grinned in triumph at the tinkle of shattering glass from below, though her smile faded when some unfortunate passerby screamed a curse immediately after.

"One more day," she repeated, shutting the window. Then she grabbed her rucksack and bow, checked her gear, and burst out her front door.

The sudden bang startled Jynn so thoroughly that he nearly dropped the nornstone wand. He juggled the device as a storm of Ruskan curses thundered from the apartment next door. "You magic my apartment!" Mrs. Ur'Kretchen shrieked through the wall. "You magic my apartment and scare cat! Why you hate cat? Horrible wizards!"

Jynn took a deep breath and hollered back, "I feel nothing for your cat, Mrs. Ur'Kretchen!" This was not entirely true; Jynn held a good amount of pity for the cat, considering the poor beast was forced to share a tiny apartment with an ancient swamp hag. Yet he thought better of saying as much; given that the ancient harridan nearly hammered through the wall at imaginary provocations, he didn't want to know what she'd resort to if he actually insulted her.

The thunderous assault subsided, leaving Jynn to turn his attention back to the wand. He had assigned several students the task of repairing the defunct device, and after several weeks of their efforts, he was pleased to see that the young omnimancers hadn't managed to destroy it.

The archmage ran his hands over the gemstone runes inlayed in the ebony wand. The sigils were intact, as was the sorcerous projection matrix woven around them. The correct spells were arrayed through the prophetic latticework. As far as Jynn could see, it should have been a simple weave to get the wand to accurately measure the latent fate in the immediate area. Yet any channeling produced nothing but a brief flash from the wand and shouts from the neighbor.

He drummed his skeletal fingers on the worktable. The matter of the olives and the serendipitous convergence of his own purposes with Gorm and Heraldin's had initially convinced the wizard that the city was a hotbed of manifest destiny, yet now he wasn't so sure. In the subsequent weeks, he'd taken so many walks by the royal archivist's offices that Patches had begun to groan whenever the wizard reached for the leash, yet all he had to show for his efforts was a new set of blisters on his calloused feet. Jynn wondered if the coincidences surrounding his meeting with the Dwarf and bard were just run-of-the-mill happenstance, rather than the early drops of a coalescing destiny. The only way to know was to measure the latent fate around the city, and the only way to measure latent fate in a given area was through the use of a nornstone device.

Jynn flexed his fingers, ready to channel more magic into the wand, but reconsidered at the sounds of heavy footsteps and a yowling cat next door. It has been said that the definition of insanity is trying the same approach repeatedly and expecting different results, but the archmage felt that a more immediately relevant definition of insanity was howling like a banshee and trying to knock a wall down with a broom handle whenever the neighbors made a sound. With that in mind he stood up, wrapped the wand carefully in an old cloak, and headed to his own chambers, a modest apartment down on the third floor.

Patches wilted and stared fixedly at the wall as Jynn fetched his heavy cloak and boots. "No, boy. You don't need to come this time," Jynn told the dog. Patches' tail thumped on the floor a couple of times at the reprieve, but he kept averting his eyes until Jynn left the apartment.

The Order of Twilight was too small and ill-funded to have amenities like dedicated training chambers or well stocked laboratories or even a tower that wasn't also inhabited by several elderly and perhaps infernal tenants. A Device Support Department was far out of the realm of budgetary possibility. Yet strolling a few streets Wallward and up a tier brought him to the Tower of the Sun within the hour. The ivory spire stood wreathed in golden filigree and crowned with a statue of Musana. The goddess of light held an orb that burned with sorcerous flame and was locked in a stare down with the silver statue of Alluna that topped the Tower of the Moon across the street. Omnimancers were no more welcome in the Order of the Sun's national headquarters than noctomancers, but the Order of Twilight's arrangement with the Academy of Mages gave Jynn and his staff access through the service entrance to the basement.

The musty cellars beneath Musana's glimmering perch housed the Order of the Sun's Device Support Department. Portly solamancers, acne-encrusted apprentices, and a couple of theological support friars in bright yellow robes moved laconically amidst tables laden with enchanted objects. Huge tomes with titles like *Liber Usus* and *How to Handle Your Rod* lay scattered amongst the wands and amulets, as well as a conspicuous army of mugs half-filled with cold coffee.

The Human behind the front desk could have been mistaken for an Ogre, were it not for the solamancer's robes he wore and the care with which his handlebar mustache had been waxed into perfect shape. The huge man hunched over a sputtering sprite stone, weaving precise threads of fire and light into it with hands like bear paws. He wore a wooden name tag engraved with a small sun and lettering that said "Hello! My Name is Jesh Watters." Mr. Watters apparently felt this accessory satisfied any social obligations he had to the customer, as he did not so much as look up from his work when Jynn approached the desk.

"Hello, I'd like to—" the archmage began.

"Ticket," said the attending wizard absently, sliding a slip of paper across the desk.

"Of course. Where are my manners?" Jynn muttered. He took a pencil stub from a small tin cup and filled out his personal information, a brief summary of his challenges with the wand, and checked the box that indicated the job should commence with urgency.

Mr. Watters frowned down at the ticket. "That's an omnimancer relic."

"Yes."

"I'll have to get a noctomancer in here to work on it with us." The massive wizard didn't look up from the slip of paper.

"Yes."

Watters scowled at the paper. It took a certain sort to devote all their time and energy to the maintenance of magical devices, and that sort somehow managed to maintain a reputation for poor interpersonal skills amongst the Academy of Mages—an institution best known for settling petty grudges with reality-warping blasts of sorcery. Jynn suspected the attendant taking his ticket had been selected to man the front desk for his ability to form complete sentences that directly related to the current conversation.

"It'll need a week," said the solamancer.

"I thought service on a wand takes two days."

"We're getting a lot of stuff like this in." The attendant affixed the completed ticket to the wand with a ball of wax and set it on the counter behind him. "And so are the noctomancers. There's a queue."

"A lot of what stuff?" asked Jynn.

"Omnimancer relics," said the wizard, shuffling various enchanted devices around the shelf. "Nornstones. Theological support monk tools. That sort of thing."

"Ah." This marked the usual spot in a conversation to thank the attendant, and to receive a wish of a good day in reply. Yet the archmage was lost in a sudden flurry of thoughts, and the attendant's attention had never really been on the customer, so the exchange sputtered and died like a campfire deprived of logs.

The omnimancer's brow furrowed as he made his way up the stairs. Simultaneously malfunctioning nornstones across the city could have been a coincidence, of course, but the coinciding failure of so many devices used to measure coincidences seemed too... coincidental to ignore. The breakdowns themselves might have been an indicator of heightened levels of latent—

"Jynn?"

The archmage looked up from his pondering and found himself staring into a familiar set of dark eyes. "Oh! Laruna! What are you doing here?" he blurted.

The solamancer glanced around at the conspicuous number of mages in bright orange, yellow, and red robes moving in and out of the Tower of the Sun's main gate. "Taking a class." She shrugged, and a slight blush bloomed in her cheeks. "But what about you?"

"I... uh..." Jynn glanced about, wishing he'd brought Patches along, then realized that the truth could be framed in a fairly innocuous manner provided he didn't ramble on about his father's research. "I dropped off a device for repair."

"Another magical accident?" Laruna asked.

"Not this time," said Jynn. "My nornstone wand is acting up."

"Oh?" She flashed her teeth in an amused smile. "Working with latent fate? You must be trying your hand at divination."

"Something like that," said Jynn. "I have noticed an increase in the amount of coincidental or serendipitous events recently."

"We do seem to be running into each other a lot."

"Ah, yes. Ahaha. But I'm more interested in... well, it just seems that lately events have been funneling together. Specific needs suddenly being met at exactly the right moment, circumstances lining up in just such a way, funneling people toward something... that sort of thing."

"What other—?" Laruna began, but she was cut off by a red-faced bannerman wearing a courier's feathered cap.

"Laruna Trullon! And Jynn Ur'Mayan?" he boomed. "Must be my lucky day! I thought I'd be up and down the halls of at least two mage's towers finding you, and here you are right on the sidewalk, havin' a chat! Guess this means I can give you both your messages at once."

The mages shared a wary look as they accepted two sealed scrolls from the courier. "What is this about?" asked Jynn.

"The biggest quest of the age," said Gorm Ingerson, his beard shining like copper in the lantern's light. "Slayin' the Dragon of Wynspar."

Burt waved his cigar at the Dwarf. "You said the dragon was the biggest ruse in history."

"Which makes this the most obvious trap in history," Heraldin added.

The party nodded in agreement. Six Heroes of Destiny and one irate Kobold sat around a small table in the dim taproom of Moira's Tavern. Six scrolls of royal mandate and one ashtray sat in front of them.

"And ye know what that means," said Gorm.

"This could be the opportunity we've been waiting for," said Laruna with a grin.

"You've been waiting for him to send you into a trap?" said Burt.

"We been waiting for the right moment to talk about the dragon," said Gorm. "Now he's back with no evidence of the dragon, and we can make a case against him directly to Andarun's nobility and guildmasters and business leaders."

Burt exhaled a long, silver-blue stream of smoke. "S'probably exactly what he wants," he said.

The heroes' smiles faded a little. Laruna shook her head with the sort of perplexed smirk one might reserve for a child asking pointed questions as to the whereabouts of royal undergarments. "Well, no, he wouldn't want us exposing this on stage. You can't let that sort of accusation go unanswered, and all of the evidence is on our side."

"Well, sure, but what's to stop him from answering with an accusation of his own?" asked Burt. "Maybe say you faked all of it."

"Maybe it gets messy on stage," Gorm conceded. "But at the end of the day, a full investigation will have to be opened, and the facts are on our side."

Jynn grimaced. "That's seldom enough," he said, nodding to Burt. "Consider who will appoint the investigators."

"I see what you're saying," said Kaitha. "But there are certain norms that govern the nobility. They have to appoint impartial lawyers."

"The guy who lit his own subjects on fire and blamed a made-up dragon to jack up the hoard's market valuation is gonna follow norms and ethics." The Kobold took another drag of his cigarette and chuckled mirthlessly at some hidden joke. "Yeah, all right. Thing is, Lightlings have been playing at decency for as long as Slaughs have liked slime, and all that time they've been murdering and pillaging our people and each other every way you turn. No matter how firm an ethos is, someone will always find a way to bend or shift it until there's a good angle for them.

People don't want to be ethical. They want to believe they're ethical, and there's a lot of skeletons in the gap between those two."

"Can't say you're wrong, but what else can Johan do?" asked Gorm.

"Blame it all on you," said the Kobold. "Say you fabricated the evidence in a plot."

"We got proof that he an' his temple were behind the scheme to kill Freedlanders."

Burt waved the idea away with his cigarette, sending trails of smoke zigzagging lazily into the air. "Proof is no better than a lie if people don't want to believe it. And even if they were willing to accept the Golden King as a murderer, you're making them accept that there's no dragon too."

"And that the dragon's hoard they've been investing in is worthless." Kaitha sucked in a deep breath through her teeth. "How many billions of giltin are invested in the Dragon of Wynspar's hoard?"

"Enough to collapse the whole economy," said Laruna.

"Or they can believe your shiny king," said Burt. "The people love him. The temples see him as one of their own. The Wall is having its best run in years. And we're going to march in and say we have a few documents that show it's all a lie?"

"Such things are hard for people to believe, especially if they're true," Heraldin said.

Gaist nodded.

"Now you're seein' it," said Burt. "All Johan has to do is offer a different story that people like better."

"So they can find a new villain elsewhere," said Jynn softly. "Like the six standing before him on stage."

A thought struck Gorm. "It's one of them empirical offenses."

The others gave him a confused look. "A what?" asked Heraldin.

"Ye know. The bit from thrones—a big obvious line of attack with a clever one behind it."

"The Imperial Offense?"

"That's the one. We saw the big attack, the fake quest into the dungeon. But I'm bettin' that one's the ruse, and Johan wants us to try to dodge out of it by showin' what evidence we have." He squinted his eyes until they were thin slits, as though he could see the scenarios play out in front of his face if he just focused hard enough. "The king gets all of us on stage so everyone hears our accusation and we make it as big as we can. He denies it, and acts shocked it was us who attacked the Tandosians. Easy enough to clean out the facility in the Winter's Shade and make it look like it was a simple monastery or somethin'. Some loyal bannermen will be happy to declare there's no evidence of wrongdoin' by the Tandosians. Suddenly, we're vandals and cowards, and then we all get thrown in the Guild Enforcement Office's dungeon. And with the public turnin' against us, Johan can have us hanged or strangled in our beds without losin' face. And then he can have his fake dragons kill with impunity, but without us muckin' up his plans."

"That... makes sense," said Kaitha.

"The trap behind the trap." Heraldin nodded.

"Thank ye, Burt." Gorm nodded to his friend. "Ye've saved us again."

"What can I say? I've got a knack for reading people's motivations," said the Kobold.

"You're a savant at thinking like an evil bastard," said Heraldin.

"It's the company I keep," Burt shot back.

Kaitha ignored the Kobold and bard. "I'm not so sure we're saved," she said to Gorm. "It's good that we know what Johan plans to do, but whether or not we make our accusations, he can still bribe the bannermen and clean out the facility."

The Dwarf smirked. "Oi! Bard! Don't ye use the Imperial Offense in thrones all the time?"

"Long ago. It was my favorite tactic when I was young. But when you play against a skilled opponent, it doesn't work." Heraldin looked at Gaist askance. "Someone who knows the game well can counter it every time."

"And how do they counter it?" asked Gorm, eyes still locked with the ranger's.

"The key to defeating the Imperial Offense is not to fall for the ruse or try to cover your flank. If you play defensively, the game is already lost. But if you call the opponent's bluff and push straight... through..."

"Aye," said Gorm softly.

The bard's eyebrows made a sudden break for the safety of his hairline. "You madman," said Heraldin. "You can't mean…"

Kaitha shook her head. "Gorm…"

Gorm grinned and bared his teeth at the same time.

—CHAPTER 19—

"We accept the quest," said Gorm Ingerson.

"Pardon?" asked Johan the Mighty, staring down at the six heroes kneeling at the base of the throne's podium.

"We'll answer the call of duty and slay the Dragon of Wynspar," repeated the Dwarf.

The king rallied so smoothly that even Gorm almost believed Johan had a bit of trouble hearing. "Ah, yes! Ha haaa! Wonderful!" The king threw his arms out wide, and the assembled nobles, bannermen, and town criers took it as a cue for enthusiastic applause. Gorm watched the king bask in the adulation of the crowd, studying his face carefully. The Dwarf had to fight back a smile when the king's eyelid twitched.

"And so, you must have a plan to deal with the beast," said Johan, turning back to the party.

"Aye," said Gorm.

The king's smile faded for just a heartbeat. His eyes flicked into a sidelong glance with Weaver Ortson, whom Gorm noticed was looking unusually pale. "And what is the plan?" he prompted.

"Wouldn't want to give away all our trade secrets, Your Majesty," said Gorm.

"Right. Right."

"So, at Your Majesty's pleasure..." Gorm let the sentence trail off.

"Uh... there's nothing else to discuss, then?" asked Johan. "Nothing you'd like to share with everyone?"

Gorm shrugged and looked at the eager faces leaning in from the gallery. Many wore the hungry, malicious expressions of onlookers at a public execution. Someone had clearly promised them a spectacle more exciting than a ceremonial contract signing. Their collective anticipation was as sure a sign of a trap as a raised flagstone or an innocuous grid of holes on the walls of a corridor. If he gave Johan any excuse to take offense, the king could make a counter-accusation, and soon the whole kingdom would be discussing the dueling allegations. It would be Gorm's word against the king's, and given that the king's word was law, it was easy to see where that would go.

A classic Imperial Offense. And the only way out was straight through it.

"Ye can count on us, my king," he said, raising his axe in a carefully calibrated gesture of solemn bravado.

"We always get our foe," added Kaitha.

Johan's grin was frozen, but his eye twitched again. "And that's it?"

"I believe we're supposed to sign the contracts," said Jynn.

"Right! Right. Bring them forth! Ha haaa..." Johan punctuated the order with his trumpeting laugh, but it lacked its usual resonance, as though someone had shoved a sock down the instrument.

Guild clerks carried thick binders, writing implements, and small desks to the crimson carpet in front of the heroes. They moved with a rigid ceremony that appealed to Gorm's Dwarven sensibilities, though their colorful tights and frilly ruffs were even more offensive to the same part of his nature. They set up small desks in front of the heroes, then deposited a neat folio, inkwell, and quill on each one.

The contract's cover sheet was fine vellum covered in calligraphy, illuminated illustrations, and royal seals. The king had already signed the order, and the details of the quest were exactly as expected. They were to start their expedition within the week, the king would require proof of the dragon's death, and they were entitled to a ten thousand giltin fee plus one one-hundredth of the dragon's hoard. Even that small fraction was estimated to have a lot of zeroes at the end. The problem, Gorm suspected, was that the sum would be all zeroes at the beginning as well.

"Everything look in order?" asked Johan. "Terms are good?"

"A kingly sum." Gorm smiled brightly and flipped the page.

The rest of the pages were set in the neat type of a Gnomish printing press, occasionally interrupted by neat script filling in an intentional blank. Gorm's grin grew as he glanced over the document; it was the guild's standard contract, the same one a rank one hero might get when asked to clear rats from an inn's basement. The mages had worried that Johan could sneak in aggressive nondisclosure clauses or harsher penalties for substandard performance, but the king hadn't bothered to alter the terms at all. These were documents that were never meant to be signed.

"So, nothing to discuss then?" The desperation was audible in Johan's voice now, even to the crowd of onlookers. Sibilant whispers rippled through the audience, and Gorm could almost hear the mob's focus shifting from himself to the king, like a school of piranha aligning on an explorer wading into the river.

"Everythin' looks straightforward to me," said Gorm truthfully. He took the quill from the gilded inkpot and scrawled his ceremonial signature on the cover sheet. His eyes met the king's as the other heroes signed their copies, and Gorm couldn't help but grin at the sweat beading on Johan's brow. They both knew what was down in the depths of Mount Wynspar's dungeon.

The truth.

It has been said that a lie can make its way around the world before the truth gets its horse saddled. To be sure, when complicated facts or counterintuitive principles are involved, lies and rumors get a head start. Yet it shouldn't be ignored that a simple truth can move as fast or faster than a convoluted lie. It's also pertinent to note that the proverb is often cited by people unhappy with the current state of public opinion, as it may be true that false allegations about a noble's infidelity will spread like wildfire, but—to the distress of many nobles—so will true allegations. The idea that lies are more rapid or mobile is often uttered in the hopes that people will begin to accept a story's pervasiveness as evidence of its untruthfulness, which just goes to show that a clever idiom can walk through many gates where facts and rational arguments will be detained, questioned, and hung in the morning.

Any town crier in the Freedlands knows that what really propels a story, true or not, is that spark of human interest, that *il'ne se la*, that potent alchemy of drama and passion and scandal that drives deep into the brain and grabs the mind's eye with both fists.

Today's story, reflected Heren Hillborn, had it all. Mighty heroes. A massive monster. A desperate plea from a king who failed to slay the beast. And obscene sums of gold that many, many people were entitled to a share of. Abundant variables and angles to speculate on and argue about.

Heren took a deep breath of crisp mountain air and smiled. It was going to be a good day.

She settled on a promising corner on the upper slopes of the city. There was a stone wall to lean against, a steady flow of hillward folk headed into Mistkeep's center for market day, and no other town crier in earshot. She took a couple of deep breaths to limber up her lungs, gave her bell a firm shake, and let her final exhalation grow into a full-on shout. "Heeaaah-EX-tra! Extra! Another party to face the Dragon of Wynspar! Monster that nearly slew King Johan to be tested again! Are your investments safe?"

A Tinderkin in opulent robes rolled her eyes as she passed, but Heren ignored her. more people were coming down the lane. Heren perched on the corner like a bear at a salmon run, and bellowed with just as much volume. "Learn why the fate of the Freedlands and your pension hang in the balance! Extra!"

A silver-haired Human in a blacksmith's robe sidled up to her. "When's all of this supposed to be done with?" he demanded.

"That's extra," Heren reiterated, jangling the coin pail she wore around her neck. "They're to set out within the week," she added when he deposited tuppence into the bucket.

"And this party's got a chance to succeed?" asked an old Halfling doubled over beneath a load of firewood.

"'Course not!" snorted the blacksmith. "King Johan nearly died on this mission."

"Ah, but this time—"

"Five reasons why the new party is doomed! Extra!" said Heren loudly.

There was a thoughtful silence as the wood gatherer and the blacksmith considered the offer.

"How much extra?" asked the wood gatherer.

"One shilling, or five pence if you'll listen to a special offer from the General Store."

The Halfling produced five copper coins and listened patiently as the town crier told her about the General Store's commitment to quality rope, hatchets, and stepladders. Heren gave her a blue, wooden chit worth five pence off her next purchase, and a one-shilling commission to Heren if she used it. She gave another chit to the blacksmith, and a third to the round woman who had joined them before launching into her list.

"The first and least reason," began the town crier, "is that dragons are the most deadly monster the Heroes' Guild has ever categorized. A dragon is big enough to eat a man in one bite, has scales like thick armor, and can fly faster than any horse. But worst is their fire. Experts at the Zoological Society of Monchester say that dragonfire is a flame so pure it can burn anything outside of a dragon. Legends tell us that the Weeping Rocks of Eastern Daellan were a mountain until the dread dragon Pyritax melted them with a gout of his flame."

"See?" said the blacksmith.

"Heroes' got potions for dealin' with fires," said the wood gatherer with the deep-seated confidence of the truly ignorant. A couple of more recent onlookers nodded in agreement, though most of the small crowd gathering around the town crier were clearly on the blacksmith's side.

Heren handed out General Store chits to each newcomer without skipping a beat, as though her hands and head were being operated by different people. "The second reason is that Johan the Mighty and the Golden Dawn failed to defeat the monster. King Johan is arguably the most fearsome hero on Arth, and even he couldn't defeat the dragon."

"See?" said the triumphant blacksmith. "That ought to be the end of it. If Johan can't do it, none can."

"He couldn't kill the liche," said the wood gatherer.

"He killed Detarr Ur'Mayan the first time," snorted the blacksmith. "'Sides, a dragon's different, innit? You heard the girl; a dragon can eat your armor in one bite, and fly better than your horse can."

"Um, my horse can't fly," offered an onlooker. Heren reflexively flipped him a blue chit.

"Flies better than even them winged horses," corrected the blacksmith. "And its fire will toast any hero before they get close enough to shoot an arrow."

"Not if they got a potion," insisted the wood gatherer.

Heren quickly moved to cut them off; a little debate was good for business, but you had to stop the comments before things got out of hand. "The third reason the heroes are doomed," she said loudly, "is that a third of their party hasn't been adventuring in almost a year. Among the heroes to face the dragon, only Kaitha of House Tyrieth, solamancer Laruna Trullon, and Gaist the weaponsmaster have consistently quested. Gorm Ingerson has only run one job, and—"

Heren would have noted that the party bard had not worked in a year, but at that moment the stone wall she was leaning against exploded outward in a shower of shale and dust. A hulking form stepped into the street, small stones dripping from its gray fur. Two crimson eyes locked with Heren's, and a voice like an avalanche roared at her. Amid the screams of the fleeing townsfolk and the pounding of her own heart, it took Heren a moment to realize it was shouting words.

"Did you say Kaitha?" bellowed the Troll again.

Heren found that, despite her profession and training, her mouth was no longer forming syllables. Her lips flapped up and down soundlessly, and her knees buckled under even that strain.

The Troll held up a pair of gnarled hands and leaned in so close she could feel its hot breath. "No! No. Look, you're having a physiological reaction. Perfectly normal! Just breathe. Relax!" To emphasize the need for calm, it flashed a set of teeth like a Goblin armory at her.

Heren sobbed.

"Now, listen. Stay calm," said the Troll with the slow deliberateness of someone swaying on the edge of panic. "Did you say Kaitha of House Tyrieth is going to fight a dragon?"

The now-literal town crier managed to nod as she wiped her eyes.

"All right. Stay calm. Just breathe," said the Troll slowly, though it wasn't entirely clear he was talking to Heren. "And... and you think she and her party might not... they all might... not make it?"

The desperate timbre of the question triggered an instinct seared into the grain of Heren's entrepreneurial soul. Slowly, automatically, she extended a trembling hand clutching a small blue chit worth five pence off the Troll's next purchase at the General Store.

The Troll stared at the chit.

Heren followed its gaze.

Their eyes met again. The rest of Heren's instincts, the elder senses used to keep primitive Man alive amid the primordial monsters and spirits of old, kicked back in, and she lowered the chit slowly and squeaked an answer.

"What?" said the Troll.

"They say it's certain death!" squealed the town crier, squeezing her eyes shut.

The Troll's pupils dilated, as though focusing on something far away. "Certain... death," he repeated in a tone so flat, so level, that for a moment Heren thought whatever panic had propelled him through the stone wall had ended.

She was wrong.

"It's a complete meltdown," said Feista Hrurk. She pointed to a vellum chart next to her. It looked like someone had attempted to draw a line up and to the right, but then decided to scribble in half of the parchment instead. "It's chaos. The Wall panics one moment and it's manic the next. Shares of the Dragon of Wynspar spike and drop on any rumor. If Gorm Ingerson so much as sneezes, half a billion giltin appears or evaporates."

Asherzu Guz'Varda steepled her fingers as she considered the graph. Around her, Warg's board wore various shades of concern and avarice. "And have the fundamentals changed?" she asked.

"Not that I can see," Feista said. "The dragon hasn't been on a raid or slain any heroes since the Golden Dawn, so its hoard can't be any more or less valuable than the equipment Johan's party carried. The only change is in the trader's heads."

"And so it can be used against them!" said Izek. The Goblin wore an eager grin. "Their cowardice weighs them down! Now is the time to strike with cunning trades!"

Asherzu looked doubtful. "I think the advantage is to not make trades," she said. "We were wise to be rid of our shares of the dragon's hoard."

"When the enemy is panicked, you strike!" insisted Izek.

"Not when they are panicking because their war barge is sinking," countered Pogrit. "That is the time to sit back and watch them founder."

Izek shook his head. "But surely there is some device we can use to our advantage here. Some derivative fund or Heroes' Guild procedure that can be leveraged?"

"I am proud of our traders," Asherzu said. "They have grown swift and cunning in their time roaming the Wall. But the Lightlings have many more years of experience than us, and their derivatives are often traps laid for the unwary. We lack the skill to exploit this opportunity."

"What if the dragon has much gold?" said Freggi. "Not as much as the inflated price of its hoard implies, but still much. Even if other funds sink, will not their institutions get a sudden infusion of... uh, how do the Lightlings say *skib'dibarg*? Molten gold?"

"Liquid assets," corrected Feista.

"Yes, that," said the Goblin matriarch.

"Can we afford to miss out on being as molten as the other banks?" asked Izek.

"Liquid," said Feista.

"Our balance sheet is wet enough, since we divested from the dragon's hoard," said Guglug.

Feista rubbed her forehead. "Just the one word. Liquid."

"We had to sell shares in every financial institution and reinvest directly in commodities and non-combat sectors," continued the Slaugh.

"And the timing was right," said Asherzu. "Our stock price touches the sky, and our cash reserves are as full as the sea. All of our foes envy our stability and untainted balance sheets."

"But, Great Lady, there is a risk to inaction," insisted Izek.

"There is wisdom in your words, Izek of the Li'Balgar. But there is a greater risk in holding shares of the dragon, beyond that which Feista

Hrurk has already told us." She looked at Burt. "Our sources do not think that Gorm Ingerson's party will find a dragon at all."

The Kobold pulled a drag from a ratty cigar. "They're betting on it. And if they're right... well, no dragon, no treasure."

The other Shadowkin exchanged worried looks.

"I have heard such a rumor on the Wall," said Pogrit. "Yet none give it much thought."

"Nor will they," said Asherzu. "As long as everyone believes the dragon is wealthy beyond measure, they are rich. If everyone was to say there is no dragon, their fortunes would be as dust in the wind. The cautious among them will try to quietly divest of the dragon's hoard, and those who cannot accept the possibility will buy the stock up, though I cannot say if it is because they believe in the hoard's value or if they wish their illusion to live a little longer. The indecisive will do both, at different times."

She gestured to Feista's chart. "And it will be, as was said, a complete meltdown. Chaos."

The board stared at the jagged lines of the graph, which looked like the outline of a forest fire, and imagined the turmoil and panic behind it.

Another thought, tired of patiently waiting in the queue, struck Feista. "Wait," she said, shaking her head. "If Gorm Ingerson's party doesn't think there's a dragon, what are they doing down there?"

"Survival is priority number one," said Kaitha. "And frankly, it's going to take everything we've got."

The Elf paced in front of a large map nailed to the oak wall. It profiled Mount Wynspar, with the tiers of the city running up its left side and a maze of corridors and ancient chambers running through it like the innards of some bizarre shellfish laid bare on a dissection table. Toward the city, the drawing was a map with specific rooms and caverns noted, but closer to the heart of the mountain, the map trailed into vague outlines around particular regions and woodcuts of monsters, traps, and nightmarish cavescapes. "There are no safe zones in Mount Wynspar.

No shops of traveling merchants, and nobody to come if we need help. If we get caught in a bad situation, if we lose focus for just one moment, someone will die."

The other heroes nodded grimly, glaring at the dungeon map as though it was covered in offensive graffiti.

"Successful parties follow five rules for survival," continued the Elf. "First, be prepared. Bring the right gear, check and make sure it's in the right place, and always be ready to fight or flee. Preparation is everything."

"That's why we're here." Gorm swept out an arm to encompass the room. The sales consultation room at Creative Destruction's main shop had several fine chairs arrayed around the map, two reinforced podiums for demonstrations, and shelves filled with every sort of adventuring gear, from silksteel rope to explosive vials. "To get geared up!"

"Hear, hear!" said Boomer from the back. A tattooed Scribkin built like an Orc, Boomer was half of the duo that ran Creative Destruction Incorporated, Andarun's most prestigious and innovative adventuring consumables company. His co-founder and partner, Buster, was a scaled Gremlin in a white coat that smiled and quietly raised a fist in the air.

"I thought we were here so we could use their map," murmured Heraldin.

"That too," Gorm whispered out of the side of his mouth.

"The second rule," Kaitha continued loudly, "is don't split the party. Stay together as much as possible, in the most literal way. Third, keep moving, but don't rush. Dawdle and the big dungeon predators will come. Get reckless and we risk falling into traps. We camp light and quickly. We keep marching when we're up. Fourth, fight smart. We'll be in enclosed spaces with hostile, unfamiliar terrain. No brash moves." She leveled a glare at Heraldin, then shifted her steely gaze to Laruna. "And no fireballs! Nothing explosive at all."

The solamancer rolled her eyes and gave a begrudging nod.

"And fifth..." Kaitha's bravado and shoulders dropped in one long sigh. "Fifth is that we finish the job, whatever happens. If I fall, mourn me when the quest is done. If you fall, I will do the same. But if we let grief or pain or rage cloud our judgment for even a moment, it can mean another of us dies. Or all of us. We all know the risks. We all know what's at stake if we fail. So no matter what, we keep moving. We take the next step. We finish the job."

A solemn silence filled the salesroom for a moment.

"Aye," said Gorm, leaning back in his seat. "No matter what, we see this through to the end."

"To the end," said Laruna, raising a fist.

"No matter what," said Jynn.

Gaist nodded.

"Just make sure they only say good things about me in my ballad," said Heraldin.

"Gonna be more of a jingle, then," said Gorm.

"If we stick to these rules and follow the plan," Kaitha said, "we've got a shot at finding the truth, facing whatever's down there, and making it home. If we don't, we'll be lucky to have any bard mention us."

"The principles seem sensible, but what is the actual plan?" asked Jynn.

Kaitha pointed to the edge of the map closest to the city. "After we enter the Dungeon Gate, we'll be in the Lower City. Standard subterranean ruins, and it shouldn't be too dense as the Golden Dawn cleared them out a couple of weeks back. Expect Dire Rats, your basic slimes and oozes, scargs, and bandits."

"What about... uh..." Laruna turned to Buster. "What's the polite thing to call Shadowkin who may rob or kill you?"

"What? Oh, I wouldn't worry about addressing anyone who's trying to kill you," said the Gremlin, looking up from a clipboard.

"She means, what should she call 'em now?" said Boomer.

"That makes more sense, I suppose." The Gremlin turned back to the solamancer and adjusted his spectacles. "I'd say 'bandits' covers it."

"Right, but how do I distinguish Orc and Goblin bandits from, uh... other bandits?" The mage's question wilted near the end, and she wore the expression of a rafter looking down the river at an ominously roaring cloud of mist.

"How do you distinguish Elf and Halfling bandits?" asked Buster.

Kaitha came to the mage's rescue. "Expect a diverse variety of bandits," she said firmly.

Laruna shot an apologetic wince to the Gremlin. Buster waved the offense away.

"We'll head through the northern passages instead of downward, so we can skip the sewers, the Reeking Deep, and the Fungal Passages entirely," the Elf continued, tracing a horizontal line from beneath the Fourth Tier to just underneath the Seventh. "If it's still clear after the Golden Dawn, that should bring us to the Low Way within the first day. If foes have crept back in and started rearming traps, could be up to two days.

"The Low Way will take us on a steep descent, and when we're down far enough we'll hit the Necropolish, and that's a labyrinth." The ranger drew a line down a straight corridor into a maze of thin passages positioned roughly beneath the Ninth Tier to the area below the Pinnacle. The area was decorated with woodcuts of tentacled monsters and imposing subterranean buildings.

"We need to focus on pressing northward through the Necropolish, and—"

"Excuse me, but are you saying 'Necropolish'?" asked Jynn.

The Elf paused. "Yeah, the Necropolish."

"I believe it's pronounced—"

"Technically, it's Stennish Site Nineteen, the Suspected Necropolis, Druidic Site, or Temple City," Kaitha interrupted loudly. "It's a group of underground buildings that nobody can define, but it's got similarities to a lot of temples and everybody who lived there is dead. It's like a necropolis. It's the Necropolish."

"How clever," said Jynn, though his face said the opposite.

Gorm shivered despite his heavy cloak. "Only been there once, and years ago, but I can still remember all the creepy broken statues and huge carvings."

"The important point is that it's deadly." Kaitha pointed to the illustrations around the region. "There are traps. There are monsters that haven't been categorized yet, dark things that crawl up from the Underheart. There are high pathways over chasms you can't see the bottom of, but if you fall, pray the drop kills you because the gods alone know what kind of horrors are down there. Most of the heroes that go questing in the Necropolish never return. And those of us who have returned... well, I haven't talked to anyone who didn't lose a party member along the way."

"Me either," sighed Gorm.

"And outside of Johan, nobody has ever claimed to see the other side of it," said Kaitha, sweeping her hand to the blank heart of the dungeon. "Beyond the Necropolish is the Black Fathoms, and somewhere within that darkness is where the dragon is supposed to lie." Her finger came to rest on a large woodcut of the sleeping wyrm. "But nobody can say where, or how deep."

Heraldin traced the air with his fingers, lining up some basic geometry. "Wouldn't it make more sense to climb up the mountain, find a cavern, and make our way down? We wouldn't have to be much higher than the Pinnacle before we'd pass the Necropolish."

Kaitha pointed at the blank area at the top of the map, just inside Andarun's Pinnacle. "If we were to try to make our way through unmapped stone, we'd as likely find a dead end as a straight drop all the way to the Underheart. The slopes are riddled with unmapped passages, and outside of the city the mountain is riddled with gnurgs, Frost Reavers, Snow Drakes, Dire Goats, and worse. Guild heroes have been trying to map the upper entrances for decades, and they rarely come back. It's far too risky to take an unknown route."

"Besides, Johan may have cleared a path for us," Laruna added. "If we can stick to his route, we can move much faster."

"True. Our best chance of a path to the mountain center is the Low Way," Kaitha affirmed. "And even then, it'll likely be a dangerous slog filled with deadly foes."

"And for that, you'll need gear!" Boomer rumbled from the back.

Gorm grinned. "That we will. Ready to show us the latest?"

"Thought you'd never ask," said Boomer, hopping up from the desk.

"Not without prompting, apparently," Gorm heard Buster mutter as the pair took Kaitha's place in the front of the room. "Have a little patience."

"I can't wait—we... there's no time!" Thane roared, running across the yard in a panic. "I need to pack! I need my things!"

"I know. I know." Duine Poldo spoke in his most soothing tones from the shelter of the house, but it was like trying to calm a passing thunderstorm. "Can you tell me why, though?"

"She's in—they're all in danger!" The Troll rumbled past, carrying his bandolier and several small satchels across the yard. A Wood Gnome clung to the fur on Thane's back, with another hanging from his feet, and another from hers, and so on, forming a chain of Domovoy that trailed after the Troll like a banner.

"Who is? What?" Poldo leaned out the cottage door, but he didn't dare walk out into the courtyard while the Troll was in such a state. Already, the rock wall had two massive holes in it and the lean-to was more of a slump-down thanks to Thane's hysterics. It wasn't safe to be underfoot.

The Wood Gnomes clearly agreed. As Thane threw the packs down in the lean-to, the chain of Domovoy dangling from his fur swung low enough to grab their kin emerging from the bushes. It stood to reason that the safest place to be during a Troll rampage was behind the Troll.

As Poldo watched the rescue effort, he felt Red Squirrel crawl up his shoulder. "What is all this about?" he asked the Wood Gnome.

Red Squirrel chirruped in his ear.

"Oh, the Elf? She and her party are in some danger?"

Red Squirrel chittered a response. Thane charged past, the streamer of Wood Gnomes waving in his wake.

"The Dragon of Wynspar?"

The response was an extended sequence of squeaks, chirrups, and piping notes.

"My gods. The Heroes of the City sent to slay the dragon..." Poldo trailed into a thoughtful silence. He turned to look into his little farmhouse and through the hall door at the small office he'd set up. It was still sparsely furnished, but cozy and warm nonetheless. More importantly, it was safe. Escaping the Hookhand and coming to Mistkeep had given him a new lease on life, and one with most favorable terms. With the Wood Gnomes' aid, an office like this, and the resources he held in the bank, he could be running a successful hedge fund in a month or two. He had everything he needed to start all over again.

Which meant he had a chance to do everything differently.

"Come on. We'll go too," he said to Red Squirrel.

The Domovoy rocked back on his heels and nearly fell from Poldo's shoulder. Rapid-fire protests squeaked in Poldo's ear.

"Yes, I know. But we only made it this far with his help. And now he needs our help."

Across the yard, Thane tripped in his panic and spilled the contents of his bandoliers. With a roar of frustration, he fell to his knees.

"Clearly," said Poldo. "He'll wind up getting branded a foe for sure if we can't calm him."

Red Squirrel chirruped sullenly.

"And there will be hazard pay for all of you, of course."

The Wood Gnome leapt to attention and chittered something across the yard. A cheer went up from the diminutive crowd clinging to Thane's back as Poldo tramped over to the muddy spot where Thane was gathering up his dropped papers and purple trinkets.

The Troll caught the Gnome's eye as Poldo approached. "I have to go." Thane's voice shook with desperation and apology. "I have to help them. Help her."

"I know," said Poldo, bending over to pick up a string of purple beads. "We're here to help pack."

——CHAPTER 20——

"Packing is three-quarters of preparation, and preparation is ninety percent of success," said Boomer. The tattooed Gnome and his Gremlin partner beamed at the heroes from behind the sales podium. "Nothing's more crucial to a successful trip than having the right gear, and Creative Destruction offers a line of dungeon delver packages designed to maximize your chances of completing your quest. Now, your basic adventuring package consists—"

"Save the basics, Boomer. We'll take the deluxe," Gorm said.

"Eh?" said the Gnome.

"The deluxe. The big package. The kits with all the premium potions and sealed provisions and unbreakable ropes and waxed matches for the smokeless torches."

"We use glowstones now," said Buster.

"Great! Whatever ye say. Ye two know what adventurers need, ye always have a special, deluxe kit ye try to sell parties on, and we're on the kingdom's coin today, so get us the best ye got. And then," Gorm leaned forward in his chair and growled through his grin, "show us your good stuff."

The Gremlin protested. "But you're buying our best—"

"None of your mass produced pre-marketed packages." The Dwarf waved dismissively at the shelves of product lining the walls. "I want to see the really good stuff! The stuff that ain't for sale yet. The stuff ye ain't sure the guild regulators will allow!"

"But—" Buster began, but Boomer wrapped a silencing arm around his shoulder and interjected.

"Ah, see! I told you it would be a good day when Ingerson comes!" The Gnome's grin pushed the curled tips of his mustache up until they nearly reached his bushy eyebrows. "And if he wants to test our new work, let's not stand in his way," he added meaningfully.

The Gremlin's eye ridges creased in worry. "But—"

"Come on. Ye can show them the thing you've been working on," said Boomer, giving his partner a squeeze.

"Oh, yes!" Buster's eyes widened and a colorful crest extended from the top of his head. "Yes, this could be perfect for it!"

"Come on! We'll get Marda and the team to help," said Boomer. Hand in hand, the pair scurried from the room.

"This should be interesting," Heraldin said to Gaist.

"If we're looking for really powerful artifacts, I've already offered the Gray Tower's collection," Jynn told Laruna.

"I'd say we need every advantage we can get," said the mage.

Kaitha followed Gorm to a side table with light refreshments. "Are... are Boomer and Buster together?" she whispered, still peering out the door that Boomer and Buster had left through.

"I ain't heard anything about them splittin' up." Gorm poured himself a glass of water from a tin pitcher.

"Really?" The Elf's eyes were as wide as her grin. "I never suspected. And you never mentioned it."

Gorm eyed the ranger warily. "Why would I?"

"Well, I thought... I mean, good for you."

"What? How?" Whatever was good for him, Gorm suspected its net benefits were canceled out by the conversation.

"You know, you just..." Kaitha moved her head as though trying to wriggle through a knotty issue. "I just thought that you might have a problem with it."

"Hardly see how it'd be my problem," grumbled Gorm.

"Exactly."

"What?"

Kaitha sighed. "Look, some people would find a Gnome and a Gremlin in love to be... I don't know, what is it you Dwarves say? Shameful. I thought you might say it's shameful."

"It is shameful," Gorm said, popping a tart into his mouth.

The Elf reared back with a little gasp. "How can you say that? I mean, how can—how can you just say that?"

"I didn't just say it!" said Gorm. "Ye asked me!"

"But, I mean, they're your friends!" said Kaitha. "And how are they any worse than Jynn or Laruna? Or me and... well, or any other couple?"

"They ain't any worse. It's no different at all!"

"Exactly!"

"Aye, exactly!"

"What?"

Gorm rolled his eyes. "Look, all ye surface folk spend every day prancin' about together, fawnin' over each other, and publicly twistin' yourselves in knots over private matters. It's all shameful. I'd never do any of it, and I'm clanless. An honored Dwarf would lose face for doin' the least of what ye folk do every day. Even most *arak'nud* show more restraint than your people."

"So we're all just supposed to—"

"Ye ain't supposed to do anything," said Gorm. "If I couldn't make peace with surface folk not adherin' to my customs, I'd have stayed in the clanhome. There ain't no point in tryin' to make all of me friends into Dwarves, and there ain't any point in tryin' to keep me from bein' one."

Kaitha opened her mouth, then closed it. She gave Gorm a prolonged stare. "We'll call it progress," she said eventually.

"Call it whatever ye like, so long as you're talkin' to somebody else," grumbled Gorm. "Gods knows I don't want to talk about any of this. It's shameful."

"If you say." Kaitha shook her head. "How are the pastries?"

"Ain't bad," said Gorm, grabbing another grundant tart. "Boomer must have set up the meeting. Buster always cheaps out on the snacks."

When Creative Destruction's founders returned, they led a procession of Gnomes, Humans, and Gremlins wearing white coats and carrying several sealed cases. Each box contained new marvels yet to be wielded by any hero or encountered by any foe, save for some unfortunate test dummies and laboratory monsters.

"Goop arrows!" announced Boomer, holding up a quiver full of arrows. "Sometimes the only way out of a sticky situation is to create another one!"

"Funny you should say that," said Buster, peering into the quiver.

"Eh?" Boomer tried to draw an arrow, but the shaft was half-encased in a sleeve of viridian ooze that stretched as the muscular Gnome pulled. The arrow snapped back into place with a warbling twang as soon as he released his grip. "Uh, still in testing," he said with an apologetic grin.

"We'll pass," said Kaitha.

For the next demonstration, attendants lined the top of the podium with several paper trays of eggs. A Goblin in a white jumper carefully set a red, covered rucksack on top of them. "Now then," said Buster as the attendants placed more eggs inside the bag. "You may be wondering how you can reduce the risk of accidental fire or detonation when you're carrying around so many firebombs and volatile potions."

"At least, you will be once you see how many firebombs and potions are in the deluxe package!" laughed Boomer.

"That's why we've designed the RED bag, or Reduced Explosive Damage bag." Buster's arms performed some grandiose choreography in the direction of the rucksack.

Gorm's brows, which had been drifting into a deep furrow as he considered the strange setup, flew up as Boomer lit the fuse on a vial of alchemist's fire. "It's got similar enchantments to your standard extra-dimensional satchel, but with the ability to expand almost infinitely when force is applied in the direction of the walls of the bag," the Gnome explained.

"Yes, Boomer," said the Gremlin, watching the fuse burn.

Gorm shared a nervous glance with Kaitha.

"And as everything is bound to its position from the edges of the extra-dimensional pocket, all your valuables will also be safe from any explosive—"

"Boomer!" said Buster as the heroes dove for cover.

"Oh. Right," said Boomer. He dropped the explosive into the bag as the last of the fuse burned down. "The point is, the RED bag will prevent all collateral damage."

Fwump.

Flames fountained from the mouth of the satchel, searing a hole through the oak ceiling. The force of the eruption slammed the red bag against the podium in a spray of yolk and shell that showered the Gnome and Gremlin.

"Provided you close the cover!" barked Buster.

"Drat." Boomer wiped thick threads of egg from his mustache as he stared up at the showroom's new skylight. "But still, we're all unsinged, right? Nobody's on fire, hey? And look!" He reached into the bag and produced three unblemished eggs. "Perfectly safe. Provided you close it."

Gorm whistled as he climbed back into his chair. "We'll take six."

"There's only three in existence." Boomer accepted a towel from a helpful attendant. "You can have two."

"Fair enough," said Kaitha. "Got anything exciting to put in it?"

Boomer and Buster stopped cleaning the egg off themselves and shared a sidelong glance.

"Should we?" asked the Scribkin, a hint of a smile twitching his mustache.

"If it wasn't the dragon..." Buster said uncertainly.

"But it is!" laughed Boomer. "Wait here!"

Buster addressed the mages as the Scribkin darted from the room. "You're familiar with the principles of arcane oscillation?"

"That's the theory that you can use low magic to send waves along threads of sorcery," said Laruna.

"If done correctly, some mages believe it may have exciting applications," said Jynn. "But it's just theory."

"And if you do it wrong..." Laruna made a worried face.

Buster nodded. "Exactly. Except it's not doing it wrong if you're hoping for a chain-enchantment to create force distortions in the weave."

"Ohhh," Jynn and Laruna said in unison, their voices dipping low and their eyebrows rising high.

"We found that you can prime an oscillating reaction along threads of magic within an occult sphere," said Boomer.

"What's an occult sphere?" asked Kaitha.

"An occult circle in three dimensions," said Jynn.

"Like this one!" Boomer returned carrying a small, shimmering ball, bound with two grooved, brass bands crossed over each other at the poles and covered in runes and mystic symbols. The surface of the sphere between the bands alternated silver and gold in a checkered pattern. "I give you the Occult-Primed Arcane Oscillation Explosive. This one's inert, of course. Just a demonstration model."

On the edge of perception, Gorm heard the gentle whisper of every muscle in the room relaxing a hair.

"To arm it, you twist like so until the colors are aligned." Boomer gave the ball a turn, and the brass band around the sphere allowed the halves to rotate. Another twist, and the explosive was half-silver, half gold, bisected down the middle. The Gnome set it on the podium. "Once it's ready, all it needs is an external stimulus to detonate."

"Like what?" asked Heraldin.

The Gnome shrugged. "Almost anything. A fire. A smaller explosion. Drop it. Cast a spell on it. Look at it cross-eyed, ha! That last one wouldn't set it off. Probably. But it won't take much."

"So... can we throw it?" asked Heraldin.

"Oh no, the OPAOE ain't for a fight. You want to be well away from it when it goes off. Very limited combat applications. Like a suicide mission."

"Or tossing it down a deep chasm," suggested Buster.

"Or if you come across, say, a cavern with a hive of Dire Spiders, this will take care of it."

"The entire hive?" asked Gorm.

"The entire cavern, I should think," said Jynn.

"If not the entire mountain," said Laruna.

Heraldin whistled.

"Well, that's a bit extreme," Buster said, then thought for a moment. "But I wouldn't set it off under the city," he conceded.

"Or anywhere in sight of people you care about," said Boomer.

"So how do we use it if we can't throw it or look at it?" asked Gorm.

"I thought you'd never ask! Let's go to the next podium." Buster's crest quivered with excitement as he scurried to another station, where attendants had set up a small blast shield and a flat, brown box set on the podium.

The Gremlin flipped the top of the box open and selected a cigar bound with gold foil and topped with a rounded red cap from a row of identical cylinders. "This may look like an ordinary cigar," he told Gorm, "but it's actually a remote detonation device. You just twist the blast cap off like so, and place it next to your charges." He expertly removed the red tip of the cigar and handed it to an attendant, who hurried off to set it in place behind the blast shield. "Then, travel as far away as you like—the enchantment will hold anywhere from here to Chrate or Ruskan. And when you're ready, you smoke the cigar down to this red line." He pointed to a thin strip of scarlet foil a little way down the cigar. "Like so. Boomer?"

"With pleasure!" The Scribkin accepted the cigar, then gave it a few deep puffs as his partner lit the end with a small wand of flame.

"Once the enchanted foil ignites, the blast cap will detonate, and so will your payload." Buster shook out the wand. "You can detonate a bomb from anywhere!"

The heroes turned to the blast shield in polite anticipation.

The blast shield remained unmolested by fire or force. An intermittent chorus of uncomfortable throat clearing began after a while.

Gorm glanced at Buster. "How long does this usually take?"

"Two or three minutes, depending on how vigorously you puff," said Buster. "I call it the smoke bomb!"

"I'm pretty sure that name is taken," said Heraldin.

Boomer shook his head, sending clouds of blue-gray smoke twirling around his mustache. "I told you. I told you people would think of the other one."

"It's not trademarked!" snapped Buster. "Marketing can deal with the name when we get closer to wide release."

"I like 'exploding cigars,' myself," said Boomer.

"Does the cigar explode?" asked Jynn, leaning away from the Gnome.

"Aha!" Buster's crest and dorsal ridges extended in triumph. "See? I told you people would think that!"

"But... why a cigar at all?" asked Laruna.

Gnome and Gremlin turned the full force of their flabbergasted scorn on the solamancer. "What do you mean?" asked Boomer.

The mage shrugged. "Wouldn't it be better to just have a vial you break or a slip of paper you tear to detonate? Why all the waiting? And why something that you need to inhale?"

"For style! For panache! For that... that il'ne se la that every hero needs in their brand," said Buster.

"Imagine walkin' out of a bandit lair with a cigar clenched in your teeth just as the whole place explodes behind you! Or imagine surveying a dark temple with a thick cigar in your hand and havin' the whole buildin' explode just as you take a puff!" Boomer pantomimed inhaling from a cigar and tossing it away. "Nothin' left of it but a geyser of flame and dust just after you say 'all that ceremony, up in smoke.'"

"The quips practically write themselves!" said Buster.

"Though we're makin' a book of 'em, just to get the creative juices flowin'," said Boomer.

An attendant handed Gorm an open pamphlet. He glanced down at several alleged witticisms printed in thick lettering. "'Guess I'll light up. Everyone else here is going to,'" he read.

Boomer and Buster's twin grins radiated hopeful enthusiasm. "See?" said Boomer. "It all comes down to style."

"Style can tell us a lot. The little flourishes. Common expressions. Frequent hallmarks of sentence structure."

"The fact that it's scarg-spit crazy," said Pathalan, High Scribe of the All Mother.

"Indeed," murmured Scribe Beryn distractedly. The ancient Human hovered over the scroll like a reptilian mother over her clutch of eggs, tongue darting over his lips as he studied the text. His skin was the same mottled brown as his robes, just with more wrinkles and a rougher texture, and he wore a pair of pie-plate spectacles that made his eyes look like the huge orbs of some nocturnal lizard.

"I mean it's supposed to be nonsense," said Scribe Pathalan, ill at ease in the tiny, wooden chair next to Beryn's desk. The darkness of the old scribe's windowless chambers pressed in around the tiny light of Beryn's glowstone, so that he and the old man seemed to be alone on a starless night. Pathalan could only tell they were surrounded by old scrolls and books by the smell of old parchment. He shivered and pressed on. "Or at least it's usually nonsense. But this... it's not like the All Mother at all. That's why I brought this to you."

It was an ill-kept secret that Scribe Beryn knew the All Mother's scriptures better than any other scribe. This was impressive for a Human who, near the end of his life, had a mere seven decades of study under his belt. Since his youth, Beryn had been drawn to Al'Matra's writings like a moth to a candle, all the while eschewing the less scholarly trappings of being a temple scribe such as holy feasts, holidays, fully-funded retreats to a lake in the Green Span, greater feasts, ritual dances with the priestesses, unsanctioned cavorting with the priestesses, and holiest feasts. Pathalan couldn't fathom what sort of tiny, precise madness would cause a man to forego the best parts of his job, but the All Mother's temple took all sorts—indeed, they took anyone they could get—and Beryn was admittedly the useful sort.

The old man blinked and turned the massive lenses upon the Elf. "Short sentences... direct, first-person direction... notes of sadness. It sounds like the All Mother to me."

"But it makes sense," Pathalan protested.

Beryn glanced at the page, then turned his gaze on the high scribe, brow furrowed in concern. "Does it?"

"Well, not exactly, but—"

"'Don't make me remember. I don't want to remember,'" Scribe Beryn read the text with a slow, pedantic rhythm. "'I am sorry for what I've done, but don't make me remember it. Stay away.'"

"Yes, fine, not a lot of sense," conceded the high scribe. "But it's coherent in a way, right? She's not mentioned olives or fish once. And she keeps coming back to this. I mean, three, four times a week I'm getting this sort of... of willful forgetfulness. And when she does it's very... intense. Unusually so."

This was an understatement. Normally, the All Mother's scripture ready to be penned was like a faint itch at the back of the high scribe's mind, and simply relaxing his wrist and letting them write themselves solved it. These words felt more like a burning rash that had already been scratched too much. They wouldn't be ignored; his wrist leapt for a pen of its own accord sometimes. Once he'd woken from sleep to find that he'd walked to his desk in his nightclothes and scrawled several verses.

"Well, her holiness does work in more mysterious ways than most," said Beryn.

"It's more than that." The Elf pursed his lips. "Perhaps it's some sort of... attack?"

"You think it's demonic?" asked the Human.

"I was thinking more mnemonic..." said Pathalan. There was no need to suspect an extra-dimensional demon when the All Mother had more than enough inner ones to account for any strain of madness. "She's upset about something."

"Sadly, that's not unusual," said Beryn.

"Right, but... I'm just wondering if there's something we can do to ease her mind," said Pathalan. He consciously did not say, "so that she'll stay out of mine."

Scribe Beryn gave Pathalan a flat, fascinated look, like an entomologist might consider something with too many legs emerging from a chrysalis. "You know that finding the wisdom in the All Mother's words takes years. Decades." He extended a leathery arm and gave the Elf a pat on the hand. "I'm still working through the ontological significance of the thematic patterns in the early books of Jeph, and I had much more hair and teeth when I began that. You can't take any of it at face value."

"Right," said Pathalan, though doubts lingered.

"Are you feeling all right, Holy One?"

He let out a long breath through his teeth. "It's probably just that business with the statue. I think it's starting to get to me."

"Oh? Have they not fixed the sculpture of High Scribe Niln yet?" asked Beryn.

Pathalan felt a chill run from the tips of his toes to the points of his ears, and he couldn't stop himself from shuddering. "It feels like he's watching me, like he's laughing at me. I can't even go in the sanctuary anymore with him grinning like that. I just... I mean, something's coming. I just don't want to remem—I don't want to know what it is."

Concern sent deep wrinkles spiderwebbing across Beryn's liver-spotted features. "Perhaps some rest would be good for you, High Scribe."

"Yeah. Or maybe a feast. At least Acolyte Penna could bring me another cup of tea." Pathalan's voice quavered as he stood on shaking legs. "Something to take the edge off."

"That sounds nice," said Scribe Beryn. "A nice cup of pugwort and honeysuckle, I should think."

The high scribe nodded. Yes. Pugwort was strong. "After I... after I get back to my desk."

"Yes, I'll send her up," said Beryn, watching the Elf stumble back toward the doorway. "All Mother guide your words."

"May she take a break for a while," muttered Pathalan in reply, though he knew that sentiment was hopeless. Already he could feel the burning beginning at the back of his skull.

"At least stop for the night!" Poldo hollered over the rushing wind. "You need a rest!"

If the directive held any sway over Thane, he didn't show it. The Troll thundered on through the swirling snow, even as the sun threatened to slip behind the black brambles of the Green Span's winter canopy. The driving wind bit at Poldo's skin, and clumps of ice built up in his mustache and tugged at his lips.

Several Wood Gnomes took what shelter they could in the fur on the back of the Troll's shoulders. When they caught Poldo's gaze, Red Squirrel shrieked a tiny imperative at the top of his miniature lungs. It was barely audible over the howl of the frosty wind.

"I'm sure he just didn't hear me," said Poldo.

"Hello, Kaitha." Thane's breath was a white cloud against the deepening blue of the winter evening. "My name is Thane."

As one, the Wood Gnomes shot Poldo a look of uniform apprehension; when you are being carried through a blizzard at breakneck speed, it is best to be carried by someone of sound mind.

"He's just rehearsing, I think," Poldo assured them.

"We've met before... though not like this," Thane managed labored breaths. "But I've helped you before... and I'm... here to help again."

Red Squirrel chittered again.

"No regrets at all!" said Poldo. "Listen, if nothing else, it's clear that he needs our help. He's in no state to deal with the bannermen or the guild. Besides, he shall have to stop eventually!" Poldo's attempt to reassure the Domovoy was weakened by his own doubts. The Troll ran with the single-mindedness of a golem, sprinting past every limit of endurance that the Gnome imagined for him. He moved faster than a carriage, sometimes galloping, sometimes sprinting, always pressing northward as fast as his huge muscles could carry him.

"Probably," Poldo conceded, pulling his cloak tighter around himself.

"Hello, Kaitha. My name is Thane." The Troll breathed the words like a mantra. "Hello, Kaitha. My name is Thane."

Kaitha waved.

The crowd roared from all around her. Banners hung from windows and the deep crags of the Ridge. People in the throng held up handmade signs with words of adulation and encouragement, though it was apparent that some had been repurposed from when the Golden Dawn had marched to the Dungeon Gate mere weeks ago. The laziest sign bearers had simply painted a streak through the words "GOLDEN DAWN" but left the signs otherwise unchanged. It looked like some crazed editor had gone on a redlining bender through the city.

"Smile, too," Gorm growled from her side. He stood with her at the head of the Heroes of the City as they paraded toward the Dungeon Gate.

"You first," said the Elf.

"I am smiling!"

"Is that what that is?" Kaitha gave him a dubious sidelong glance.

"Aye! We're doing 'triumphant heroes marching to victory.'"

"Ugh, no. That's what the Golden Dawn did," said Heraldin from behind them.

"I thought we were doing 'grim and determined stoical heroes walking to the job,'" Kaitha said, as the small procession came to a halt next to a hardwood stage covered in banners of every hue. King Johan walked up to the podium and the crowd erupted in cheers.

"Right," said Laruna.

"Wait, have I been the only one smilin' and greetin' folk since we got here?" Gorm asked.

"Is that what that was?" asked Jynn.

"I thought you were baring your teeth and menacing them with an axe," said Heraldin.

Gorm looked nonplussed. "What? No! How could ye think that?"

"You did make that baby cry," said Laruna.

"I assumed you were doing 'grim hero with a dark past.'" Heraldin thought for a moment. "Or at least a drunk past."

"Nobody else thought we were doin' 'triumphant heroes.'" The Dwarf grimaced in a way that was almost distinguishable from his smile. "Nobody else has been smilin' and wavin'?"

Kaitha thought back over arriving in guild coaches to the square, their rousing introduction by guild promoters, and their parade to the final podium. "I waved when you asked me to," she offered.

"Well, ain't that a fine thing," grumbled Gorm.

Johan launched into a speech like a lunar cycle; it had bright and dark parts, a tide of applause flowed in and out with its rhythm, and it kept going around in circles. The king spoke with conviction and scintillating energy, but when he paused in between themes Kaitha could see a sheen of sweat on his brow and his eyes darting about like a cornered animal. She smiled, completely spoiling her stoic effect.

Gorm's almost-grin grew as the speech neared its end. The king seemed to be inviting correction with increasing desperation.

"The dragon—and there definitely is a dragon—is the greatest threat to our nation. These heroes know it. They know what they're about to face, don't they?" Johan looked down at them with wretched anticipation, waiting for some sort of lifeline.

But the heroes had planned for this. Gorm and companions nodded respectfully and looked back up at the king with blank, expectant smiles. Denied a last chance at a fight over the truth, Johan was left alone with the facts. And the fact was that it was ten minutes past time for the quest to begin. With a final, empty wish of good luck and gods' speed, Johan ordered the Dungeon Gate opened.

The heroes continued their parade toward the yawning portal. They walked two by two, uniformly determined and stoic, past the cheering crowds. Flower petals were released, as was customary, but this deep in winter the only blooms available on the mountain were frostgarnets. Their crimson petals looked to Kaitha like a spray of blood drifting through the air at the lazy pace of a memory. Just like the fountain from a Troll's jugular as an arrow pierced it. And his eyes filled with pain in the instant before she fled, but she should have—

"Lass?" said Gorm. "Your glowstone."

Kaitha snapped from her reverie just as they passed under the shadow of the gate. The other heroes already had small points of light hovering above their heads like tiny guardian angels. She took her own glowstone from her belt pouch and blew on the milky crystal. The stone began to glow with increasing intensity as it flew into place by her head.

She took a deep breath. The air smelled of damp stone and moldering bones and an adventure about to start. "Ready?" she asked the others.

"Whatever comes," said Gorm.

"Whatever comes," Kaitha agreed, moving into a scouting position as the other heroes got in formation. The gloom deepened as the massive Dungeon Gate began to close behind them, pushing the last of the daylight into a thin sliver of silver in the dark.

—CHAPTER 21—

The reverberation of the door slamming behind Weaver Ortson rang through the stone halls of the palace. He felt like a man just arrived at a party that has already ended; the palace was empty save for a lone guard standing in the middle of the cavernous entryway. The bannerman gave the guildmaster a quiet nod and averted his eyes as Ortson hurried toward the throne room.

The hallway was as silent and empty as an old tomb. Ortson caught a glimpse of a maid in the antechamber, like a deer in a dusty glade, but she fled quickly. He took the chance to produce a flask from his tunic and, with a generous swig of liquid courage, pressed on.

Weaver had heard rumors that the palace had become somber since Johan's return, but he'd been too busy avoiding the place to see for himself. People said that the bolder and less scrupulous among the nobility and executives still clamored for the king's attention by day, but the king's spirits fell with the setting sun. Andarun's court read the king's emotional state like seafarers watched the clouds, and departed before the storms rolled in. The lack of court intrigue was notable, but logical.

Ortson felt much more concerned by the lack of servants.

His clerks said many of the palace staff had resigned. Without a lady to serve, Marja's handmaidens had departed for their native Ruskan. The queen's honor guard resigned as one, ostensibly for failing to stop the queen's last, reckless act of devotion. The bakery staff was almost completely cut without Marja's appetites to keep them busy. Just over a week after Johan's return, and half of the staff had left the palace.

Some of them didn't make it home.

Ortson didn't need rumors to know what had happened. Over the king's short reign, he'd helped Johan find people who were poking around the northern project and the truth about the recent dragon attacks. After they disappeared, it was up to the grandmaster and High Councilor of the Heroes' Guild to limit any investigation that could cast suspicions on the king.

Ortson paused by a tapestry depicting the Fifth Age siege of Highwatch, and thought back to his last fight at the ancient fortress. He'd been on the inside of the king's inner circle back then, building the bureaucratic barricades that kept secrets in and prying eyes out. Yet those defenses were falling, and there were new secrets to keep quiet. Secrets that Ortson didn't know. He worried that he was on the same side of them as the missing servants.

After all, some of the palace staff must have noticed Johan's final words to his wife, and could have recognized them as a device from the books she infamously devoured. Some bannermen likely recognized the warped but familiar laugh amid the messenger sprite's approximation of the Golden Dawn's dying screams. And anyone with half a brain could tell that the timing of the king's dramatic emergence at his own funeral was too well-coordinated, too clearly choreographed, to be a coincidence.

Perhaps the best evidence that the servants suspected the king had anticipated—even instigated—Queen Marja's death was that there were so few of them. There weren't even enough staff for a proper dusting, apparently; a cluster of spiderwebs lurked behind a ceremonial suit of armor, and the ceiling above it was crowded with cobwebs.

Ortson took another swig from his flask and made his way to the doors of the throne room. The guildmaster didn't have much regard for Marja, but neither had good King Handor, and it'd never crossed their minds to do the queen any harm. It was like kicking a dog; needlessly cruel, and whatever evils Ortson had done, they had all been for a purpose. They had all been part of a plan, he reminded himself bitterly, because Weaver Ortson had always believed the ends justified the means. He'd just never been on the wrong end of the means before.

Everything had started to spiral when the king and the Tandosians started... whatever it was they were doing down in the Royal Archives. Ortson made a face at the distasteful thought and sanitized his tongue with another draught of whiskey. What was the king doing down there? Why did he assemble the Golden Dawn, only to kill them? If they needed to die, why bring them into the dungeon at all? He had so many effective means of eliminating problems up here. If something down in the dungeon drew the king into Wynspar, why kill his own heroes? The questions haunted him until the moment he walked into the throne room and realized with a start that they all shared a common answer.

Johan was clearly mad.

The paladin king perched upon the throne of Andarun, his mailed fingers digging into the wood like talons. His bloodshot eyes stared at an empty spot on the floor with all the hungry intensity of a vulture watching a marooned caravanner crawl across the desert. A joyless grin split his scarred face, and his lips twitched as he growled a one-sided conversation through his pearly, almost luminescent teeth.

"It can still work. They haven't found... they might die. They aren't that... no, there aren't enough of them... Trust me, it can still work. We just need more time... just a little more time..."

Ortson walked carefully around the empty space that occupied Johan's gaze. "Majesty?" he said tremulously. "Y-you summoned me?"

The paladin blinked and straightened, inflating with a sudden good humor. "Ah, yes. Weaver! Ha! I wanted to talk to you about the plan!"

The guildmaster's mind frantically ran through the various initiatives the king might be referring to. Most of them weren't the sort he'd speak of in a public place, even without any public around. "The, uh... which plan, Your Majesty?"

"Why, the plan to stop Ingerson, of course."

"I... I don't know what you mean." Rivers of sweat poured over the floodplain of Ortson's brow.

"Ha! You must!" said the king. "After all, you didn't come up with a reason why Ingerson's quest couldn't move forward—"

"I beg your pardon?" asked Ortson.

The king's smile froze, but his eyes were like hot embers. "I wanted you to find a reason to bypass all this business with the dragon."

"But.... but you asked if there was a legal rationale... there wasn't one." Ortson dabbed at his forehead with a sopping handkerchief, though it had all the effect of an umbrella in monsoon season.

Johan pounded the abused armrest of the throne. Cracks spiderwebbed through the venerated wood. "You're the thrice-cursed Grandmaster of the Heroes' Guild!" he roared. "If you can't find a good rule, make one up!"

Ortson sputtered at the sudden reversal. "B-b-but you... I had just done that to allow the quest in the first place! It took all I had to set up two no-bid quests for the largest hoard in history in weeks. W-we bypassed so many protocols to get your quests—"

"Ingerson was supposed to try to accuse us! He was supposed to reveal that he raided the northern site!"

"I, uh..." Ortson tried to follow the king's line of reasoning, and kept tripping at the same point. "Why would we want that, sire?"

"So we could deny everything!" said Johan, leaping to his feet. "We should be arguing about who the real criminal was! Why would I want him to go on a high-profile quest? Why would I want to send him down to investigate the dragon? And now that you've let him and his cohorts into the dungeon, I assume you have a plan to stop them from coming back!"

"Ah..." said Ortson. "Well, sire, I assumed that the actual dragon, or whatever else you fought down there, would make short work of them. Right?"

Johan's eyes narrowed. He studied the guildmaster with the disgusted fascination of a child who has found a bloated, spindly-legged creature under a log. "I'd prefer to leave nothing to chance," he said eventually.

"B-but if they return without slaying the dragon, we can say they were derelict in their duty for fear of the dragon," said Weaver. "And if they do actually succeed, you can still deny that you killed the, uh... we can still deny all wrongdoing."

It was a poor recovery, and Weaver didn't need to look at the king's face to see that it hadn't been enough. He did though, and saw that Johan's perpetual grin had faded into a determined grimace. The almost-unspoken accusation hung in the air like a sword above the guildmaster's head.

"Do you think I killed someone, Weaver?"

"Of course not, sire."

"You said I'd need to deny it. You think I killed someone?"

The guildmaster searched for an escape, but it was hard to see one through the haze of alcohol. "Not... uh, not directly," he tried.

"Not directly?"

"I mean, I saw her eat... the poison..." Ortson's eyes were beginning to water. "It... it was suicide."

Johan's shoulders fell, genuine disappointment pulling his face into a deep frown. "I... I really did love Marja," he said.

"Of course, sire—"

"The princess I saved. The damsel that needed a hero. That needed me." Johan held a hand up as he descended the stairs, as though reaching out to touch a memory. "It was a tale out of storybooks: a hero, a wicked wizard, a maiden in distress, a daring rescue. Lovers kept apart for years... decades... by caste and fortune, reunited at last. I loved our story, Weaver. I loved her."

Ortson stepped back from the descending king. "Sire, I didn't mean—"

The king closed his hand into a mailed fist. "But I have important plans, Weaver. More important than you could ever comprehend. Failure is... it's not an option. It's not even a possibility!" He growled the last remark, as if to cut off an unheard dissent. It took a moment for his snarl to fade back into a mask of melancholy. "When she threatened those critical projects, I... I knew we couldn't be together any longer. The best I could do was give her a happy ending."

"She went mad with grief and killed herself," said the guildmaster, backing away.

"For love. The way she always wanted to. It really was the best I could do for her, once she got in the way. I don't have a choice in this. I cannot fail." Johan turned his eyes on Ortson. "I can't tolerate failure."

"Sire—!" Ortson started to back away, but Johan was on him in a flash of golden armor and ivory teeth. A gauntlet like an iron vice clamped onto his arm.

"I needed a plan. I needed Ingerson stopped. You didn't do that. You... let... him go into the dungeon, when I needed... him... stopped." Johan's voice was level even as his face reddened and veins throbbed on his forehead.

"Sire, I... I've served the crown loyally... for many years." Ortson's words were a whining wheeze. The king's grip sent waves of agony through his arm.

"Ha haaa! Indeed you have, Ortson. For many years. Long enough to know that in this business, there's two types of people."

"Not the speech," Ortson sobbed, trying unsuccessfully to pull his arm from the king's grasp. "Not the loose ends speech—"

"Ha! I see you're familiar with the basic concept." Johan wrenched his arm and grinned as the guildmaster screamed.

A few moments later, the lights in the eyes of the shrine of Mordo Ogg at Sculpin Down flashed with sudden brilliance.

"Ooh!" Ignatius cooed, watching the crimson glow fade away. "Another big one! And so soon after Her Majesty. And she after..."

The old man pursed his leathery lips and stroked the thin, ivory strands of his beard. He didn't know much about math—serving in Mordo Ogg's priesthood didn't require much arithmetic beyond counting the departed. Yet he could see a logarithmic pattern in the interval between major deaths lately, even if he had no idea what logarithms were.

Ignatius licked his lips, deep in concentration. He glanced suspiciously at the sky. Something in the clouds sparked a decision in the old priest, and he quickly opened a small compartment beneath the shrine and drew out a small wooden placard. He carefully placed the sign in the stone skeleton's lap. It read:

Attendant away. Service continues.

Moments later, Ignatius made his way toward the Pinnacle, clutching his robes close against the chill as he ran through the streets. People hurried out of his way, perhaps because he was a clergyman in service of the god of death, or perhaps just because he was an old man in tattered robes laughing and muttering as he sprinted up the road.

The old priest knew of an observation tower on the Fifth Tier where a sightseer could pay a shilling to look out over the lower tiers of the city. People lined up by the dozen to see the city in the summer, but in the frosty Highmoon air nobody stood by the tower door but a dour-looking Goblin minding an empty till. Ignatius dropped a silver coin into the tin bucket and ran up the stairs to the observation deck.

The winter wind carved through the old priest's robes as he stepped up to the railing, but he paid the cold no mind. The sky above the city was chill and clear, but to the south, clouds drifted toward the western coast as though pulled along by the Tarapin. His gaze followed them Ridgeward, where he saw a cluster of cumulus puffs drifting north up the coast. He looked back toward the Wall, and on the eastern horizon saw thin wisps of vapor teased south by the wind. The upper tiers and Mount Wynspar blocked the northern sky, but he could guess that winds toward Scoria were trending east, pulling the clouds into the beginnings of a very large spiral.

"More to come," he whispered, watching the sky. "Much bigger things to come."

"I'm sorry, but I can't deal with anything else at the moment." Feista Hrurk waved Aubren away without looking up from her memo. "You'll have to see to it."

"Yes, ma'am, but—" The young Human was barely audible over the war drum, manned now by two Wood Gnomes bouncing up and down in turns.

"It will have to wait. I need these numbers. Next, do the Plus-Five Corporation!" Feista barked at the Wood Gnomes. Teams of the diminutive workers moved furiously across various spreadsheets laid out over the desks of Warg Inc.'s analysis office. Swirling patterns shifted in the crowd as the Domovoy calculated and marked figures to the rhythm of the war drum. Around them, Goblins and Orcs shuffled papers and checked figures. "This report is due by the lunch hour!"

"But ma'am—" Aubren hovered by the office door, a dusting of snow on her winter shawl.

"If this is about the shoddy work in the kitchen, you have to handle the contractor." Feista glowered down at the stubborn numbers on her parchment. Reams of untouched paperwork lurked behind the page, metastasizing within her inbox as she struggled to concentrate.

A messenger sprite landed atop the pile of papers, it's faint pink glow literally highlighting the daunting workload in front of her. "Feista Hrurk?"

"I'm busy," snapped the Gnoll.

"Message from Asherzu Guz'Varda."

Feista carefully recalibrated her demeanor. "Yes?"

The sprite began to speak with the deliberate cadence that Asherzu reserved for ceremonies or important meetings. "Feista, I know that you have much work, but honor me with your opinion on J.P. Gorgon's liquidity versus its holdings in the dragon's hoard. I must have this by sundown."

"*Spug!* Thrice curse Grund's cudgel!" swore Feista. "She probably had someone from J.P. Gorgon in the room with her when she sent that!" She brushed the report away and turned to the Wood Gnomes. "New report! Put these on hold!" she said.

A loud groan went up from the Wood Gnomes.

"Ah, but Mrs. Hrurk..." Aubren still hovered by the desk.

Feista felt her hackles rising. "Aubren, I can appreciate your challenges, but you cannot come all the way to my office every time—!"

"I know, but it came!" Aubren shoved a large envelope into her employer's paws. "The letter finally came!"

Feista felt the weight of the thick envelope, transfixed by its seal. The red wax bore a sword crossing a falling fireball, the seal of the Heroes' Guild.

White Rat scampered up on her desk to see what distraction could cause every other shred of paperwork to be so forgotten. The Wood Gnome apparently recognized the significance of the envelope, because she shooed Feista and Aubren from the room with reassuring squeaks.

"I... uh... I need to go home," she told one of the clerks.

"Now?" asked the Goblin.

"The letter," said Aubren.

"Oh! Go! I shall tell Lady Asherzu, and we will get the numbers to her!" cried the accountant.

Feista walked home as if in a trance, guided gently by Aubren's steering hands. The girl took the Gnoll to her own apartment near the top floor of Mrs. Hrurk's Home for the Underprivileged, then left her alone with the most anticipated and dreaded letter of her life.

Mrs. Hrurk sat down at her table, opened the letter, and began to read.

To Feista Hrurk, NPC #SKGN12838432,

We have reviewed the file for the encounter between Kriss Rodgerson, Hero License #920911960; Moxie Glum, Hero License #369741082; James Greensleeves, Hero License #885027606; and Drif Matuk, Hero License #900272314, operating under the party designation of the "Fearless Four," hereafter "the heroes" and Hristo Hrurk, NPC #SKGN12838431, hereafter "the F.O.E.," on the 6th of Tandos, 7.373.

There was no quest contracted for slaying the F.O.E., and the F.O.E.'s NPC papers were in good standing prior to the 6th of Tandos. However, the heroes engaged the F.O.E. under random encounter protocols after they witnessed the F.O.E. committing criminal activity, pursuant to HG4.23.1b. The F.O.E. did not dispute violating Andarun's civil foot traffic code ACS2.455.223, subsection b, unlawful crossing of a public road without use of specified crossing, also known as "jaywalking." The F.O.E.'s noncombatant papers were revoked for disregarding the law, pursuant to HG4.23.1f. Civic traffic codes are for everyone's safety.

Your appeal contended that the F.O.E.'s summary execution upon losing his NPC papers was undue and that the F.O.E. did not pose a threat to the heroes. However, guild law leaves discretion to heroes to determine what does or does not constitute a threat. Hundreds of professional heroes are killed every year—sometimes by Gnolls—and heroes in the field must make life-and-death decisions in a split second to survive.

This review finds that the heroes acted appropriately and in accordance with guild law, as well as applicable laws of Andarun and the Freedlands. The loot from the random encounter amounted to one (1) tunic, one (1) pair of Gnoll breeches, one (1) loaf of bread, three (3) tea cakes (lemon), and one (1) satchel containing sundries and coin worth three (3) shillings, nine (9) cents. The loot was divided between the heroes and the guild pursuant to HG4.23.2c.

You have now exhausted your civic appeal. This decision cannot be further appealed without written approval from a master of the Heroes' Guild. Please remember that repeated requests without proper paperwork can be considered harassment of guild personnel, punishable by revocation of your NPC papers under HG4.23.1d.

We wish you well in your future endeavors.

Taness Tenderfoot, Senior Arbiter, Internal Arbitration

Fat tears splashed on the heavy parchment. Every detail of the letter cut through Feista like a hot knife, and memories poured through the wounds. Hristo always brought tea cakes home to the pups, no matter how tight money got. She'd argued about that with him, but she could never stay mad at a father for doting on his litter like that. She remembered the crazy futures he'd dream up for their children, and the random laughter that erupted from him whenever they came running to him.

The sight of his body seared across her mind, broken and charred by weapons designed to slice and scorch steel armor or drake scales. The pups hadn't spoken for weeks after they buried him. She remembered the nights weeping to herself in dark alleyways.

And now she was here, living a future too wild for even Hristo to dream up, a leader at a thriving bank and a proprietress of a charity, living with more money than he'd ever made. All without him; he'd never see the marvels his children would, never watch them grow, because the guild had reduced him to a footnote in some Lightling's paperwork. The guilt and the sorrow crushed her, and the only breaths she could manage were choking sobs.

Aubren must have heard her, because someone sent the pups in to check on her. They said nothing, but crawled into her lap and held her tight. She squeezed them back and wept into their soft fur.

Much later, after there were no tears left to cry and the pups had gone to bed, Feista sat in the kitchen while Aubren stewed over a simmering pot.

"It's a travesty! It's disgusting!" The Human waved a gravy-laden spoon at Feista. "You should find a guildmaster and demand he approve another appeal!"

"It's not like that." Feista sighed into her mug of tea. "I can't just go up and make demands."

"Well, I would!" said Aubren. "I'd give him a piece of my mind while I was at it."

"You could, but that doesn't mean I can," said Feista. "You're a pretty young Human. You could call him names while you're at it, and nobody would strip you of your papers and kill you in the streets for doing it. But a Gnoll?" She shook her head. "I won't have the pups orphaned."

"Surely they wouldn't—" Aubren caught herself and pursed her lips in thought. "Well, they shouldn't."

"They shouldn't," agreed Feista gently.

Aubren ladled out some thick stew for the Gnoll. "So... what happens now? And how can I help?"

"I don't know," sighed Mrs. Hrurk. "It will take a lot of planning to get an approval for an appeal, and I don't know when I'll be able to find the time. And I'm just so... so tired of it all."

"Yeah, but... but we can't let those heroes just get away with it, right?" The girl put the bowl in front of Feista.

"It's not just the heroes." Feista stared into her bowl and stirred up the steam. "It's just... the way you have to deal with Lightlings. With the guild, at the bank, on the Wall, in the thrice-cursed restaurants. We can't just say what we mean, what's true. We have to be so... so *careful* around Lightlings, we have to work so hard to not hurt their feelings; to not do anything that they could find fault with.

"And the whole time, we have to listen to them complain that we're... that we're here! That we're out of place, not down in some dungeon where they think we belong. We get the rude comments, the cold shoulders, the jokes about our appearance, the mockery of our culture—my grandfathers' heirlooms on a restaurant wall! And our families... my Hristo... killed!

"But we're the ones who have to look past all that, for the sake of peace and our lives. We have to put on a smile, and forgive everything we endure, and look past all these insults, and then we still have to treat Lightlings with such careful respect. It's exhausting, carrying that much. I don't know if I can do it again. Hristo forgive me, even for him."

She set her spoon down and gave a sidelong glance at Aubren. The girl's face was a portrait of pained consternation. "But... but we're not all like that, right?" asked the Human. "I mean, I'm not like that."

Feista suppressed a sigh that might have come out a scream. The girl meant well, even if she didn't—couldn't—recognize the way she had seized Feista's anguish and used it as a mirror. And so the Gnoll smiled, and forgave the girl, and looked past the insult. "No, you've been a good friend to me," she said, patting Aubren's hand as she delivered the absolution. "Thank you for the stew."

Aubren beamed. "I'll get you some bread," she said.

"Thank you," said Feista. She didn't let her smile fade into a long sigh until the Human was out of earshot, lest she offend her again. Sometimes the most earnest among them could be the most easily offended, and it was always best to handle Lightlings delicately.

"The slightest twitch can set one off. One errant movement, a misplaced breath, anything can trigger their defenses." Heraldin carefully maneuvered a twisted lockpick toward an ancient padlock. "Could be poisoned darts. Deadly gas. Magical lightning. Anything. A delicate touch is everything with a Baronson and Knock."

Kaitha took a step back next to him, eyes scanning the huge cavern. "I appreciate that, but—"

"If there's a 'but,' you don't appreciate it. Baronson and Knock were the greatest locksmith and trapmaker of the Sixth Age." The bard's voice rose into the high, strained timbre of a truly dedicated fanatic. "Nobody has ever come close to their ingenious craftsmanship. This was probably installed back when the Dark Ones occupied Wynspar over five centuries ago, and it's still operational! It's a—"

"Shut up and pick that thrice-cursed lock!" roared Gorm, wrestling with a small, amphibious monster clinging to his shield. The creature stood no taller than his thigh, with damp blue skin covered in slime from the tip of its tail to its blunt snout.

Kaitha loosed her arrow. The creature on Gorm's shield flashed with orange light, stiffened, and bounced into a pack of its compatriots. A moment later, it clambered to its feet and resumed its advance.

"What in the hells are these things?" hollered Laruna. She conjured a wave of flame at several of the salamander-like creatures, sending the survivors scampering back toward the black pool on the far side of the cavern.

"I believe they're called newtonians." Jynn waved the Wormwood Staff, and a nearby specimen withered and crumpled like a slug under salt. "A monstrous race of amphibians that has never managed to acclimate to—"

"Nah! Ain't newtonians!" Gorm interrupted as he moved to intercept a pack of creatures before they reached the mages. "Newtonians are like squishy, slimy lizardmen with half the brains!"

"Amphibians, yes," said Jynn.

"That sounds like these!" said Laruna.

Gaist caught a nearby assailant with a low swing from his mace, sending it arcing through the cavern like a flare before plunging into the black water. He turned to Laruna and shook his head.

"They ain't squishy like newts. Watch!" Gorm delivered an expert slash of his axe that should have bisected a nearby specimen. Instead, the creature glowed orange and went totally rigid for a split second, and Gorm's axe bounced harmlessly off it as it tumbled away. It snickered as it righted itself, mocking the futility of the Dwarf's assault. "See? Newtonians don't do that."

"So, what do we do?" asked Kaitha. She fired another arrow, but the non-newtonians were gathering in greater numbers now.

"It'd help if we could get through that bloody door!" Gorm yelled over his shoulder.

"It'd be faster if I could concentrate!" Heraldin shot back.

Gorm gritted his teeth and weighed his options. Magic was effective against the salamander-like humanoids, but the mages' reserves were already dwindling. The journey into Wynspar's depths had already set the party against walking skeletons, festering blightbats, several irate Rock Drakes, a gang of bugbears, a swarm of bearbugs, and a Viscous Rhombohedron, all of which had required considerable strength and sorcery to overcome. The party needed rest, but there was no telling how much farther they needed to fight before the next empty chamber. He weighed the costs and the benefits, and signaled Laruna to stand back. Surviving the morbid accounting of a dungeon quest required careful budgeting of one's death dealing resources, and vaporizing the salamander-people was a luxury they couldn't afford.

He scanned their surroundings for other opportunities, but the cavern was totally bereft of pit traps, acid vats, precipitously swaying stalactites or lighting fixtures, or anything else that could be used to advantage by an enterprising and creative hero. The cave's only feature was the pool, a black mirror in the gloom, but given the dark shapes still emerging from it, Gorm doubted that the non-newtonians could be harmed by the water.

A bold forerunner leapt at Gorm. He swatted the amphibian away with his shield. The creature went bright orange—practically luminous in the dim light of the glowstones—and bounced into one of its compatriots. The second non-newtonian also went rigid and vibrantly amber, and the two fell together.

Within the whirling gears of Gorm's mind, an idea sparked. Trajectories and forces lined up in his mind's eye as he looped his axe onto his belt and made a sudden charge. In one swift motion, the Dwarf seized a surprised non-Newtonian by the neck and slammed it into the ground. He felt the jelly-like flaps of its neck become as solid as oak in an amber flash, and its body went as straight and stiff as a javelin. He hurled it into the front ranks of the creeping horde, which glowed and went rigid upon impact. These non-newtonians, in turn, tumbled into the ranks behind them, and so forth until waves of orange light were cascading through the throng of amphibious monsters.

"Yes!" shouted Jynn. "If enough force triggers their sudden increase in density, we can create a chain reaction to—"

"Don't overcomplicate it! Just hit 'em hard!" Gorm grinned as he leapt toward another unfortunate non-newtonian.

Kaitha kicked the front-runners into the crowd with deadly precision. Gaist wielded a victim in each hand, sweeping the stunned salamanders through the ranks in graceful arcs. Gorm bowled into the ranks of slimy soldiers, using his shield to knock waves of foes back. Even Laruna and Jynn got in an odd punch or swat with a staff. Orange light and confused squawks filled the room as the non-newtonians tumbled over each other.

Yet despite the success of Gorm's tactic, their enemies weren't actually being felled, or harmed at all. Within a few seconds of impact, the non-Newtonians would return to their natural flaccidness and begin disentangling from each other. Some began to break away and head back for the pool, but most immediately resumed their slow advance on the heroes.

"We can't keep this up forever!" Kaitha hollered. "When's that door going to open?"

"Still working on it!" Heraldin knelt by the only path forward, deftly moving his lockpicks.

As Gorm sent another wave of light and chaos through the non-Newtonians with a punch of his shield, he noticed that the group that had returned to the pool weren't resubmerging. Instead, they stood at the edge of the inky water and joined in a low chorus of guttural, rhythmic cries.

"*Oobleck! Oobleck! Oobleck!*"

"What's an oobleck?" asked Laruna.

Gaist shrugged.

"I have some theories, but I'd rather not see them proven." Jynn pointed toward the pool with the Wyrmwood Staff. "Look!"

Gorm's eye caught it then, a hint of a huge bulge in the pool. As the non-newtonians' chants rose, so did the black mass in the water, revealing a glint in an eye bigger than Gorm's shield.

"What is that thing?" cried Laruna.

"How deep is that pool?" Jynn wondered aloud.

"How's that thrice-cursed lock coming along?" Kaitha shouted.

"I'm doing my best!" Heraldin gave a deft twist of his pick.

"Do better!" yelled Gorm.

Water and ooze poured from the oobleck's head as it rose above the pool. An arm like an ancient, slime-covered oak emerged from the muck and found purchase on the stone ridge. The non-newtonians cheered at its emergence and gestured at the heroes with malicious delight.

"I'm not sure we can hit that one hard enough," Kaitha said to Gorm. "Any ideas?"

"I'm about ready to feed him the bard if he doesn't hurry up and—"

"Open!" yelled Heraldin over a metallic clank.

"Go! Get goin'!" Gorm waved them to the exit while holding the horde at bay with his shield.

Kaitha was first through the door, scouting the next cavern. Heraldin and the mages followed, hurrying through while Gorm and Gaist brought up the rear, bashing any non-newtonians that came within range.

The oobleck's back was emerging from the pool now, arching up to the ceiling of the cavern like a snake preparing for a strike. It launched toward Gorm as he backed toward the door, barreling forward like a siege weapon and sending a spray of amber non-newtonians flying in its wake. The Dwarf and Gaist dove through the door and Heraldin slammed it shut. A moment later, the cavern wall boomed with sudden impact and orange light flared beneath the door. Dust and pebbles rained from the wall.

"Are we clear?" Gorm asked.

"We are." Kaitha nodded to a corner where a couple of dead scargs bristled with silver arrows.

"Where do you suppose we are at this point?" Laruna asked.

Gorm took a deep breath. He felt the weight of the mountain around them, and judging by its pressure and their orientation, he'd estimate they were below the Seventh or Eighth Tier by now. The stone walls of the room were stone blocks rather than hewn stone or cave walls, and the doors on either side of the chamber were built with distinctive, if plain, arches. "Looks to be an entrance to the Low Way," he said.

"Thank the gods," said Heraldin.

Jynn frowned. "A day behind schedule."

"It's not behind schedule," said Kaitha. "We said it'd take two days to make it here if monsters had returned to Johan's path through the dungeon, and they certainly have. Assuming this is his path at all."

"You think we've lost his trail?" Laruna asked.

Kaitha shrugged. "Monsters don't repopulate a dungeon like this in days. These creatures have been here for months at least. It takes years to spawn that many newtonians, or whatever they were, in a pool that size."

"But we encountered those blightbats in, what, the third room of the dungeon?" said Jynn. "How could we have lost his trail that fast? And if we did, where did he actually go?"

"Only one way to find out." Gorm drew his axe and nodded to the door. "We keep movin' forward."

——CHAPTER 22——

Alone in the common room of Mrs. Hrurk's Home for the Underprivileged, Feista Hrurk couldn't see where to go from here.

Another guild appeal on Hristo's death could take years, assuming she could find a guildmaster to approve one. A dull, buzzing pain thrummed in her chest at the thought of regularly revisiting old injustices and salting the old wounds in her soul. Despair crushed the air from her throat, choking down sobs that never emerged. Even if she set her career and the pups aside to fight her way through the darkest depths of the Pit and back, she'd probably lose her appeal again. It would take everything she had to fail once more. She wasn't sure she had anything left to give.

But then what? Normally, when the ache of missing Hristo overcame her, she could turn to her children or get lost in her work. Yet if her husband could be murdered in the street for a petty violation, where did that leave her children? Her friends at the home? Her house and her career? What did she have that couldn't be taken away with a minor infraction and a flash of a hero's sword?

She might have spent all night paralyzed by such thoughts had it not been for the knock at the front door.

A flash of panic lanced through her spine as she wondered if the guild had come for her, if her pushing for an inquiry had exposed some issue with her papers. Or perhaps her allegations had run afoul of a rogue hero, and they'd fabricate the paperwork after she—

Feista shook her head and hurried to the door before the knocker woke up Aubren or the pups, because she knew that there was little good in letting fear bind her. She still looked through the peephole before opening the door, however, because she was sure there was even less good in letting foolhardiness kill her.

She blinked. The view outside was totally black, as though all of the streetlamps had gone out and no candles or glowstones lit the windows.

Then a familiar voice cut through the darkness. "Hello? Is anyone there?"

Feista threw open the door and caught Duine Poldo in a deep embrace. Poldo's contingent of Wood Gnomes poured into the house around their feet, and from the floorboards and furniture Mrs. Hrurk's team rushed to meet them. The Gnoll and the Gnome towered over many happy reunions as she wept into the dewy tweed of his suit coat.

She composed herself quickly, and pulled back enough for propriety. "I am so glad to see you, Mr. Poldo."

"And I you, Mrs. Hrurk," said Poldo. "But I am afraid I must ask you for a favor."

Her smile froze, her perception caught between a dear friend and the face of a Lightling asking her for yet another thing. She took a deep breath. "I... yes, of course, Mr. Poldo. What do you need?"

"Oh, it's not for me, my dear." Poldo gestured to the area behind him and, notably, far above his head.

Feista gasped. In the light pouring out through the door, the darkness behind Poldo had the texture of matted fur. Her eyes followed the wall of flesh and hair up to a slack face. A Troll swayed as he stared vacantly at the second story of her house, like a man who had won a pyrrhic victory in a drinking contest.

Poldo squeezed her paw. "Thane and I are in the city on pressing business, but he needs rest. I wonder if he might make use of—"

Thane toppled with the slow groan of a falling oak. Wood Gnomes leapt from his fur like sailors from a sinking ship before he crashed to the pavers. Startled cries rang out from several windows, nearly drowning out the thunderous snoring of the Troll.

"Uh... use your front steps, I suppose," Poldo finished. "Just for the night."

Feista took a shaking breath through a grin she couldn't hold back. "You're a good man, Mr. Poldo. Of course, you're welcome as long as you like. Won't you come inside?"

"I would love that, but I worry what the bannermen will think if they find Thane sleeping here." The Scribkin sat down on the top step and wrapped his coat around him. "He's in no state to deal with the king's law. I think—oof—I think it's best that I watch over him from here."

"Good idea," said Feista. "I'll keep you company."

"But it's so late, and I'm sure you have much to attend to in the morning," Poldo protested as the Gnoll fetched a shawl from its hook and stepped out into the chill. "Mrs. Hrurk, please, you don't need to do this."

Feista looked at the prone Troll the Gnome was helping, and remembered what Poldo had done for her and her children when the rest of the world had left them in the rubbish. "But I do, Mr. Poldo," she said, sitting down next to him. "I truly do."

"There isn't a choice in the matter," said Garold Flinn. "When the king sends one—or two—a direct order, it carries all the weight and force of the law."

"We break the law all the time," said Benny Hookhand.

"When we can escape notice. When we can stay underneath the scrying spell." Flinn shook his head. "Do you think King Johan will ignore such an offense?"

"You don't know."

"We both do. He said he needed somebody reliable."

"That's more threat than compliment in our line of work."

"Exactly my point."

From the outside, it might appear to a proverbial onlooker that the Gnome was having an argument with himself as he slouched by his dimly lit desk. On the inside, the Tinderkin was locked in a vigorous debate with the other consciousness currently residing in his skull.

"He wouldn't dare move against us," said the Hookhand.

"Oh? And have your sources turned up anything on the fate of Weaver Ortson? Or is his disappearance just as mysterious as the vacant palace staff?"

"Well, I..."

Benny trailed off, giving Flinn the opportunity to seize control again. "Even Goldson and Baggs have fled the city on the pretenses of a business trip. The king is best avoided, but failing that, we must act swiftly."

"I still don't like it," Benny grumbled. He nodded at the black box on the desk. "Feels like old magic. Really old. The dangerous stuff."

Flinn felt it too. He suspected the king's courier had experienced a similar sensation, given the speed with which the man had dropped the package and unceremoniously scuttled away. "I think we will have need of as much danger as we can get, given our task."

"What is in the box, anyway?"

"I know you read the king's letter." Flinn glanced over the missive that Johan had sent alongside the parcel. "I was there."

"I don't do paperwork, and I don't read orders," said Benny Hookhand. "That's what lackeys are for."

"Sadly, we find ourselves bereft of lackeys."

"Speak for yourself. I have you," smirked Benny.

Flinn sighed inwardly as Benny laughed outwardly. "The king has provided us an artifact from the Leviathan Project."

"The what?"

"An old experiment funded by King Felik the Fourth and King Lojern of Ruskan. Its participants dabbled in forbidden magics, as I understand, so it was kept secret. And just as well; Felik and Lojern wound up feuding with the wizards they had hired."

"I remember that. Detarr Ur'Mayan and the rest, back before they got branded as foes. Lot of henchmen ran a lot of contraband for them. What were they doing again?" asked Benny.

"It was not entirely clear," Flinn replied. "Something about making guild heroes stronger. Or more cost effective. Or both. I suspect they would have known what they were looking for had they found it, but as best I can tell, all of their efforts ended in failure."

"Yeah, getting beheaded by Johan doesn't seem like much of a success."

"A timely observation," muttered the Tinderkin. "But who can say what the mages accomplished before they were disbanded? All records of the project are kept locked in the Great Vault, as are most of the artifacts used by the rogue noctomancers."

"Until now," said Benny, tapping the box with the tip of his hook.

"Until now," agreed Flinn.

"So what's in the box?"

"The last experiment of Teldir of Umbrax," said Flinn, opening the package. Several loose sheets of paper covered its contents. The top page showed a drawing of three malformed skulls clustered together, each with a third eye staring from its forehead. Arcane diagrams and a long verse were scrawled in the margins around the grim sketch. "The Stone Skulls of Az'Herad the Mad."

Beneath the paper, a red lacquered box contained a trio of carved stones. They were a perfect match for the drawing, with bloodred gemstones set in the eye sockets of each grim face. Despite the dry satin they lay on, the stones glistened as though perpetually moist, and smelled faintly of rot. Flinn glanced over subsequent pages of notes. "Teldir discovered the ritual to activate them."

"But you said the experiments all failed," said Benny.

"With spectacular violence in this case, it seems," said Flinn, flipping to a guild audit. "But some failures are more useful than others."

Benny tapped their nose knowingly. "Ah, we like to call that sort of thing a happy accident."

"I doubt that Teldir of Umbrax would use that term, were he still alive."

Benny twisted his lips into a frustrated scowl. "One thing, though. How do we know all this stuff?"

"It's in the king's instructions."

"Yeah, fine, but how does the king know all this stuff?" Benny gestured impatiently with himself. "I mean, this was all before Handor, before Johan was 'the Mighty,' right? Back when he was some farmboy dreaming of slaying gnurgs. How'd he figure out which secret wizard uncovered which forgotten relic?"

"I... uh..." Flinn frowned at the unpleasant sensation of finding himself momentarily speechless. "Well, the king has access to all of the Royal Archives and learnings. The Leviathan Project must have the letters, memos, reports, invoices... the sort of detritus that piles up around any project, secret or not. Surely he could find the information."

Benny shrugged Flinn's shoulders. "Could, maybe. But would he? Johan strike you as the kind of person to do a lot of late-night scribe work?"

"He doesn't strike me as the kind of person to welcome such lines of inquiry," said Flinn, checking over the letter again. "Nor as the patient sort. Now that we have the stones and the rites, all we need is a few corpses. And I happen to know where the king left a few."

"What about what happened to that wizard?" said Benny. "You think it's safe to use the stones?"

"Safer than angering Johan," said Flinn, placing the stones back in the box. "Besides, just because we'll perform Teldir's incantation doesn't mean we'll repeat Teldir's mistake."

"And what was that?"

"Sticking around to observe the results," said Flinn.

"Ha! So we head down, set the stones up around the stiffs, read some magic words, then bolt like a Gnome on fire," said Benny.

"We'll also need to draw some diagrams in salt and blood, set a trigger spell, that sort of thing." The Tinderkin slipped the parcel into a rucksack. "Still, you've captured the essence of the plan."

Benny nodded Flinn's head. "Seems easy enough."

"Seems like trouble," said the bannerman. She wore the red and blue heraldry of a member of the Fourth Tier's regiment of the city guard, though it was stained with the viscera of a midnight ten-cent beef roll.

"Very suspicious," said her partner, a Sun Gnome in pristine but otherwise identical livery. He studied the scene before him with dark eyes set in a brick-brown face. He must not have liked what he saw, because the silver mustache beneath his long nose drooped into an extended frown.

"I'm sure I don't know what you mean," said Duine Poldo. "Is there a problem with his paperwork?"

The Troll snored loudly behind him.

"The paperwork looks all right," the Human officer reluctantly offered, but her scowl said she wasn't one to trust appearances.

"NPC papers don't mean you can sleep in a public street," said the Sun Gnome.

"He's sleeping on private property," Mrs. Hrurk said, loudly enough to be heard from her perch on the stoop. "Those are my steps."

"So he was trespassing then?" A note of hope sounded in the taller bannerman's voice, but her face drooped when she saw the expressions Mr. Poldo and Mrs. Hrurk's wore.

"I'm sure I don't know what you mean," the Scribkin repeated.

The bannermen scowled and glanced at each other. Poldo suspected they were used to getting their way through a combination of quickly spoken jargon and implicit threats. Yet Poldo was more than familiar enough with the law to see through their jargon, and nobody out-threatens a Troll. He almost pitied the poor guards. It was clear they were looking for the sort of patrol that ended in a mug of coffee and an egg pastry, and instead they were stuck here with only unpleasant options. If they backed down, they'd lose face. If they tried to arrest Thane in this state, they might lose limbs instead.

The Sun Gnome snorted. "Still, we should interview the Troll."

"Of course," said Poldo, stepping aside.

The bannermen stared at the recumbent behemoth. Arth didn't have a proverb about letting sleeping Trolls lie, but the two guards clearly felt such an axiom should exist.

"Someone should take down his name and a statement," said the Human.

"Someone is welcome to," said Mrs. Hrurk.

The two bannermen stared at each other expectantly. An awkward silence stretched and twisted in the cold wind.

Eventually the Sun Gnome relented and, with no small amount of trepidation, approached the sleeping Troll. "Sir?" he whispered, nudging the tip of Thane's finger with the butt of his spear.

Thane's awakening was a tectonic event, forecast only when his bloodshot eyes snapped open. Arms like tree-trunks slammed the pavers and pushed him upward, and he rose with the force and roar of a mountain growing from colliding continents. "What time is... how long did I sleep?"

Poldo raised his hands in supplication. "Just a few hours," he said. "But I—"

That was as far as he got. The Gnome may as well have tried to placate an avalanche. With a roar like a rockslide, Thane barreled onto the street and sprinted Ridgeward.

"Someone should go after him," said the taller bannerman.

"Someone should," agreed her partner.

"I will," Poldo harrumphed as he adjusted his coat. "Though I doubt I'll catch up with him."

The Sun Gnome shot him a sidelong glance. "Know where he's going?"

"The Black Fathoms," breathed Gorm, staring into the gloom.

"It's almost enough to make you miss the Necropolish," said Kaitha.

"Aye," said the Dwarf.

"You miss the deadly traps, the razor-toothed horrors, and the predatory slimes?" Heraldin pointedly pulled an incisor like a dagger from the tatters of his cloak. "Really?"

"I miss knowin' what I was up against," said Gorm. "Traps and monsters and evil goo are part of the job. But this is... this is... what in the Pit is this?"

They stood on the edge of a bridge's sheer drop. The suspended pathway looked to be carved from solid stone with a precise grace that rivaled the Khazad'im's greatest ancestors. The path led to a walkway circumnavigating a massive pillar, as wide around as a watchtower, that rose from the black depths. The walkway had similar bridges spanning away from it to other pillars, which had similar walkways and ramps branching to yet more of the great towers. Above and below the party, similar networks of paths connected the pillars to each other and the walls of the cave. Some of these trunks were capped with ornate domes, while others had broken off near the top. The great monoliths stretched into the distance, filling a cavern wide and deep enough to fit all of Andarun inside.

All of this was illuminated by a wan, blue light that emanated from somewhere beyond the great pillars, like a moonrise through a titanic forest, a sacred glade for the gods of the earth and stone.

"I'd have thought the Black Fathoms would be... blacker," said Jynn.

"Look down," said Laruna.

Jynn glanced down at the cavernous depths below them, stretching farther than the thin light could reach. He looked back up again. "Ah," he said.

"Do we trust the pathways?" asked Heraldin.

Something far behind them gave a long and feral roar. Gorm suspected one of the dungeon's apex predators had found the trail of carnage they'd left through the Necropolish. "Do we have a choice?" he asked.

"They seem sturdy," said Kaitha, taking a few experimental steps over the pathway. "Probably magical, judging by the... runes?"

"Just carvings," said Gorm. The long, geometric grooves carved into the pathway and columns looked like someone had tried to draw a logical map of old oak bark.

"Possibly ritualistic," said Jynn. "This is all clearly made by the Sten."

"Careful, then," said Gorm. "We'll take it slow."

The ominous bellow echoed through the Necropolish again, though notably less distant than before.

"But not too slow," he added.

They filed across the bridge, eyes averted from the chasm yawning beneath them. On the far side of the platform ringing the closest stone trunk, two more branching paths led to another pair of pillars. There was also an archway set in the pillar itself, beyond which a set of stairs spiraled up to the next level of paths.

Kaitha scanned the stone bridges above them. "Good place for an ambush," she murmured to Gorm. "Keep your eyes up."

"Well, I sure ain't lookin' down." Gorm yearned for the feeling of solid mountain beneath his feet again.

"Although there are paths down there as well," said Jynn, peering over the edge.

"Where do you suppose all of these bridges go?" Heraldin pointed to a spot where a distant pathway led to an arch in the wall.

Gorm shrugged. "Elsewhere in the Necropolish, probably. The lower branches could lead to the Underheart, or even have secret passages back toward the Reeking Deep. And some of the upper paths..." He paused, feeling the weight of the mountain around him and gauging distances as the old stonesmiths had taught him as a lad. "They could be passages to pockets above the Pinnacle, or even to some of the unexplored caves on the surface."

"Those holes could certainly account for some of the alleged bottomless drops in the surface caves." Laruna gestured toward the top of a crumbled pillar in the distance. Above it, a wide circle in the ceiling clearly marked where a staircase had once led to some unknown heights.

"So where does that go?" asked Kaitha, nodding. Directly ahead of them, one pillar extended from all the way to the ceiling of the cavern.

Gorm ran through his mental map of the mountain, and his eyes narrowed. "Let's head that way," he said, setting out across another bridge.

"Why? Where does it go?" asked Heraldin.

"Can't say for sure without climbin' the steps." Gorm glowered at the spot where the trunk of the stone tree met the cavern's granite canopy. "But if I had to guess, I'd say somewhere behind the palace."

Laruna scowled. "But... there isn't anything behind the palace. It's just solid rock."

Gorm shared a meaningful look with Kaitha. "Solid rock, and wherever that staircase goes," he said.

"No. I understand what you mean, but there is no way for you to enter the dungeon there." The guard captain's voice was deliberate and, with the exception of a nervous crack at the end, calm.

"There's a door!" thundered the Troll, with enough force to nearly blow the slight man from his feet. He gestured furiously at the giant door set in the Ridge.

To his credit, the officer stood his ground, a feat that most professional heroes would not have attempted when staring up into the face of a raging Troll. "Y-yes, b-but the Dungeon Gate requires several keys and-and-and a lot of paperwork to open."

"And oxen!" called a less bold guard from behind a grandstand.

The Troll loosed a furious bellow, prompting the guards to take a step back. "Why?!" Thane yelled, shaking his fist at the city proper. "Why would it take paperwork to open a door?"

"W-well, it's for s-s-security," said the bannerman, whose conduct was beginning to slip over the thin line between bravery and natural selection. "It's d-dangerous to open the door. There are all... all sorts of horrors and monsters b-b-beyond... uh... it."

The Human's explanation died in his throat as the Troll squatted down, and he found himself staring into a pair of bloodred eyes above a mouth like a cutlery drawer. "Then which side do you think I belong on?" Thane growled.

"Oi, Captain!" came a holler.

Troll and bannerman swiveled their eyes up to the top of the southern watchtower, where several helmeted heads peeked out over the top of its ramparts. Most of the Dungeon Gate's contingent of guards had retreated to relative safety to learn from their leader's example or, failing that, get a good view of the consequences.

"Why not tell him about the other passages?" hollered down a lieutenant.

Thane's diamond-hard stare swiveled back to the captain, who cleared his throat. "Uh, right. Right. If you climb the Ridge and head up onto the mountain, there are numerous caves that theoretically..."

But the Troll was already away. He leapt past the dumbfounded guard, ran toward the Ridge, and then vaulted up onto the rock. The huge Shadowkin climbed quickly, punching handholds into the stone when there were none. By the time the other guards joined the stunned captain on the ground, the Troll had disappeared over the top ledge of the Ridge and sprinted off up the mountain.

"Think we should have warned him about the monsters?" asked the lieutenant.

The captain shook his head slowly, still staring at the holes in the solid rock that the Troll had made as he climbed. "Better to warn the monsters about him," he said. "I pity anything between a Troll and whatever it is he's after."

"Poor, stupid bastards." Gorm shook his head. "Never saw it coming."

"The only question is what 'it' was," said Laruna.

The corpse of Grettel Sparklit, also known as Bettel Torkin, lay face down on one of the narrow bridges that crisscrossed the Black Fathoms. She was split from the shoulder to the middle, black blood staining her gold-inlayed leather armor and the stones around her. Jynn knelt by the body, probing around the corpse with currents of sorcery.

"It's obvious," said Gorm. "That's a sword wound. A monster would have eaten the body, and a bandit would have looted the armor. This is intra-party violence."

"You're likely right," murmured Jynn. "Though I find these irregular puncture marks on her neck and face strange."

"Johan's armor has plenty of spiky bits," said Heraldin.

"These weren't from armor. Listen, we agree on the culprit," said the archmage. "But there are troubling questions about the means."

"Can't you just, you know, ask her how Johan did it?" said Heraldin. "Some light necromancy."

Jynn eyed Laruna the way a bayou deer might watch an apparent floating log drifting its way. "There are those who would frown on that."

The solamancer shrugged in a manner that suggested that, while she was certainly unwilling to participate in such abominations as necromancy, she could be elsewhere if someone was going to do it.

"But even if we do find room for... moral flexibility in this situation, I'm afraid Bettel cannot be communed with or otherwise summoned, as she's been sealed against such magics." Jynn sent a strand of amethyst sorcery at the body by way of demonstration. It crackled and fizzled out in a golden flash as it reached the body. "Another troubling event is that her body has been consecrated. This whole area has. It'd take powerful artifacts or... unacceptable measures to defile it sufficiently for necromancy to work."

Gorm sighed. "I suppose we should have assumed Johan would cover his tracks."

"It's easy to see why he'd do it, yes," said Jynn. "Consecration is one of the best ways to ensure that dead men tell no tales. But it isn't sorcery. It has to be done in the service of one's god, and what god would help cover up an intra-party murder?"

"Maybe." Gorm waved away the concern. "Ye don't have to quest with too many clerics to know the gods are fine with intra-party violence, especially if their folk are winnin' it. They can always come up with some reason for justifyin' it. All it'd take is Bettel here crossin' her eyes at a statue of Tandos or bein' insufficiently faithful to earn the whole crew some divine wrath. Or at least some divine complicity in Johan's crimes."

"Perhaps," said Jynn, doubtful. "Maybe we'll find some additional clarity when we locate the rest of the Golden Dawn."

"I wouldn't count on any easy answers," Kaitha called from the edge of the path. She and Gaist stood on the walkway running around the tall staircase in the middle of the cavern. "You're going to want to see this."

"Somethin' wrong?" asked Gorm, trotting toward them.

"Many things," said the ranger.

Gaist nodded with uncharacteristic emphasis and pointed to the other side of the pillar.

"Of course it is. It always..." Gorm's grumbling died in his throat as he walked around the pathway and into a paradox.

The cavern beyond the pillar was the cavern behind them. That is to say, the next bridge from their walkway, and indeed every other path extending northward, ended suddenly in a smooth, slightly curved barrier that extended from the ceiling down into the depths as far as the eye could follow it. Its surface was black and smooth enough to perfectly reflect the stone trees and pathways behind them, but—impossibly—it was also the source of the pale blue light that filled the cavern. Gorm could see an azure glow from behind the reflected stonework, though if that light was reflected as the trees and pathways were, it should have been somewhere behind them. The expanse they had been walking toward was an illusion cast by the monolithic sphere. Gorm had the sensation of looking forward and backward at the same time.

"What is it?" breathed Laruna.

Gorm approached the strange field, watching his own reflection approach across the narrow bridge. He gave the surface an experimental prod with his axe. Silence rang out, a ringing quiet spreading from the point of contact. He set his axe down and touched the strange wall with a gloved hand. Warmth radiated from the smooth surface through the leather of his gauntlet.

"It's like one of the prophecies you had in your lab, Jynn," said Heraldin. "Only bigger."

Judging by the slack-jawed grin the wizard wore, the omnimancer had already reached the same conclusion. "A prophetic vault!" he gasped. "The whole chamber is one giant Stennish artifact designed to channel low magic! Look at the patterns of pillars! The sigils made by looking at the paths from key angles! The—"

"The strange machine with that corpse," said Gorm. He nodded across the eastward path. A strange contraption of brass and iron had been set up along another path leading into the magical field. It reminded him of a Gnomish drill engine, but instead of a bit, the front was fit with several stone tablets, each of which was covered in strange runes.

"Umbraxian make," said Laruna, reading from a small plaque on the side of a machine. She stood back and shook her head. "Their artifice is usually as untested as it is dangerous."

"I doubt the machine did that." Heraldin pointed at the body of an Elf in golden armor, presumably Fenlovar of the Golden Dawn, slumped against the strange device. Her back and arm were hewn by several sword blows, but her own blade was still in its sheath.

"Another one cut down with a blade," said Kaitha.

"And another one with the strange puncture marks." Laruna nodded to the distinctive wounds around the dead Elf's neck.

"And another one consecrated, I'd wager," said Gorm.

Jynn nodded, kneeling next to the body.

"So where are the others?" asked Laruna.

"Presumably dead," said Kaitha.

"Yeah, obviously. You can see where they got slagged." The solamancer gestured to a brick-red stain on the blue-gray stone behind Fenlovar's corpse. "One went there. And another over on the other side of the machine. And one of them really got nailed." Here she pointed to a large splatter on the side of the pillar. "But where'd they go? They didn't run away—at least, not far—and bodies don't disappear into the air."

Gaist gestured at the vast chasm surrounding the walkways they stood on.

"Aye." Gorm peered over the edge into the inky depths. "There's a lot of air for a body to disappear into here."

"Maybe," said the solamancer, glaring at the red stains. "But it doesn't make much sense."

"None of this does," said Gorm. "Why they came down here, why Johan killed 'em, and what they were doing with this thrice-cursed contraption."

The other heroes looked at the machine. Its exact purpose was inscrutable, but to the extent that it meant to be aimed at something, it was clearly aimed at the heart of the gently glowing barrier.

"They wanted to pierce the vault. To bypass the prophecy," Jynn murmured, inspecting the machine. "They wanted to undo the knot without unraveling the weave around it."

"That even possible?" asked Gorm.

"I don't know." Jynn stepped around the machine. "Whatever is sealed in the prophetic vault could have been here for ages. Perhaps since the Sten. Whatever's on the other side of— auugh!" A line of crimson light seared across the stone beneath Jynn's feet. Smoldering graffiti spread across the ancient walkways as the sinister glow burned an arcane symbol over the face of the path.

Gorm shielded his eyes from the sudden glow. "What in the Pit is that?"

"A magical trigger!" Laruna pushed past Gorm as she rushed to the wizard's side.

"A trap?" Heraldin had to shout to be heard over a sudden cacophony.

"Ain't a trap!" Gorm hollered, but his words were lost amid the horrible, sibilant roar. His ears filled with a wet whispering, thick and sick and susurrant, as three shadows detached from the dark heights of the cavern and dove toward the heroes' platform. "It's an ambush!"

——CHAPTER 23——

The Alpine Gnurg is a master of ambush. Members of the monstrous species wait patiently in caves or crags for weeks at a time, nearly dormant until some unlucky or foolhardy creature stumbles over their dens. And though it is impossible to truly understand the mind of a hideous amalgam of titanic centipede and fleshy nightmare, it is easy to imagine something akin to anticipation flowing through their neuron clusters whenever their antennae detect the vibrations of approaching footsteps.

The specimen lurking on the southern slopes of Mount Andarun clacked its mouthparts and tensed its many appendages in just such a facsimile of eager glee. Something approached from the lower slopes—at a full run, judging by the vibrations—and it felt large.

It never occurred to the Alpine Gnurg that this might not be food. Ancient sorcery and subsequent evolution had collaborated to tune every part of the creature, from its multitude of powerful legs to its rock-shredding mandibles, for leaping out of deep tunnels and making alpine climbers wish that they'd taken up boating instead. Gnurgs that passed up opportunities to feed never passed on their genes; there weren't enough wayward hikers and careless goats around to sustain a population of cautious apex predators. If it moved and it was on a mountain, an Alpine Gnurg was built to assume it was food.

And so it was when the entrance to its tunnel was eclipsed by a shaggy figure, the gnurg lunged immediately, and subsequently discovered how an invasive species could disrupt an isolated ecosystem like the crags at the top of a dungeon mountain. This was in part because magic and nature had also conspired to make Trolls into unstoppable killing machines, and in part because the gods had yet to dream up anything that could stop this particular Troll from getting into this particular mountain.

Natural selection quickly rendered its grisly verdict. Every battle has a tipping point, beyond which it's not so much a struggle as a grim certainty playing out over the loser's protest. Once the Troll punched through an eyehole and got a grip on the faceplate of the gnurg's armor, the creature's fate was sealed. The Alpine Gnurg's final scream cut off with a grim crack.

The Troll hardly paused long enough to slick the ichor from his eyes. A moment later, he charged down the monster's burrow at a full sprint, the wounds and gashes in his skin already closing. The smarter nightmares would stay out of its way. The more foolhardy ones would share their fates with the gnurg. Neither would give Thane much pause.

Nothing on Arth could stop him from getting to her.

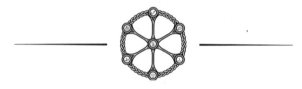

"Bloody stubborn," Gorm growled at the thing that had once been Dagnar Firdson, the Golden Dawn's resident Dwarf. This observation was only half true; the desiccated husk of a Dwarf before him was the farthest thing from bloody that a corpse could be. It didn't have a drop of fluid remaining in it. Dry heat radiated off the creature like a desert wind, and Gorm felt his own skin cracking under the withering glare of its empty eye sockets.

But the dead bastard was surely stubborn, as obstinate as a tectonic plate. Gorm punched his axe through his opponent's face. Dagnar's head exploded in a cathartic cloud of dehydrated flesh and brittle bone, run through with a web of wiry beard hair. Yet the grim particulate left gravity's call unheeded. A buzzing noise filled Gorm's ears as the cloud slowed to a stop in midair and, after pausing just long enough to mock the other laws of physics, coalesced into Dagnar's face once more, grinning mirthlessly beneath his empty eyes. The thrumming in the air took on the stilted, irregular rhythm of laughter.

"What are these thrice-cursed things? They're too tough to be zombies!" Gorm shouted to his party. Dagnar took a clumsy swing at him, and the berserker barely felt the blow in his shield. "And too weak to be revenants!"

A silver arrow burst through Dagnar's chest, and he staggered back as his torso re-solidified.

"Too solid to be a ghost!" Kaitha called, taking aim again.

"Too ugly to be vampires," Heraldin added. He parried an attack from the powdered shade of Rod Torkin. The dead man staggered back into the arc of Gaist's mace and was pulverized from the shoulder up, if only momentarily. "And too crumbly," the bard added.

Jynn stepped behind Gorm, back-to-back as Agatha of Chrate's corpse advanced. "It's a novel form of necromancy," he said over his shoulder.

"You said necromancy can't work here!" Gorm blocked another blow from Dagnar.

"I didn't think it could!" the omnimancer insisted.

"Well, there are some things you need to be thrice-cursed certain of!" Gorm shouted, punching his axe through Dagnar's skull again. "Can ye unweave the enchantment?"

"It'd be hard to, because most necromancy doesn't work here!" Jynn's voice had the shrill timbre of a man about to set aside rational thought for a moment, but any rant he was about to embark on was silenced by a sudden gout of flame. Agatha disappeared within the wall of fire, and a moment later a similar blast enveloped Dagnar.

"Fire does!" Laruna wore a smug grin as she waved from the center of another walkway.

"But only for a moment," Gorm countered. Already Dagnar's ashes were swirling back around the small stone—

The stone!

Gorm grabbed the small idol, carved in the shape of a three-eyed skull, and thrust it into the air. "The stones!" he shouted. "The stones are the source of their magic!"

"Aha! A powerful artifact!" said Jynn.

"Right!" said Heraldin. He turned back to the abomination in front of him, who was advancing on the bard with a cudgel. "Now, I just need to—"

Gaist's fist erupted from Rod Torkin's chest, clutching the stone. The weaponsmaster pulled the sorcerous heart from the corpse and, with a swift punch, sent Rod's crumbing body plummeting over the edge of the walkway into the darkness below.

"That was way too smooth," Heraldin said. "Like this wasn't your first time punching into a man's chest and ripping out his... well, whatever drives him."

Gaist shrugged.

"Really? I'd assume the rib cage gets in the way," said the bard.

Gaist flattened his hand and demonstrated a short, piercing jab by way of morbid illustration.

"That is both awesome and terrifying," said Heraldin.

"All right." Jynn held up Agatha's stone. "Now what do we do?"

"You're the wizard," said Gorm. "I thought ye'd know."

"Oh, researching the right spell to use on an artifact can take days. Weeks. And... uh... we have much less time than that." The wizard nodded to Gorm's hand.

"What do ye—thrice-cursed bones!" Gorm cursed as he looked at the ash swirling around his hand like a cloud of flies. "Drop 'em!"

He hurled the stone out into the black depths of the cavern. It dropped, as stones do, followed by those thrown by Gaist and Jynn. The air thrummed as three clouds of dust and ash swarmed after the artifacts down into the darkness, like bees after their queens.

Gorm and the heroes took the moment to join ranks as the clouds bore their stones back to their platform. "They just keep coming back," he growled.

"So how do we stop them again?" Heraldin asked.

"That's the million-giltin question," said Kaitha. "It's a trick fight."

"Thrice curse it," swore Laruna.

Jynn shook his head. "A wha—"

"A trick fight," snapped Gorm. "Ye wizards are always makin' traps and artifacts and weird creatures, right? And you're always trying to make 'em invincible and foolproof and all that, right?"

"If you mean wizards generally try to make their creations succeed, then yes," said Jynn.

"Right. Only nothin's invincible. Nothin's foolproof. A potion of fire resistance washes off in water, right? A spear keeps cavalry at bay, but it ain't so useful once the enemy's in close."

"A knight's armor has holes in front of his eyes which, as it turns out, is a great place to shoot a knight," Kaitha offered. "And sometimes a wizard gets close enough to perfecting their creation that there's only one or two ways to kill it. You can't overpower the threat. You have to know the trick. They're very dangerous"

"They're thrice-cursed obnoxious, that's what they are," said Gorm. "Only silver lining is that usually the trick is killin' all the wizards."

"I doubt that would help in this case," said Jynn.

"Not directly, anyway," Gorm grumbled.

Kaitha ignored him. "Heraldin, try hitting one with water. Gaist, see if the stones have any loose bits or carvings that come off. Jynn, go through our potions and your spells for ideas. Laruna, can you get a stone hot enough to melt it?"

"Maybe?" said the solamancer. "It depends on the enchantment around the carving."

"Well, it's worth a shot." The Elf fired off a silver arrow for emphasis. "We need to figure it out before we tire."

"And if we don't happen to be fortunate enough to be lugging around whatever their weakness is?" asked Jynn.

A thrumming, buzzing chuckle filled the air as the corpses of the Golden Dawn advanced.

"Then start praying to any god listening that Gorm and Niln had a point with all their talk of destiny." There was no humor in the ranger's smirk as she shot Gorm a sidelong glance. "Because we'll need some help from above to survive this."

"Please! Please! A little longer!" Thane's aimless prayers rode on ragged breaths as he barreled down the twisted passages of Mount Wynspar. He sprinted past the nameless horrors and lesser monsters that scrambled unheeded from his path. He leapt bottomless chasms with barely a thought. Traps fired and misfired as he trampled their ancient mechanisms; their darts and arrows bounced from his thick hide, their blades bent and broke against the force of his charge.

Still he ran on, gasping words to someone who could not hear him, and running all the faster so that she might. "I'm sorry... I'm sorry I left... I will be with you soon... hang on."

Sometimes he ran in total darkness. Some of the corridors he traversed were illuminated by glowing fungus or shimmering crystals. Ahead, his eyes caught a faint glow that seemed both fainter and larger.

His foot crushed an old pressure plate, causing stone walls to slide in place around him. Presumably the tiny chamber would soon start filling with sand or water or poisoned gas, but the Troll didn't pause to find out. He crashed through the wall with a punch like a rockslide, rounded a corner—

And bounced off something more solid than the mountain around him.

Thane shook his head and looked up. A wall of emptiness blocked further passage. The barrier glowed faintly the color of an evening sky, and behind its sorcerous light he could see the rubble of the trap wall and his own panicked face staring back at him.

The Troll leapt to his feet and pounded on the barrier. It rang with a sort of distorted silence whenever he hit it, but otherwise his blows had no effect. His impotence was as alien as the wall itself, and an unfamiliar panic began to well up inside him before he remembered a side passage.

It took a precious minute or so to double back through the broken trap room, where green acid was dribbling from broken pipes in the hole Thane had punched through the wall. He turned down the side path, ground through the machinery of a crushing wall trap, blew through a scarg nest, and found himself face-to-face with the same enchanted surface. This barrier had a slightly different curve than the previous one, bending back and toward the top of the hallway like the edge of some massive sphere. Otherwise it was identical to the other wall, and just as immovable.

"No!" he cried, pounding on the wall, and the resulting boom of silence drowned out his own sobs. "I need to get to them! Let me pass!" On the last command, he swung his fist at the barrier for emphasis, but it never connected. The barrier began to disintegrate at his words, beginning at the point where his fist would have slammed it. The hole widened rapidly, shedding particles of faint light that twinkled like miniscule stars before falling like snow. The momentum of Thane's punch carried him stumbling through the gap to the other side. By the time he looked back, there was nothing left of the barrier except a line on the floor where the dust and mold stopped, leaving only pristine stone carvings that put Thane in mind of his old garden.

It was confusing and unsettling, but there was no time for it now. With a weary groan, Thane hurled himself down the passageway as fast as his tired legs would carry him.

Exhaustion kills.

It was one of the first axioms Gorm learned as a professional hero, a painful if not terminal lesson that every young adventurer comes to grips with quickly in the field. A shield offers no defense without the strength to lift it. A sword is just a sharp accessory without the energy to swing it. Armor is more weight than protection for a hero at the end of his reserves. There were potions and enchantments and magical gear to help prolong a hero's endurance, but even they had their limits, and when they reached their end the hero using them tended to as well.

That was the worst part of facing the undead. Worse than the unsettling smiles, their stench, and the stains they left everywhere, was their unholy stamina. They might have been slow, clumsy, weak, and predictable, but the restless dead did not tire.

And if he couldn't put them down before he did...

"Doesn't look good," Kaitha panted beside him.

"Keep tryin' things," he said, glaring at the undead half of the Golden Dawn on the other side of the walkway. "What about acid? We tried acid?"

"Three varieties," said Heraldin. "Now they'll burn your skin if you touch them."

"But they're still coming," said Jynn.

"What about somethin' sticky? Can we glue 'em down?" said Gorm.

"Shouldn't have passed on Boomer's goo arrows," said Kaitha.

"And we can't melt the stones?" Gorm asked. "Felt like we got really close with that one." Dagnar's flesh, as it were, was blackened and charred around a faint orange glow in the center of his chest.

Laruna shook her head, her hands balled into fists beside her. "I can try again, but powerful magic is binding the stones together."

An idea struck Gorm. "What about the—"

"She was using the Wyrmwood Staff," said Jynn.

"Burn it!" And then, in an unwitting example of Nove's sixth principle of universal irony, he added, "Any other way we can get the stones hot enough?"

Nove's principles of universal irony actually document their own greatest flaw. Nove penned his sixth principle after a series of high-profile demonstrations of the first four principles in the academies of Essenpi catastrophically failed. When the watched pot incident resulted in fatalities, the high chancellors of academia forbade Nove from further experiments.

Disheartened, Nove worked out a mathematical proof that showed that even if his principles were accurate, they could not be measured or relied upon. Nove's Bidirectional Paradox proved that if his principles were ever validated enough to become laws, they would make the universe too predictable and thus immediately disprove themselves. Or, put another way, a person cannot avoid saying things that might be ironic, because it's actually more ironic when an unexpected statement or behavior leads to unexpected consequences. The theory, proofs, and full ramifications of the sixth principle took Nove a full year to pen. These volumes are seldom cited or read, however, because he eclipsed the work when he famously summed it up over a beer with colleagues afterward as, "the gods are bastards."

Gorm was certain that some deity must have a cruel sense of humor, because the moment he uttered his question, a bright blue light flared near the uppermost reaches of the cavern. In a few heartbeats the prophetic vault dissolved into a cascade of sparkling particles, draining away the cool blue light that had filled the cavern. Behind the falling barrier, high above their heads, a crescent of flame carved itself from the blackness, dripping white-hot gobbets of molten doom. The fire cast a crimson light that illuminated a serpentine neck as thick as an ancient oak, ending in a reptilian head that was the same size as a Gnomish harvest machine, though with significantly more sharp bits. Titanic wings unfurled like a galleon's sails as two luminous green orbs looked down. The Dragon of Wynspar rumbled like a long-dormant volcano as it regarded the living and undead heroes assembled on the walkway beneath it.

Gorm felt his spine melt and his legs turn to jelly under that molten glare. "It can't be..." he breathed.

"The dragon!" Heraldin punctuated his cry with a trio of glass orbs that burst into cobalt clouds. The sudden explosion startled Gorm enough that his survival instincts bypassed the malfunctioning circuits of his brain, hardwired his legs, and sent him sprinting up the nearest walkway.

The smoke startled the dragon as well. It reared back as its scales flared with crimson light, painting the cavern the color of blood. The beast pulled in a lungful of air with a sound like a hurricane wind, and then held its breath as its head aligned on its target.

Gorm was holding his breath too, even as he ran, and that instant stretched out over a tiny, agonizing eternity as the whole world seemed to hesitate for a moment.

Then a stream of fire, white-hot and blistering, poured from the dragon's maw. The undead members of the Golden Dawn shambled along the walkway as fast as their decaying legs could carry them, which meant that they made it two steps before the spray of molten death engulfed them. The enchanted stones within them audibly popped, and three wailing souls rose like ghoulish, glowing smoke from the center of the inferno. When they dissipated, there was nothing left of the undead heroes but a glowing hole in the stone walkway.

"Run! Get to cover!" Gorm hollered, but even as he ran for the nearest pillar he doubted it could provide much shelter from the dragon's flame. The other heroes scattered.

"You said there wasn't a dragon!" screamed Jynn as Gorm overtook the mages on the narrow walkway around the stone tree.

"I didn't think there was!" Gorm shouted.

"Well, there are some things you need to be absolutely certain—"

"Shut up!" Gorm shoved Jynn and Laruna toward the pillar and away from a lance of dragonfire. Heat like the center of a forge rolled over him as the flame passed, blistering skin and singeing hair. He might have succumbed to the heat anyway had Laruna not managed to deflect the stream with a weave of fire magic.

"Are you all right?" the solamancer gasped as the dragon's flame faded.

"Aye, thanks." Gorm scrambled to his feet, already scanning the cavern for the others. "Where is everyone?"

"There are Heraldin and Gaist." Jynn pointed across the black chasm to the next pillar. The bard waved while Gaist peered around the stone trunk to watch the dragon.

"Good," said the Dwarf. "And the dragon's focused on us."

"No." Laruna peered around the pillar. "It's turning away."

"What?" Gorm's heart plunged into the pit of his stomach as he scrambled for a better view.

The dragon picked its way through the stone branches of the petrified trees like an eagle climbing through a bramble. Its almost-feline body could move with fluid grace, but its giant wings made maneuvering through the tangle of stone an ungainly task. It unfurled them for balance, then tucked them back in to squeeze under a path, then flapped them to avoid tipping over the side. Yet as awkward as its progress was, it was still gaining on the figure sprinting along the paths ahead of it.

"Kaitha!" Gorm screamed.

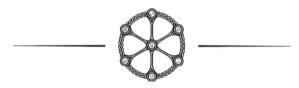

The ranger slowed as she reached what was, appropriately enough, an effective dead end. The path ahead ended at a broken pillar housing the ruined remains of a stone staircase, with no path around it and no branching turns. The pathways crisscrossing through the air above her were far out of reach, and the blackness below held no hope of a safe landing.

Her own walkway shook with a sudden violence as something heavy landed behind her. By the time she regained her footing and turned, the dragon was already rearing up, scales flaring bloodred as it pulled in a breath. Hot doom bubbled behind its dagger teeth.

Kaitha knew, even as she drew her bow, that it wasn't enough. Her life would be cut short and cauterized as well. The best she could say was that she went down fighting. She breathed out her regrets, nocked an arrow in one fluid motion, and set her sights on the dragon's baleful eye. The entire world seemed to hesitate for a moment.

With the exception of one Troll.

Thane plummeted from the heights of the cavern with a roar like an avalanche and landed squarely on the end of the dragon's muzzle. The sheer force of a rapidly descending Troll to the face cannot be ignored, not even by an elder dragon, and the creature's head was snapped down and to the side just as the spout of dragonfire came rushing from its maw.

Thane screamed as white-hot flames caught him directly in the midsection. The dragon screeched as the struggling Troll punched through scales and bones, tearing flesh and breaking horns and teeth. The air was rent with the cries of two of Arth's most fearsome titans experiencing new and unfamiliar pain.

The dragon's flames sputtered and died, but the Troll kept up the assault, sending loose scales and hot blood raining down on the stone. In desperation, the beast slammed its own head against the stone pillars, and Thane cried out as his bones snapped under the crushing force. With a final shake of its head, the dragon flung its assailant away and careened over the edge of the walkway in a motion caught between a dive and fall. It unfurled its wings and glided beneath Kaitha's path like a great red whale passing beneath a fishing skiff as it fled back toward the entrance of the cavern. Other stone trees in the path of the beast shuddered as the dragon collided with them in its reckless, panicked flight.

She turned back to her own walkway, where Thane writhed on the stone. He lay at the center of a splatter of black, viscous blood, his arms and legs tracing erratic pathways as they flailed. His torso was a mess of thin, charred tendrils of flesh that waved around in a futile dance as they tried to weave themselves back into a Troll. His mouth was open wide in a scream that she couldn't hear, though Kaitha couldn't tell if he was silent or the blood pounding in her ears had drowned him out.

Then he looked at her with eyes like a sunset, crimson flecked with gold and fiery orange, and the pain and shock seemed to drain from him. The most beautiful smile Kaitha had ever seen bloomed on his face, and he opened his mouth to greet her.

But rather than words, thick, black blood welled up from his throat. The light behind his irises faded, and he slumped lifeless to the floor.

——CHAPTER 24——

"Another one goes!" laughed Ignatius. The priest cackled as red light flared in the eyes of the shrine of Mordo Ogg. "Big or small, all are the same in death!"

The red light grew brighter, and did not fade.

"And you were a big one!" snickered the priest.

"Hey! It's not funny," said a small voice. "You shouldn't laugh, you meanie."

Ignatius was not used to being addressed as such, or even addressed at all. Most people averted their eyes as they walked hurriedly past Mordo Ogg's shrine near Sculpin Down. The dark-robed priest turned to see a small Gnoll child leaning on a cane. "What?" he asked.

"Losing someone hurts," The boy looked at his feet with his tail tucked beneath his legs as if remembering a distant pain. "A lot. Laughing only makes it worse."

"I... uh... well, death is a part of life—the last bit, aha, and... I... well, it's good to not make it more than it is..." Ignatius found it difficult to explain himself to the small child because, like so many people called out by children, his rationale was stupid. Much of what passes for wisdom are actually attempts to paper over faults and weaknesses with pithy slogans. The priest tried another one. "I think it's important to find humor where you can in this life."

"Well, I think it's important not to be a smelly old coot whose brain is turning to cheese!" snapped the Gnoll, demonstrating the limits of the innocent wisdom of children. He hobbled off to another pair of giggling pups, who hoisted him up to support him. The trio ran laughing from the square.

Ignatius snorted as he watched them go. Being laughed at did hurt, as it turned out. Still, none of Mordo Ogg's clients had complained in all of Ignatius' years of service. He giggled at the thought and turned back to the shrine.

The crimson light in Mordo Ogg's skeletal eyes hadn't faded.

"Are you still here?" asked the priest, leaning in close to the statue. "Don't fight it. Don't fight. It happens to everyone."

The light remained unmoved.

After a while, Ignatius stepped back. "Usually it doesn't take this long, though," he added to the unwavering glow. "What's keeping you?"

Kaitha cradled Thane's head in her lap, stroking his fur as she wept. The Troll's glassy eyes stared up at the sobbing Elf.

Gorm blinked back his own tears. He'd assumed there was a finite list of friends he might see perish in the depths of Wynspar, and Thane was the last person he'd have put on it. To see his old companion now, after so long, just to watch him die was a new and awful kind of ache.

But it didn't change the rules of the dungeon delving.

"Come on lass," he said, resting a hand on her shoulder. "Come on. We need to go."

Kaitha didn't seem to hear him. "You came back," Kaitha sobbed to the Troll. "You came back for me... why?"

"Because he couldn't live in a world without you," said Heraldin softly. "I think... I think he knew that some treasures you cannot keep, no matter how much you wish it was different. But they are still worth everything. And he gave everything for you." The bard drew in a ragged breath and looked at Gaist with red-rimmed eyes. "I see that now."

Gaist nodded solemnly.

"You came back," the Elf repeated. She kissed Thane's forehead, and her lips came away with a thin coat of gray dust. Thane's face had turned the gray of old ash, his skin cracking and brittle.

"Not to be insensitive," Jynn murmured in Gorm's ear. "But is such rapid desiccation normal for a Troll that has... you know..."

"Don't know," said Gorm, wiping his eyes. "Ain't never seen a Troll... you know... before. But it ain't the time for that sort of question. Ain't even time for mournin'. The dragon's still about." He could still hear the beast thrashing around in the depths of the cavern. "Let's go."

"We'll take him to a temple healer..." Laruna forced the words through a throat choked with tears. "They have old magics and rites that could... that might... we have to try if there's a chance that—"

The mage's hopeful words were lost in a sudden gale that howled through the cavern with the force of a tempest. Thane's body blew apart like a great, gray sand dune in a desert wind. The last of his remains blew through Kaitha's scrabbling fingertips and swept into the abyss. As soon as he was gone, the wind died as fast as it had come, leaving only traces of gray dust on the bloodstains and a mournful wail echoing through the broken hall.

"No." Kaitha doubled over under the weight of her grief, her tears mingling with the dust and the blood. "No!"

"Come on." Gorm put his hand on her shoulder, though it was as much to steady himself as to call her back to the quest. Elsewhere in the cavern, the dragon still raged. "We see it through to the end, remember? No matter what. We need to move before we lose any more."

Kaitha didn't seem to hear him. "He came back," she sobbed. "He came back for me, and he... and I never got the chance to... I never got to tell him..." The Elf broke off, overtaken by her sorrow.

"He already knows, lass," Gorm told her. "I'm sure he knows."

"Don't give me empty words!" The Elf finally looked at him then, her eyes bubbling with agony and tears. "He's dead! How could anyone be sure of what he knows?"

"The light won't fade!" Ignatius slapped the side of the stone skull as if to dislodge a stubborn particle, but the ruby glow remained in each of Mordo Ogg's hollow sockets. "Why won't you go?"

The illumination burned brighter in mute protest, then faded back to its strong, steady crimson.

"It never takes this long. It—oh, wait! What?" Ignatius clambered into the lap of the statue and leaned in close to its face, like an oversized child demanding attention from a stiff and stoic parent. "Are you going?"

The glows in the skull's eyes appeared to be dimming for a hopeful moment, but closer inspection revealed that they were just contracting. Even as the lights got smaller, their glow grew more intense, until they were two pinpricks of a diamond-hard, white-hot glare.

"What are you—" Ignatius began, and then the lights exploded.

The blast was no bigger than the firecrackers that alchemists sold to revelers and miscreant children, but it was enough to blind any priest within a nose-length of the shrine. Ignatius tumbled off the statue, smoke trailing from the singed remnants of his eyebrows and the overpowering smell of ozone ringing in his nostrils.

It took him several befuddled moments to untangle his limbs, and once he did, he found it difficult to stand. It wasn't just that the blast left him blinded, half-deaf, and bleeding from his nose; now a howling wind was descending from the mountain with enough force to rip banners from their polls and topple careless pedestrians. Ignatius slid back along the cobbles as he braced himself against the gale. A flurry of paper blew in from the Third Tier, followed by a gaggle of clerks bouncing down the stairs in pursuit. The clouds above began to flow in a far more pronounced spiral.

Then the wind was gone, or at least diminished enough for Ignatius to stand again and the administrators to chase down their fleeing paperwork. When he finally looked back to the shrine of Mordo Ogg, the priest saw two azure flames blazing in the eye sockets.

It had been a long time since Ignatius knew the cold prickle of fear; he'd made his peace with death years ago, and since then he'd grown friendly with it. Yet where a familiar warmth should have kept rhythm in time to life's cycle beating against the edge of oblivion, now there was only a frozen blue flame.

Icy terror bloomed in Ignatius' chest, and hot tears cut through the soot staining his face. He shook with horror and fury as he stared at the offending gleam in his master's eyes. "Why won't you move on?" he rasped. "It's time to leave."

Timing is everything.

There is an old adage that timing is most important in comedy and in combat. This lends itself to a humorous series of observations about how jesters are like professional heroes, though such statements are usually made by the jesters and in the absence of said adventurers. Other professions might take umbrage as well, though only because they feel an equal claim to the significance of timing. A day trader on the Wall can make or lose a fortune on the speed of their trade sprites. Seconds can literally be the difference between life and death for a healer's patients. And any pastry chef in Andarun could tell you that the shortest increment of time in the universe is the span it takes a perfect soufflé in the oven to become a misshapen lump.

Yet professional heroes live and die by timing like no other profession. A good adventurer must know how to move in sync with swinging pendulums, release the rope at just the right moment to land on the far ledge, and dance through the rhythm of a group melee. A hero needs to be able to sense when it's the right time for a dramatic line, or a sneak attack, or a show of force. And more important than any of that is knowing when it is time to leave.

It was past time to leave.

Gorm could see the Dragon of Wynspar clambering from the dark depths. It can be difficult to read expressions on a face as long as a chariot and full of teeth like claymores, but something in the crimson dragon's eyes suggested that it had moved on from its flight response and was ready to give fight a good show of it. It unfurled its broken wings, tattered and ripped by its fall, and began to advance on the party in a limping, stumbling clip.

"Get movin'! Find cover!" he shouted to the other heroes. He watched the dragon build up figurative steam and literal smoke as it charged through the cavern. "Go! We'll be right behind ye."

The party didn't need much encouragement, or at least much more than a rampaging dragon, and they ran down the branching pathways toward the heart of the cavern. The beast roared behind them.

"All right, lass. See it through to the end, remember? Bein' professional saves lives. And, he didn't..." Gorm swallowed the lump in his throat and tugged gently on the Elf's arm. "He didn't die so ye could throw yer life away."

He meant it to be a gentle reminder, but the ranger flinched as though physically struck by the words. Still, whether it was shock or pain or reason, something he said got Kaitha on her feet and they sprinted after the others. Whatever the Dwarf's stout legs lacked in reach they made up for in vigor, and he was gaining on the mages when he heard the sound of a rushing wind. The dragon's enraged bellow paused long enough for a sharp rush of air behind him, like Ad'az filling the great bellows of his divine smithy. The other heroes scrambled behind the next stone tree, but it was too far for Gorm to make in time.

Adrenaline lanced through Gorm like lightning through an oak, activating instincts honed over decades of not being skewered, disintegrated, or eaten by monsters. He leapt out over the void just as the dragon breathed a wall of fire toward him.

Gorm watched that frozen moment, that tiny eternity where time seemed to slow to a standstill, over and over again in his mind.

Several things went right for the Dwarf. The first was that the dragon, having been subjected to a Troll to the face and subsequently tumbling through the stone glade like a flaming pinball, was clearly wounded enough to diminish its capacity for violence. Its fiery breath came out as more of a smoldering cough.

The blobs of mucus and magma that Wynspar's guardian hacked up were still enough to roast Gorm in his armor, but the Dwarf had timed his leap perfectly, judged the gap with an expert eye, and been nudged in the right direction by the sort of air currents that form when stale dungeon air is stirred by an ancient elemental spirit of fire on a murderous rampage. The uninitiated might have called it luck. A veteran hero would say timing is everything. Either is a euphemism for the fact that in any given life-threatening scenario, some adventurers beat the odds.

Yet, odds being what they are, some don't.

He looked back as he hit the ledge and saw Kaitha had made the same calculation, attempted the same leap, sought safety in the same walkway. Yet she must have been a step behind him, or miscalculated the gap in haste or grief, or perhaps caught a less favorable wind, because her trajectory wasn't leading to the same destination. Gorm's eyes met the Elf's in that frozen fraction of a second while she hung in the air, and his stomach dropped as time resumed its horrible march. The ranger dropped as well, and then she was gone.

"Kaitha!" Hot tears streamed down Gorm's face as he shouted. He scrambled to look over the edge; a yawning black void stared back at him impassively.

He wanted to search the darkness for her, to call out again, to figure out a plan to get her back. But dragons are nothing if not difficult to ignore, and the monster still bounding toward him was sufficient reminder of how quickly and easily two dead party members could become three if he lost sight of the mission.

He scrambled back from the edge just as the dragon rushed past him, still dribbling molten slobber from its wounded maw. The dragon's advance hadn't been so much a final charge as a push past enemy lines to get back to its lair, and now it limped and stumbled back toward wherever it had come from.

Gorm set his grief aside, next to his mourning and regret. There would be time to sit down with them later, unpack them, and attempt to drown them in a barrel of ale. But now, he rejoined the remainder of his party with a grim look in his red-rimmed eyes.

"Where's Kaitha?" Laruna asked.

The Dwarf shook his head.

"No," whispered Heraldin. "She can't be—"

"Later," Gorm growled. "There'll be a time for questions and tears and raisin' glasses to the fallen later, but only if we survive. We've got to finish this."

"And what 'this' are we finishing?" Laruna demanded. "We were down here to prove there was no dragon. I'd say that ship has sailed!"

"We wanted to prove Johan was down here for something besides killing the dragon," Jynn offered.

The solamancer shook her head. "Was he? He and his party tried to break through that wall that the dragon was hiding behind, before some of them turned undead."

"You don't believe that," Jynn said

Laruna shrugged. "Doesn't matter. The people will."

"I thought we were avoiding being executed," said Heraldin.

"That doesn't seem to be working out either," Laruna growled. "Not for all of us."

Gorm chewed on his lip and watched the light of the dragon's flame shrink as it fled to the mountain depths. It was true that this adventure had significantly more giant, fire-breathing reptiles than he'd anticipated, and of all the projections a hero made when planning a quest, the number of dragons seemed like the worst one to underestimate.

Still, professional heroes encountered unexpected monsters all the time, and it wasn't cause for uncertainty. The guild's standard course of action was to kill and loot the foe or, failing that, retreat, regroup with other heroes, come back with better gear, and then kill and loot the foe. Besides, the dragon wasn't unexpected. Everybody on Arth expected there to be a dragon. The markets had quite literally bet a fortune on it. They had bet everyone's fortune on it. And now they expected Gorm to do what Gorm did best.

Get in, get angry, get violent, get out, and get rich. It was practically a reflex for the berserker after all of these years. He was already in, and with two dear friends lost, he was far past angry. If he could get violent enough to make it out of the dungeon, riches were a given. Even Johan couldn't touch him.

Doubts tugged at his mind. They had strong evidence that the Golden Dawn were killed by Johan, and not a monster. They'd been sent into a trap with some hideous new form of undead waiting for them. They had the paperwork to prove that the dragon wasn't responsible for any of the recent attacks in its name, and the old Stennish magic had hidden the dragon from everyone. And when he put it all together... well, when he put it all together he had far more questions than answers. But the one answer he did have had always worked before, and it would satisfy his growing itch for vengeance. Gorm's wrath, his paperwork, and his purpose were totally aligned. What came next was obvious.

Gorm drew his axe. "We keep going."

"Where?" demanded Laruna.

"Not entirely sure on the destination, but we've got a contract, and that gives us a direction." Gorm blinked back his own tears as he pointed an axe in the direction of the fleeing dragon. "We're in a dungeon, we're fightin' a dragon, and there may still be a treasure. That's as basic as quests come. Much as it hurts, no matter the cost, we swore we'd see it through to the end. And this ain't over."

"There's still time," said Johan the Mighty. "I still have time."

Garold Flinn couldn't say for sure if that was true. He wasn't entirely clear on what the king was referring to, or even if Johan was addressing him. Yet the assassin smiled and said "Yes, sire," as he approached the throne, because not agreeing that Johan had more time would likely increase the odds that Flinn didn't.

The king sat perfectly still on the throne, staring into nothing with eyes as wide, round, and mad as the full moon. His cornsilk hair spilled in unkempt tangles over his golden armor; the pallid skin of his face stretched into a rictus sneer. It was unclear to Flinn how long the paladin had sat motionlessly watching the air, though he found a worrying sign in an enterprising spider that had found time to spin a web from the king's pauldron to the royal armrest.

"I sent the Stone Skulls of Az'Herad the Mad. They'll... they'll work," said Johan. "I still have time. It has to work."

"Indeed, sire," said Flinn, glancing around the empty throne room. He had seldom ventured into the chamber, but these days there weren't many prying eyes within the palace. There didn't seem to be anyone at all, yet his eyes settled on a thick rolled rug inexpertly propped in a dark corner.

"It will work. It has to. Mr. Flinn did what I asked," said Johan.

The king said it to the empty air with total conviction, as one might tell a garden hedge about a bedrock truth.

"Absolutely, sire. Every detail to your specification."

"Every detail," said Johan. "It will work. I have time."

"Indeed, sire." Flinn's eyes were locked on the rolled-up rug in the corner. There was something familiar in the fat bulge at the center of the carpet, and even more so about the slipper extending from the bottom of it. He weighed his risks carefully and added, "And I'm sure Mr. Ortson's plan will work as well."

The king didn't startle. He barely flinched as a shadow of doubt flickered over his sweating face. "Flinn followed every detail," he reiterated.

Benny's questions swirled in the recesses of his mind, but Flinn pushed them aside as he pulled together a plan.

It is distressing for anyone to discover that their boss has been secretly outsourcing part of their portfolio, but this is especially true for assassins. In murder and in marketing, if you're not buying or selling, you're the product. If Johan had someone else kill Ortson, or even if the king had bloodied his own gauntlets in the act, it was yet another sign that Garold Flinn was becoming less indispensable. Good assassins, or at least upright ones, never stick around long enough to become dispensable.

"And on top of that, I have a contingency plan, Majesty," he said.

Johan's eyes finally flicked to the Gnome. He said nothing, but sat breathing heavily as flecks of spittle gathered on his lip.

"To buy more time," said Flinn smoothly. "Shall I set it in motion?"

"Yes. The contingency. Ha ha…" The king's gaze slipped back to the space in front of him. "I have time. I planned it perfectly. We can stop… stop everything. This will work. It has to."

"I'd bet my life on it, sire." Flinn bowed as he backed away from the throne. It was unclear if the king even noticed his departure, but he still waited until he was out of the throne room before turning on his heel and fleeing down the hall.

"What was that?" Benny Hookhand asked as they ran. "I don't even know what the king's talking about!"

"Nor do I," Flinn breathed, darting back into a servant's hallway.

Benny scowled. "Then how is your plan going to buy him—"

"I didn't say I'd buy him time. I plan to buy us time," said Flinn, turning his frown into a smile. "Primarily by being elsewhere."

Elsewhere, water pooled in the dust.

This is very common and usually not worthy of note, except in stories of bad plumbing or mold infestations. Water pools in the dust of caves and caverns all the time, in accordance with several laws of physics and chemistry.

Except this water was treating the laws of physics and chemistry as general suggestions. For example, most water evaporates and disappears shortly after landing on a dusty surface, and all the more so if the cave it occupies is subjected to extreme heat. Yet the Elven tears that had fallen into the powdered remains of a recently deceased Troll endured despite the proximity to a raging dragon and its flaming breath.

If anything, the puddle of tears seemed to be slowly expanding. Its edges bled along the stone, lifting the gray-blue dust and swirling it around in faint patterns that did not glow, but held the edge of a glow, like the sky above the horizon at twilight.

The pool kept expanding, coursing from some unseen spring. Water and dust ran through grooves in the stone, tracing patterns carved by long-dead hands. And the more the water spread, casting faint echoes of sigils into the dark, the faster it poured from nowhere. Soon, the tears flowed like a river, tracing azure lines along the ancient pathways of the stone glade.

"That's not normal, right?" said Laruna. "They don't usually do that."

"Don't know," said Gorm. "Ain't fought a dragon before."

"Legends say dragons lie on great hoards of treasure," said Heraldin.

"Aye, but that's before ye wake 'em up," said Gorm. "They don't keep lying down after ye make 'em mad. I think." He peeked around the scarred and battered pillar that served as cover for the five remaining heroes. Beyond him the dragon lay with its back to the party on a large platform suspended over the deep pit of the Underheart. The creature's hide had dulled to the flat black of a charred log, with amber traces of latent heat glowing in the grooves between its scales. "Besides, I don't see any treasure."

"It's using its own body as a barricade," said Jynn.

The stone platform certainly looked like an excellent site for an enterprising dungeon designer to store a massive hoard. It sat in the dustless, pristine space beyond the fallen magical prophetic vault, near the rear of the cavernous stone forest and yet somehow feeling like the center of it, if not the center of the whole mountain. The stone trunks and branching paths were arrayed around the dais in patterns that subtly drew the eye back to the center. This was where any hero would expect to see the golden monkey idol, or the weapon of destiny, or dunes of gold coins and gems punctuated by the occasional overflowing chest. They still might be there, Gorm thought hopefully, obscured by the dragon's massive backside.

As he watched, the dragon's reptilian head snaked up from behind its torso, like a bannerman poking up from behind a rampart. Its scales flared a furious crimson when it saw the Dwarf staring, and it managed to cough a flaming loogie at him.

Gorm watched the gobbet of fire hurtle past him and into the darkness below. "Not much of a fireball," he told the others. "Can't have too much left. We just wait it out a bit before we go on the attack. Gaist, ye'll need to get the drop on it, if ye can find a way up to the paths that—"

"But what is it defending?" Laruna asked, peering around the pillar.

Heraldin shrugged. "Probably a treasure. Maybe a nest."

"Right," said Gorm. "So, once Gaist is in position—"

"It's scared," said Laruna.

"It should be," said Heraldin.

The solamancer stared at the dragon as a student might peer at a particularly complex equation. "No, I mean I think it's scared of losing something. I don't think that's just a treasure. It could have fled down to the depths to escape us. Something else is motivating it."

"So a nest then," said the bard.

"Don't think of it like it's a person," said Jynn. "It's really an animal driven by needs like greed and self-preservation in equal measure. I'm sure it gets confused sometimes."

"Sounds like most people to me." Laruna returned her gaze to the other heroes. "I don't think it's a nest. This isn't about instinct."

"It's a flying fire-breathing lizard the size of a barn!" said Heraldin. "You can't know what it's thinking!"

There was almost an audible slap as the same thought struck them all at once.

"Yes, I can!" said Laruna.

"The Eye of the Dragon!" said Jynn, shuffling through his enchanted satchel.

"How does it work?" the solamancer asked as the wizard produced the gemstone.

"The Tandosians just stuck it on a hat," said Gorm.

"I'm fairly certain that's not how it works," said Jynn, looking over the crystal.

"Besides, we don't have any hats," said the bard. "None to spare, anyway," he added when he noticed Gaist eyeing his wide-brimmed headgear.

Gorm pulled the solamancer aside as the others examined the gem and discussed the terms of surrendering a hat. "Lass, I see where you're goin' with this. Ye're wonderin' what it's thinkin', or if it has baby dragons, or some other reason for delay. But that thing killed our friends. It's tryin' to kill us right now. If we hesitate... if we don't do what we need to, we could all go the way of... of..." He shook his head. "I trust ye, but are ye sure about this?"

"No," said Laruna, and Gorm was surprised to see tears running down the woman's face. She wiped them away when she caught him looking. "I wish it was simple too, you know. I hate all the cloak and dagger drake spit in the city, and I hated not knowing what we'd face down here. And now we know, and finally it seems so straightforward. That thing killed Thane, and then it killed Kaitha, and I want to kill it. I want it to be wrong, to be evil. I want it to deserve everything I throw at it."

Gorm had to take a deep breath to loosen his white-hot grip on his axe. "Aye," he croaked. "I want that too."

"But I can't have another Bloodroot on my conscience," said Laruna, gulping back more tears.

The words were like a lance of fire through Gorm's heart. He couldn't speak, but shook his head.

The mage continued, "I want vengeance. I want a way to... to win... for all we lost to not be in vain. But I need to be right about it. And this feels wrong. So I... I can't give into the fury, Gorm. I don't know what we should do. I don't know if I'll make it worse. But if I stay in control and... and try to feel as the dragon feels, I think I can find the way forward."

"Bloodroot wasn't your fault. It was mine." Gorm's voice was ragged and labored after fighting past the hot lump in his throat. "I should have suspected what the guild was up to, and I charged ahead into Johan and Handor's trap, and all them Orcs and Niln and Tib'rin paid for it."

A firm hand gripped his shoulder. Gorm looked up into Gaist's eyes, dark and sorrowful and, above all, understanding.

"We all should have seen it," said Heraldin.

"We all charged ahead," agreed Jynn. He handed Laruna the gem. "We all fell into the trap."

Laruna lifted the glittering crystal to her head, faint weaves of fire twisting around her fingers. The gem hung in the air in front of her, every facet alight with a sudden, inner flame. "And we all can be better," she said.

Gorm nodded. "Go," he whispered, eyes squeezed shut. "Find us a way."

"And watch out for the dragon's fire," said Heraldin.

Laruna didn't glance back. "I am the fire," she said. Then the solamancer walked around the stone and toward the dragon, the gem above her head glowing with enchanted light.

——CHAPTER 25——

Thin strands of illumination stretched out into the void, a bridge of blue dusk in an otherwise impenetrable darkness.

Kaitha had expected something like this, though she recalled from temple lessons that there was supposed to be a light at the end of the passage, and possibly flying children with stringed instruments. What she did not expect was the sensation of flaming centipedes ripping up and down her body. For a moment she wondered if this indicated that her soul hadn't met some sort of metaphysical standard to walk the path, and then the pain became so sweeping that it was all she could do to squeeze her eyes shut and breathe.

After a brief and excruciating interlude, three things became clear.

The first was that she was not dead yet, as evidenced by her labored breaths. The second was that this came with some drawbacks. The third, and this was directly related to the second, was that emergency surgical sprites were in no way as addictive as salve. Emergency surgical sprites weren't as addictive as self-administering salt to the eyes. Emergency surgical sprites were less pleasurable than the injuries that triggered their frenzied, fiery ministrations. She wasn't sure they were preferable to the death that they had arguably prevented.

The best thing about emergency surgical sprites, in her opinion, was that they expired with tiny, wistful sighs as soon as their work was done. Yet once they were gone and the pain had receded enough for her senses to come back, Kaitha found herself alone in the darkness with her thoughts and recent memories. A deep heartache rolled over her, pushing aside the agony of her injuries and their treatment. Fresh tears rolled down her face.

Thane came back for her and he died. He looked in her eyes, and never heard her speak, and now he...

He didn't die so ye could throw yer life away.

The memory of Gorm's words cut through the crush of grief. She might meet Thane some day in the afterlife, after all, and if she wanted to be able to look him in the eye—or do whatever disembodied souls did to regard each other with mutual respect—she couldn't tell him that she used the time his final sacrifice afforded her to fall down a hole and starve to death.

Even the thought of moving forward, of a time when something could be different, helped a little. "I don't want to remember," she murmured, and opened her eyes.

To her surprise, the bridge of blue light was still there. The shimmering pathway hadn't been a vision of the afterlife after all. Instead, luminous sapphire fluid was pouring down from the heights above her and running through the channels that Stennish craftsmen had carved ages ago.

On either side of her, the walkway she stood on fell away into total darkness. Looking up, she could make out the amber light of a distant flame through the tangle of stone pathways, like looking at a campfire through a thicket. It occurred to her that she must have hit most of the stone glade's branching pathways on the way down in order to survive such a fall. It certainly felt like she'd hit most of them when she struggled to her feet.

That left her with a choice between following the strange light or walking away from it into the darkness. On the surface it was a straightforward decision; her glowstone was gone, her healing items were recently expended, and she couldn't survive another fall like the one she'd just endured. The only sensible choice was to stay on the glowing trail.

Yet there was something horrible and familiar about the light. Looking at it made her feel as though she'd stepped into a scene from a half-remembered nightmare. Cold dread welled up from her depths, and she felt like it would be better to fling herself into the darkness than follow the flowing light. "I don't want to remember," she said, almost reflexively. She wanted to forget the pain, his screams as he died, but more than that, she wanted to never find out the secret of the glowing water. "Don't make me remember. I—"

He didn't die so ye could throw yer life away.

"He came back," Kaitha growled, shoving the despair away. "He came back for me. I can do this. I will do it. I owe it to him."

Her bow was lost in the fall, presumably on a ledge above her or broken in the depths below. She drew an arrow from her Poor Man's Quiver and held it like a dagger as she set off. She did not know where she was, or what lay ahead, or the reason for the terror that gripped her heart. Yet she was sure of what had been done for her, and what it cost, and it gave her the strength to walk down the path.

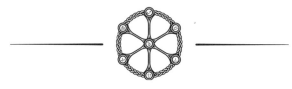

High above the Elf, Laruna was also slowly making her way along a stone path, though her leaden pace had little to do with uncertainty and more directly pertained to the angry dragon hissing at her. But Laruna was also propelled forward by the sense of recent loss, and beyond that, a white-hot rage that she had only recently tamed.

The dragon was only making things worse.

The massive reptile seemed incensed by the idea that a mortal would approach it alone, and even more so by the deliberate steps she took toward it. It spat at her while the tip of its great tail whipped back and forth like a perturbed cat's.

"What's it saying?" Jynn hollered from behind her.

"I don't know. It's angry!" she shouted back.

"I can see it's angry!" The wizard ducked behind the pillar as Laruna waved away another blast of dragonfire. "I meant, what's it saying through the Eye of the Dragon?"

"Nothing!" Laruna flicked the gemstone as one might tap a thermometer to settle the mercury. "I'm not sensing anything."

"You should be able to tell how it's feeling!"

"I believe we've established the anger!"

"Maybe you should get closer?" Heraldin said.

The thought gave the solamancer pause. Flames held little fear for her, not even dragonfire, but teeth like swords and scything claws were another matter. She wasn't exactly sure how far the creature's serpentine neck could stretch, but it seemed like the sort of thing you only got the opportunity to misjudge once.

Yet as Laruna tried to gauge the creature's reach, she saw a flash of panic in the simmering eyes, and it occurred to her that watching a furious mage advance through a firestorm was likely a frightening sight; it was the last thing many a deceased monster saw before it was summarily executed-slash-cremated. And while she couldn't bring herself to feel pity for the creature that killed Thane and Kaitha, she could carry herself far enough in that direction to see there was only one way forward.

It was an enlightened thought, and apparently one the dragon had yet to reach. Dorsal spines rose like hackles along its serpentine neck, and it looked ready to strike.

"I see that you are angry," the mage called to the dragon. "That's good." She spread her open palms in a gesture of peace.

The dragon leaned back and snorted, like a schoolboy preparing to do something unpleasant to a teacher. With a flash of crimson along its blackened scales, it vomited forth a dribbling ball of flame, the last of its reserves thrown into one final assault.

There was nowhere to run, no side to dodge. Laruna's vision went white as the dragonfire rolled over her, and her world was a sea of fury and flame. It felt like both of them would consume her, and she loosed a shriek that almost drowned out the despairing cries of the heroes behind her. Yet Laruna's wasn't a scream of pain, or even frustration, but of effort—a grunt of exertion as she beat back the rage—the justified, righteous fury—that threatened to overwhelm her.

Laruna's universe was a white-hot ball of fire and anger. Yet she was not the anger she felt. She was separate from the anger, and in control of it.

"I am the fire," she said.

The heat was as warm and welcoming as a blanket; the blistering flame felt like an extension of herself. It didn't matter where it came from or who conjured it or how much of it was dragon snot by weight—the fire was as much a part of her as she was of it. And like her anger and herself, when she controlled it, it could not harm her.

The hottest flames on Arth coalesced into a small, blinding ball in the mage's palm, leaving her unscathed but not unchanged. Amid the receding dragonfire, rubies and black pearls boiled to the surface of her robes amid streams of molten gold. The fabric bloomed in black and crimson splotches, like parchment falling on hot embers. When the last of the fire coalesced in Laruna's hand, she wore the red and black robes of a pyromancer.

"Laruna?" said Jynn from somewhere behind her.

She ignored his questions, eyes locked on the stunned dragon as she stepped over the invisible line that she imagined marked the edge of the dragon's reach. All it would take was a quick flex of the dragon's neck, and she'd give the beast a very short dental examination in passing.

"We share the anger and hurt, if nothing else," said Laruna, still advancing.

The dragon snapped and clawed at the air in a way that didn't appear very sympathetic.

"You killed my friends!" Laruna took another step forward. "And I ache to get vengeance, but I know that if I let these mortals pass, they'll shatter the dear stones!"

Her words echoed off the cavern walls, which were otherwise filled with a confused silence. The dragon stared down at the mage as though she'd grown a second head, which didn't seem that farfetched given the sudden swirl of alien thoughts in her mind.

"Uh, what was that last bit?" Jynn called.

"The mortal can hear a heartstone in my head!"

"That's not much better!" Heraldin shouted.

The mage shook her head. "I mean I wear its thoughts as of old!"

"Still not there!" Gorm shouted.

Laruna clutched her temple and tried to disentangle her inner voice from the inner voice that wasn't hers. Memories swirled through her mind, though not in the sort of convenient slideshow of pictures and snippets of voice that could be pieced together into a pertinent montage. It was like standing in the eye of a sandstorm, and she could no more read an individual thought than she could focus on a single grain of sand whipping by in the gale. Emotions, pain, facts, words of languages long dead, faded dreams and musings on their meanings; she was caught in the center of a vortex that threatened to sweep her away, and it was all she could do to keep her balance.

She might have fallen, had the gemstone not failed first.

Laruna became aware of the high-pitched whine in front of her forehead when it crescendoed in a sudden pop. The stress of a dragonfire bath and an ancient dragon's rage and confusion was too much for a crystal that had heretofore been used primarily for cowing lesser dragon-kin. The remains of the Eye of the Dragon showered in an amber fountain all around her, and the dragon's memories and thoughts drained away. She tried to hold on to the ideas but it was like snatching at the receding tide, and all she managed to clutch were impressions of hatching from an egg and the primal joy of hunting wild boar and frying bacon in situ. Even that slipped away quickly, and she was left staring up at an equally confused dragon. The great reptile regarded her with wide eyes, and its scales were shifting in hue from a brilliant red to a warm yellow.

Though Laruna's connection with the dragon was gone, the great dragon's memories had carved a canyon through her mind when they flowed away, and in it she could see the contours of the dragon's perspective. A name hovered at the edges of her recollection, like a name she'd heard of a distant aunt having, and it felt like it would fit.

"I see you... Kulxak," the mage said.

Kulxak's yellow color took on a metallic, golden quality for a split second at the mention of her name. Laruna saw hesitation in the dragon's great emerald eyes, but also a spark of comprehension. The dragon understood the Human on a basic level, even if it didn't necessarily speak the language. It reminded Laruna of the time she'd bartered with an Arakian peddler; the man didn't speak a word of the Imperial tongue, but through body language and tone he still managed to fleece her out of half her purse for a fake grimoire. Or...

She glanced back at Gaist. The weaponsmaster gave her a barely perceptible nod that somehow conveyed that he was confident in her ability and that she had chosen the right path, and perhaps even that he was a little proud of her. If the doppelganger could convey all that in a nod, Laruna could convey that she very sincerely did not want to fight a dragon using body language as well. The pyromancer spread her hands wide in supplication. "I see you, and you see me. Right, Kulxak?"

She took another step forward. "Peace," she told the dragon. "I want peace, and I think you do too. You're protecting something. I don't know what it is, but I don't want to hurt it."

Kulxak stared at her, sparks drifting from her flaring nostrils with each labored breath.

"I just want to find a way forward."

Laruna noticed the dragon glance back to Gorm and the others.

"They do too. We just want to move on."

The dragon regarded her again for a long while. Then she nodded her massive head, as though some decision had been reached, and shifted her weight. With painful effort, the dragon unfurled enough to give the pyromancer a glimpse of her treasure.

"What is it?" shouted Jynn.

"Is it a hoard?" asked Heraldin.

"Must be eggs," Gorm said. "Look how hard it fought to get back here."

"It might be," Laruna murmured, craning her neck. There were seven piles of oblong, milky-white shapes, each with a larger specimen sitting behind a neat stack of smaller ones. The objects had an egg-ish quality, but their faint translucence and the way they stood on their short ends put her in mind of the eggs of insectoids rather than reptiles. Their shapes were wrong too, irregular and, in the case of the larger specimens, broader on the top. As she drew closer, she grew more certain that these weren't eggs at all. Most eggs, she was confident, didn't have pectorals or breasts.

She looked up at the dragon. "What are they?" she asked.

"Odd stonework is nothing new. It's just part of some threatening dungeon architecture." Kaitha told herself. She tried another deep breath, but it came out a rattling hybrid of laugh and sob that told the rational part of Kaitha that the unsettled bits were still driving the chariot. "You've seen dozens of these. Maybe hundreds. Standard operating procedure for class B dungeons over five hundred years old. TDAs are just part of the job."

Just as poisonous insects display bright colors under threat or venomous reptiles flash their crests to intimidate rivals, ancient tombs and dungeons are often outfitted with old mechanisms whose only purpose was to ward off spelunkers and grave robbers. Any hero knew it was a safe bet that a long-lost culture willing to fund the construction of doors that open based on the position of giant mechanical star maps or sunlight shining through an array of intricate crystals would have also made investments in things like spring-loaded crushing ceilings, dart-flinging tripwires, and stone guardian golems. Similarly, chances were good that any dead civilization that hadn't thought to implement such deadly traps had long ago had the last vestiges of its existence dismantled, hauled off, and sold to the highest bidder.

So it was that anyone on Arth who wanted a career in heroics, or at least a long one, couldn't lose her nerve at the sight of threatening dungeon architecture, or TDAs in the vernacular of the guild. Most heroes viewed them as a useful tool for identifying weak links in a party; one knew it was time to rethink the engagement strategy if the newblood was going wobbly-kneed at the sight of rune-encrusted interlocking disks the size of city gates, skull-faced doors that opened along the hinge of the jaw, or any of the other mysterious constructs that ancients had used as a way to keep future generations off the lawn of the dead. Kaitha had seen plenty of TDAs, and had judged more than a few colleagues on how well they handled themselves in the presence of otherworldly edifices.

But now... now she found it almost impossible to keep up her professional stoicism in the face of, or perhaps the faces of, whatever she was looking at.

She could think of several explanations that might account for the glowing water, from resonant sorcery to tiny, bioluminescent organisms living in the strange flow. But unless nature had also granted the tiny creatures bioantigravitance, that couldn't explain how the water was flowing up, and to the sides, and in all directions through the narrow passage she had been led into. Its thin, even streams formed a web of azure light that covered all parts of the surrounding tunnel. And even if she could explain the water's blatant disregard for the law of gravity, that didn't come close to accounting for the shapes it was twisting into.

No, not the shapes. The people. The shimmering water running through the ancient channels formed very clear figures, each no taller than her forearm and drawn in lines of blue light. And they moved, working and walking and speaking as the water switched from channel to channel in swift, staccato jumps that reminded Kaitha of raindrops running down a windowpane. Around and above her, a city of watery ghosts of every shape and size walked and shopped and smithed and went about their silent lives. The streams babbled with high, tinkling notes, and behind them, the stones hummed like an orchestra warming up.

Despite her initial suspicion that the images were a TDA, none of the figures were actually threatening her. There was no more violence on the walls than in the average market of Andarun. In fact, there was considerably less of it, as none of the fluid people appeared to be shouting, brawling, or trying to sell blood-stained goods off the back of suspicious-looking wagons. It was as peaceful a scene as one could hope for, yet watching the walls filled Kaitha with a deep dread.

The dancing images showed a time before the Agekeepers were the Agekeepers. She could tell in part because the stocky Humans were in the minority to the Elves, Dwarves, and Gnomes flowing through the hallway. Even more telling, she could see many strange figures in the crowds; tall and barrel-chested, like Dwarves stretched to Elven height.

The Sten.

Something about their presence on the wall made her uneasy in a way that the remnants of their artifacts and architecture never had. It was one thing to know that they once moved among the races of Man, it was another to watch one buy a bundle of carrots from a glowing effigy of a Gnome. And as she watched the figures move, something tugged at the back of her mind; a memory of a memory, a whisper of something forgotten.

The idea brought the panic welling back up from her hidden depths. "I don't want to remember," she murmured, almost reflexively. "Don't make me remember."

One of the Sten, as though having heard her utterance, looked at the ranger and smiled. With a few steps he grew to three times his size, as though stepping to the foreground of a painting, scattering droplets as he blocked out the figures behind him. He gave a friendly wave and beckoned down the hall, as though she had asked for directions. As though there was anywhere else to go.

"N-no," Kaitha gasped. "No, stop."

The Sten's broad features grew softer, almost sympathetic, and in the expression Kaitha saw the hint of a smile on a dying Troll's face. *He died for me. He came back.*

And that settled it. She nodded to the Sten, not to say that she trusted him, but to let him know that the professional was back in charge, and she could handle whatever the aquatic light show would throw at her. Slowly and deliberately, she started down the hall, ignoring the screams of protest from the voice deep within her.

Don't make me remember! I don't want to remember!

"I don't want to make you remember," High Scribe Pathalan whispered. Sweat beaded on his brow as he stared with sleepless, bloodshot eyes at the scripture he had just written. The high scribe sat at the epicenter of a storm of papers, every one of them covered in similar denials of recollection. Even as he considered the countless lines of protestations scribbled across the pages, another scripture seared across his mind. Reflexively, his hand jerked out and scrawled.

No! Stop! The other way! I don't want to remember!

"What other way?" sobbed Pathalan. His mind searched frantically for something, anything, he could do differently. Anything to get the blaze of angry protests to cease. He had to—

No. That was madness. Pathalan set down the quill, slapped his unshaven cheeks, and reminded himself that insanity was an occupational hazard for those who worked in the Temple of the All Mother. If he actually started believing what the goddess said, he'd wind up wearing a jacket with sleeves that tied together.

He needed something to calm his nerves. Tea. Tea always helped. He dug a small, silver bell from one of the drifts of parchment lying across his desk and rang it.

This would pass, he told himself. The unpleasant business with the bronze statue of Niln would resolve itself, as his rivalry with its subject eventually had. The gods knew that Al'Matra's fancies were as transient as they were inscrutable.

The trick, he knew, was to mentally box these scriptures up and pack them away. Just like the silly rituals, and the monthly fasts, and the holy wars with better-armed temples. Pathalan found religion much more palatable when it was stripped of all the belief and obedience, and all that remained was unquestioned authority, free meals, and a complete lack of accountability. The life of a clergy member was a comfortable one, provided you set aside the gods.

The problem was that it was hard to set aside someone who was screaming fire into your brain every few minutes. Pathalan groaned as another scripture erupted from his quill.

The thing that had brought Pathalan to Al'Matra's service rather than the richer, more prestigious temples was the All Mother's benign absentmindedness. Whereas other gods took an interest in the observance of rituals, conduct in line with their divine ethos, and the balance of the temple coffers, Al'Matra was usually too preoccupied with stone fruit and mollusks to bother her high scribe. The High Scribe of Tandos wore a king's ransom in jewels around her neck; the High Scribe of Musana liked to boast about his feasts with nobles; but Pathalan had freedom and time to relax in a way they and every other scribe in Andarun envied.

Or he had. Now he was chained to a goddess thrashing angrily in the weave, and unlike the more coherent gods, she couldn't tell him what she wanted. Or how to stop the burning.

Another scripture erupted in his mind's eye, searing the back of his eyeballs until he released the heat and pressure through his quill.

I don't want to see them! I didn't know! I couldn't know! Don't make me remember!

Pathalan straightened his features as he regarded the little verse. Intense? Yes. Insane? As always. But harmful? No. It was just another string of nonsense. It would pass when the goddess' mood finally shifted. He took a deep breath and reminded himself that he could get through this.

Acolyte Penna set a saucer with a cup of tea on the high scribe's desk and scurried away. The aroma of steeping blue manabloom and honeycomb brought a smile to Pathalan's parched lips. If pugwort took the edge off, blue manabloom beveled it down to a cylinder. A tea brewed from its cobalt petals was inner peace and tranquility in a cup. A sip or two, and he'd be fine.

As he reached for the cup, his inner mind suddenly flared with the red heat of new scripture, and he felt his hand reflexively reach toward his quill. He grunted as he resisted the urge and reached for his tea instead.

His arm jerked back toward the page, doggedly moving to write the scriptures. Pathalan scowled. Not every verse had to be inscribed the moment it was relayed, of course. High scribes needed time to sleep, or use the chamber pot, or partake of some refreshments. It was only reasonable that this scripture could wait a moment, and so—grimacing with effort—the high scribe reached for his tea.

When Pathalan regained consciousness, he could smell damp pages and see the faint blue splodge across his parchment where the tea had spilled. There was a charred scent in the musty air as well, and the paper darkened and scorched around the edges of his latest, monosyllabic screed. The high scribe choked back a sob as he stared in horror at the single word scrawled around the edges of the page.

No No No No No No No No No No No No No No No No No No No No No No No No

"No, no, no!" cried Ignatius, slapping the stone skull of the shrine.

The sculpture of Mordo Ogg stared impassively back at him, unswayed by the assault. The same electric blue light that had scorched its brows and sent molten tears dribbling down the god's cheekbones still hissed and spat from the recesses of its eye sockets.

"Everything dies! You're no exception!" barked the old priest. "You've got to know when to quit! It's all part of the cycle! The cycle of change! You can't stay the same forever!"

And then, quite horribly, something changed.

The shift wasn't the sort of jolting surprise that had brought so many elderly people briefly passing through the shrine. Ignatius barely noticed it at first; there was just an odd quality in the air as he berated the stubborn light in his god's eyes. The strange sensation resolved into a sound, a thin whine barely audible over the priest's shouting. It grew in volume and pitch, as a teakettle left on the boil too long, and as the priest fell silent under its shrill protests he noticed wisps of smoke curling around the corners of the skull's eye sockets. An overpowering scent of ozone curled the hairs in his nose.

Ignatius took a step back and regarded the skull. "This isn't right," he muttered. Worse still, it was wrong in a way he didn't recognize.

He darted forward and opened a small compartment at the statue's base. The heat rolling from Mordo Ogg's face was intense enough to crack his lips and singe the charred stubs of his eyebrows. Frantically shuffling some old armor aside, the priest grabbed a lacquered ebony box from the cubby and darted back to a safe distance. With a deep sigh, he opened the box at a small hinge.

The top half of the case contained a paper note, on which someone had written "FOR EMERGENCY USE ONLY." The bottom half was a velvet pad, occupied by a single, greenish crystal. It flared with emerald light and gave a small chime when Ignatius pressed his index finger to it.

"Somethin' wrong?"

Ignatius startled and looked at the speaker, a young Halfling in a courier's cap. Where there's smoke, there's fire, and where there's fire, there's an audience. The lad stood at the fore of a group of assembling onlookers staring at the shrine. The courier nodded at the trails of smoke pouring from the shine's blazing blue eyes. "'Cause it looks like that might be bad."

"Very bad," muttered Ignatius. His mind followed the implications and then, like a lost child who follows a trail of candy to a gingerbread house, wished that he had not. He jammed his finger on the crystal a few more times for good measure. "Worse than you can imagine."

——CHAPTER 26——

"It's hard to imagine this being any worse," Heraldin sputtered. "Everyone thinks there's some amazing treasure down here. People are counting on there being mountains of gold and gems! And we found what? A handful of broken statues?"

Gorm looked at the ring of seven marble figures at the center of the dragon's dais. Their torsos were tall and barrel-chested, but notably deficient in extremities. The arms and legs of the figures were neatly stacked in front of their respective midsections, and each pile was topped with a head wearing a melancholy expression. But the terminal ends of their arms, legs, and necks were rounded and smooth.

"Not sure they're broken, per se," he said.

"These are Stennish artifacts preserved by low magic and guarded by a dragon." Jynn carefully inspected the impeccably sculpted head of a woman with her hair up in elaborate braids. Her stoic features were broad and soft, despite being carved from the stone in sharp, fast cuts. It was an effect that Gorm had only seen on one other statue, and that stood in a square in Andarun's Pinnacle Plaza. "They're some of the best examples of Stennish sculpture I've ever seen, and perhaps the first fully rendered representations found of their leaders outside of the Dark Prince. They're priceless."

"No! No, they're *not* priceless," Heraldin ranted. "The problem is that they're priced—very definitely priced—down to the last copper, and bought and sold by every bank, broker, and investor on Arth. By any estimate, each one of these statues needs to be worth a king's ransom in order to not bankrupt half the world. And I doubt anyone can or would pay much for a bunch of make-your-own sculpture kits that—"

A low rumble from the heights above reminded the bard that every good hero—or at least every hero who intends to see the inside of a tavern again—must always take their proximity to a dragon into account.

"That are masterfully crafted treasures nobody could dream of selling," he squeaked, looking up into Kulxak's fiery eye. "But still."

"We can't sell them anyway," said Laruna, tending the dragon's wounded scales. "They still belong to her, and we aren't slaying this dragon. We don't need any more bloodshed today."

"Aye." A pit opened up in Gorm's stomach as he thought of Kaitha and Thane. He pushed the grief down beneath the surface; not to smother it, but to plant the seed that would bear the fruits of justice. He loosed the white-knuckled grip that his hand had subconsciously wrapped around the handle of his axe, and let out a long breath between his teeth. "But the problem's still the same. There's supposed to be a treasure, and there ain't."

"That puts it in line with the rest of this quest. There wasn't supposed to be a dragon, and there was." Heraldin's voice dripped resentment.

"We're supposed to kill her, and we won't." Laruna scratched under Kulxak's chin, and the great dragon's scales turned a satisfied golden hue.

"All true." Gorm's mind raced down the twisting path of memory that had brought him to this point. "Then again, we were all supposed to be dead, and most of us ain't."

"Were we?" asked Jynn.

A grin split Gorm's beard. "Aye, far as Johan's concerned. I'd bet my beard he was the one who sent them fancy undead to kill us just before the dragon broke through that big spell. The king didn't want us to get this far, to see what we saw, to..." His mind reached the end of the thought before his mouth had time to catch up. "We need to go."

"Where?" asked Heraldin. "We can't go back to—"

"Back to the city," said Gorm.

"Of course you'd say that." The bard threw his hands in the air and gave Gaist an exasperated look. "Of course he'd say that. I should just stop talking altogether!"

"That's what we've all been saying, yes," said Jynn.

Gorm had no time for such bickering. He was already stomping back across the narrow stone bridge between the dragon's dais and the stone grove. "We need to get back to the surface before Johan realizes his trick with the Golden Dawn ain't worked. There's only a narrow chance..." He paused and looked at the others. "Come on! And Laruna, tell the dragon to stay here, for her own safety."

"I can't talk to her," protested the pyromancer. "The gem shattered. I mean, I get a vague idea of her mood and I think she understands us up to a point, but there's a language... barrier..." The mage fell silent as Gaist didn't speak over her protests. Wordlessly, he stepped up in front of the dragon and crossed his arms.

The dragon regarded him coolly. Its scales turned a cold gray, tinted amber around their edges.

"Did he just interrupt me?" Laruna asked.

"Hush," said Heraldin. "I don't want to miss this."

"Miss what?" Gorm asked, watching the exchange, or lack thereof, between warrior and dragon.

Gaist nodded. Kulxak shrugged her titanic shoulders. The weaponsmaster opened his hands. The dragon flashed a brilliant ruby, then yellow. Gaist tapped his temple. The dragon reared back, its scales a vibrant citrine. They continued the discussion, or perhaps argument, in total silence.

"I think it's working," Heraldin hissed.

"And that's strange, right?" said Gorm.

"Right?" said Laruna. "It shouldn't work."

Yet it was. The basics of body language were far older than Mankind itself, let alone the dragon, and so Kulxak seemed to understand Gaist's meaning well enough. Likewise, reading the threat displays of dragon-kin was etched into the primordial brain of every hero, and since every display that a reptile the size of a barn makes is at least a little threatening, the weaponsmaster held his own in the debate.

Eventually, the weaponsmaster turned to the bard and shrugged, then moved to follow Gorm off the dais.

"The dragon will stay," Heraldin said, trotting after him. "She wanted to anyway. Some sort of unfinished business or something."

Gorm glanced behind him. "And how can ye get all that from—"

He caught Gaist's eye, and the weaponsmaster gave him the most absolutely clear glare he had ever been on the receiving end of. More than a werewolf's predatory sneer rejoiced in a hunt; more than a giant's confident grimace boasted; even more than a gazer's central eye said "death beam," Gaist's face said that if Gorm was so thrice-cursed dense as to not understand basic nonverbal cues, he should just shut up about it and accept the wisdom of those who could.

"Oh. Right." Gorm was both mollified and mortified. "Well, good. We'll see her on the other side." He managed an awkward bow to the dragon, and the others followed suit.

Kulxak inclined her head toward them.

"We'll be back," said Gorm, "Once this is all settled."

The dragon looked at Gaist, who shrugged and made a very succinct gesture. Then, apparently satisfied, she curled around the ring of statues and wrapped herself in her huge, battered wings.

"So can I assume there's some sort of plan here?" Jynn asked as the heroes charged through the great grove of stone pillars.

"More like an idea and a deadline collidin'," said Gorm.

"That's more of a plan than we usually have," said Heraldin.

"Does it account for that strange blue light?" asked Laruna.

"Uh," said Gorm, slowing to a trot as he rounded a pillar.

Several of the stone trees were covered in glowing azure liquid that ran up and down the better part of their trunks through the intricately patterned carvings on their surface. The luminescent flow drew similar designs along the walkways surrounding the pillars before pouring off them in shimmering waterfalls that lit the endless darkness below.

"It ain't acid," said Gorm, withdrawing the toe of his boot. "Let's go."

"You're just going to run over it?" asked Jynn.

"Well, I ain't drinkin' it or splashin' it on me skin," said Gorm, already stamping through the stream. "And we should be quick, in case there's fumes."

"But we don't know what this water is," said Jynn. "This could be powerful magic, or latent prophecy, or the work of divine or demonic agents, or—"

"Could be anything. Could be the residue of that barrier fallin', or some ancient trap halfway to bein' sprung. But I ain't got time to sit here studyin' it, because the one thing I'm sure of is that it could attract attention from above."

"You think it's divine, then?" asked Laruna.

"Nope." Gorm stopped at the largest of the stone grove's pillars. He pointed to the doorway on a landing with a stone spiral staircase at its base, and followed the masonry all the way to the ceiling of the great cavern. "I'm more confident than ever them stairs wind up somewhere in the mountain behind the palace."

"Johan," snarled the pyromancer.

"Aye. I been wonderin' how that bastard and his Golden Dawn got that magic contraption down here," said Gorm. "The one they tried to use on that magic barrier. I mean, they didn't carry it into the dungeon. Not by the path we took."

"It didn't seem like anyone walked the path we took at all... oh!" said Heraldin.

"Exactly!" said Gorm, tracing the pathways branching out above them. "Also explains how Johan pulled off that surprise entrance at his own funeral. Ah. There!" He pointed to one of the archways out of the cavern and followed the path all the way back to the large spire. "That's our way out. Quiet now. I bet there's a bloody huge echo in here."

The heroes fell silent as they started up the spiral staircase. Gorm was relieved to find that the glowing water had remained outside the tower, and they progressed quickly and quietly up to a second landing, where he led them out onto dry stone.

"If Johan knew about the barrier, that means he's been here before," said Laruna as she exited the staircase.

"But why did he want to get into the prophetic vault?" asked Heraldin, following.

"No idea." Gorm pulled a thick, square packet wrapped in brown paper from his red rucksack. "Safest to assume it's for no good, and that we've only so long before he knows it fell. We alert him too soon, and he can go after the dragon, frame her for burnin' all them citizens, get whatever he was after, and get away with it all."

"Then we probably shouldn't take these stairs into the middle of the palace," Laruna noted.

"Aye." With the package appropriately positioned by the rear of the bottom step, the Dwarf stood and tucked a small, brown cylinder into his belt pouch. He pointed to several upper walkways extending from the staircase. "We'll take a side passage to somewhere above the Ridge, sneak back into the city, and get ready to strike a decisive blow."

"How does one prepare to fight a king in his own castle?" asked Heraldin.

"With numbers." Gorm was already headed along the path.

The bard and weaponsmaster shared a puzzled glance. "Numbers?" said Heraldin.

"We just reached the heart of the biggest dungeon on Arth and found out there's no loot." Gorm took a deep breath, and felt a spark of excitement travel down his spine. "It's time to get finance involved."

"It all comes down to the money. That's the thrice-cursed unfairness of it, but it's a truth nonetheless." Duine Poldo's whiskers bristled as he spoke. "With a paid advocacy team and a—"

Feista Hrurk shook her head and set the arbiter's letter down on her desk. "The guild won't take my case, Mr. Poldo," said Feista. "I spoke with Jirada of the Bone Eaters at work; her son was slain by gold-hounds two years ago. She spends every giltin she earns on lawyers and advocates, and the guild won't take her case. They protect their own, Mr. Poldo. The pups and I are not their own."

"Perhaps," said Poldo. He sat and listened to the laughter of the children playing Orcs and Humans outside, broken by occasional shrieks as one side inflicted mock atrocities on the other. His hands curled and uncurled at the thought of Hristo Hrurk's death, and the loss it had inflicted upon Mrs. Hrurk and her pups. There had to be a way to help. "Perhaps if I reached out to my acquaintances at Fordrun and Hawks, we could—"

"No," said the Gnoll, shaking her head.

"Well, it might work," the Gnome said. "It really is all about who you know."

"No, Mr. Poldo. It really is all about what you are."

"My dear, I—"

She silenced him with a glance. For a long time, they sat unspeaking as the sounds of the bustling home wafted up from beneath them.

Mrs. Hrurk spoke first. "You are a good man, Mr. Poldo. The very best Light—the very best of the Children of Light that I know. And I know you mean to help. You have helped so much, and we are all grateful. I am grateful. But there are some things you cannot fix. If you could... if you could snap your fingers and bring my Hristo back, and punish the heroes who took him away, if you had that magic and used it for me... then I would still be as a pebble caught in a wheel, bouncing wherever your people sent me. You would just be bouncing me in a better direction."

She stared out the window down at the street below. "My Hristo died because he crossed the wrong Lightlings; no, because he crossed the street in front of the wrong Lightlings. My children and I were given a second chance because I met the right one. At times it feels like everything we lost and had and lost again came not from what we did, but what your people did. And though I have worked my paws to the bone, and though I have built two careers and raised three beautiful pups, at these times I still feel that I live in a Lightling's world, and that I can only have what a Lightling chooses to give me."

She turned back to him, the fur around her eyes damp with tears. "You cannot fix that, Duine. It speaks well of you that you would try, but you need to know that it hurts just that you would have to. If you bring in the best lawyers, it is another reminder that I could not. If you get justice for Hristo, it is another thorn in my heart. You cannot give me victory, because a victory unearned is not a victory at all."

Poldo tried not to bristle, but he was unaccustomed to problems that he could not solve. "So you just, what, sit here and think of how unjust everything is?"

She looked at him with kindness and mercy; the look a priest gives a wretch with a self-inflicted wound on the temple's doorstep. "Every day. I do my best, I fight on, I work as hard as anyone I know, and then I sit down and think about the injustice of it all every day."

The Gnome bit back his response, his reasons that he could be more effective, and swallowed them all in a ragged breath. He recalled telling Thane that the evil that was hardest to spot was the one lurking in his own good intentions. It took a bit of thought to come up with words that felt right. "I am sorry. For the things I can't help, and the ones I could do better. May I... may I sit with you for a time?"

She smiled and took his hand in her paw. "I'd be glad if you did."

They sat together for a moment—just a half minute or so of somber reflection and welcome companionship. And then, because the universe is just as full of cruel irony as any other kind, there was a rapping on the windowpane. They tried to ignore it for a time, but the messenger sprite was determined enough that the glass panes began to rattle and shake under the weight of its siege.

"Perhaps the sprite has an extra-strong seeking enchantment," Poldo mused.

Feista frowned and stood. "Her lady must think it's urgent," she said, but when she opened the latch the pink sprite buzzed past her and landed on the desk in front of the Gnome.

"Duine Poldo of Silver Guard Securities?" squeaked the sprite.

"Formerly of Silver Guard Securities, yes," said Poldo.

Upon that confirmation, the sprite placed its hands on the area its belt might be and leaned back. When it spoke, its tiny voice had dropped an octave and developed a hint of Scorian brogue. "Mr. Poldo, I ain't got many connections in securities, and I need one now," it said. "I saved your life once in the lair of Benny Hookhand, as ye'll recall, and now I'm callin' in a favor. Meet us at the main offices of Warg Inc. It's a matter of urgency."

The sprite hadn't stopped speaking before another, this one from Lady Asherzu herself, flew in the open window and landed in front of Feista. "You are needed at the main office," the tiny, pink figure intoned in the Orc's voice. "And I know you have contact with the Gnome called Duine Poldo. If you can find and bring him, make every effort to do so."

Three more sprites were already lining up behind it. Feista looked at Duine with regret in her eyes. "I think we had better leave, Mr. Poldo," she said.

"Yes, Mrs. Hrurk," he said, finally releasing her paw. "Whatever this is about, it seems rather important."

"Oh, it's always important. Always urgent, they say. Everything's the worst thing. Every priest thinks a loose toenail on their idol is the end of the world." Theological Support Friar Brouse's grumbled litany did not pause as he marched up to the back of the crowd gathered around the square in Sculpin Down. Cowl down and shoulders hunched, he trundled into the mob, a dingy phalanx breaking the siege line. "And who do they want to fix it? Who else? Sprites all hours, screamin' crystals, everyone wailing like it's all on fire, and it all comes down to me. And I tells 'em, I says it needs to be high priorities. I says, but they never listen. They just says—"

"Yes! Finally! Come quickly!" The gaunt face of Ignatius loomed as the onlookers suddenly parted. The old priest's long beard swayed to and fro as he did an impatient dance over the cobbles. "Hurry! You must hurry!"

Brouse paused long enough to bunch his face up into a deep scowl. "Yeah, that's what they all say," he muttered as Ignatius started pushing his way through the citizenry. "I'll remind you, mister sir, that the crystalline matrix is for emergencies only!"

The old priest suddenly whirled and grabbed the friar by the shoulders. "This is an emergency!" he shrieked. "Someone isn't dying!"

Brouse's scowl deepened. "That sounds like the opposite of an emergency. That's a good definition of something that isn't an emergency."

"Gah!" Ignatius practically spat in irritation, jerking his head as if to ward off a fly. "I mean, nobody might be dying!"

"Still not seein'—"

"Look!" The old priest pointed ahead of them. Smoke was rising from the epicenter of the murmuring crowd's attention. Thick black clouds of it rose in a spiral pattern to join the cyclonic clouds darkening the sky from the mountain to the horizon. "The shrine... the soul! He won't leave! The master won't—can't—send him on!"

"Well, could be..." Brouse mused, scratching his whiskers. "Could be that your QRCs got unmoored from the BOAT."

Ignatius' features scrunched up in confusion. "We're nowhere near the river—"

"The Being of All Things?" said Brouse impatiently, as though this was the most common and reasonably assumed definition of the word "boat." "The essence of reality? It's a technical metaphor, and if your shrine's quantum resonance crystal gets out of alignment with it, you can get little puffs of smoke or squeaking noises or red liquid that looks a lot like blood. See it all the time."

"And have you seen it do this?" asked Ignatius, stepping aside. Brouse squinted in the sudden glare.

The onlookers had left a wide gap between themselves and the smoking shrine of Mordo Ogg in an effort to balance their natural curiosity with their instinct for self-preservation. Every spectator would hate to tell their grandchildren they missed out on whatever interesting thing was about to happen, but that imperative carried implicit requirements regarding their survival to a time frame that included said grandchildren.

The shrine of Mordo Ogg's head was nearly engulfed in the white-hot glow of its eyes. Behind the blueish corona of the skull's incandescent glare and the black smoke pouring from the shrine's stricken head, Brouse caught brief glimpses of orange, bubbling stone. The air around the statue shimmered with heat, creating the illusion that Mordo Ogg's head was waving back and forth like a man suffering from a headache.

"Is that anything to do with your boat?" demanded Ignatius.

Brouse's grimace pulled his bushy brow down and his stubby whiskers up until his face was a ball of prickly hair with a pair of dark eyes glaring out of it, like a hedgehog in a yellow cowl. "Could be," he said, honoring the support professional's creed of death before admission of error. And then, to hedge his reputation against inaccuracy, he added, "Could be something else."

"Pretty sure that covers everything." Gorm looked around the finely furnished executive conference room of Warg Inc.

"Let's check the list." Jynn stood next to the Dwarf, considering a sheet of parchment on a clipboard. He rapped his pencil on the first item on the page. "We have capital."

"Lady Asherzu and her board assured me that this company of theirs has plenty of money if the offer is right." Gorm nodded and waved to the chieftain and her retinue. The lady smiled at the heroes and gave them a gracious nod. "And given that I don't see how anyone can refuse, I'd say we got the capital."

"Very well. We have the Heroes' Guild."

"Aye, Vordar Borrison, guildmaster and emissary of the Dwarven Heroes' Guild." Gorm eyed a rusty-haired Dwarf exchanging pleasantries with a pair of Goblins. A cadre of Dwarven clerks stood behind him, carrying leather cases embossed with the seal of Khadan'Alt's guild. "He's second only to Grandmaster Korgen, and says he speaks with his authority."

"And you're sure the Old Kingdoms will be on board with this?" Jynn asked.

"I'm sure they won't have much of an alternative. Just like everyone else," said Gorm. "'Sides, after all the business with Detarr Ur'Mayan, Korgen owes me a big favor."

"Didn't they do us a favor?" asked Jynn. "We had to beg them to conscript the Red Horde."

Gorm snorted and shook his head. It was amazing how well-educated people could be so unfamiliar with the basic economics of favors. "Aye, they did us a little favor, and I'd have been indebted to them if that was that. But it paid off like a silver seam for 'em, what with the liche's loot and their new negotiations with Johan, and now they owe me a big one."

The wizard's brow furrowed. "And if they do well from this favor? Will they owe you again?"

"Of course," said Gorm.

"This just seems like a way of getting them to do what you want indefinitely," said Jynn.

The berserker grinned. "So long as it's mutually beneficial," he said. "This is how civilizations are built."

"This is how crime organizes," murmured Jynn.

"Not too far apart, more often than not. Speakin' as such, ye got legal on your list?"

"Yes. I believe that's the two lawyer-monks by the refreshments table."

"Oh?" Gorm craned his neck. "Oh, the ones in robes who... what's she doing with a quill and scroll?"

"I believe she's filling out a receipt-of-gift form for the puff pastries," said the wizard.

"Lawyers," grumbled Gorm. "Well, they're here."

"And I suppose Adchul must owe you a big favor to be here."

"They do, but nothing works the way it should with lawyers involved." Gorm glowered at the pair of monks. "They'll fill out paperwork for a tart, but for a hero who saved their whole monastery back in three forty-three? Nothin'. We'll be payin' full hourly rate plus expenses, I suspect."

"Can we afford them?" asked Jynn.

"Like everyone else in this room—"

"We don't have an alternative," the archmage finished with the Dwarf. "Right."

"We need this agreement to hold, and more important, we need people to think it'll hold," said Gorm. "The seals of Adchul ward off litigants and questions like a priest's symbol wards off the undead."

"I suppose you're right." The wizard ticked legal off his list. "Diplomats?"

"Laruna and Gaist are seein' to the Ember of Heaven's retinue now. The diplomats and emissaries that travel with her can speak for the empress, and they'll better know how to reach out to Daellan and Ruskan."

"Public relations?"

Gorm pursed his lips and nodded. "Heraldin says a well-worded story and a few whispers to the right town criers will have the city abuzz and rallying to our cause."

"And you think the bard is right for such a delicate job?"

The shadow of a grimace flitted over Gorm's face. "I don't think there's a job the bard is better suited for."

"That isn't the same," pressed the wizard.

"It's as good as we'll get," Gorm said. "Ye offering to go help him?"

"My skills lie elsewhere," said Jynn. "And my time is better spent investigating the metaphysical implications of these developments."

"The what now?" Gorm wasn't sure where this was going, but his brow had already furrowed in anticipation of a discussion he neither understood nor liked.

Jynn leaned in for a conspiratorial conference. "Consider all of the signs that we've seen. The background low magic thrumming through the city. The strange coincidences that brought us together on Johan's trail. The way Thane's body desiccated and explosively decomposed in an instant. Where have you seen that before?"

"Nowhere," said Gorm. "No, wait... it was kinda like them... soul-bound critters your father made."

"Exactly. His death is connected to a phenomena that I am the world's best known living expert on, and I just happened to witness it. Consider the prophetic barrier around the dragon's lair, and the nature of the dragon's hoard! These strange happenings and coincidences point to some low magic that goes beyond the work of any coven of hedge witches. This is the shape of the loom beneath the weave, signs of the ebb and flow of destiny or the will of the gods."

"Destiny and the gods tend to sort themselves out," Gorm retorted, but without vigor. He had a sense that something big was happening, and now that the archmage put words to it he felt a growing sense of unease in his gut.

"Perhaps, but if we want to be sure our party and our city survive whatever these cosmic forces have set in motion, we would do well to at least understand what we are up against. I wish to return to my lab for a few things, and I need some time to study this."

"Time is the one thing we ain't got much of," said Gorm. Still, he couldn't deny that it would be good to understand what the thrice-cursed cosmos was getting at. "But I'll let ye have what I can spare. Help me get this set up here, and then ye can slip out and get to yer work. Just don't be seen."

Jynn nodded. "Agreed."

"What else is there on the list?"

"Just a broker to bring it all together," said the wizard. "Somebody with deep experience in securities trading, professional heroics, plunder funds, market culture, structuring a venture, and negotiation."

"And he just arrived." Gorm nodded to where Mr. Poldo was hanging a coat for a Gnoll he didn't recognize. "Who's that he's with?"

"It's Mrs. Hrurk, Warg's new finance hotshot," interrupted Burt. The Kobold popped up next to Gorm and waved a cigar toward the pair. "She and Poldo are friends and business partners."

"How long ye been down there?" Gorm checked around his seat for the Kobold's hiding spot.

"Don't worry about it," said Burt.

"So you didn't hear us talkin'?" Jynn asked.

Burt grinned and took a drag off his cigar. "Oh, I did. But it's just best to assume the lady and I know everything. No sense worrying about it."

"Were ye smokin' in here?" Gorm dug into his rucksack and pulled out some incriminating specks of ash. "Bones! Now me gear stinks!"

"How can you tell the difference?" Burt barked back. "You smell like someone grilled an old sock."

"I smell like I came from a dragon's lair, on account of we did."

"Speakin' of which, where's the Elf?" Burt looked around the room. "You didn't mention where she went to."

The question hit like a warhammer to the gut. Gorm swallowed the sudden ache in his throat and shook his head. "Kaitha didn't make it."

Burt's ears drooped, and the cigar dropped from his muzzle. "What? Oh... oh bones. She... I'm so sorry."

Gorm managed a curt nod. "Time for mourning will come. She'd want us to carry on."

"Excuse me, Mr. Ingerson," said a nasal voice. Gorm turned to see Mr. Poldo standing near the edge of the group, flanked by Mrs. Hrurk. "Did I overhear you say that an Elf named Kaitha has perished on your quest?"

"Aye," sighed Gorm.

"Oh dear. My condolences," said the Scribkin sadly. "And I am sorry to pry. But we have a mutual friend who went looking for your party, and he'll be devastated when he hears the news. I'm sure you remember Thane the Troll."

Another blow nearly knocked the wind from Gorm. He sucked in a gulp of cold air through his teeth, ignored the stinging tears in the corner of his eyes, and broke the news about the Troll to the group.

Burt howled, Mrs. Hrurk gasped, and they barely caught Poldo as the Scribkin fell backward.

"It... it can't be," Poldo breathed, staggering into a chair.

"Afraid so," said Gorm. "And believe me when I say he'll never be forgotten. But their losses are meaningless if we don't press on and finish what we started."

"I... I just... I... of course you must," said Poldo, wiping his eyes with a silk handkerchief. "But... forgive me. I know you must be familiar with losing comrades, but I have seldom dealt with this in my profession. Excuse me."

The Gnome hurried away, audibly sobbing. Mrs. Hrurk went with him, her paw on his shoulder.

"You need to give us a moment." Burt wiped a tear from his eyes. "It's a lot to process."

"Ain't time enough," said Gorm. "Once ye start workin' through the loss, ye never really stop."

"If we delay much longer, Johan may get his way and send the rest of us to the next life as well," Jynn added.

"Aye. Let's call the meetin' to order." The Dwarf sighed as he stood and knocked on the table a couple of times. Naturally, several attendees took this as a signal to visit the refreshment table one more time before the meeting really got going, and so when Gorm spoke it was with a voice raised over the clink of spoons in coffee mugs and the clatter of plates.

"Friends, acquaintances, and lawyers, thank ye for gatherin' on short notice. As most of ye know, our party descended into the depths of Wynspar not a week ago. Most of my companions and I returned this morning, though two dear friends did not make it."

A solemn silence fell over the room, broken by the clattering of crockery from the refreshments table. The lone lawyer-monk by the coffee winced sheepishly and hurried over to sit beside her brother in law.

"We've no time to mourn, though," Gorm continued. "We ain't reported our quest to the guild yet, and only a few souls know we survivors have returned. We need your secrecy, and your help, for the good of the kingdom."

The assembled attendees exchanged uneasy glances. "Will it be legal?" asked one of the lawyer-monks.

"You're here to make sure it is," said Gorm. "Now, will ye commit to speak none of this to the outside world until tomorrow?"

Most of the attendees voiced their agreement, but the lawyer-monks insisted that all parties execute Adchul's standard mutual NDA. This took several minutes of shuffling, reading, discussion, and finally signatures. Once the paperwork was executed, Gorm continued, "First of all, we didn't kill the dragon."

Concerned murmurs filled the room. Gorm waited for them to die down before dropping the flaming oil down the mineshaft.

"But we did find the beast, and it has no treasure."

The room erupted in gasps and startled cries. An accountant fainted. A financier began to softly weep.

One face at the table, however, did not seem so upset. "And what is this to us?" asked a large Orc.

"Borpo Skar'Ezzod – Junior Elder of Finance" was engraved on the nameplate in front of him. "Have we not wisely divested from the dragon's hoard? This is to our advantage!"

"You speak out of turn, Borpo," said Asherzu Guz'Varda. "All of the economy hangs on the hoard of this dragon. If there is no treasure beneath Wynspar, we shall have no customers. Nobody shall pay rent. Loans shall go unpaid. Money will be both precious and meaningless. The system itself shall break."

"The Lightling's system is already broken," Borpo retorted, and a few of the Shadowkin nodded. "We can reforge the world into something better!"

The beads in Asherzu's braids rattled as she shook her head. "If we throw everything back into the forge, it is our people who would feel the fire the most. Did you learn nothing of my father's teachings? If we cannot conquer each other through business and commerce, are you so naive as to think all people will stop striving to advance? And how will they strive and fight without an economy to do it in? How do you think the Lightlings will behave if we have all of the giltin in the economy?"

"It will be different now," Borpo insisted. "We have many gold-hounds in the guild. Many Lightlings will flock to our banners if we have the gold. We could win such a war!"

"We may, and we may not," Asherzu said. "But what would we lose in the fight? How many children would never see parents again, or die hungry? How many widows and widowers will roam the streets? How many lives would we destroy to make the system better for a few? And would a system built on such pain and loss be any better than the one we have?"

She shook her head. "The world must change, but you cannot separate what it will be from how it will be made. My father did not choose the path of the aggressive seller because he had never been wronged by the gold-hounds, nor was it because he feared to fight and die as his father before him. No, it was for my siblings and I that he laid down his axe and picked up his counting scales. For the way of the Wall and finance is brutal and unjust and merciless, but Mankind was all of those things before the first coin was minted, and it will be so after the Wall and its banks crumble to ruins. My father knew that if he waged war with coin, if he followed the path of the aggressive seller, he would see his sons and daughters grow up. And though he and our clan were dealt a great injustice by the king and his guild, Zurthraka Guz'Varda saw all of his children come of age. I cannot say the same for my mother, or their parents, or their parents. Has any other chieftain in our tribe's sagas done as much?"

"And so must we sit back and endure more, just to preserve a system that has taken so much from us?" asked a Goblin executive.

"No. I know as well as any that this world is flawed. My father, my tribe, were unjustly killed, and they are but grains of sand on the shores of the dead." The chieftain and CEO stared at each of her kinsmen and employees in the eye, one by one. "But for all of its faults, our path to glory and honor lies along the Wall, not over its ruins. If we wish to give our children a future that is a gift and not a curse, we will follow the path of the aggressive seller. We will hear of every opportunity to deliver value for our people."

Borpo stared at her a moment after she finished speaking, and Gorm braced himself for the Orc's retort. It never came; the burly financier hung his head. "Your words ring true, Chieftain. I wish to see my Druella grow mighty and wise. Let us hear the Son of Fire's proposal."

"Thank ye," said Gorm. "We've a plan to save everything, but to do it, we'll need all of ye. Warg Inc. brings capital and manpower. I'm told Duine Poldo may be one of ten brokers on Arth with enough experience to pull it off. The guild and the lawyers make it all legitimate. Every one of us has a part to play if there's to be a future for any of us."

"We will hear your entreaty, friend Gorm Ingerson," said Asherzu. "The Guz'Varda Tribe and Warg Incorporated remember the help you have given our people."

"As does the Heroes' Guild of the Old Kingdom," said Vordar. The Dwarf nodded to Gorm. "I shall consider your offer most favorably."

"Hearing your request does not initiate an attorney-client relationship," intoned the lawyer-monks.

Gorm looked to Mr. Poldo. The Scribkin stared back with red-rimmed eyes, and his words came in a short gasp. "I will help. For the sake of friends lost, and those I still hold dear, I will help."

"Good." Gorm grinned and nodded to Jynn, who began to pack up. "Now, I'll tell ye the outline of me plan, but ye'll need to carry it out. Work together, respect each other, and don't falter for a moment. This is literally to save the kingdom, if not the world."

Burt piped up. "And what are you heroes going to do? Where's the rest of your party? And where's the wizard going?" The Kobold pointed to Jynn, who was already heading for the door with his cloak drawn tight around him.

"Oh, we all got our parts to play." Gorm's grin was like a Flame Drake's, all teeth and malice. "Ye focus on buildin' the future. We'll right the wrongs of the past."

——CHAPTER 27——

Arth's history played out on the passage walls, outlined in luminous liquid dancing over the damp stone.

Kaitha watched the people of the old world flow through the dark hallways. The tiny figures performed familiar scenes from legends she'd been told since days she could no longer remember. The sounds of the streams and the hum of magic flowed together into a haunting melody, and each watery figure moved to the music's rhythm. They repeated the same actions over and over, as though caught in eddies of time, allowing Kaitha to follow their tale like a book as she slowly made her way down the passage.

A part of her didn't want to look. The rest of her couldn't look away.

She knew some of the stories. Her eyes fixed on the Dwarves mourning the loss of their wives in the Age of Legends. The gods Baedrun and Fulgen came up from the heavenly depths to deliver a plan to save their people from dying out. Some Dwarves' heads flashed up and down in acceptance of the divine plan, others flickered from side to side in rejection. These dissatisfied clans walked away from Baedrun's offer and journeyed to a patch of marbled lichen, where they made a pact with a cloaked figure. Kaitha recalled that temples taught that the figure was Noros the Nightmare King, then still Noros the Dream Maker, and the pact he was making was to give them new women to replace their fallen wives. Another scene showed that the lost clans of the Dwarves had married the women

Noros introduced them to, and their children were the first Goblins. Any priest would tell you this was their punishment for disobedience to their gods, and most would follow that bit of moral instruction with a reminder that tithing your wealth was also a prominent commandment.

Yet the story on the wall continued past the advent of the baby Goblins, first among the Shadowkin, into the province of heresy. On the walls of the dark passage, the first of the Shadowkin were greeted with joy, as the first children born to Dwarves in a long time. Even when more Dwarves were born from Baedrun and Fulgen's scheme, they joined their green cousins on the wall without any apparent conflict. The watery citizens of the passage resumed their mundane tasks, now with Goblins alongside them.

Kaitha squinted in confusion at the glowing figures. She was sure that everybody knew that Goblins and Dwarves had been ancient enemies since the Second Age. Yet according to the glowing water, the Goblins and Dwarves of the Second Age seemed blissfully ignorant of their enmity. One Goblin tribe held a great feast for all the other peoples of Arth in one image, with the Sten taking a place of honor at their table.

It didn't stop with the Goblins. Further down the hallway, equally confusing vignettes showed the first Orcs born to the Elves, cursed with mortality and new forms by the magic of Mannon and his demons. Yet the Elves on the tunnel walls welcomed their new children, mourned the deaths of the first Orcs, and built cities with their green kin. She saw the Gnomes collaborating with Gremlins and Gnolls, witnessed the Naga rise and be welcomed by Humans and Halflings. Every time the magic of Noros or the demons created a new type of Shadowkin, the people of old moved to welcome them. With each new addition, the walls became more crowded, more vibrant. Some of the streams shifted in color as the demographics of the liquid mural changed, flowing toward violet or emerald, and even on to ruby or golden. Soon the passage was a glimmering rainbow that stretched farther than she could see.

Tears brimmed in Kaitha's eyes as she walked beneath the scintillating lights, in part because of the beauty of the dancing colors and the joy they portrayed, and in part because of a sensation, undeniable and undefinable, lurking at the back of her mind. A memory of a memory, a whisper of a long-forgotten thought, tugged at the corners of Kaitha's consciousness and filled her with an uneasy sorrow that didn't feel entirely her own. That alien melancholy crescendoed as she witnessed the first Troll born to Stennish parents. The parents seemed unable to find a suitable bassinet, given the hairy arms and legs extending from it, but otherwise they were clearly enamored with the first of the most deadly of the Shadowkin.

"They were at peace," she said, though just voicing the thought ached in depths she didn't know she had. "For a time, at least." The water on the wall seemed to sense her doubt, even react to it. Even as she recalled stories of the War of Betrayal, she began to notice the fissures running through the illuminated streams; jagged slashes of dark, dry stone where the water and the light would not touch. Citizens whispered and schemed at the edge of the darkness, faces dour and eyes narrowed to suspicious slits. Once she focused on one of the swaths, she saw more, until all she could see was the web of shadowy fractures running through the mural of light. Kaitha felt her stomach drop as she stared at the malignant gloom spreading through the dancing luminance, a sense of growing dread and certainty festering in her core. The histories may have been wrong about how the Third Age began, but there was no question as to how the War of Betrayal ended.

"They lost it all," she rasped, staring at the beautiful, breaking mural wrought in water on the walls. "Why? Why would they throw it all away?"

"It doesn't make any sense at all," Meryl Sabrin told Jynn as she handed him the wand. "The technician said your nornstones are in perfect condition, the projection matrix is untouched, and the whole wand is sound."

"It just isn't functioning." The archmage grimaced as he set the wand down on a table filled with arcane instruments. The Twilight Order's instructional laboratory made up for what it lacked in students with a plethora of artifacts, relics, and enchanted devices. Several pages of Jynn's notes were scattered about as well, though it was hard to make anything coherent of them in the scant minutes he had. The readings and research felt like a four-dimensional puzzle, and the nornstone wand should have provided a key piece.

"That's the strangest part. Mr. Watters said it worked fine in a pocket dimension—even gave a normal reading." The young omnimancer tapped a notch halfway up the wand. "Yet nothing they tried got it working in the city. That flash you see when you start channeling is the indicator light generating at the nexus, but instead of traveling along the projection matrix it... flashes out."

"Indeed," said Jynn. He picked up the wand again and channeled a bit of sorcery to give it a hopeful try. There was an azure flash, and then the wand lost all of its light save for the tiny threads of magic still connecting it to Jynn's hands. "Still, it seems odd that—"

He was cut off by a sudden thundering that shook the walls of the lab and rattled the beakers and crystals on every desk. "You magic! You magic scare cat! Make cat crazy!" bellowed a familiar, guttural voice.

Jynn sucked his breath in through his teeth. He had neither the time nor the patience for his neighbor's nonsense. "Mrs. Ur'Kretchen! I can assure you we have... done... no... such..." The archmage's shout trailed into a confused murmur as a sudden thought occurred to him.

He looked at the wand. Meryl looked at the wand. They looked at each other.

"To the roof!" Jynn cried, scrambling from the table. The pair of omnimancers rushed to the staircase that took them to the small platform used by the building's resident manager to clean the gutters and feed the gargoyles. A few of the stone-skinned creatures grumbled and scurried away as Jynn aimed the nornstone wand out over the empty street and channeled sorcery into it, squeezing his eyes shut against the expected flash of blue light.

When he opened them, his mouth fell open as well. Meryl gasped.

A blue orb of cobalt light hovered like a mute sprite above the street directly in front of the smoking tip of the wand. It trembled and jittered with a manic energy that could easily frighten or provoke a bored house cat; it took Jynn a moment to realize that the trembling of his own hands was causing the shaking wand. Still channeling, he swiveled the wand to point up, and the glowing sphere rose into the gray winter sky like a tiny sun. He swung the wand back and forth, and his stomach sank as he watched the tiny blue comet streak across the sky above him.

"Keeps a consistent distance," the archmage muttered. "Somewhere between twenty and thirty wand lengths away. Sustaining the indicator appears to be causing strain on the wand's pyromantic bindings, resulting in smoke trails."

"What does it mean?" asked Meryl.

"I'm not sure," Jynn murmured, his eyes locked on the glowing sphere. "But I'm certain whatever it is, it's huge."

"It's a Circle of Nations," said the olive-skinned pyromancer. "It's mages from across Arth gathering to discuss matters of national import. These are the pyromancers who speak directly to kings and queens and the empress, the highest members of our circles."

"It's perfect," said Laruna, looking beyond the guard to the gilded doors he blocked. "Let us pass."

"I'm afraid you can't go in there." The pyromancer was a short man with a thick mustache. His crimson robes bristled with gemstones and onyx and other indicators of well-earned rank.

Laruna held up a hand to stay Gaist. "You should be afraid, because I am going in there, and you can't stop us."

The guard's eyes narrowed, and amber flames engulfed his hands. "You must be new to the Order of Pyromancers if you don't recognize... uh... my—" His threats spluttered and died along with the flames around his hands.

"New and upcoming within the order, yes." Laruna smiled as the guard's flames wove around her fingers and dissipated into nothing. Already new rubies and black pearls were growing from her robes as some of the decorations receded within the fabric of the stunned guard's. It hadn't been a formal mage's dual, but both of their garments seemed to recognize that one wouldn't be necessary. "Now, step aside."

The guard responded with a noise caught between a squeak and a sob.

Gaist reached out and took hold of the stunned guard's shoulder. Sweeping his arm as one might do to push open a gate, the weaponsmaster moved the pyromancer off to the side. He gestured for Laruna to proceed with a bow.

"Thank you," said Laruna, and she pulled the ornate doors of the chamber open.

The room within was plush and warm, done in motifs of brass and crimson. Heavy braziers glowed with the amber light of simmering coals, and heavy velvet pillows cascaded off every bench and sofa. Half a dozen pyromancers sat around a central table, enjoying tea and spiced meats. Their robes were done in different styles, from the high angular shoulders of Ruskan tailors to the loose, sweeping garments of the Empire, to the wrapped silks and linens of the far continents, but all of them bore the ornate decorations of the most senior archmages. Their eyes swiveled to the door as Laruna walked through it.

"Laruna Trullon." The Ember of Heaven appraised Laruna's red and onyx robes. "I see that you have mastered yourself and become one with the fire."

Laruna stepped forward. "I have."

"And given what you've done to poor Gerrun out there, it seems your power has grown considerably."

"It has."

The Ember of Heaven smirked. "And given that you have interrupted this most high circle of your new order, I assume you have something important to tell us."

Laruna grinned. "Archmage, believe me when I say that you don't know the half of it."

"This is the biggest deal the Wall has ever seen. Perhaps the largest trade in ages. Be about your tasks!" called Duine Poldo. The Scribkin stood at the center of the conference room, a furious if diminutive conductor guiding the paperwork to a dramatic crescendo. Warg employees, lawyer-monks, Wood Gnomes, and Dwarven guild clerks swirled around him like dancers.

Feista Hrurk couldn't help but wag her tail as she watched the Scribkin at the height of his craft from her desk near the back of the room. She could hear the hitch in his breath, smell the perspiration on his brow, and yet the Gnome pressed on, totally in command of one of the most elite business teams in Andarun.

"Has the quest for the dungeon of Wynspar been voided?" Poldo called.

"The arbitration is executed and on its way to the guildhall," Vordar of the Heroes' Guild answered. "Workin' on the guild injunction now."

Poldo nodded as a crew of Wood Gnomes carried him a bundle of papers. The Domovoy swarmed around the Scribkin like bees around a hive. They stamped out letters and memorandums with tiny, lead blocks, sorted them into neat piles, and surfaced the odd document when it warranted the maestro's attention. Poldo accepted one such document offered by a small crew of Gnomes and adjusted his thick spectacles. "How is the NPC application coming along?"

"We do not know the spelling of the beast's name," cried Borpo Skar'Ezzod. "This complicates matters!"

"Refer to it as the Dragon of Wynspar," Poldo directed, "and attach an addendum to your motion for emergency consideration stating you'll file a correction after sentience is established and provisional papers are granted."

"I shall draft it!" Borpo raised his quill in a meaty fist.

"What about the court motions?" said Poldo.

"We shall file a motion to find the king is not a neutral party in matters of the dragon," chanted a lawyer-monk, "and send him notice as an adverse party to strengthen our case. He will not have the authority to reverse our work unilaterally."

Yet Poldo was already signing a new batch of contracts, dancing along to a project plan that only he could see.

Feista sat on her tail to keep it from thumping against her chair as she watched the Scribkin work. It was impressive, and inspiring, and a reminder that she had a complex market valuation to complete if the plan was to succeed. Determined not to fail Poldo, she turned back to her own parchment and was startled to see Asherzu Guz'Varda standing next to her.

"Now I see the stone upon which you sharpened your business skills," said the Orc chieftain, her eyes locked on the Gnome at the center of the paper maelstrom. "Truly, he is a sight to behold."

Feista felt her tail trying to creep between her legs, and she cleared her throat. "Uh, indeed lady. I shall tell my grandchildren of this day," said Feista.

Asherzu smiled and gripped a pendant hung round her neck. "It will be so if the gods shine on us and we triumph. But first, we must see this through to the end."

"It's not over yet!"

King Johan's sudden eruption froze Ahri Mizen in her tracks halfway across the throne room. The royal guard swallowed hard, eyes flicking warily around the gloom of the cavernous chamber. Thick spiderwebs filled the room, hanging from the tapestries and spreading between the columns, choking the window light. The threads of viscous silk extended all the way to the royal dais, where they tugged at the greaves and vambraces of the armored figure slumped motionless on the throne.

The guard watched the king for a few thundering heartbeats, trying to see if the outburst was directed at her. But the paladin didn't stir, save for the rise and fall of his pauldrons with each labored breath and a bulbous, black spider that scuttled across his breastplate. The guard could see other black, round shapes lurking in the shadows of the room. She'd seen one as big as her hand yesterday. Petri claimed he saw one as big as a cat. Then he had gone missing halfway through his shift, and nobody could find him.

Ahri had dismissed the rumors initially, of course. Skepticism of grim rumors was practically a job requirement for those still working at the royal palace. You couldn't believe what they said about why the queen killed herself, or the death of that Heroes' Guild bigwig, or the staff disappearances, or any of them really. The Mizens had served the kings of Andarun for generations, and it was as much familial duty as honor that bade her to brush aside all of the grisly chatter.

Something small but substantial dropped atop Ahri's head. Some frantic swatting and brushing set a thick clump of webbing down into the dust, still tangled around several strands of her dark hair. She glanced up. The torchlight gleamed off several dark, swollen shapes creeping between the rafters.

It occurred to Ahri then that the line between healthy skepticism and dangerous delusion probably lay several hundred paces behind her. Suddenly eager to be done with her errand and get to work on a resignation letter, the guard took two more steps, dropped to one knee, and cleared her throat.

Johan's golden helmet snapped around to stare at the royal guard. She could practically feel his gaze on her, could feel every crawling thing in the room staring at her from the darkness.

"Sire, a thousand—" The guard swallowed a scream as a huge spider covered in black bristles pulled itself from beneath the royal dais. "Sire, a thousand pardons, but I bring news from the ramparts."

Protocol demanded that the king bid her continue, and the rumors regarding the unpleasant fates of petitioners and palace staff who broke protocol had an unsettling new credibility in the wan light of the enwebbed throne room. Ahri squirmed while the king pondered her announcement. The king's gaze sank, and he murmured half a conversation to his own knees. "No... no, if he succeeded, he would just come here the back ways... so if it's from the ramparts..."

"Sire?"

"It's not over yet," growled the king. "What does he want?"

"Uh..." The guard glanced around for some help and, finding only spiders, decided to rush through the message as delivered to her. "There's a hero at the palace gates, sire. It's—"

"I know who it is!" Johan leapt to his feet, sending errant strands of webs and flailing arachnids flying from the throne. "What does he want?"

Gorm let the king's question hang in the air. Instead of acknowledging the paladin, he pulled a thick cigar from his belt.

"I said, how dare you make demands of your king?" Johan shouted, leaning over the ramparts of the palace. "What news is so important that you could not bring it to my throne?"

Gorm stood alone on the slate cobbles outside the palace walls. Pinnacle Plaza was mostly deserted, swept clear of shoppers and professionals by a bitter chill and a biting wind. The hardy souls that did remain were beginning to hurry over toward the royal gates in the hopes of catching a glimpse of the king, or a spectacle or, ideally, both.

Gorm struck a match. A tiny amber light flared outside the palace like the lone campfire of a miniature besieging army. "I come to parley," he said, putting the flame to the tip of the cigar.

"Parley?" the king sneered.

"Aye. Negotiate. Discuss. Come to terms as quickly as possible."

Johan rocked back on his heels. "You speak to your liege, Dwarf! Why would I need to negotiate with the likes of you?"

The berserker smiled. He knew he had Johan by the cape now, and all that remained was to keep the king's focus where the party wanted it. He took a deep breath to savor the moment, which unfortunately meant savoring a lungful of acrid smoke from the cigar. His witty retort died in a fit of choking.

"What's that?" asked Johan. "Speak!"

"I come—*ahem*—to—*cough*—make you—*cough*—I—*hack*!"

"What?" demanded the king. "What are you getting at?"

Gorm lost his words entirely in a cloud of expectoration and bluish silver smoke. His throat burned and tears welled in his eyes.

"Something wrong?" asked Johan, cruel amusement creeping back into his voice.

Doubled over and about to cough up a lung, Gorm inwardly cursed Boomer and Buster's convoluted design sense. *Il'ne se la* indeed! Through his tears, he could see that the cigar had only started burning toward the ring of scarlet foil.

"You had better have a good reason to behave this absurdly, Ingerson!" Johan leaned over the ramparts, desperate glee cracking his voice. "Do you realize what legal jeopardy you've put your party in? I'd have heard if you reported your quest to the guild offices! Not only are you disrespecting your liege—you've abandoned your duty!"

Gorm cleared his throat and took a deep breath. "Debatable," he said.

"What debate is there?" Johan demanded. "I sent you to kill a dragon, and—"

"And we fought it." Gorm's throat was still on fire, but the thrice-cursed cigar burned too slowly for him to catch his breath. He put the wretched device to his mouth and gave it a cautious puff, careful not to inhale the smoke.

A smug smirk split the king's scarred face. "Ha! We both know that's not true!" And then, remembering the gathering crowd, he added, "We, uh, would have heard the battle. And you would look worse for wear!"

Smoke drifted from the edges of Gorm's grin. "We fought your dragon, and then we talked things out with her."

"Talked things out? Ha ha!" Johan gestured down at the Dwarf as though inviting the rampart guards and growing crowd of onlookers to join in his ridicule. "What nonsense is this? Did you get the beast to sign a contract? Did the mountain itself serve as witness?"

"Nope." Gorm puffed at the cigar, watching the ash burn toward the red foil circle. "Just talked to her."

"Nonsense!" said Johan, leaning over the ramparts. "You can't talk to dragons!"

Gorm puffed out a cloud of smoke, cleared his throat, and pulled a smooth shard of crystal from his belt pouch. "We both know that ain't true," he said, holding it up. The fragment caught the last of the light in the deepening gloom, reflecting a distinctive, scintillating shade of amber. "You're familiar with the Eye of the Dragon, I'm sure."

The crowd gasped, though Gorm doubted anyone beside himself and the king knew of the gem. Rather, he suspected they were shocked by the way Johan visibly recoiled from the sliver of the gem, like a vampire stumbling upon gauze drapes. The king caught himself and tried to hide his reaction by feigning a confident shrug, but the muttering of the crowds said the onlookers had seen the flinch.

Gorm puffed the cigar. The edge of the red foil finally curled in the flame. A thundering rumble echoed from the north. The Dwarf smiled and flicked the thrice-cursed cigar away.

"And I know you're thinkin' this is some game or trick, since neither you nor I thought there was ever a dragon down there. Ye been to the center of the mountain too, I know."

"You lie! I don't know what you speak of!" snarled the king.

"I wonder if that's true," said Gorm. "I wonder if ye thought there was an old weapon or mounds of treasure past that magic barrier ye couldn't get through, or if ye knew it was just a few old statues."

A couple of screams rang out from the crowd at the revelation, and many quick-thinking residents rushed off to find their broker or their sprite stone.

Any pretense of confidence dropped from Johan's face. "You... you saw..."

"I did. Don't much matter now that your staircase down to the Black Fathoms is rubble. Turns out there was a dragon on the other side after all, guardin' them sculptures for some reason."

"You... that's not..." Johan shook his head slowly. "You couldn't... I mean, there's no drag—there's no way you spoke with a dragon!" His eyes darted across the murmuring crowds staring at him from every corner of the plaza. "He lies!"

Gorm shrugged. "The dragon will say otherwise, once we get her NPC papers sorted. And she'll also deny burnin' a single village or caravan."

"That... that doesn't prove anything," said Johan.

"Maybe not," said Gorm. "That's why we'll bring the documents from your facility up north. Lots of interestin' readin' there, including orders that you—"

"This is slander!" shouted the paladin. "You betray your king! It's... it's treason!"

"Ah, no. Those are different." Gorm's voice was as cold and hard as steel. "Slander is tellin' everyone the good folk of Bloodroot were to blame for stealin' them Elven Marbles. Betrayal was murderin' the hardworkin' Orcs and Goblins there because of your greed. Treason is killin' your own citizens in fake dragon attacks to cover up your crimes. What I'm here for is justice."

"Bloodroot?" Johan's face twisted up in confusion, and then split into a mad, incredulous grin. "You—you're accosting me on behalf of the Orcs? Ha! That's right! I forgot you had a thing for greenskins! This is all because that little Goblin you ran around with was put down!"

"It's about so much more than that," said Gorm. "It's about all the peoples everywhere ye killed, directly or not. It's about those ye put bounties on and those ye let starve in the street. It's about a priest ye had murdered, and about Kaitha and Thane, and all the others who died on account of your treachery. It's about all the crimes I don't know about, the victims we'll never find."

The Dwarf unslung his axe from his belt and leveled it at the king. "And aye, it's about Tib'rin, the best thrice-cursed squire a hero could ever ask for. And if his was the only blood ye had on your hands, I'd still be here."

"And where exactly do you think you are?" Johan growled. "You stand alone in a street, making empty threats against your king!"

"Not threats. An offer to parley," said Gorm. "I'll take ye peacefully. We'll choose a panel of magistrates. Ye'll get a fair trial, and lawyers, and—"

"Who do you think you're speaking to?" shrieked the paladin, suddenly apoplectic. "I'll not submit to the law of commoners! I am the King of Andarun! The Champion of Tandos! The mightiest warrior Arth has ever known! An army waits at my command! This palace is a fortress, built and stocked to withstand a siege, and our vaults hold the greatest weapons on Arth!"

Gorm's lips pulled back in an ambiguous grin that could have just as easily been a predatory snarl. "So what you're sayin' is, you're a big threat sittin' on top of a lot of wealth."

Johan's mouth hung slightly agape, as though his next sentence had lodged there on its way out. Realization struck the confusion from his face just as a horn trumpeted in the distance, playing the Heroes' Guild call to arms.

──CHAPTER 28──

"The new quest declares King Johan a Force of Evil, and the Palace of Andarun his dungeon," Duine Poldo explained. He gripped a leather armrest to steady himself, but their carriage was designed for an Orc, and he still slid across the wide seat as they careened up the streets of Andarun. "That means the Palace of Andarun is now officially a dungeon, and the treasures within it are officially loot."

"And you believe the guild and the nobility will accept this new quest?" asked Asherzu, seated across from the Scribkin. Darak Guz'Varda and Borpo Skar'ezzod were wedged into the seats around her, framing the chieftain in a wall of pinstripe silks and green flesh.

"The Dwarven guild has already affirmed it. And as for the nobility and the judicial..." Poldo gripped the seat with both hands as the carriage made an especially wide turn. An unfortunate pedestrian screamed from somewhere outside. It took a moment for Poldo's stomach to drop out of his throat. "Well, the key will be to get the people to want it to be true, and their desire will put pressure on institutions to make it so."

"And with so much of the economy tied up in this fight, that shouldn't be hard." Feista Hrurk slid across the seat next to Poldo's. "Everybody's fortunes are resting on this quest."

The Gnome nodded. "As in so many things, the government will follow where the market leads."

Asherzu nodded. "Does the palace have so much treasure?"

"Not in the palace itself, no. There will be valuables, to be sure—a king's ransom—but in the grand scheme of things it's a relatively small sum." Poldo glanced out the window and saw several more of Warg Inc.'s carriages in formation behind them. The brigade of black-clad coaches careened through the streets of Andarun like a squad of knights charging a foe, and it struck him that their mission had far greater stakes than that of a hero fighting any beast. He turned back to the Orcs. "The real treasures lie in the Great Vault of the Heroes' Guild, below the palace. The artifacts stored there are worth more than all the gold in the Freedlands—half of which is in the vault anyway."

Asherzu nodded, thoughtfully. "But does your vault possess the same value the hoard of the dragon was thought to?"

"It can't possibly," said Mrs. Hrurk. "There isn't enough gold on Andarun to be worth what the Dragon of Wynspar was valued at."

"But perhaps a sizable percentage, if the gods are good," said Poldo. "Many firms have more than half of their assets directly or indirectly in a dragon's hoard that turned out to be empty. For them, the difference between losing a sizable chunk of those holdings and losing all of those holdings could be the difference between their worst day as a business and their last day as a business. Our mission is their only chance of survival. With those stakes, they'll act now and let the lawyers justify it later."

"The key is to get them invested in the new quest," said Mrs. Hrurk. "Literally."

"Exactly," said Poldo. "Once I register the quest with the Andarun Stock Exchange, we must get the shares out and into circulation before the heroes complete their quest. That's why we need the full Warg Inc. staff at the Wall. I'll sell Warg the shares at a copper a piece, with the understanding that you'll act as a clearing house to exchange them with any buyer at a one-to-one rate."

"Minus a three-percent processing fee," interjected Asherzu.

"And once the transfers have begun, we'll need to signal..." Poldo paused as the chieftain's statement finally boarded his train of thought. "Wait, what?"

"A three-percent processing fee on all transactions," said Asherzu. "Warg Inc. shall withhold three percent of the Palace of Andarun shares as payment, or charge for smaller transactions directly in giltin."

The Scribkin smiled in sudden realization. "Ah, surely you mean three basis points, my dear. Three percent would be a hundred... times... that..." His smile faded as he saw those of the Orcs, their tusks and eyes gleaming.

"Indeed it is," said Asherzu. "I think two hundred and ninety-seven basis points an appropriate markup given the market's condition."

"What condition?" asked Poldo.

"Desperate," said the chieftain. "Warg Inc. has the least exposure to the dragon's hoard of any bank. Our staff is ready and en route to the Wall—who else can assemble their host of clerks before the king dies? As you said, many banks will fall this day. If any are to stand, they need us. They will pay three percent."

"But... but it's outrageous!" burst Poldo. "Most clearing house fees are a basis point on the high side! Three percent is extortion!"

"Oh no, Mr. Poldo," said Asherzu. "This is business. My colleagues and I would never dream of harming you."

Borpo looked about to speak, but the chairwoman silenced him with a deadly glare.

"We will stop our carriages if you wish," Asherzu continued. "You can get out and run to Maiden Street and register your stock and negotiate with another bank to act as clearing house. I do not think you have time, but you may. If the market collapses and you are too late, well..." The Orc gave a small, apologetic smile.

"But..." Poldo reeled at the very idea of what it would take to succeed without the Shadowkin at this point, and what it would cost to fail. "This rate is... it's absurd. Nobody will accept it!"

"I doubt that, Mr. Poldo." The chieftain smiled. "They do not have much choice, unless they wish their whole economy to collapse."

Poldo scowled. "You pretended you don't want the economy to fail any more than we do!"

"We did not pretend. We have no wish for such a collapse, but we fear it less," said the Orc. "Warg Inc. has no exposure to the dragon. Our balance sheets will not tumble as others. And if the economy falls, we Shadowkin have more money and more experience living a hard life in the wilds. We will feel the pain, but we are used to such pain. My people will find a way. Your people... well, I worry for many of them."

Anger flared in Poldo at the betrayal. "I just thought we were on the same side," he snarled.

"Did you?" Asherzu seemed surprised. "How much did your portfolio grow when your Goldson Baggs sent heroes to kill my father? How much gold did you make when my brothers and sisters died? The blood of my ancestors and my friends runs through these streets, and for centuries your people justified the slaughter by saying we would do the same to you. When did you think we joined you in this?"

Poldo opened his mouth, but thought better of it and swallowed his protest. "But surely things are different now."

"They are," said Asherzu. "My kin and I have joined you on the path of the aggressive seller. No longer do we fight; now we compete! We wield briefcases instead of axes, and plunder accounts instead of homes! And even as we triumph, as fortunes rise and fall, all of the parents will return to their children at the end of the day. Conquest without orphans. Battle without bloodshed. Everything is different, Mr. Poldo, even if some things stay the same." A fire burned behind the chieftain's eyes. "And if you cannot accept this, perhaps your problem was never how we fought, but a fear that we might win."

Poldo shook his head. "I see your point, madam, but with so much at stake, now is not the time to..." He trailed off at the gentle weight of Mrs. Hrurk's paw on his own hand. He turned to look into her big, brown eyes.

"Then when?" the Gnoll asked.

Duine Poldo thought for a moment before his shoulders fell. "Seventy-five basis points," he said. "It will make you one of the richest banks in Andarun."

Asherzu's grin widened. "Two hundred and twenty-five. We do not strive to be 'one of' anything."

"One percent," said Poldo. "Any more will break some firms."

"Such firms will be broken anyway. Many businesses fall this day. Two percent."

"One hundred and twenty-five basis points!" snapped Poldo. "Over a hundred times the going rate! Leave me a shred of my dignity!"

Asherzu considered the Gnome. "One hundred and thirty."

"Done," said Poldo, and held out his hand.

"A pleasure, as you say," said Asherzu, wrapping her hand around his and shaking it. "Mr. Borpo shall have the contracts—"

Borpo had already thrown the door of the carriage open and, holding a rail to steady himself, leaned out of it with a fist in the air. "One hundred and thirty basis points!" he shouted.

"One hundred and thirty basis points!" an Orc roared from another carriage. Another took up the call, and then a Goblin's reedy voice joined in, and then the Gnolls began to howl it. Soon the whole host of carriages had taken up the cry, whooping like warg riders as they descended on the Wall.

Gorm could see fear on Johan's face as they approached.

Heavily armed bystanders began moving toward the front of the gathered crowd, wearing bladed armor and wicked grins. They were just the vanguard, those heroes lucky enough to catch an early rumor of the job of the century, if not the age. Parties of adventurers crested the steps from the tiers and marched across the Pinnacle. Enchanted trinkets rattled against polished armor. Arcane runes danced over sorcerous robes. Flames and lightning and white auras of frost crackled over blades and long spears. Soon the Pinnacle was crammed with heroes, all armed to the teeth, all eager to storm the palace and take its treasures. As numerous as locusts. As certain as the grave.

"What's with the king?" asked Laruna, stepping up to Gorm's left.

"Just gave him his options," the Dwarf muttered. "Don't think he likes 'em."

Gaist nodded, falling into place on Gorm's other side.

If the king heard them speaking, he gave no indication of it. The king stared with wide eyes at the advancing heroes. His lips twitched as though muttering something, but if he made any sound it was too low to be heard down on the cobblestones.

"So when are we going in?" Jynn joined the pyromancer beside Gorm. The Wyrmwood Staff glowed with gray light in the archmage's hand.

"Waitin' on the signal," said Gorm.

The omnimancer nodded. "We'll have plenty of backup, it seems."

Other parties were clustering around the four Heroes of Destiny, arranging themselves according to the order of their arrival. The Shadow Stallions had reached the palace surprisingly early, with their Great Eagle circling above. The Night Panthers managed to get a spot just ahead of the Gutter Dogs, and now the rival parties growled and snarled at each other. Gorm caught sight of Mr. Brunt towering over his own party; a one-eyed woman and a pair of Gnomes clustered around the Ogre like soldiers around a siege engine. He waved to the Ogre, and thought perhaps he got something approaching a nod in response.

Heraldin emerged from between the Obliged Corpses and the Spinning Rocks just as the trumpets blared again. "Is it time?" the bard asked.

"Just waitin' on the signal. And an answer," Gorm added loudly, looking up to the ramparts.

Johan shook his head, a snarl curling his scarred lip. The pitch and volume both skyrocketed as he sputtered accusations down at the party, "If you hadn't killed... no, if you hadn't... You said..."

"We're here 'cause of what ye done, not us," Gorm called out to him. "Are ye comin' peacefully or not?"

Yet the king didn't seem to notice the Dwarf at all. He shook his head. "There's still time!" he screamed, turning to fly across the ramparts. "I can still win! There's still time!"

The palace guards along the wall glanced back and forth, weighing the situation. On the one hand, their king was fleeing, and on the other, a legion of heavily armed professional killers was coalescing in the plaza. Those most familiar with guild practices must have realized that they were currently mid-demotion from defenders of the crown to evil henchmen, because they began stripping their armor and weapons off as they broke ranks and fled into the courtyard.

Gorm grimaced. He'd hoped to keep the king occupied near the front gates a bit longer. If Johan had enough time to make it back to the ruined steps, he could still find a way down into the dragon's lair and attack the wounded creature. But they couldn't start the new quest before—

A white comet suddenly flew from one of the upper tiers, like a falling star headed back home to the sky. It rose high above the Pinnacle and popped, flaring into the grinning, giant face of a Goblin shaman glowing faintly against the dark clouds. The strange visage took a moment to orient itself downward, then smiled and winked with exaggerated enthusiasm as it dissipated on the roiling winds.

"They've registered the quest at the stock exchange," Heraldin said.

"Do we need to give them time to transfer all of the shares?" asked Jynn.

"Ain't time for that," said Gorm. He looked to each of the other heroes. "Ready?"

Heraldin nodded grimly and extended a hand into the center of the group. "For Kaitha," he said.

Gaist put his hand on the bard's and nodded.

"For Thane," said Laruna, adding her hand.

"For the people of the Freedlands," said Jynn, placing his unmarred hand on the pyromancer's.

Gorm nodded and placed his calloused hand on top. "For all of 'em, and for Niln and Tib'rin too. Let's slay the king and save the dragon."

They locked eyes with one another, each face reflecting a steely resolve. Then Gorm gave a curt nod, and they broke apart and turned to face the queue of heroes still forming behind them.

"Heroes!" the Dwarf barked, raising his axe above his head. "Colleagues and acquaintances from across the realm! I'm Gorm Ingerson, formerly the Pyrebeard!"

A silence fell over the Pinnacle, save for the footfalls of civilians vacating the plaza. It is well-known that professional heroics is a spectacle best enjoyed far from the range of any errant fireballs.

"I slew the Hydra of Hangman's Grotto. My party saved Andarun from the Liche Detarr Ur'Mayan. And most recently, I led an excursion to battle the Dragon of Wynspar!" Gorm said, banging his axe on his shield to emphasize each accomplishment. "But this quest is the most foul I been on yet. I could tell ye of a bastard king whose lies killed citizens as he seized power. I could tell ye of injustices and deceptions that span back years, of men and women murdered to slake his lust for power. I could show ye evidence—damning evidence—that would prove that he and his lackeys are behind all of the so-called dragon attacks plaguin' the Freedlands!"

Thousands of eyes stared back impassively from the eye-slits of ornate helmets and beneath enruned hoods.

"But half of ye wouldn't listen to me back story, and most of the rest wouldn't care," Gorm conceded. "And I ain't time for it anyway. All ye need to know is that our cause is just, that our payout is certain, and that I'm declarin' this quest…"

The air crackled with anticipation as the berserker took a deep breath. Gauntlets tightened around sword grips and magical staves.

"This quest is a guild raid!" Gorm shouted. "All parties share the work and glory!"

A shout like thunder erupted, a cacophony of excitement and war cries blending into one roar from the throat of the guild. Gorm and his party were carried forward on a surge of charging heroes. Crackling clouds of flaming gasses erupted from the palace as spells and potions collided with its walls. The main gate was a bent and ruined husk by the time Mr. Brunt ripped it from its freshly corroded hinges. With another shout, the wave of adventurers swept into the courtyard and crashed down on the contingent of palace guards and Tandosian clerics therein.

A melee swirled around Duine Poldo.

Bodies pressed against the Gnome from all sides. Distant screams of anguish and despair pierced the air, usually from traders only now fully grasping the actual value of their portfolio given the price of the Dragon of Wynspar's hoard. They screamed offers and demands and desperate pleas as they pressed down upon the assembled brokers of Warg Inc., waving purchase slips and fighting to get closer to the trading kiosks. Cries of triumph rang from those who successfully swapped their shares in the dragon's hoard for a stake in the new quest to bring King Johan to justice. Wood Gnomes streamed past, ferrying reams of paper back and forth between the roaring giants all around them.

An Orcish broker thrust a contract at Poldo. He signed it after only a cursory glance; the lawyers would sort it out later anyway. This business was desperate and fast, every transaction a messy skirmish. Corporations teetering on the brink of collapse were pulled back up from the edge of bankruptcy, while others fell and were consumed. Arth shook as the economy of the Freedlands took a sideways step.

Behind Poldo, Mrs. Hrurk perched on a small platform. The Gnoll beat a war drum while minding a complex spreadsheet of her own design. The Domovoy had set up a large chalkboard behind the Gnoll. A Wood Gnome in a chipmunk pelt used a piece of twine to rappel down to a long rectangle drawn on the middle of the gray slate. As shares of the dragon's hoard were transferred, Wood Gnomes below the makeshift chart chittered details of the transactions up to the suspended Gnome, who filled in more of the graph with a piece of chalk as long as her arm.

Yet as innovative as this system was, there was no time to marvel at the Domovoy's ingenuity. Just the first third of the makeshift meter was full, and already the sounds of fireballs and lightning bolts were ringing on the Pinnacle. Poldo felt his stomach turn, and grimaced. They needed more time and faster sales if they were to have any hope of success. "Keep on!" he shouted, grabbing another contract and signing it. "Keep going!"

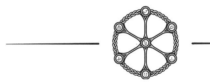

"Hurry!" Gorm thrust his hand forward as if trying to haul his companions along with an invisible rope. "The vault and Royal Archives are just up ahead."

"Right," said Laruna, unmoved by the Dwarf's pantomimed tugging.

"And I'm pretty sure Johan's staircase to the Black Fathoms is at the back of the vaults." Gorm did a sideways shuffle toward the doorway, a motion that was less a mode of ambulation and more an encouraging dance for his fellows.

"Yeeesss." Jynn had to squeeze the concession from between his clenched teeth. "And yet..."

The shriek of sorcery rending steel and a scream of agony rang out from somewhere above them. A palace guard or Tandosian cleric had either decided to put up a fight or failed to disarm fast enough, and the results were the same. Some defenders of the palace believed in their cause enough to stand against the guild heroes pouring into the palace. Those who managed to survive the carnage quickly realized that the difference between a noble guard and a hapless henchman was public opinion of one's boss and, more pressingly, that the difference between a henchman standing against guild heroes and an oily smear on the cobblestones could be measured in seconds.

Some of Johan's guards accepted their fate and fought until the bitter end. A few fools tried to flee. Yet most were familiar enough with guild protocols to drop their weapons, strip off anything of value, and feign unconsciousness, thus forestalling any possible incentive to dispatch them. Gorm's descent into the palace basement brought them past at least a dozen prone figures lying in their undergarments next to neat piles of loot.

"We want... to catch... Johan." It was all Gorm could do to speak rather than scream; rage and anticipation were squeezing his chest until his heart burned and his gorge rose in his throat. A red mist was hanging at the edge of his vision, begging him to release his fury.

"True," said Heraldin.

"So we need... to... hurry!"

Gaist shook his head and pointed at the doorway ahead.

The heavy door wasn't ornate, but it was covered in enough reinforced hinges, intricate locks, and clear signs of traps to give the impression of decoration—exactly the sort of door one would expect to guard Arth's greatest treasures. It was open, supporting Gorm's theory that Johan had recently fled this way. He had not, however, anticipated the massive cobwebs framing the entrance, swaying around a Johan-shaped hole in their middle. A hand-sized spider stared with undisguised malice from the desiccated corpse of a royal clerk just inside the threshold.

"We need to be careful here," said Laruna. "Slow it down."

"Like the others," added Heraldin. The bard nodded to a couple of other exploring parties. Newbloods swarmed the palace upstairs, chasing guards and harassing servants, but seasoned heroes knew that the biggest threats and best loot were likely to be deeper in the newly declared dungeon. Grizzled veterans double-checked top-shelf gear, readied potions, and wove sorcerous wards in anticipation of moving through the ominous doorway.

"What? That?" Gorm asked. The red mists were closing in, inviting him to let go and give himself over to reckless pursuit. "All for a little spider?"

"I wouldn't say little," said Heraldin. The spider raised two legs as long as the bard's fingers and waved them menacingly.

"There's probably some simple explanation for all them webs anyway," Gorm said, looking to Jynn.

The wizard looked at the Dwarf askance and shook his head.

"No?" Gorm felt his own unease rising. "I mean, a king's about to die, right? Maybe that much destiny, I don't know, compresses bugs' breeding cycles or otherwise attracts spiders?" His shoulders fell at the omnimancer's blank expression. "No simple, rational explanation for... for all this?"

He gestured at the spider. An even larger and hairier specimen leapt from the shadows to pounce on the distracted arachnid. In a matter of seconds, it covered its struggling prey in webs and, with an eight-eyed glare at the heroes, dragged its meal back into the shadows.

"No," said Jynn. "This is just creepy."

"There's so much malignant sorcery here," said Laruna. "And the transformation must have happened quickly. You don't see this sort of infestation every day."

Gorm deflated with a long sigh. The corruption ensnaring the palace in thick webs was disturbing, but it wasn't unfamiliar. "Not every day, but I have seen it before," he said.

All eyes turned to the Dwarf. "Where?" asked Heraldin.

"In my nightmares, mostly," said Gorm. "But before that..."

"In the dungeon of Az'Anon the Spider King," Jynn finished for him.

"Aye." The Dwarf gripped his face in a mailed hand and grit his teeth. A nagging suspicion tugged at the back of his mind. "Gods, he must have brought it back."

"Exactly. Help from beyond," said the omnimancer.

Gorm took a deep breath and dropped his hands to his sides. "Explains a lot."

"I wish you'd do the same," said Laruna. "Who brought what back?"

"Johan brought something back from the dungeon of Az'Anon," said Gorm. "Something big and evil and with an affinity for spiders. Back when Az'Anon killed some of the best heroes I knew and sent me runnin', Johan of Embleden was just a young hotshot with more ribbons on his tabard than quests under his belt. But afterward, Johan started taking on solo quests to slay the most powerful wizards on Arth."

The omnimancer nodded. "In a few years he was the guild's most celebrated hero, and some time after that the Champion of Tandos, and then the King of the Freedlands. His rapid rise suggests aid from something supernatural."

"The only question is what that somethin' is," said Gorm.

"I'll bet it's epic, whatever it is." Heraldin grimaced and shot Gaist a meaningful look.

Gorm ignored the bard. "Could be a coven of dark magic users, or any kind of demon, or a spider totem, or even Az'Anon's ghost. Not sure how we can figure out what."

"I believe I can answer that," said Jynn.

"Ye know what's behind all this?" said Gorm.

"No," said the wizard. "But I believe whatever it was also made Az'Anon the Black into the Spider King. My father and the rest of Az'Anon's associates from the Leviathan Project were frightened of it, and I suspect they had theories about its nature. And I am nearly certain their letters on the subject are somewhere in the Royal Archives, near the back of this very vault."

Gorm saw where this was going. "We ain't got time for readin' through an archive! I'll allow that we need to be cautious, but Johan's makin' his way toward the stairs now."

"The stairs we destroyed," said Laruna.

"He seems to think he's got a chance, and I ain't willin' to risk him bein' right." Gorm snorted. "If he can find a way down to the dragon, who knows what he and whatever's pullin' his strings will do?"

"Then go on ahead," said Jynn. "Help me reach the archives, and I'll find the letters while you make your way to Johan. If you stall for time, I should know what we're up against before it reveals itself."

Gorm considered the proposal as he checked over his gear. "We get him started on a monologue, maybe test his strength a bit, play up the final confrontation... I still don't think ye'll have more than ten minutes before the bastard either summons his helper or true-forms or some such."

"Then I'll make the ten minutes count," said the omnimancer. The gemstone in the Wyrmwood Staff flared a little brighter at its master's determination.

Heraldin stepped in. "It does make sense, my friend. We need to know what we're up against."

Gaist nodded and watched another party of heroes make their way into the vault. Their weapons gleamed in the amber light of their solamancer's flame.

"Jynn can do this." Laruna locked gazes with the wizard. "And we need him to."

"Aye, fine." Gorm hefted his axe and shield. "Last time I faced... whatever this is, I ran screaming. Knowin' what we're up against is the best chance we have not to do that again. We'll get ye to the archives, and then the rest of us will clear a path to Johan. But ready yourselves."

Orange light flared and shouts rang out from within the vault. Something inhuman screeched in pain, and the shadows of spindly, hairy appendages waved through the light of the fire.

Gorm nodded to the other heroes as they readied their weapons. "It's gonna be rough goin'."

——CHAPTER 29——

Gorm's warning turned out to be the sort of understatement that Jynn Ur'Mayan hated.

The phrase "rough going" implied a trek through brambles, or perhaps climbing over cumbersome rocks. "Rough going" conjured visions of a hike that turned out a bit sweatier than normal. "Rough going" suggested the sort of aches that a good beer and hot meal could ease.

Jynn reflected that, had he been asked to describe their journey into the Great Vault of Andarun, the fabled home of the Heroes' Guild's greatest treasures and stockpiles of loot, he would not have used such an innocuously broad term. Wizards prefer precision. Accuracy is a survival skill for those who make a career in magic, where a mispronounced phrase or clumsy gesture can be the difference between levitating a ham sandwich across the room and ripping a hole in space-time. As such, the archmage would have been much more exact when describing their descent into the black marble fortress beneath Andarun's palace, making liberal use of phrases like "a nightmarish flight through a labyrinth of arachnid horror," or "a grueling slog under constant assault from spidery abominations," or even "the most traumatic experience that the gods have yet to curse me with."

Thick curtains of webbing hung in front of locked doorways and dangled from vaulted ceilings. Gauzy tendrils waved from every glowstone lantern like the limbs of tiny ghosts reaching out for the adventurers. Spiders with the size and temperament of angry terriers leapt from the shadows and dropped from the ceiling, green fluid dribbling from their daggerlike mandibles. Flashes of sorcerous flames and crackling lightning cast baroque, spindly shadows on the black walls. The air rang with the screeches of burning spiders and the cracking of steel hacking through exoskeletons.

Most of the adventurers down here were seasoned enough to handle giant vermin, even if the spiders were unusually numerous and well-coordinated. The lurking arachnids were beat back with grim efficiency. Yet as routine as killing giant spiders was for veterans, being a professional hero is always dangerous. Jynn witnessed an unnamed warrior pulled away from his teammates and carried off by a swarm of rat-sized spiders, and some shouts down a side hallway indicated that another group had lost at least one member.

These other parties split away from Jynn's party in the front rooms of the vault, drawn by chambers filled with mountains of giltin and piles of arcane artifacts like moths to candles. Soon the archmage could see no sign of any other heroes, save one. Johan had left a clear trail of carnage through the vaults. If the mad king and the spidery denizens of the vault had any relation, it couldn't be called an alliance. Various chunks of arachnid littered the halls around the Johan-sized holes burned through the webs. The morbid trail left a mess on the boots. On the other hand, Gorm swore he could gauge how close they were to the king by the intensity of the twitches and spasms of the dying spiders in his wake.

They continued along the paladin's path until Jynn found a door with a small placard indicating the Royal Archives lay beyond.

"I hate to split the party in the middle of a dungeon," the Dwarf grumbled.

"You'd hate letting Johan get away more. And you'd hate a surprise in a fight with him even more than that," the archmage reminded him. "I won't be long."

"Don't be," Gorm said.

Jynn turned to enter the archives, but a hand caught his arm. He turned to find Laruna holding him, but she dropped his sleeve as soon as their eyes met. "I'll come with you," she said. "It's not safe to run solo on a high-level quest."

"Aye," said Gorm. "If we're to split, ye should at least be a pair."

"B-but what about you?" asked Jynn.

Heraldin and Gorm gave him a quizzical look. "We've got Gaist," the bard said.

Gaist flourished a blade for emphasis.

"We'll be fine," said Gorm. "Just find out what Johan's got down his britches and follow us. We'll be at the end of the trail of dead spiders."

Jynn looked back at Laruna. A gust of emotions howled at the windows of his mind, but he closed his eyes and shuttered his mental space with a deep breath. "Very well," he said. "Let's be quick."

The interior of the Royal Archives was organized and opulent. Rows of leather-bound books and neat stacks of scrolls lined mahogany shelves that covered every inch of the walls. A fine desk with a velvet blotter sat at the front of the chamber, marking the line between a reception area and countless rows of free-standing filing cabinets extending back into the darkness. A library with plush reading chairs might have been a welcome sight, were it not for the sticky gray strands woven between the shelves or the spiders swarming over the remains of the unfortunate royal archivists.

The archmage dispatched the closest arachnids with a few threads of elemental death. Another swarm skittered forward, only to be engulfed in orange flames.

As Jynn watched Laruna step over the piles of former spider, it occurred to him that many people would assume a pyromancer was the last type of spell caster one would want in a room full of priceless parchments and books. But now that he saw her at work, there was no better mage to have here with him. The fire was an extension of her will, burning away arachnids and webbing while leaving paper and wood untouched.

Then she caught him staring, and he turned his attention to draining the tiny souls from a nest of spiderlings rushing toward his flank.

"I wanted to talk to you," said Laruna. "Though I suppose this doesn't seem like the right time, either." She sprayed a wave of flames at a bulbous spider dangling from a bookshelf.

"We are a bit preoccupied," Jynn said, driving the point of the Wyrmwood Staff into a particularly large spider's eye. It recoiled and melted as his magic liquified its exoskeleton.

"It seems the right time never comes." Laruna gave a sad smile and hurled a fireball into thick webs heavy with sinister, bulbous silhouettes.

They shrieked as she turned to Jynn. "But I'd rather say it at the wrong time than never say it."

"Laruna, I—"

"I'm sorry," said the pyromancer. She roasted a spider in its own juices with a wave of her hand. "I'm sorry that it took me so long to thank you for saving my life." A stream of flame from her fingertip set a massive web alight. Its oversized residents tried in vain to flee the blaze racing along the strands. "I'm sorry that when you gave up your hand for me, I got too wrapped up in judging how you gave it rather than appreciating what you sacrificed." A lone arachnid escaped the blazing web and, with an uncharacteristic sense of self-preservation, fled for the shadows. It only made it a few steps before erupting in a pillar of flame. "I'm sorry that my judgment frightened you, and most of all I'm sorry that I proved your fears well-founded."

Jynn listened, his own emotions roiling behind the thin walls that he had erected. He stared at her, his lip quivering, his heart pounding, his hands casually weaving eldritch sigils that melted nearby spiders into puddles of green goo. "Thanks. I forgive... I'd already forgiven you," he said eventually.

"Thank you," she said. A charred leg near her twitched and was engulfed in another fireball.

"And... is that all?" Jynn asked as he fried a fleeing spider with a lightning bolt.

"Should there be something else?" she asked him, burning the last of the webs away.

Jynn's mouth was dry, and his palms damp. He glanced to one side and saw, to his disappointment, that they were near a rather extraordinary filing cabinet. It was covered in bands of metal, huge rivets, and the sort of sigils normally reserved for a demonologist's basement floor. It had only one drawer, and just above the lone handle a brass plaque bore a familiar etching of a fish with tentacles wrapping up around its tail—the sign of the Leviathan Project.

Laruna followed his gaze. She took a deep breath and forced a grin. "Probably not the right time for this," she said.

"We did tell Gorm that we would hurry." Jynn smiled in apology as he turned his attention to the drawers.

There were enchanted locks and wards all over the cabinet, of course; magical wards and locks are best for keeping out skilled thieves and overcurious apprentices. Best practices called for complex spells of both noctomancy and solamancy, so that no one individual could open the spell. This policy operated under the presumption that there were very few powerful omnimancers around anymore, and if there were any it was unlikely that they'd be trying their hand at safecracking.

Jynn noted the Novian irony and filed it away mentally as he swiftly dismantled the spells with his own weave and popped the drawer open. A cloud of dust billowed as it slid out.

"What are we looking at?" Laruna asked, conjuring a brighter light above Jynn's head.

"The sealed files of the Leviathan Project," Jynn said, glancing at a sheet of parchment. "And judging by the archives' access records, we're the first people to do so for over two decades. And before that... it's just Handor and his father. Almost nobody alive knows what's in here."

The pyromancer nodded. "But you think it will help us fight Johan?"

"I do." The archmage picked up a thin file covered in the stamps and seals of the kingdom's most secret documents. "Before Johan claimed to have slain him in triumph, Az'Anon the Black stumbled upon something that terrified every mage working on the Leviathan Project. We need to learn what it was."

"I don't want to know," Kaitha murmured as she stared with vacant eyes at the glowing images flowing over the doorway. "I don't want to remember."

It was unclear to Kaitha how long she had stared at the door, caught between the ancient magics that compelled her forward and something deep in her soul that forbade her from taking another step. These opposing forces, along with a probable concussion after her drop, left her in a fugue state, murmuring ignorance and denials at the watery figures on the doorway.

The glowing water and the vacant shadows combined on the door, with the dancing figures clearly cut into two camps. The hum of magic in the air had grown deep and ominous, like the thunder of a distant army on the march. On the one side, the water painted the Sten and the Shadowkin, yes, but also many Elves, Dwarves, and Humans. On the other side, a golden figure wearing the crest of Tandos and carrying a long spear led a force of all the peoples of light, with spears and blades protruding from the mob like a half-melted hedgehog. Kaitha thought the figure must have been Issan, the legendary Elven general and champion who led the Children of Light to victory in the war to come. A rift of dark stone stretched down the seam of the double-sided door, and in the middle of the darkness...

"Don't make me," Kaitha said. She sensed something dreadful beyond the door, something that terrified her in her core. A faint scratching beyond the stone was occasionally audible, like some distant rodent gnawing at the edge of perception. "I don't want to remember."

Yet she couldn't forget, not when her eyes fell on the limp forms drawn in glowing water in the middle of the dark swath. Most of them were of indeterminate origins, but some pointed ears indicated there were Elves among the dead, and one form was unmistakable: a hulking corpse of a Troll.

Her eyes jerked away from the Troll's face, but it was too late. One glance at the watery features, and memories welled up within her. She saw Thane's smile, his eyes, the way he looked at her when he—

"Don't make me remember!" Kaitha repeated, with more force than a trance would usually allow.

But she did remember, another part of her growled from the corner of her psyche. She had to remember. She wouldn't let him be forgotten. Her determination returned, along with the frenetic scratching at the doorway, and she took a step toward the door.

Something in Kaitha's mind shrieked in protest. She reminded herself of the moment that Thane died in this gods-forsaken dungeon so she wouldn't have to, and she kept moving forward. Her eyes scanned the massive door for a mechanism to open it, but it quickly became apparent that wouldn't be necessary. The door creaked open as she approached, its unseen hinges driven by some hidden mechanism or sorcery. And once the stone doors had parted enough for her to see into the room beyond—

A mass of hair and claws and whirling eyes launched from the doorway, gibbering and shrieking. Kaitha dove to the side, splashing into a wall and scattering a glowing group of Elves into tiny droplets. She drew her knife and dropped into a fighting stance, but the creature—or creatures—were already fleeing back up the tunnel as fast as their distinctive hobbling scamper would allow.

Scargs. Variegated ones, judging by the streaks of yellow, red, and mottled greens running through the bat-like creatures' fur. Judging by the way they continued to shriek and hiss at the glowing watery murals on the walls, Kaitha surmised that whatever magic had drawn her in had terrified the nest of them. She watched as one last, tiny inhabitant of the nest bounced after its family, chirruping in displeasure, and then the gaggle of them was gone.

A part of the ranger wanted to follow them, to flee screaming from the tunnel and its sorcerous mural. Yet scargs could fly out over the deep chasm behind her, and an Elf could only plummet into it, so her only option was to go forward.

Setting aside the wild protests from the back of her mind, Kaitha stepped through the door and onto the scene of the War of Betrayal.

She expected to see battles. She expected there to be bloody armies cast in glowing water, and mounds of dead depicted in dripping currents. Yet instead, in the small circular chamber beyond the door, she saw a negotiation. To Kaitha's left, azure and emerald water showed a Stennish king and queen with a toddler at their heels. A delegation of diplomats or advisors swirled into existence in front of the royal family and bowed low—one Orc, one Sten, one Elf. On the ranger's right, Issan and the generals of the Army of Light gathered at a table in discussion. Nodding in agreement, Issan himself set out with a Human, a Dwarf, and a Gnome. The diplomats and the generals moved toward the middle of the room, drifting along a tide of water until they met their counterparts directly in front of Kaitha. A tent bubbled up around them, and they began to talk.

As the tiny emissaries haggled, Kaitha carefully walked into the chamber. The room was like a cistern, a smooth stone cylinder that extended higher than her vision could see. A few vents and rotted steps were visible in the shadows above. The air was damp and musty here, and the floor covered with all the disgusting trappings of a scarg nest: fur clumps, rat bones, and mounds of scarg guano that were all being slowly pushed about by the rivulets of glowing water streaming into the room from the tunnel behind her.

To Kaitha's surprise, the water showed the negotiations on the wall working. As the current drew crowds of anxious onlookers on either side of her, the parties shook hands. The Sten raised her hand into the air, and Kaitha half-smiled in a reflection of her tiny, pantomimed triumph.

It was too good to be true. It wasn't true. Already she could see the dark shadows spreading down the walls, blackening the stone behind the dancing lights.

The darkness touched Issan, and he stabbed the Stennish woman through the back. Kaitha covered her mouth to choke back a cry as one of the greatest heroes of her people then killed the Orc and, taking up the warrior's axe, fell upon the other members of his own party. Bloodred water dripped from the bottom of the tent as the general finished his grisly task. When Issan emerged alone from the tent, he was cast in a crimson light, and as he gestured back to his own party, the angry red seared across his army. Issan's crimson forces fell upon the Sten and their allies, slaying warriors and women and children alike.

Kaitha watched the carnage with wide eyes, biting the back of her hand until a trickle of blood flowed down her arm. The Sten hadn't betrayed the Children of Light. They had been betrayed. She was certain of the truth of it; no, she *remembered* the truth of it, and with the memory an unbearable anguish pressed down on her heart, like the pain of losing Thane a thousand times over. She fell to her knees, and tears streamed freely down her face, falling to mingle with the ruby river flowing over the stones.

The river of tears flowed on.

It had no deep aquifer to burble up from, no snowmelt to feed it from on high, nor any slope to guide its impossible flow. Yet it bubbled along in happy defiance of physics, humming as it flowed through the Black Fathoms at the mountain's heart. The sound echoed through the massive chamber, bouncing off the treelike pillars and their branching pathways. The stream's music filled the air as the water rushed over the pathway into the dragon's lair.

Kulxak the dragon, Guardian of the Stones, ordained Warden of the Future, regarded the oncoming stream warmly. The water flowed up to her back where it paused, burbling musically just behind her wings.

With a pained and labored grunt, the dragon lifted herself and shifted her massive weight to the other side of her precious charges. The stream waited patiently for her to settle down, then proceeded into the deep grooves encircling the ring of dismembered statues. Patterns and sigils glowed with sudden vibrance as the luminous liquid sluiced through ancient channels. Matching symbols began to glow on the stone statues as well, faint characters cast in blue that seemed to light up from just beneath the surface of the marble. A new sound joined the stream's music, a deep thrumming echoing up from the stony depths of the cavern. This tectonic tala began to beat in a staccato pair, like the heartbeat of the mountain itself.

As Wynspar's isorhythmic pulse strengthened, the scattered sculptures in the glowing circle began to move. The disembodied head of a Sten shifted suddenly to the side, as though shaken by the swelling of music around her. Another beat and the statue's head lurched a finger's width away from the stone beneath it, as though dislodged from the floor by the rhythm. One more pulse from the depths and it was free, drifting into the air with the lazy grace of an unmoored boat. Beneath it, other parts of the sculpture began to shake and float.

Borne on a languid tide of music and light, the stones slowly began to rise.

"They need to move faster!" Duine Poldo cried as he stared at the Domovoy's chalkboard. A Wood Gnome in a chipmunk pelt was coloring frantically as her colleagues squeaked numbers at her, yet the chalk graph showed that only half of the known shares of the dragon's hoard had been exchanged. The Scribkin glanced up at the Pinnacle. Andarun's top tier flashed and smoked like a waking volcano as blasts of sorcery and exploding alchemical potions flew about the palace. "We won't have time if we can't move the shares faster!"

"My employees labor with all haste," Asherzu called back. "We cannot do more!"

She was right, of course. They needed more hands. And Poldo could only think of two. "Mrs. Hrurk!" he shouted.

The Gnoll looked down from her perch by the slate, still keeping perfect rhythm. All around her, swarms of Wood Gnomes sloughed their pencils across spreadsheets or ferried rivers of paper around her feet. Messenger sprites swarmed overhead, bathing the one-woman concert in a flickering rainbow of light. She looked to Poldo like a master of her element, a sorceress commanding the seas and sky. He smiled as he said, "I'm afraid I must impose on you to mind things yet again."

"Why?" the Gnoll shouted down, her head cocked to one side.

Poldo grabbed a stack of boilerplate contracts from a nearby Warg Inc. clerk. "I thought I might try my hand at day trading."

"You can lose a fortune that way," she warned him, but he could see her tail wagging.

"That is the idea," he said.

"Go," she called down. "I have this under control."

"Indeed you do," he shouted with a wave. Then he drafted a quick memorandum delegating his signing authority to Feista Hrurk, filed it with a passing lawyer-monk, and pushed through the press of Warg's brokers, accountants, and processors toward the front lines.

Further Baseward, Warg's staff had managed to form a beachhead in the chaos. A vanguard of Orcs and Gnolls had established a small perimeter, a thin ring of flimsy transportable tables that, along with the imposing glare of Darak Guz'Varda, stood between the delegation from Warg Inc. and an army of desperate brokers and bankers. The crowds outside pushed and shoved and jockeyed for position, straining to get to the salvation offered by Warg clerks.

Every stool suited for a Scribkin of Poldo's stature was occupied by a Goblin or Slaugh, and he could not reach the tabletop well enough to write without one. Poldo reasoned that if he had to lose his dignity, he might as well do it to good effect, so he found a spot between a Gnoll and a Naga and clambered up onto the table. Once he was situated on his knees, contracts and forms spread around him in a semicircle, he beckoned to the nearest banker, a stocky Human with a mustache the shape and color of a hay bale.

The man gripped his spectacles as he jostled forward, clutching a folio of papers to his chest. By way of greeting, he thrust a business card at Poldo and recited the neat text on it word for word. "Nik Demilurge. Senior Vice President of Investment Banking. Consolidated Acquisitions Unlimited LLC, a Goldson Baggs Company."

"Duine Poldo," the Gnome replied, handing the man his own card. "How many shares will you be trading?"

"Well, assuming we can negotiate a deal, we have over half a million shares of the dragon's hoard, not including exposure from our other investments—"

The Scribkin cut him off. "We can't help you with your other investments, unless they've sent their own bankers here to divest themselves of the dragon. And there is no negotiation. It's a one-for-one exchange in stock; you give us the Dragon of Wynspar, we swap back the Palace of Andarun with Warg Inc. retaining one point three percent as a transaction fee."

"A hundred and thirty basis points?" Demilurge huffed. "That's outrageous!"

The Gnoll next to Poldo began to wag his tail.

"That is the offer, and I doubt you'll find better," said Poldo.

The man's face reddened, and his hay bale mustache bristled. "But that expense—"

"Is cheaper than the cost of inaction, I'm sure. But if you want to go try and sell shares of the dragon's hoard elsewhere..." Poldo looked beyond the man pointedly.

"No, wait!" Demilurge shifted to block the Scribkin's view of the herd. "I just... I mean, they say it's unlikely the Palace of Andarun has a third of what the Dragon of Wynspar was valued at. And now another fee on top of that—it's a shocking loss for our firm. Investors will be furious."

"They usually are, but I doubt they'll find better options among those who didn't take our deal," said Poldo.

Demilurge tried again. "People will lose jobs."

"Only if you take them away," snapped the Gnome. "Sir, I am beginning to lose patience."

Beads of sweat formed on the man's crimson brow. "I... I'll sign..." he said. "I just cannot believe the shares of the dragon's stock would retreat like this."

"Retreat?" said Poldo, starting to fill in details on the contract. "My dear Mr. Demilurge, the dragon has no hoard. It has become an NPC. There is no quest. This is not a retreat, sir. The stock is shattered. It is panicked flight. It is a total rout."

"I prefer the term tactical repositioning," grunted Garold Flinn. He kicked back off the wall and let the silk rope glide through his gloved hand for a heartbeat before his black boots touched the palace wall again.

"I bet you do, but it's still running away," Benny Hookhand growled through Flinn's mouth.

"Postponing my victory in light of ongoing circumstances," murmured the Tinderkin. A cacophony of battle cries, explosions, and clashing blades blared from the courtyard as he rappelled down the dark stone face of the palace. He kept one hand on the rope, and let the hook dangle in the other by his side. His line descended into a hidden corner of the palace gardens, a small nook where the queen's tower met a wall in a tangle of dark ivy.

"You got a lot of euphemisms for the coward's path," Benny sneered.

"A little fear can be healthy, and excessive courage is a liability," said Flinn.

"I'm sure many elite assassins think that way."

"Only the ones that last." Flinn wished, not for the first time, that he could drop the uppity weapon into the shadowy patch of bushes below.

"So you're gonna just slink out of here?" Benny asked. "No stabbin'? No gutting anyone?"

Flinn shushed himself. "I'll probably have to kill a guard or two on my way out, for the sake of passing as a guild hero. But yes, generally the idea is to be stealthy."

"And you think it will work?"

"If you can keep my mouth shut!" hissed the assassin.

"Yeah, 'cause listening to you has done us a fat lot of good," muttered Benny.

"Shut up!" Flinn growled. He glanced around for anyone who might have heard his outburst or seen his descent from the palace and, finding noone, moved out into the courtyard. The Tinderkin affected a grin and muttered through his teeth. "Honestly, it isn't that hard to pass as a professional hero. One only needs to stalk around acting confident and murdering people. And given that we saw Ingerson and his party pass into the vault, I doubt anyone here will recognize me," he added; a statement which, according to Novian philosophy, made what happened next practically inevitable.

"Mr. Flinn!" The voice didn't so much say the Tinderkin's name as rumble it, like thunder over the plains. The assassin froze, cursed all of the gods, and turned slowly to find his old associate looming over him from a doorway.

"Ah, Mr. Brunt!" said Flinn. "We meet again! What are the odds?"

The Ogre stared vacantly into the air several feet above the Gnome's head. "Flinn... hero?" A touch of uncharacteristic uncertainty rumbled in Brunt's voice.

"Yeah, yeah," said Benny. "I'm a hero. Doing good, murderin' evil chumps, all that stuff."

The Ogre's bloodshot eyes swiveled downward, clearly nonplussed.

"Ahem, excuse me." Flinn cleared his throat as he reasserted control. "What I meant to say is that I am indeed pursuing your noble occupation."

"Brunt?" A woman with olive skin and an eyepatch stepped out from behind the Ogre. She looked around, confused. "Do you know these... oh, sorry, I thought I heard two people."

"You didn't hear nothing!" Benny snapped, pointing himself at the woman.

A rumble of eminent displeasure echoed from the heights of Mount Brunt.

"I'm pretty sure I did hear something," the woman retorted, squaring her shoulders and giving Flinn a steely glare. "How do you know this man, Brunt?"

"What's going on?" More heroes, presumably the remainder of Brunt's party, approached from somewhere behind the Ogre.

"This guy's giving Brunt trouble," the woman replied.

Benny tried to seize control again, and Flinn jolted with the effort of keeping the hook's mind at bay. "Will you let me speak!" The Tinderkin's patience leaked from him in a high-pitched hiss like steam from a tin kettle. "I know how to handle this idiot!"

"Idiot?" The hero at Brunt's side looked up at the Ogre and then back to the Gnome. "I don't know who you're talking about, but—"

"Keep your mouth shut or I'll open your throat!" Flinn snarled with a flourish of his hook. "I don't need you—"

But he never finished the sentence, because at that moment Brunt finally reached a conclusion. The Ogre wrapped a hand like a leathery vice around the assassin's torso and head. "Flinn... bad!" he growled.

Flinn tried to argue as he was lifted, but his mouth was covered by the massive hero's grip. His arms were pinned to his sides, and his legs kicked uselessly at the air around him. His muffled protests died away when he was level with the Ogre's face. There was a finality in the Ogre's tiny, angry eyes.

"Justice... Brunt style!" growled Brunt, and squeezed.

——CHAPTER 30——

A damp crunch filled the air, and then again as Gorm Ingerson swung his axe once more. The giant spider's face flew off in a spray of green and black ooze. "Works well if ye cut their heads off!" he shouted to his companions.

"How?" Just down the hall, Heraldin held a spider the size of a large dog at bay with his rapier.

"Just chop it off!" Gorm hollered, turning to square off against another specimen.

"Chop what off?" the bard screamed. "There isn't a head to chop! There's no neck! It's just eyes and fangs and then legs!"

"No, ye—hmm..." Gorm paused, considering the spider warily advancing on him. There was no neck or head discernible on what a more educated hero would have called the spider's cephalothorax. "Well, ye can... chop the body at the right angle to slice off the face."

"How is this helpful?" Heraldin shrieked, just before the spider in front of him exploded in a font of black ichor. Its relatively decapitated corpse spasmed and rolled up like some sort of spring-loaded golem. Behind it, Gaist cleaned his sword and nodded to the eyes and mandibles twitching on the ground.

"See? Gaist gets it." Gorm pulled his axe from the face of the final arachnid. "That the last of 'em?"

"The last of the big ones, anyway." Heraldin stepped on a hand-sized spider as he considered the piled corpses of its larger kin. He nodded to the long hallway at the rear corner of the vault, still flickering with orange light. "Could any be left alive in there?"

Gorm shook his head. The hallway ahead was narrow, unlabeled, and, until very recently, choked with spiderwebs. It was the sort of passage that seasoned heroes avoided and younger heroes never came out of, and Gorm would have happily skipped it had Johan's trail not clearly led straight into its darkened maw. After a brief consultation with the bard and the weaponsmaster, the party decided to use the last of Heraldin's flaming oils to clear out the passage. One thrown vial later, the doorway began belching thick black smoke and huge, hairy spiders. Gorm considered the de-faced corpses of the arachnids, and then the smoldering pathway ahead. "Not much can survive a conflagration like that. Bigger question is if the smoke's clear enough to pass."

Gaist checked the hallway and gave a quick nod of affirmation. Almost everything in the passage had burned away, including whatever carpets and tapestries had adorned the walls. Now the tunnel was nothing but blackened stone, empty save for a couple of charred spider corpses and trails of black smoke drifting toward the thin grates of the vault's ventilation shafts.

Gorm's heartbeat thundered in his ears as they made their way down the hall, but the red mist had retreated entirely from his vision. Sweat beaded on his brow, and his axe twitched with a tremor in his hand. He started when Heraldin whispered to him.

"Is everything all right?" the bard asked.

"I... I'm fine."

"It's just that you've stopped moving."

Gorm followed Heraldin's gaze down to his own boots, which were indeed stationary. "I... I have a bad feelin' about this."

"Me too," said the bard.

The Dwarf smirked despite himself. "Ye have a bad feelin' about everything."

"And I'm usually right." Heraldin tipped his hat with a grin. "But that's never stopped you before. What's wrong?"

Gorm took a deep breath through clenched teeth. There was an oily feeling in the air, a miasma of dread that he'd felt in his nightmares for over two decades. He'd felt it only once before in waking hours, when that foul viscosity and the accompanying tendrils of thorny midnight had chased him screaming from the dungeons of Az'Anon the Spider King. Sweat poured from the Dwarf's brow. "Somethin' ain't right... all around us," he said. "There's something... *wrong* down here."

"Something besides the giant spiders trying to eat our faces?" asked the bard.

"Aye," said Gorm.

Gaist nodded.

"Of course there is," said the bard with a dour grimace. "Should we wait for the mages then? It might be good to—"

"Ha haaaa!" Somewhere ahead of them, Johan's laughter rang out. It sounded strange, like an out-of-tune trumpet blown by an asthmatic herald. Yet as warped as the laughter was, it still carried an unmistakable note of triumph.

Gorm swallowed his rising gorge and took a deep breath to steady himself. "There ain't time to wait any longer. Whatever Johan's up to, we can't let him finish it. Let's go."

The door at the end of the hallway was still partially open. The heroes heard sounds of frenetic activity as they drew close to it: heavy breathing, labored grunts, clanking metal, and the intermittent grating of stone on stone. There was soft muttering too, punctuated with a muted version of Johan's signature laugh.

"Just a little farther," the king gasped. "Just a little more.... to... hrrngh... go! Ha! This can still work. I just need to get low enough, and then I finish off whatever's down there. Then I kill the witnesses, and I emerge the triumphant king! Ha ha! It still works... No witnesses, no problems. Who could argue? I still have time... I still..."

Gorm pushed open the door a crack and looked into a small, circular chamber around what looked at first glance like an empty cistern. A bent iron railing and a few chunks of rectangular stone protruded from the sides of the dark pit like broken teeth—the remnants of a spiral staircase that led down into the black depths of the mountain. Johan knelt at the edge of the pit, using his sword and mailed fist to chip away the mortar around the cobbles on its border. He'd already moved several, carving a thin first step into the rim of the circle.

"What do you see?" Heraldin whispered in Gorm's ear.

"Just Johan workin' by a broken staircase." The Dwarf scanned the shadows for any sign of a lurking spider demon or dark altar. "No sign of the big bad."

"What does that mean?"

Gorm considered what could have brought the arachnid plague and the oily miasma in the air both to the dungeon of Az'Anon decades ago and now to the palace. "Could be he was keeping some otherworldly horror down the stairs. Or maybe his patron is off fightin' the other heroes. But if he's made a pact with a shadow creature or demon, it could still be in there, invisible."

"What's our plan, then?" asked the bard.

"Tactical therapy," the Dwarf murmured.

"What?"

"Common tactic for dealin' with villains, especially the ones in charge," whispered Gorm, readying his axe and shield. "Ye get 'em talkin' about their plan, and why they're doin' it, and soon enough they're in a monologue about how they had a bad childhood or their mommy didn't love 'em. And all the while, you're minin' 'em for clues about what you're up against and repositionin' yourself tactically, or even stallin' for time. Or all three, in this case." He signaled Gaist, who acknowledged with a curt nod and slipped into the shadows of the chamber.

"And that works?" asked Heraldin.

"Ye'd be surprised. Let me do the talkin'." With that directive, Gorm pushed through the door and called to the kneeling king. "That'll take a while. I'd guess those stairs went down half a league before I blew 'em up."

The king swore under his breath as he worked a chunk of mortar loose, but he didn't look up from his futile work.

"I knew ye had to have stairs connecting back to the palace." Gorm walked into the room slowly, his shield held high to deflect any sudden attack. "How else could ye have gotten back to yer own funeral so quick? And once we found the dragon behind the prophetic vault, that just about confirmed ye knew there was really a dragon in Wynspar all along."

"It can still work," Johan muttered, choking back a sob.

"That's why ye went on the first quest." Gorm shared a meaningful look with Gaist and Heraldin as they took up positions on either side of the king. "If ye could get through the barrier and kill the dragon, ye'd clear yourself of any suspicion and keep your reputation. Better an impoverished kingdom than a hangman's noose, eh? But ye couldn't get through the barrier." He let the prompt hang in the air.

Johan turned a little, his gaunt features glazed with sweat. Within the sunken sockets of his eyes, a hatred burned for Gorm for a moment. "And you figured that out just by seeing the dragon?"

"Once I saw the prophetic vault and your failed machine, I realized ye actually couldn't get what ye wanted down there. And once we met the dragon, I figured we were your backup plan. If we killed the dragon, ye got away with all the false dragon attacks. If we died, we'd never get to make our accusations. And if we failed as ye did, ye'd have us face guild justice for abandoning a quest."

Johan stood slowly, eyeing Gaist and Heraldin around him. "And instead, you applied for the dragon's NPC papers and pushed some branch of the guild to declare me a foe?"

Gorm grinned. "A little more paperwork to it than that, but aye. We had the guild designate the palace as a new quest, one that we owned the bulk of. Then we turned it into a raid. The palace is overrun with hundreds of heroes."

Johan nodded. "And this was your plan all along."

Gorm opened his mouth, then paused. His brow wrinkled. "No, this was *your* plan all along!"

"What makes you think I would plan this?" the king asked, readying his sword.

"What makes you think I would?" demanded the Dwarf.

"Are you certain you didn't?"

Gorm's forehead knit as his mind's eye replayed the last few moments of conversation. "Wait... are ye tryin' tactical therapy on *me*?"

Johan grinned. "What makes you think tha—"

"Ye are!" Gorm was incredulous. "You're tryin' to get me to monologue!"

"I'd say more than trying," said the paladin.

"You have been doing most of the talking, my friend," Heraldin admitted with an apologetic shrug.

Gorm's heart was filled with shocked disbelief even as his mind searched for ways to get the villain talking. The two of them arrived at the same conclusion, and asked the same question in unison. "Do ye really think you're the hero?"

"Aren't I?" laughed Johan. "You plotted against the crown, stole kingdom secrets, allied with a monster in our deepest dungeon, executed a coup on paper, and now you're threatening to assassinate the lawful monarch of the Freedlands! Ha!"

"But... but ye know none of that's true!" Gorm protested.

"Of course it's true!" snapped Johan. "It will be true because we say it's true! Truth is what everybody knows, what everybody wants to know! They want their king to be good, to fight for them, to be on their side! They want to be certain of who the forces of darkness are, and they want to know they're kept at bay! They want their heroes to triumph! The hero always triumphs!"

"Ye ain't no hero," Gorm snarled back. "You're a coward who had good people killed and then tried to frame a dragon. Ye'd kill an innocent creature and topple a kingdom's economy just to clear your name—"

"Clear my name?" laughed Johan. "Ha ha! Clear my name! My name is King Johan! My title is all that matters! You still don't even know what this is all about, do you? You still think it's all for kingdom's laws and petty courts and avenging... avenging a Goblin, for Tandos' sake! You have no idea!"

Gorm saw the opening, and pressed. "It's so ye can escape justice and play the hero."

"You fools!" laughed Johan, a hint of mania creeping into his voice. "Cosmic forces beyond your comprehension are at work! Gods and Mankind alike will tremble at my feet when my work is done! You are but ants nipping at my ankles, tiny flies giving a final whine before you're swatted!"

Heraldin grimaced. "Epic," he mouthed to Gaist.

Gorm fought hard to suppress a smile as the king fell into a monologue. Johan had gone full villain, ranting like a run-of-the-mill dark lord. Soon enough, that would create an opening. The warrior gripped his axe tighter and feigned a look of perplexed concern, goading the paladin to reveal his secrets. With any luck, the king would inadvertently expose his link to the palace's malodorous aura and arachnid invasion. The trick was to keep Johan talking.

There was no stopping the tide of words. Ink spattered as High Scribe Pathalan's quill scrabbled furiously over the parchment, yet he still couldn't get the scriptures out fast enough.

And I! I stood by!
I watched my beloved children be slaughtered!
I let them be killed!
I was blind to their innocence!
I betrayed my beloved!

The goddess' grief was palpable, heavy, crushing. Words of anguish and guilt came faster than he could write, or even comprehend. The verses were angry shouts and mournful wails, long-forgotten truths and new revelations that upended centuries of dogma. The All Mother's memories, all of them, had returned. And she was pouring them into Pathalan's mind like an ocean being run through a paper funnel, threatening to tear him apart and wash the shreds away.

Pathalan felt his second hand grab another quill and start writing on another piece of parchment. One paper shifted, and his head slammed down onto it to hold it steady. When the page was full of scrawlings, his neck spasmed, involuntarily lifting it from the parchment and letting a sudden wind from nowhere blow it from his desk. Another page slid onto the desk beneath it as his head thudded against the pages once more, and the writing resumed.

And still he wrote, his fingers covered in ink and blood, his knuckles twisted and cramped. His back arched in agony, pulling at his arms in a vain effort to stop his hands. His mind searched for something—anything— that could shelter him from the flaming words that thundered down upon his consciousness. His lips pulled back as his eyes rolled skyward, and an earsplitting cry erupted from his parched lips.

"Ha-HAAAAA!"

Gorm considered Johan's triumphant laugh as a sommelier might test a new vintage; the rising timbre, the robust volume, the notes of despair playing among various flavors of confidence and fury. A good hero could tell a lot from a villain's laughter; and the paladin sounded like he was about to break. Still, the Dwarf thought hopefully, there was still a chance that some advanced tactical therapy could stall him until Jynn and Laruna returned. At least the king wasn't talking about the party being too late or—

"You're too late!" crowed Johan, his flaming sword held high. "Too late!"

Gorm cursed Nove under his breath and shared a dark look with Gaist. Their confrontation with the king was running headlong toward the intersection of wordplay and pyrotechnics that marked the end of most stand-offs with villains. All it would take was one more pun, one more opportunity for a final proclamation, and Johan would launch an attack.

"I'm pretty sure we have a little more time," he said lamely, prolonging the standoff at the cost of his professional dignity. Where was that thrice-cursed wizard?

Johan scowled. He clearly knew as well as Gorm that the Dwarf's response to his ultimatum was an embarrassing break of custom on par with excessive quipping, looting during a fight, or forgetting the rope. Good manners and good business demanded heroes strike at the moment of maximum tension during a conversation; properly timing the clash made for better ballads and celebrity for the victor, and it prevented anyone from dying with embarrassing, mid-thought last words like "there's one thing I can't figure out" or "I never liked my brother."

"You're stalling." The king's grin was all teeth and triumph; he saw through the berserker's ruse. He glanced back and forth to Heraldin and Gaist. "You're just buying your party time."

"Ye still haven't told me what this is all about," Gorm countered, and this was true. Johan's speech had covered some pedestrian embarrassments suffered as a boy, his dreams of being the greatest hero ever, his belief that it was his right to rule; all fairly standard components of the resentful villain's psyche. Yet nothing he had touched on explained the nameless dread lurking in the shadows, the spidery denizens lurking in the archives, the palpable gloom that hung in the air. He decided to push his luck. "What'd ye face down there, in the dungeon of Az'Anon?"

Johan's smile twisted into a sneer. "You'd know if you hadn't run!"

"It's here now, ain't it?" pressed Gorm. "Ye brought it, didn't ye? Ye made a deal with the darkness."

"Lies!" snapped the king. "You're jealous because I slew Az'Anon!"

"Never understood how that happened," said Gorm. "We fought the undead all the way into Az'Anon's lair, and ye were barely strong enough to take on a few skeletons on your own, and half as bold as ye were strong. I saved your hide more times than ye made yourself useful. And then ye suddenly killed the Spider King on your own? No, I don't think so. I think whatever gave Az'Anon his power offered ye the same deal, and ye took it."

The accusation drained the blood from Johan's face and twisted it into a resentful sneer. "I found the strength within myself!" he cried.

"Drake spit!" Gorm snarled back. "Where are ye hidin' whatever it is? We'll not rest until we find it!"

It took Gorm a split second to realize that he'd inadvertently delivered an ultimatum, and by the time he did, Johan was already upon him. "Then die!" hissed the paladin, his blade a burning arc in the air.

The sudden force of the attack caught Gorm off guard. He barely got his shield up in time to deflect the blow, and it knocked him off-balance enough that he had to awkwardly parry another. Yet awkward, last-second defenses weren't enough to withstand an onslaught from the Champion of Tandos. The paladin's sword was blessed by the god of war, and Gorm felt a hot searing in his forearm as the end of Johan's blade slipped past his defenses and cut through his mail. A sudden cloud of green smoke erupted around them, giving Gorm just enough time to scramble away, and Gaist clashed with the king.

Johan was a streak of gold with a manic grin, a toothy comet blurring between the three heroes. Golden crescents flashed in the gloom as he struck at them, his hungry blade seeking their hearts and heads. Yet there was no finesse behind the king's force. The paladin's lurching strikes and lightning motions blurred the boundary between the supernatural and the unnatural. It almost looked as though his body was dragged through each charge rather than lunging, and his strikes came in staccato, jerking steps that roiled Gorm's stomach.

Gaist parried, Gorm blocked, and Heraldin dodged and swerved like a pig at the fair to avoid the paladin's unnerving onslaught. They feigned attacks on him as well, darting forward whenever his back was turned, never letting on that they didn't want to strike. Not until Jynn and Laruna returned. The heroes needed to be cautious, to take the fight slow.

And they might have been able to, had the paladin kept his mouth shut.

"You've done it now," snarled Johan, darting to take a swipe at Heraldin. Gaist caught his blade, and then the bard and weaponsmaster flitted away amid a cloud of vermillion smoke. The paladin growled and then ripped through the air back to Gorm. "You should have left well enough alone."

Gorm caught the paladin's blade with his axe. "It wasn't well enough," he growled.

"And what was wrong with it?" demanded the king, taking a swipe at Gorm. "I could have left you alone after the liche attacked. You had fame. You had wealth. You were comfortable. Why weren't you satisfied?"

"Comfortable?" Gorm growled, trying to hold the paladin's blows and the crimson mist behind his eyes at bay. "Ye killed so many! Ye built your fame and treasure on the blood of innocents! Burn your bloody fame and wealth! I'm here for justice."

"Oh, right. The Goblin!" The flames from Johan's blade cast his diabolical grin in a hellish light. "I almost forgot you think this is about your little greenskin friends. Do you think they'll be better off after your little rebellion? I'm going to find every one of them that ever spoke to you and revoke their NPC papers. I'll outlaw every stinking Orc and Goblin in this city, and see them all declared foes. Everyone you ever cared about is as good as dead and looted. They just don't know it yet! Ha haaa!"

In his mind's eye, Gorm could see the bodies in the street, hear the screams of the dying, feel the agony of so much loss over his own broken oath. It constricted and twisted his insides until the air was wrung from his lungs and hot tears squeezed from his eyes. He tried to reply, but could only manage a short bark, like he was choking on his own voice.

"Are you scared? Are you ready to run away?" Johan sneered, taking the Dwarf's reaction for fear. "You won't get away this time!" he cried, lunging forward to strike at the opening in Gorm's defenses.

"No! Gorm!" cried Heraldin, but it was too late. In a professional hero's world, one can't hope to survive if they make many sloppy mistakes.

And Johan had just reached his limit.

Gorm's hand caught the paladin's vambrace and held it fast. The king tried to wrench his arm back, but blanched when he looked at the Dwarf's face.

The berserker bared his teeth at the king, or perhaps grinned at him. He gave another rattling cough, choking on the laughter bubbling up from his core. White-hot rage seared away any of Gorm's lingering fear, leaving a burning purpose glowing at the center of his core. The pure joy of it washed over him in an irresistible wave, and he began to cackle as the crimson mists closed around him and painted the world red.

"I can't see anything," murmured Jynn, glancing over a memo from Aya of Blades to the Order of the Moon. "Nothing relevant, anyway."

"We don't have long," Laruna called back over her shoulder.

"More spiders?" asked Jynn.

"Well yes, but—" The pyromancer paused briefly to immolate an advancing spider. "But listen!"

Jynn tilted an ear. The palace was filled with the sounds of heroes at work; clanging steel, dying screams, and the gentle ringing of sacks of gold being hefted over meaty shoulders. Yet above the distant din, he could also hear a familiar voice lifted in manic soliloquy interspersed with triumphant, two-note bouts of laughter. "Ha haaaa!"

"They're fighting Johan already," said the omnimancer.

"Someone is," Laruna agreed. "We need to hurry."

"Right." Jynn flipped through the file and tried not to think of the tantalizing secrets and forbidden knowledge dancing past his fingertips.

"I've seen a few allusions to a letter that circulated between Win Cinder, Aya of Blades, and my father in the final days of the Leviathan Project."

"And you're sure it names whatever allied with Az'Anon?"

"No. Nothing I've read discusses the letter's contents in any detail." Jynn pursed his lips as he reached the end of yet another folder. He was almost through the file of canonical evidence. "But it's the best lead I have. Assuming I can find it."

"And fast." Laruna fried another spider creeping from the shadows to a smoldering crisp.

Jynn paused at a letter bearing a few official seals. It wasn't *the* letter; this one was addressed to a young King Handor, from High Priest Ayathan Ith'Issan. Jynn didn't recognize the name, but the seals and sigils stamped all over the document in crimson and gold wax indicated that he was a very senior member of the inquisitorial arm of the Temple of Tandos, and Az'Anon's name caught his eye. The letter began with the proper formalities addressing a king, followed by overwrought assurances that the king's request for secrecy and discretion would be treated with the same obedience as scripture. But the passage that followed was more significant.

> After careful inquiries and prayerful consideration, the Temple of Tandos has found that the allegations made by Win Cinder in the unfortunate letter you referred to me are undoubtedly false. The mages employed by your father may have believed their blasphemous allegations, but their reasoning is as flawed as the results of their so-called Leviathan Project.
>
> Ask yourself this, Your Majesty: if our scriptures are all wrong and Az'Anon really consorted with such a being as his fellow necromancer alleged, could any hero ever have overcome the Spider King as Johan the Mighty did? We do not doubt our young champion's power, but the answer is so obvious, the alternative so ridiculous, that we are certain you will reach the same conclusion as our holy inquiry.

We have burned our copy of the heretical mage's writings and thank the holy warrior that your father saw fit to send the Heroes Guild after those dark and foul sorcerers. I understand that the laws of Mankind forbid your archivist from following our example, but I nonetheless implore you to direct him to treat Win Cinder's missive as he would a sheet of disreputable propaganda or a scrap of trash. It is of no value to anyone.

"That's it," muttered Jynn. The Temple of Tandos' denial of Win Cinder's message held no weight for him, but their recommendation was an excellent clue as to the letter's location. He pushed past the reams of paper to expose the very back of the drawer where, as per the custom of every Agekeeper and kingdom archivist in this hemisphere, a thick, red file sat behind the other folders. It held a sheaf of loose sheets and scribbled notes; some incoherent, some discredited, and some just not relevant enough to warrant a place in the official narrative, but all too valuable for any faithful keeper of records to throw away. Between a page of illegible shorthand and a sheet of fine vellum covered by a large tea stain, Jynn found a slim black envelope.

A distant shriek that could have been laughter or a scream rang out. "We need to hurry," Laruna repeated.

Jynn licked his lips as he lifted the envelope. His hands trembled as he opened it and unfolded the thin parchment within. His hands were shaking violently by the time he reached the end of the note.

The pyromancer glanced back at the archmage. "Jynn?"

The archmage sucked in a breath and braced himself. Then he read the last passage again, wherein Win Cinder provided evidence to confirm the worst fears of Az'Anon's compatriots in the Leviathan Project. Jynn's stomach roiled and his knees were turning to jelly as he read the old noctomancer's dreadful conclusion.

"What is it?" The concern was plain on Laruna's face as she looked at the wizard.

The blood thundered in Jynn's ears. His mouth was dry and his palms were damp. "We have to stop them," he gasped. "We have to stop them now."

—— CHAPTER 31 ——

"Y ou're welcome to try." Heraldin threw up his hands in exasperation. "There's no talking to him when he gets like this."

Gaist nodded as he stared into the maelstrom of steel and laughter that blew around Johan the Mighty, threatening to knock the king from his feet. Gorm moved too fast for even the weaponsmaster's eyes to follow, a red and silver blur amid the dust; the best way to follow the berserker was to watch the sparks that erupted from the paladin's enchanted armor with every axe blow. Johan screamed something, though the other heroes couldn't hear it above the king's laughter and the ringing of axe on plate mail.

"We're supposed to be stalling!" Heraldin shouted above the din, but he knew it was pointless. If Gorm noticed the bard's warning, it didn't alter his furious course at all.

Gaist tried stepping into the berserker's path, raising a palm to halt the Dwarf's fury. The weaponsmaster's cloak kicked up in a sudden rush a split second before another shower of sparks erupted from Johan's vambrace; Heraldin couldn't see if Gorm had dodged around the doppelganger or if Gaist had just miscalculated his trajectory. Gaist shifted his footing again, and again his cloak snapped back in the Dwarf's wake. The weaponsmaster tried a third time, and then another, and soon he was leaping about as though part of some complicated dance with the berserker, but he could not intercept his friend.

Heraldin turned his focus to the paladin currently experiencing exactly the opposite problem. No matter where Johan dodged, no matter how fleet his steps, Gorm was already there when he arrived. Violet and aquamarine flashes—the bright flashes of dying spells—marked wherever the Dwarf's cruel axe hacked against the paladin's golden armor. The ensorcelled charms and wards were all that kept the paladin on his feet. Leaking motes of magic danced around the ruptured ley lines in the plate, making it clear that the enchantments couldn't hold out for long.

Johan swayed to and fro, a gilt tree buffeted by an uncouth storm. The tattered remnants of his crimson cloak dangled from his back, and scraps of it pooled around him like the blood of a dying beast. The king opened his mouth to shout another challenge when a vicious blow ripped his entire left pauldron from him in a spray of sparks and ozone. He staggered back and swung his sword in the general direction of the attack, but Gorm was already gone. A heartbeat later, another strike brought colorful sparks erupting from Johan's back, knocking him toward the yawning pit at the room's center.

It was obvious that the king was losing ground. What was less obvious initially, but was becoming more and more undeniable, was that he was losing strength as well. Every slash of the axe, every missed parry, every swipe of the flaming sword through empty air; it all seemed to sap a bit of Johan's might. His movement had been as fast as an adder earlier; now he stumbled about sluggishly, and seemed to struggle to lift his sword. Heraldin surmised that the paladin's mind must have been addled as well; instead of watching for incoming blows, Johan was staring into nothing and shouting nonsense.

"No! It can still work! I can still find a—rgh!" The king choked on his protest as a hack of Gorm's axe decapitated a decorative eagle emblazoned on his remaining pauldron. But he kept ranting in between blows. "There's still time! When I beat them—argh! When I beat them, the people will thank—oof... There's still time!"

Now the king was shrieking, his wails so loud and piercing that Heraldin almost didn't hear the shouts from the hallway. He turned to see Jynn and Laruna sprinting into the chamber, their faces flushed and panicked. "Stop!" Jynn shouted. "Stop fighting!"

"Yes, we've been over that." Heraldin gestured toward Gaist, who still ducked and rolled around the king in a futile attempt to intercept the berserker.

"You can't..." Jynn doubled over, gulping for air. "You can't kill him. Whatever you do, just don't kill—"

He was cut off by a final-sounding *chok*. Bard and mages alike turned to the king, whose enchanted protections had finally succumbed to Gorm's fury. A great gash rent Johan's armor from where his left pauldron belonged to the opposite hip. Gorm landed in front of the king, eyes wild and axe bloody, still grinning and laughing like a madman.

Johan watched his life leak from the fissure in a flow of crimson and black. His mouth opened and closed as though trying to push out a word, but all that came out was a strained "hah" and a spray of blood and spittle. He dropped to his knees, and a final choking breath escaped his lips in a long, sighing, "Haaa."

"No," moaned Jynn, backing toward the door. "Oh no. No, no, no..."

"What?" Heraldin asked, unnerved by the archmage's terror.

"This is bad," said Laruna.

"What is?" demanded the bard, just as it dawned on him that the laughter echoing about the chamber wasn't entirely Gorm's anymore.

Heraldin turned. Gorm's crazed grin was fading, and a shadow of fear fell over his features as the guttural laughter echoed through the chamber. Gaist backed away from the king's body. Johan still wore an expression of final shock, his eyes vacant and glassy, his mouth slack and dead. Yet he was laughing, or at least something was laughing through him. The king's skin spasmed and twitched with each stomach-turning guffaw. His body began to shake and distend, and the fluid seeping from his fatal wound was now a black, shimmering tar.

"What's happening?" Heraldin asked, taking a step away from Johan. All five heroes shuffled toward the edges of the room, their eyes locked on the king's convulsing corpse. The tremors stopped suddenly, leaving the body still for a pregnant pause.

Heraldin shuddered. "What—"

Johan burst like a lanced boil, sending spirals of black fluid curling toward the ceiling. Tendrils of spraying ooze became vines of black thorns that lashed the floor and gripped the ceiling. An impossible fountain of mucilaginous darkness erupted from the empty armor, running in an oily mess in some places, firming into coal-black chunks in others, growing to fill the room. A leering face emerged from the torrent, as though a skull was pushing through a curtain of oil, but even as it grinned down at the party a pair of jaws took shape around it, and it was swallowed by a visage even more hideous. Other faces were taking shape, bubbling to the surface of the muck like gray meat from a black stew. Some were Human, some animal, all laughing even as they bit and tore and swallowed one another.

The bard choked on his own rising bile. "W-what—what is—?"

"Keep it together," snarled Laruna. She squared her shoulders and ignited her fists as she stared. "The bastard's true-forming."

"I can see that," said Heraldin. "But into what? A shadow beast? A greater demon? How bad is this?"

"As bad as it could possibly be," said Jynn.

"All is lost," Kaitha sobbed, staring at the bloodred walls. "It's all lost."

There were few figures left on the wall now. The War of Betrayal was nearing its grim end, with all armies shattered and civilization nearing the brink of collapse. The lights that formed the watery people on the walls faded as their bodies fell; the darkness closed in, running down the walls in a malevolent tide. She could feel the void's smugness, she could see how it advanced and slaked its foul thirst on the blood shed as the people of Arth slaughtered each other.

Beneath the creeping evil, Kaitha saw the siege of Andarun cast in the dying light of its fallen defenders and citizens. The remnants of Issan's armies were at the gates of the Palace of Andarun. Beneath the mountain, Stennish magic users carved stones and painted murals with the frenetic energy that more sensible defenders might have used to erect barricades. Outside the gates, a crew of Stennish priests carved a statue with similar determination. They finished the sculpture just as Issan's forces cut them down as they marched toward the palace.

The deepest rooms of the palace suddenly illuminated, where the last cadre of wizards and priests stood around the king and queen of the

Sten. The royal family held a young child, who cried while the gathered Sten worked some strange magic over him with desperate urgency. This cluster of royals and advisors were, as far as Kaitha could tell, the last of the Sten; Issan's forces had scoured the ancient city clean.

Her eyes turned upward, where the colored water twisted to form new shapes on the wall. These figures were larger, and instantly recognizable. She saw Musana stepping from beams of light, and Fulgen with his lantern, and Maeneth, and Kaedna, and all of the gods of Arth battling in a great melee. The deities of Elves and Dwarves fought those of Orcs and Goblins and every other manner of Shadowkin, and all of them fought against the gods of the Sten. At the center of the maelstrom, she could see Al'Thadan, the All Father, battling a grinning Tandos. And on the edge, staring back at Kaitha with sorrow and pain that the ranger felt more than saw, was the All Mother. The queen of the gods seemed unsure what to do, or whom to side with as her husband battled her son.

"Stop," Kaitha whispered, though she knew the queen wouldn't listen. "Don't—"

But Al'Matra did. The darkness cast a shadow over the Falcon Lady's face, and she closed her eyes as she reached out a hand toward her son. Empowered by his mother's blessing, the god of war glowed a little brighter as he surged forward, and below him Issan burst through the last doors of Andarun's palace. Kaitha sobbed as the king and the queen of the Sten fell, dropping in sad splashes from the wall. And as Issan's cruel spear found its mark in the toddler prince, Tandos' weapon struck true at Al'Thadan's heart. The water on the walls glowed with a sudden searing redness before all light in the chamber winked out. The water fell from the walls in a sudden shower as whatever magic that had suspended it left.

Kaitha knelt alone in the damp darkness. Pain and grief pressed down on her; a weight like Wynspar itself was set atop her chest. This was her doing. She had sided with the traitor god Tandos, worshipped him when she worked as a hero, blessed him when he and his army had betrayed Al'Thadan. She had lent the power that felled her love, loosed the arrow that stuck in his throat, driven him away with her mistrust. Her guilt twisted and stretched between consciousnesses, through the veil of reality, across millennia, until her mind threatened to snap under the strain. The sweet oblivion of madness called to her again. Tears poured down her face anew as she felt herself falling back into the welcoming embrace of insanity. She might have tumbled into it forever, but a thought caught her.

"He came back," she whispered.

She saw Thane's garden again and remembered his familiar presence, felt the warmth of his arms when he carried her across the Plains of Aberreth, saw his final smile as his last breath slipped away. And it ached to remember, ached in the deepest parts of her soul, but it was a different kind of pain, as different as ice is from fire. He had returned for her. He had given everything for her. He had forgiven her. He loved her still.

She seized on to that thought, and the world snapped back into focus around her. The shame and madness fled, and sudden clarity took their place. Her grief was still with her, next to a growing rage. He loved her still. They could have been together. They never should have parted. And they might not have, had it not been for the vile force that had tricked her, had brought her to this dungeon, had seduced her son and blinded her to her husband's nature.

An emerald light flared in the darkness, and some distant part of Kaitha recognized that it came from her own face, that the tears running down her cheeks were alight with jade flames, pooling in growing green fire beneath her. But that was just a small part of the ranger's consciousness, and she was just a small part of the mind staring out from her green, glowing eyes. Her mouth turned into a furious sneer and her hands balled into crackling fists as she stared down the darkness that had taken everything from her and driven her into the shadows. When she opened her mouth again, she called the evil by its foul name.

"Mannon!" roared Al'Matra.

"That can't be," Gorm told the mages with a confidence he wished he felt. "Mannon's dead. Or missing. Or... or..." He trailed off as the impossibility of what Jynn said and the impossible horror unfurling before his eyes mixed together into a foul possibility that he didn't want to acknowledge.

"See?" Heraldin said to Gaist. "Epic. This is why I hate being right."

Gaist was too preoccupied with Johan's transformation to so much as glance at the bard.

Mannon, Nemesis of the Creator, Foe of the Gods, Father of Demons, Destroyer of Worlds... the great enemy had amassed enough superlatives for an entire foul pantheon. Yet when Gorm visited temples, they didn't talk about the Felfather as a being so much as a concept. The name Mannon was synonymous with Evil; encountering him in a dungeon was like having Hospitality over for dinner or meeting Travel on the street.

Yet Gorm could think of no other name for the horror rising from the shattered remnants of Johan's armor. The geyser of liquid malice flowed and twisted up to the ceiling, where the darkness pooled against the stone like the cap of a great black toadstool. Innumerable mouths laughed softly from its moist, undulating body. The same thorny tentacles that had haunted Gorm's nightmares for decades wreathed its bulbous crown. The Pyrebeard had fought greater demons back in the day; he knew what they looked like— and he even saw their visages among those in the melee of faces twisting through the black morass above them. But this was something different, something ineffably worse than anything he'd faced before.

Gorm looked back to the mages. "We can't—" he began, but a tentacle the size of a tree trunk slammed down against the stone between them. The force of the impact dislodged the rubble at the edge of the pit, and it widened like a broken-toothed maw as the stonework plummeted into its depths. Above the hole seven other tentacles had peeled away from the trunk of the oozing mass, so that it almost resembled a great spider. The largest head that pushed from its round, full body, however, was that of a ram's skull as big as a wagon, with misshapen horns and a single leering eyeball that locked onto Gorm as it opened its mouth to speak.

It said, "Baa-aaah."

"Come again?" said Gorm, some of his icy fear retreating.

A small tentacle unfurled from the bulk of the black mass and, after growing a handlike appendage, extended a single finger toward the ceiling, as a coughing person might ask for a moment to clear their throat. The creature seemed to be doing the opposite, however, as another huge face was already emerging from the morass, closing around the protesting ram's skull. The new visage was like a Human skull, but with bloodred eyes and curled horns growing from its top. It swallowed its predecessor, cleared its throat, and spoke in a voice as smooth and cheerful as the rainbow on an oil slick. "Ahem. Excuse me. Hello, adventurers! By way of introduction, I am the one they call Mannon, and I've come to parley."

Gorm considered the ancient, world-shattering evil that had just bleated in his face before requesting an audience. "What?" he managed.

"Negotiate. Discuss. Come to terms as quickly as possible. I know you're familiar with the concept, Gorm Ingerson." The demonic visage kept speaking as the face of an Elven woman emerged from the mass around it, mouth agape to consume the speaking face. "You proposed it to my associate just a while ago."

Gorm had trouble processing the Felfather's words, if only because it was difficult to concentrate on anything but the huge face of the Elven woman working her lips around the demon skull like an ambitious snake tackling a griffon egg. "Ye... ye mean Johan."

"Yes, an old business partner." Mannon paused as the Elven face closed her lips over the diabolical skull, swallowed, and licked her teeth with a grimace. Then she seamlessly continued the discussion. "We had quite a run together, he and I. I took him from farm boy to king. Did some impressive work together. Good guy." Tentacles wrapped around Mannon's current face and pulled it back into the emerging maw of some nameless creature that was both canine and squid-like. It swallowed noisily and wiped its greasy maw with a tentacle. "But things happen. We move on. The past is the past. Let's talk about the future."

"We don't bargain with evil!" Laruna shouted.

The faces covering Mannon sighed and rolled their eyes at the pyromancer's declaration. "Evil?" sneered the squid face. "What a silly, outmoded term. I am self-interested, and self-interest is practically a virtue. It inspires people, drives them to moral labor, and powers the thriving economy that builds all of our wondrous things! Why, imagine what life would be like if every person stopped eating, stopped bathing, stopped caring for themselves in general. Madness. No, there's little better for Mankind than self-interest. Especially when two reasonable beings can come to an arrangement that's... mutually beneficial."

"Mutually beneficial?" snorted Gorm. "All ye want is conquest and destruction!"

"Conquest? Destruction?" Mannon's faces all began to laugh like the audience in a mummer's play. "What is left to conquer, little Dwarf? What would I destroy? This world is mine. It bowed to my plans ages before I planted my king upon its greatest nation's throne. The gods elevated my most faithful servant even as they reviled the deities I bargained with long ago. And the people who claim to wish to stop me chase markets all day long for the sake of self-interest! This world is everything I could want it to be, and it's totally mine." His visage looked thoughtful for a moment, and he raised a finger on the handlike appendage again. "With one little exception. I do have a few loose to ends to wrap up. Mostly just the thrice-cursed ones my associate and I were working on."

Threads of magic wove around the statues in the ancient lair of the great dragon Kulxak, dancing above the glowing streams of water to a haunting melody. They swirled and wove around the bodies of seven stoic figures; the statues of the Sten now stood fully complete upon the dragon's dais. Glowing azure water gathered wherever snowy marble torsos and extremities joined together, so that they gleamed from every point of fluid articulation.

And they sang.

No sound came from their watery throats, but every stone in their glowing forms vibrated with a magic as old as blood and bone. They thrummed and hummed in a haunting melody of seven notes that repeated over and over as they regarded each other, one by one.

When their greetings were finished, they turned as one to the dragon on the dais. Kulxak craned her neck and bowed her head to the seven, and they bowed their heads to her. Her duty complete, the wounded dragon lay back down to rest, and the Sten, with slow purpose, began to walk along the glowing blue path set for them.

"The Sten, they were always so difficult. Stubborn!" Mannon said with the face of a bearded man. "When I needed some healthy competition amongst the gods' peoples, I got half of 'em with some promises of advancement or glory, or even just a longer life. Most of the others came around once I made the Shadowkin look different. You can get good competition along any line you divide people by—open conflict too, if you're lucky—and the more obvious a line the better. But the Sten... the Sten never wanted to play the game. Even when I made their kids into Trolls, they just... well, let's say they couldn't adapt to the changing times."

Gorm's mind reeled as world-shattering revelations lined up to dance past his mind's eye. He was still struggling to reconcile the idea that Johan had been in league with evil incarnate, and now it sounded as though the people blamed for Mannon's rise were the only ones to consistently resist the dark one's corruption. The gods revered Mannon's faithful servant... was Tandos the traitor god, and Al'Thadan innocent? It explained how Johan rose so fast within the Tandosian ranks after bargaining with the presence in the dungeon of Az'Anon. And it sounded like the statues beneath Wynspar, sealed away by prophecy, were somehow the key to the unholy alliance's success.

The face of something warty and reptilian consumed Mannon's active head. Its eyes stared at Gorm as it swallowed. "So I needed the Sten gone. And they almost are. It's just some old statues, some ancient prophetic nonsense, some threads to be broken. And after that, you know, there's really nothing else that can threaten my vision. I can stop hiding down here on the mortal planes, and go pay the holdout gods a visit. Maybe I make a few changes down here—get it a little more to my tastes—but believe me when I say Arth is almost there already. It's so close. I am so close!" The last bit was rasped with fierce determination, and the reptilian face looked embarrassed by the outburst for a split second before the head of a skeletal bird swallowed it. "Johan and I worked so hard to get down there behind the barrier. I mean, you don't know half of the planning and logistics you guys messed up with that stunt in the northern site. Your findings forced Johan to try out the prophecy cracker before it was ready, and when that failed we had to scrap the whole project—including the workers."

"The Golden Dawn," said Heraldin.

"Exactly," gurgled Mannon. "I think they could have cracked it in another year or two if we didn't have to change the timeline. But here we are, right? Barrier's down, the Sten are exposed, should be easy to wrap things up. The only thing I need is a new partner to help, well, to help people adjust until I'm ready to reveal myself. Big opportunity for the right person."

"We'll never side with you!" Laruna snarled again.

"Yeah, most of you won't," agreed Mannon, his eye sockets still locked on Gorm. "I can't have all five of you running around knowing my secret. It takes a lot of work to hide from the gods. A lot of magic, energy... it's hard enough when just one person knows. It's like they say, when you're conquering the mortal realms, there are two kinds of people—useful subjects and loose ends. And sadly, four of you are loose ends. The question is, which one of you isn't? It takes two to make a dark pact, folks. Who wants to get a deal done?"

Gorm didn't glance at his companions; he didn't have to. He knew their answer. "We ain't bargaining," he growled, trying to keep his voice steady despite his rising terror.

Mannon's face looked as nonplussed as a bird skull can, but a moment later a smiling Halfling visage swallowed the face and took over. "Look, I get it," he said. "Watching your friends die is a high price to pay. But consider what you get! One of you gets to walk out of here the hero who slew the mad king and stopped his insane scheming! You'll be rich beyond riches, you'll be revered by all. Whatever you want, it'll be yours."

The party was silent. Gorm glanced at his companions, looking to see if there was any plan that could get them out of this.

Jynn nodded toward the door. Should they run?

Gorm gave a slight shake of his head. They'd never make it to the hallway; all they'd manage is turning their backs on Mannon.

Laruna raised her eyebrows. Perhaps a fight?

Gorm winced. Mannon fought gods and entire armies in the legends. Five heroes didn't stand much chance. They needed to retreat for now. He glanced over at Heraldin and Gaist, who were locked in their own pantomimed conversation.

Mannon squeezed his eyes shut and shook his many heads. "Okay, okay, look, after so many years trapped down here, my omniscience isn't what it used to be, but I can still read faces, body language, maybe a bit of your minds. You're planning. You're trying to do that noble last stand thing. And I get it; you're professionals and you have good habits and all that, but you've got to look at the big picture here. I've won. It's done. One of you might as well reap the benefits."

He turned to Gorm, and the Dwarf felt the stares of countless malicious eyes bearing down on him. "You! What do you want, Gorm Ingerson? Power? A place in your clan? Vindication for the last time we met? I can give it to you."

"I want nothing ye can offer," Gorm growled into the many faces of evil.

"Try me."

"The people free and safe, justice for the downtrodden, and the rights of all people restored," said Gorm.

Mannon's multitude of eyes stared at him for a moment. "Yeah, not my thing," he said, turning his gaze to the mages. "You! Wizard! What do you want?"

Jynn smirked and stepped forward. "The truth revealed, and the information used to govern fairly."

"Funny," growled Mannon. "What about you, pyromancer? You want power, right? Power I got!"

"To stand against oppression," said Laruna, taking a step to bring her next to Jynn. "To serve the light. To—"

"Yeah, I get it," groused Mannon, now wearing the face of a snarling dog. "Maybe you'll come around. What about..."

The dark lord turned his myriad eyes upon Gaist.

Gaist stared back with the stoic determination of a military statue.

"Yeah, never mind," said Mannon. "But you!" The dog's head broke into a happy grin as it turned to the bard. "You, Heraldin Strummons; you know all the pleasures this good world has to offer. What do you want?"

Heraldin stepped forward. "I want them to write a song about me."

"Yeah? Fame? Fame I can do," said Mannon. "We can work with this."

Gorm started to shout to the bard, but a look from Gaist silenced the berserker.

"A whole ballad, at least sixteen verses." Heraldin spoke in level tones as he walked toward the waiting maws of the demonic entity. "And make sure it's one with an original tune, not some rehashed drinking song. No pan flutes."

"Yeah, something with lutes and percussion." Mannon stared at the approaching bard with the hungry gaze of a spider watching a curious fly. "That's what you want. And people everywhere singing about you. We can get that going. And they'll call it 'the ballad of—'"

"*Zahat'emptor!*" Heraldin shouted.

Gorm's heart froze as the bard sprang into motion.

A head that was both like a frog and fish emerged from Mannon's tar-ball body to consume the canine head, and in the distracted moment, Heraldin pulled something small and shimmering from the RED bag at his side. The Occult-Primed Arcane Oscillation Explosive gleamed briefly as Heraldin deftly twisted its core and hurled it at Mannon. The dog's head looked surprised as the metallic sphere stuck in the tarry ooze of its forehead just before the frog-fish mouth closed over it.

"Run!" screamed Heraldin. "Tell them everything!" Yet he and the weaponsmaster ignored his own directive. Their weapons were drawn in futile bravado as Mannon reared up in fury at the betrayal.

Gaist darted forward, twin blades drawn, his slashing at a leg a graceful dance. Mannon countered with a thick vine of black thorns erupting from his bulk, a dark tentacle of the same sort that Gorm had seen kill Iheen in so many nightmares, and striking the weaponsmaster full in the chest.

"No!" shouted Heraldin, echoed by screams from the others. Mannon tossed the doppelganger's limp form into the black pit at the center of the room, and all of his eyes rounded on the bard just as the explosion came.

Even contained within the body of evil incarnate, the OPAOE sent a shockwave rumbling through the room. The force of the blast expanded Mannon to twice his size, knocking Gorm from his feet. Bright green ooze and blue flames erupted from ruptures in the Felfather's straining form. Every one of the thing's foul mouths screamed in unison as it staggered and fell into the yawning black pit, its tentacles still clawing to keep it from plummeting the rest of the way down. Gorm saw one of them grab the bard and pull him toward the pit.

"Heraldin!" the Dwarf cried as he stood, but he felt a tug at his shoulder.

"Come on!" Laruna shouted. "We have to warn the city!"

The bard caught the very edge of the pit, gripping it desperately. His eyes caught Gorm's as the Dwarf scrambled for the door, and Heraldin managed to put on a brave smile. "I hate being right," he said, just before the tentacle ripped him from the edge and pulled him into the dark fathoms.

CHAPTER 32

"As in, all the way down," said Sister Varia. "As deep as it goes. The sub-sub-basement."

"Down where Sister Felani found the nest of scargs when she was looking for some sacred wine," said Alithana, a young Elf in white and green robes.

The scribe standing before the door didn't make eye contact with the two women. He stared out the window opposite the door he guarded so intently he was practically sweating. "Didn't we wall off the lower basements?" he said hurriedly, clearly hoping to rush them away. "Call for a tradesman. The high scribe is... he's indisposed."

Varia scowled. "This is an emergency, Brother Tuomas!"

"Some bumps in the basement is hardly an emergency," said Tuomas.

"Not bumps. Screaming. In Root Elven," said Alithana.

"And a weird light coming from down there," Varia added.

"It can't be that bad," insisted Tuomas.

"Bad enough that old Scabbo ran off."

Tuomas scowled. "He can't have."

"I saw it."

"That old rat was too fat and decrepit to run anywhere."

"Bolted out the front doors and ducked down into a hole in the Ridge," said Varia, nodding.

Tuomas sucked his teeth. "That is bad."

"Why do you think the high priestess sent Sister Alithana and I to fetch High Scribe Pathalan?"

The scribe's eyes snapped to the acolyte. "The high p-p-priestess?" he stammered. "But I sent Brother Cheesemonger to fetch her here twenty minutes ago."

"Yeah, well, she's got bigger problems, doesn't she?" said Sister Alithana. "Lights and screaming in the basement. Urgent messengers from the other temples. And now that statue of the last high scribe has started acting strange again, hasn't it Varia?"

The acolyte shuddered. "I'd swear the bronze git is grinning right at me."

"Bigger problems," Brother Tuomas repeated. His eyes were still vacant, but his voice had taken on the sour edge of a man pushed too far.

"Yeah, I'd say so," said Alithana. "Though it's not for you and I to decide, is it? We're on the high priestess' orders."

"Well then, who am I to block servants of the goddess on an important mission?" Tuomas' voice was equal parts sugar and venom, and he wore a smile that gave the sisters pause. They might have reconsidered their request, but the scribe was already pulling open the heavy door to the high scribe's office.

A wave of heat and emerald light washed over the three. Green flames danced over the holy texts and scrolls that lined the walls and covered the shelves, burning but not consuming. There was no crackling of flame either, but a susurrant sound like the wind through the reeds, or the whisper of countless angels reciting the All Mother's scriptures.

Pathalan was at the center of the jade inferno, suspended in the air above his desk, surrounded by a swarm of parchment that danced and swooped on currents of heat and divine power. His frame bent at odd angles, his eyes stared at the ceiling, his mouth warped in a silent scream of agony. He held a quill in each hand, and they wrote on the parchment that obediently floated to him, as if eager to receive the scriptures.

Sister Varia shrieked and pushed the door shut. A few flames and errant pages escaped as she did so.

"Still want to see him?" asked Brother Tuomas with saccharine malice.

"Uh, no. No, I think we'll be going." Sister Varia smoothed her robes to hide a stifled sob.

"We need to tell the high priestess," breathed Sister Alithana, reading one of the sheets of parchment that had sailed through the door.

"Brother Cheesemonger was supposed to have already—"

"Not about High Scribe Pathalan." The priestess held up the errant parchment. It was covered in scripture, with emerald flames still dancing along the edges of the text. "About the goddess' words. This says Tandos is revealed a traitor. I think... I think the gods are going to war."

"It's your basic armageddon scenario." Brouse rolled himself a cigarette and nodded up at the maelstrom of black clouds and crimson lightning spiraling over the Pinnacle. "Prophetic visions coming to pass, magic and destiny crashing into each other, and gods settlin' old scores on the mortal planes as well as the higher ones. See it all the time."

Ignatius gave the technical monk a sideways glance. "You do?"

"In books, yeah." Brouse struck a match and lit his cigarette. The grizzled monk stared down his stubbly beard at the instruments lining the plaza. Devices whirled and whistled. His briefcase sat open on the ground, and every crystal set in it flashed with panicked urgency. Brouse grunted, satisfied with his interpretation of the signs. "Classic armageddon."

"How can you tell?" Ignatius asked, uncertain if the monk was right but absolutely convinced that Brouse's confidence was unwarranted.

Brouse rolled his eyes. "See that string of holy beads dancin' and jumpin' like it wants to escape that silver hook I hung it from? That'd be swaying gently if someone's premonition was about to come to pass. We've got dozens, no, hundreds of prophecies and counter-prophecies competin' to become reality."

Ignatius was still skeptical. "Well, yes, but—"

"And see that clay fat fellow whose sweatin' like a guilty man before the magistrate? Statues of the false monk Titus Ur'Sloot only sweat when gods or their influence are nearby. And I know it's reading right, because the Umbraxian fertility idol has rolled behind a potted bush, and it only gets modest when divine eyes are focused nearby."

"I suppose," conceded the priest of Mordo Ogg. "But—"

"Your magical currents are up, your causal wavelengths are compressed, your metaphysical index is all over the place…" Brouse rattled off indicators as he pointed to the various devices, totems, and meters that he had arranged around the square. "Your cosmological flux is everywhere, your ontological connections are all tangled up, your probability curve is inverting, and then there's that." The monk pointed triumphantly to a simple device consisting of a chicken foot set upside down in an iron candlestick. All of the foot's bony digits were curled up like a fist save the middle one, which was extended toward the sky. "That one tells me we're totally—"

"Yes, fine, a classic armageddon," snapped Ignatius. "But what do we do?"

"Have a smoke. Keep our heads down." Brouse offered a rolling paper to the old priest. "Might want to head inside at some point, mister sir, but… nah, your guy's a neutral party. Probably no trouble for you."

"No, what do we do about the master's shrine?" Ignatius' voice cracked. The death priest found himself on the eve of a world-shattering crisis without use of his shrine, and was experiencing the sort of desperate anxiety normally only seen in mages whose crystal balls malfunction right before the Academy Dueling Tournament.

Brouse considered the shrine of Mordo Ogg. The sculpture's skull hissed and bubbled from the heat of its searing eyes, and molten tears ran down its stone cheeks. "Hmmph. Seems like some stubborn soul might've got ol' Mordo Ogg stoppered up, like a Gnomish music box with sand in its gears. Or maybe a dog choking on a chicken bone."

"But what do we do about it?" whined Ignatius.

"My job's fixin' relics and artifacts, not their patrons. Not much we can do but step back and wait for things to get moving again." Brouse gave a shrug, then cocked his head to the side. A keening whistle scraped at the razor's edge of hearing, like a teakettle about to boil over a few blocks away. "Although we should give the shrine a healthy distance."

"Get back! Get away!" Gorm waved his axe at other adventurers as he was sprinting through the spider-spattered halls of the Great Vault. He could hear Mannon's screams behind him, the scrabbling of claws and teeth on stone. The Felfather wouldn't stay down for long. "Run!" he screamed at the bewildered adventurers emerging from the side chambers and passageways of the expansive treasury.

To a man and woman, the other heroes ran. Among the many unspoken rules of professional heroics is that when one hero calls for flight, everyone of the same rank or lower should bolt in the same direction as fast as possible. So when the adventurers looting the Great Vault saw the hero once known as the Pyrebeard sprinting alongside the Archmage of the Gray Tower and one of the most famous mages in the Freedlands, each hero's risk-reward analysis reached the same conclusion in the blink of an eye. Sacks of gold and gems hit the floor and heavier artifacts were tossed aside as the crowd of heroes poured for the exit, taking up the cry for retreat.

"What's the plan?" Laruna huffed.

"Don't know. Do ye believe that thing is actually Mannon?" Gorm asked, still struggling to wrap his mind around the nature of the threat.

"Perhaps there's another demonic entity powerful enough to corrupt Tandos and his temple, subvert the kingdoms of Arth, and evade detection by all the mages and priests in the nation for centuries," said Jynn. "But that doesn't seem much better!"

Gorm grunted. How did one make a plan to combat something on the scale of gods and demons and destiny?

If the old berserker had a destiny, if there was some grand purpose in his life, it needed to show up soon. Niln had told him the scriptures would show him the signs, and signs couldn't get much clearer than this. But his old friend had also said that he'd know what to do when the time came, and here at the intersection of now and never, Gorm couldn't fathom what to do.

"This is just like him!" Jynn ranted. "This is typical Detarr Ur'Mayan at his finest!"

"An apocalyptic battle with the source of all evil is typical of your father?" Laruna asked dryly.

"The secrecy!" Jynn snarled. "He knew that Johan didn't defeat Mannon in Az'Anon's lair, or somehow deduced that Johan and Mannon had entered a dark pact. And he could have warned us, or the kingdom, or anyone else. But no! Instead he set out to kill Johan himself and everyone on Arth in the process. The man would literally rather destroy the world than open up to his own son! He never told me..."

Jynn trailed off, lost in a new thought.

Destroy the world. The phrase stuck with Gorm. He recalled that Mannon said the world was exactly as he wanted it, that he owned it. To defeat him would be to... to overthrow the ruler of the world. It might tear down the kingdom. It would mean revenge for the Sten. Niln's scriptures attributed all of those goals to the Dark Prince.

And suddenly Gorm realized why the scriptures never talked about the Seventh Hero of Destiny and the Dark Prince fighting. They never were meant to fight. The Dark Prince was destined to strike down the king, sunder the powers that led the kingdom. The Seventh Hero was to save the good people of Arth and stop evil from triumphing. Since the crowned King of Andarun was currently an ancient entity made of oily goop and hate, their goals were one and the same.

"It's the same person!" Gorm exclaimed.

"Well, maybe I'm a little like him," Jynn said. "But I—"

"Not what I mean, and not important," the Dwarf barked. "I've got a plan! I just need to get to the plaza."

"That might be a problem," Laruna shouted, looking over her shoulder.

Gorm glanced back and into a nightmare. The hallway behind him ended abruptly in a coal-colored mass of snarling faces. Luminescent green oozed from innumerable gashes in Mannon's oily membrane. Mercurial tendrils covered in sharp thorns whipped from the Felfather's bulk and clung to the stones. They dragged the shapeless malice through the hall in bursts of fluid motion, like ink dripping across a parchment.

"Go!" screamed Gorm, looking forward. The door to the Great Vault was just ahead, illuminated by the receding torchlight of the fleeing heroes ahead of them.

"I can hold him here," Jynn breathed as they stepped through the entrance.

Gorm shot him a sideways, "What?"

"Help me close it!" The wizard stopped running and leaned against the heavy iron door to the vault, straining to push it shut. "I can hold him—" He stumbled as Gorm shoved the door shut with one hand.

"Metal and stone ain't going to hold him!" Gorm gestured angrily at the door.

"Wards will buy you time," said Jynn, already weaving. Magic danced from the tips of his gloved hand and the end of the Wyrmwood Staff as he waved them over the portal. "You won't make it to the plaza if someone doesn't slow Mannon down. Just go."

"But—" Laruna began, but she was cut off when several inhuman mouths screamed from within the vault.

Gorm grimaced. "Ye sure?"

"Yes." Jynn kept weaving, sorcerous runes dancing from his fingertips and melting into the door like snowflakes. He turned from his work to call over his shoulder. "And Laruna?"

The pyromancer looked at Jynn uncertainly.

"I always loved you," the archmage said, then turned back to the door as if to leave it at that.

"Gods," Laruna growled, rolling her eyes as she turned back to Jynn. "Go on, Gorm. We'll hold him here."

Gorm only paused for a moment, then nodded. "Thank ye." They wouldn't have made it this far had it not been for Heraldin and Gaist's sacrifices, and it would take more than even that to get to the Pinnacle. A party wipe and the fate of the world hung in the balance as he raced up the stairs.

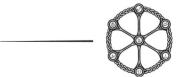

"You have some sense of timing, Jynn Ur'Mayan," Laruna said as Gorm's footfalls receded. "Now? After all the times you passed this conversation by, now you want to talk?"

Jynn's lips curled up in a small, sad smile. "Well, it—"

The wall shuddered as Mannon collided against the door. Jynn's runes flared with aquamarine light under the impact, but the spell held and the door remained shut.

"It doesn't seem we'll get another chance," the wizard finished.

Laruna joined him at the wall, adding her own weaves to the wards he'd set over the door. The portal reverberated and flashed again as Mannon heaved his unholy bulk against the doorway. "I wish things had been different," she said.

"I wish I had been," sighed Jynn, still weaving. "I should have told you, Laruna. I should have said many things long ago. I've always hidden things from you; my heritage, my omnimancy, my feelings—I always had some excuse for why sharing my life with you wasn't necessary. And yet I'd get so angry when my father kept things from me, and I'd take every secret as a rejection."

"The wards won't hold long," said Laruna. Mannon slammed against the vault door again, rattling the walls and bringing powdered mortar and stones raining down from the ceiling. A couple of runes flared and flickered out.

"It's easy to spot your parents' flaws. It's much harder to avoid inheriting them," said Jynn, replacing the lost runes. "I should have told you I loved you. I should have fought to keep you. I should have done so many things differently. But I'm grateful I still have a chance to fix one of my mistakes."

He smiled at her. "You make me want to be a better person."

Tears like diamonds gleamed at the corner of her eye. "All of my happiest memories are with you."

The omnimancer turned his attention back to the groaning doorway. "I'm glad that in the end, I let you know how I feel."

The wards on the door flickered and sizzled like roaches in a lightning trap. Iron and stone groaned under the massive pressure of Mannon's will. Black and green ooze burbled between the stones of the wall, shorting out more enchanted wards in bursts of amber sparks.

"This isn't how to do it!" Laruna said.

"Delaying Mannon or talking about my—" Jynn began, leaning on the Wyrmwood Staff as he stood.

But he didn't get to finish. Laruna grabbed him and pulled him into her, pressing her lips against his so forcibly that he couldn't have resisted if he wanted to. The pyromancer wrapped one arm around Jynn, pulling him closer, and she intertwined the fingers of her other hand with those on the omnimancer's skeletal hand. Jynn felt the warmth and the heat rising in him, threatening to overtake him.

And then she began to channel.

If Laruna's wrath was a bonfire, her love was like a sun. Flames poured from the hand that held Jynn's, burning away the wizard's glove and exposing the skeletal digits underneath. The fire bloomed and engulfed both the mages, and yet still more magic flowed through the pyromancer, burning, urgent, all-consuming. Jynn felt noctomantic power surge through the Wyrmwood Staff, the artifact desperately working to prevent the tide of unrestrained solamancy from overwhelming its master. Tears filled his eyes, though he couldn't tell if they were from joy or agony as the sorcery threatened to pull him apart.

Laruna pressed her body even closer to his and moved her hand from his fingers to clutch his wrist. "Weave," she murmured, without taking her mouth from his.

"Mmmpth," agreed Jynn. He had a vague idea of what to cast, but it was almost impossible to craft a spell while distracted by the heat of Laruna's sorcery and the softness of her lips. A memory of his father's work crystallized amidst the heat and fire, and he began to work it into the rising spell. His fingers danced and his hand rose, weaving threads of shadow from the staff into a matrix of the pyromancer's flames. Still embracing her, still locked in a kiss, he lifted their hands to focus the weaves. The threads of magic above them wove into a complex structure that bent the magic around itself and amplified it into a cyclone of flame and darkness.

A plume of fire and molten stone erupted from the grounds of the Palace of Andarun, transforming the eastern tearoom and surrounding garden into a pillar of light and heat. It rose high over the palace, an obelisk of flame that towered over the city and drew frightened screams as far away as the Base and the Riverdowns.

Duine Poldo only paused long enough to glance at the conflagration rising from the palace. He couldn't tell whether the blaze boded well or ill for Gorm and his companions, but his eyes kept flitting back to the slate where the Wood Gnomes tracked the stock transfer in white chalk. The meter indicated they were just over two-thirds done.

His eyes met Feista Hrurk's across the trading floor. Their efforts to move an entire economy a step sideways would be for naught after the palace quest was complete, and their time was growing short. Gorm and his party had their part to do; those on the Wall had to do theirs. "Faster!" Duine cried, attacking his paperwork with renewed vigor as Mrs. Hrurk began to drum louder. "This is our moment! It's now or never!"

"Now," Laruna murmured, guiding Jynn's wrist. Together, they brought their hands swiveling down and toward the door, falling like an executioner's axe. The pillar of sorcery followed the arc of their arms, a blade of blazing shadow that carved through stone and wood, through the walls and the iron vault door, and into the ancient demon beyond.

Mannon's multitudinous mouths howled as searing flames and hooks of shadow tore through the center of his dark mass. Faces emerged from his charring membrane only to be burned away or ripped apart by barbed hooks of darkness that flickered amidst the flame.

The more magic Jynn wove, the more Laruna sent burning through his arm. The crystal in the Wyrmwood Staff whined in protest, like lake ice about to crack. Still the magic poured on, boring a hole clear through Mannon's center and carving off one of his eight main legs. Green ichor and smoking, oily ooze dribbled onto the floor of the Great Vault of Andarun.

It was several long, burning, precious moments before the demonic faces' screaming ceased and the reserves of Laruna's magic finally exhausted themselves. Jynn tied off the weave as the pyromancer pulled her lips away. "That was…" The omnimancer trailed off, still holding her, still looking deep into her eyes.

"I know," Laruna said. "I—"

But she didn't finish. The mage went suddenly rigid as a tentacle of black thorns lashed across the pair. Jynn staggered back, his staff falling as Laruna was flung back against the wall. He tried to scream her name, but another of Mannon's tendrils grabbed him about the head and swung the mage like a fleshy hammer against the opposite wall.

—CHAPTER 33—

The sheet of parchment slammed against the wall of the shrine of Tandos near Mauggin's Row on the Fourth Tier. A priestess of Musana beat a nail into the edict, pinning it to the mantle of the wide door. It was a simple shrine; an ornate building no larger than a small shed featuring all the typical trappings of a place of worship of the warrior god: an altar with room for two to pray, a bronze spear wrapped in silken flame, icons of great heroes and champions, and an interfaith mob of furious clergy carrying torches and holy weapons at the door. The most senior priests and priestesses carried scrolls to nail to the doorway; writs of judgment or proclamations of holy wars against Tandos and his faithful.

Tandos the traitor god. Tandos the god of the Dark Ones. Tandos the deceiver. Tandos the servant of Mannon. In every temple across Arth, from the Imperial Seat to the frozen north of Ruskan to Enolia and the Dreadlands and all the far continents beyond the seas, high scribes and oracles still reeled from sudden revelations. The All Mother's memories had returned, and with them some spell had broken over the pantheon. The texts of Musana and Alluna talked of webs of darkness falling from the gods' eyes; Fulgen's scriptures said the silent god was angered enough to use his voice; the Deep Gnomes claimed that even Dewen had no more patience for the warrior god. Gnolls and Goblins and Orcs bearing symbols of Grund, Gathra, and Gich were among the mob, proclaiming that their gods had turned from Mannon's lies long ago and would see justice for those who hadn't. Even gods who weren't particularly interested in a war between good and evil—feral Fengelde, murderous Sitha, greedy Az'ilgar, fickle Uldine—had sent clergy to bring the fight against the Lying God.

Most of Tandos' clergy fled. A few of the war god's Elven champions laughed as they leapt into their last, brief battle, showing their dark nature at the end. Some acolytes had the sort of sudden epiphanies that only a well-armed horde of clerics and paladins can inspire, and opted for conversion rather than martyrdom. The players changed, but the scenes were the same as all of the temples across Arth came together to stand against the traitor god.

Almost.

The one temple conspicuously absent from this brief holy war was the same one that had been prosecuting battles against Tandos for centuries. The Temple of Al'Matra in Andarun had no time to participate in its vindication; its clergy had more pressing matters to attend to. Such as the emerald flames consuming their sanctuary.

Priestesses, scribes, and the rest of the All Mother's displaced clergy watched the otherworldly fire from the courtyard. They stood in small clusters, little islands of priesthood arranged by seniority, trying to work through the madness playing out all around them.

"Doesn't make any sense," Sister Varia told a cluster of her fellow third-year acolytes.

Sister Alithana struck her most beatific pose. "Well, the All Mother—"

Meni cut her off. "Don't you tell me the goddess works in mysterious ways. We've all seen mysterious. I can handle mysterious. Inscrutable, even."

"Downright crazy," offered Brother Tuomas.

The others shot Tuomas a sidelong glance; even if the All Mother's memories had returned, it seemed too soon to lift the ancient taboo on saying the c-word in the All Mother's sanctum.

"But not... not harmful. Not dangerous," insisted Sister Meni. "Not to us."

Brother Cheesemonger nodded. "I once heard High Scribe Pathalan say he liked his gods like he liked his chocolates: sweet, readily available, and set neatly in a pretty box."

A few of the junior scribes gasped at the irreligious notion. Most of the priestesses in training smirked and exchanged knowing glances.

"Some people are saying the fire is to punish the high scribe for not being devoted enough," said Sister Piniana, an emissary for the sixth-year acolytes on a mission to spread gossip among her juniors.

"More like for pinching so many bottoms at holy feasts," said Sister Varia.

"Do you think he's all right in there?" Brother Filks wrung his hands.

The other third-years exchanged winces. Brother Filks was the sort of gentle soul who saved bread crusts for sparrows and stopped to let caterpillars cross his path. Whatever dam held back the tears behind his red-rimmed eyes was already leaking.

"I suspect he's in a better place," said Sister Alithana diplomatically.

The acolytes watched the temple burn and ruminated on High Scribe Pathalan's famously hedonistic lifestyle.

"Hopefully," said Alithana, mustering her beneficence.

"The fires are probably less green there, anyway," sniffed Sister Varia.

"Is anybody going to put it out?" asked Sister Lemba.

"Oh, I heard the senior priestesses tried," said Sister Piniana. "All it got the bucket train was some singed eyebrows and a face full of steam. Besides, it's not actually burning much."

"It looks like it's burning everything," said Brother Cheesemonger.

"Yeah, it looks that way," said the sixth-year acolyte, rolling her eyes. "But it doesn't burn paper, or carpets, or wood, right? It's holy fire, not like... real fire."

"So it's a metaphor?" asked Brother Filks.

"Something like that. We just need to stay back here and let it play out, and we'll be fine," said Sister Piniana, happy to share her expertise. Unfortunately, her observation acted upon Nove's first principle in the same way a lit match might react with a fireworks warehouse.

The explosion rent Al'Matra's ramshackle temple into a fountain of flaming stones, wooden beams, and sculpture. The shockwave sent Al'Matra's clergy flying through the air. Chunks of stone columns and support beams embedded themselves in nearby buildings. A flying statue of a shrimp missed crushing the high priestess by a hand's breadth.

As acolytes helped each other to their feet, Sister Alithana shrieked in fear and pointed back at the crater where the All Mother's temple had stood. Jade fire still erupted from it, but in the flames, a shape was visible.

The bronze sculpture of High Scribe Niln stood amidst the inferno like a sea captain bracing himself against a storm. His hands were balled into fists, and his sculpted robes flapped against him as though blown by the backdraft. Yet his face... his face radiated pure joy, grinning wildly, empty eyes staring toward the Pinnacle.

And behind him, another figure rose from the rubble.

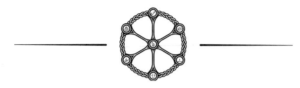

The stones shifted, then began to grind over each other like a horizontal rockslide borne on currents of glowing water through the towering pillars and branching walkways of the Black Fathoms. They bobbed and weaved to the spot where two broken bodies lay beneath the blasted remnants of a stone tower, without any credible path forward.

But magic, especially low magic, is the triumph of destiny over credulity. The song of the Sten was rising, and the stones would not be stopped. And without any possible way to go, the stones and streams took an impossible one.

Granite slabs bobbed upward as though borne on a rising tide. The water flared with light as ivory statues approached the shaft of the ruined staircase, illuminating the edges of the great stone tree forming at the top of the cavern. The dancing masonry bobbed in the glow, swirling around the point where the fallen ascended.

Gorm's heart pounded with the frenetic force of a war drum as he raced toward the top of the staircase. Ahead of him, heroes and Tandosian prisoners alike scrambled to heed his cries of retreat. Behind him, Mannon's screams grew nearer with every step the Dwarf leapt over.

His mind raced as he ran. The statues were the key. The Sten had protected them with old magic, even a dragon. Mannon and Johan had plotted and schemed and turned the kingdom on its head just for a chance to destroy them. The old Stennish sculptures had to be the one thing Mannon feared. And while most of the sculptures resided at the bottom of a deadly drop on the opposite side of the King of Demons, Gorm's brain alighted on the one Stennish sculpture that he knew was central in prophecy.

The Dark Prince was supposed to bring back Al'Thadan and the Sten. Everyone who bothered paying any attention to the old Al'Matran prophecies assumed that meant the Seventh Hero would stop the Dark Prince. But if the Sten were Mannon's foes, if Tandos was the true evil, and Al'Thadan wasn't the traitor everyone thought, then bringing back Al'Thadan to stop Mannon and saving the world were the same thing. He just needed to...

It occurred to Gorm that he had no idea what to do when he reached the statue, but he quickly moved on to more pressing thoughts, such as: "There's the door toward the exit," and "Mannon sounds very close," and "Why am I airborne?"

Gorm suspected the last two were related right before he hit the wall opposite the stairs. He picked himself up just in time to scramble away from a clump of black, thorny tendrils that poured from the staircase. The oily brambles of a thousand of his nightmares waved at him with menace, and Mannon's faces were crowing eagerly somewhere just out of sight. Yet Gorm could see green ooze dribbling and pooling at the top of the stairs. Mannon bled. The fact that evil itself could bleed suggested that it was theoretically possible—if philosophically challenging—that it could be killed. Of more immediate importance, it could at least be forcibly dissuaded with an axe.

Gorm slashed, and several tendrils fell. They quickly slithered back to join the oily bulk pushing through the door from the stairs, but Gorm was already running. He struck wildly at another probing tentacle and ducked through a doorway.

The Dwarf's flight through the palace was a blur. Raking spines and gnashing teeth tore his cloak, snagged his armor, slashed across his face. His axe spun and twirled as he ran, splitting leering faces and severing thorny tendrils in sprays of green and black ooze. The cacophonous sounds of Mannon's pursuit thundered in his ears; the howling of hungry maws, the snaps and crunches of chairs and end tables dragged beneath the creature's bulk, the creaking protests of stone and timber as the foul ooze pressed itself through doorways. Gorm's face and beard were sticky with sweat, blood, and whatever foulness Mannon was made of by the time he staggered from the front doors of the palace.

The courtyard was in between its metamorphosis from a battlefield to an administrative field office. Eager adventurers had already begun preparations for guild carters to loot the palace. Claim notices hung from the marble plinths and brightly colored inventory flags flapped from every golden fixture, patio furnishing, and corpse. This premature postmortem paperwork likely only contributed to the courtyard confusion when fleeing heroes came spilling from the palace and whatever spell the mages had used left a smoking crater where the Wallward gardens used to be. Now heroes milled about and shouted questions at each other.

"Run!" Gorm rasped as he stumbled down the palace steps. "It's comin' this—"

And then it arrived. The front gates shuddered and buckled as Mannon erupted from the stone facade of the palace in a shower of slate and chartreuse slime. Screams rang out as Mannon's many faces leered down at the guild heroes, and then the doom of Arth sloshed after Gorm again.

He was already running for the courtyard gates in a straight line. His lungs ached, blood streamed down his face, and his ears rang with the cries of adventurers caught in the wave of vile ooze that roared behind him. Yet nothing could take his focus from the mission. He had one chance, one idea to stop Mannon, and everything else was a distraction—

A warrior in silver armor crashed into the ground by his feet, nearly knocking Gorm over. It stopped him short, which was all that kept a golden sculpture from smashing into him. He glanced back and saw Mannon preparing to hurl a sundial and a struggling ranger at him next.

"Bones!" swore Gorm, already running again. He sprinted in a jagged pattern, trying to evade the lawn ornaments and adventurers that rained down around him. The projectile heroes were easier to avoid; they announced their imminent impact with screams and curses. Gorm was almost to the gates of the courtyard when he heard a surprised bellow, and the clouds above him were briefly eclipsed by the airborne form of Mr. Brunt. The Ogre sailed over the wall and landed like a trebuchet stone somewhere on the Pinnacle.

It was a Halfling rogue that finally clipped Gorm, catching his leg just as he made it to the courtyard gates. It took him a moment to right himself, disentangle from the cursing thief, and get them both back on their feet. He made straight for the gate, while she darted to the left, perhaps hoping to dive out of Mannon's path. A split second later, her muffled scream confirmed that the ooze was still hot on his heels.

He could see the Dark Prince standing with his back to Gorm in the middle of the empty plaza. The shops and cafes of the Pinnacle stood empty; a line of thugs and goons contracted by the Heroes' Guild held Andarun's citizenry at the far end of the Pinnacle, far from the danger and loot. They milled about with the casual confidence of spectators; making predictions, buying ten-cent beef rolls from shouting vendors, and searching for some sign of excitement. Half of them were looking away from the palace, watching an emerald glow flaring from the lower tiers.

The crowd's demeanor changed as Gorm ran from the gate. Mannon roared behind the berserker, and the faces of the enforcers and onlookers shifted from excitement to surprise. As one, their gazes swiveled upward. They gave a collective gasp and took a synchronized step back. Yet fear can only unify a people for so long, and soon it was everyone for themselves as they ran screaming for the steps.

Gorm's chest burned like it was on fire, his throat was raw and ragged in the frost-kissed air, and his legs did not feel like anything at all. The Dark Prince was just ahead, and for a brief and glorious moment, Gorm was sure he was going to make it.

A vine-like tentacle whipped around his arm and wrenched it back so hard that he dropped his axe. He spun around and pulled his hand free, but another tendril had snagged his leg. Still more ooze wrapped around his waist, thick enough for a leering face to grow from it and start gnawing on his torso. The many bleeding facades of Mannon leered down at Gorm, wearing faces of triumph even as they consumed one another. Gorm roared, his voice shaking with rage and terror and the exertion of trying to stay on his feet, until a shockwave blasted him.

Emerald flames washed over the plaza. Patio chairs and racks of merchandise flew away from the epicenter of the explosion, shattering the windows and splintering the walls of the abandoned shops lining the Pinnacle. Mannon reared back, his manifold eyes squinting in the glare of brilliant green light, his tendrils dropping Gorm. The Dwarf grabbed his axe and turned to the impact site where a viridian comet had struck the cobbles between himself and the Dark Prince. At the center of the shattered and bubbling stone, a familiar figure rose.

"Kaitha?" Gorm rasped. "It ain't possible!"

At high enough population destiny, concepts such as "possibility" or "probability" break down. One-in-a-million chances become near certainties, and even more outlandish odds become the norm.

In the halls of the Palace of Andarun, for example, time and space had given up any attempts at enforcing the laws of nature. Wan light filtered into the stone depths of the palace's basement through the ceiling's recently seared skylight, yet those beams were almost entirely lost in the azure glow of the streams running through the cobbles and over the carpets. The waters pulsed and burbled in harmony with a haunting melody, sung by stones cursed ages ago. The singers strode purposefully toward the stairs, where the luminous river was already beginning to creep up the steps.

The music rose, and as it lifted, it called. Two more singers joined the chorus and the glowing figures marched toward their fate. With every step, their song and the light grew stronger and more brilliant.

Gorm had to squint to look at Kaitha, and not just for the blinding halo of emerald flame that danced around her head. Her whole form was blurred and shifting, as though reality itself couldn't decide whether she was an Elf or a goddess. Her hair was both waves of auburn and silver locks webbed with pearls. Her eyes were reddened by the tears flowing from them and also blazing with the same emerald fire that danced around her. She wore Kaitha's familiar leather armor and also the divine mail of a goddess, covered with dancing filigree and green flames. The avatar of Al'Matra nocked an arrow like a lightning bolt in a bow older than the mountains and sighted it on Mannon.

A large head, squid-like and burbling with sinister laughter, emerged from Mannon's mid-region, green and black ooze dripping from it. "Interesting," it burbled, sounding almost like laughter. "I see the Mad Queen herself has—"

The arrow screamed from Al'Matra's bow and into the head's bulbous eye. The tentacles waved and the beak beneath them wailed as Mannon shrank back.

"Not mad," said the goddess and Kaitha. "Just angry."

"Kaitha?" Gorm said again. Most of his mind worked feverishly to catch up with current events, but it was difficult to process the arrival of a fallen friend and the metaphysical implications of Al'Matra's appearance. Still, a professional hero doesn't last years in the field without developing a keen instinct for self-preservation, and that instinct told Gorm that while the theological and ontological connotations of a goddess incarnate battling the progenitor of all evil in the mortal realms were staggeringly complex, it was a fairly straightforward deduction that standing between them as they fought was a really dumb idea. He dove aside just as another of the All Mother's arrows rent the air, a lethal comet blazing toward its mark at the black heart of the animated sludge.

Mannon caught it.

The bolt still crackled with power and vibrated in the clutches of Mannon's thick tentacle, as a bee might struggle in a mantis' claws. A new head was laughing as it swallowed the squealing squid face, a guttural, gulping sound. "Oh, no dear. You must be mad," chuckled the new face, like that of a frog with razor teeth. "How else could a single god hope to defeat me in the seat of my power?"

"Deceiver!" cried Al'Matra.

"I only lie when I need to," slurred the frog head. "But you know as well as I that you can't stand against me."

The goddess replied with a single shot that split into three as it arced toward Mannon's bulk. Tentacles whipped around two of the bolts, but the third struck home in one of the demon lord's smaller faces. It gave a tiny wail as it slumped over, black tongue lolling.

"Not for long, anyway," snarled Mannon. Several of his other faces loosed hoarse screams as he charged at the All Mother's avatar.

Gorm scrambled along the Wallward side of Pinnacle Plaza toward the sculpture of the Dark Prince, ducking behind a patio table upended in front of Sigil's Cafe. Broken crockery crunched beneath his boots as he ran to the cover of another upturned table, then dove behind a tangle of wrought iron chairs.

Mannon had been determined to stop him from getting to the sculpture, which was reason enough to think reaching it was a good idea. The trick was finding the right moment to run across the wide-open expanse of the plaza. He glanced up over the edge of the table.

The black mass of malignance had closed the distance with Al'Matra's avatar, and the goddess had cast aside her bow in favor of smiting the evil with her fists. Every punch sent a ball of holy fire scorching toward Mannon. His foul tentacles managed to deflect some of the blasts, while others seared bubbling seams into the demon lord's viscous membrane, sending gibbets of green and black ooze spraying over the cobblestones. Gorm was most concerned, however, with the fireballs that Mannon managed to dodge.

Errant projectiles arced over the plaza, their divine power unmoored by mortal errancy. One burned through a jeweler's tent before immolating the Restored Tambour Cafe. Another set a ten-penny beef roll cart alight and sent it careening into the flagship store of Bugbeary Limited, whose luxury enchantments and alchemical reagents turned out to be just as explosive as their more austere counterparts.

As Gorm watched, another fireball flew high into the air in the general direction of himself. In his professional opinion, it looked like an excellent time to be on the opposite side of the plaza. He sprinted around the debris and ran toward the Dark Prince as the flaming projectile sank almost lazily down to crash through the window of the cafe. The Dwarf leapt for the sculpture just as Sigil's Cafe went up in a billowing cloud of flame behind him, creating the sort of dramatic look that normally took an expert pyromancer and several expensive glamours for a hero to achieve.

The effect was dashed, and Gorm nearly was as well, as the shockwave from another explosion knocked him sideways and sent him skidding across the cobbles. Dazed, he looked up to see Kaitha rising from the unrecognizable ruins of several small shops and restaurants, a thick trickle of blood dripping from her brow. With another cry she launched herself back at Mannon, a viridian comet burning toward the darkness.

Gorm turned back to the center of the plaza and found that he was nearly at the statue of the Dark Prince. "Still got time," he muttered as he scrambled to his feet and stumbled over to the sculpture. Unfortunately, he was out of plans.

"What do I do?" he asked, half expecting the statue to answer. The Dark Prince stared over his head, as though avoiding an awkward question. Gorm felt around the sculpture's base and the boots for a hidden switch or lever, checked the horizon for any wayward structures that might have formed significant silhouettes at sunrise or sunset, and probed for recesses where some conveniently available gemstone or artifact might fit neatly. There was nothing.

Al'Matra shrieked. Peering around the sculpture, Gorm saw that Mannon had caught her leg in one of his thick tentacles. She struck back with searing fists, and several of Mannon's faces burned away with wails of pain and despair. Yet they all grew back, leering and hungry as more tendrils of darkness wove their way toward the All Mother.

"Come on!" Gorm slapped the side of the Dark Prince's leg as one might rouse a dozing student late for class. "Come on! Dark Prince, we need ye! We know the Sten ain't what we thought—ye ain't what we thought!"

The statue was stoic. Al'Matra screamed somewhere behind it.

"I don't know what ye want!" Gorm shouted at the impassive stone. "I'm sorry! I'm sorry I doubted all this destiny and prophecy nons—er, stuff! It's new to me! But I believe in ye now! You're the Seventh Hero and the Dark Prince! You're the one of legend! And if you're gonna come to save anyone, now's the time, 'cause there won't be much to save soon!"

If the statue was concerned with a Dwarf's faith in it, it gave no indication.

Gorm's mind raced, grasping at straws. "Do I need to say your name? Sten? Sten king?" He didn't know any Stennish names, though as far as Troll names went... A flash of memory in his mind showed him Thane's body bursting in a cloud of dust, decomposing in the same violent way the soul-bound minions of Detarr Ur'Mayan had many years ago. "Thane? Is it ye?"

Something wet spattered over Gorm as a shadow briefly eclipsed the clouds above. He glanced at the blood and ichor dribbling over his hands just as Al'Matra crashed into the cobbles behind him. He glanced back, anticipating another barrage of green fire, but Kaitha lay motionless in an expanding pool of crimson.

"Come on!" Gorm cried. "Thane or Dark Prince or whoever ye are! I believed! I showed up! You're supposed to save the world. Do your destiny stuff! Work your prophecy! Just do it fast!"

The statue was still. The black tentacles whipping around it were not. Thin tendrils of shadow and malice caught Gorm about the leg and the arm. He hacked at a couple with his axe, but the fluid limbs wrestled his weapon away and threw it to the ground. More and more rubbery limbs wrapped around the Dark Prince, crushing Gorm against the stone, pressing the air from his lungs. A tentacle wrapped around his face and—

And he saw himself taking up his axe and driving back the darkness. Felt Mannon grow limp as he clove its last head from its vile body. Heard the cheers of his name from a beloved populace. They would call him Pyrebeard, demon slayer, the greatest hero of the guild's long and storied history. He could be made grandmaster of the guild. Perhaps the throne was in reach. An end to the pain crushing his lungs and a gift of everything Arth had to offer. All he had to do was accept the pact, to make the bargain, and he could be the savior of the world.

Gorm ripped the tentacle from his mouth with the last strength he could muster. "Al'Thadan!" he screamed. Two more tendrils of thorns wrapped around his face and slammed his head against the stone, and there was only darkness.

——CHAPTER 34——

It can't all be darkness. Not according to Nove's seventh and final principle of universal irony.

Many assumed the philosopher-scientist would be bitter and angry late in his life. After the academies banned testing on his first five principles, he penned a sixth that effectively postulated that his life's work could never be verified. This well-documented failure ensured that Nove's principles would never become Nove's laws. To the people of his time, it was apparent that Nove would never join the ranks of Essenpi's greatest minds.

That is the sort of failure that drives many almost-great people to villainy, or at least curmudgeonly hermitry. Yet Nove's contemporaries and students found him to be cheerful, even jovial. In the forward of his ultimate work, Nove noted that many people's surprise at his contentment was what prompted him to study and document one final principle.

Nove's seventh principle of universal irony notes that there must be some good in the universe, because irony could not exist otherwise. Irony relies on the expectations of sentient beings. If everything was always the worst it could be, there would be no sentient beings at all, nor any expectation that there ever would be anything good to disrupt, and thus no irony. The universe is often cold and cruel, but if it was always horrible—if the worst always came to pass—nobody would have reason to expect anything else. Nobody would be around to expect anything.

In the vast emptiness of space, chemical processes began that would lead, over inconceivable eons, to creatures discussing justice and altruism and the greater good. Despite the worst instincts of humanity, civilizations rose and endured. Beauty and art, kindness and intelligence, love and life itself; none of these things should exist in an uncaring, entropic universe. And yet, against all reasonable expectations, they do—even if only for brief, brilliant moments.

For Nove, hope wasn't a wish. It was a mathematical fact.

You have to consider the best possible scenario.

Several notable things happened as the darkness closed in over Gorm.

In Sculpin Down, the shrine of Mordo Ogg split from the top of its stone skull to the base of its throne, sending a cloud of hot steam rolling into the empty square in front of it.

In the museum of Andarun, the Spear of Issan suddenly buckled and kicked like a fish on a boat. Its struggles were brief; the ancient weapon exploded before a bannerman could investigate, embedding splinters in the glass of its display case.

In the ruined Temple of Al'Matra, the statue of Niln now looked like it was laughing with joy, his eyes upward and his hands extended toward the sky.

Any of these phenomena would have normally caused a small uproar, but save for an old priest weeping at the ruptured shrine of death, they went almost entirely unnoticed. The citizens of Andarun gazed at the center of the cyclone above the city, where an azure light hung in the air like a shooting star pausing to check its directions. A moment later, the errant glow dropped and struck Pinnacle Plaza with an incandescent explosion that threw every shadow on the mountain into stark relief and blinded citizens up and down the tiers.

Mannon shrank back from the light, from the pedestal at its epicenter. When the dazzling glare burned away, a Sten stood in the place of an ancient sculpture. He was tall and barrel-chested. Swirling tattoos and beads of sweat covered his slate skin, and his long, blue-gray beard blew in the wind.

In one hand he held a blade of singing steel; the other was clenched in a tight fist. His broad shoulders rose and fell in ragged breaths as he stared in horror where his beloved lay broken and bleeding on the cobbles.

Thane, the Seventh Hero, the Dark Prince, Champion of Al'Thadan and hope of the Sten, turned to face the ancient foe with burning eyes.

"You!" the many faces of Mannon snarled in unison, his dark mass slopping away from the statue and the light that still emanated from Thane's blade.

The Sten raised his sword by way of response, and the Felfather shrank back like a cornered rat. The wind sang through the ruined buildings, and the stone of the mountain itself seemed to thrum in harmony with the blowing storm.

"It doesn't matter!" Mannon drew himself up again, like a swelling wave of darkness and glowing green ichor. His many faces gibbered and snarled as they consumed one another. "Prophecy or not, you cannot defeat me in the heart of my realm! Not against my full power! Not alone!"

Thane considered Mannon, whose malleable shape was marred by countless rends and tears that oozed luminous, chartreuse fluid. His middle was split so wide that he could no longer stand, and instead his remaining large tentacles dragged his bulk after him. Even as the Felfather reared up, corpulent globs of ooze dripped from his bulk and spattered on the cobblestones.

"You don't look like you possess your full power." The Sten nodded at Mannon's wounds, then paused. He cocked his head to the side, listening.

"What are you—?" Mannon began, but then his faces froze in horror.

The wind still howled and the stone still thrummed with latent power, but the song in the air was more than just a harmonic coincidence of natural sounds. Behind the Seventh Hero, the All Mother's voice lifted to join a chorus echoing from somewhere behind Mannon. The demon's faces wailed, but their discordant voices were swept away in the rising melody.

Thane smiled. Blue light was spreading over him now, tracing the spiral patterns of his tattoos and the curved edge of his blade. His whisper thundered over the mountain. "And I am not alone."

Gorm Ingerson felt the music before he heard it.

At times in his life, usually when he thought himself near its end, Gorm had become conscious of the pounding of his own heart, or the flow of air in and out of his lungs. This song was the same sound; the music had always been there—always been a part of everything—but now in the darkness it welled up in his bones and hummed in his throat and rang in his ears, sending tears streaming down his cheeks.

He opened his eyes and saw a glowmoth flapping through infinite darkness. Its shimmering blue wings flashed in the light of its bioluminescent belly as it danced before Gorm's face. When it saw him staring at it, it fluttered a short distance away and came to rest on an old Dwarf dressed in simple robes. He held a candle that sparked to life as more glowmoths lit up around him. The old man reminded Gorm of the shrines set on the deep roads beneath the Ironbreaker Mountains, each bearing an icon of the god of light in dark places.

"Fulgen?" Gorm asked.

Fulgen smiled at Gorm, and opened his mouth as if to answer. He took a short breath, as if unused to speaking and unsure what to say. And then, without warning, the Silent Underglow roared.

The sound washed over Gorm, burning like fire and blinding like light, and part of him wanted it to stop but the other part of him was roaring, or rather singing, adding his voice to the song that had always been there, that would always be there.

When Gorm's eyes snapped open, he saw Kaitha rising in front of him. Not standing, but rising into the air on currents of green fire and blue sorcery. The Dwarf looked down and saw that he was borne on similar strands of magic, weaving and dancing to the all-encompassing tune. The magic turned him around and gently set him down on the shattered cobblestones. When he stepped forward, he was near a tall Sten carrying a gleaming blade. Opposite him, Kaitha stepped into place. Beyond her, more figures were walking into the middle of the Pinnacle. Gorm recognized many of the figures as the marble sculptures they'd left in Kulxak's lair, animated by the streams of enchanted water flowing through their joints and over their smooth surfaces. But the others...

Jynn and Laruna's faces were familiar, but their robes were unlike any he'd ever seen. Laruna wore the searing light of the midday sun, lit by a brilliance that never touched the omnimancer walking beside her. Jynn's garments were the blue-gray of a lake at twilight, and they reflected a gibbous moon from a different sky. In one hand he held the Wyrmwood Staff; the other was intertwined with Laruna's fingers. Behind them, Gaist glided across the cobbles, his cloak as black and shifting as a shadow. Three ghostly lanterns hovered above his head like a foxfire banner. Heraldin brought up the rear, holding an unremarkable wooden staff and wearing a scowl that suggested he was aware of the discrepancy in ordained armaments.

Mannon snarled in every direction as the figures walked past him, shrinking back like a rat from a flame. All of his faces glared at the adventurers and the shimmering figures standing beyond them. "You can't be here!" several of his grotesque mouths chorused. "You can't!"

Yet they were. The Heroes of Destiny took up positions around the Sten in the center of the plaza, glowing water rushing around their feet. Gorm looked down and found the ensorcelled currents flowing around his own boots, and saw that the streams were connecting him with his old companions to form a perfect circle. Once the ring closed, new luminant tributaries split from the ring beneath the heroes and rushed to the center. The azure glow swirled around the Dark Prince and flowed back out to the heroes, so that he stood at the center of a great, glowing wagon wheel, with one hero standing at each of the spokes. A symbol Gorm recognized instantly.

"There weren't enough!" screeched Mannon. "It can't be the prophecy!"

His foul breath was wasted. Destiny flows like a river, running across the rough and uneven horizons of possibility. Its flows join and split as they make their way through time, but when probability and prophecy channel enough fates together, it becomes as unstoppable as a flash flood tumbling through a canyon.

Mannon fought back. His thick tentacles whipped in vicious arcs, sending horrible, leering faces screaming toward the heroes. Other faces detached themselves from his viscid mass and scuttled forward on thorny legs. A face like an oil-drenched vulture emerged to consume Mannon's dominant visage, its beak opening in five different directions to swallow its predecessor. Three crowns of black iron perched upon its head, a yellow flame hanging in the air above each one. It opened its star-like mouth to loose an ear-shattering scream, and choked on the silver shaft of an arrow protruding from its mouth.

The being that was both Al'Matra and Kaitha nocked another arrow as she darted over the broken stones. The Felfather's tentacles swatted at her, but they may as well have tried to catch the wind. She leapt and danced as she dodged away, and another volley of her arrows found their marks in several of Mannon's free-roaming, ambulatory heads.

The shots cleared a path for Heraldin as he danced over the battlefield. Flames billowed from his staff wherever it struck, whether he was bashing one of the faces pursuing him or planting the staff into the cobbles to vault over incoming strikes. He supplemented these bursts of fire with a barrage of glass spheres that exploded into clouds of brilliant smoke, choking and blinding the foe until he was away.

The smoke also concealed the shadow that was Gaist. The weaponsmaster emerged from the mists in flashes of steel and crimson silk. He sliced limbs and screeching faces from the black morass of evil, then melted back into the shadows before the severed blobs splattered against the cobblestones. His blades burned with a ghostly light during their brief appearances, and the wounds they left in Mannon's side glowed like heated metal.

These smoldering wounds marked targets for Jynn and Laruna's sorcerous strikes. The mages stood at the outer edge of the battlefield, launching spells into the fray. Encroaching tentacles and creeping heads groped toward the spellcasters, but sending swarms of expendable troops to battle a pyromancer is as effective as using snowballs to hunt a Flame Drake. Laruna seared Mannon's progeny to a screaming crisp with one hand, while her other clasped Jynn's palm and channeled power into the balls of fire and shadow he wove. The omnimancer's potent spells bloomed into flame wherever they slammed into Mannon, and as they burned away they left violet hooks of shadow embedded in his viscous flesh. These sorcerous hooks seemed to hamper Mannon's motion, as though tethering him to the stone, and his movements became slow and uneven as the barrage continued.

Sluggish movements and uneven strikes are fatal mistakes, and Mannon paid for every one. Gorm Ingerson sang through the air all around the demon lord, his axes carving through tentacles and sending spouts of glowing green gore skyward. He felt something like the berserker's rage, but there was no red mist, only the music. Its rhythm pulsed in Gorm's heartbeat, his muscles vibrated with every chord, and his axe struck with the rhythm. Gorm's onslaught reached its crescendo in time with creation's symphony, just as Thane reached Mannon's dominant head.

Flashes of desperation played over Mannon's faces as he tried to stop the Seventh Hero's advance. A tentacle like an oak tree swung at the Sten, its faces' opening maws filled with oily teeth. Thane's blade flashed, a stench of ozone filled the air, and the limb fell wailing into a limp puddle. The tattoos on the Dark Prince's skin glowed with power and anticipation, and his eyes burned with raw fury.

In the face of such an onslaught, Mannon fled.

He didn't get far.

The Felfather convulsed and shook in a manner that suggested he was trying to fly away and shrink into nothing at the same time. A moment later, his amorphous bulk splattered back onto the ground. "What?" his mouths shrieked as he convulsed again, but this time Gorm could see the hooks of shadow embedded in his flesh glow more brightly as Mannon strained against them. The sorcerous tethers held and dragged Mannon back to the ground with a wet thud. His manifold eyes flashed with budding horror, and then they all rotated to stare at the omnimancer across the plaza.

"I first saw that binding when my father tried to pull you from Johan," Jynn called. "Later, I found I could even kill a demon when it is so restrained. I doubt that even you have a way to leave the mortal planes now."

Laruna grinned wickedly. "Although, there's always the standard route. The one that mortals use all the time."

"Wait!" Mannon cried with a cyclopean face. Several of his smaller heads echoed the plea. "Wait! We can make a deal!"

Gaist emerged from a cloud of turquoise smoke, his hard eyes set in a way that said that heroes did not, as a matter of policy, negotiate with interdimensional manifestations of evil, and that even if they were open to such discussions, the current conflict was too far along for a peaceable resolution. It was a very succinct and effective facial expression, and the other heroes let it speak for them as they advanced.

"You don't know what you're doing!" Mannon wailed. "I gave you all of this! People prospered! Other evils will rise up in my absence—far worse for you! Far worse!"

Yet the foretold time had come. Thane raised his blade and charged, and the other Heroes of Destiny followed. For a pristine moment, crystallized in Gorm's memory forever, they were a force of good protecting the innocent by slaying evil.

Then blades and arrows and spells struck deep into Mannon's wounded flesh with the force of ages. The cuts and gashes along his slimy body flared with searing light, and the world disappeared in a brilliant flash.

The goddess' power receded from Kaitha like the outgoing tide, leaving her coughing and sputtering in the sun. A thin blanket was beneath her, but the cold of the cobblestones beneath it cut through the fabric. She tried to open her eyes, then quickly squeezed them shut again in the sudden glare of the winter sun. Someone placed a mug of warm water in her hand, and she drank it eagerly.

"Glad to see you're up," said a friendly voice. Kaitha blinked a few times, and her blurred vision resolved itself into a plump Dwerrow wearing the white and red robes of a medic among the bannermen. She was one of several overseeing a triage camp set up next to the smoldering ruins of Bugbeary Limited. Most of the other makeshift cots were empty. Only a few wounded heroes still lay convalescing in the sun.

The medic noticed her glance. "Oh, the only ones of you lot left are the ones with your, ah, sense of fashion." The Dwerrow tapped her wrist, and Kaitha glanced down at her sobriety bracelet. "Anyone able to take a draught of salve is already up and on their way."

A sudden thought cut through the haze in Kaitha's head like a sunbeam through the clouds. "Gorm?" she croaked. "Laruna? The others?"

"Oh, your party is fine, Miss Kaitha. Have some more water, dear," said the medic, and waited until the ranger was drinking to continue. "All your fellows are out helpin' with the clean up, and I'm sure there will be paperwork after that. You can join them once you've rested up. The whole city is talkin' about this one. Ha! They'll be talkin' about it on the far continents by next week!"

Kaitha was only half listening. Memories streamed through her mind; she could recall entering the chamber beneath the mountain perfectly, yet when the goddess had come upon her, everything became clouded and confusing. She could only catch glimpses of the exploding temple, and fighting alongside Gorm, and Jynn taunting an ancient evil, and...

The mug slipped from Kaitha's hand and cracked on the cobblestones.

"Miss Kaitha? Are you all right? No, sit back down! You can join your friends once you—Miss Kaitha! You need rest!"

Yet the ranger was already walking out of the medic's camp, her eyes locked on the rubble of a boutique armorer across the plaza. Fjordstorm Pinnacle looked like it had been hit by a siege weapon, and now several people searched through the rubble. Gorm was one of them, and also Heraldin, and a one-eyed woman who seemed familiar, but all of Kaitha's attention was focused on the tall figure in their center.

He was built like a bear, with a thick beard that spilled down over a chest like an oak cask. He leapt with limber grace when Gorm shouted to him, but had the strength to lift a thick beam and cast it aside like a child tossing a stick. When he reached into the wreckage and helped a dazed Mr. Brunt to his feet, he was only a head shorter than the Ogre, yet somehow he seemed bigger. And when Gorm saw the Elf and said her name, the Sten turned around with a smile that outshone the dawn. He slapped Mr. Brunt on the shoulder and remitted him to the care of the one-eyed woman, then bounded over the ruined timbers toward Kaitha. He stopped short after hopping down from the wreckage onto the cobblestones, and for a moment it looked like he might jump back up into the rubble.

He didn't, though. The Sten took a deep breath, ran a meaty hand through his hair, and spoke as she approached. "Ah, hello Kaitha," he said in a voice as deep as a mountain's roots. "My name is Thane."

She stared at him with a gazer's focus, as if her eyes could peel off this new facade and see beneath his skin with enough intensity. He looked different from... well, from anyone who had walked on Arth in the last five ages. But there was something familiar in his smile, something that she could feel rather than see.

"Uh, I know... I—I think you know me. We've met. In a way," the Sten stuttered a bit as the Elf drew closer to him, and worry flashed in his eyes before he remembered his next line. "B-but I'd like to get to know you better. Would you care to join me for tea?"

Kaitha squinted at the tattoos on his exposed arms. There was something familiar about the spiral tattoos that cascaded over his muscles, a pattern reminiscent of the fur she'd seen on a dying Troll beneath Wynspar.

"I'll buy the tea," Thane added hurriedly. "I know a nice place. Spelljammer's. It's right over... uh..." Thane's voice faltered as his eyes fell on the smoldering ruins of Spelljammer's Cafe.

"Aha, that's unfortunate. Still, I've heard the Astral Plate is... is..." The Sten turned to the other end of the Pinnacle, where a team of Academy mages were working to extinguish the fire that still raged through the wreckage of the Astral Plate.

"Well, maybe Sigil's could—oh no..." The panic in Thane's voice bloomed into despair as he turned to the smoking crater where Sigil's had been. Words failed him entirely as he turned to the Restored Tambour, which would need to be restored again before anyone could walk inside, let alone order tea there.

"Is there nowhere to get a cup of tea!?" Thane cried, hands on his head. "Or a coffee!? Anywhere I could heat some water and put some leaves in it!? I just can't believe... I need... uh..." The Sten's lament fell silent as he caught Kaitha's gaze, and he smiled as he remembered himself.

Kaitha studied his eyes as she drew close. They were the same; faceted amber orbs flecked with crimson, like a sunrise.

"Maybe lunch?" Thane ventured.

But by that point, he was within reach. Kaitha seized the braids of his beard and pulled him into a kiss that somehow exceeded every expectation.

——CHAPTER 35——

orm rolled his eyes and looked away once the kissing started.

He'd watched Thane and Kaitha meet with a grin on his face, wondering what they'd finally say to each other after overcoming dungeons and death and an evil from beyond time. As it turned out, nothing. The Sten just asked the Elf for a date, and then she latched onto his face like a leaping swamp leech. Jynn and Laruna had done pretty much the same thing once Mannon was dead and gone. Now the mages had run off somewhere, and he knew better than to go looking.

Grumbling inwardly about the perpetual indecency of tall folk, the Dwarf turned his attention back to the rescue at hand. Heraldin and Gaist were still tending to Mr. Brunt and his party, though their discussion had oddly turned from relief at finding the Ogre mostly unharmed to concern over his wardrobe.

"You need to get rid of that, Brunt." Magriss pointed up at the Ogre's head. "It's not an accessory. It's dangerous."

Brunt rumbled something unintelligible, but also clearly uncooperative.

"It's beyond dangerous," said Heraldin.

"He's taken a shinin' to it," said a Scribkin engineer. "He likes it now."

"Burn what he likes!" snarled Heraldin. "It's—"

Brunt rumbled again, like a volcano about to evict the local villagers.

"It's something we should reconsider," Heraldin finished with considerably less force.

Gorm walked around the Ogre, trying to get a better view of the subject of controversy. His eyes caught the twisted piece of black iron in the Ogre's ear just as a psychic imperative rolled into his mind.

Hey! Get me down! Brunt's earring shouted in Gorm's head.

An iron hook hung from the Ogre's cauliflower earlobe, with the crossbar of the hook wedged through one of Brunt's piercings and the sharp crescent of the hook dangling. The ends of the crossbar waved about like iron worms in a futile struggle to wiggle out from Brunt's flesh.

Gorm squinted up at the protesting jewelry. "Is that—"

"Who else would it be?" Heraldin said, glowering. "How many sentient hooks are there?"

A vision of a criminal mind, or really anything approaching an average one, in Brunt's body brought a scowl to Gorm's face. "So is he—?"

"No," said Heraldin, shaking his head. "Mr. Brunt seems... resistant to Benny's command."

This idiot has a mind like a greased slug! Benny Hookhand wailed. The tendrils of iron flexed suddenly, and a palpable sense of exertion filled the air.

Brunt loosed a thunder of short, staccato booms. It took Gorm a moment to realize it was laughter.

A few seconds later, the hook went limp. *I can't get a grip on it. I can't even tell if he hears me!*

Gorm grinned. "Looks like Benny finally met his match."

"Mr. Flinn did as well, they way they tell it." Heraldin shrugged. "He still can't—uh—shouldn't keep the Hookhand. Benny is a menace."

"Who's going to take him away?" Gorm asked.

Anyone! Benny snarled, waving his iron tendrils anew. *Someone get me down!*

"Tickles!" Brunt's face, which had been perpetually set into a vacant scowl every time Gorm had seen the Ogre, twitched under the strain of reconfiguring itself into a broad grin.

"Still, I've never seen Brunt so happy," said Magriss thoughtfully.

"It doesn't matter how he feels," Heraldin insisted. "You can't wear a sentient weapon as jewelry!"

"Fashion... forward!" said Mr. Brunt.

"I suppose that's up to the authorities," Gorm said with a grin.

"Ah, that's the trick," said one of the adventurers with Brunt. "What authorities? The king and queen are dead. There's no clear line of succession."

"No line of—gods, it'll take months to sort out," Gorm said, again inwardly cursing the senseless tall folk once again. In Dwarven society, every Dwarf knew his place in the line of succession, from a king's sons down to the lowest beggar on the street. There were constant squabbles over such rankings, of course, but they were handled well in advance of the king's death. The Dwarven system led to a lot of extra conflict over scenarios that would never come to pass, and it could make family meals very awkward, but it also eliminated any uncertainty in times of transition. "This could mean war among the nobles and houses."

Someone tapped Gorm on the shoulder. He turned to find Gaist pointing at the Heroes' Guild field arbitration station near the palace gates. A large cluster of oak folding tables were set up for guild clerks and arbiters to process the mountains of treasure scattered about the palace, but currently the paperwork seemed to be on hold. A large group of people standing around the station were engaged in a heated debate with several statues.

The Stennish walking sculptures were still ambulatory and, now that they had stopped singing in harmony with the universe, were also capable of speaking in Root Elven. Gorm hadn't understood a word the statues said when he thanked them, but now that some Elves had been located to translate for the sculptures, people seemed to wish they were quiet again.

"It seems like Andarun's old tenants have something to say about that," Heraldin said.

"Looks like things are gettin' complicated," grumbled Gorm.

Gaist nodded as they headed for the scrum.

To their credit, Jynn and Laruna were amid the gathering, though it was unclear whether they were more interested in contributing to the discussion or studying the Stennish sculptures.

"What they are saying," Laruna said loudly, "is that there is no basis in today's laws for your proposal."

This was relayed by an Elven hero to the sculptures, who spoke amidst each other in a tongue Gorm had never heard before. Eventually, the foremost of the stone Sten turned back to the gathered lawyers, clerks, nobles, and heroes. The marble woman wore her ivory hair in an ornate braided bun, and the eddies and currents of glowing water running over her stone body suggested the same swirling patterns tattooed on Thane's gray skin. She spoke in a reedy, flowing language that sounded like Elvish, and as she did the water around her eyes and throat flared with extra light, like a beacon sending out sailor's code.

"Uh," the Elf said, "she says that he is still the rightful king. They're being very forceful about it."

The crowd grumbled at the announcement. "The nobility will not stand for this!" snapped a Human wearing a conglomeration of tights, ruffs, and frills that had to be expensive; only the very rich could afford to look so ridiculous. "House Gedral least of all!"

"Golems are not people in the eyes of the law," stated a lawyer-monk flatly. "As such, this opinion is of no consequence."

"Yes, exactly!" shouted the presumable lord of House Gedral. The crowd muttered in agreement.

"These aren't golems." Jynn corrected the lawyer as he peered closely at the nearest specimen. "They're phylactoric mobile constructs fulfilling a preordained function in the lower theurgosphere."

The crowd stared at the archmage with the mute apprehension of people who know they've heard something important but have no idea what it is.

Jynn sighed. "What I mean is that these are the reanimated essences of the last of the Sten. They've sent themselves through space and time using prophetic manipulation and carved vessels."

"Not golems, then?" ventured a knight.

"They have souls," growled Laruna. "Not golems. Souls."

"Ah, they're the undead, then!" said a guild clerk. "And the dead don't have rights. Right?"

All eyes swiveled back to the lawyer-monks, who hunkered down in fervent consultation. Eventually one raised a hooded head. "Settled law holds that some rights are held in perpetuity or reinstated upon rematerialization on the mortal plane."

"See Scoria v. Dead Lord Mordun in 7.314," intoned another monk.

"It doesn't matter!" snapped Lord Gedral. "We don't have to listen to these walking rocks! They'll stand down or my armies will—"

The threat in the noble's voice was strong enough to crash through the language barrier, and in reply all seven of the walking sculptures turned their baleful stares on him in unison. Their eyes crackled with sudden, crimson energy, and a high-pitched whine filled the air. The noble deflated in the face of impending vaporization, his jaw slack and his ruff drooping.

"They really are very forceful about it," said the translating Elf.

"Forceful about what?" whispered a low voice in Gorm's ear.

"Gah!" Gorm burst out, leaping back. "Don't sneak up on me like that!"

"It's a bit of a habit." Thane grinned apologetically as he stood up straight.

"What is everyone arguing about?" asked Kaitha, leaning against the Sten's arm.

"And why are they all looking at me?" Thane muttered out of the side of his mouth. All eyes were on the Dark Prince, including the fading red gazes of the Stennish sculptures.

Gorm smiled up at his friend. "They want to make ye king, lad."

Thane's face fell. "They want to... what?"

One of the Sten interjected in Elven, and the translator obliged. "Uh, he says that Thane Thrice-Born is already king. He always was. It was written in the loom when his, uh, stone vessel was prepared, and now... now he and his line are high kings of the land."

"Right, but dead people writing on rocks is no basis for a system of government," said the guild clerk.

Another sculpture spoke up.

"She says it's his birthright," said the Elven translator.

"Birthright? Who cares about who begat who?" demanded the clerk. "There's got to be a better way to determine who runs things!"

"Now, hang on—" began Lord Gedral, doubtlessly the latest in a long streak of begetting.

"No, he's right," said a guild arbiter. "A king needs to be familiar with how things work. An expert on the law, and diplomacy, and economics. A figure who can inspire the masses and manage the powerful. And we're just supposed to believe that this fellow who popped out of some rock is going to be good at all of that?"

"I'm not!" Thane's eyes had a hunted look, and he glanced around like a cornered animal trying to find some means of escape. "I'm not good at any of those things!"

"I, for one, am not going to be ruled by some reanimated statue," said Lord Gedral.

Gorm didn't spend much time around the nobility, but it didn't take much to see where this was going. He took his axe from his belt and grabbed a rag from the nearby wreckage.

"We don't even know where he came from!" interjected a noblewoman. "He could be a demon himself, for all we know."

"He's not a demon!" Laruna shot back. "He used to be a Troll!"

A collective gasp from the crowd suggested that this was not an effective argument.

"Hardly any better!" sneered Lord Gedral. "We can't be governed by someone whose only work experience is living as a monster in the wilderness. Gods, he must have been practically raised by wolves!"

"Wolves were afraid of me!" Thane's voice had risen to a panicked pitch, despite Kaitha's best attempts to calm him.

"Indeed. Hardly a fit ruler!" snapped Lord Gedral.

"So who else?" asked Gorm quietly, polishing his axe.

The crowd fell silent.

Lord Gedral took a moment to straighten his ruff and adopt a humble facade. "Well, ahem, I'm sure that a suitable noble of good pedigree and means could be found."

"I'm sure ye could find enough to fill the palace courtyard. That's the problem, ain't it?" Gorm checked his reflection in the steel of his Orc-forged axe-head. "It'd be a war for sure, assumin' any of ye survive war with the Sten there. Though given what their magic did to the King of Demons and the entire plaza in an afternoon, I don't like your odds."

The crowd looked back to Lord Gedral, whose eyes were locked on the statues and their Elven translator. The noble's mouth opened and closed wordlessly, like some frilly tropical fish pulled from the Teagem Sea.

"Maybe ye'd prevail. Maybe one of ye would be king next. But I doubt there'd be much of a Freedlands left to rule over. I doubt the guilds and banks and all the rest will stand for that. A poor king is certainly bad, but most businesses I know will take a bad certainty over a big, dangerous unknown."

The clerks and lawyers in the crowd began to nod and mutter. Even the less ambitious nobles looked thoughtful.

Deep furrows knit Thane's brows as he stared down at Gorm. "What are you saying, Gorm? I don't... I don't want this."

"I'm sorry, lad—er, Your Majesty," Gorm corrected himself. "Nobody wants it. But what a king needs most of all is legitimacy, and ye've more of that than anyone else. Without ye on the throne, we may lose all the lives we just fought to save."

Thane looked at Kaitha, and then the crowd, and then the bard stepping forward.

"Thane, my friend, if I may... have you considered a regency?" Heraldin asked.

"A what?" Thane eyes lit up with hope.

"If you were to appoint a trusted regent, he or she could rule in your stead while you learn more about the role," the bard went on. "You'd still be king, of course, but the actual governance could be handled by someone more... experienced until you feel ready to take up the mantle."

"Ad hoc administration formed for the indefinite interregnum," said a lawyer-monk. "It sounds legally defensible."

The statues conferred as well, and eventually delivered a statement through their translator. "The Sten would accept that arrangement."

"You see?" Heraldin grinned up at Thane. "You don't need to understand the law or diplomacy or business. You just need someone you trust who does."

Thane thought for a moment, and then broke into a wide grin.

When it was over and done, Duine Poldo surveyed the carnage.

The Wall was littered with the wreckage of business on an epic scale. Broken quills and empty ink pots littered the ground. Loose sheets of parchment blew across the Wall. Poldo himself was sitting on a briefcase sized for an Orc or Elf that had been abandoned to the flagstones amidst the melee. Dazed clerks staggered about, trying to make sense of what had just happened. A few interns and low-level employees folded up the last of the temporary trading desks, but most of the brokers and day traders had fled to the bars and taverns along the Broad Steps to mourn their losses and drown their sorrows.

A young Halfling in a rumpled suit staggered across Poldo's path and looked at the Scribkin with bleary eyes. "Did... did we win?"

Poldo sighed and looked up at the Wood Gnome's slate swaying forlornly in the wind. The white chalk line had filled about four-fifths of the bar. "We gave the economy a chance to survive, but almost a fifth of Andarun's wealth is still in a fund that is now worthless. It's like the gold just evaporated. Many workers just lost their jobs, or pensioners their funds. They just don't know it yet." He sighed heavily and shook his head. "There are no winners on a day like today."

An enthusiastic whoop rang out further up the Wall, followed by ringing laughter.

"There are few winners on a day like today," Poldo corrected himself as he turned to look at the leadership of Warg Incorporated.

The Shadowkin stood in a circle some distance away. Someone had carried in a massive keg of Orcish grog, and the senior leaders sipped it from elegant gazelle horns as they celebrated their massive gains. What had been a rout for Andarun's established business community had been a triumph for Asherzu and her team. With a portfolio untainted by the dragon's hoard and a near monopoly on the transaction fees from the largest sell-off in history, Warg had become one of the wealthiest banks on Arth over the course of the afternoon.

Poldo saw the chieftain raise a toast to Feista Hrurk, and another celebratory cry went up. A small smile crossed the Gnome's weary face. "It will be all right," he said as Mrs. Hrurk raised her own glass. He noticed her tail tucked between her legs in embarrassment.

"Yeah," said the Halfling. "But I was asking if they killed King Johan? There was all that screaming and the strange lights up on the Pinnacle."

"Oh. I'm sure," Poldo said. "It's usually loud and messy, but some hero inevitably gets the job done. If they hadn't, I doubt we'd still be here. All that's left now is to see what it cost us. The cost... the cost was so high..."

"You financed the expedition?" asked the young broker.

"No." Poldo's shoulders sagged. His thoughts drifted back to Thane, and the future they might have made in Mistkeep. The Halfling mercifully hurried along, and Poldo cradled his head in his hands and wept.

A while later, Mrs. Hrurk sat down next to him on the briefcase, and improper as it was, took his hand in her paw. Poldo rested his head on her shoulder and let the tears flow. He wasn't sure how long he sat there, leaning on the Gnoll and wrestling with grief. Eventually, his memories were interrupted by the clip of footsteps on stone.

"Mr. Duine Poldo?" asked a nasal voice.

"Another time," said Mrs. Hrurk, shooing the interloper away.

Yet the visitor would not be deterred. "I found him!" the man shouted. Poldo opened his eyes to see a young clerk from the Heroes' Guild jumping and waving.

"No, you haven't," growled Mrs. Hrurk. "Let the poor man rest."

"Sorry, ma'am," said the clerk. "I'm on orders from the king."

Poldo looked up with a start. "I thought the king was dead."

"Well, yes, the old king. And the new king was too, they say. But only for a while, and he's better now." The clerk paused, his lips moving as he walked back through that scenario. "It's complicated, sir. But there is, in fact, a king, and he's called for you."

"Young man, I do not have much patience for this," Poldo said wearily. "It has been a very long day, and I just lost a dear friend."

Then Gorm Ingerson eclipsed the clerk, grinning ear to ear and offering the Gnome a hand up. "Aye, about that last bit," said the Dwarf. "I've got good news."

There was a reunion of the very best sort; both unexpected and joyous, where the only tears were of joy and the laughter flowed freely. Friends who had thought their goodbyes were final, found each other whole and hale. Insurmountable challenges had been surmounted. A future that had seemed impossible was here, and with everyone together to see it.

It was followed by a coronation of the very worst sort, both frenetic and confused, where nothing was planned and there was no precedent to cite. The new king was awkward and unsure; he ducked under arches and doorways that were far above his head, and often crouched down as if he could shrink into the background entirely. He would only address the attendees with frequent reassurances from friends and ancient guardians, and even then his words were punctuated with fits of hyperventilation and mild panic attacks. Nobles seethed and businesses fretted at the timid oration; the city was already reeling from the financial ruin wrought by the Dragon of Wynspar's plunder fund evaporating and the loss of two monarchs, and sentiment was not helped by the dragon herself emerging from the mountain to attend the ceremony. The future was uncertain and terrifying once more.

Yet then came a ceremony of a completely new kind. Andarun's history had few regencies, and never a voluntary one. The new king entrusted his authority to a Scribkin trailed by a swarm of Domovoy in tiny suits. The new regent gave a perfunctory speech outlining his top priorities for the city, and his diminutive cohort set about executing them before he had walked off the stage. The gears of governance ground back into motion.

Jynn Ur'Mayan and Laruna Trullon watched history flow by from the side of the makeshift stage, seated together on a mostly intact bench. His arm was wrapped around her shoulders, and she idly played with his fingers. "What happens now?" the archmage asked, watching a gaggle of Wood Gnomes skitter past.

"I suppose we rebuild what was broken," the pyromancer said. "It will take time, and hard work, but I know we can come back from all of this stronger than ever."

Jynn gave her a wry smile. "I was talking about what happens next for you and me."

Laruna grinned back at him. "Me too."

——CHAPTER 36——

Time passed.

By Dewen's month, the Palace of Andarun had been restored enough for royal audiences to resume. New banners hung from the walls, alternating purple and gold with green and silver—a gift from the newly reopened Temple of Al'Thadan and Al'Matra United. A new royal throne with enough height and heft to accommodate a Sten sat at the top of the royal podium, carved from finest ebony and inlaid with gold and precious stones. It was, of course, more a symbol than a seat, as it was always empty. At the base of the steps was a much smaller chair, set behind a simple but well-made desk. A chair fit for a regent. It was also usually empty, as Duine Poldo preferred to work in a small office in the western tower of the palace. The room had a magnificent window, originally made for Princess Xandra the Fifth in the Sixth Age, offering an unparalleled view of Pinnacle Plaza and the city beyond it.

Poldo stared out the window as he listened with waning patience to the latest petitioners pleading their case. "I understand your concerns, gentlemen," he said at length. "But as I have said, I am confident that your institution has the reserves to survive the battering it received in this winter's volatility without tax relief. The executive bonus pool, for example, doubtlessly has some available funds in it."

Fenrir Goldson's eyelid twitched, but otherwise he and Bolbi Baggs maintained their composure. "Indeed, sir," said the ancient Dwarf.

Baggs made an obsequious gesture with a gloved hand. "However, that alone will hardly—"

"Yes, I realize," Poldo cut him off. "Still, I know that if there is anything to stand on at Goldson Baggs Incorporated, it's the creativity of your accountants. I remain certain you will find a way to survive. Unemployment is at near-historic levels, new job creation is down, and even those who work cannot make enough to make ends meet. The kingdom's coffers have been pillaged—quite literally—and all that remains within them are the funds that we taxed back from the guild and beneficiaries of Johan's quest. And in such dire times, influence of nefarious groups such as the Red Horde or the Power of Light grows. We are working through a convergence of crises, and the kingdom's aid must go to those with the greatest need."

"As you say, Regent," Baggs said through a grin. Poldo thought he heard the old Halfling's teeth grinding.

"And now, gentlemen, I'm sure you are as busy as I am. I have an appointment at the Heroes' Guild before the ceremony this afternoon. Perhaps I will see you at the unveiling."

"Ah, I should hope so," said Mr. Goldson. "But before we go, there was another matter we hoped to discuss..."

"Oh?" Poldo feigned surprise as he glanced over his planner. "I don't see anything else on my agenda."

"Ah, we must have left it off our petition," said Baggs. "Careless."

"Regardless," said Goldson smoothly, "as we are here, we hoped to discuss the inquiry into our company regarding the Elven Marbles and the unfortunate business at Bloodroot."

"It really is getting silly," said Baggs. "The town criers are suggesting that there may be criminal charges in a business matter! Ridiculous!"

Poldo took a deep breath. The topic was as predictable as gravity; in corporate physics, every action has an equal and opposite effort to avoid consequences. "Ah, I am sorry, gentlemen, but you must realize that I cannot discuss an ongoing investigation with any member of the public, let alone two affected parties. General Gurgen will doubtlessly make you aware of the bannermen's findings once they're ready."

"Oh, we wouldn't dream of talking about the particulars," said Mr. Goldson. "We just wanted to discuss the principle of the thing."

"While we certainly share in the sorrow for the unfortunate demise of the Orcs of Bloodroot, this inquiry does more harm than good. Probing into the past only prevents healing," simpered Mr. Baggs.

"Not so much as letting the responsible parties go without consequence." Poldo stood and retrieved his long coat from a hook next to his desk.

"An interesting philosophical point," said Mr. Baggs. "Perhaps we could discuss it over dinner?"

"I'm afraid not, gentlemen," Poldo replied brusquely. "I welcome your input as much as any other citizen's, but all of our communications must happen through official petitions and follow regular procedure. To do otherwise might create the appearance of impropriety. And now, gentlemen, I really must be along. The royal guard will show you out." A few Wood Gnomes darted off to fetch the bannerman at a nod from the Scribkin.

For the first time, cracks appeared in the calm facade of the two bankers as they exchanged nervous glances. "Uh, Mr. Poldo," Baggs ventured. "I appreciate the need to maintain appearances, but since Handor's days our firm has enjoyed a... ahem... special relationship with the crown."

Poldo turned to the magnificent window and gazed out over the city, trying to hide a smirk that he couldn't restrain. "Indeed you did, gentlemen," he said, clasping his hands behind his back. "But I've solved that."

"*Lady, I bring ill news,*" said Ugmak of the Zabbagar. The wise-one wore a long mustache that denoted his caste and seniority, and a well-fitted suit that denoted his recent promotion to middle management.

Asherzu Guz'Varda grimaced. Below her, charts and spreadsheets were splayed across her mahogany desk, held in place by paperweights made from the skulls of her father's enemies. "*Speak,*" she said.

"*It is the Red Horde, lady,*" said the wise-one. "*They have refused our entreaties for, uh, a short time for rest between our fights.*"

"*For* peace." Asherzu emphasized the Imperial word.

"Yes. That," said Ugmak, whose grasp of Lightling tongues was still limited.

Asherzu stood and walked to her office window as she considered the message. *"And did they say why they rejected our offer?"*

Ugmak faltered a bit. *"They say... they say that you have become as a Lightling, my chieftain. That you are unwilling to do what must be done to bring back the ways of our people. They dishonor themselves with such careless slander,"* he added hurriedly.

Asherzu allowed herself a small smile. "Necessity is most subjective, is it not?" she said, switching to the Imperial language.

"Lady?" asked Ugmak, uncertain of what she'd said.

Asherzu thought about translating, but shook off the idea. Shadowtongue had no word for a subjective idea; the closest it came was *labbo ri'zabbadad*, or the reason for a war yet to be fought. Yet subjectivity was a wonderful concept, as were peace treaties, and trials that weren't by combat, and corporations. For all the pain and suffering they caused, Lightlings were also the source of so many fantastic ideas. As were all peoples, Asherzu reflected. Fulgen taught that every soul held the capacity for works of evil and destruction, but also the seeds of beauty and creation. Anyone's path to lasting glory led them to stand against the vile within and work to foster the good throughout.

She watched the river of people flow below her window. Two figures stood out like great boulders among the rapids; Darak had taken the afternoon off to court Gizardu the Mountain. In the days of her childhood, wooing an Orcess of Gizardu's power would have meant traveling together to slay a great foe or raid a village. Instead, Asherzu's brother was bringing Gizardu down to the Second Tier for a kebab and grog. Asherzu grinned at the thought of nieces and nephews in years to come.

Ugmak cleared his throat behind her. *"Chieftain, what must I do?"*

"Tell me of your approach as you met with the Red Horde."

"We told them of our desire to reconcile the tribes, and entreated them to see that our people divided are weaker than we are together, and told them we were willing to work for a short time for rest between fights."

"Ah," said Asherzu. *"That would be the problem."*

Few of her people truly understood the path of the aggressive seller. Some believed that the path took their kin far from the Old Ways. Some, like the Red Horde, would call her a coward, soft and weak. They had before, when she grew in her father's shadow, when she kept to his path after his death, and when she took his place. Yet she was still here, and many of her critics had joined her on her path. And at the end of the day, her people went home to fat and happy children each night.

A knock at the door interrupted her thoughts. A Naga receptionist poked his head through the door. "Lady, it isss almossst time for your hot ssstone massssage."

"Ah, good," said Asherzu. "It is most needed today." Massages were another great innovation of the Lightnings. And satin pillows. And chocolate. All three awaited her now, and every night. Such were the perks of the path of the aggressive seller, when you were good at it. And with Warg Incorporated's meteoric rise to market dominance, few would say there were any better than Asherzu Guz'Varda. "Tell Mitsy of the Gentle Hand I will be down shortly."

"And, uh, what of the Red Horde?" asked Ugmak.

Asherzu smiled at the wise-one, then looked back out the window. He was one of those who also misunderstood her way. Ugmak and his ilk thought that the path of the aggressive seller followed the high-minded ideals that Lightling's talked about when they spoke of selfless concern for the greater good, and of the good in all people invariably triumphing when shown a better way. Asherzu would like to walk life's journey in such a world, but she did not. The path of the aggressive seller guided her through this one, where people could be irrational and fearful and greedy, and those impulses often got the better of the good within them.

"Find the mightiest chieftains among the Red Horde. Tell them of the success of Warg Incorporated," she told him, watching the people swirl through the street below their mighty office building. *"Boast of the plunder we took from the Lightlings on the day Johan the Deceiver was slain. Send a drummer to chant the saga of our mighty brokerage, which inspires fear and trembling upon the Lightlings' Wall. And then..."* Asherzu's tusks flashed in a predatory grin. *"And then offer them jobs."*

"Saying goodbye?" Kaitha asked. The curtain whispered as it closed behind her, shutting out the rays of sunlight and noises of Pinnacle Plaza.

Gorm gave her a quick nod of acknowledgement before he turned his gaze back to the statue of Niln. The high scribe was cast in deep blue by the azure tent set up around him. He wore a serene smile, hands clasped behind his back, gazing down benevolently on the cobbles before him.

"They say the statue of Niln moved..." Gorm said, his voice hoarse. "He must have, if this is the same one they hauled up from the ruins of Al'Matra's old temple. The Al'Matrans told me he'd been doin' it for weeks, scarin' the acolytes and all that."

The Elf shrugged. "It's not the most unbelievable thing we saw last year."

"It ain't even in the ten most unbelievable things," said Gorm. He looked at Kaitha with red-rimmed eyes. "But it means that he was here, lass. He was with me—with us—when we went through all this. When I lost my way fighting the liche. All of it. And now..." He shook his head and looked back up at the bronze face of his friend.

"Now he's just a statue and a memory," said Kaitha sadly.

"Aye," said Gorm. "Just like Tib'rin, and Iheen, and all me other friends. And when ye came back after I thought ye died, and Thane turned out to be a soul-bound Sten, I... I guess anything seemed possible. Anyone could come back. And selfish as it is, maybe I thought... I just hoped the rest of 'em could too."

His eyes trailed from the bronze figure of Niln to a smaller, newer statue next to him; a brassy Goblin with a wide smile and a noble dagger. The sculptor had done his best based on Gorm's description, but without the small plaque saying so near its base, nobody would recognize it as Tib'rin Had'Lerdak. "That I might see me old squire again."

Kaitha put a hand on his shoulder, and for a quiet moment they stood and regarded the statues.

"In a way, we are together. Always," the Elf offered eventually. She nodded to the other sculptures grouped behind Tib'rin and Niln. Gorm's own visage stared back at him from behind the Goblin's shoulder, with a grinning Burt leaning out of his rucksack. Laruna and Jynn stood behind them, their hands raised as though weaving spells. Niln was flanked by Heraldin and Gaist, standing back-to-back. Behind them all, elevated on the old plinth that had been the Dark Prince's perch, Kaitha and Thane stood hand in hand. A small plaque in from of them read:

THE SEVEN HEROES OF DESTINY
&
OTHER SAVIORS OF ARTH

"That we are," said Gorm, giving the statue of the Goblin a fond tap on the shoulder. "In many ways."

"In many ways," the ranger agreed as they turned to leave.

Gorm nodded up at the bronze Elf and Sten. "Public artwork must add a bit of pressure to the relationship, eh?"

"Oh, yeah, but that's nothing," said Kaitha, shaking her head. "It's the old Stennish sculptures that are trying to rush things, with all of their talk of rebuilding populations and keeping the lineage going. Gods above. We're not even thinking about the future yet."

"Won't be long, I imagine," Gorm grumbled. "Everything's fast with ye tall folk."

"Don't you start," the Elf warned him.

"What? That's how it usually goes." Gorm pulled the curtain back and let Kaitha walk past him out next to the stage. "Ye and Thane make each other happy, ye know how the other feels, and ye got more history than most Humans who get together."

"The history is the problem," Kaitha said with a shrug. "I always wonder how many of our inexplicable feelings were ours and how many were just an echo of the gods' relationship—a famously rocky relationship, I'll remind you. And now there's destiny and prophecy and governance and everything coming all at once. And yeah, a statue of us doesn't help. It's a lot for a young relationship, and I want to make it work, so we're taking. It. Slow." She emphasized the last point with a finger jabbing into Gorm's mailed shoulder.

"Aye, fine. Fine," laughed Gorm. "But I will say I still have a good feeling about ye two."

Her eyes scanned the people milling about the plaza in advance of the statues' unveiling, and found Thane speaking with several attendants. The king noticed her as well, and gave her a besotted grin and enthusiastic wave. "A very good feeling," she said, waving back. "I'm going to go rescue him from whatever that conversation is."

"Will I see the two of ye before your journey?" he asked.

"Definitely," Kaitha said. "We'll have everyone up to the palace for a sending off."

"I look forward to it," Gorm told her, and then she was away.

Finding himself alone, the Dwarf searched the plaza for familiar faces. Bannermen and royal servants bustled about the stage. Beyond them, crowds of onlookers gathered like thunderheads, drawn by a rare opportunity to see the new king and the rumors that his speeches tended to be a spectacle. Jynn and Laruna sat with delegations from all three orders of the Academy of Mages. The assembled spellcasters were engaged in a heated discussion about some doubtlessly obscure and arcane matter, and so when his friends waved him over, he shook his head apologetically and feigned an urgent need to walk in the opposite direction.

His path took him to Heraldin and Gaist, who were seated behind the stage and locked in a one-sided discussion.

"I don't know why we'd start in Scoria. It will be cold and damp up that way for months. Chrate is much warmer in the spring," the bard told the weaponsmaster as Gorm approached. "We should begin down in the Teagem. I'm not backing down on this one."

Gaist remained absolutely motionless.

"Fine," said Heraldin. "Scoria, and then Chrate, and then we make our way down through Knifevale to the Teagem coast."

"Plannin' a quest or a vacation?" said Gorm.

"Neither. Or perhaps both," said the bard. "We're taking our respective talents on the road to put them to good use. And while we're about, we'll enjoy the sights! The foods! The women! The music! The world awaits us!"

Gaist nudged the bard with a gentle elbow.

"And of course, we'll be doing good work while we're at it," the bard amended. "Free music for needy children. Defending the defenseless. Maybe help liberate some downtrodden souls, should they present themselves."

"Sounds like quite the adventure," said Gorm.

"Of the very best kind," grinned the bard.

"With a friend?"

"And without anything trying to kill us."

The doppelganger nodded at Gorm with a question in his eyes.

"Oh, I don't know." Gorm drew in a lungful of the cool mountain air. "The Feast of Orchids comes in Fireleaf this year. Might see if the Khazad'im will let an old clanless like me take part. Or maybe I put in for reinstatement, and see if I can make the festival in 378."

"If there is a 378," said Heraldin. "By the time the Agekeepers sort through all the history we just unraveled and remade, they're sure to declare this the Eighth Age."

"By the time they sort all of that out, it'll be 380." Gorm grinned. "And beyond that... well, time will tell."

"You're welcome to join us, of course," said Heraldin.

"Appreciate it, but I ain't much of a musician, and ye and I have different ideas about what's fun. Or helpful. Or legal. Or necessary for basic decency."

"True enough. We'll see you at the ceremony then."

Gorm bade them farewell, then wandered back out into the current of bustling clerks and attendants. He felt aimless, adrift on a sea of possibilities. Where would he go next? What was his purpose now that Johan was gone? What was left to conquer after you helped slay the greatest evil the world has ever known?

Lost in this reverie, he almost stumbled over another figure who was suddenly in his path.

"Ah, Mr. Ingerson. I've been looking for you."

"Excuse me, Mr. Poldo," Gorm said. "Er, Your Regentness."

"Mr. Poldo will do." The Scribkin checked a silver pocket watch, then snapped it shut. "We should have enough time before the unveiling. Come with me. I'd like to discuss a proposal with you."

"Uh, yes. Of course." Gorm followed the Gnome with a disconcerted nod. "Where?"

"Just over here." Mr. Poldo cut through the crowd like a shark through a reef, unconcerned and serene as startled bystanders hurried out of his way. He looked, at first glance, to walk alone ahead of Gorm, but on closer inspection the Dwarf saw bannermen silently moving into place all around them, and a multitude of Wood Gnomes weaving between the feet of the onlookers.

The regent led the hero and his invisible retinue to the backside of the scaffolding that held the curtains in front of the new statues, where a royal carriage waited with an open door. "If you'll join me in my makeshift office, we can speak privately," Poldo said over his shoulder.

The inside of the carriage was more office than makeshift, complete with a regal desk and several trays overflowing with paperwork. Gorm sat on the plush bench opposite the desk at Poldo's behest.

"I hope I found you well, Mr. Ingerson," said the regent.

"Aye, and you?"

"I feel honored to work for the people of this great kingdom, which is good, because there is a lot of work to do." That apparently accounted for all of the pleasantries the Scribkin required, as he opened a thick file on his desk and consulted its contents. "It occurred to me, Mr. Ingerson, that although our fortunes have been linked more than once, in very significant ways, I do not know you very well. I hope you'll forgive me, but I decided to do some research on your background."

"Ah." Gorm shifted uncomfortably in his seat. "So that would be my..."

"Your Heroes' Guild personnel file, yes," Poldo said.

"Right." Gorm cleared his throat while the regent read from the sheet. "Am I in, er, trouble?"

"If you were, I suppose you'd be accustomed to it." Poldo's thick mustache bent upward around a brief smile. "No, Mr. Ingerson. As I said, I have a proposal for you. You are doubtlessly aware that the late Weaver Ortson has vacated his seat on the Guild Council of Andarun. I think you would make a fine guildmaster, and would like to appoint you to the position."

Gorm felt his stomach drop into his iron-soled boots. "Ye... ye want to make me the grandmaster of the guild?"

"Oh, no. No. Of course not." Poldo shook his head and waved a hand dismissively. "The guildmasters appoint their own officers and leaders. I would not dream of interfering with their process. But each master serves at the king's pleasure, and as I speak for the king, it falls upon me to appoint a new member to their ranks. I'm especially confident that His Majesty would be pleased with this decision, should you accept."

"But I... but why me?" said Gorm.

"A seasoned hero who helped slay the lord of evil and has a personal friendship with the king?" Poldo shrugged. "It seems an easy case to make."

"Oh, aye, I can kill things, but I've no talent for diplomacy. Or politics. Or not offendin' people at fancy parties," said Gorm. "None of the things a guildmaster needs. Ain't even sure what a thrice-cursed guildmaster does! Beg pardon."

Poldo stared at him for a moment, then sniffed. "Well, a master has many duties. Voting on matters of guild governance. Sponsoring initiatives within the adventuring profession. Proposing and commenting upon regulations. And, of course, reviewing civic appeal cases and internal investigations within the guild—a practice that has been woefully neglected of late. Why, take a recent case brought to my attention by a friend and mutual acquaintance."

The Scribkin held out a hand and a sheet of parchment flew from a tray into his grasp, borne by a pair of silent Wood Gnomes. He glanced over the sheet, then offered it to Gorm. "The case of one Hristo Hrurk."

Gorm took the paper and started to read. "Papers revoked... traffic code... summary execution? For a traffic violation? Discretion?" As he read, Gorm's curious muttering descended into indignant sputtering and then further into the depths of rage. "Ye can't discretion away all the engagement guidelines! There still has to be an immediately witnessed act of villainy, or else there's a grace period where ye can only apprehend the foe! This arbiter don't know what she's on about. And Drif Matuk was involved! There's a bastard if I ever knew one. I bet ye'd find loads of cases like this one in his file."

"A guildmaster might," Poldo agreed.

Uncertainty momentarily interrupted Gorm's anger, and he faltered. "I... I mean, there's laws and protocols. I'm familiar, but I ain't an expert—"

"You'll have experts on staff, and lawyers, and clerks. Sometimes they might even give you useful information. But I am not nominating you to follow them. I'm nominating you to lead them."

"I just ain't sure why," Gorm said honestly.

Poldo smiled and looked back to the papers in front of him. "When I looked in your file, Mr. Ingerson, I found an interesting anecdote. You may recall the incident. It seems that a couple of years ago, you violently assaulted a guard at an Elven embassy over an insult to a Goblin."

Gorm's smirk was rueful. "Aye, I doubt I'll ever forget that one."

"You saw an injustice, you didn't let prejudice color your judgment, and you took emphatic action," said Poldo. "The Heroes' Guild needs all of that, and more."

"So ye want me to beat the snot out of that arbiter and some rogue heroes?"

"Of course not," said Poldo. "It would be improper to suggest that any one case warranted your attention—let alone your violence—just because of my personal connection."

"Oh," Gorm said, chagrined. "I guess I—"

"I want you to review all of the civic appeal cases, Mr. Ingerson," said Poldo, gesturing at the overflowing stack of papers. "Over eight hundred of them last year alone. And I want you to treat all of them exactly the same. I want you to listen. I want you to care. And, when injustice has been done, I want you to take appropriate action, even if it ruffles the feathers of those puffed-up cockatrices on the guild council. You are good at those things. The rest will follow."

Gorm looked at the stack of paperwork, then back to the report in his hand, speechless.

"Thousands of people are hurting, missing loved ones that were cruelly taken away," the Scribkin pressed. "Someone's world will always need saving, Mr. Ingerson. Someone will always need help. The challenge changes shape, but the work will always be there, if only someone will take it up."

Gorm gave a small smile. "Me," he said.

"I hope so, Mr. Ingerson," said Poldo, snapping the file shut. "I truly do. I am certain His Majesty will be most pleased when I tell him of your imminent appointment. But now, we must go and watch the United Temple unveil their new monument to you and your fine fellows. Tomorrow is a new day, and you can begin saving the world anew then."

Saving the world anew began with breakfast at the Sculpin Down Road Brothers' Diner.

Gorm tucked into a pile of seasoned potatoes and sausage smothered under runny eggs and a thick slab of buttered toast. It was the sort of breakfast that his da used to say would put hair on his chest, served with coffee strong enough to burn it off again. In the throes of such greasy bliss, Gorm felt that his cup was running over, and not only because the waitress was distracted while pouring.

Across the booth, Burt worked at a plate that was half the size but all of the calories. "I still think they got my ears wrong," grumbled the Kobold in between bites of bacon. "I mean, yeah, it's an honor, but how much work is it to count the notches in a guy's ear? I look like my cousin Herbie. They should have hired a Shadowkin sculptor for me and the Goblin."

Gorm grunted in assent and mopped up a bit of egg with a bit of toast.

"But what do you expect? They put a Gnome in charge, and he forgets about us. I'm still miffed at Thane about that."

"Oh?"

"Oh yeah, I'm thrice-cursed furious," said the Kobold, his ears twitching in agitation. "We worked for years fightin' injustice. We moved all the tribes in Warg Incorporated to capture the markets. We deposed a king and killed the thrice-cursed demon god behind everyone's problems, and at the end we finally—finally—get a Troll turned Sten on the throne. And what's he do? He turns his power over to a rich old Lightling."

"Mmmph—" Gorm said through a mouthful of potatoes.

"No, no, I'm serious. When do we win? When do we come out ahead? Lady Asherzu and the tribal heads are richer, but all us grunts working in the bank, what do we see of that? My buddy Folbo got a hundred giltin bonus check and a three silver an hour raise. How's that get him ahead? It doesn't. He still can barely afford an apartment with his six brothers. He still has to work extra hours to make ends meet. He still has the same thrice-cursed knight outside his tenement every morning, checking all the Shadowkin's NPC papers and letting all the Lightlings pass. He's still behind. All of us are. Everything that helps us, helps you Lightlings too. It just helps you more. We never get ahead, and we never win."

Gorm felt his gorge rise atop a ball of indignant sentiment. He wanted to say that Mr. Poldo and Thane were doing their best, just as anyone was, or to remind Burt how much worse things could be if Mannon had won. But he washed those unwise words back down with a swig of bitter coffee, and reminded himself that none of those facts made what Burt said any less true. "Aye. It's drake spit," he said.

"It's total drake spit," agreed Burt, sipping his own coffee.

"Pass the ketchup." Gorm pulled a small notebook and a pencil nib from his belt pouch.

The booklet didn't escape Burt's bulbous gaze. "Oh, you workin' the new gig already?" he asked with a smirk.

"Startin' today," said Gorm with a smile. "Should be made official by lunch. Now tell me about this knight down by Folbo's apartment."

The Kobold looked warily at the page. Gorm couldn't fault him for not trusting anything associated with the Heroes' Guild. "And, what? You just write it all down?"

"And compare it with other notes in his file. And whatever Folbo will say. And then I open an investigation."

"Pssh." Burt champed at his cigarette. "It's not gonna help. You think some paperwork is gonna fix ages of problems, just 'cause your doin' it? Doesn't make sense."

"Doesn't matter if it makes sense," said Gorm. "It's standard procedure."

The Kobold looked at him thoughtfully, and shrugged. "Fine. Guy calls himself Tychus of Copper. Real ugly."

And so Burt related the story of his friend's struggles, interspersed with streaks of profanity stronger than the coffee. And Gorm listened, and wrote things down, and cared.

Everybody jumped back when the bottle shattered on the broken cobbles of Borskin Way. Accusatory shouts rang out from the children on either side of the street, alongside the biggest and most taboo cuss words that each group could muster. The Orcs and Goblins had an advantage here, as the Human children could only swear in Imperial. Swearing was the only situation where Recky Figgs envied his Shadowkin neighbors' bilingual skills. Only Belnitha Potts could compete, as her father was an Elf and she could swear in Root Elven. But Elven swears were less expressive, and took too long to say, and nobody else could understand them anyway.

The Orcs insisted that Boggs Fuller threw the bottle just to start a fight. They were right, of course. Boggs was the oldest kid this side of Scoria's tannery district, a thick mass of muscle and acne with a smattering of wispy hairs around a chip-toothed smile. He took special delight in starting brawls with younger children, and even more delight in finishing them. It was a given that Boggs had thrown the bottle, and it was equally certain why he did it, but no Human of any color was going to admit that; siding with the Orcs on anything was a sure way to find yourself on the wrong side of Boggs' fists when the fighting started.

Instead, Recky accused Scubgar, a weedy little Goblin who always cried and ran home rather than fighting back. Scubgar teared up and looked ready to bolt, but that only made the remaining Shadowkin angrier. Things were headed for a brawl, and just to make sure they got there quickly, Boggs began shouting slurs at the Shadowkin children. Recky saw Throg Gub'Zubba grab a thick branch that would make a nasty club. The young Human searched for a good throwing rock, just in case Throg got a chance to use it.

Thardu, a young Orcess with warg-fang bracers, screwed up her face and sneered at the older boy. "What'd you say?"

"I said you're a swamp-pelted wolf-loving greenskin!"

"No, I heard that!" said Thardu. "I meant the part about not fighting."

Boggs' brow wrinkled. "What?"

"*Tra lee, tra la! Let's not fight! Let's hear a song!*"

"Is that a song?" asked Rax.

"It's genuinely hard to tell," said Belnitha.

"Oh, har-dee-har." An adult Human rounded the corner into the alley. His clothes were bright, his hat was floppy, and he was, for lack of a better term, playing a lute. "Perhaps not a song, but a story! A tale to amuse and amaze and, if possible, de-escalate."

"De-what?"

"I believe that stories have the power to change young minds, as they're so impressionable!"

Unfortunately, another trait of young minds is that they often have underdeveloped impulse control, and at that moment several children from both sides of the street gave in to the natural inclination to throw things at an obnoxious bard. A hail of stones, bottles, and broken sticks sailed through the air.

Then the shadows moved with a sound like silk whispering in the wind, and something huge passed in front of Recky. The child ducked instinctively, and when he opened his eyes again, a massive Imperial man in a dark cloak and a red scarf stood in front of the bard, holding a green bottle. A heap of other projectiles were stacked neatly on the street in front of him.

"Allow me an introduction," said the bard. "I am Heraldin, and as I mentioned, I believe that stories have the power to end violence. Metaphorically. This is Gaist. He believes in stories too, but should they fail, he also has the power to stop violence. Physically."

Gaist crossed his arms.

"He wants me to tell you a story."

"He... he does?" asked Scubgar.

"Believe me, I'd rather be performing at the Curious Milkmaid, but he—oof!" The bard grunted and shot the huge man a loaded glare, but he said, "I mean, yes, we both want you to hear our story."

"Yeah?" Boggs demanded, sensing that the moment for a good brawl was passing. "And what if we don't?"

Gaist's eyes locked on the boy.

Boggs froze in that black-diamond stare. Sweat beaded on his brow as he tried to meet it, but he couldn't hold the gaze for long. "Yeah, all right," he said, sitting down.

As if on cue, every other child in the street dropped to the street or clambered atop one of the barrels and crates scattered about the alley.

"Now," said Heraldin. "How many of you have heard the tale of a Goblin who befriended a Dwarf?"

The children's confused stares were ambiguous.

"None of you, right? You shouldn't have. I own the exclusive rights to—ow!" The bard shot the weaponsmaster a dirty glare and rubbed his elbow.

"A Dwarf chummin' with a Gobbo? That'd never happen!" protested Boggs. "Who'd want a Goblin for a friend?"

"Anyone wise!" said the bard. "Goblins are famously loyal creatures. A Goblin's heart is brave, and they'll do anything for their friends even when they're misunderstood or underappreciated—which is almost always the case. Like a good beer—ow! I mean, like a good tea cake, they make almost any day better."

"But a Dwarf?" protested a child. "Liked a Goblin?"

"It's true. They became the very best of friends."

"Really?" said Scubgar.

"Oh yes. It's part of the tale of the Troll and the Elf who fell in love."

"Ew!" said Thardu, but she scooted closer to the bard.

"Is that true?" asked Belnitha, casting a sidelong glance at Throg.

"Every word of it. We saw it ourselves," said Heraldin. "And it all started when a particularly brave Goblin lost his family, but still found the courage to befriend a curmudgeonly Dwarf..."

——EPILOGUE——

"**C**rag will smash you!" the Troll growled. Thick cords of muscles rippled under his shaggy fur, and his wicked teeth gnashed dangerously. "I'm gonna beat you into a paste!"

This display would normally be enough to send any traveler running, but Crag's captor hardly seemed to notice. Thick, damp arms wrapped around the Troll's shoulders and held the back of his head, so that he couldn't reach behind him. His legs scrabbled for purchase on the path, but they were weak after days of being dragged through the woods. "I'll kill you..." Crag croaked, but much of the strength had left him.

The walking statue said something else in an unfamiliar tongue; the same one it had spoken in when it wandered into Crag's den days earlier. The Troll had originally tried to extort treasure from the strange rocks. When robbery failed, Crag tried to intimidate the sculpture into leaving. It didn't react at all, save to repeat itself in its strange tongue with infuriating patience. When Crag finally lost his own and threw a punch, the sculpture casually let him shatter the bones of his hands against its face before it grappled him in an iron hold. The Troll had been on a forced march since, despite struggling with all of his strength.

"Athor?" a voice called out from the trees ahead. "Athor, is that you?"

Crag looked up as the sculpture spoke again. He had been hauled to a strange archway of Myrewood brambles and white dogwood. In the center of it, a strange man with spiraling tattoos stood smiling up at the Troll.

The insolence of the man brought Crag's fury back. "Crag will grind your bones!"

The man considered him thoughtfully, stroking his long, braided beard as he did so. "Perhaps," he said. "Let him go, Athor. Uh, *rilyanethe*."

The sculpture's hold on Crag released, and the Troll dropped to the ground. He was back on his feet immediately, though his exhausted legs buckled and confusion roiled his thoughts. "Run! I'll kill you!" he roared. "I'm a Troll!"

"So am I," said the man. "And I am a Sten, as are you. My name is Thane."

"I... I'm a Troll!" Crag reiterated, in case Thane had not heard him. When the Sten didn't react, he added, "You should run. People are scared of Trolls."

"Don't I know it." Thane laughed as he turned and walked deeper into the tunnel of brambles and dogwood. "Come with me."

"I'm a Troll!" Crag insisted, pounding the ground. "Trolls kill! Trolls murder! Trolls are horrible! Mean! Nasty!"

"So I've heard. But we've found otherwise." Thane gestured as he walked into the clearing beyond the archway.

"I'll—" Crag shouted, and then words failed him.

He was in a huge clearing, bounded by white trees and brimming with flowers. Fragrant blooms and earthy mosses spilled over rocks and covered every surface, even twining up the trunks of spiraling fruit trees. Verdant pools harbored flotillas of colorful lilies.

Most notably, it was full of Trolls.

Crag had learned that Trolls lived alone. Crag had been told that nobody wanted to be near a Troll, not even another Troll. Yet here Crag saw them working together, tending plants and reading books and speaking with the same strange statues that had dragged him here. Some looked at him and smiled. A few waved.

"Who's this, Thane?" asked an Elf, bounding up beside the strange man.

"Kaitha, everyone, this is Crag," said Thane. "Crag, welcome to our home."

"I... I'm a Troll," Crag said, reverting to what he knew while the rest of his world spun upside down.

"Yes, and a Sten," said Kaitha.

"I's mean!" Crag insisted. "I's hurts people!"

"That's a choice," said Thane. "You can choose differently."

"I'm a monster," insisted Crag, his voice cracking.

Thane reached out and clasped his fellow Sten on the shoulder. "Maybe you were," he said. "But you don't have to be. You can be more. And we want to help."

Words failed Crag, and tears threatened to overtake him, but he managed to nod as the Sten pulled him into a burly hug that took his breath away.

THE END

ABOUT THE AUTHOR

J. Zachary Pike was once a basement-dwelling fantasy gamer, but over time he metamorphosed into a basement-dwelling fantasy writer. His animations, films, and books meld fantasy elements with offbeat humor. A New Englander by birth and by temperament, he writes strangely funny fiction on the seacoast of New Hampshire.

Learn more at **www.jzacharypike.com**.

Say "Hello"

Email: **zack@jzacharypike.com**

Support me on Patreon: **patreon.com/jzacharypike**

If You Enjoyed This Book...

Word of mouth is the biggest factor in any author's success. A review on your favorite online bookseller, Goodreads, or any other site could make a huge difference, and would be very much appreciated.

Get Another Free eBook by J. Zachary Pike

You'll get a free digital copy of The Cabal of Thotash when you join J. Zachary Pike's email list. You'll also get monthly emails with exclusive content, short fiction, news about upcoming releases, cover reveals, and more. It's quick and easy to sign up here: **www.jzacharypike.com/ newsletter/**

GLOSSARY

Agekeepers: A sect of esoteric historians who keep and update the official records of Arth. It is the Agekeepers who define when an age begins and ends.

Al'Matra: Technically the highest-ranked Elven god as the queen of the pantheon, the All Mother and her followers are really impoverished outcasts. The scriptures say she went mad after the All Father's betrayal.

Al'Thadan: Formerly called the All Father, the highest Stennish god was once the king of the pantheon. He is said to have been Arth's greatest defender against the forces of Mannon until he colluded with the dark lord during the War of Betrayal in the Third Age. According to the Agekeepers, Al'Thadan was struck down along with all the Sten at the end of the war.

Andarun: The greatest city on Arth, at least according to most of its citizens, and capital of the Freedlands. Andarun was built on ancient ruins on the southern slope of Mount Wynspar.

Arak'nud: The Dwarven term for a Dwarf who has elected not to be a Dwarf. A tiny population, arak'nud leave Dwarven society for any number of reasons, from wishing to live in another culture to falling in love with a Gnome or Elf. They are not clanless, nor are they above or below any Dwarf, because as far as any Dwarf or arak'nud is concerned, they're Human.

Arth: A world much like Earth, but with more magic and fewer vowels.

Bannerman: The bannermen are the town guard, armies, and other armed officials of the Freedlands. Every branch of every civic organization within the Freedlands is required to maintain some number of armed men who may be called to arms when fealty demands it. Each bannerman is loyal to such a company, which is loyal to a city, which is loyal to Andarun, which is loyal to the Freedlands. In this way, each bannerman serves his or her country.

Class: Professional heroes fall into a variety of classes (e.g. warrior, mage) and sub-classes (e.g. swordsman, pyromancer), largely distinguished by the methods they use to kill monsters.

Domovoy: See Wood Gnome.

Doppelganger: A widely distrusted race of shapeshifters, commonly believed to have been created as infiltrators for Mannon's armies in the War of Betrayal. Doppelgangers would make ideal diplomats were they not such ideal spies, double agents, and assassins as well.

Dragon: Great reptiles that command the elements, most famously fire. It's well-known that dragons slumber deep beneath the earth atop great mounds of treasure, and universally agreed that it's always best to let sleeping dragons lie.

Drakes: Dragon-kin that are much like full dragons, except smaller, weaker, and nowhere near as smart. Drakes still pose a significant threat, however, especially when encountered in their native element.

Dwarf: Dwarves are shorter than Elves and Humans, but as Dwarves stand almost twice as wide at the shoulder and are famous for violent grudges, it's generally best not to mention that. Rigid, industrious, and usually stoic, Dwarves live in massive clanhomes dug under the mountains. To the puzzlement of many of the other races, there are no Dwarven women.

Dwerrow: The Gnomes of Clan Erdin, or Hill Gnomes, are often mistaken for Dwarves. They're just a head shorter than Dwarves, but otherwise have similar stocky builds, long beards, and muscular frames. Other key differences from Dwarves include narrower shoulders, rounder features, and (perhaps most significantly), the presence of female Dwerrow. They are also usually heavily tattooed with spiral patterns used to indicate heritage, standing, and fealty.

Elf: The most enigmatic of the Children of Light have sharp, angular features, but flowing, graceful movements. They live in tree huts, and most have accumulated untold wealth. They are immortal and yet innocent, playful yet powerful, whimsical yet wise. Above all, they are infuriating to almost everyone who is not an Elf. Elves all belong to houses, each of which swears fealty to a great house. Of course, Elven fealty shifts frequently, and so the Elven houses are forever in flux, playing games of intrigue and power.

Elixir: A miraculous healing potion brewed by magical means, elixir or salve can close wounds, restore organs, and even regrow lost limbs if consumed soon enough after an injury. It's nearly as effective as it is addictive.

F.O.E.: Short for Force of Evil, the official Heroes' Guild designation for an enemy of the people and a legal target for heroic slaying.

The Freedlands: The most powerful nation on Arth, the Freedlands is a federation of semi-autonomous city-states. The Freedlands has a small centralized government, ruled by a king set in Andarun, that regulates the powerful guilds, associations, and corporations that do business in the Freedlands and beyond.

Fulgen: Fulgen, also called the Silent Underglow or Father Tinderhope, is the Dwarven god of light. He rules over candles in the darkness, purity among corruption, and truth amid lies. Among the Dwarves, he is a favorite of miners and heroes.

Giltin: The currency of the Freedlands, long considered the standard for all of Arth. The common symbol for giltin is G, as in 5G. One giltin is ten silver shillings. One shilling is ten copper cents.

Gnoll: A race of Shadowkin with canine traits, once known as Clan Galden, or the Golden Gnomes. Gnolls were bred for a variety of purposes in the War of Betrayal, and many of these breeds (technically known as Demi-Gnolls) are still around today.

Gnome: Gnomes take as many shapes and sizes as the clouds in the sky. While their legends hold that all Gnomes once shared a common ancestor, the great Gnomish clans have all become their own subraces. Be that as it may, it's proper to refer to any of them as a Gnome, be they a Halfing, Tinderkin, or Deep Gnome. Said subraces are often used interchangeably with clan names. All Gnomes stand shorter than most Humans, and most are shorter than Dwarves.

Goblin: A race of Shadowkin that descended from the lost clans of the Dwarves. Goblins are short, scrawny, potbellied Shadowkin.

Golem: Enchanted automatons originally created by the Scribkin, golems have been refined and adapted to serve many useful purposes across Arth.

Gremlins: A race of Shadowkin with both feline and lizard-like qualities, once known as Clan Remlon, or Moon Gnomes. Gremlins are known for their inquisitive nature, their mastery of bioengineering, and their tenuous grasp of ethics.

Griffin: It is said that a griffin is a lion with the head, talons, and wings of an eagle, but the Zoological Society of Monchester has determined that a griffin is, in actuality, a Giant Eagle with a lion's butt.

Halfling: Halflings are Gnomes of Clan Haughlin. They have round features, pot bellies, and curly brown hair (even on the tops of their feet.) While generally good-natured, Halflings are averse to manual labor, or indeed anything that isn't comfortable. Unfortunately, they're often very comfortable with petty theft.

Hardvaark: A ground-dwelling monster with a long, pig-like snout and a thick, metallic carapace. Its tenacious nature made it the namesake of one of the Freedlands' most prestigious universities.

Heroes' Guild: An international organization of professional adventurers who specialize in monster slaying, treasure acquisition, hostage retrieval, and more. The Heroes' Guild is among the largest and most powerful organizations on Arth. Its wealth rivals that of the city-states of the Freedlands, and even some small countries.

High Magic: The elemental energy woven through the universe, high magic is called the great weave. High magic is divided into two sides— solamancy and noctomancy.

Human: Y'know. Humans. Originally mixed-race men, the first Humans were children of Gnomes and Elves and Sten. In time, they became so common that they married amongst themselves and spread throughout Arth. Now they are the most populous race of Man, outnumbering all of the old races combined.

Issan: A legendary Elven Champion of Tandos in the War of Betrayal, notable for slaying the Dark Prince's first incarnation.

Kobold: Kobolds are a diminutive breed of Demi-Gnoll, standing just below a Human's knee in height. They have big eyes, a short muzzle, thin limbs, and a severe case of small dog syndrome.

Lawyer-monks of Adchul: A reclusive sect of monks who believe that discipline, law, and study represent a non-exclusive method to obtain enlightenment, with no guarantee of enlightenment or of any other goods and services made by said monks.

Leviathan: A legendary sea monster said to be born of the ultimate evil.

Liche: A mage that rises from the grave through necromancy and extensive planning. Liches are the most powerful form of undead.

Low Magic: The oldest laws of the universe, the rules of life and death, love and hatred, blood and bone.

Mankind, Man, Races of Man: Legends say the Creator made the four races of Man—the Dwarves, Elves, Gnomes, and Sten—to make Arth more interesting, and has regretted it ever since.

Mannon: Malice incarnate, the ancient foe of the Creator who deceived Mankind, created the Shadowkin, and even corrupted some of the gods in ages past. Depending on the temple one visits, it is said that Mannon is either dead, in hiding, or a little bit of him lives in all of our hearts.

Mage: A person able to see and weave high magic, usually through years of dedicated study and social isolation.

Magic: The essential forces of the universe as understood by those who fiddle with them. Magic is divided into high and low magic.

Mercenary: A killer for hire. Specifically, mercenaries are the killers for hire that are not professional heroes. Assassins, soldiers, thugs, goons: they all fall under the general headline of "mercenary." While more common than professional heroes, mercenaries are less regulated. With some assassins and thugs aside, they're generally thought to be weaker as well.

Monstrous Races: Humanoids bred for various combat roles by Mannon and Noros to fight in the War of Betrayal, the monstrous races are distinguished from Shadowkin in that they didn't descend from the races of Man. Examples include Ogres, doppelgangers, and lizardmen.

Musana: Musana is the Elven goddess of light and life. She encourages purity and grace, and honors simple living. Musana's high ideals make her popular, especially among the Order of the Sun, but many followers often misunderstand her teaching: Musana's most famous stories depict her humbling those followers who think themselves more pious than others. She is twin sister to Alluna, the Elven goddess of the moon.

Naga: A race of Shadowkin with serpentine traits, Naga were once Clan Nagata, the Iron Gnomes. They resemble scaled men and women from the waist up, but their lower halves are those of serpents.

Necromancer: While all noctomancers can touch the shadowy side of high magic that binds the dead, the word necromancer is reserved for those who have created undead for nefarious purposes.

Noctomancer: A member of the second great order of mages, the Order of the Moon. Noctomancers are Humans and Gnomes that can weave the elements of air, earth, and shadow.

Noros: Once the Gnomish god of dreams, Noros became Mannon's greatest lieutenant.

NPC: A Noncombatant Paper Carrier is a Shadowkin or monster who has secured noncombatant papers, removing his, her, or its status as a F.O.E. and thereby preventing professional heroes from killing them (legally).

Omnimancer: A mage who wields both solamancy and noctomancy. Omnimancers once comprised the third great order of mages, the Order of Twilight, but they have fallen from grace. Now, omnimancers are the spell casting equivalent of lepers, living on the margins of society.

Orc: A race of Shadowkin, Orcs were once Elves that sided with Mannon. Hulking, bucket-jawed, green-skinned, and ferocious, Orcs have a war-torn history and a legacy of brutality.

Order of the Moon: See noctomancer.

Order of the Sun: See solamancer.

Order of Twilight: See omnimancer.

Owlverine: All the deadly ferocity of an owlbear, packed into a beast no bigger than an owlhound.

Ogre: One of the monstrous races, Ogres are like clubs: big, simple, and made for violence.

Poor Man's Quiver: An enchanted quiver that always contains exactly one enchanted arrow, no matter how many are pulled from it. After purchasing one, any man would be poor.

Rank (Heroes' Guild): There's no way to measure the value of a life, except the life of a professional hero, in which case their rank is an effective metric. As a hero attains ranks in different classes by killing things, it's essentially a measure of how deadly, and therefore how valuable, a hero is.

Scarg: A vaguely humanoid bat-like creature, the origins of scargs are unknown. Some say they're naturally occurring monsters, while others say scargs are a monstrous race or a Gremlin experiment gone wrong. They come in many varieties and breeds, most of which are more annoying than threatening to a professional hero.

Scribkin: The Gnomes of Clan Tinkrin, or Scribkin, stand half as tall as most Humans, with stocky builds, bulbous noses, and thick, bushy hair. Industrious and curious, Scribkin are Arth's most innovative inventors, enchanters, and engineers.

Shadowkin: Legends hold that by the Third Age, many of Arth's people followed Mannon or the gods loyal to him. Before launching the War of Betrayal, Mannon and Noros corrupted these lost people into more aggressive, poetically ironic shadows of their former selves.

Slaugh: Picture a Gnome-sized frog walking on its haunches. Now imagine it has a foul temperament and a fouler odor. Technically, they're Shadowkin descended from the Gnomes of Clan Slaughin, but many other Shadowkin are loathe to admit as much.

Solamancer: A member of the first great order of mages, the Order of the Sun. Solamancers are Humans and Elves that can weave the elements of fire, water, and light.

Sten: The great traitors. Legends say that members of the fourth race of Man were long considered aloof and enigmatic before they followed the traitor god Al'Thadan and colluded with Mannon. Gray-skinned and as tall as Elves and as broad as Dwarves, Sten were masters of low magic. The Agekeepers confirm that they were wiped out in the War of Betrayal.

Tandos: The Elven god of war and glory, Tandos is the greatest son of Al'Thadan and Al'Matra. It was he who finally struck down his traitorous father, and it was Tandos' servants who defeated the Sten. Today, he rules over the pantheon as the divine regent in the place of his mother, who is unfit for rule.

Tinderkin: The Gnomes of Clan Kaedrin, Tinderkin are taller than any other Gnomes, standing a little taller than even a Dwarf. They are lithe, graceful figures with sharp, slender features. Tinderkin are nomadic, traveling in small, familial bands. They take their name from the fires they build for nightly gatherings, which are often elaborate visual spectacles.

Troll: Trolls are massive, apelike creatures, the corrupted remnants of the now-extinct Sten. A Troll is a gray-skinned Shadowkin with a flat, broad-nostrilled face and a shaggy coat of thick fur. They have peerless regenerative abilities and can shrug off mortal blows or regrow limbs within minutes. Originally bred for war and killing, they are regarded as good for little else.

Undead: The bodies and/or spirits of fallen mortals, animated by foul magic to haunt and/or hunt the living. They take many forms, including ghosts, ghouls, liches, skeletons, vampires, wraiths, and zombies.

Ward: A magical barrier, shield, or other protective spell woven by mages.

Wizard: A title given to male mages. Its counterpart, witch, fell into disuse during the Age of Darkness.

Wood Gnome: The most diminutive of Gnomes, members of Clan Fengeld stand just over most men's ankles. They grow long beards, but all of their hair tends to get lost in the tangle of pelts and scraps they wear. They're fiercely territorial and will often refuse to surrender land even after another race has built a city atop it. Their squatting habits have led many modern citizens to regard them as a particularly obnoxious form of vermin, and one that is remarkably difficult to get rid of.

Wynspar: The mighty mountain that Andarun is set into. It is riddled with caves, tunnels, dungeons, and various other dark places for monstrous horrors to lurk.

Wyvern: A variety of drake with leathery wings instead of forelegs, much akin to a bat, and a barbed, venomous tail, much akin to a scorpion. It's every bit as unpleasant as it sounds.